OLD MEN in LOVE

John Tunnock
1940 – 2007

OLD MEN in LOVE

John Tunnock's posthumous papers

introduced by
Lady Sara Sim-Jaegar

edited, decorated by
Alasdair Gray

BLOOMSBURY
LONDON 2007

First published in Great Britain 2007
©opyright 2007 by Alasdair Gray

Bloomsbury Publishing Plc, 36 Soho Square, London W1D 3QY
www.bloomsbury.com

All papers used by Bloomsbury Publishing are natural,
recyclable products made from wood grown in well-managed
forests. The manufacturing processes conform to the environmental
regulations of the country of origin.

A CIP catalogue record for this book is available from
the British Library

ISBN 9780747593539

Helen Lloyd's secretarial work and research, Richard Todd's
draughtsmanship greatly helped this book.

Typeset by Joe Murray of Glasgow

Printed in Italy by L.E.G.O. SpA

FOR
ALEXANDRA

Offshore

Iona, August 2005

One beginning and ending for a book was a thing I did not agree with. A good book may have three openings entirely dissimilar and interrelated only in the prescience of the author, or for that matter one hundred times as many endings.
— *At Swim-Two-Birds* by Flann O'Brien

TABLE OF

Introduction by Lady Sara Sim-Jaegar   Page **1**
1   *Tunnock's Diary, 2001*   **9**
2   Citizens   **14**
3   State Funeral   **23**
4   Domestic Interior   **29**
5   A Statesman's Day   **32**
6   At Aspasia's   **37**
7   *Tunnock's Diary 2002*   **46**
8   Prologue to a Historical Trilogy   **52**
9   *Tunnock's Diary 2002*   **61**
10 In a Florentine Monastery   **70**
11 In a Florentine Nunnery   **75**
12 Somewhere in Rome   **77**
13 Angus Calder's Letter   **83**
14 *Tunnock's Diary 2002-3*   **87**
15 Wee Me   **102**
16 Early Sex   **113**
17 Further Education   **133**

CONTENTS

18	My World History: Prologue	Page	141
19	*Tunnock's Diary 2004*		148
20	The Young Prince		158
21	Lampeter		162
22	From Br. Prince's Journal		171
23	Charlinch		182
24	The Growth of The Spirit		193
25	Stoke, Brighton and Weymouth		207
26	The Abode of Love		222
27	Hepworth Dixon's Report		237
28	Tailpiece		247
29	*Tunnock's Diary 2006*		249
30	The Trial of Socrates		264
31	*Tunnock's Diary 2007*		295
32	Socratic End Notes		299
33	The Denoomong of the Imbroglio		302
34	Tunnock's Crossword Testament		303
Epilogue by Sidney Workman			304

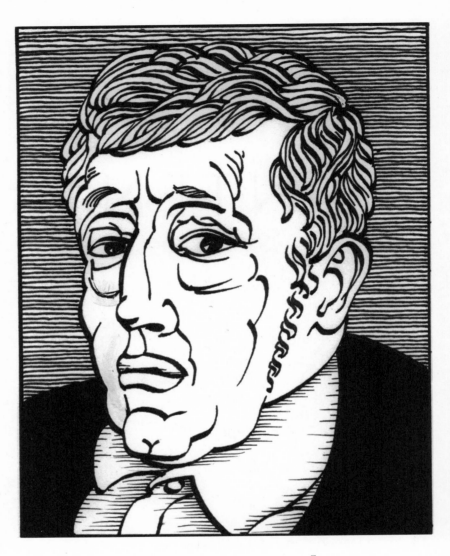

Francis Lambert
2007

Lady Sara Sim-Jaegar's Introduction

We Sim-Jaegars are a widely scattered clan. Though born and educated in England I am now resident in Los Angeles with all the rights of a United States citizen. The Edinburgh Festival has twice drawn me to Scotland, yet I never dreamed I had a distant cousin there until a solicitor's letter arrived "out of the blue," as they say. It told me John Tunnock had died intestate, that I was his next of kin, and asked how I wished to dispose of his estate – some thousands of pounds in a savings account and a large terrace house in Glasgow's Hillhead district. The current sale price of such houses was anything between half a million and a million. Furnishings, domestic appliances, ornaments, pictures and books had not yet been professionally valued, but a Glasgow agent of Christie's (the well-known auctioneering firm) had written expressing interest in a stained glass panel representing Faith, Hope and Charity in the stairwell window, since records of the William Morris workshop indicated that it was designed by Burne-Jones. If I wished to view my cousin's former property without residing in it (which was perhaps likely, given the circumstances of his death) I would easily find accommodation in a neighbourhood Hilton hotel.

This letter had clipped to it a Herald newspaper cutting dated three weeks earlier. It said that John Tunnock, retired schoolteacher, aged sixty-seven, had been found dead at his home in Glasgow's Hillhead district, and the police were appealing to the public for information about anyone seen entering or leaving his home before the morning of Saturday, 28th April. Attached to the clipping was a further note from the lawyer saying the police had taken all evidence the house could yield and no arrests would be made. He had ordered the removal of blood stains and the place was now thoroughly tidied and cleaned, all locks on doors were changed and a new up-to-date burglar alarm installed. He awaited my instructions.

Well! God knows I have all the money I need but a

businesswoman can always use more. My investments are safe because I work closely with my brokers and lawyers – not that I suspect them of corrupt practices, but when professional men's judgement is at fault (and no financial arrangement is ever flawless) they sometimes automatically ensure that the cost is borne by inattentive clients. This canny attitude brought me to Glasgow against the advice of American and English friends who said I would be in danger of criminal violence, and pointed to my cousin's fate as a warning. My omniscient insurance advisor disagreed. Glasgow, he said, certainly had the greatest density of European poverty, ill health and crime west of the former Communist empire – in one district the average life expectancy was seventeen years less than that of those living in the Gaza Strip before the recent Israeli-Lebanese war – but the murder rate was still three quarters of that in most United States cities. Statistics show that in Glasgow's Hillhead area a woman is marginally safer than in Beverly Hills, especially if she does not wear bright blues or greens while watching television football in crowded pubs. These colours, that sport, such pubs do not tempt me. To Glasgow I came.

Next morning at the Hilton hotel I had a business breakfast with the solicitor, Alasdair Gillies. He could tell me nothing directly about my cousin, never having met him. Legal documents in the possession of his firm, letters in the Tunnock family home had enabled him to trace me through a distant relation who had emigrated in Victoria's reign. They had also revealed a family secret. John's mother Griselda was youngest daughter of Murdo Henderland Tunnock, for many years minister of Hillhead Parish Church. Like her two sisters she never married. Unlike them she had left the family home, first becoming a typist in a local tax office before promotion in 1936 to a superior post in London. Four years later at the age of forty-one she gave birth to John, her first and last child. The birth certificate gives a line of unpronounceable consonants as the father's name, gives his occupation as Polish naval officer, which seems improbable. Griselda brought her baby to Glasgow a week later, deposited him with her sisters (whose parents were dead) and returned to London. Soon after she too died, crushed by a falling wall while cycling to work after a night of heavy bombing by the Luftwaffe.

John's subsequent life with his aunts seems to have been

unusually cloistered. He attended Hillhead Secondary then the
University of Glasgow, both near each other and less than ten minutes
walk from the family home. He trained as a teacher at Jordanhill
College, a short bus ride to the west, after that becoming a teacher,
then headmaster of Molendinar Primary School in Robroyston, a
longer ride to the east. He never owned a car. Mr Gillies suggested
that his aunts "kept him on a very short leash". They were his
housekeepers until 1977 when he took early retirement to look after
them, helped by house cleaners and visiting nurses. Before then he
had holidayed with them in hilly or coastal parts of Scotland. The
last aunt died aged ninety-seven in 1998, after which he seems never
to have slept outside the family home. On week days his social life
was mainly evening visits to Tennants, a pub at a corner of Byres
Road where the usual clients were students, academics, several long-
term unemployed and a few owners of small businesses who avoided
declaring their earnings to the Inland Revenue. Here John was well
known though his quiet ways drew very little attention. His main
acquaintance was Francis Lambert, a retired university lecturer and
more robust figure with whom John Tunnock gossiped and discussed
crossword puzzles. On Saturdays and Sundays John walked briskly
to pubs elsewhere, some in the city centre or south of the river or
further east, seldom drinking more than a half pint of lager in each,
and stopping at cafés for cups of tea or snacks. His visits to these
places were not exactly predictable, but regular enough for people
he met to assume he lived locally, though most of the pubs were
over a mile apart. None of those he talked to thought him interesting
or unusual before they heard of his death.

I brooded on this information, then asked if any of these
pubs showed football matches on television? Had John worn
noticeable colours? Mr Gillies understood more by my question
than I knew it contained. The police had investigated that (he
said) and found John Tunnock never wore team colours, supported
neither Rangers nor Celtic, was neither Orangeman nor Fenian,
Mason or Knight of Saint Columba. When asked what football
club he supported Tunnock always said Partick Thistle, which in
Glasgow is a code name for agnostic and might inspire contempt

in Protestant or Catholic bigots but not murderous rage.

"Had he no sex life?" I asked. Apparently none before 1998, said Mr Gillies, but his diary indicated he had then "lashed out a bit". I asked what that meant. He said I should read the diary to find out. I said his silence on the matter suggested dealings with prostitutes, or homosexuality, or paedophilia – the last now so notorious that one fears to show kindness to any child anywhere. What had the police discovered? Gillies told me that the women who cleaned his house said he was "a nice wee man who wouldnae hurt a fly or say boo to a goose." He seemed not to have visited any pub on the night of his death. His cleaners found the body next morning on a staircase landing and a forensic report indicated he had died suddenly of a fractured skull about ten hours earlier, the fracture caused by abrupt contact with a step. There was no alcohol in his blood, though the state of the living room upstairs, together with fingerprints on glasses and bottles, indicated some kind of party with several individuals, one a drug user known to the police. He (Mr Gillies) had been privately informed that the drug user had confessed to pushing John away during an amorous struggle on the staircase when she tried to leave, a push resulting in his fall. The Crown Office had decided not to make a respected citizen's sex life public by accusing the girl of culpable homicide, especially when a jury would almost certainly bring a verdict of not proven. Only Scots law allows this, which a cynic has suggested means, "Go away and don't do it again." The most famous beneficiary of this verdict is Madeleine Smith, charged with poisoning an inconvenient lover in 1857.

"Well," I said, slightly disgusted with my cousin, "since you have the keys to his house please take me there." I do not mention the address because houses tainted by suspicion of murder are harder to sell, but I found the surrounding architecture, gardens and parks pleasanter than many pleasant parts of London, because less grandiose. This did not prepare me for the interior.

The only part of John Tunnock's diaries I have read mentions a robbery that deprived his home of expensive bric-a-brac. I doubt if I could have faced it before that robbery. The clutter of dark mahogany furniture with dark, slightly threadbare upholstery, dark oil paintings in thick gilt frames, heavily ticking pendulum clocks, glass-fronted

book cases full of bound sermons seemed pressing in to crush me.
The day was overcast. We switched on electric lights with frosted
glass shades that had been converted from ancient gas fittings. Over
tables in the main rooms were chandeliers that could be raised or
lowered by adjusting a central brass cone-shaped counterweight.
The lavatory was the biggest surprize. I had expected Victorian
plumbing to be primitive, but here it was palatial, complex and
gloomy in a way recalling Edgar Allan Poe. The vast bath was housed
in a panelled chest ending in something like a sentry box with its
own little vaulted ceiling. It had a dozen big brass taps, each with a
label giving temperature, angle and force of a different spray. Their
position suggested a servant was needed to turn them, a detail that
struck me as weirder than the death on the staircase outside. The
water was heated by gas burners under a tank in a wardrobe-like
cupboard lined with what must have been asbestos. A smaller
wardrobe-like structure in the living room had no visible doors but
something like a glass porthole at eye level. Mr Gillies said this was
the house's most modern article, being a 1938 television set
manufactured by John Logie Baird's company. It did not work of
course. There was no other television set, no telephone or record
player. There was an upright piano with an unusually thick case: a
pianola or (as they say in the States) a player piano operated by rolls
of perforated card. A player could work it in person using pedals
and stops, or switch on an electric motor to play it automatically. A
stand like a huge wine rack held about three hundred rolls of work
by composers from Bach to Gershwin, as I could see from labelled
disks at the roll ends. There was also a radio in a two-foot-square
cubical wooden case.

Despite my dislike of the place I saw it was a better example
of nineteenth century interior decor than many in well-endowed
museums. I considered offering it to Glasgow District Council to be
maintained as a small local history museum, but Mr Gillies told me a
similar house, more representative since not as opulent, was on show
in a tenement near Sauchiehall Street, so Glasgow's museum service
would not want another. After careful consultation I decided to sell
through Christie's the Burne-Jones window and two dull landscapes I

was told belonged to the Barbizon School. Through Sotheby's I sold the most valuable furniture, including the Baird television set, the pianola with its rolls, and even the Edgar Allan Poe shower-bath. Through a local firm, West End Auctions, I sold everything else. Mrs Manning, owner of the firm, tells me the portraits of clergy and volumes of sermons will decorate a public house in Saltcoats called *The Auld Kirk*, in a building that was once indeed a Church of Scotland. These transactions will finally raise more cash than the million I expect for Tunnock's empty eight-room-and-kitchen home.

John Tunnock's papers were now all that remained to embarrass me. After old letters, receipts and bills were destroyed I had a mass of typescript and a large desktop notebook two-thirds full of undated entries in tiny, clear, almost sinisterly childish calligraphy. It would have been heartless to discard all that as waste paper, but what else could I do? The typed pages were historical novels, which I detest. I also dislike reading diaries, even those written for publication, and a sample of John's miserable confessions made me think them unpublishable – I now know this idea is old-fashioned and out of date. On Mr Gillies's advice I put the lot in a suitcase and left it at the University of Glasgow's Scottish Literature office, with a letter offering a donation to the department of a few hundred pounds in return for an honest assessment of the contents. Did anything in these papers deserve publication? I asked. Would a publisher consider them a commercial proposition if I paid for the printing? Or would Glasgow University, which in 1962 had awarded John an honours degree in the Humanities, find room for these papers in its archives?

A fortnight later the head of the department, Alan Riach, sent a courteous and helpful reply. He thought the historical fictions well written and entertaining, but the one set in classical Greece lacked chapters connecting start and finish, the one set in Renaissance Italy was three loosely linked dialogues with neither beginning nor end, and the fictional biography of the Victorian clergyman had already been novelized by Aubrey Menen in a 1972 Penguin paperback called *The Abode of Love*. No reputable firm would undertake to publish such work by an author who was unknown, Scottish and dead. For the same reason no public archive would

want them. If university and national libraries became repositories
of unpublished fiction by unknown authors they would soon have no room for anything else. The notebook diary and notes for an autobiography were another matter. Their account of a life that had ended violently might interest a publishing house, especially if I paid part of the production costs and the book was introduced and edited by a known author. With my permission he would show the papers to Alasdair Gray, a writer who lived locally and, with some success, had edited and published the papers of a Glasgow public health officer.

It was thus that I met Mr Gray whose response to all John's papers was enthusiastic. The diary and personal notes and historic fictions should be published together (Gray said) thus casting light on what he saw as a major theme, men in love. Tunnock, like many of his generation, was an old-fashioned Socialist and had at first planned the novels as a trilogy with a name suggesting the Marxist theory of surplus value, but had then changed it to something more frivolous. A better, more eye-catching and more accurate title would be *Men in Love* for it would connect Tunnock's love life with those of his heroes, and balance them. The patriarchs of Classical Greece, Renaissance Italy and Victorian England loved their idea of truth or beauty or God more than any woman, but the women in Tunnock's love-life had certainly ruled *him*.
"If you can call it a love life!" I said grimly, "I have known many men, but none like John Tunnock. If you manage to get his diary published along with the rest I insist the book be called *John Tunnock.*"

Mr Gray, not very graciously, seemed to accept this but said the final choice of title would probably be decided by the eventual publisher's marketing department. He said that if I paid for the printing out of John's estate the book, edited as he envisaged, would certainly be distributed by Bloomsbury Publishing of London, a highly successful firm that had done well out of J. K. Rowling's Harry Potter books. Mr Gray (who clearly has a high opinion of his own talents) said he would design and provide the book with decorative illustrations, "in colour, if the money stretches so far". He indignantly refused my offer of payment for his editorial work because, "It is a privilege to be midwife to so unique a volume." John Tunnock would never be a popular success (he said) but he would "claw back" something from Bloomsbury in royalties if I signed a paper granting him possession of copyright. This I was pleased to do.

He differed from Alan Riach, however, by insisting that I write the introduction, because his reputation as an occasional writer of fiction often led critics to doubt the value of his serious work. But Lady Sim-Jaegar (he gallantly declared) was both known in United States business circles and remembered in Britain as the glamorous wife of a popular American ambassador. My introduction would publicize the book better than anything by him if I described my discovery of the material and his editorial method: he would use the undated diary entries to introduce and connect the fictions, thus annoying purists but making the book more entertaining. He had also found a verse among the papers that would give the book a cheerful end, and as editor, he would provide notes explaining details that some readers might find puzzling.

"Footnotes or endnotes?" I asked. He said, "Marginal notes. I like widening my readers' range of expectations."

I saw no sense in that but let it go.

Writing this introduction has so saturated me in what seems a bygone era (though actually modern Scotland) that I am tempted to say that I now lay down my pen, satisfied in having done all I can for my unfortunate cousin's memory. But I dictate these words to a secretary sitting with her wireless-enabled laptop on the sunny patio of my Los Angeles home. It only remains to add that the publishing director of Bloomsbury, or perhaps her marketing department, insists for commercial reasons that the book be called *Old Men in Love*, which is certainly more accurate than Alasdair Gray's original idea. I will now do my best to forget John Tunnock while hoping that Mr Gray manages to "claw back" more money from the publication than he has led me to believe possible.

Beverly Hills, California
28 July 2007

One
Tunnock's Diary
2001

The time is now three in the morning after the most bemusing hours of my life. They started yesterday when I arose and as usual on days when cleaners come, had to start by tidying away signs of female presence scattered over my floors from living room to lavatory: discarded garments, cosmetic tools, photographic magazines about the sex lives of beautiful rich people. The women I once knew kept a tidy house – why are young things who stay here different? I begin by showing them cupboards, drawers and the newspaper rack but when I suggest they tidy things into them they snort and ignore me. They love their messes like cats that have not been housetrained so claim a new territory by pissing over it. When serving breakfast to Niki yesterday I told her so. Her reaction was violent and I came near to apologising for my honesty. Our parting was acrimonious. Worked all day at University Library on Athenian economics, left late, called in at Tennants. It was buzzing with the communal elation that usually follows Scottish football victories, though the TV kept showing what seemed a Hollywood disaster movie. I joined the Mastermind who told me suicidal terrorists had made two passenger planes crash into the World Trade Center, totally destroying it and killing hundreds. He thought the elation in Tennants resembled the delight of mobs in Berlin, Paris and London who in 1914 cheered the start of the first great modern war – they knew the world would now change unpredictably, which gave them a brief illusion of freedom. I disagreed. The Twin Towers have been the main financial house of an Empire State whose bankers and brokers (according to New York writer Tom Wolfe), think themselves masters of the universe although they do nothing but enrich themselves by manipulating international money markets. They do not care what this does to other nations, but know they control them, and such capitalists should

Mastermind is Tunnock's invariable nickname for Francis Lambert, who in the 1970s achieved some fame through BBC television by doing well on a general knowledge quiz show called *Mastermind*.

not *be perfectly safe. The destroyers of the Trade Center must have thought like John Brown and the blacks who attacked the United States armoury in Virginia and those who in 1916 flew the Irish Republic flag above the central Dublin Post Office: they knew they would die but thought their example would change history in a way years of appealing for justice had failed to change it. Mastermind is an old-fashioned Tory since his father was a landowning squire in the north of England. After a thoughtful silence he said the atrocity would not even slightly damage Capitalism, which is fully insured against the worst conceivable losses of life and property. The calamity was an act of guerrilla warfare by folk without an army and air force to fight the U.S.A. – folk from several lands where the U.S.A. have propped dictatorships, usually to let the U.S.A. buy natural products cheaply – Iran had been one before the recent war. This propping had been done secretly with British assistance, so most Americans and Britains knew nothing of it. If President Bush reacts by declaring war on much poorer nations another Vietnam situation will arize, which the terrorists probably want. Bush's richest supporters will want that too, as their wealth gathers interest from an expanding war economy. It will also excuse them for seizing dictatorial powers unthinkable in peace. "Interesting times," concluded Mastermind, having turned my temporary elation into worry for the future.*

I came home and was pleasantly surprized at first, thinking Niki had recovered from her huff and tidied the house more thoroughly than I had ever seen it since she moved in. Several minutes passed before I saw she has finally moved out, helped by a systematic partner or partners who own or have hired a van. They have removed enough from this house to equip another, also many small, valuable ornaments. I wandered from room to room in a kind of daze, wondering what to tell the police. My fondness for young things could lead to difficulties if Niki is under the age of consent. What is the age of consent? (Memo: find out.) Such thoughts, troublesome at first, are now eased by blissful relief not caused by sipping this brandy the robbers failed to discover under the pianola lid.

Yes, my life suddenly feels wonderfully simplified by the disappearance of Niki and familiar objects I now realize I never liked. The silver-framed photographs were especially depressing.

Inside them our family history flowed through three misleadingly respectable generations: the grandparents I never knew, then my mother and aunts in their younger days, finally me standing between Nell and Nan clutching my Ph.D. scroll, capped and gowned, plump and po-faced like an alarm clock between two candlesticks. My aunts said that was the proudest moment of their lives but I hate being reminded of my appearance. I hope Niki and partners get good money for those frames. The rising crescendo of our quarrels over the last month has been exhausting. Yvonne, equally messy, heralded her departure in the same way. I keep forgetting how each unexpected disappearance restores me to the hopeful freedom I first enjoyed after Aunt Nan's funeral. Once more I am a man again. In fact more than a man – a writer! Remember the words of Vasari that inspired that bashful university student, poor wee John Tunnock: Nature has created many men who are small and insignificant in appearance but who are endowed with spirits so full of greatness and hearts of such boundless courage that they have no peace until they undertake difficult and almost impossible tasks and bring them to completion, to the astonishment of those who witness them. The years of school teaching and running a home for elderly invalids only allowed time to collect raw materials for my book. Since Nan died I have sketched out many adequate chapters but completed none. Niki, Yvonne etcetera. were wildly distracting but necessary, for without the sexual pleasure they gave I could not convincingly describe passionate people. True, I found passion late in life, but so did Fra Filippo Lippi, also orphaned at an early age. He too was in his forties when he helped a young thing escape from a nunnery and began his great paintings in Prato Cathedral. But at last, thank God, I am exiled from fleshly distractions. Silence, exile and cunning will now let me reveal, here in Glasgow, the European Erdgeist to the world in a vision of three unique civilizations. It will be called WHO PAID FOR ALL THIS? and when that Great Book Booms, none other will be left upstanding. Tomorrow, Tunnock, to work!

This sentence introduces Brunelleschi in Vasari's *The Lives of the Great Artists* translated by Julia and Peter Bondanella in the Oxford World's Classics edition.

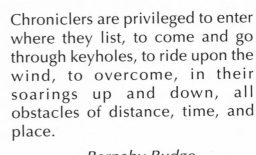

Chroniclers are privileged to enter where they list, to come and go through keyholes, to ride upon the wind, to overcome, in their soarings up and down, all obstacles of distance, time, and place.

– *Barnaby Rudge*
by Charles Dickens

THE GADFLY

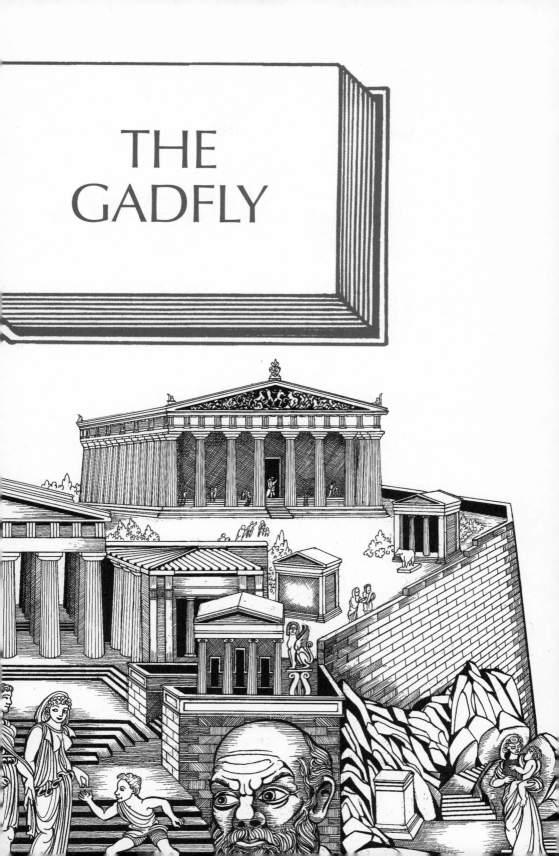

2: CITIZENS

HUNGER AND DREAD MAKE SLEEP DIFFICULT within this seaside city but no lamps are lit at night: they would burn oil that is part of a precious, dwindling food supply. Above and around it myriads of lights glitter from the height of the Milky Way down to the dark fields outside the city walls, but the vast random constellations differ from evenly spaced lower lights which also flicker more, being watchfires of a besieging army.

By a hilltop fire a soldier huddles within easy reach of his short sword, round shield and heap of fuel. He dozes when the flames are high, wakens cold when they sink and, yawning, feeds the fire with sticks and handfuls of dry goat dung. He sometimes glances at a comrade standing on a low limestone ridge behind him. Both soldiers verge on middle age but the first seems younger, being thinner with a trim beard. His face, melancholy in repose, has fine lines suggesting many different expressions, for it is an actor's face. The other soldier – short, pot-bellied, bushy bearded – is almost menacingly ugly, his partly flattened nose having the tip tilted like the snout of a small pig. With wide-open mouth and eyes whose fixity suggests total absence of mind he faces east to where a dark sea reflects the lowest stars.

Two more soldiers arrive on the ridge, the foremost carrying a bundle of branches. Jumping down beside the fire he drops them on the fuel heap and in a voice that sounds aimed at

many people declares, "While scavenging yonder I bumped
into one of our gallant Ionian allies. Like the rest of his nation
he's a bit of an idiot – you *are* an idiot aren't you?" he calls to
his companion who stands staring curiously at the ugly soldier.
"Yes, a bit of an idiot but a thoroughly decent chap, also a
farmer like me when he's at home. He gave me a nip from his
flask so I asked him back here for a bite and a heat."
"He's barefoot without a cloak," says the Ionian, still staring
at the ugly soldier, "and not even shivering."
"O yes he's tough! And given to fits like that, but only when
there's nothing else to do. How long this time?"
The question is for the seated soldier who mutters "Since the
moon went down."
"Is he religious?" asks the Ionian.
"Not more than the rest of us. Some folk say a lot less."
"Because he looks…you know…a bit like the priestess on the
tripod when the god goes into her."
"It isn't a god *he's* got inside him. It's a demon!"
"What kind?"
"A little one that gives him advice."
The Ionian cups a hand behind his ear, brings it close to the
ugly soldier's chest and says slyly, "It isn't doing that now. I
can't hear a word."
"Leave him alone – it's his way of thinking!" cries the seated
soldier impatiently.

The Ionian climbs down beside the farmer who, having
warmed his hands at the fire, rummages in a pile of satchels
under the ridge. Pulling out a string of onions and grey lump
of cheese he lays them on a flat-topped boulder, contemplates
them gloomily, draws his sword and hacks the lump into
smaller lumps. With a gesture inviting the Ionian to do the
same he wrenches off and bites an onion and crams cheese
into his mouth. They stand side by side for a while, stolidly
chewing and looking downhill across lower watchfires to the
dim walls of the lightless city. Perhaps exasperated by a coarse
mouthful the farmer swallows it and growls, "Why doesn't
that stupid little state surrender?"

"Why don't we pack up and go home?" says the seated soldier.
"You tell him," the farmer orders the Ionian who slowly clears
his mouth then says, "I don't go home because my government
ordered me here. It sent me because it's afraid of your
government."

"If that's your attitude hand over that flask," says the farmer
grumpily. The Ionian brings a bulging goatskin from under
his cloak. Seizing it by the neck the farmer loosens a cord
there, tilts his head back, squirts a jet of wine into his mouth
and swallows. Ignoring a hand the Ionian has stretched out
for the flask he points the neck at him and declares, "You
have just said a very ignorant thing. You referred to *my*
government. I don't have a government. I *am* the government
your government is afraid of – I and all the free citizens of
Athens. That city refused to pay us the tribute we need to
defend Greek civilization. We discussed this defiance
thoroughly and voted for war. That is why your government
sent you and your kind to help the free men of Athens attack
Potidia."

"I voted against attacking," says the seated soldier.
"So did he I believe," says the farmer, indicating the ugly soldier
with his thumb, "but you're democrats so you obey the will of
the majority, otherwise the Athenian state would fall apart."
He drinks again from the flask then murmurs to himself, "Good
stuff," still ignoring the outstretched hand of the Ionian who
says, after a moment, "I heard that Pericles governs Athens."
"Nonsense! He's rich enough to be useful so we elect him to
do some important jobs and sometimes take his advice. We
can get rid of him any time we like."

"He's been head of state for thirty years," says the seated soldier.
"He's not a tyrant! He's not even popular! He's a pompous,
cold-hearted selfish snob who loves nobody but himself and
a foreign prostitute! But he's the best man for the job because
he knows what we want and gives it to us."

"If you ever visit Athens," the seated soldier tells the Ionian
pleasantly, "you will find everyone with prominent jobs are
like those in any other Greek city – they are rich."

"Blethers!" says the farmer hotly. "The rich have more time

than the rest of us to do public work, but at every parliamentary session our president is picked from the electoral rolls by lot, so ANY Athenian citizen has a chance at being president. If the Alopeky District wasn't here on military duty, tomorrow *I* could be president of Athens, or that stonemason, or a comic showman like you. Why are you grousing? Do you hate our political constitution? Do you want to live under another?"

"No," says the seated soldier.

In a following silence the farmer sees his companions watching the ugly soldier. Annoyed by the loss of their attention he says roughly, "Ignore him. He can stand like that for hours. He carves marble into statues and the twiddly bits on top of columns. You need toughness for that."

He swigs from the bottle again and mutters, "Not very good statues. Too stiff and mathematical. Nothing at all when compared with the best modern stuff. The great statue of Athena on the Parthenon, seventy feet high. Sailing toward the city on a clear day you see the head in the golden helmet, the shining point of her spear come up over the horizon before you see anything else, and when you stand at her feet and look up…she breathes! No other nation in the world has a goddess like her."

The farmer may be exaggerating the height of Athena's statue by Phidias. A popular website says it was only 12 metres or 38 feet high.

Finding himself still ignored he taps the Ionian's shoulder with the flask's neck and says pleasantly, "Listen Ionian, I am going to cheer you up. I will prove to you. By dialectics. That your father. Is. A dog."

The seated soldier sighs impatiently. The Ionian stares. The farmer ties the flask to his belt saying, "You're a farmer like me so you have dogs at home, right?"

The Ionian nods.

"Think of one. One that's had puppies but isn't a bitch, right? Is that dog a father?"

The Ionian nods.

"Is that dog yours?"

"I said so."

"Then that dog…must be your father!"

The farmer chuckles but the Ionian is not cheered up.

"Quackery," says the seated soldier, throwing a branch on the fire. The farmer glares at him, growls, "What did you say, grocer-boy?"

"Quack-quack-quackery."

"You are wrong. It is a dialectical demonstration of a misconstrued syllogism. I've learned from experts," says the farmer with dignity, then asks the Ionian, "Know what an expert is?"

After a pause the Ionian says, "Someone who advizes a government?"

"Correct! But all the free citizens are the government of Athens so we have hundreds of experts! Hundreds and hundreds attracted by our wealth from all over Greece – experts in rhetoric, semantics, politics, history, physics, land measurement, sword fighting, wrestling and interpretation of dreams. They teach the rich for so much a lecture, but on warm evenings poor men like me…well, I'm quite prosperous really…on warm evenings clever men like me go to the marketplace where a lot of experts stand on the pavement lecturing *each other*! Wise men with a good new idea usually keep it to themselves and rent it out carefully a bit at a time, but *their* ideas seem to breed by being argued over, so if you stand nearby you can pick up all kinds of useful tips."

"That bit about my dog wasn't useful."

"Not to you! Your state is either a tyranny or a plutocracy or a phony democracy where a ruling boss and his gang are elected every year or two, but in Athens even law courts are democratic. Anybody can prosecute anybody they want or defend themselves before a jury. When you're doing that it's very handy knowing how to twist words and do you see something moving and glittering between the first two watchfires there?"

He points downhill. The Ionian peers.

"That," says the farmer, "is an officer on a tour of inspection and he'd better not find you this side of the hill."

"O," says the Ionian and pointing to the flask at the farmer's belt asks, "Can I have back my…?"

The farmer says firmly but kindly, "I'm sorry lad. No."

The Ionian leaves. After a moment the seated soldiers says,
"You stole that wine."
"Can I help it that I am a Greek?" cries the farmer, slapping his chest with his fist, "The blood of the great Odysseus flows in these veins and we know what a scoundrel *he* was. Like a drink?"
"No. Who's the officer?"
"The Darling. Yes, The Darling," says the farmer, looking.

The young man who joins them is so strikingly beautiful that the farmer stares frankly at him and the seated soldier turns away to avoid doing so. Though officers of the Athenian democracy mostly belong to the richer class not many dress to show it. This officer's brilliant tunic and armour show it without inciting mockery because fine clothing suits him and he is popular. A slight lisp and hesitation in speech indicate a conquered stammer which most folk find charming in so masterful a man.
"Cheers," he says, warming his hands over the fire. "Fourth Alopeky Distwict are you?"
"That's right," says the farmer boldly,
"How are you off for wations? Their quantity I mean, not quality."
"*Quantity's* all right. Any news?"
"Weports say they'll soon be eating each other in that little city. Their Spartan fweinds seem to have abandoned them."
"Like a drink?" says the farmer, offering the goatskin.
"Thanks."
The Darling drinks, brushes his lips with a finger, then points and asks, "Why doesn't that man move?"
"He often goes like that when on guard. He is – "
"The stonemason, yes. I know about him. He visits parties given by my uncle's whore."
They watch the figure on the ridge for a while. The Darling says, "That mason is a fweind of Heavenly Weason."
"Is any Athenian NOT a friend of heavenly reason?"
"I'm talking about Anaxagoras, the physics expert. We call him Heavenly Weason because he says the world was formed

by heavenly..." (with an effort he manages to say) "...*reason. And that's why it's weasonable.*"

"Too abstract," says the farmer shaking his head. "If the world is a solid ball like some people say then it must have been punched into shape by something tough. A physics expert! Is he one of those who say the sun and stars are made of the same stuff as the ground?"

"Yes," says The Darling, drinking again.

"That's idiotic! The ground doesn't shine. The stars do."

"What about meteorites?" asks the seated soldier.

"Well, what about them, grocer-boy?"

"My mother gave up the shop years ago," says the other, standing and stretching his arms, "and how do you explain meteorites? Little lumps of white-hot iron that sometimes fall out of the sky, usually at night. The country folk call them falling stars."

The farmer frowns. The Darling and other soldier grin at each other. The farmer suddenly snaps his fingers and says, "Criminal little beetles occasionally say something blasphemous about Almighty God so the Eternal Father uses a little tiny thunderbolt to squash them flat. So be very careful, you comedian!"

The comedian laughs, hugs him and reaches for the flask saying, "Give me a swig of that."

The Darling hands it over, smiling and saying, "No wonder Athens is named after the goddess of wisdom."

"Yes," says the farmer cheerfully. "Not every nation has common citizens as wise as the head of state and his nephew!"

The Darling stops smiling and a moment later says dryly, "I'll leave you now. The sun's coming up."

All three look eastward. Under the brightening sky a tiny line of piercing golden light is widening along the sea-sill. As if talking to a friend the mason says, "Welcome great Apollo, God of Day, Light of Life, Giver of Harvest and Harmony."

These are the first words of the Greek hymn to the sun. The others recite along with him saying "Thank you for overcoming chaos, the dark and cold in your bright chariot. Give truth to your oracles, peace to your shrines, wealth and grandeur, wisdom and victory to Athens, her people and allies for ever. Amen."

The mason stretches his arms, skips to exercize his legs, jumps down from the ridge. Taking the last onion from the rock he removes the withered outer skin, sits down and chews it with appetite. The Darling, having paused to watch this, says jauntily, "I thought you experts believed the sun was a ball of white-hot iwon bigger than Peloponnesia."

The mason looks steadily at the beautiful young man, clears his mouth and says quietly, "When a body gives me warmth and beauty I want to thank him, whatever he's made of."

His shyly teasing tone is flirtatious. The Darling sees the farmer and comedian watching with amused interest. He gestures farewell and strides away.

"Hard luck old chap!" says the farmer, chuckling. "You're too ugly for him."

He reclaims the flask and rummages again in the satchels.

The stonemason finishes eating the onion. The comedian asks, "What did your demon say this time?"

"I'm to sell the stoneyard."

"Give up your business? Why?"

"I don't know. He gives orders, not explanations. He seems to have grown tired of questions that recently fascinated me. What is the essential substance of the universe? Water, as Thales thinks? The fire of Heraclitus? The single solid unchanging globe of Parmenides or the eternal indivisible atoms of our friend Anaxagoras?"

"I prefer the Pythagorean Brotherhood's idea," says the comedian, grinning. "They say numbers make the shape and sound of everything from the earth to the strings of the harp, twing twang twong."

"How do such things influence our conduct?"

"They don't. Only gods do that."

"Not much! Eros, Mars and Dionysus can certainly drive us mad, but they let us act how we want if we respect their shrines and titles like our neighbours do. So if even gods do not teach us to be better men they are as small a part of earthly wisdom – as little earthly use in scientific theories of the universe."

"Priests and poets need gods and experts need theories."

"Yes, as a source of income, but the wisdom of the state – the wisdom that keeps us alive and comfortable – is in the skill of labourers and craftsmen, the abilities of weavers, smiths, sailors, merchants…"

"You need my skills most!" says the farmer. He has placed a loaf like a small boulder on the rock, has hacked it with his sword into three equal parts and is moistening them with the last of the Ionian's wine. The mason nods to him, says, "True. And what unites all people in a healthy state is honesty and mutual trust, things taught by our mothers when we are tiny children, not by priests and experts."

"Perhaps," says the comedian, smiling, " though my mother taught me it was right to cheat customers if they never found out. But why sell the stoneyard if there's more wisdom, more virtue in being an honest tradesman?"

"I don't know," says the mason frowning and picking up his share of the breakfast.

"And how will you live?"

"I don't know."

"Well," says the comedian with a sudden air of great gaiety, "since Pericles introduced payment for parliamentary attendance *and* jury service it isn't hard for an unemployed Athenian to scrounge a living."

The mason twists his mouth as though tasting sourness but again nods agreement.

3: STATE FUNERAL

NATIONS AND SINGLE PEOPLE are only happy when feeling as good as their neighbours or even better. Five centuries before Jesus was born Israel was proud of having the one true God, Egypt of having the oldest history and buildings, Phoenicia the greatest merchant navy, Persia the biggest empire. Though lacking all these things Greece – especially Athenian Greece – had the first people proud of being most modern. Greek historians agreed that everything Grecian except the poetry of Homer and Hesiod had been shared with, or learned from, surrounding nations a century or two earlier, but the Greek states had so improved their governments, laws, town planning, art, medicine, philosophy, athletic games and ships that these were now the best anywhere. But like all other people, tribal or civilized, nomads or settled, ancient or modern, they believed funeral services make the dead less liable to haunt the living. Battles between Greek states were followed by a truce to let each side retrieve their dead and give them decent funerals.

The bodies of those killed in early warfare between the Athenian and Spartan leagues had been returned to their families for private mourning. The Athenian remains would now be publicly entombed in a cemetery beside the cliff of the Acropolis. Each electoral district had brought the bones of its dead in a single big coffin, and these now lay in a row beside an empty coffin representing bodies that had not been recovered. All would be placed in the mausoleum designed by Phidias, sculptor and master of public works, but first a speech must be made. In Athens no priest had more authority than a minister of state. Pericles, the state's chief minister, normally avoided public speaking because many Athenians resented conspicuous men so much that they sometimes voted to banish them for that reason only, but today Pericles had to speak because his political programme was in danger. Anti-war speeches were increasingly heard in the marketplace, in parliament and in the comedies of Aristophanes. If he did not speak now, whoever did would be thought a mouthpiece he was hiding behind, or a politician bidding to replace him.

From the shadow of the mausoleum he saw what seemed all Athens assemble. Like every large Greek gathering outside parliament (which only men attended) it was dividing sexually. On one side were men not abroad on military service, and since many were abroad the wives, daughters and mothers on the other side were a larger crowd. Women could not vote – were supposed to be powerless – but Pericles did not doubt their influence and knew that among them anti-war feelings were strongest. For a moment he envied the leaders of Sparta where mothers were proud of sons who died fighting for their country, ashamed of those defeated in battle. He was relieved to notice the male side being increased by an influx of resident aliens – shipwrights, builders and experts who had found work in Athens since the United National Greek defence fund had been brought there from Delphi. The aliens, like women, could not vote but they certainly supported his war policy. His speech would have to respect every shade of opinion present without verging a fraction from that policy. He sighed, climbed upon a rostrum overlooking the crowd and coffins, then stood patiently until those who saw him fell silent. When silence was complete his firm, even voice reached everyone in his audience without seeming to shout.

"I will start by begging all the gods for help. May potent
Zeus, fertile Ceres, earth-shaking Poseidon – may
harmonious Apollo, lovely Aphrodite, swift Hermes, chaste
Selena – may the wise virgin Athena who names our city
and The Kindly Ones who guard it in their cavern under the
Acropolis – let all these unite to stop me saying anything
false or unsuitable.

"The death of these men we are mourning has deprived
this year of its Spring. They have become like the gods –
great beings we will never see again, but must never forget
while holding them in the greatest honour and respect. But
I cannot praise them without also praising the city that bred
them. This Athens they died defending is unique.

"We call ourselves a democracy because we are not
ruled by a king, or by the rich, or by a political clique elected
every year or two. We rule ourselves, all the free men of
Athens meeting daily or weekly to discuss and vote upon
the business of the state. We make our own laws, gladly
obeying the will of the majority. When a leader must be
elected to do a special piece of business, what counts is
not wealth but ability – nobody with great abilities is denied
power because he is poor. And our private lives are as free
and open as our politics! If our neighbour wants to enjoy
himself in a way that is not our own we do not sneer or
throw him black looks – we are tolerant, and friendly. Our
homes and public buildings are comfortable and beautiful,
but that has not made us soft. Our Empire brings us goods
from all over the world, but that has not made us
extravagant. In civilized living Athens is recognized as the
teacher of the world. Our Spartan enemies are taught to
fight from infancy. They do without all the good things of
life, in order not to be afraid of death. Yet we, who enjoy
every reasonable pleasure, fight just as well as they! We
know that happiness depends on freedom, and freedom
depends on courage. Which is why these men died. Their
death has not made them greater men than you here who

fought and still live. But let their bones remind us that this war must not end before we win it.

"Many grief-stricken folk are understandably angry with me. In arguing for war I voiced the will of the majority, but my voice was most outspoken. We knew then that we would lose sons, brothers, fathers, neighbours, yes! perhaps our own lives. And now it is happening and some have forgotten why we went to war. Let me remind you.

"Fifty years ago the Persian king, having conquered Babylon, Arabia and Egypt, decided to add Europe to his empire, beginning (of course) with Greece. He built a bridge of boats over the Hellespont and crossed it with the biggest army the world has ever seen. Greek states collapsed before that army while his mighty fleet accompanied it along our coasts – every Greek state surrendered to him except Athens. We knew that a great city is not made of houses, streets, temples: it is the people! The Athenian citizens went into their ships and fought back while the Persians in futile rage wrecked our buildings. Whereupon the rest of Greece, starting with Sparta, followed our example, and joined us against the invaders. The Gods also joined us – they were tired of Persian successes. They sent a storm that wrecked the enemy fleet. Asia retreated.

"It retreated, but only a strong Greek alliance can stop it returning. Every Greek state once knew that. Only one state is fit to lead that alliance: ours. Sparta did not want the job. The military class who rule it are too busy holding down their serfs to lead the united Greek nations. So the defence of Greece was handed to Athens by every Greek state, whether democratic or not. Ship-owning cities put their vessels under our command. Those without ships, or who do not want the trouble of maintaining a ship, pay us taxes to defend them – except one or two who take us so much for granted that they want us to defend them for nothing! Which is cowardly and unjust. They complain because we use part of the defence

fund to rebuild Athens better than it was before the Persians
demolished it. Yes, people who kept their own cities intact by surrendering to barbarians are jealous of our magnificence. Are they right to be jealous? These dead men did not think so.

"To those who are not convinced I will put the argument differently. You rightly think our wartime sufferings may grow greater and still not bring us victory. Why should half of Greek civilization fight the other half for the right to tax some coastal cities? Let these cities join the Spartan alliance if they wish! Make peace! But if these small cities are allowed to leave our Empire you can be sure that three or four bigger ones will also abandon us. Making peace now will not end this war, it will lead to a bigger war on a larger front, a war we would lose. Making peace now means giving up our Empire. Some people, in a mood of political apathy or sudden panic, think this a fine and noble thing to do. But it is now impossible to give up our Empire. It may have been wrong to establish it. It would be suicide to let it go. We have roused too much hatred in the states we are – "(he pondered for a moment) " – protecting. Which is also why these men died.

"It remains for me to say what the wise among you already know: we need not dread the warfare ahead while we, the free citizens, stay brave, cautious and united. Look at the hills surrounding us on three sides – see those rocky summits and well-farmed slopes planted with vines, olives and fig trees. Yes, they send our market delicious produce. But if Spartan armies were camped on every one of these hills our democracy could not be defeated, even if they camped there for years. Impregnable walls now join Athens to the harbour and the ships bringing us everything necessary to life and enjoyment. Athens still rules the sea as we did when ours was the solitary state that, with the help of the gods, saved European civilization from Asiatic barbarism. The courage and unity of our fathers made that victory. These dead men are their worthy sons. Let us entomb them with all the honours they deserve."

Applause was not part of the funeral rite but a deep murmur in the crowd showed the speech was widely approved. As he left the rostrum young women pressed forward to clasp his hands, two with flowery wreaths they tried to put on his head. With upraised hands he prevented that, pointing to coffins they should adorn instead.

"A noble speech, Pericles!" shouted a stern voice from a group of older women, relatives of a famous dead patriot. "You deserve crowns of sweet-smelling flowers! My brother fought for Athenian freedom against the Persians and Phoenicians! You have led our brave men to destroy a Greek city that was recently our ally, and gained nothing for Athens but the corpses of our men and the hatred of fellow Greeks!" "Then why add perfumes to a grey old head Elpenice?" he asked sadly, then hurried into the male crowd at its thickest.

4: DOMESTIC INTERIOR

SOCRATES, NO LONGER SOLDIER or mason, sat at home mending a sandal. Being skilled with edged tools he neatly sliced off the frayed end of a strap and cut threads binding it to the buckle. With an awl he pierced a line of holes in the strap's clean new edge and prepared to stitch on the buckle, using a bone needle and strong thread from his wife's sewing box. He knew the buckle should be both stitched and knotted to the strap, but how tie the knots? The other sandal would show. Bending to remove it from his foot he came face to face with a small boy playing under the table. The boy stared at him solemnly, a clay model of a little man in one hand, a model of a ship in the other.

"Boo," said Socrates.

He placed the whole sandal on the table beside the other and studied the knots round its buckle, sighing slightly because they were intricate and because free Athenian males were not used to sewing. His wife, suckling their youngest child across the table from him, had been silent all day. He knew why she was angry, had not broken the silence between them because it would start an argument he could not win. He hoped to leave the house without argument, perhaps going barefoot, as many thrifty yet respected Athenians did. But that would provoke remarks from friends who thought him henpecked and knew he normally wore sandals. He gripped the needle and started stitching.

"You're going out again," said his wife.

"Yes, Tippy."

"To the gymnasium again."

"Yes, Tippy."

"Where you will chat to a lot of pretty young men."

"I talk to any who will listen Tippy, but beauty adds zest to conversations."

"And from the gymnasium you'll go to that prostitute's house and mix with dirty sluts and foreign experts and rich young loungers like The Darling."

"Yes, Tippy."

"Get them to give you money!"

She stood, laid the baby in a cradle and put a bone ring between its gums. He murmured, "Surely the larder isn't empty?"

"It will be tomorrow."

"But market people trust you."

"Yes, because I pay what I owe whenever I manage to screw money out of my famous, feckless, useless husband. O I hate being a poor man's wife. Give me that."

She sat beside him, seized sandal and needle and deftly worked with them, saying through clenched teeth, "I wish our slave had not died."

"She was old, Tippy. You had to do more for her than she could do for us."

"She stopped neighbours seeing that I am the only slave in this house. Their helpful little advices madden me even more than the worry of paying for food. 'Get your husband into jury service! Get him into parliament – the pay is good and all he need do is vote,' they say. 'He's pally with men who could get him a government job,' they say. 'A foreign embassy even. Think of the bribes he would get on top of his pay,' they say. 'He can't do any of those things,' I tell them, 'his demon won't let him. It wants him to do nothing but teach all the time.' 'What does he teach?' they ask. 'I don't know,' I say, 'He doesn't talk to me about it, I'm just a stupid woman.' And I laugh as if our marriage is a wonderful joke. Which it is not. It is not. It is hell. What

do you teach those pretty boys you keep meeting?"
"I teach them not to be so sure of themselves, Tippy."
"They *like* you for that?"
"The reasonable ones do."
"Put on your sandal!" she said, handing it over. "Go to your pretty, reasonable friends. Get money out of them." The child on the floor, upset by her tone of voice, made a mewing sound and folded its arms comfortingly round her leg.
"Tippy," said Socrates beseechingly.
She looked and saw his face so full of misery and love that, after biting her under lip, her own face took on much the same expression. In a voice mingling tears and laughter she said, "They call you the wisest man in Greece!"
"They know no better, Tippy. I can't teach you anything because you only know facts."
"Yes. Women can never escape from those."
He bent down and buckled on his sandal, telling the boy
quietly, "Please be kinder to your mother than I am."

5: A STATESMAN'S DAY

SOON AFTER DAYBREAK PERICLES came to the Athenian port and for nearly three hours conferred with harbourmasters, dockers and seamen, occasionally scratching notes on a thin wax tablet backed by wood. He then returned to the city, striding swiftly uphill between two great new walls joining the port to the Athenian citadel. The sky was clear and blue, the air warm yet fresh, the big marketplace more than usually busy. He crossed it, entered the council chambers and stood in a corner of the big lobby, glancing over his notes but able to see those who entered or left. Most councillors were as familiar to him as he to them. He steadily ignored knowing looks from many who shared his views and enquiring looks from some who did not, but beckoned to his side one at a time new councillors whose opinions were not exactly known. He talked to them about revenues to be voted for dock maintenance, for equipping warships and for building new ones. Each councillor tried, usually successfully, to hide his elation at being singled out by the nation's greatest statesman. He listened to them as carefully as they to him, giving different reasons for increased expenditure. He told a merchant it was needed to protect trade from barbarians and pirates – an arms manufacturer that it would maintain Athenian military supremacy – a landowner that it would reduce local unemployment – a patriotic farmer that it would spread democracy abroad. Pericles thought all these reasons valid but did not expect others to be so broad-minded. He ended each speech by saying how the expenditure would profit dealers in

timber, metal, sailcloth, cable, earthenware and food. All
councillors were chosen from the electorate by lot so only one of his hearers belonged (like Pericles) to The Few who owned big estates. The rest were from The Many, but all Athenians profited by some commodity the navy needed and his final appeal to the profit motive clinched every previous argument. By its fourth utterance Pericles was sick of that argument and almost sick of himself. He regarded Athenian democracy as an example to every nation, present and in future, so regretted that what most united his fellow citizens was greed.

"You're tired! Come and eat with me," said the fourth councillor, pleased to see the great statesman show signs of weakness. He gestured toward the excellent restaurant where councillors dined at public expense and could entertain guests.

"Impossible. Goodbye," said Pericles regretfully. He was hungry but always avoided flaunting his privileges.

It was now afternoon when most Athenians had lunched and were enjoying a siesta. He liked the streets at this time for there were fewer people to greet or stare at him. He ignored starers and answered all greetings with the slightest of nods: a manner that led some to call him Zeus or The Olympian, though he knew he had coarser nicknames. The only people he sometimes spoke to in the streets were sausage sellers – fast food peddlers thought socially inferior because they sold the cheapest parts of animals in a shape supposed to be used as dildos by sexually frustrated women and impotent men. From a market stall he bought two sausages and ate them sitting on a stool in the shadow of an awning.

"Where's your man today?" he asked the sullen woman who sold them.

"On a bender."

"Hm?"

"Getting sloshed out of his tiny wits by drinking with equally rotten mates."

"A pity."

She resumed a silence in which he calmly finished his meal then went to inspect public building work.

Which was no more his business than that of any other Athenian, but by listening to complaints of tradesmen, foremen, artists and architects he left most of them in a happier frame of mind. The walls of the new concert hall had been completed but not the steep pyramidal roof. Though designed by an acoustics expert it was the subject of jokes that amused the workmen but alarmed the architect who said, "A roof like this has never been built before. It may echo worse than the inside of Dionysus' quarry."

"It didn't echo in the model."

"A wood and clay model, no matter how big, cannot accurately predict the acoustics of a vast building."

"Then all you can do is build it," said Pericles. "Remember that you'll be praised if it sounds good, I'll be blamed if it does not."

He walked back to Aspasia's house before sunset, brooding with some satisfaction upon the day's events. As he passed a group drinking outside a tavern one of them bawled, "Pericles! Smy pal Pericles!"

Pericles neither paused nor looked aside. Behind him a stool was knocked over, then came stumbling steps and a yell, "Don't you know me, Pericles? Have you no word for your pal the good old sau-sau-sausager? Sausagist? Sausalogistical expert?"

Pericles resisted an urge to walk faster. After a few more maudlin appeals the drunkard behind lost his temper and yelled "Onionhead! Onionhead! You think you're the Lord God Almighty yet your balding head is shaped exactly like an onion! You damned Olympian onionhead who thinks he runs the whole city! – the whole empire! Nya! Onionhead!"

Excited children and some interested citizens now accompanied the prime minister and his critic. They excited the sausage seller to a greater range of insult.

"Skinflint! Miserly skinflint! *And* the richest man in Athens! He spent so much money buying our votes with plays and processions that his sons had to dress like commoners! No wonder they hated his guts, the damned miser. Listen to me,

Dionysus' quarry was a cavernous space called The Ear of Dionysus, because there was a point where the owner, without being seen, could hear every word spoken by slaves working there.

Onionhead! Stop pretending you're deaf! You're a miserable, miserly, onionheaded skinflint and whoremonger! Yes! Whoremonger! You live with a foreign prostitute and kiss her every morning before going to work, you unmanly queer old queen! You rotten ugly onionheaded miserly skinflint whoremonger!"
The enlarging crowd accompanying them stimulated more insults in a louder voice.
"*And* an atheist! You believe a damned foreign physics expert who says heaven and earth were made by accident! You don't believe in Zeus because you think you *are* Zeus! For nearly thirty years you've tricked us Athenians into letting you do what you like with us but you're a guttering candle now, my friend! We're beginning to see through you – our democracy now has a REAL spokesman in parliament! – Cleon, a man of the people who'll soon sort out you and your foreign pals and foreign experts and that foreign whore of yours, the brothel-keeper! What a hypocrite you are, passing laws against poor bastards and living in a brothel with your mistress! No wonder your two wives divorced you! No wonder your first son was a rogue and the second an idiot and God killed both of them you onionheaded, foreigner-loving, blasphemous, hypocritical, miserly multimillionaire tyrant in commoner's clothing! But you can fool nobody now, you indecent, whoremongering utterly incompetent war leader!"

The sun had set when Pericles reached the yard before Aspasia's house and turned round. The sausage-seller fell as silent as the watchful crowd behind him. Pericles looked thoughtfully at the dark sky overhead. A servant came from the house and stood near him.
"The moon won't rise for another hour," Pericles told the slave. "Fetch a lantern and show this citizen home."
He turned his back upon a great explosion of laughter and applause and entered the house. The sausage-seller also turned and, facing the jeering mob, stroked his beard for a while then raised his hand in the parliamentary gesture requesting permission to speak. An interested silence followed. To the

slave he cried imperiously, "Lead the way, boy!" and advanced upon the crowd with a grotesque expression of lofty disdain and a swagger that caricatured the stride of Pericles. The crowd, laughing, parted to let him through, a few humorists bowing low on each side.

Inside the house Pericles embraced Aspasia and stood a while with closed eyes and his cheek against hers, sighing sometimes because the past quarter hour had been a strain. She murmured, "A bad day?"

"A good one till near the end. Now I will wash. And then enjoy, please, you. And then can we eat and be intelligently entertained? Who comes tonight?"

"Heavenly Reason. And our greatest artist and greatest playwright and wisest man."

"Our wisest man. You mean Socrates."

"That's what the Priestess of Apollo called him."

"I wonder why. He was an honest though not great stone carver. He is certainly a brave soldier and talks amusingly, but he has done nothing else I know toward the welfare of the state."

"You think The Oracle should have mentioned you."

"I do."

"You're jealous of poor old Socrates!" she said, laughing.

"Yes. Thanks for letting me admit to a weakness. You're the only one I can do that with. Anyone else coming?"

"The Golden Mean, High Anxiety and Critias."

"Rich men should not come here," he said wearily. "If The Many find out they'll think The Few are plotting against them. And The Many will be right."

"The Few are worried about Cleon. They say he's now too popular, too powerful."

"I wish they would leave their political worries to me who knows how to handle them. Please come to bed. I'll wash afterwards if you don't mind."

6: AT ASPASIA'S

THE EVENING WAS LESS AGREEABLE than Pericles wished because Alcibiades arrived and insisted on talking politics. Pericles listened with an air of polite attention that his nephew vainly tried to make serious attention. Socrates and Aspasia watched them from across the room. Aspasia said, "You love our Darling?"

"Yes."

"Then maybe you can help him – I can't because he doesn't trust women. Yet he won't grow up properly without the love of someone he admires. He knows it, too. Most of his lovers have been intelligent older men of good character, but he shatters them. After a week or two they grow servile and pathetic. So the only man he can admire is Pericles."

"Who can only love Athens."

"And Heavenly Reason," she suggested.

"And you."

She smiled, smoothing the dress over her breasts and murmuring, "I think so. I wish more women would come here, my girls are too few. I've asked our cleverest men to bring their wives but they won't."

"Housewife talk is mostly limited to household matters."

"Yes, because Athenian husbands treat them like slaves. When a man's friend calls on him, even during a meal, the wife retires to a back room with the children. Which is barbaric. No wonder the men here prefer boys and prostitutes."

"In Sparta," said Socrates thoughtfully, "boys *and* girls are educated by the state."

"Educated to wrestle and fight! So Spartan women grow up as harsh and brutal as their husbands. But in Aolia the women walk the streets in brightly coloured gowns and meet in colleges where they practise every beautiful art from embroidery to poetry and love. Which is why the greatest Greek poet is an Aolian woman."

"Sappho?"

"You disagree?"

Socrates said gently, "Some think highly of Homer."

"A killer's poet. The pains and glories of warfare are the best things he knows. But Sappho sang of the wounds love inflicts and love is the best thing of all."

After a pause Socrates said mournfully, his eyes still on The Darling, "Yes."

"Listen," said Aspasia urgently, "His talks with Pericles always end badly. When that one stops he will go to the wine table to make himself drunk. Can you prevent that?"

"I'll try."

"Let me tell you how to woo him. You must – "

"No no no. If my little demon won't tell me how to do it nobody can."

"The Oracle at Delphi says our war with Sparta will last thirty years," said Alcibiades urgently.

"For once the Oracle may be right."

"You cannot deny that the Persian Empire is in decline."

"Maybe," said Pericles.

"Not maybe. Certainly. A nation that conquers beyond its own natural boundawies must keep spweading and spweading because if it calls a halt it inevitably shwinks. Our people have halted Persian expansion so it's time for a new world empire to awize. And if we twy we can make it – " (he hesitated and with an effort said,) " – *Grreek*. Because Gweek technology and social organization is better than anywhere else and Athens has the biggest fleet in the world!"

"You're quoting one of my speeches."

"Our democwacy can send an iwesistible fighting force against any countwy in the world!"

"Only one country at a time."

"But with all Gweece behind us Athens could wule the Meditewanean – though not while we are fighting each other! A master *strrroke* of policy is needed to weld us into unity under Athenian leadership. A stwoke that must first take in Sicily because . . ."

"My dear nephew," said Pericles placing a hand on the young man's shoulder, "That bright idea is a very old one. I had it when I was your age."

"I wish I had known you when you were worth talking to," said Alcibiades icily, shaking off the hand.

He went to the wine table and lifted a full flagon.

"You mustn't drink that terrible stuff," said a voice at his elbow. Startled he looked sideways and saw nobody at first, being a head taller than the speaker who, with a surprisingly strong grip, took the flagon from Alcibiades' hand, tilted back his head and emptied the wine down his throat in one long continuous swallow.

"Now then," he said, placing the flagon on the table with no sign of breathlessness and the air of someone getting down to business, "You look at yourself a lot in the mirror I hope?"

"Yes I do," said the young man coolly. "Why do you hope that?"

"It should help you to become what you appear to be."

"Which is?"

"Good."

"You believe beauty encouwages virtue?" said Alcibiades incredulously.

"Yes! A soul that doesn't fit its body is as uncomfortable as a foot that doesn't fit its shoe."

"And ugliness?" said Alcibiades, staring at the hairy face with the broken nose.

"Ugliness encourages virtue even more. If we don't cultivate our virtues nobody will talk to us . . . will they?"

Alcibiades smiled and relaxed a little. Socrates raised a forefinger saying, "Listen! Beautiful people envy your beauty, brave men admire your courage, clever folk respect your intelligence. This city dotes on you. Everything you do has become fashionable, from lisping to horse racing. And if you thought you would be like this for the rest of your life you'd kill yourself."

"Yes. I want to be ... *grrreat!*"

"I'm glad. But there are many false kinds of greatness. You must learn to discard those."

"What do they look like?"

"I don't know," said Socrates, smiling and shaking his head. "I'm ignorant, I'm no expert. But you want to enter politics in a big way?"

"Yes."

"And become a statesman like Pericles?"

"*Not* like Pewicles. You know how he wants us to win this war. 'Fight the Spartans when we have to,' he says, 'but do it as seldom as possible. We're wicher than them, so if the war lasts long enough they'll go bankwupt first.' How vewy wise! How abominably mean!"

In another corner of the room three of Athens' richest men were gathered, each having discovered that Pericles would not speak to them. One was Theramines, nicknamed The Golden Mean, being a moderate politician who kept changing his political allegiances on grounds of political principle. Nicius, nicknamed High Anxiety, dealt largely in slaves. He was a cautious, successful general and diplomat whose wealth and political success had not incurred the envy of The Many, who regarded him with genial condescension because he was as full of superstitious fear as an ignorant peasant. Critias, a younger man, had inherited a big estate and was not yet eminent enough to have a nickname. He said, "Think of it! A stinking skin-merchant like Cleon leading the Athenian empire! It could happen."

"He's a free citizen like you and me," said the Golden Mean mildly. "If he won't see reason we should bribe him."

"Bribing a demagogue is like pouring sacks of salt into the sea," said High Anxiety glumly. "Twenty-five years ago The Few could get rid of Cleon through a quiet little street accident –" (he made an upwards stabbing gesture) "– The same thing today would start a revolt. Nobody's property would be safe."

"We're more civilized nowadays," said the Golden Mean

cheerfully.

"The Many are like spoilt children!" said Critias fiercely. "Pericles has given them far too much – full employment! Disabled workmen's compensation! Pensions for widows and public sanatoriums. Nowadays you can't even tell a slave from a freeman by the clothes they wear."

"Sports festivals," said High Anxiety, sighing, "religious festivals with drama and music. I've paid for a lot of that. Prominent men aren't safe if they don't make themselves popular."

"Most social welfare is paid for out of the United Greek Defence Treasury – not from our pockets," the Golden Mean pointed out. They brooded on that for a moment then High Anxiety said, "The refugee camp – have you heard the news from there?" They had not. He told them that two days before some refugees had died of black putrescent swellings in the armpits and groin; Dr Archileos had attended them and had died that morning of the same illness.

"A plague," said the Golden Mean slowly, "could compel us to negotiate peace with Sparta. I doubt if Pericles could survive that. He acts like a god but he's not immortal."

"The fates are tired of him," said High Anxiety, "A sheep on his farm near Megera has given birth to a unicorn – a black ram with a single horn here –" (he touched the centre of his brow) "– instead of two. It was born blind in the early hours of the morning and died six hours later at the height of noon. You see what that means?"

The others smiled and shook their heads.

"It means Athens will be destroyed if it continues to be governed by one man. A well balanced state needs two leaders, one for The Many, another for The Few. Well, The Many have their Cleon. If you speak out for The Few, Theramines, you will get my vote."

"And mine," said Critias.

"You are more suited to that job," the Golden Mean told High Anxiety, "since you read the omen that way. Has Heavenly Reason said anything about the unicorn?"

"Yes. He opened the skull and found the brain was distorted. Instead of two lobes like a walnut it had one that came to a

point, like an egg. He said it was one of those freak births by
which Nature sometimes produces new species. Most distortions
are unhealthy so the brute dies, but when a new shape is useful
to a beast it lives and gives birth to more with that shape. It's
useless arguing with Heavenly Reason of course. He may be
absolutely right, scientifically speaking, but I believe Nature is
governed by Fate so is full of warnings for us. The unicorn was
born on Pericles' farm so is obviously a warning to *him*."

"What are you plotting, my fellow citizens?" asked Aristophanes,
joining them.

"Do you think we'll tell a popular political satirist that? Think
again," said the Golden Mean, smiling.

"Behold!" cried the dramatist, pointing to the couple at the
wine table. "Our Darling is adding philosophy to his empire."

"I hope Socrates doesn't suffer by it," said Critias. "Nobody is
better company – he's amusing as well as wise."

"Socrates *suffer*?" said the comedian chuckling, "He's incapable
of suffering. His demon protects him against attackers from
every quarter of the compass."

Socrates was saying, "So you feel able to advize the
Athenian state?"

"Yes."

"On shipbuilding? Or where to dig a new harbour?"

"Of course not. Shipwrights and surveyors know about those
things. I would advize on the largest political matters – war
and peace."

"So you know the right times to go to war."

"Yes."

"And the right people to fight."

"Yes."

"What do you mean by 'right'?"

"I mean – " said Alcibiades, paused, then sat down, pressing a
finger to his lower lip.

"That's not a hard question," said Socrates helpfully, "What
reasons do we give when we go to war?"

"We say we're wesisting a wicked thweat, or haven't been paid
what we're owed."

"So when you advize people to make war you're talking about justice? A war is *right* when it is *just*?"

"Not...always. Though when it is not just we have to pwetend it is."

"Then you might advize the Athenian people to fight an unjust war?"

"Yes," said Alcibiades boldly, "Because I love my land and her laws and any action which incweases her safety or power will seem wight to me!"

"Well said. And if a friend meant to increase his safety or wealth by killing or robbing a neighbour, what would you say if he asked for advice on the right time to do it?"

"You *know* what I would say," said Alcibiades groaning. "But one citizen is not an entire state. What is bad for the first *can* be good for the second."

"Hum. Tell me, which people do you admire most: those who risk their lives fighting injustice or those who increase their power by unjust fighting?"

"You *know* what I would admire most. Usually. Under normal circumstances."

"But there are political circumstances when you would urge the people you love most to do the thing you admire least?"

"Yes!" said Alcibiades desperately. "Yes, because it is customawy political behaviour."

Socrates, who had been leaning tensely forward in pursuit of the argument, clapped a hand to his brow and staggered back as if from a stunning blow.

"By Zeus I never thought of that! You're right, you know. You argue beautifully. You've really driven me into a corner, Alcibiades. I don't think there's an answer to that one."

His hearer stared at him suspiciously. Socrates said in a very ordinary voice, "So you plan to be one of those customary politicians? The kind that do what most people would do in their position? But didn't you start by saying you wanted to be great?"

Alcibiades rubbed the side of his face ruefully while Socrates watched him keenly, kindly. Aristophanes the comic playwright had been listening to them for some time. With a forefinger he prodded Socrates in the chest saying, "I spy, with my little eye, something beginning with S."

They looked at him enquiringly. He appeared to be slightly drunk which was not the case but enabled him to talk more freely at parties. He said, "Sssseduction. You, Ssssocrates are trying to sssseduce our Darling."

"I'm hoping to make a friend of him."

"No, you're fishing for another disciple. All this man's friends are his disciples, Alcibiades. You must have seen them around the marketplace. There's a fat drunkard who makes money by telling rich folk that the goal of life is happiness, and a thin man in rags who says he's a realist and would rather be dead than happy. There's Chaerephon, a scientific democrat who investigates the guts of beetles and wants total equality of income, and Critias, that mine-owner over there who says only the rich should be allowed to vote. There's even a cobbler who acts as unpaid secretary and writes down their conversations! A very peculiar crew."

"What do you teach them, Socwates?" asked Alcibiades.

"Nothing," he said smiling, "Nothing but what I learned from my mother, Phaenarete, the midwife."

"I don't understand."

"She wasn't a prolific woman. With my father's help she made only one human being – " Socrates slapped his chest "– but she helped a lot of others into the light who would never have opened their eyes without her, and aborted some that weren't wanted. Have you heard of my voice? My demon?"

"Who hasn't?" said Aristophanes.

"It's nothing special," said Socrates, ignoring him, "Everybody has one and it's the best, the truest bit of them, but a lot of folk can't hear their inner voice because of loud *ideas* shoved at them by friends and experts, greedy cliques and governments. Good ideas are a gift from God. He doesn't send me any so I try to rid my friends of ideas that don't fit them. I want to hear your voice, Alcibiades, telling me the fine godly things you really believe. But before I hear that voice you'll have heard it first: inside yourself."

"How do you rid folk of bad ideas?" said Aristophanes. "Do you use a flue-brush?"

"I use dialectics," said Socrates, smiling at him.

Alcibiades stood up and told the comedian, "I'm going to a very different party from this one, but I want to see this ugly little wisest man again. May I, Socwates?"

"Please, yes."

Alcibiades left. The comedian chuckled, helped himself to wine, said admiringly, "You really are a demon. I was trying to spoil your game but I helped you with it. I helped you with it!"

"Have you money to spare, Aristophanes?"

The comedian produced a small leather bag, tossed it up and caught it overhand with a chinking sound.

"Can I have some?" said Socrates humbly. The comedian untied the mouth of the bag and held it out. Socrates removed four silver coins. His friend said, "Take more".

"This is enough. A little at a time from a lot of different people stops them crossing the street to avoid me."

"You'll soon wish you had taken the whole purse because I am going to mock you in a play."

"Why?"

"Because I am sick of clever buggers hanging about the market spouting smart ideas that leave ordinary, sensible people confused."

"I am not a bugger Aristophanes and, as I've just said, I do my best to weed out what you call smart ideas."

"Perhaps, but there are still too many clever buggers around and if I mocked the others they would sue me for libel. You won't. Will you?"

"No."

"Because your demon won't let you!" cried the comedian, laughing.

"That's right," said Socrates sadly.

Seven
Tunnock's Diary
2002

Depressed. I need a chapter describing a performance of The Clouds, but no matter how hard I study that play I cannot get the jokes. It caricatures Socrates as a sly meteorologist enriched by spreading fog through the minds of disciples. Aristophanes, as in all his plays, is satirising part of the democracy – in this case experts who taught fashionable young men the most modern ideas. He is surely attacking a very pernicious idea, like our recent one that Capitalism has abolished Socialism and brought world history to a satisfactory end. He is probably also mocking fashionable jargon, like our own dysfunctional instead of bad, vertically challenged for short, chronologically gifted for old, downsizing for dismissing a lot of workers, outsourcing for employing more poorly paid foreigners, spin doctor for writer of speeches that make lies seem truthful. In another fifty years such speech will sound meaningless along with comedy satirising it, not because folk will be talking more sensibly, but because the spin doctors will have invented a new truth-concealing jargon. And The Clouds was written two and a half thousand years ago! Yet I am sure Brecht or Ibsen COULD have made a funny, cutting, relevant modern version of it.

Remember, Tunnock, you are not a Glaswegian Brecht but a retired schoolmaster with literary ambitions inspired by Plato's Symposium, which has Socrates joking about love with Aristophanes and Alcibiades, and rejecting all pretence to wisdom, preferring "right opinion", which he describes as a referee between wisdom and ignorance. Scottish Enlightenment philosophers called it common sense. Socrates was therefore a sceptic like Diogenes, Voltaire, Hume, Nietzsche, not a system-builder like Plato, Aquinas, Descartes, Kant. And he defended

common sense with uncommon courage. After the Shining Sands
sea battle a huge parliamentary majority voted for the mass execution of sea captains who had not reclaimed the bodies of the dead. Socrates was president that day and Xenophon writes that he declared the vote illegal under Athenian law, which said everyone accused of a crime should be tried for it separately. Socrates ruled that a parliamentary majority, no matter how great, must not break its own laws. Courage was needed for that. Alas, next day the lot made a coward president who legalized the mass executions. Thucydides writes that Socrates, after the majority voted to invade Sicily, went through the streets shouting that this would lead to disaster. It did. Like Aristophanes he was of the anti-war minority, but strongly opposed majority decisions because democracy dies without that opposition.

Yet Plato's later dialogues have Socrates advocating government by a clique of celibate academics who employ military police to manage productive people, rewarding the chief policemen by letting them rape who they like – an adolescent fantasy. And Aristophanes dramatized him as a money-grubbing obscurantist homosexual who sits on a rooftop to seem nearer heaven until an enraged pupil burns his house down. Was the play a flop because Athenians disliked the jokes? Or because Socrates went to every performance and stood quietly in the audience, showing the difference between himself and his caricature on stage? Or is Nietzsche right in saying Socrates started the decay of noble Athenian thinking by making men doubt their manliest instincts?

I cannot solve these problems, nor can I condemn to obscurity chapters on which I have worked so hard. Having given a copy of them to the Mastermind I have posted another to Chapman, hoping Joy Hendry will print one or two.

Late afternoon saw from behind, outside Kirklee corner shop, young thing inadequately dressed for cold winter weather. Short bright purple hair twisted into spikes like sea urchin's. Naked zone round waist tattooed with scorpion holding flower. Tight

Chapman: A Scottish literary magazine founded in 1970 by Walter Perrie but edited since 1976 by Joy Hendry.

wee denim jacket above nude zone, broad belt of square metal studs under it, belt holding up denim skirt with frayed hem, not much wider than belt. Net stockings, high-heeled sandals, not plump anywhere. Repulsive. Dislike thin lost pathetic girls, however tartily dressed.

Entered shop, bought milk bread biscuits Sunday Herald then lingered in the warmth. Brooded over magazine display. Every cover seems designed by the same agency using the same women with perfect figures and complexions. They wear less on male pornography mags, more on female fashion and scandal mags, those on motorcycle and computer covers are irrelevant to contents, yet still catch the eye shouting sex sex sex sex sex. The big Byres Road newsagents Barrett's has some unsexy covers, but The Economist, Scottish Field, House and Garden are hardly visible among shelves of glamorous repetitive women-baited cover photos – always photos, perhaps because art schools no longer teach drawing and painting. And nearly every cover lists an article with sex in the title: "Twenty Ways to Dress Sexy for the Under Fifties!", "Are Beattie and Blanko Still Having it Off?", "The Men Who Make Me Come, by Gwendoline", "Sixty Celebs Tell You Their Dirtiest Bedroom Secrets".

Had forgotten the girl outside shop when, leaving, saw her from in front. A fierce accusing scowl showed she was no helpless waif. It halted me, dazed and breathless. A moment passed before she noticed me, said, "Who do you think you're staring at?"

I muttered, "A good looking lassie."

"I cannae say the same about you."

"Of course not, I'm an old man."

"A fat wee ugly old man."

"But harmless," I pointed out.

"So what?"

I said she seemed to have waited a long time for someone, if they didn't turn up she could come to my house nearby for a heat and something to eat and drink.

"That isnae all you want to give me," she sneered. I said anything else she got was for her to say, and gave her a card

with my address. She asked why my name was not on it and I said, "No name, no pack drill ".

She looked across the street, then behind her, then sucked in her purple-stained under lip, then said, "Can I bring a friend?" "Not if he's a man," I said firmly. She said bitterly, "Don't worry, he won't be."

"See you later perhaps," I said and skipped briskly home, my blood buzzing. At such times, thank God, a glorious excitement fills me that no memory of past disappointments can spoil.

Upstairs I turned on the gas fire, regretting that since the city went smokeless in 1969 I could not build in the grate a blazing heap of coals. I made a cosier space inside the room by pulling the sofa up to the hearth rug, placing the armchairs at each end and, on the coffee table between, the three tier cake-stand with plates of Abernethy biscuits, chocolate biscuits and strawberry tartlets. On the sideboard I laid out glasses, brandy decanter, open bottle of red wine, then took precaution of locking other wines and spirits in bathroom geyser cupboard, leaving one bottle of red in kitchen. I put a ragtime roll on the pianola, sat down and waited. And waited. And waited. Then fell asleep.

I was wakened by doorbell shortly after pub closing time, jumped up, switched on pianola, rushed to open door. A troop of girls marched in, led by a bulky older one in a military khaki overcoat, my wee urchin-head coming last. They stood in the lobby looking around as if I was not there, but followed me upstairs after hanging coats on hall stand. I was not alarmed. There were only four and I always feel safe with women. Men sometimes punch each other for no good reason but petty theft is my worst experience of women. They wanted wine. I served it and sat sipping brandy, the commander of the troop beside me, the rest as far away as possible and whispering to each other while beasting into the biscuits. The commander said, "Have you nothing modern?"

I deduced she was speaking of the music and said, "That's Scott Joplin, he's modern."

She said, "You don't know what modern is. Have you no more booze?"

"Some," I said and went down to the kitchen, she following. I

No name, no pack drill is British Army slang suggesting namelessness ensures freedom. Pack drill is punishment any senior officer can impose on a soldier of lower rank, but only if he knows the soldier's name, rank and number.

was glad only one other bottle was visible. As I uncorked it she said, "What do you want Is for?"

"Is?" I said, puzzled. I know that young folk sending text messages on mobile phones shorten their names to one syllable, but was confused by such savage brevity.

"That pal of mine you picked up."

"That is none of your business," I said.

She said, "Things will go easier if you come clean. Do you want her to tie you up and spank you?"

"Tut tut," I said, "No no."

"Do you want to do it to her?"

"Certainly not."

"So what do you want?"

I lost my temper and shouted that I wanted pleasant female company and whatever that naturally led to, which (I repeated) was none of her business! None at all! She frowned, nodded thoughtfully and said "You shouldnae be dealing with Is. You should deal with me."

I stared at her and she stared expressionless back. Her face was freckled, without make-up, not glamorous, not ugly, not exactly plain. She wore a leather jacket and baggy jeans with cuffs turned up to show laced-up, thick-soled boots. I said coarsely, "Sorry hen, you're no my type."

"You don't know that."

Her impudence was not surprizing. All women think they know me better than I do. I groaned, shoved the bottle into her hands, rushed back to the living room where the three others sat giggling and drinking the last of the brandy. I changed the ragtime roll for the first Wagner that came to hand, sat down and, pedalling furiously, played the overture to The Meistersingers as loud and fast as possible. Someone shouted, "So you want rid of us?"

"Yes," I said, standing up. They had finished the wine and still sat round the fire, the three youngest staring at their boss who, without moving, said slowly, "I think you owe Is more than biscuits and three swallies of booze."

"You mean money," I said, "Here's what's on me, there's no more in the house."

I dropped my wallet open on the coffee table so they saw the notes inside, then chucked coins from my pockets on top. Isabel and the other two stared at me, then at their boss, then at the money. One (not Isabel) stretched a hand toward it. The boss said, "Leave it. Come on yous, we're going."

She stood up and led them out. I hurried before them to open the front door. The boss took longer to put her coat on and left last, saying as she passed me, "You havnae heard the end of this."

I lost my temper, thrust my face close to hers and with what felt like a thoroughly evil grin whispered, "If that's a threat, I'm no feart."

We stared at each other for a moment then I slammed the door on her.

And went upstairs weary to bed. Why did I say that last thing to her in the voice of a tough Blackhill schoolboy? I understand myself as little as the young things I pick up. I'm sure life is easier for Italians, or was before the Counter Reformation.

This morning received letter from Joy Hendry saying she will print a special edition of Chapman with all my first chapters of Who Paid for All This? *as a work-in-progress, if I give her a prologue explaining and outlining the whole book. Very encouraging. I will tackle it at once, giving it an epigraph from my favourite novel.*

Blackhill: a Glasgow housing scheme built in the mid 1930s, known as a Slum Clearance Scheme because folk from the poorest areas of central Glasgow were put into it. The school where Tunnock had worked was there. The scheme was notorious for its high level of crime so was mostly demolished in the 1970s and given another name.

8: PROLOGUE TO HISTORICAL TRILOGY

"The scope and end of learning is to allow perfection to distributive justice, giving everyone his due, procuring good laws and causing them to be observed: an achievement really generous, great, deserving the highest praise."
— from *Don Quixote* by Miguel de Cervantes

WHEN A STUDENT of the Humanities in 1958 I intended to become a great writer. My ambition was as strong (I thought) as any that had driven Shakespeare, Burns or Tolstoy, but private efforts proved I was a poor versifier and could never be a playwright or novelist, because though able to write brisk dialogue I was incapable of inventing a plot. I was therefore only fit to become a historian, a biographer, or perhaps a blend of both in the manner of Plutarch. I had not yet tried to write anything of that sort because the available material was the whole of literature, religion, science and philosophy – the complete records of the human race, so any selection from them would be accidental if not harmonized by a mighty idea. Gibbon's mighty idea showed the slow ruin of the Roman empire making room for the nations of Christian Europe and Arabic Islam. Marx showed all history as a struggle between social classes for the ownership of surplus wealth. My own schooling had described history as a forward march from an age when low-browed cavemen killed their meat with stone clubs. To my own time when every sane British adult could vote for the government of their welfare state which had achieved a full employment, abolished abject poverty, and made good health care and education and legal justice available to every citizen. I did not doubt the essential truth of such big ideas, but knew I could write nothing worth reading unless excited by a big new idea of my own, or else by a new way of making an ancient truth look like new.

One Saturday morning I visited Renfield Street, a short street of shops in central Glasgow. It joins Sauchiehall Street, Bath Street and Argyle Street to the main bridge over the Clyde, so is always throng with pedestrians and vehicles. It is now almost

incredible that second-hand books were once sold from flat-topped wheelbarrows at the corners of blocks on the western side. The spate of private cars must have swept these away in the 1960s, but in my second university year I found on one a tattered Penguin paperback of 19th century verse called *Hood to Hardy*. Opening it at random I found it had work by poets my teachers had never mentioned, and as I read the street noises seemed to withdraw, leaving me in a silence with these words:

> *This Beauty, this Divinity, this Thought,*
> *This hallowed bower and harvest of delight*
> *Whose roots ethereal seemed to clutch the stars,*
> *Whose amaranths perfumed eternity,*
> *Is fixed in earthly soil enriched with bones*
> *Of used-up workers; fattened with the blood*
> *Of prostitutes, the prime manure; and dressed*
> *With brains of madmen and the broken hearts*
> *Of children. Understand it, you at least*
> *Who toil all day and writhe and groan all night*
> *With roots of luxury, a cancer struck*
> *In every muscle; out of you it is*
> *Cathedrals rise and Heaven blossoms fair;*
> *You are the hidden putrefying source*
> *Of beauty and delight, of leisured hours,*
> *Of passionate loves and high imaginings;*
> *You are the dung that keeps the roses sweet*

I did not know what amaranths were or why they perfumed eternity, but that verse shook my intelligence awake by contradicting everything I had been taught about history, literature and life, and would be officially taught for years to come. Since then evidence that this grim view of civilization is strictly true keeps hitting me in the eye. Recently I found this passage in a second-hand paperback called *Who Killed Tutankamun?* by Bob Brier, an American Egyptologist:
The density and quality of bones reveal a person's social status and occupation. For instance, manual labour increases muscle

size which causes bone to thicken, so a single arm can tell us if the dead man was a labourer or a man of leisure. In the remains of a queen from 4,000 years ago I had never seen such delicate bones; it was as if she had never lifted her hand and travelled everywhere in her sedan chair. The cemetery of the workmen who built the pyramid at Giza held the bodies of men who moved heavy loads. Their spines were severely deformed, especially the lumbar vertebrae which ultimately bore most of the stress.

This quotation is from *Antigone* by Sophocles.

Forget the Pyramids. Suddenly all I had been so blandly taught made new, better sense and included all the great Athenian tragedies of sexual and political conflict lasting from generation to generation, with more than one great chorus bitterly chanting "Not to have been born is best." Every nation in the world – Jewish or Roman, Spanish or British, German or American or Russian – has been made by a devil's bargain, usually a war of conquest, letting a well-organized lot master arts and sciences while treating the defeated as shit. Deep thinkers have never stopped worrying about this devil's bargain. Buddha and Jesus tried persuading people to withdraw from it. That is why early Christians believed Satan was Lord of the Earth so all nature was damnable, especially human nature that let a minority enjoy earthly possessions – no wonder the first Christian Jews converted so many women and slaves whose lives had been cheapened by Roman conquest. Nietzsche despized them for trying to obey Jesus by loving those who hated them, blessing those who cursed them and willingly giving what little they owned to whoever needed it more, or merely demanded it. I am too weak to despize them. This doctrine let them exert the only moral authority in the power of the otherwise powerless. Nietzsche had no right to scorn them for using it.

This pure sad Christianity was warped when well-provided powerful folk adopted it. Early Roman Emperors thought it a conspiracy to undermine their Empire and tried to extirpate it. A later one made it the Empire's official religion, partly because it was spreading but also because its doctrines stopped slaves

and poor folk rebelling, so the faith spread far and wide, many
of the poor accepting Hell on Earth because they hoped to
change places with the rich after death. Then states arose in
Renaissance Italy where life for many became pleasanter. They
revived the old pagan idea that the human body and its
appetites were more Good than Evil, so the natural world was
God's handiwork and not inherently damnable. European trade
and conquest increased with experimental sciences, now
called natural philosophy. In the 17th and 18th centuries Kepler,
Galilio, Descartes, Newton and Leibnitz were both Christians
and great mathematicians who believed the natural universe
with its infinite multitude of suns and worlds was created and
managed by God down to the very last detail. Only Pascal – a
devout Catholic whose faith was close to Calvinism – found
the idea terrifying. Most educated people were comforted by
it. There have always been atheists – rich and poor folk who
saw that bosses used religion to exploit others, and thought it
a fraud. It became possible for prosperous people to say, at
least in private, that if the natural universe was a huge machine
running as Newton described, no god was needed to keep it
going. *But only a god could create it, and start it running so
beautifully!* was the reply of those who thought the only evil
in the universe was human greed and stupidity. In his *Essay
on Man* Alexander Pope set out, like Milton, *To justify the
ways of God to man*, and after finding human pride the only
source of evil concluded that *Everything that is, is right.* Leibnitz
tried to show that every form of evil was essential to the
workings of a splendid universe so *Everything is for the best
in the best of all possible worlds.*

Some great intelligences disagreed – Dean Swift and Doctor
Johnson, Christians with some faith in God and common sense
but none in philosophical systems, Christian or scientific.
Johnson said of the *Essay on Man*, "Never has penury of
knowledge and vulgarity of sentiment been so happily
disguized." And Voltaire thought the machinery of the universe
imperfect. He cartooned Leibnitz as Dr Pangloss who travels

through Europe with his innocent pupil, Candide. They find Protestant states brutalized by wars for the glory of a Prussian king, Catholic states where questioners are tortured and burned by the Inquisition, Holland where all religions are tolerated but it is a crime to be poor. Accompanied by a sailor they arrive at Lisbon, capital of Portugal, in time for the 1755 earthquake.

They felt the earth tremble beneath them. The sea boiled up in the harbour and broke the ships which lay at anchor. Whirlwinds of flame and ashes covered the streets and squares. Houses came crashing down. Roofs toppled on to their foundations and the foundations crumbled. Thirty thousand men, women and children were crushed to death under the ruins.

The sailor chuckled: "There'll be something worth picking up here."

He rushed straight into the midst of the debris and risked his life searching for money. Having found some, he ran off with it to get drunk; and after sleeping off the effects of the wine, he bought the favours of the first girl of easy virtue he met amongst the ruined houses with the dead and dying all around. Pangloss pulled him by the sleeves and said, "This will never do, my friend; you are not obeying the rule of Universal Reason."

"Bloody hell," replied the other. "I am a sailor and have trampled on the crucifix four times in my trips to Japan. I'm not the man for your Universal Reason."

Candide had been wounded by splinters of flying masonry and lay helpless in the road, covered with rubble.

"For heaven's sake," he cried to Pangloss. "Fetch me some wine and oil! I am dying."

"This earthquake is nothing new," replied Pangloss, "the town of Lima in America experienced the same shocks last year. The same causes produce the same effects. There is certainly a vein of sulphur running under the earth from Lima to Lisbon."

"Nothing is more likely," said Candide, "but oil and wine, for pity's sake!"

"Likely!" exclaimed the philosopher. *"I maintain it's* 57
proved."

**TUNNOCK'S
PROLOGUE**

Yet something in humanity refuses to lie down under disasters and injustices, hence the French and other revolutions aiming to make a just world for everyone – no wonder great poets welcomed it. In Britain the revolution was purely industrial, making big landowners wealthier and enlarging the middle class. Dickens and Hardy showed how miserable this made life for most folk, though Dickens usually softened that message by giving happy endings to pleasanter characters. Wealth gained or sought by evil means inspired most great masterpieces – Goethe's *Faust*, Stendhal's *Red and Black*, Wagner's *Ring*, Dostoevsky's *Crime and Punishment*, all Ibsen's plays. Strangest of all, best-sellers about supernatural, evil bargains were written by folk without faith in the supernatural – *Frankenstein*, *Dr Jekyll and Mr Hyde*, *Trilby*, *Dracula*, *A Picture of Dorian Gray*, *The Wild Ass's Skin*. The last is Balzac's only supernatural novel. His realistic ones indicate that criminal bargains are well worth striking if you are smart enough to keep the gains. I did not want to believe that. I was sure that all great efforts to achieve liberty, equality and fraternity in Cromwell's Britain, Robespierre's France, Lenin's Russia had been good efforts, though powerful cliques had spoiled them by helping dictators seize power, power they mainly obtained in 1789 France and 1916 Russia when foreign armies invaded to stop the revolutions.

Despite which most children of even poor people have enough to believe life is basically good, and on this basis teachers and governments promote the lie that we need not question those running our states, because they are *good* states, and in safe hands. I decided to examine closely some states widely advertized as good and, without cynicism, show how the goodness was purchased by badness.

I did not glimpse all this in Renfield Street as I held in my hand the tattered book I bought for ninepence. The jacket told

Davidson's *Runnable Stag* is in many anthologies. T.S. Eliot was influenced by his *Thirty Bob a Week*. Hugh MacDiarmid, 18 when Davidson's body was left by the tide on a south coast beach, said it struck him like, *a bullet hole in the lands-cape, God seen through the wrong end of a telescope.* In *The Sign of Four* Holmes gives Watson *The Martyrdom of Man,* saying "let me recommend this book – one of the most remarkable ever penned."

me the price when new had been 2/6, meaning half a crown, meaning 30 pence when 12 pennies made a shilling and 240 a pound. How queer that old money now seems! I still have and love that book. Among notes at the end I read that the author of the poem had been: *John Davidson [1857-1909]. Born at Barrhead, Renfrewshire, son of a Dissenting Minister, Schoolmaster in Scotland until 1889 when he settled in London and published various plays and volumes of verse. He died in circumstances that suggested suicide.* Barrhead is a small factory town in the Renfrew Hills six or seven miles south of Glasgow. It made lavatory pans, and I think could be reached by tram before 1963 when the trams were scrapped. I began thinking that another obscure individual in the west of Scotland (me) might write something great that would *open people's eyes* as Davidson had opened mine. Great writers had been trying to do so for centuries but their works were taught by teachers with eyes firmly shut, so the eye-opening effort was endless. When I tackled it I would be recentest in a line of great tacklers. The job was obviously endless.

At first my book was going to be a broad historical survey until a remark by Sherlock Holmes directed me to Winwood Reade's *Martyrdom of Man*, which showed that survey had been written. Reed describes mankind originating in Africa when climate and land made clothing no problem and food come easily. Overpopulation drove us into the valleys of Egypt and the Euphrates, where we could only feed our great numbers by inventing complex irrigation systems maintained by an intellectual minority. These were the first civilizations, since when civilizations had been ruled by elites using religion and armed forces to control the majority. The continual spread of humanity had ever since formed nations where warfare was unending. Both poverty and refusal to suffer it constantly drove folk to invent new means of livelihood, or plunder their neighbours, or do both at once. Scientific knowledge (said Reade, writing in 1872) was replacing religion as a way of mastering folk, which was why Europe had come to dominate the world. Men and women would only be freed from lives of torture by finding how to make good food cheaply out of minerals, and by solving the overpopulation problem through emigration to other planets.

The accuracy of Reade's account cannot be improved and is not much hurt by ending in a glimpsed utopian future, just as the accuracy of Karl Marx's view of history as class warfare is true despite his prophecy of a workers' revolution creating a classless world where all government withers away. If global businesses ever make food or any essential thing cheaply they will always sell it as dearly as possible, to keep riches and poverty eternal. Davidson was not a Socialist and would have taken that for granted. I could never write a broad historical survey as good as Reade's and Marx's, so I decided to select three triumphant historical periods and show both their virtues and the devil's bargain that created them from the viewpoint of real people. Plato's *Dialogues* showed how Periclean Athens might be dramatized round Socrates. Browning's poem *Fra Lippo Lippi* showed a way into Renaissance Florence. I took longer finding a guide into the glories and miseries of Victoria's reign. What real person would help me to dramatize that over-weaning, self-satisfied nation brilliantly described by Dickens, George Eliot and Hardy? Even Sherlock Holmes' tales are mostly about private fortunes created or inherited through crimes in India, Australia, America or piracy on the high seas. My only chance of a story that would not be adversely compared with theirs was to make it factual – not entirely factual for I would invent conversations – but factual enough to be supported by the historical evidence.

One day in Voltaire and Rousseau's second-hand bookshop, then at the corner of Gibson Street and Park Road, I found Aubrey Menen's novel *The Abode of Love*, about a sect created around 1845 by Henry James Prince, a former Church of England curate. Menen describes Prince as a smart hypocrite who exploits rich dupes with the help of a lawyer. I knew that could not be true, since all who successfully fool many for a long time have first fooled themselves. I searched Glasgow University library's special collections and found Prince's published diary, sermons, and some contemporary accounts of him. These told a stranger story than Menen's.

What have these three in common? Each was too eccentric to be typical of their nations, but their effect on typical people showed how their nation worked. Each was guided by something sensible people reject. Socrates, the most rational and humane of them, had his demon. The painter Filippo Lippi was inspired by Catholic beliefs that sensible Catholics today reject as superstitions. Henry James Prince, a devout, self-lacerating Anglican, strove hard to serve such an impossibly stern idea of God that at last he weakened by believing he and God were identical. The Socratic demon generated European moral philosophy, Filippo Lippi's Catholicism inspired beautiful paintings, Prince's faith achieved only a large rest home for a privileged few. Prince will be the least creative of my heroes being nearest today, when local and national governments openly promote private company profits instead of public welfare.

Nine
Tunnock's Diary
2002

Several weeks ago Mastermind returned my Athenian chapters with comments on my translation of names. Expert, he said, was a good modern equivalent of Sophist, The Darling was suitable for Alcibiades, Olympian and Onionhead for Pericles, except that Athenians likened their prime minister's head to a sea-onion, a marine growth. He regretted that Heavenly Reason was such a lengthy translation of Nous, Anaxagoras' nickname, yet could suggest nothing better. And where had I got The Golden Mean for Theramines and High Anxiety for Nicias? I said I had invented these names to indicate their characters. He grunted then told me that buckles for footwear were a medieval invention – Roman helmet straps had them, but sandals were tied with thongs for centuries after Christ. Having got that detail wrong annoys me more than my trouble with Aristophanes' Clouds. Mastermind had no helpful suggestions about The Clouds.

Between sleep and waking this morning imagined my naked body spread out flat like a landscape beneath me with many wee black circular openings like rabbit holes. I descended and entered one in my chest, then found myself talking to Lorenzo de Medici about the love that led God to make the universe. That dream is a reminder that when writers cannot write something, they should write something else. In the Library I found a Yale Publication on Filippo Lippi's art with good big colour reproductions. It shows two frescos in which Filippo has a self-portrait. He is not the lean, sharp fellow I imagined but dumpy, with swarthy face and morose expression, more like a plumber or butcher (which his father was) than a womanising Bohemian. This reassures me. Apart from Whistler and poor dear Oscar, only amateur artists play at being narcissistic butterflies. Good artists, until struck down by disease or accident, are hard workers with great staying power.

One Sunday a fortnight ago I was searching Encyclopaedia Britannica for clues to how the Medici funded Brother Filipo's monastery when the doorbell rang. In walked Yvonne, as suddenly as she walked out in 1999. She did not say how long she will stay this time, or why. Suspect she is estranged from a partner, as steady fuckers are called nowadays, and will stay until reconciled or finds another. Why do none of the women in my life tell me about themselves? (Memo: try to find out). Though she now refuses me full sexual intercourse it is good being back in bed with a woman again, however indifferent or rude to me they are out of bed. When asleep they sometimes snuggle up close and make me feel part of the universe again. Niki used to do that, clinging to my back like a sensual wee papoose or koala bear clinging to its parent. I would stay awake enjoying that for an hour or longer.

Alas, Yvonne now lies in bed as far from me as she can. Distressing. She was the first I ever had sex with easily, pleasantly, without worry. I can only feel her body now by moving carefully against it when she is sound asleep. It is better than no contact at all. Had I been fool enough to marry her she would now certainly be insisting on a separate bed, probably a separate bedroom. But her presence now, though not erotically fulfilling, does me good. When womanless I often lie abed glooming to myself until noon. Now, like when Nell and Nan were alive, I rise promptly at 7 a.m., bath, shave, dress, make breakfast and eat it in kitchen after serving Yvonne hers on a tray in bed. Then four hours of writing in living room, then off to pub lunch at the Rubaiyat or Aragon, then four more hours of research in university library, then homeward by way of Tennants. There I usually discuss my book with Mastermind. (Memo: he says Lisa Jardine's Worldly Goods, Schama's The Embarrassment of Riches, d'Eramo's The Pig and the Skyscraper show concordance of art, architecture and successful capitalism.) Then home. Yvonne rings the doorbell some time before midnight, I make supper and to bed we go.

She has never asked for her own key, saying that being in the house alone without me gives her the creeps, perhaps the natural reaction to Victorian décor of someone who, a century ago, could only have been a scullion here.

Before closing time last night I was moving through the crowd toward

the door when a man embraced me saying, "My old pal! Do ye still
love me pal?"

"I don't know you," I said, detaching myself. I thought he was drunk.
Outside the pub he started walking beside me saying, "You don't
know me, pal, but I know you. Because of my daughter."

I saw that he wasn't drunk but had pretended to be as a way of
introducing himself. I asked if she had been to Molendinar Primary.
"What you talking about? You know who I mean, pal!," and he
tried to nudge me. I asked who he was talking about.

"Don't pretend you don't know!" he said, exasperated. I stood still
and faced him. We were at the corner of Ruthven Street. The pavement
was busy with people who knew me but even without them he would
not have seemed physically threatening, being only half a head taller
than me with a haggard face, broken nose, and so thin that, from
armpits of denim jacket to turned-up cuffs of grubby jeans, his sides
were perfectly straight, without bulges indicating where waist, hips,
knees were.

"Are you Yvonne's father?" I asked, determined not to be intimidated.
He asked me who the fuck Yvonne was. I said, "Are you Niki's dad?"
He shook his head. I said, "If you are the father of Is, she came to
my house with friends over two years ago and ate my biscuits and
scones and left without saying a word to me."

He said, "Who the fuck is Is?"

I told him our conversation was pointless since neither of us knew
who the other was talking about. I strode away and he followed me
bleating, "Come on, pal! Come on! You know I'm talking about
Zoe."

"I don't know a Zoe."

"You must, pal! She keeps talking about you – says you're the most
cultured man she ever met. Zoe's mad keen on culture – wanted to
be a muralist when she was wee. Even now she keeps hanging around
fuckin musicians with rings in their ears and noses."

I faced him again and said I had never met a Zoe in my life and I am
not a liar, so either she was or he was. He protested that Zoe was
the straightest, honestest girl in the world – she never told fibs. He
said, "I'm honest too, though I don't pretend to be a saint. I've done
drugs, pal, and been done for drugs, been in and out of jail ever
since I left school. I'm telling you straight, I've never did an honest

Polis is
Glasgow
phonetic
dialect for
police.

day's work in my life – that shows you how honest I am."

I asked if he was trying to frighten me. He shouted "Not at all, pal! I can see you're no feart. I'm no feart either. I don't care if I get done by the fuckin polis or by my fuckin mates because I'm used to it – in fact, tell you the truth, I quite like it being a bit of a masochist. I'm no feart of jail, I'm used to that too. I'm no feart of death because what difference will it make? None. The world will continue without me. Business as usual. Zoe cares for me a bit but I don't fool myself, me dying would be a weight off her mind. But you, you're a prosperous cultured gentleman and a scholar, pal. Surely you can spare me a tenner or two for Zoe's sake?"

He was so abject that I gave him a fiver, saying that I knew no Zoe and adding that he would get no more money from me. He went away mumbling that I hadn't heard the end of this. I wonder about Zoe. How can a man like me have made a strong cultural impression on a woman I cannot remember? The woman Henry James Prince raped in the year of the Great 1851 Exhibition was a Zoe, but the Florentine Quatracento is a far more satisfying period. Concentrate on it.

Spud is
demotic for
potato: a
popular
article of
British
working-
class diet,
usually
served boiled
with meat or
fried as
chips. Being
commonplace
yet
comfortably
nourishing, it
is sometimes
used as a
mild term of
endearment.

Found note from Yvonne tonight saying, "Thanks for helping in a hard time but things have improved so I am off. You will not see me again but you are a decent old spud a lot decenter than I expected when you first picked me up. All the best and good luck from, Your Pal, Yvonne." – a better goodbye note than none at all or a curse, which is what most nymphs leave me with. She has left the place tidy and seems to have taken nothing but a cake of toilet soap and tube of toothpaste. Still, it is a blow. I solace myself by concentrating on my amazing Brother Filippo.

The mural in Prato cathedral shows him last in a queue of folk attending Saint Stephen's funeral, with beside him Diamante, the monk who was his painting assistant. Their dark grey gowns contrast with the red robes of an adjacent cardinal. Filippo has the glum face and wry mouth of a child suddenly deprived of a sweet or favourite toy. The head of Diamante looks toward his master with a firmer, more dignified expression. This was painted in the early 1460s when Filippo was about fifty-five. In 1469 he paints himself more prominently in the cathedral of Spoleto among attendants at the death of the Virgin. Here he wears a white robe open over his dark one, facing forward but his eyes looking sideways to the bier where the Virgin peacefully expires. His hand points her out to a fair-haired boy of about twelve who stands in profile beside him, holding a tall glass candlestick. This is a portrait of his son Filippino, and the boy's clear, handsome, thoughtful face is very different from his dad's worried, uneasy gaze, depressed mouth and dark chin. Filippo obviously regarded himself with interest but without admiration, a proof of high intelligence. In the same cathedral his finely carved head and shoulders, with the same pointing hand and wearing the same Carmelite robe, lean out of a roundel above the tomb Filippino designed twenty years after Filippo's death, when the son was an artist as famous as his dad. Lorenzo the Magnificent commissioned that memorial. The bronze head and pointing hand in this carving are like those in the Spoleto mural, except that the face looks wise and kind. Was Filippino's memorial to his dad more truthful than dad's self-portrait? Can that pleasanter portrait of him also be true to side of his character he himself ignored? Of course it can.

---

*I live in strange, strange times. Newspapers and broadcasts would make study and calm writing impossible if I attended to them, and they still erupt on me from pub television sets, from Mastermind, from headlines glimpsed on newsagents' billboards. Shortly after Thatcher's reign I saw billboards yelling **LOONY M.P. BACKS IRISH BOMBERS!** Mastermind, an old-fashioned Conservative, told me an English Tory M.P. had examined evidence presented at a trial of Irishmen jailed for a murderous I.R.A. bombing, and decided there had been no evidence to convict them, because a new law by a panic-stricken government had let the police arrest people on suspicion, and also use anything they said or signed after arrest as evidence against them, even if they later denied it in court. The British politicians, police, judges, newspapers and public wanted some Irishmen arrested for the crime, wanted that so much and so fast that the real bombers were never found. The "loony" Tory re-opened the case and the jailed Irish were proved innocent, "which could never have happened in Scotland," a woman I met yesterday told me. She was intensely agitated by injustices and said, "Scottish*

M.P.s and lawyers are the most corrupt and cowardly in Britain. Hardly one of them has the guts to challenge a judge, a sheriff, the police or anyone with some authority. I'm a Socialist and Irish, so I naturally hate the English, but I have to admit some of them have a sense of fair play I see hardly anywhere in Scotland."

Heraghty's is
a public
house on
Kilmarnock
Road about a
mile south of
the Clyde.

I met her on the way back from Heraghty's around lunchtime. On Gorbals High Street I entered an eating place called Hasta Mañana and found a seat opposite a small woman with a large nose questioning a waiter about his private life. Her voice was penetrating yet so fast I could hardly catch her words, though they were friendly. The waiter left after taking my order and she told me, "A very good man, that!" and a long story about his courage and decency. He was Spanish Moroccan and owned the place. One night he saw a stabbed man staggering on the pavement outside and rushed out with towels and staunched the wounds, saving the man's life. "Not many Glaswegians would have the guts to do that," she said. "Most of them would cross the road to avoid helping a stabbed man, afraid of being stabbed by his enemies. What do you do?"

I said I was a retired school teacher and asked what she did. "A criminal lawyer," she said. "My clients pay me through legal aid, which of course the government is steadily abolishing. They only want justice for people rich enough to buy it. A teacher! What do you think of the Labour Party giving away all our schools?"

I said I had retired more than ten years ago and knew nothing about that. She said hardly anyone in Britain knew about it because Blair was continuing a Margaret Thatcher policy. When the Labour Party was in opposition it complained about such things and they were reported in news stories, but the New Labour measures had Tory support, so there was no discussion when the government created Private Finance Initiatives to transfer the grounds of schools and hospitals to private businesses who promised to build new schools where and when they are needed: "So of course more and more schools, especially primary schools, are being shut and pupils concentrated in fewer and bigger buildings far from their homes. Smart, eh? A great boost for the property market. Hospitals are being treated the same way. Each week Glasgow councillors give more and more public land to private businesses. Local people complain like hell, but with Tory support the Labour Party ignores

them. Britain was never much of a democracy but it's now becoming
positively Fascist. Do you agree?"

I said the closing of schools was regrettable because for at least a century Scottish schools with very few pupils and teachers had given good starts in life to many professional folk from poor homes. I also said she was surely wrong to call Britain Fascist because we had no concentration camps or government hate campaigns against racial and religious minorities; and I avoided discussing contemporary politics because that interrupted my studies of Medician Florence. She said, "Well, you're a nice old ostrich. There must have been a lot of decent Germans like you after Hitler came to power. I don't suppose you want to know about the Bouncing Czech, the Enron rip-off and how British and American lawyers, bankers and governments connive to help millionaire company directors steal their employees' pension funds."

She went on to tell me about these things in great details until I paid for my meal and rushed out. I am not an ostrich but a Scottish Renaissance scholar whose spiritual home is Medician Florence.

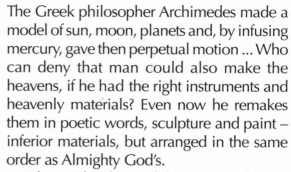

The Greek philosopher Archimedes made a model of sun, moon, planets and, by infusing mercury, gave then perpetual motion ... Who can deny that man could also make the heavens, if he had the right instruments and heavenly materials? Even now he remakes them in poetic words, sculpture and paint – inferior materials, but arranged in the same order as Almighty God's.
– *Plato's Theology of the Immortal Soul* by Marsilio Ficino

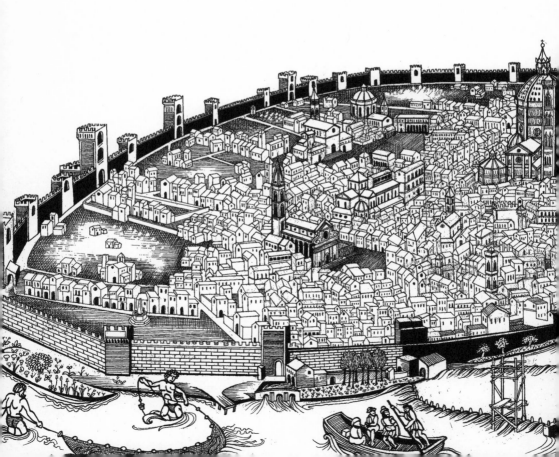

BROTHER
FILIPPO

10: A FLORENTINE MONASTERY

FLORENCE, two thousand years after republican Athens, became a republic almost as wonderful. Unlike most cities when the Roman Empire dissolved Florence had not been ruled by a dynasty of war lords, so masterpieces of European literature were much later written by Florentine Dante, Boccaccio and Petrarch. The city was ruled by a parliament of craftsmen and tradesmen who excluded all noblemen, only admitting landowners enriched by trade. It imported silk from China, dyes from India, wool from England, turning them into rich fabrics sold all over Europe. This trade needed an international banking system, so the parliament of Florence was dominated by merchant bankers who manipulated the trade unions, priests and mass of people by a combination of bribes and by funding a high level of social welfare only approached by some neighbouring republics. The chief bankers were the Medici family who had branch offices in Milan, Venice, Rome, Geneva, Bruges, Antwerp, London; also agents in Baghdad and Constantinople. The Catholic Church still condemned capitalism as a sin but tolerated the Medici because they paid for bigger and better churches and monasteries which ran schools and hospitals. These splendid new buildings were designed and decorated by astonishingly fine artists born in Florence, and many attracted by its prosperity.

A wall of the Carmine Monastery was being painted with a brown rocky wilderness where hermits wearing Carmelite robes prayed singly or conversed in couples. Brother Filippo applied the colours while Brother Diamante ground and mixed them. These two had a dispensation that allowed them to run their painting business from a house outside the monastery, and over breakfast that morning Filippo had again blamed Diamante for insufficiently haggling down the price of market vegetables. Though unwilling to greatly anger Filippo (a dangerous thing to do) Diamante wanted to be slightly disagreeable. He heaved a deep sigh.

"Regretting what you paid for those tomatoes?" said Filippo pleasantly.

"I was remembering Brother Guido's wall in the chapter house of San Marco," said Diamante on a melancholy note. "Nothing regrettable there! Guido painted it excellently if we remember the over-abundance of saints, abbots and popes he had to include."

Brother Guido, christened Guido di Pietri, received the monastic name Giovanni da Fiesole, but is better known as Fra Angelico, 1387-1455.

"Yes, the preaching friars have many saints; we Carmelites, alas, only two."

"Why alas? Their saints are all modern: our founders are in the Scriptures."

"The other orders say the prophet Elijah and John the Baptist are as much their progenitors as ours."

"They envy our antiquity," said Filippo smiling pleasantly. "They are newcomers founded two centuries ago, more than a millennium after the Crucifixion. The Prophet Elijah was a Carmelite a thousand years before Jesus was crucified. John who baptized Him was a hermit on the slopes of Mount Carmel. We came through Sicily to Italy a century ago, but our first monastery is still in the Holy Land."

"Other orders say our rules have changed so much since we came to Italy that our order is now as modern as theirs."

"They are right to say so Diamante, but when facts are at variance with Truth we should cling to Truth."

Diamante stopped mixing a colour, looked hard at Filippo and asked, "Is a fact not a truth?"

"Yes, but it is first of all a *thing* – a piece of our imperfect fallen world, therefore not perfectly substantial. Only truth is perfect, unchanging, eternal, Heavenly. On earth it is only found in our Holy Scriptures, in Catholic traditions, and in history. Brunelleschi, Ghiberti and Donatello think it is also in geometry because measured designs help us make beautiful architecture and convincing perspectives. They may be right, but there is no doubt that Holy Scriptures, Catholic traditions and history support Carmelite antiquity. Forty years ago the Saracens broke into our monastery on Mount Carmel and martyred our brothers as they sang the *Salve Regina*. That is why the Virgin appeared to our Pope in a dream and told him that when a Carmelite dies, after only one day Mary Mother of God will visit him in Purgatory and escort his soul straight to Heaven. We can both take comfort in that, Diamante. Certainly I do."

"You would doubt it if you were a Franciscan or Dominican."

"Of course. And if I were a Turk I would doubt God's Holy Trinity and Virgin Birth and be adorning the walls of mosques with patterns of coloured tiles. Instead I can paint God, His Mother, Son, angels and saints with bodies looking almost as solid, colourful and well-dressed as God Himself could make them. God is very good to me."

Filippo was now applying paint to the robe of a tubby hermit who sat in a rocky cleft, hearing the confession of a handsome young man kneeling in profile. Diamante noticed that the older hermit was as tubby as Filippo and had his occasional sly smile. Unable to let the conversation end so smugly he murmured, "They say Fra Angelico will be beatified one day."

"Unlikely. People qualify for sainthood by martyrdom, or miracles, or deeds of astonishing charity. Angelic John has achieved none of these."

"But he has saintly virtues. He kneels in prayer while painting the Holy Family. Has never broken his vows of poverty. Or chastity."

"Unlike me. But Brother Angelico comes from a rich family. Finding he did not want money and women he chose to join the Franciscans when a grown man. Aunt Mona made me a Carmelite when I was eight because she could not

feed me. Poor soul, she could hardly feed herself. I do not
envy Guido's lack of appetite for some good things God
places within my reach. I do not even envy Angelic Guido's
remarkable talent, for his work has taught me a lot. Apart
from my master, Messy Tom, Angelic John is the best of the
older painters. His weakness is an absence of various
expression. *ALL* his holy figures are delicate, sweet and
benign. Were it not for the energetic design, harmony of
colour and masterly chiaroscuro his greatest works would
make me feel I was facing a banquet of twenty courses
marinated in honey. Think, Diamante, of that poor haggard
ugly gap-toothed Magdalen made by Donatello! Think of
Eve's weeping, grief-distorted face painted by Masaccio in
this monastery! It is the finest thing Messy Thomas ever
did! Nobody can paint better than that."

Messy Tom is
an English
translation of
Masaccio,
Italian
nickname of
the mural
painter
Tommasso
Guidi, 1401-
28?.

"The public prefers Angelic John."

"Naturally. Among the vulgar public only those made ugly
by suffering appreciate pictures of those also made Holy
by it. But artists of talent – artists great enough to lead instead
of follow vulgar taste – such artists will always come here
to learn from the work of Messy Thomas and me. Angelico,
despite great virtues, is a Gothic manuscript illuminator
enlarged and modernized by the great examples of
Florentine art, especially sculptures in bronze. The great
paintings of the future will grow from we who are achieving
in paint the spatial depth Donatello has mastered in his
great door panels, and are learning even more from nature."

"Yes," said Diamante thoughtfully, "Your grief-stricken faces
are as natural as old Giotto's. And your Christ childs are
very natural, sturdy little ruffians. And your virgins are
always dressed in the height of fashion, which in young
girls is natural I suppose."

Fillipo looked hard at Diamante who said, without raising
his eyes from colour grinding, "And the Medici appreciates
Angelico as much as the public do. Perhaps more."

"That shows Cosimo's breadth of vision. He discovered
Angelico years before I became a painter and now
commissions work equally from us both. He prefers having

me in his house because, unlike Angelico, Cosimo and I are sinners. Cosimo is the worst because his crimes are against nature. He breeds money out of money so like other bankers will finally sit in Hell scratching himself among the sodomites. I am only . . . only . . ."

"Avaricious?" murmured Diamante, "A fornicator? Forger?"

There was silence for half a minute in which Diamante braced himself for a wrathful explosion. Instead he heard Filippo warble in sing-song, "We have been companions since our novitiate Diamante! You have learned all you know of fine arts from me Diamante! Let us concentrate on our work Diamante! I promise not to say more about your foolish, ridiculous, extravagant, insane, unChristian expenditure on tomatoes."

11: A FLORENTINE NUNNERY

I N A CONVENT CELL LENT TO HIM for a studio Filippo painted a young nun, Lucrezia Buti, lent to him as a model for his Virgin Mary in Glory. As usual he had begun the session by sinning with her carnally because, he said, that let him paint without the distraction of carnal lust. He had then worked for nearly half an hour in silence before she murmured between rigid lips, "Filippo, if I have a child?"

"Have you already missed a period?" he said, frowning and mixing a colour.

"No."

"If God wills you a child," he said, applying his brush carefully to the panel, "six or seven months will elapse before your appearance announces the advent. Plenty of time."

"But Filippo – " she cried.

"Don't move! Imagine that I am the Archangel of the Annunciation. Imagine the little baby God is perhaps making in you. It is a wonderful thought, fearful also! What will people think? You are a virgin, and unmarried, yet the child will be God's as well as yours, so He is bound to save you from harm. You know how God saved the Holy Virgin from scandal – He got old Joseph to marry her before she bore His Son. Wedding a jobbing carpenter must have been the first of her sorrows. You need not stoop so low."

Between rigid lips she murmured, "I am afraid."

He said cheerily, "Don't be. You have me."

"Not often."

He stroked colour into the Madonna's robe then said firmly,

"When I have finished this you must leave here. I will help you escape on a holy day, a sacred festival when the Mother Superior is looking elsewhere. Come and live with me."

"As your wife?"

"Of course not. I am a priest. STAY SERENE!" he shouted, "You are to be my Virgin in Glory, not my repentant Magdalene."

"My convent will be dishonoured," she said mournfully. "My family will be dishonoured."

"Your noble brothers are not as rich and powerful as my friend Cosimo Medici. They made you and your sister Spinetta nuns because they could not afford dowries that would fetch you noble husbands. You will be happier when not quite married to me, a butcher's son, yes, but also a great artisan and priest. There is room in my workshop for you and Spinetta also, if she too wishes to escape. A couple of women will be useful. Brother Diamante does his best but is not a good housewife."

"This makes me weep, Filippo," she said and wept, uncertain whether from sorrow or joy.

"Weep joyfully," he urged, "Despair is the one sin God cannot forgive because it prevents repentance. He easily forgives other ones, even murder, which is a nasty big sin. Making babies is hardly a sin at all. In the beginning God commanded all his creatures to be fruitful and multiply. Stay serene Lucrezia!" he pled, but her weeping became sobs until he yelled, *"Stay serene or I cannot paint you!"*

With a great effort she mastered the sobs. For a while there was silence but for the soft strokes of his brush, then he said casually, "You will often be painted when we live together. There will always be a market for Virgins with your face and eyes."

Lucrezia's convent was a small one with only four other nuns. The house was of a kind later denounced by the republican friar Savonarola because of a grill in the door behind which young nuns sometimes stood flirting with young men in the street outside. On a day of Holy festival when the Mother Superior led out her Brides of Christ to see the Girdle of Our Lady displayed it was easy for Lucrezia and Spinetta to escape in the crowd.

12: SOMEWHERE IN ROME

Aᴿᴇᴠᴏʟᴛ ʙʏ ᴛʜᴇ ɴᴏʙɪʟɪᴛʏ ᴏꜰ ʀᴏᴍᴇ in 1434 forced a
Pope (like several of his predecessors) to flee the
city in disguize. For ten years Eugenius IV was a guest
of Cosimo de Medici in Florence, usually residing in the
Medici palace where he met Brother Filippo. In 1443 the
support of foreign kings let the Pontiff return to Rome and
soon after he commissioned an Annunciation from Filippo.
Sometimes he relaxed while watching the painter at work
and grumbling about his problems. One morning he said
gloomily, "Strange times, strange times! I have healed the
thousand-year-old schism between Roman Christians in the
west and Greeks in the east. The Byzantine Emperor John
Palaeologus and the Holy Roman Emperor Sigismond
recognized my supremacy, and now so does Emperor
Frederick. I have signed agreements with Copts in Egypt
and Nestorians in Mesopotamia, so Christians in Africa and
Arabia will be restored to Roman Christendom. What do
you think of that, my Pippo?"

"No previous Pope has done as much, my Pontiff," said
Filippo politely, "except Saint Peter, perhaps."

"Has done as much on paper. Potentates sign agreements
with me and go on doing as they please. Palaeologus signed
because he needs me to organize a crusade to save
Byzantium from the Muhammadans – they have cut his
empire down to a circle of suburbs round Constantinople.
But that damned remnant of the Council of Basel still
supports Antipope Amadeus Duke of Savoy, who is not even

a priest! Antipopes are *always* Antichrists! I *cannot* raise a crusading army from a schismatic Europe, so in a few years Constantinople will be conquered by pagans. The last of the ancient Roman Empire will be destroyed and Greek Christianity extirpated. O O O I *detest* the ambition that dragged me from my monastery. I weep tears of rage when recalling the profound peace I once enjoyed as a young monk."

"Don't return to your old monastery, my Pontifex Maximus," said Filippo, chuckling. "A previous pope threw up the job because it was damning his soul so Dante describes him eternally racing round the outer walls of Hell, one in a crowd of souls hated equally by God and Satan. Continue being as good a pope as you can in these strange strange times and you need only suffer a few years in Purgatory."

"More than you expect to suffer!" said Eugenius grimly.

Filippo stiffened the corners of his mouth to prevent a smile and with a modest shrug murmured, "Well, I am a Carmelite."

A little later he wiped his brush clean, laid it down, stirred crimson powder into a pot of medium while saying, "Surely several Christian kings would join a crusade if your Holiness raised his own army to fight against Islam?"

"A papal army is a dissonant concept, both theologically and pastorally."

"Yet Martin V, your great predecessor, defeated Braccio da Montone in the battle of L'Aquila and crushed Bologna by force of arms. He regained the lost papal treasury. The Papal States now dominate central Italy."

"Pope Martin belonged to the Colonna family, chiefs of that gang of noble scoundrels who forced me to flee Rome twelve years ago. He enriched his relatives as much as he enriched the Vatican treasury, which is not inexhaustible. My only possible armies now would be lent me by French or Spanish kings whose troops would probably sack Rome while passing through."

"Hire soldiers from outlandish nations who would only

demand their soldiers' wages – Switzerland, the Baltic
countries, England and Scotland."

"I say again, Pippo, our treasury is not inexhaustible."

"Will your Holiness forgive the prattling tongue of a bird-brained monk who imagines a new way to make your treasury inexhaustible?"

"Speak, parrot."

"In Mainz upon the Rhine there is a wonderful German engine with a lever which, pressed down once, stamps a sheet of paper with inked words more clear, regular and legible than the finest penman can write."

"I know that very well," said Eugenius gloomily. "Already German bishops are buying letters of indulgence in bulk from the engineers, each with a blank space for the name of the soon-to-be-forgiven, and room at the foot for the bishop's signature and seal. Twenty good scribes working for a week in my chancellery could not write as many letters of indulgence as this engine stamps in an hour."

"Then your Holiness should hire a German engineer to build this lettering machine in Rome, and announce *ex cathedra* that only indulgences signed by you and cardinals in the papal college are valid. The vastly enlarged revenue you received would never stop pouring in."

"Do not tempt me, Filippo. I am a Venetian so no enemy of commerce, but I fear this clerical engine will effect the Church in unforeseen ways, just as gunfire (another German invention) is changing warfare. I will not use or ban or try to control these engines until I see clearly what their effect is liable to be."

Filippo silently resumed painting. Eugenius said, "This picture has more domestic furniture than most Annunciations, also more browns. I suppose oil paint allows that. I am glad you have confined your usual wild forest to a narrow view through the arch."

After more unhelpful remarks that Filippo ignored the Pope said, "God's mother is not usually approached from the left."

"Yes, entrance from the right is customary. My previous Annunciations have that."

"You are trying something new."

"Your Holiness perfectly understands me."

Eugenius sighed and said, "Yes, Florentines must always be innovating. It produces brave new art but also heresy. Too many of your scholars learn Greek, study Plato, start doubting the theology of Aquinus and à Kempis. Nicolo Granchio is a splendid administrator. As my legate in Constantinople he persuaded Paleologus to meet me in Italy, which was not easy. Like several German priests he makes a surprisingly uncorrupt cardinal, neither simoniac nor nepotist, not an adulterer, sodomite or pederast, not even given to impatience or anger – my own worst sins. Yet he thinks Christendom and Islam could unite! How can a member of the Sacred College indulge such a cloud-cuckoo idea? Luckily he puts ideas into abstruse Latin jargon that hardly anybody understands. He tells me Muslims believe in the Jewish Old Testament as we do, that the Koran accepts the Virgin Mary as Christ's Mother. It seems the Koran also says Jesus is a God-inspired prophet and forerunner of Muhammad! Blasphemy! Muhammadans who do not believe Jesus was God's Only Begotten Son are as damnable as Jews who reject Him."

"But not as damnable as atheists who call Moses, Jesus and Muhammad the three impostors," said Filippo, adding with a long brushstroke a bright crimson plume to the archangel's wing. Eugenius shuddered and said, "Your artistic confidence makes you dangerously jocose, my son."

"You are right to reprove me, Papa, but Cardinal Nicolo is also right to think the Turks are not exactly barbarians. I was once the slave of a Turk."

"How did that happen?"

"On a boating trip off Livorno I was captured by corsairs and sold with the rest of the crew in Morocco. My master, though pagan, was a man of humane and liberal views and my skill in portraiture entertained him. He certainly did not think all Christians would go to Hell. He quoted an

Granchio, better known as Nicolaus Krebs of Cusa, was the best Renaissance philosopher. He rejected Aristotle's doctrine that mathematics deal with large and small things by saying everything was infinitely divisible in the eyes of God, so all size is relevative. Also that only God was eternal and infinite with His centre everywhere and limits nowhere – so the world and everything else was contained by God, and never at rest.

Arabian poet who said that when our souls stand before
the judgement seat of God we will find Him so infinitely
merciful that we will gnaw our fingers in rage at the sins
we might have committed on earth without offending Him."
"I see why that heresy delighted you," said Eugenius,
laughing. "But God's mercy is only for the repentant."
"I know that Your Holiness, of course I knew my master's
words were a blasphemy leading to the circle of Hell where
schismatics are repeatedly hacked in two. But some
Christians are over-obsessed with their sins and God's
judgement. When you consider the scope of His work –
the great dome of the stars and clouds, the seas and snowy
Alps, the brown and green and flowery lands surrounding
our cities of splendid men and women, our glorious
churches and palaces, rich markets of fruit, vegetables,
meat, cloth, furniture and all other fine goods – why, it is
perfectly obvious that God spends more time creating lovely
things than he spends condemning bad ones."
"You are making a God in your own image!"
"No father, I promise you, it is the other way round."
Eugenius shook his head, rolling his eyes in an Italian way
indicating despair and resignation.

Vasari says that when a slave in North Africa Filippo interested his owner by sketching him in charcoal, the Muhammadan never having seen a portrait before. Eventually Filippo was ransomed and returned to Florence by way of Naples.

And after more silence asked, "Are all your Virgins derived
from the figure and face of the same woman?"
"I almost think so, Papa." said Filippo, dreamily. "The Virgins
I painted before I met Lucrezia must have been prophecies,
because on seeing her in the parlour of that little convent I
recognized her at once. Yes Father. Yes indeed, Holiness."
"That is another Greek heresy," said Eugenius, not severely.
"Plato or perhaps Socrates (they are practically the same) said
souls are eternal as God who made them, so birth is not the
making of a new soul but a reincarnation, and those who love
at first sight recognize their mates from an earlier life."
"As you say, Father, a heresy. Only God knows how such
miracles happen."
"Brother Filippo, you are too amorous for a priest. I have
power to dispense you of your clerical vows. You now have

a son by your Lucrezia. Little Filippino will not be a bastard if I make you a layman able to marry her."

Filippo dropped his brush and stared at the Pope, open-mouthed and shaking his head in many small vehement negations. Then he cried, "Holy Father, you must not deprive me of my priesthood! My link with Holy Mount Carmel! My promise of release from Purgatory by God's mother!"

It is queer how glibly I write speeches for folk whose language I do not know, and who painted wall pictures I have only seen in books, and were inspired by a Christianity in which I have no faith, in a land I have never visited. All of them are highly educated. How can I write convincing speeches for ordinary peasants, shopkeepers and craftsmen without going to Italy and learning the language?

13: ANGUS CALDER'S LETTER

Old Grindle's Bookshop
Spittal Street, Tollcross
Edinburgh
2003

Dear John Tunnock Mate,

I call you Mate because that is a common English way of sounding friendly and I am English. Like you I am a middle-class Socialist of the Robert Owen-John Ruskin-William Morris kind, but would feel pretentious if I called you Comrade. Have just read your first chapters in Joy Hendry's special edition of Chapman. Great stuff, Mate! I would not be saying this to a Glaswegian I have never met if I were not a bit drunk (Smith's Glenlivet Malt) and moved almost to tears. I've read nothing so good since Alasdair Gray's Lanark. Most writers are shy introverts with a very narrow experience of both public and private life, so learn about it by reading each other's books. They usually compensate for this by inventing tougher, richer, sexier heroes than themselves. I ain't referring to low-class fantasy heroes like Fleming's James Bond but to historic figures worn like masks by better writers – Mary Renault's Alexander the Great, Marguerite Yourcenar's Hadrian, Graves' Claudius and our own dear Alan Massie's Roman emperors. Your Pericles and Alcibiades are more believable because you confront them with convincing common citizens like your farmer and sausage seller and show through them how the greed of the Athenian Empire led it to destruction. This is relevant to continual wars started in eastern oil-bearing nations by U.S. presidents and our own dear Tony Blair, on the pretext of defending justice and democracy. Congratulations!

But (I must be very ve-e-e-e-ry drunk to say this to a writer I have never met) how can you keep this level of relevance in a book ending with an eccentric Victorian clergyman? As your prologue says, his century was an age of industrial and social revolutions. What can an Anglican priest getting rich by fooling

This letter was stapled to a page of John Tunnock's diary between the last entry and the next. The writer is a left-wing historian and literary critic who taught at the Universities of Sussex and Nairobi before settling in Edinburgh, and author of *The People's War: Britain 1941-1945* and *Revolutionary Empires: English Speaking Empires 1400–1780s.*

wealthier people tell us about the British Empire in India, Africa, Egypt? About women and children slaving 14 hours a day in mines and factories? About the fight to legalize trade unions and Cooperative Socialism? I don't want Who Paid for All This? to end by showing as little of the 19th century as Bertie Wooster's antics in Blandings Castle show the 20th. If it ends like that you had better call your book Money at Play.

Instead of provincial England why not show the Golden Age of a third famous city much the same size as Periclean Athens and Medician Florence? A city whose main citizens became intellectual world leaders? Why not use late 18th century Edinburgh? It had Hume, founder of modern philosophy; Adam Smith, founder of political economy; Hutton, who made geology a modern science; Boswell who wrote the first modern biography. Burns, a world-famous poet, was its honoured guest. These and many others of slightly lesser genius all knew each other socially.

Mind you, mate, I'm not pretending Scotland in those days was all sweetness and light. The landowners and merchants of Edinburgh and Glasgow owned cotton and tobacco plantations in Florida, Virginia, Carolina, and sugar plantations in Jamaica, so used slaves as much as English merchants. Scottish coal miners, like Russian serfs, had been their employer's property for a couple of centuries under laws making it a crime to help them escape, and sometimes had iron collars riveted round their necks. In England the parliamentary system was managed on behalf of the aristocracy and rich merchants by several magnates; in Scotland it was managed by one, Henry Dundas, nicknamed The Uncrowned King of Scotland, being most recent in a line of uncrowned kings appointed by the London government. Fewer Scottish householders were entitled to vote than Englishmen in the county of Suffolk, and as nobody got a government job in Scotland without Dundas approving, the law courts, the county and town councils were completely Tory. He enriched his family and friends, normal practice then as now, and of course blocked all attempts at political reform.

But you need someone remarkable whose life reveals this
society. Why not James Watt, born in Greenock, maker of
musical and scientific instruments who turned engineering into
a science that transformed the world? He and his apprentice
Murdoch (who invented gas lighting) and partner Matthew
Bolton were members of the Birmingham Lunar Society. So was
Josiah Wedgewood. Bolton and Wedgewood's factories
anticipated Henry Ford's production lines. These men were
political radicals who supported the American colonists' fight
for independence, and welcomed the French Revolution.

Or take Thomas Muir, who Dundas thought the most
dangerous man in Scotland. Surely you know about Muir of
Huntershill? The Glasgow stickit minister who became an A *stickit*
Minister is
Edinburgh advocate? And started Scottish Friends of the People Scots for a
Societies demanding political reform? And talked with leaders student
of the French National Assembly in Paris? And joined the clergyman
who fails to
Society of United Irishmen? And was tried in Edinburgh for qualify.
lending Tom Paine's Rights of Man to a weaver? Was
transported to Botany Bay, then escaped from there in an
American vessel with the connivance of George Washington?
After shipwreck and sea battles he was received back in Paris
with acclamations by the French National Assembly. He would
have been president of the Scottish Republic had the proposed
French invasion succeeded, did you know that? Why so many
rhetorical questions? It's the Glenlivet talking.

Your excellent Prologue says your teachers discouraged
prrronouncing the r in worrrds to stop you sounding Scotch. Calder is
here over-
Has your education made you, like the Scottish Labour Party, modest. He
indifferent to the land where you live? Are you writing with an is a
competent
eye on London and its book reviewers? I am not, alas, a creative poet with
writer, just an English historian in Edinburgh. Historians, of three
published
course, enjoy escaping into the past as much as fiction writers. books of
Many are like Ibsen's Dr Tesman who spends his honeymoon verse, the
first of them
studying cottage industries in medieval Brabant and ignoring translations
his fascinating wife. In a humble way I have tried to emulate of Catullus
into Lowland
Herodotus, Xenophon and Marx instead of Tesman and show Scots.

how the nation where I live has happened. I also know that some fiction writers have done it better. Scott and Tolstoy's greatest work was set a few generations before their own time, but the kind of people and class conflicts they described were and are still contemporary.

I must be daft as well as drunk to criticize an author I've never met for something he has not yet written, but believe me mate, your first chapters have enthused (oh God I hate that word but cannae think of another yes I can) have inspired me to this insolent diatribe.

I am, believe me,
my dear dear sir and mate,
your apologetic,
humble,
and very urgent well-wisher,
Angus Calder

Fourteen
Tunnock's Diary
2002-3

Damn Angus Calder. Through Joy Hendry's Chapman the greatest encouragement I ever received ends by demanding that I abandon years of research and invent a new ending to my masterpiece. Had a Scottish Enlightenment setting occurred to me twenty years back I might have used it but I CANNOT now fling aside years of research and undertake more. How can I possibly write well about life in Edinburgh around 1780 – 90 when I hardly know Glasgow in 2003 though surrounded all my life by detailed information about it? I could write nothing after reading that letter yesterday and went for a meditative stroll that ended in another bad shock.

The weather was neutral, neither cold nor warm, wet nor sunny, the sky one ceiling of smooth grey cloud. I love such dull days, perhaps because I am a rather dull man. I wandered through the University grounds, crossing Kelvin Way and entering the park. Mastermind tells me Glasgow parks are now dangerous places, infested by gangs of youths from District Council housing schemes who, when Glasgow was productive, would have been apprentices learning to build or operate ships and machines, but now live on Social Security benefits while stealing money for drink and drugs. Casual violence is their main recreation. Some openly call themselves Nazis and patrol the inner public parks, maiming or murdering folk who seem homosexual or foreign, and folk with darker skins are the usual victims. The chief Kelvin Park terrorist calls himself Hitler – how does a quiet, erudite, stay-at-home body like Mastermind know such things? I saw that the monolithic bust of Carlyle facing the old park bridge had its nose smashed off again. Ten

Carlyle's *Life of Frederick the Great* tells how King Fred's Prussia was about to be conquered by a trio of nations when the Russian Czarina died, at which Fred's other enemies made peace with him. Goebbels was reading this in 1945 when he heard of President Roosevelt's death. He rushed to Hitler with the good news that history was repeating itself, and though Russian troops were in the suburbs of Berlin, Britain and the U.S.A. would now join Germany to fight the U.S.S.R. (The top Nazis believed the U.S.A. was mainly fighting them because Roosevelt was a Jew.)

years ago it was restored in ciment fondu after a similar act of vandalism by people who (judging by words spray-painted on a nearby statue of a soldier commemorating the Boer War) were feminists defying patriarchal authority. This time the nose was probably removed by one of Hitler's henchmen who did not know Hitler the First was encouraged by Carlyle.

When writing hard I often find sentences in an accidentally opened book that help the work forward, so on leaving the park I visited Voltaire and Rousseau. This big low-ceilinged shed (probably once a livery stable) has all kinds of second-hand books stacked in high cases and in piles on the floor. In a box of dog-eared paperbacks I found Picture This by Joseph Heller, published by Pan Books of London. I had never heard of it, though Heller's Catch 22 is one of the three great novels about World War II. Glancing into Picture This I was stammygastered to find it a one volume trilogy about (1) Socrates and Athenian democracy, (2) Rembrandt and the Dutch Republic, (3) the modern New York art market. Paid 50p, brought it home, read, digested it before sleeping.

Picture This reports on Periclean Athens more than dramatising it, but tells much that I missed. Socrates went barefoot. Heller also shows the rapacity of Dutch capitalism better than I show that of Florence. His presentation of Rembrandt is masterly – he knows more about oil colour than I do about tempera and fresco. His third section shows modern capitalism working through millionaire art deals in New York and refers to the Vietnam war in a way that exposes my writing as antiquarian exercizes. I have not shown the ignoble sweat, toil and mercenary warfare that PAID FOR the freedom and confidence that let Italians make astonishingly lovely towns. Why does modern Capitalism, despite commanding much more wealth, only produce more cars, motorways, pollution, drugs, weapons and warfare? What is it doing to Britain? To Scotland? To Glasgow? Why did that never occur to me as a subject?

Doctor Johnson said the only measure of a good nation is how well it treats the poor. Surely orphans, the sick and disabled, homeless and unemployed and unemployable are treated better now in Britain than in Italy five centuries ago? Perhaps not. I once read that British travellers used to greatly admire schools, orphanages and hospitals for the poor in Italy. These, of course, were attached to monasteries and staffed by monks and nuns. Britain had such places until Henry VIII first nationalized monastic lands and buildings, then sold them to private owners, thus destroying what had been (no doubt) a semi-corrupt welfare state, but one which was meant to care for the poor. Henry's Protestant reforms kept him and his greatest supporters rich, made many in the middle class richer while increasing the number of beggars. Why does this sound familiar?

I was deluded to think I could know Athens and Florence as well as Dickens, Balzac, Dostoevsky, Joyce knew London, Paris, St Petersburg, Dublin. Making Socrates go barefoot won't change that. Mastermind tells me tomatoes were impossible in Filippo's Florence because they came from America which Columbus reached twenty-seven years after Filippo died. Changing them to artichokes won't help. The Mona who put him into the Carmelite monastery, I have discovered, was his mother, not his aunt. Diamante assisted Filippo until he died, but Filippo had a sister who did the housekeeping. And Pope Eugenius died five years before Filippo seduced Lucrezia. And perhaps she seduced him. And I haven't the faintest idea how ordinary people made their livings in the weaving sheds and dye-works that made Florence rich. Maybe most lived fairly satisfactory lives, like fully employed, well-paid British workers between 1945 and 1970.

I am haunted, oppressed by feeling I should write about the life I know, but what do I know about life? What has life taught me about Glasgow? How can an old man of very little experience put the world where he lives into a good story?

Think about it, Tunnock. You have nothing else to do.

Unable to start thinking about it. After penning last entry around two in the morning I bathed, changed into clean pyjamas slippers dressing gown and was enjoying small whisky-toddy nightcap by livingroom fire when doorbell rang and rang and rang until I opened door to large crying baby upheld by woman *saying hysterically, "Can I come in Johnny? I've nowhere else to go." In she came and it was Niki. Not knowing what else to do I led her into kitchen. She sat down at table, burst into tears so I had two weeping females (the wean was female) in this house where to my certain knowledge nobody since I was a baby has wept. I tried quieting them with tea and warmed milk which she put into bottle for baby. I made cold beef pickles tomato cheese sandwiches because she was hungry and stiff hot toddy that she gratefully drank after to my horror adding some to baby's bottle. Between bursts of hysterical tears in phrases I did not try to fully understand she spoke of being beaten deserted involved in vague unspeakable crimes by someone who then attempted murder and suicide with or without success. Only two of her sentences were clear and often repeated, "Don't throw us out Johnny, we've nowhere else to go," and, "Please don't send for the polis."*

I escaped from her by rushing upstairs to make a bed. Luckily wardrobe in main bedroom still has thanks to Nan big drawer of sheets blankets pillowcases I never needed so quickly made up bed in small room opposite so now Niki and Mo (what is Mo short for? Surely not Moses or Moloch) are sleeping there. I hope. How long will they stay?

During our session in kitchen Niki produced photograph from pathetic little knapsack that had held Mo's bottle, gave it me saying, "This is yours, sorry there's no frame." Without pleasure recognized young self in gown and mortarboard between Nan and Nell. Asked why had kept it she said, "I sometimes liked looking at it." This suggests she sometimes liked remembering me how strange. I hardly gave her a thought after she vanished two years ago.

In the wee small hours last night, perhaps around three o'clock, I heard the tapping on my bedroom door that I had been dreading for over a week. I unlocked and opened it a few inches and saw Niki in nothing but her knickers. In a voice low enough not to wake Mo in the room behind her (Mo wakens horribly easily) she asked if she could join me? I whispered, "Sorry, not with a baby in the house," and cautiously shut and locked the door again, feeling terribly guilty. I have never before had the chance of comforting a young thing and gratifying myself at the same time, but have no sexual appetite for pitiable women.

Cannot work on my book with Niki and Mo in the house and am afraid to leave them alone here for longer than it takes to run to the Byres Road shops and back. She won't go out because she says people are after her. I do not ask who or why because her answers would certainly be lies. For three weeks she has hardly left the bedroom. I am sick of carrying trays of food upstairs, sick of the queer looks shopkeepers give me when I buy disposable nappies, women's underwear (since she brought no change of clothes) also lipstick, mascara and false eyelashes. When asked why she who wants to see nobody must doll herself up she said her face in the mirror was all she had to look at, and why didn't I have a television set? I answered that television is a drug that added nothing to life, that it distracts, deludes, insulates people from reality and she yelled, "That's why I want it!" When I said it was unhealthy to keep a baby in one room all day she said I could take it out as often as I wanted. I do NOT want to take it out. If Mo starts liking and trusting me I will start feeling responsible and be stuck with the child until it is old enough to support itself, which will not happen before I die of natural causes.

A dull dreadful day. Having paid one of the cleaners to buy Niki and Mo warm coats with big hoods, also the modern equivalent of the sling-seat squaws used to carry papooses, I got my lodgers out of the house by going for a taxi, using it to collect them from the house and take us to Anniesland station. Here Niki was sure nobody would recognize her if I carried Mo and she kept her head well back in the hood and a scarf over her mouth as if she had toothache. We took a train to Helensburgh, walked along the esplanade, looked in shop windows, had tea and ice cream in café, took train and taxi home. They enjoyed the outing. I would have enjoyed it too had I been a character in a sentimental Victorian novel. I did not enjoy it.

My life a hopeless nightmare. Now nearly a year since she came. Work on my book at a standstill. Whole idea of it awkward, wrong, impossible. Can sometimes snatch half hour in library reading dull social histories of Glasgow, half-heartedly meaning to write another. My former womanless, childless existence used to make me feel outcast from life's feast – know now it was a paradise of freedom and hope. An implacable force, probably Nature herself, has enslaved me to a selfish bitch I neither love nor have sex with. Only a masochist could stand more of this. I was not a slave when I shopped, cooked, cleaned for Nell and Nan – they had done as much for me before taking to their beds, and I knew they would one day leave me by dying. Niki and Mo won't die unless I

Have never never never lost my temper because nothing annoying used to happen, but for weeks now am containing with difficulty rage that must end in bloodshed and infanticide when it finally overwhelms me. This diary will prove I was driven to it. I may only be suffering what many married men endure but they must have been immunized against weeping women, screaming infants by miserable childhoods full of frantic mothers and blubbering siblings. I was spared that normal-family-life shit and am too old to take more. Am on brink of breakdown, verge of insanity. Another day of this life will drive me to

---

Amazing improvement. This morning overheard cleaners casually refer to me as Mo's father! Cross-examined, they said Niki told them so. I thanked them politely for that news, went upstairs, and to stop myself grasping Niki's throat seized an ornate vase I have never liked and hurled it to smash in the

fireplace. Then I stamped around the room clawing the air with
hooked fingers, howling like a wolf, growling like a tiger,
spitting at Niki the filthiest names I knew – "Inconsiderate
mother! Untruthful parasite! Selfish manipulator!" I only went
quiet when starting to enjoy this undignified performance. Its
effect was remarkable. Baby Mo stopped wailing and watched
me with obvious delight. Niki stopped weeping and when silence
fell asked in a plaintive but sensible voice what I wanted? I
pointed to the mess in the fireplace and said, "Clean that up,
bitch, and you'll hear!" – using an American accent which
somehow seemed appropriate. She has now agreed to take Mo
out after breakfast each morning when I go to the library. She
will not be given a key to the house but receive twelve pounds a
day for expenses and be let back in when I return after five to
make dinner. In the evenings she and Moloch will be left in the
house if I go to Tennants, but if I find she has let people in
when I am out she and infant will be evicted, and if she robs me
again I will call the police. She knows I will keep my word so at
last, with peace of mind and enriched experience, I can devote
myself to a new and better book. What kind will it be?

I am starting to glimpse something truly original, like a great
figure emerging from a fog, a narrative uniting global and
Scottish history and my own without fictional masks, an
immense task. Hurrah and onward, Tunnock, while keeping your
eyes on the world around you.

Last week, on the way back from Heraghty's around noon, called
in at the Hasta Mañana on Gorbals Street and saw the small
big-nosed lawyer I met there over a year ago. Perhaps I was
looking for her. I took an empty chair opposite as she talked into
a mobile phone with her usual speed and intensity. She spoke to
people about impending court appearances for over fifteen
minutes without seeming to see me. I finished an excellent bowl
of soup and was starting on a salad when she switched the phone
off and said, "Well John Tunnock, how's Medician Florence?"
I told her I had been forced to abandon it and was embarking
on something that would also show visions of the local and

This long
dash
indicates the
only friend of
John Tunnock
who has
refused
permission to
let their
name be
printed.

This
demonstration
was on
February 15th
2003.

contemporary. She asked why and after pondering my very wordy answer thrust an unclenched fist at me across the table. I stared at it, puzzled, until I saw she was offering to shake my hand. I allowed this and found my new book has made me a new, very useful friend. Her name is ———— She gave me her phone number. I gave her my address.

Yesterday I received her postcard telling me Tony Blair (though she spelled him Bliar) would be addressing the Scottish Trades Union leaders in Glasgow Conference Centre, that folk from all over Scotland would be marching there to protest against another Anglo-American war with Iraq. Other big protest marches would be happening in London, most European capitals and New York and Sydney, so she would call in a taxi at nine today and pick me up to take part. This frightened me. I approve of people publicising their ideas in peaceful protest marches, whether they are workers who don't want their industries shut, or pacifists who want nuclear missiles banned, or even Orangemen who think the world's worst menace is the Catholic Church. Freedom of speech needs everyone to openly show what they believe, even if their beliefs are stupid and wrong. Without public discussions and demonstrations the only alternative to government by millionaire politicians is terrorist bombings. But I am emotionally incapable of public appearances. When the taxi came I went out and began explaining this, but before I had said two sentences through the taxi window this implacable woman opened the door and said "Stop talking, ostrich! Get in!" I did. It was a bright, fresh, sunny morning so I had no excuse to even go back indoors for a coat.

So by taxi to Glasgow Green where not one crowd but many crowds were moving between triumphal arch before High Court, the Clyde to the south and People's Palace Museum in the east. In many demonstrations weirdly dressed people are noticeable and reported by the press as typical. This multitude had hardly any. Most folk were pleasantly un-uniform and of every age. Young parents pushed toddlers in prams. Two boys of ten or eleven, with no apparent presiding adult, walked carefully side by side to display a single cardboard sandwich board with peace slogans written in fibre-tipped pens. The Eurydice Women's

Socialist Choir sang peace songs. A nice woman held up a sign saying I Trust No Bush But My Own. There was a group with a banner saying, Dumfries Ageing Hippies Against The War, a group of older folk whose banner announced THE TAYSIDE PENSIONERS' FORUM. ———— told me Blair is proposing to abolish old age pensions because workers' contributions are now too small. So New Labour will undo the Liberal Party's People's Budget of 1909? I am worse than an ostrich, I am Rip Van Winkle. Many held up printed placards saying Make War on Want, Not Iraq, Not In My Name Mr Blair, No Blood For Oil, and white cut-out polystyrene doves on the ends of little canes, and distributing radical party news sheets against the war and demanding Palestine liberation. Light brown people (who I refuse to call blacks) were over five per cent of the crowd.

There were no visible organizers so we joined the people at their thickest beside Greendyke Street where the march was scheduled to start, edging in until pressure of other bodies made movement impossible. In this cheerful, good-humoured crowd ———— seemed to know everyone, pointing to musicians and actors I never heard of, besides the novelists A.L. Kennedy and Bernard MacLaverty, poets Aonghas MacNeacail and Liz Lochhead, the writer Angus Calder who was too far away for me to introduce myself. At last guidance came from the police who stood in a line between the crowd and the street. A small number moved aside and let us gradually through in numbers that started walking ten abreast, filling the width of the street without overlapping pavements on each side. We entered the procession about half a mile behind the leaders, from Greendyke Street marching up the Saltmarket to Glasgow Cross. Occasionally those around us burst into wild cheering inspired by folk waving encouragement from upper tenement and office windows. The stream of the march split neatly in two to pass the gawky clock tower of the Tollbooth, all that remains of Glasgow's 17th century town hall, magistrates' court and city jail.

John Prebble's book about the Glencoe massacre mentions that in 1692 two British Army officers were jailed in the Tollbooth. Before reaching Glencoe village they opened their sealed orders and, finding themselves commanded to put men, women and children to the sword, broke their swords, marched back to Fort William and told their commander that no decent officer should obey such an order. They were sent south by ship for court martial, but Prebble says there is no record of one so they may have been released without punishment. It occurred to me that a great anti-war memorial should be set on that tower commemorating soldiers who had bravely refused to obey wicked orders. Scotland's city centres, castles, cathedrals, public parks are so full of war memorials to heroically obedient killers that visitors might think warfare had always been Scotland's main export. Some of the most elaborate put up before 1918 commemorate a few officers and men who died in Africa, Egypt and Asia where they were part of regiments killing thousands of natives fighting on their own soil without the advantage of gunpowder. The company of so many people who wanted peace suddenly filled me with enthusiasm for this anti-war memorial. I thought it could also carry the names of the four British officers who resigned their commissions during the 1991 Bush war on Saddam Hussein's Iraq – they were protesting against bombing Iraqis who could not fight back against cluster bombs "that minced up everything living within a three-mile airstrip." I started explaining my great idea and it hardly left my mouth when –––––– said, "Don't waste time thinking about it. No local government, no public body in Scotland will ever allow it." But surely many folk in Scotland and England admire brave refusers and would agree with Berthold Brecht (or was it Heinrich Böll?) who said the worst German vice was obedience. Yet in 1991 I read that British and U.S. airmen enthusiastically queued to airstrike Iraqi ground troops. One bomber said that from above they looked like swarms of cockroaches.

From a helicopter that crossed back and forward above our march must also have looked like cockroaches as we went via Ingram Street to George Square. Our biggest roar went up as the Civic Chambers came in sight. Why were no Glasgow Town Councillors waving encouragement from the windows? Why were none in the procession holding up a banner saying GLASGOW COUNCILLORS AGAINST THE WAR? They could

have marched behind the banner of Unison, the local
government employees' trade union. But in that case the Labour
Party leaders might not let them stand at the next election, so
they would lose their wages. From George Square we saw a
silhouette of our procession crossing the summit of Blythswood
Hill far far ahead.

I have always been a stranger to group emotions, fearing
and disliking even the idea of them, and was surprized by a
warm relaxed friendliness spreading through me because I was
part of this miles-long peaceful procession of folk I have taught
or drunk with in pubs all my life, the Scottish workers,
tradespeople and professional folk I feel at home with. This
sensation became so strong that it brought tears to my eyes,
perhaps because a small brass band not far behind was playing
familiar melancholy tunes, The Floo'ers o' the Forest, The Auld
Hoose, The Bonnie Banks of Loch Lomond. I began describing my
sensations but ———— said, "Yes, all these folk will suffer if our
businessmen listen to an expert in Scottish Enterprise, a
government body once called The Scottish Development Agency.
He is advizing Scottish businesses to have their goods made by
workers in eastern Europe or Asia. But crying about it won't help."

At last we arrived in a desert of car parks covering the site
of the former Princess Dock, a basin surrounded by cranes
where giant ships unloaded cargoes when Glasgow was a big
international port and centre of manufacture only fifty years
ago. The crowds already seemed more of a multitude than they
had been on Glasgow Green and confronted a shining white
building locally nicknamed The Armadillo, a huge apparently
windowless metallic structure whose arched sections seem
sliding out of each other. A line of yellow-jacketed policemen
was looped protectively around it and I realized The Armadillo
is the Scottish Conference Centre where Blair would now be
addressing the Scottish Trades Unions. We stood listening to
occasional storms of applause from a crowd around an open-
topped double-decker bus near the river. That speech was
inaudible to those not near the bus because loudspeakers had
been banned, so the orator may have been a spokesman for the
Church of Scotland, or for Scotland's Asiatic Communities, or

for the C.N.D. or for the Scottish Socialist Party because later I heard all of these made speeches and so (amazingly) did Glasgow's Labour Lord Provost, a woman. After half an hour we left, moving against the flood of people still coming because the procession was much longer than its three-mile route.

I walked back home alone, needing peace to think about this wholly new experience. It cannot be ignored but how can I use it? Kelvingrove Park was crowded with others who had left the procession so I crossed it feeling safe from Hitler the Second. I called in at Tennants where Mastermind told me Blair had rescheduled his speech, delivering it before 10 o'clock when the procession left Glasgow Green and flying back to England before it arrived, adding, "No doubt when Blair dies the obituaries will praise his moral courage in ignoring the electorate's opinion."

Home by 2.30 where Niki served me with afternoon tea as she has done regularly since I lost my temper last week. For the first time she had got the amount of sugar and milk in my cup exactly right. I praised her. She seemed pleased. Could I train her to become, not a mistress or wife, but a helpmeet who shops, cooks, serves nice meals? A companion who will help make my descent through senility to death a comfortable passage after I have published my masterpiece and enjoy the fame and fortune it cannot fail to bring?

Protestants instead of **protesters** may be a hint that anti-war protesters are heirs to the traditions of the 15th century Reformation.

My lawyer friend phoned this morning and, her voice harsh with indignation, told me BBC television reports of Blair's Glasgow speech yesterday were inter-cut with views of the protestors outside the building, thus suggesting he had delivered his speech as he had planned, instead of fleeing before the protestants arrived. I told her my book would correct that account of our march at the very end, unless I lived to see Blair arrested for his lie that Iraq is nearly ready to atom bomb Britain in 45 minutes.

Am confirmed in my new plan for the book by Nicolai Gogol's life who, like Burns and Walter Scott and me, was first inspired by the songs and ballads of his homeland, the Ukraine. He spent years attempting a history showing how different it was from the rest of Russia because Ukrainian Cossacks had kept Islam out of Christian Europe in the south when Polish Catholics were doing the same thing in the north. But he was no provincial! His Taras Bulba, fruit of that historical research, owes much to a Russian translation of the Odyssey. His Dead Souls, the first great Russian novel, owes much to his reading of Don Quixote and The Pickwick Papers. He tried to complete that vision of Russia (as a Hell of grotesque souls) with a Heavenly modern conclusion in which his fraudulent hero is redeemed by a good Russian prince and Orthodox Christianity. He failed, but with his friend Pushkin, generated all Russian literature between the failure of the December revolution of 1825 and the Soviet revolution in the 1920s that is great, unique and worth world-wide attention. My book will fail to present a vision of self-governing Scotland becoming a unique example of good Socialism, but may manage to show why it could and should be. Forget fame and fortune. I recently read a story about young American students asked, as a psychological test, to say what inanimate thing they would like to be. A black girl upsets everyone by saying, "a revolver". I asked myself that question and immediately answered "a molecule". Why? Molecules are invisible, anonymous, invulnerable and essential. My book will almost certainly appear after my death when I will be invisible and invincible.

Start it tomorrow.

This story is *Drinking Coffee Elsewhere* from Z Z Packer's collection of that name published by Canongate, Edinburgh, 2004.

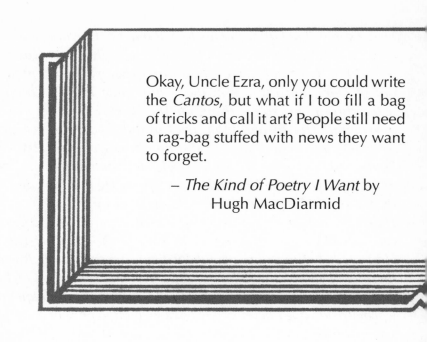

Okay, Uncle Ezra, only you could write the *Cantos*, but what if I too fill a bag of tricks and call it art? People still need a rag-bag stuffed with news they want to forget.

– *The Kind of Poetry I Want* by Hugh MacDiarmid

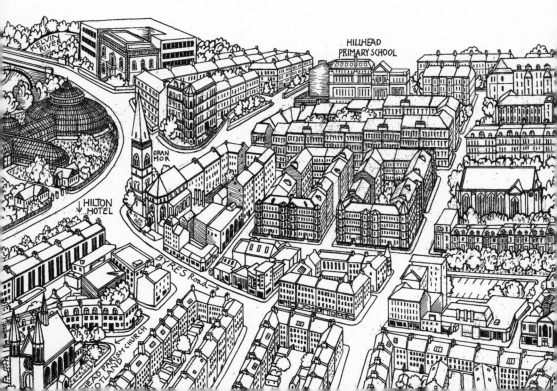

TUNNOCK'S
PLACE
AND TIME

UNIVERSITY
LIBRARY

UNIVERSITY
of GLASGOW

RIVER KELVIN

E
Hillhead
Glasgow
N viewed
from the West
2007
W

TENNENTS
PUB

← Byres →
Road

15: WEE ME

MY CHARACTER WAS SHAPED by two gentle, unmarried women who mothered me from infancy, providing all I needed and almost all I wanted without a word of reproof or complaint. If I am not now monstrously selfish it is because I loved them as dearly as they loved me, so tried to save them from the trouble a dependent, growing boy might cause elderly women. This was usually easy as I only felt perfectly safe and happy at home with them. The unsatisfactory parts of my world were outside it. Each Sunday we attended services in the church where a grandfather who died years before my birth had been the first Minister of God. I enjoyed the hymns, had no objection to prayers but would have found the sermons boring had Nell, the youngest aunt, not fed me a chocolate cream or liquorice allsort or peppermint humbug whenever I fidgeted. Too much sugar rots the teeth so I was only given sweets during Sunday sermons, blissfully sucking while my eyes dreamily explored the great interior like a spacious lantern. The church had been modelled on the gothic Sainte-Chapelle in Paris so there was no pillar or gallery to prevent a clear view of the coved ceiling and tall stained glass windows. I was too young to consciously enjoy its beauty but now believe it enlarged my soul like all truly good things we meet when young.

But I stopped enjoying the Sunday schools held by a church elder in a comfortable part of the undercroft. She was a retired school teacher as kind as my aunts. She told us simple Bible

stories chiefly about Jesus at first, but at the age of seven started
teaching the early history of mankind and God's chosen people with straight readings from *Genesis, Exodus, Numbers, Deuteronomy, Joshua, Samuel* and *Kings*. She omitted dull *begat* chapters and sexually explicit ones like Abraham's fraudulent prostitution of his wife in Genesis chapters 12 and 20, but did not censor the genocidal wars by which the children of Israel replaced the original inhabitants of Palestine. I thought the Lord God who ordered the Israelites to *"smite them, and utterly destroy them; and make no pact with them, nor show mercy unto them"* was cruel and unfair. I said so. The teacher was a gentle soul. She told me the war was not a fight for land between Jews and those earlier settlers, the Ammonites, Midianites, Canaanites and Philistines; it was a "life-and-death struggle between truth and falsehood for the cultural development of God's people". I asked what that meant. Becoming a little flustered she said God *needed* to order the slaughter of men, women and children who did not believe in Him, so that the Jews had a homeland where His son Jesus, Prince of Peace, could be born to preach the religion of peace for everyone. I did not then know that Christian nations had been as warlike as pagan ones, and had used the Old Testament for centuries after the crucifixion to justify the invasion and massacre of foreigners. But the teacher knew this, so skipped from the spread of Christianity by Saint Paul to the recent victory over Fascism by Britain and the U.S.A. She did not mention the essential help nations got from the atheist U.S.S.R. but said the German defeat was a Christian victory and had established a United Nations Organisation that would oppose warfare from now onward. Yet this explanation did not stop me thinking the Israelites had been cruel, greedy and unfair. I told my aunts so and Nell looked at Nan in a slightly guilty way. After a brief pause Nan her elder sister said firmly, "You are right to think that. Most of what the Bible says Jesus said should be believed. Some of the rest was written by poets as good as any you will find in Palgrave's *Golden Treasury* and some by propagandists as bad as any in Nazi Germany. But the Bible has so changed world history that nobody will

This quotation is from the *Bible for Today* edited by John Stirling and published by Oxford University Press in 1941.

understand that if they know nothing about it. But you need not attend Sunday school if you do not wish."

So I stopped going. Nan also said, "Nell and I are faithful members of the Church of Scotland because, though agnostics like most religious people nowadays, we are also old maids ruled by force of habits drilled into us by a rigorous parent. You need not come with us to church if you dislike it."

But I liked hymns, stained glass, also the sweets which I only stopped sucking when I lost my taste for sherry. I attended church with my aunts until they were bedridden.

At school my shyness and short, stout figure made me uninteresting to both pupils and teachers though I was scrupulously clean, always neatly dressed, and did well in all my lessons except physical training and sport. The clash between life inside and outside my home was shown in my schoolbags.

In the late 1940s the children of thrifty parents still carried schoolbooks in khaki satchels issued by the government to hold gas masks during the recent war, but in posh Hillhead most of us had cloth or leather schoolbags hung by straps from our backs. Mine was of shining leather which always looked new because on Saturday mornings Aunt Nell brushed it with shoe blacking, then polished with rags until it shone. I would have preferred a schoolbag stained by accidents like those of other pupils, but could not hurt her feelings by telling her so, and eventually insisted on doing that job myself, though not quite so efficiently. Aunt Nan handled our finances. When I started at Hillhead Secondary School aged 11 Nan replaced my bag with a pigskin briefcase. I foresaw the mockery it would bring but pretended to be grateful. Only our school captain and some prefects in the final year had briefcases, none as blatantly expensive and manly as first-year Tunnock's. After the evening meal we called Tea or (if Nan and Nell had asked a friend to share it) High Tea, we usually sat in the drawing room, listening to the BBC. At the end of my first Hillhead Secondary week I brought home the briefcase full of new

Many Glasgow families called the evening meal *tea or high-tea*, and called the mid-day luncheon, *dinner*. Tea was usually eaten when the wage earner came home around 6 o'clock, and contained a large main course followed by a variety of biscuits and cakes and several cups of tea.

schoolbooks, and asked for a table in my bedroom to do

homework there in private.
"Why of course," said Nell, but Nan said firmly, "No."
We stared at her. After a solemn pause she said, "Homework
certainly needs privacy. He must have the study."
"Yes indeed," cried Nell with enthusiasm and they conducted
me there. The study was a room my aunts always kept clean
but otherwise avoided, perhaps because their father had
insisted on privacy there when writing his sermons, which
seem to have been his only work when not conducting Sunday
services. I had always assumed it was forbidden to me, though
nobody had said so. They ushered me and my briefcase inside
but stayed out, telling me to make myself at home and would
I like a cup of tea in half an hour? but I wanted nothing before
our usual supper together before bedtime.
"Well," said Nell, "If you want something sooner, strike that
twice and one of us will come running."
She pointed to a brass push-bell on a massive, leather-topped
desk. Looking strangely satisfied they left me there. Either then
or later I heard Nan say it was nice to have a man working in
the study again.

On first sitting down in the leather-upholstered swivel chair
and spreading my schoolbooks on the desk I felt daunted by
this ponderously furnished chamber, but soon came a feeling
of ease and mastery because this place was wholly *mine*. I
had no need to ensure privacy by turning the large brass door
key in the lock because the aunts never entered without
knocking and asking my permission. Nell only entered to dust
and hoover once a week when I was at school. An elaborate
ebony inkstand on the desk had a shallow little drawer in the
base where I found keys unlocking the desk drawers and doors
of glass-fronted bookcases. One drawer held a cut-glass
tumbler and a stoppered decanter three-quarter full of brown
liquid. In cupboards under the bookcases I found more of this
liquid: five bottles of Harvey's Bristol Cream Sherry and several
dozen empty ones. Tasting that sherry did not then occur to
me. In the following weeks I gradually found the delights of

From
Chambers
Biographical
Dictionary:
HARRIS,
Frank (1856-
1931), British
writer and
journalist,
born,
according to
his
autobiography,
in Galway,
but
according to
his own later
statement, in
Tenby, ran
away to New
York at the
age of
fifteen,
became
boot-black,
labourer
building
Brooklyn
Bridge, and
worker in a
Chicago
hotel, but in
1874
embarked
upon the
study of law
at the
University of
Kansas.
About 1876
he returned
to England
and entered
the news-
paper world.
Perhaps the
most
colourful
figure in
contemporary
journalistic
circles, an

the bookshelves among a mass of very dull sermons.

The first discoveries were an early *Encyclopaedia Britannica* and an 1850 *Chambers' Conversationalist's Lexicon* with engravings (some coloured by hand) of improbable flying machines that could never have left the ground, wooden warships with side paddles and smoking funnels between masts crowded with sails, grotesque creatures, plants, castles, temples and cities. These pictures and fragments of text took me to a time when the U.S.A. and Russia traded in slaves and serfs, when Japan was closed to foreigners and maps of most large continents had big blank areas inscribed *Terra Incognita*. Then I found two volumes of Rabelais' *Gargantua and Pantagruel* illustrated by Heath Robinson, Balzac's *Droll Tales* illustrated by Doré, Kraft-Ebbings' *Sexual Pathology* with photographs. Most precious was a set of four tall volumes with ornately gilded leather bindings published by The Harvard Gentleman Scholars' Press of New York in a limited edition of 150, each personally signed and numbered on the biblio page by the editor, Frank Harris. The pictures alone must have made the cost immense: Ovid's *Art of Love* was illustrated by Mantegna, Aristophanes' *Lysistrata* by Aubrey Beardsley, Baudelaire's *Les Fleurs du Mal* by Felicien Rops, Burns' *Tam O' Shanter* by William Bell Scott. I investigated the texts of these after sampling the illustrations, eventually reading all the *Droll Tales* and most of Rabelais, the latter in what I now know was Urquhart's translation. The Harvard Gentleman Scholar volumes were a constant delight. The verses in the original tongues were helped by English prose translations and the pictures which showed a lot of lively nudity.

Of course the translation of *Tam O' Shanter* was needless. Any English speaker can easily understand it. I read Burns' verses to learn the story behind Bell Scott's outline drawings of the witch Nanny leaping and flinging about in her cutty sark, and enjoyed them so much that I tackled his complete poems which were also in Grandpa Tunnock's library, beside Catherine Carswell's 1920s biography of him. She had aroused the fury of admirers who sentimentalized him as a hard-working family man (which he was) by calmly and without censure naming his lovers and illegitimate children. These Burns books filled a big gap in my education because Burns was not mentioned at school where I learned verses by Wordsworth, Shelley and Keats – *naytcha* poems, the teachers called them, being careful not to pronounce a final r. The subject matter (daffodils, the west wind, sky-lark, nightingale) were certainly natural but not human. Burns' poems are all about human nature. He loves it at its most fallible, so how could *he* be taught in schools? When I was a teacher I would have been sacked had I taught young children *The Jolly Beggars'* chorus – *A fig for those by* LAW *protected,* LIBERTY*'s a glorious feast*! COURTS *for cowards were erected,* CHURCHES *built to please the Priest.* Burns is declaring that sexual love, after breathing eating and drinking, is the most essential human activity and the most enjoyable.

> *What is* TITLE, *what is* TREASURE,
>> What is reputation's care?
> If we lead a life of pleasure,
>> *'tis no matter* HOW *or* WHERE.

> With the ready trick and fable
>> Round we wander all the day;
> And at night, in barn or stable,
>> Hug our doxies on the hay.

> *Does the train attended* CARRIAGE
>> Thro' the country lighter rove?
> *Does the sober bed of* MARRIAGE
>> Witness brighter scenes of love?

Most folk, especially children, instinctively know pleasure is the best thing we can get so distrust all authority that tries to postpone or ration or abolish it. This instinct was denounced as original sin by Fathers of the Christian church from Saint Paul and Augustine to Luther and Calvin. Most educations deliberately divert, destroy or pervert that belief – a good reason

incorrigible liar, a vociferous boaster, an unscrupulous adventurer and philanderer, with the aspect and outlook of a typical melodrama 'Sir Jasper', and an obsession with sex which got his auto-biography, *My Life and Loves* (1923-27) banned for pornography, he had a great impact on Fleet Street as editor of the *Fortnightly Review,* *Saturday Review,* *Vanity Fair* and of the *Evening News,* which became under his aegis a pioneer in the new cult of provocative headlines and suggestive sensationalism.

for academia to neglect Burns even after the 1980s, when commercial entertainment and advertizements were added to academia's raw materials.

Yet Wordsworth, Coleridge, Byron and Keats took his greatness for granted. Matthew Arnold thought his poetry second only to Chaucer's, while regretting the ugliness of Burns' Scottish subject matter because, *No one can deny that it is of advantage for a poet to deal with a beautiful world.* T. S. Eliot defends Burns for his choice of subjects because a poet should *be able to see beneath both beauty and ugliness; to see the boredom, and the horror, and the glory.* With sinister dexterity Eliot then calls Burns, *A decadent representative of a great alien tradition* – by which he meant that the great Scots pre-Reformation poets were courtiers and clergymen while Burns (like Melville and Hawthorne) never rose above the social rank of exciseman, and his poetic vocabulary was not used by royalty. Since a German dynasty was popped onto the British throne in 1714, who but Eliot has thought royalty a source or defence of profound speech? *The Jolly Beggars'* chorus and its capitalized abstract nouns are in the polite standard 18th century English Burns used when writing broad general truths. When writing about particularly Scots things – poverty, women gossiping, men getting happily drunk, a grotesque hypocrite at prayer, every kind of sexual love and also love of freedom – he used Scottish words. I am annoyed by daft Burns fans who forget his use of 18th century south British mandarin speech. The song which ought to be Scotland's national anthem, *Scots Wha Hae,* is nearly all romantic English clichés – *Welcome to your gory bed or to Victory, Now's the day and now's the hour, See the front of Battle lour* etcetera. It needs to be sung with a Scots accent because first line, *Scots Wha Hae* (the only line spelled in phonetic Scots) cannot be sung by singers who say *Scots Who Have.* Try doing it if you doubt me.

Grandpa Tunnock's library introduced me to England's national literature through three big stout leather-bound volumes of Shakespeare's *Histories, Comedies* and *Tragedies*

containing (said the title pages) *the celebrated illustrations*
of Kenny Meadows whose sinister, almost surrealistic
illustrations seduced me into the astonishing delights of
Shakespeare's language. Sometimes I went round for hours
muttering a single phrase – *sharked up a list of lawless*
resolutes also *the cloud capped towers, the gorgeous palaces*
and also *I am tame sir. Pronounce!* Yet the joyful education I
got from him, Burns, Balzac, Rabelais, Aristophanes were
mostly unconnected with the schoolwork I was taught in order
to pass exams and qualify for University. I would have hated
Latin and Greek if the Gentleman Scholar's Library had not
proved what my classics teachers never suggested – Romans
and Greeks enjoyed every kind of sex together with jokes
about it. And my enriched reading certainly got me high
marks for schools essays, persuading me writing would one
day make me famous. This had to happen because my future
fame would not come from physical strength, manipulative
dexterity and a fine appearance. Plans for a literary
masterpiece became more cloudily ambitious the more I read.
I began filling notebooks with fine sentences to use in it.
Finding so much goodness in an obscure library gave me a
taste for discarded textbooks, biographies, slender volumes
of forgotten poetry in second-hand shops and stalls. I believed
most neglected books contained at least one exciting phrase
that my great book would at last restore to general knowledge
and make ENJOYABLE. It would also include love – erotic
fantasies of a Rabelaisian and Robert Burns kind. I may have
matured late but my *sex in the head* (as D.H. Lawrence called
it) never stiffened my penis before I discovered pornography.
Kraft-Ebbing's account of sexual perversions in 19th Century
Vienna intrigued but did not excite. My happiest hours were
in the study before I learned to masturbate, but read, scribbled
and fantasised about my eventual great book. I agreed with
Keats who said, *fine writing is, next to fine doing, the top*
thing in the world.

Study and school apart, Nan and Nell and I had a rich
social life. We went to plays at the Glasgow Citizens' Theatre,

to symphony concerts at the St Andrews Hall, to Carl Rosa and D'Oyly Carte operas that came yearly to Glasgow, and to exhibitions in Kelvingrove Art Galleries. In these places we met friends of my aunts' age and sex who treated me with the deference they felt due to a respectable dominant male. But at home my aunts so worried about me having no friend of my own age that at last I invented one.

One boy in my class was as friendless as myself. His clothing indicated a poorer home than most of us. His face was pitted by acne scars and his movements were awkward and jerky, maybe from an early attack of infantile paralysis. There was a rumour that he should have gone to the *Junior Secondary School*, but had only passed the qualifying exam to the Senior Secondary because the examiners pitied him. Unlike me, who was mocked, Stewart Doig (nicknamed Stoory Doig) was simply avoided. Nobody sat beside him in class if there was an empty seat elsewhere. When there was not I had to sit beside him, at which times he would try to start conversations which I discouraged, because like most outcasts who long to be accepted by a majority I disliked others in my situation. When I said this boy was my school friend Nell and Nan, who often spoke simultaneously, cried, "Bring him home to tea!"

Stoor is demotic Scots for dust or muck, so *Stoory* means dirty.

See note on page 104.

I hid my horror of the idea by saying sadly, "Impossible. He has a widowed mother who keeps him on a very short leash. She frets a lot if he doesn't eat with her – she's a bit of an invalid who has very little company – and he's a very devoted son."

Nell cried, "O poor woman!" and Nan, "And poor boy! We must do something to help. Perhaps we should visit them?"

"No," I said, shaking my head, "His mother may be poor but she's very proud and would hate anything like condescension."

"You've met his mother?" said Nan, surprized.

"No, but he talks a lot about her, and that's the impression I get."

This sounded inconclusive and unconvincing so I added,

"I've been invited to their house for a meal once or twice, but honestly, I prefer eating with you."

"But you *must* go!" they cried and, "The poor woman will be glad to see her son has got at least one good friend," said Nell, and Nan said, "It will be a rare social occasion for her. I will bake a cake for them and you must also take a bunch of flowers."

This conversation left me astonished by the ready stream of lies I had smoothly told, but depressed by the consequences. From now on my aunts wanted reports about Doig and his mother, who really was a widow but not (as far as I knew) an invalid. Nell and Nan were so pleased with this fiction of my new friend that I had no heart to destroy it by telling the truth or inventing a quarrel with Stoory that would make reconciliation impossible. A time came when I could not postpone a visit to his home so set off one Saturday after lunch with a bouquet of chrysanthemums in one hand, in the other the briefcase containing a bottle of dry sherry and rich dark fruit cake in a cardboard box. When out of sight of the house I turned north instead of south, went quickly through Botanic Gardens to the Ha'penny Bridge, chucked the flowers into the river as I crossed and then turned upstream along a path that is now the start of the West Highland Walkway. It was a grey day and thin rain began to fall. I passed the great weir serving the west bank paper mill and under an arch of Kelvingrove Aqueduct sat down on a lump of rubble and took out cake-box and bottle. Even on bright summer days this is a dank, dreary place but few folk pass that way and that Saturday it suited my mood. I opened the box, broke off handfuls of cake and stolidly ate them between swigs from the neck of the bottle. My previous experiences of alcohol had been small glasses of hot toddy brought to me in bed with an aspirin pill when a cold looked like coming on. I had never before drunk at one sitting a whole bottle of *anything*. As the sherry went down my gloom gave way to foolish, light-headed cheer. I flung the bottle away, stood up and everything seemed spinning and tilting

Kelvin Aqueduct, Maryhill: architect Robert Whitworth, built at a cost of £8509 in 1787-90, 400 feet long and 70 high, then the largest canal aqueduct in Britain. Four rusticated arches of 50 feet carry spandrel walls horizontally arched from the massive cut-water buttresses needed to contain the waters of the Forth and Clyde Canal.

round me. By an effort of will I stopped that happening, which added a sensation of power to my strange cheerfulness. Leaving most of the cake for birds and rodents I strode up to the Maryhill Road and along the busy pavement, amazed that nobody seemed to see how drunk I was. Either my self-control was super-human or other folk had also secretly drunk too much and were too busy disguising the fact to notice my condition. This last explanation seemed most probable and enhanced my sense of total freedom.

Nobody will understand what followed
without a digression.

16: EARLY SEX

WHEN I ASKED MY AUNTS where people came from I was very very young but remember the guilty glance Nell always gave Nan when wishing her to speak for them. After a moment Nan said slowly and deliberately, "Everybody begins as something the size and shape of a tadpole. It floats in an elastic bag of fluid the size and shape of an egg and this bag is in a woman's stomach. The bag stretches as the wee fishy thing gets larger, growing a human head, arms, fingers, toes etcetera. After nine months, usually, it hatches out of the mother's stomach, just as chickens hatch out of eggs."

"You mean babies break their mother's stomachs open?" I cried, because one Easter I had been given a brown chocolate egg which, cracked open, contained a chicken made of white chocolate. Nan said, "Not at all! The narrow groove between the halves of a woman's bottom continues between her legs to the point at which males . . . men like you . . . have a . . ." (She hesitated and flushed slightly) ". . . toot. Uretor. Penis is the adult word for it. Through this groove that only women possess the baby emerges in what is technically called *birth*. Births are seldom fatal but always painful. Many women like Nan and me choose not to give birth. We have never needed children because we have you."

I brooded on this. The fact that other children had mothers and I had aunts had never before struck me as strange enough to need an explanation, but Nell cleared her throat and Nan immediately supplied one: "Your mother was a wonderful woman who left this house, toiling in a British government office until she gave birth to you. She then handed you over to us, returned to the service of her country in London and died bravely in a Nazi blitzkrieg. You should be proud of her. It has been our privilege to serve her by caring for you."

Nell clapped her hands saying happily, "O good, well done Nan, that covers everything."

I thought so too. After that my aunts often referred to my mother. The meals they made were so good that I have never enjoyed meals as much since they stopped cooking for me, but after that first mention of my mother they never served me with anything, not even a soft boiled egg, without telling me how much better it would have been if my mother had supplied it. She had also (they said) been much better than them at knitting, darning, washing clothes, lighting fires, handling money and schoolwork. My school reports gave me high marks. They would nod happily over them saying, "Yes, you have your mother's brain."

Years passed before I learned that babies needed fathers. I thought nature ensured half the animals born were masculine because women needed a breadwinner to support them by working in an office or factory, for in those days the only women I knew who worked for a living served behind counters in shops. The mothers of everyone I knew at school were housewives. In the Hillhead Salon I saw *Tarzan and the Amazons* which showed the jungle hero in South America where he is captured by a savage tribe of blonde white women, all wearing very little and in their early twenties. In those days I believed all films except Disney animations were based on truth, and decided a completely female nation would be possible if a natural fluke made the mothers incapable of giving birth to males, thus forcing the women to learn hunting. The necessity of fathers dawned on me when I was twelve or thirteen and too old to embarrass Nell and Nan with a question about a matter too delicate for them to have mentioned. When anyone asked about my parents I would say crisply, "Don't remember them. Both killed in the London Blitz."

Only when Nan and Nell were dead did I learn from my birth
certificate that I was a bastard.

Through most of my schooldays boys and girls had separate playgrounds and sat on opposite sides of the classrooms. When five or six I started noticing the girls' side contained someone fascinating – a girl who seemed *better* than the rest, and who I wanted to continually stare at and come close to, had that been possible. Her name was Roberta Piper. Nobody told me my desire for Roberta Piper was a weakness but I knew I would be mocked if I admitted it and hid this desire so completely that I am sure none suspected it. Slowly, from small signs, I realized most boys on my side of the class felt the same about Roberta Piper and were equally reluctant to admit it. We shared a general idea that girls were inferior creatures, why? I suspect we were trying to reject the power Roberta Piper and her kind had over us, without exactly knowing what it was.

In the summer holidays Nan, Nell and I always had a fortnight in an Aitch Eff guesthouse. Aitch Eff (I later learned) stood for Holiday Fellowship, an organization founded early in the twentieth century by middle- and working-class Socialists who wanted social equality for all and felt that sharing holidays was a step toward it. They leased big houses in mountainous and coastal parts of Britain where members enjoyed most of a good hotel's facilities without paying as much, and where staff and guests mingled in a friendly way I thought natural and ordinary until years later when I stayed in a conventional hotel. In our second week at Minard Castle on Loch Fyne Roberta Piper and her parents arrived. When they sat down at the morning breakfast table Nell asked me, "What's wrong?" I suppose because I was blushing or had gone pale. I whispered that the girl was in my class at school.
"How nice! Your little girl is in this young man's class at school!" said Nell, and began a cheerful conversation with Mr and Mrs Piper who agreed with my aunts that Roberta and I should sit together. We did, which I both wanted and hated. I saw she was willing to chat with me but I could not say a word, my

heart was beating too loudly and my face was too hot. "I'm afraid our young man's terribly shy!" said Nan and all the adults treated this as an entertaining joke. I hated that and hated Roberta because she was grinning too. For the rest of the holiday I insisted on us eating at a different table from the Pipers, which the aunts thought a pity. I was then six or seven.

This hopeless, helpless, useless obsession with Roberta lasted through primary school. At secondary school she was replaced by someone it is pointless to name. These fascinating girls changed as we advanced from one year to the next, but among boys in my class there was a general agreement about which one she was. I sometimes heard bolder, coarser ones discuss her and speculate on who might "get her for a lumber". By that time a new sexual distraction had entered my life: American comics.

Lumber: Scottish demotic verb, meaning to intimately caress late at night in the back yards of homes to which a girl's boyfriend would be denied entry by her parents, therefore also a noun for a girl thus caressed.

Throughout Scotland and (I suspect) Britain most children's leisure reading was printed by D. C. Thomson Ltd of Dundee. Each week before the age of ten we took *The Dandy* and *Beano*, jocular cartoon magazines with characters like Freddie the Fearless Fly, Lord Snooty and his Pals, an ostrich called Big Eggo and a kindly cowboy of immense strength called Desperate Dan, who lived in a land that was partly American West and partly a British suburb. These comics had a minimum of words, speech being printed in bubbles coming from people's mouths. At secondary school age these were replaced by *The Rover* and *Hotspur* whose every double page had a serial adventure story in printed columns, with a single quarter-page illustration in black and white under the title. No girls, no women were in these stories which were about ordinary, believable boys like ourselves assisting detectives, explorers, athletes, soldiers or scientists. The aunts ordered these comics for me from Barretts, the Byres Road newsagent. I first saw *American* comics at school in the days following examinations, when our teachers were busy marking the papers and let us read anything we liked. Some students brought in these astonishing novelties: magazines with brightly-coloured pictures on every page, showing the

adventures of super-heroic adults and villains with amazing
powers and no children at all. Women among them had faces
and figures like Hollywood movie stars but often wore less
clothes. About sex the American comic publishers were as
puritan as Thomsons of Dundee. They evaded it by showing
violence instead. Fantastic punch-ups and explosive shooting
matches were continuous, with much capture, bondage and
torture. I had never before seen anything so exciting, except in
Tarzan films. I instinctively knew my aunts would dislike these
comics and that I should never bring them to the house, but
fellow pupils had more than they could read at one time so I
borrowed a few, after which Wonder Woman and Sheena the
Jungle Girl drove Roberta Piper's successors out of my head.
With real girls I could only imagine chivalrous courtships leading
to marriage, but there was no limit to what I could imagine
doing to Sheena. I was entering the state described by a character
in Albee's *Zoo Story*, who says American men start using pictures
of women as substitutes for reality, then use women as substitutes
for the pictures. I only reached the second half of that state after
the death of my aunts.

When exam papers had been marked my chances of
borrowing these comics ended, for outside the classroom I was
ashamed to look at them when others could see me. My pocket
money would have let me buy many but I was appalled by the
thought of a shopkeeper recognizing my vicious depravity as I
pointed to an American comic or nudist health magazine and
said, "That one please!". I sometimes wished an atomic war
would kill everyone in the world but me so that I could enter
any of these shops and shamelessly gloat over all that excited
me.

But drunk with sherry on this special Saturday afternoon I
did the deed without an atomic war. In part of the Cowcaddens
that was demolished in the 1970s I stopped before the right
sort of shop and, with a thrumming excitement in my lower
stomach, stared shamelessly at the covers of paperback books
in the window. One called *Love for Sale* showed (from behind)

a line of chained-together blondes wearing only knickers and high-heeled shoes, being urged across sand dunes by a man with a whip. Beyond the display I saw the back of a customer buying something. When he left the shop I hurried in, laid my briefcase on the counter and, looking away from the shopkeeper, pointed to *Love for Sale* and said, "That one please and . . . yes, and also that . . . and er, hm hm hm . . ." (I pointed to American comics on racks along the walls) ". . . I'll take that and that and that and that too. I'm buying for a few friends."

"It's nice to have friends," said the shopkeeper pleasantly. I was horrified to suddenly see she was a small woman a bit like Aunt Nell. With a face that felt red hot I flung down some pound notes, muttered "Keep the change", zipped books and comics into my briefcase, rushed out and hurried home.

I found the aunts having afternoon tea with a friend of their own age and sex.

"How was Stewart and his mother?" said Nan as I looked round the door. Nell asked, "You look flushed, have you been running?"

"Things went quite well," I said, "In fact too well, that's why I'm flushed. Mrs Doig insisted on pouring me a glass of that sherry you gave her and I'm not used to it. I'm going to lie down in the study for an hour or two. Please don't bring me anything. See you later."

In the study I turned (for the first but not last time) the door key that locked me in, then spread my purchases on the desktop and doted over them, masturbating three times in succession. After that, sick with self-disgust, I would have burned them in the study fire had the season been cold enough for one. Instead I locked them in a desk drawer and afterwards kept the key in my trouser pocket.

Perhaps a fortnight passed before an appetite for new pornography drove me out in search of another dirty bookshop, because I never bought from the same shop twice. After drinking all the sherry left in Grandpa Tunnock's three-quarters full decanter I set out with my usual excuse of going for a walk with Stoory Doig, astonished that my aunts did not see how drunk I

was. Before every full bottle of sherry had been drunk my
pornography was nearly too many for the desk drawers. One
wet Sunday I locked the study door, spread my furtive library
on the hearthrug and went carefully through it, scissors in hand,
cutting out pictures that most excited me and burning the rest –
which reminds me what a strangely different world I and
everyone else then inhabited, a world as different from 2005
Glasgow as 1954 was from the world of mid-Victorian
encyclopaedias.

The rooms in nearly every British house were heated by
an open fire burning in *a grate* inside a *fireplace*, a cavity in
the thickness of the wall. The fire was fed with lumps of coal
from a big brass jug called *a scuttle* on a tiled section of floor
in front of the grate. In terrace houses the scuttle was filled
from a small basement room called *the coal-cellar*, and in
tenements from a stoutly made box called *the bunker* on the
stair landing. Coal-cellars and bunkers were filled by men
who carried the coal in on their backs in huge sacks from an
open lorry that usually called once a month. Did each sack
contain a hundredweight? Half a hundredweight? A quarter? I
only know that twenty hundredweights made a ton and once,
when older, I tried to lift a full coal sack and failed. The sacks
came from a great heap of coal in a yard called *a ree* in
Scotland. Everywhere people lived had a coal ree a few miles
away except in parts of the Highlands and Islands where folk
burned peat. The coal rees were on branch railway lines along
which coal-burning steam locomotives brought trucks of coals
from the mines, the last of which closed in Scotland four or
five years back why am I going into all this? Before the 1960s
almost any photograph of an inhabited British landscape
showed a trail of steam drifting across. They were so common
we did not notice them, did not even notice them vanish with
the coming of electric trains. Glasgow made coal fires illegal
around 1970 when it began losing its heavy industries. This
put an end to amazingly thick winter fogs that had been killing
folk with poor lungs for more than a century. This information
is necessary to explain how I managed to burn so much paper

without my aunts noticing. Even so, they would have smelled it had I not spread the job over two weekends. From then on I kept my special selection of cut-out heroines and suggestive pictures between the pages of Cruden's massive *Concordance of the Holy Scriptures.*

For I had begun to find the words in the books and comics repetitive. The fantasies they inspired were quite separate from the great Rabelaisian-Balzacian-Ovidian-Aristophanic romance I dreamed of making me famous one day, a romance in which the women were princesses or witches, and free agents. In my perverse alternative story they were completely managed by very kind or cruel men, all powerful aspects of ME. The cover of *Love for Sale* indicated how they could be connected in a single narrative. I was not as insatiable as some Turkish sultans. After the paper holocaust the slaves in my harem dwindled to six with two permanent favourites: Jane Russell as she appeared in *The Outlaw* film poster (still a popular male sex-icon in the fifties) and Sheena the Jungle Girl. The other four were continually replaced through my fortnightly excursions in search of yet another dirty bookshop. The absence of these shops today is another sign of changed times. Pornography that was prosecuted as criminal in 1950 can now be bought in almost any shop, and things once illegal in print are shown and openly advertized in video films. Only *child* pornography causes public outrage now, and I would be remembering this phase of my life without shame were it not for Stewart Doig.

I hated lying to my aunts about him. It is also impossible to pretend something for a long time without making it come partly true. Three times a week or more I had to share a desk with Stewart and guilt led me to reply less and less gruffly when he spoke to me. Perhaps loneliness also inclined me to want a partner in crime. One day I muttered to him, "Listen, I don't want to be seen talking to you –" (this opening was so brutal that I hastily added) "– you or anybody else here. I don't want to be thought pally with anyone in this school or in sight of this school, but would you like to go a walk with me Saturday afternoon?"

He stared and nodded. I said, "Meet me at the flagpole in the
Botanic Gardens at two, right?"
Again he nodded, open-mouthed. I bent my face close to the
jotter I was writing in and muttered, "If you say another word to
me before then I won't turn up."
What a nasty wee bastard I was.

We met at the flagpole and I took him for a walk along the
disused railway line running from the Botanic Gardens down
to the Clyde by way of two or three derelict railway stations
linked by short tunnels. I was bringing him to a dirty bookshop
I had found in Scotstoun, near Victoria Park, and meant to
prepare him for that by discussing sex. This was almost
impossible. Stoory and his mother belonged to a Christian sect
called The Brethren who disapproved of sex. Instead we
passionately discussed Evil, which Stoory thought started in the
Garden of Eden when Eve, tempted by Satan disguized as a
snake, ate God's forbidden fruit that gave knowledge of Good
and Evil. I argued that God was wrong to punish Adam and Eve
for eating the fruit, as they could not know they were doing evil
until they had eaten it. And since God had created the Satanic
serpent it must have been His agent. In such discussions every
answer to an objection raises other objections. The desire of
Stoory and me for the last word kept us arguing fervently until
at last we reached the shop where I halted and interrupted him
saying, "Change the subject! Some of this must interest you. It
interests most men and certainly interests me."
He stopped, stared and began blushing, but as long as I stood
there he could not bring himself to look away. This gave me
confidence. I said, "In my opinion none of that stuff is very
wicked – I buy some every week. My people don't care what I
buy with my pocket money. Will I buy you some?"
He shook his head slightly, meaning no, and perhaps even
whispered "No". I kept bullying him until at last he admitted
interest in a photographic publication called *Health and
Nudism*, with a cover advertising an article inside called *Eves
on Skis*. More boldly than I had entered such a shop before I
went in and emerged with *Health and Nudism* and much more

in my briefcase. I handed over two magazines in a quiet corner of Victoria Park. He pushed the lower half of them down his trousers and covered the top half with his jersey, saying miserably, "My mum will murder me if she sees any of this."

"Have you a bedroom to yourself?" I asked, suddenly worried. He had. I suggested he hide them under his mattress or a carpet. He said, "Maybe they could go behind the coal bunker on the landing. But then I couldn't get looking at them. Please take them back John!"

I said implacably, "Certainly not".

"Alright, I'll try the carpet."

We resumed our theological discussion and separated before reaching a conclusion. Stewart's last sad words, "Are we going a walk next Saturday?" were answered by a lofty, "I'll think about it." O I was nasty, nasty, nasty. And when the aunts later asked (as usual) about Stewart I said, "Frankly, I'm finding him a dreary soul. I can't stand the Old Testament religion he goes on and on and on about."

Nan sighed and said, "Yes, religion *does* have a dreary side." She went on to say something about the state of Israel being founded by modern Socialists, people nothing like the old Children of Israel because centuries of persecution by Christians and others had taught the Jews tolerance, so they would eventually treat Muslims within their national boundaries as equals, despite the enmity of those outside it.

This was on Saturday evening. I was only slightly worried when Stoory Doig did not come to school on Monday morning because he was often off sick. But he joined the class after lunch break and alarmed me because I saw he was avoiding me. The subject was science which split the class into groups of four or less at separate benches. Stoory and me had always shared a bench by ourselves, but today the teacher (we called him Tojo because he looked slightly Japanese) said, "Make room for Doig here," and put him on the far side of the room so I had a bench completely to myself. This was unprecedented and noticed by the rest of the class. A little later Tojo, passing near, murmured, "Feeling lonely, Tunnock?", with a glance that may have been whimsical but made my blood run cold. For the rest

of the afternoon I expected every moment to be summoned to
the headmaster's office and receive half a dozen strokes of his
Lochgelly tawse, three on each hand. I had never been belted
but had seen it done to others, and hoped the pain of the first
stroke would make me faint. Nothing of the sort happened. As
I left to go home some boys overtook me and asked what was
up between Doig and me? I said, "Ask him."
They said, "We did and he won't tell."
I hurried away from them saying, "Neither will I," and one
shouted after me, "Don't worry, we'll find out!"

Tawse of
extra hard,
thick leather
manufactured
in Lochgelly,
Fife.

   I passed that evening sick with fear and dread, refusing to
answer my aunts' anxious questions but finally yelling, "I can't
tell you anything."
I locked myself in the study, removed my paper harem from
Cruden's Concordance, masturbated furiously several times,
burned all of it while drinking the final bottle and a half of
grandfather's sherry, then managed to put myself early to bed
without falling down. I slept so soundly that I either outslept a
hangover or was still drunk when I wakened at the usual hour,
for I felt bright and cheerful. I had no memories of the previous
day until halfway through dressing they recurred like an ugly
dream. At breakfast with Nan and Nell I tried fooling myself
into thinking the whole business might have no further
consequences, especially since the aunts said nothing about
my queer conduct the night before. In the 1950s an efficient
General Post Office delivered letters twice daily, the first delivery
before breakfast. Between porridge and boiled eggs (ours was
always a two course breakfast) Nan took a letter from an
envelope, read it more than once then said, "John, your
headmaster asks me to visit him at eleven o'clock this morning.
Do you know why?"
This plunged me again deep into a nightmare that made
intelligent thought and connected speech impossible. I muttered
over and over with increasing violence, "I can't tell you
anything" or "I will NOT go to school today," which alarmed
them. Nell, the youngest, pled with me and wept, whereupon

Nan said loudly and sternly, "Very well! You will NOT go to
school today as usual, but you WILL come to school and see
the headmaster with us!"
She had never spoken severely to me before. I could not argue
back and later, sick at heart, walked drearily school-ward
between them. On one side Nell attempted some feeble,
encouraging chirps but Nan stayed grimly silent, gathering her
forces for a conflict whose nature she could not even guess.

The headmaster had always been remote from boys he did
not punish, always austere with those who were not good at
sports. He greeted my aunts with grave politeness, leaving his
office desk to do so and offering them chairs before it. I was not
greeted at all and left standing. He sat down and told them, "I
am sorry I have had to ask you here. We have never had trouble
with John before, but he has now done something that the
mother of a fellow pupil brought to my attention yesterday,
denouncing it as downright wicked. She provided me with such
evidence that I was reluctantly forced to agree."
He paused. Nan said coldly, "What evidence?"
From a drawer in his desk he produced and laid on top *Health
and Nudism* with its cover photograph illustrating the Eves on
Skis article, and a number of *Sheena the Jungle Girl* with Sheena
on the cover in a state that made me shut my eyes tight. I heard
him explain that according to Mrs Doig, Stewart always told
the truth when confessing his sins before going to bed, and had
confessed that John Tunnock had led him into temptation and
had thrust these vile publications upon him. The dreadful silence
following these words was broken by Nan asking crisply, "John
gave these as a present to poor Stewart Doig?"
"Yes, John persuaded Doig to accept this unmitigated filth."
"Is that all?" cried Nan in a voice so loud with gladness and
relief that I opened my eyes wide and saw her lean forward and
lift *Health and Nudism*. After glancing quickly inside she put it
back saying, "My dear sir, when we received your letter this
morning John became so speechless with shame and horror
that I feared he had made a girl pregnant, or been discovered in
some act of adolescent homosexuality, or had publically

exposed his genitals. Do you really believe pictures of undressed

female bodies are unmitigated filth?"

"Of course not, but trading in pornography is filth."

"John did not trade in these publications. You admit he gave them as presents."

"It is no mitigation for a rich boy to gain no money while deliberately using his own to corrupt a very poor boy!"

"My dear man, you are in charge of a teaching establishment founded in Queen Victoria's reign but this is 1954. You surely know that boys over the age of twelve have adult sexual organs and appetites. My nephew John is thirteen. In a tribal society he would be earning his living and selecting a mate in a year or two. Civilization makes that impossible. Our schools *must* fit young adults for modern life by suppressing their natural instincts, but you cannot expect to completely suppress them, especially when they are outside your school."

She paused and stared grimly at the headmaster who sat with hands clasped tightly on the desktop, frowning and chewing his under-lip. A short silence was broken by Nell saying faintly, "In France, I believe . . ."

"Yes, be quiet Nell," said Nan. "In France until recently brothels were licensed and kept free of disease by medically-qualified municipal inspectors, so unmarried youths with some cash could easily obtain sexual relief, often with parental approval. In modern Britain, alas, most adults are still too Victorian to teach their children the facts of sex. Nell and I are examples. We read Marie Stopes and D. H. Lawrence yet were too shy to tell our nephew John about the act of penetration and use of contraceptives. Your science teachers are equally reticent. I entered this office today fearing the worst and am glad to know John has only been purchasing aids to masturbation. Every woman who washes teenage boys' underwear knows how often they masturbate. You must have done so when you were that age. There is no point discussing something so commonplace or making a fuss about it. Modern doctors now know it does not induce blindness or soften the brain."

This speech made me realize there was some connection between the pale grey jelly with which I stained my underpants four or five times a week and the phenomenon of birth. After quite a long silence the headmaster pointed to the two magazines and in a distant-sounding voice said, "You think these aids to masturbation should be openly passed around among my pupils?"

"No. It was silly of John to trust poor Doig with them, but please bear in mind that this was on Saturday when the boys were not legally under your administration. He will not give such publications again to Stewart Doig or anyone else – will you John?"

"No! No! Never!" I almost shouted.

"Mr MacRae, I sympathize with the dilemma Mrs Doig has forced upon you. Her complaint cannot be ignored, yet a big fuss about it will be bad for the school. You know that last week a daft Church of Scotland minister made a story for the *Glasgow Evening News* by denouncing pupils of Glasgow Girls' High School for conversing with boys during lunch hour in a Sauchiehall Street espresso café. A gutter journalist could keep such a story *running* (as they say), if he heard of this equally innocuous Hillhead Secondary boy's misdemeanour. He would tell easily shocked clergy and parents about him and quote their reactions under headlines with *shock* and *sex* and *horror* in them. He would pester you for an opinion and if you did not say you had dealt with John by savagely punishing him you would be accused of being *permissive* – a cant word now current in the gutter press."

"That," said MacRae grimly, "is what I mean to prevent."

"But you cannot possibly use the tawse on such a good, obedient, hard-working pupil as John who has never defied his teachers and the Hillhead rulings in any way at all. We have told John that if any teacher so much as threatens him with the belt he must walk out of the school and come home. If he does so we will send him to Kilquhanity – a *really* permissive school – what a tit-bit for journalists that would be. I expect you will write to poor Stewart Doig's mother saying you have taken firm steps that ensure John will never again lead Stewart or anyone else into temptation. That is all you need do. Let us now agree to forget this sorry business. Please treat these publications on your desk as waste paper for their sexual aroma is not open or

Kilquhanity a boarding school, in a country house near Castle Douglas, was run on pupil self-government lines by John and Morag Aitkenhead, a kindly couple. Their discipline did without punishment. Their example was A. S. Neill's English boarding school, Summerhill.

clean. John has never brought material like that to Hillhead
Secondary and won't give it to anyone else. You have taught
him a lesson he will not forget."

The headmaster said abruptly, "Good," and stood up. So did
my aunts. He asked what class I should be attending. Maths, I
told him. He said, "Go to it then. You have a remarkable aunt,
John Tunnock," – (adding with a polite nod to Nell) – "aunts, I
mean. Don't let them down again."

I had always loved Nan but before this interview had thought
her an ordinary old lady. I was so astonished and braced by her
words that I said firmly, "Thank you Sir! Never again Sir!"

I stepped up to the desk and held out my hand to him. After the
briefest of pauses he held out his own. We shook, then he
grunted, "Off you go Tunnock."

We walked in silence from the Headmaster's office until,
turning a corner, Nell started laughing and said, "You were
wonderful Nan."

Nan said, "Yes, I astonished myself, especially with my lie about
telling John to leave school if threatened with the belt. I'm glad
you recovered your confidence at the end, John, but sorry your
pal has let you down."

I wiped what felt like a wide grin off my face and said firmly,
"He is no longer my pal."

They looked at each other and sighed because they thought I
should forgive Doig's honesty to his mother, but said no more
about the matter nor ever spoke of it again. They must have
known that discussing masculine inclinations with a male is
useless. My purchases of pornography became rarer from then
on. My erotic fantasies found enough to stimulate them in
maturer literature and visits to the Hillhead Salon and Grosvenor
cinemas. And ever since then I have loathed the taste of sherry
and drunk alcohol cautiously.

But before going home that day I approached my usual
classroom very dourly, knowing the teacher at least would know
I came from the headmaster's office and why I had been
summoned there. I later learned that the whole school knew

why: earlier that morning in the playground Doig had been surrounded by a crowd of urgent questioners and, unused to such popularity, had told everything. I entered the room halfway through a geometry lesson and the teacher fell silent in the middle of a sentence. By an effort I think I managed to look thoughtful, even absent-minded, as I walked between staring faces to an empty desk. From my briefcase I removed my Euclid and exercise book then sat with hands clasped on them (as the headmaster had clasped his) and looked enquiringly at the teacher who, with heavy irony said, "Have I your permission to continue, Tunnock?"

"Certainly, Sir! Certainly!" I said, and from that moment my reputation as a swot and a snob ended. Classmates who thought I had been savagely belted were astonished by my composure, the rest knew something unimaginable had happened. When questioned afterwards in the playground my only words were, "MacRae is not a barbarian. We reached an agreement and he dismissed the matter as a storm in a teacup."

When several boys asked me to supply *them* with dirty books and offered to pay more than the purchase price I smiled thinly and said, "No no. Once bitten, twice shy."

But how had two gentle spinsters born in Victoria's reign (Nan 1897, Nell 1900) become so broad-minded without me noticing before the Stewart Doig catastrophe? The 1914-18 war must have changed them as it changed many others. When Nell heard a pipe band playing on the wireless she was inclined to weep. Nan told me privately this was because in 1914 young soldiers marched behind bands between cheering crowds from Maryhill Barracks to the train that would take them on the first lap of their journey to the Flanders slaughterfields. That kind of public jubilation cannot have lasted much more than a year, even though most British private businesses profited by that war. I do not know if Nell lost a sweetheart in it, but many young women of my aunts' and Miss Jean Brodie's generation were deprived of potential husbands and their faith in a God praised in churches because he had made Britain victorious. Jean Brodie became a Fascist but was exceptional. More folk turned to Socialism, my aunts among them. It had broadened

their minds without changing their behaviour, hence my
astonishment when Nan firmly dominated a Scottish
headmaster. Being Socialists they were ashamed of having a
house much larger than they needed, and living upon rents
from two tenement blocks in Partick inherited from their father.
Before 1939 this income let them employ a cook and
housemaid. When these were directed into war-work they
managed without, and like most middle-class folk after the war
could not afford servants. Unlike many they never complained.
"I'm sure this exercize is good for us," Nell would murmur with
a sigh as she came home heavily laden from a shopping
expedition, and Nan would say sharply, "Of course! It keeps us
young."
They always referred to my mother as a superior being because
she had earned her own living, and also (I think) because she
had borne a child. After my first week's work as a teacher Nan
said, "Me and Nell would be two useless old women if we had
not helped to educate a useful man."
Like many Scots in those days they believed teachers, doctors
and Labour politicians were the noblest works of God because
such people (they believed) strove to reduce ignorance, suffering
and poverty. Perhaps what kept them attending Hillhead Parish
Church on Sundays was their belief that Jesus was a Socialist.
In their childhood before World War I there were many Scottish
Socialist Sunday schools for Protestant children; also John
Wheatley, though denounced by Glasgow priests, ran a vigorous
Young Men's Socialist Catholic Society. The 1979 election of
Margaret Thatcher and everything that followed astonished and
worried them. I am sorry I disappointed them by never marrying,
glad I never again shocked or disturbed them after the Doig
affair.

Soon after that I was invited to attend a school debating
society where I began voicing my aunts' Socialist opinions,
and was strongly opposed by an equally vocal Tory, Gordon
MacLean. I was his social superior because my home was in a
terrace house and his in a Byres Road tenement. He was my

social superior because one of the school's best athletes, and I
so bad at games that the physical training teacher let me miss
them. In other subjects our marks averaged out equal: he was
better at maths, science, geography: I better at English, Latin,
history, and we were equally bad at art and music. Our homes
being near we started walking to and from school together,
discussing books, films, sex but avoiding politics, which we
only enjoyed discussing before an audience. Gordon, handsome
and popular, had a complicated love life. Though not a boaster
he liked telling me about it as much as I enjoyed hearing him.
He even asked advice, which I was wise enough not to give,
but I mentioned precedents for his troubles in the life of Burns,
with relevant anecdotes from history and literature. He maybe
found this flattering but I did not mean to flatter. His dealings
with attractive girls fascinated me as much as anything I had
read about, because they were real, and I knew great writers
must study reality as well as books.

I was resigned to not directly knowing attractive girls. They
terrified me, making speech with them impossible until I was old
enough to be their father. In their presence I kept my self-respect
by an aloofness suggesting (I hoped) that I was thinking of better
things. This was easy for a boy whose manners had been formed
by the example of nice old ladies, and whose main education
was from books that had stored my mind with my grandfather's
furtive man-of-the-world knowledge. Once in the street I passed
two good-looking, giggling school girls. One rushed after me
and said, "John Tunnock, my pal fancies you rotten. In fact she'd
like you to shag her!"
I said, "Tell her she'll grow out of it."
I could be friendly and at ease with girls who did not attract
me, like those behind the counter of a Co-op grocery in Partick
where I usually shopped. One day a new assistant, a small
plump dark-haired girl, served me in a surprisingly unfriendly
way, head bent to avoid seeing my face and never speaking a
word. When I went there next week the other assistants shouted,
"Terry! Here's John," and let her attend me. I could not imagine
why. Her behaviour was still unfriendly. The fourth time this

happened she suddenly raised her head and with the manner
of someone flinging themselves off a cliff said, "What do you
do in the evenings?"
I saw a round, pleasant, pleading face with lipstick not efficiently
applied. I said, "Not much," and rushed away trembling as if
from an electric shock. Terry found me attractive! I tried bringing
her image into erotic fantasies and failed. She was too real. For
nearly a year I visited the Co-op meaning to ask her out to the
Salon or Grosvenor and each time the shock of seeing her struck
me dumber than she was. I could not imagine what I could say
about Burns, Rabelais etcetera to her that would interest Terry. I
would hand her a note of the items we wanted and before
leaving with them would mutter, "Thanks." One day when I
entered someone shouted, "Terry, here's John!" and she came
over and served me in a straightforward friendly way, like the
other assistants, but perhaps with a slight air of triumph. She
had grown out of me, and was happy to show it. I knew I had
missed an opportunity. Forty years passed before there was
another, though something else may have delayed my maturity.

The Holiday Fellowship guest houses where we vacationed
had originally been the country seats of minor aristocrats or
rich Victorian merchants, the sort of country houses that after
World War 2 the very rich kept wailing that they could no longer
afford because the Welfare State was forcing them to pay
iniquitous taxes. Nan told me that when Britain became truly
Socialist under Harold Wilson (a prime minister in whom she
had faith for nearly a year) every great country house would be
run by the Holiday Fellowship as guest homes for The People
or the elderly. I loved them for their large, unkempt, usually
neglected gardens and big libraries of books, none published
later than the middle thirties. I also liked the custom of the staff,
who were usually young foreign girls, sharing the guests' lounge,
quiet room and outdoor excursions when they were not working.
Younger guests liked helping waitresses and kitchen staff clear
tables and wash and dry dishes after meals, a custom mostly
enjoyed by young unmarried males, among whom I was always
the youngest. At Minard Castle on Loch Fyne one summer I

became sweet on a couple of lovely German girls. Leni was
tall, slim and dark haired. Ute was plump, blonde and not much
taller than me so I fancied her most, though I never met her
apart from Leni. I later realized they encouraged my friendship
as a way of avoiding older, more sexually knowing youths, but
they certainly encouraged it. Their questions disclosed that I
meant to be a writer and they saw nothing incredible in that.
Leni started talking about Goethe which I thought remarkable,
because I was sure no Scottish teenage girls liked great writers.
I remember a sunny day when the three of us climbed Ben
Nevis at the tail of a walking party. They asked questions about
Scotland and my answers naturally led me to quote various
verses by Burns that seemed to entertain them. More questions
drew from me details of his private life, which Leni said showed
he was a free spirit like Goethe, then Ute said, mischievously,
"And *your* sex life, John?"
I felt we were talking like unusually friendly equals so said
promptly, "It hardly exists. I only discovered the connection
between sexual intercourse and birth a year or two ago through
my affair with poor Doig."
"An affair? With a poor *dog*?" said Leni, grimacing incredulously.
"No! Dee – oh – eye – jee, Doig, a boy I knew. "
They wanted to hear about that so I told them. At the end both
went into fits of laughter through which Ute said, "O you funny
little boy!"
It would be wrong to say I felt she had slapped my face. I felt
like someone happily using a band saw that in a split second
takes off his hand. Shock would at first prevent pain, he would
only feel astonished that his hand was lost for ever. My shock
must have shown because at once Ute apologized, but the
damage had been done. I turned and walked away downhill
from these climbers so never saw the summit of Ben Nevis. I
am told it is a rocky plateau, a field of boulders with patches of
snow in odd nooks even in the hottest summers, and on a clear
day like that one I could have seen of every high summit between
England and the Orkneys.

17: FURTHER EDUCATION

WHEN FINISHED HOMEWORK in the evenings I began trying to turn my fantasies into a single continuous novel, always burning the results because what I wrote was obviously the work of an adolescent schoolboy. These stunted efforts still made me more of a writer than our teachers, who gave us Chaucer, Shakespeare, Jane Austen, Dickens, Thomas Hardy and only two books by Scots. Walter Scott's *Ivanhoe*, set in the 12th century, told how Norman conquerors and Saxon commoners are at last united as Englishmen – what a good lesson for a Scottish school child! Scott's best novels have Scottish folk using local speech that teachers and examiners wanted us to forget. The other novel, John Buchan's *Prester John*, told of a Scots minister's son, working for the British Empire in Africa, who thwarts a black revolt planned by a black African who has fooled the white bosses by *pretending* to be Christian.

Gordon MacLean left Glasgow because his dad got a job elsewhere. I did not much miss him, having now other friends who enjoyed discussing their emotional problems with an interested listener who seemed to have none. Before Gordon left he enlarged my political views without intending to. Hugh MacDiarmid's son, a boy of nineteen, had been jailed for refusing to do his National Service, because the 1707 Treaty of Union with England said no Scottish soldier could be ordered overseas against his will, and MacDiarmid's son refused to fight for the remains of the British Empire in Kenya,

After World War 2 healthy men over 18 years were conscripted into the British Armed Forces for two years until 1958, when the British empire was nearly extinct. Those who refused conscription for political reasons were jailed. Roughly 10,000 refused on religious grounds and were not penalized.

Crete or Malaysia, Ulster and other places he might have been sent. Gordon and I agreed his attitude was ridiculous. We thought the Treaty of Union, having merged Scotland's parliament with the English one, was now an obsolete document. We had no wish for Scottish self-government. Gordon believed Scottish people could not rule themselves; I agreed because Britain had achieved a Welfare State through the efforts of a parliamentary Labour Party founded by Scottish Keir Hardie. I also thought Scotland and England had equal representation in London – my general knowledge was good, but I had no head for numbers. Gordon explained that England had ten times more MPs in Westminster than Scotland, a fair arrangement (he pointed out) since England's population had always been ten times greater. I at once saw that a minority of Scots MPs in the midst of England's richest city *must* be constantly outvoted to benefit the southern kingdom. For many years this did not stop me voting Labour but from then on I began to see how the Union with England had warped Scotland's institutions, especially schools and universities.

Glasgow University stands on Gilmore Hill.

At Gilmorehill our lecturers were mostly Oxford or Cambridge graduates, some of them Scots. They assumed ordinary students like me would stay in Scotland to teach the next generation what we had been taught, while brighter ones – their elite – would find work in England, former British colonies or the U.S.A. Bright Scots had been doing so for centuries, and bright people will want to please foreign masters by conforming to them, so the only tutor who mentioned Burns called him "a poor man's Alexander Pope". But they agreed that Wordsworth at his best, Blake, Byron, Shelley and Keats had not just been *naytcha* poets but (like Burns) had welcomed the French Revolution as the dawn of universal liberty, equality, fraternity. This enthusiasm was presented as forgivable but out of date, since Britain had now all the liberty, equality and fraternity it needed. I also learned that most great modern poets thought monetary greed had made life ugly. Ezra Pound turned Fascist because he thought only a dictator like Mussolini could make bankers fund important public works – Yeats wanted a nation where heroic landlords ruled admiring peasants – T.S. Eliot was nostalgic for the 17th century Anglican Church where peace with God came more easily – Auden was a bouncy English public-school Communist, until World War 2 converted him to something like Eliot's Christianity. Auden also said poetry made nothing happen and our professors agreed.

I remember once mocking Shelley for writing that Homer, Dante, Shakespeare and Milton had changed people's minds more than kings, conquerors and lawgivers, therefore poets were mankind's unacknowledged legislators. Shelley (said this professor gleefully) was an atheist, Socialist, pacifist and vegetarian, and none of his writings had persuaded anyone to become these; like other great writers Shelley had found the raw materials of art in the world around him, and what he made of them was fine poems without social consequences. I should have stood up and announced that Hitler, Stalin and every successful tyrant understood literature better than Auden and my professor because these banned and burned imaginative writing, shot or jailed poets, drove them to suicide like Mayakovsky, into exile like Brecht. Instead I timidly pointed out that Goethe's novel *The Sorrows of Young Werther* had social consequences – it had been banned in Germany and France because young men, disappointed in love, had copied Werther by shooting themselves.

"Thank you for reminding me," he said, chuckling, "Yes, emotional foreigners *are* unhealthily influenced by literature, but sane people are not. Good conversation, said Dean Swift, is life's only sure source of happiness. I agree. We who have no interest in football find our happiest topics in books and art which are, after all, civilization's finest blossoms."

This thought-annihilating smugness did not silence me at first. I submitted an essay on *Hamlet* saying the plot was clumsily cobbled together in the hasty way Ben Jonson (a more careful playwright) deplored in Shakespeare. Hamlet is sent to England after stabbing Polonius but brought back just in

This statement is in Auden's *Elegy for W. B. Yeats*. Tunnock mistakenly assumes that one short quotation sums up a great poet's whole attitude.

Scott's *Heart of Midlothian* led to Scots law ending concealment of pregnancy as a capital offence; Melville's *Whitejacket* led to the USA navy abolishing flogging.

time for Ophelia's funeral by inexplicable pirates, pirates who capture his ship, let it sail on but return him to Denmark since the plot needs him there. Hamlet keeps postponing his revenge to the end of the last scene because Shakespeare, like all first class writers except Kipling, found the revenge motive too infantile to interest him, having sickened himself of it in his first and worst play *Titus Andronicus*. Of course all the Hamlet speeches are so entertaining that critics and audiences enjoy the play without question, accepting what happens as they accept the accidents of ordinary life. My tutor called me to his office and said, "Are you a Levisite?"

I told him I did not know what Levisites were.

"But you have read D.H. Lawrence's opinion of *Hamlet*."

"No!" I told him.

"Then where did this drivel come from?" he asked, waving the essay in my face. I said he had asked for an essay on *Hamlet* and I had written what I thought. He said, "You are here to *learn* – not think. Are you receiving a grant?"

Like most students in those days I was receiving a grant since the 1944 Butler Acts that paid the fees of working class students would never have been passed by parliament if the middle classes had not also benefited. The bastard said, "I do not see why my taxes should be used to support a student who does not understand the purpose of a university."

I found this professor and others had written introductions to most of the plays and poems they examined us upon, so afterwards pleased them by repeating their opinions without regard to the original texts. Luckily my main subjects were Latin and Greek, where commentary was less important than accurate translation. I did so well in them that the Snell Foundation nearly sent me to Balliol, Oxford, where my life would have become very different. But I helped a fellow student write a very funny, damaging review of Professor Fordyce's outstandingly bad edition of *Catullus*. The review was printed anonymously in G.U.M. but Fordyce was astute enough to work out who the authors were, and had enough power in the Senate to make sure we had no chance of a high academic post in Oxford or Scotland.

Glasgow University Magazine mocked this edition of Catullus' poems for omitting all explicitly sexual verses.

One Saturday morning I visited Renfield Street, a short street of shops in central Glasgow. It joins Sauchiehall Street, Bath Street and Argyll Street to the main bridge over the Clyde, so is always throng with pedestrians and vehicles. It is now almost incredible that second-hand books were once sold from flat-topped wheelbarrows at the corners of blocks on the western side. The spate of private cars must have swept these away in the 1960s, but in my second University year I found on one a tattered Penguin paperback of 19th century verse called *Hood to Hardy*. Opening it at random I found it had work by poets my teachers had never mentioned, and as I read the street noises seemed to withdraw, leaving me in a silence with these words:

This and the next two paragraphs are identical with three in chapter eight, the Prologue.

> *This Beauty, this Divinity, this Thought,*
> *This hallowed bower and harvest of delight*
> *Whose roots ethereal seemed to clutch the stars,*
> *Whose amaranths perfumed eternity,*
> *Is fixed in earthly soil enriched with bones*
> *Of used-up workers; fattened with the blood*
> *Of prostitutes, the prime manure; and dressed*
> *With brains of madmen and the broken hearts*
> *Of children. Understand it, you at least*
> *Who toil all day and writhe and groan all night*
> *With roots of luxury, a cancer struck*
> *In every muscle; out of you it is*
> *Cathedrals rise and Heaven blossoms fair;*
> *You are the hidden putrefying source*
> *Of beauty and delight, of leisured hours,*
> *Of passionate loves and high imaginings;*
> *You are the dung that keeps the roses sweet*

I did not know what amaranths were or why they perfumed eternity, but that verse shook my intelligence awake by contradicting everything I had been taught about history and poetry at school and university – all I had been officially taught about life and would be taught for years to come. Since that day I have kept finding evidence that this grim view of what we call civilization is strictly true.

I still have and love that tattered copy of the Penguin *Hood to Hardy*. I bought it for ninepence. The jacket indicated that the price when new had been 2/6, meaning half-a-crown, meaning 30 pence when there were 12 pence in a shilling and 240 in a pound. How queer that old money now seems! Among notes at the end of the book I read that the author had been: *John Davidson [1857-1909]. Born at Barrhead, Renfrewshire, son of a Dissenting Minister, Schoolmaster in Scotland until 1889 when he settled in London and published various plays and volumes of verse. He died in circumstances that suggested suicide.* Barrhead is a small factory town in the Renfrew Hills six or seven miles south of Glasgow. It made lavatory pans, and I think could be reached by tram, before the trams were scrapped in 1963.

Davidson's verses had been written at the start of the 20th Century before two world wars, huge massacres of civilian populations, and continual government-funded escalation of wars and weaponry. I discovered him when these catastrophes had left most British people feeling safe and prosperous, but what I read *for myself* and have since read confirms Davidson's tragic view of civilization. It has taken a long while for me to reach the point of asserting it here. Despite great writers working to open folks' eyes to that truth from the days of Homer and Euripides, the teachers who expounded their work did so with eyes firmly shut. The eye-opening effort is endless. In every age it must be tackled anew, but obviously it could not be tackled within the walls of a university.

I decided to support myself as a school teacher and had a practical and an idealistic reason for teaching in Molendinar Primary. Every pupil in that school except in the final year was my height or less. I also believed that good teachers are more important for primary schools than secondary schools, just as good teachers in secondary schools are more important than those in universities, because the earlier young folk get good schooling, the more it benefits their character. In those days nearly all students had their fees paid (like the armed

forces) out of tax-payers' money, because even Tories thought
the nation needed all the well-educated citizens it could get. I was enough of a Socialist to believe that well-educated teachers from prosperous districts should carry their advantages to poorer ones. Most of my pupils were from Blackhill, a Glasgow municipal housing scheme built between the wars but less well-built than the housing schemes of Riddrie and Knightswood where clerks, schoolteachers and lower-paid professional folk were neighbours of skilled workmen. Blackhill was labelled a Slum Clearance Scheme and when high unemployment returned to Britain at the end of the sixties many Blackhill breadwinners lost their jobs and the number of crimes committed there greatly increased. My most difficult pupils came from fatherless homes. The poorest children lived with grandmothers. My first years in teaching made me very unhappy but I did some good. For several years I managed to take some of the poorest on camping holidays and twice got money from a charity that let me rent an H.F. guest house for them, Altshellach, in Arran. But like most idealistic teachers my enthusiasm dwindled so I was happy to become a Headmaster (the least responsible job in any school), happier to take early retirement and hide at last in research for my historic masterpiece.

The flaw in most histories is authors who pretend to be unprejudiced reporters of fact but keep describing the world coming to a good end in their own comfortable state – only Carlyle saw that nations whose only guiding principle was economic competition were preparing a Dark Age blacker than earlier ones. In the 17th century Bishop Bossuet showed history culminating in Louis XIV's Catholic France; 18th century Gibbon thought it culminated in enlightened Europe; 19th century Hegel in Protestant Prussia, Macaulay in post-Reform Bill England. The *Outline of History* by H. G. Wells viewed it as an irregular uphill struggle toward a world government of a scienctific, humanitarian kind – a successful 20th century League of Nations. Mark Twain shot down such daftness by pointing out that if the age of the world was represented by the height of the Eiffel Tower, the not-quite million years of human history would correspond to the thickness of the paint on a knob at the very top. He wondered if those who thought the world had been created for mankind, and more especially for themselves, might believe the Eiffel Tower was mainly built to uphold the paint on the topmost knob and concluded, "Reckon they might. I dunno."

If every history had a prologue describing the education of the writer's mind, readers would know in advance why some facts dominate the narrative more than others. Dear reader you will soon see how well or badly I lay out mine. Like the Bible it starts in the only way well-educated folk now imagine the beginning.

18: MY WORLD HISTORY: PROLOGUE

A SUDDEN ENDLESS GAS EXPLOSION made all the material in this universe. Some parts collided with others, swirling into gassy clumps that got denser and hotter and became radiant globes as they rotated. Big neighbouring globes began turning round each other while smaller ones became satellites of a bigger partner. The lightest materials floated on the surface of the globes, sometimes cooling into floating plates of crust that grew bigger until their edges met, making a surface that only let out light where red-hot or where volcanoes exploded through. The air above this world of ours was of gases no life could breathe: methane, ammonia, hydrogen and water vapour. The world's crust thickened. The surface cooled until rain water could lie there without being scalded into steam. At last a sea of water covered the world except where a rocky continent, thicker than the ground under the sea, rose above it near the equator.

Tunnock acquired the knowledge in these first paragraphs from Dr Chris Burton of Glasgow University's Department of Geology.

The molten minerals under the Earth's crust had currents slowly cracking it apart, making long submarine canyons on the ocean floor with bottoms constantly restored by lava welling up through volcanic vents. Boiling water above the vents was stopped evaporating by the weight of colder water, over a mile-deep above it. In the hottest depths, in a broth of dissolved chemicals, droplets started circulating. They grew larger when they touched and merged with similar droplets, but when this made them too big for their skins they split in two and went on separately. Such droplets *evolved* into single-celled creatures we call *living* because they *sense* things outside their bodies that can *nourish* them and help them *reproduce*, having *motive power* to reach for them. The evolution from these chemical drops to living cells has never (yet?) been achieved in a human laboratory. It has to happen first in deep water because in those days lethal ultra-violet sunlight penetrated water to a depth of over thirty feet. In submarine depths the sun's rays and Earth's heat were reduced, yet still strong enough to generate and support single-celled microbes that were the only living things for at least three quarters of life on Earth before today.

Tiny primitive creatures fed on dissolved chemicals in the earliest sea, then bigger ones started also feeding on the smaller, breathing out carbon dioxide that rose above the sea, mixed with the atmosphere above and began screening out the lethal ultra-violet rays. This let larger living things evolve near the surface. More complex bacteria converted carbon dioxide into oxygen until the air above was two per cent oxygen, which let a kindlier sunlight shine on sea and land. Life now crossed the beaches, entering rivers, lakes, swamps, plains in the first great continent. Lichens, mosses, fungi were followed by primitive insects and those segmented worms that are ancestors of every lizard, fish, bird and mammal with a backbone. The whole upper Earth, fluid and solid, came to hold living things of every size – plankton, seaweeds, sponges, fish, squid, sharks in the oceans, – crawling things in submarine volcanic vents, rock pools and soil, – herbs, trees, amphibians, lizards on land, – spores, seeds, insects, bats, birds in the air. This living layer around our planet has been called the zoo-sphere. It is thinnest at the poles, thickest in tropical rainforests. There were many such forests on the swampy first continent.

The Earth's interior moves more slowly than the zoo-sphere but is never still, currents in the molten rock under the solid crust always moving huge plates of crust apart on one side, and ramming them together on the other. Mountain ranges are raised when one plate is forced over another, then rain, wind, frost and lichen starts wearing the mountains down. Rocks and gravel fall into glens and valleys, rivers wash grit onto plains, spreading it and mixing it with dead plants and creatures, creating new soil. Meteor bombardments killed great sections of zoo-sphere through sudden global winters and ice ages, spreading seas have drowned them, the world's shifting crust has covered them with new rock making underground layers of coal and metal, reservoirs of oil and gas. The world's subterranean currents broke the earliest continent into smaller ones and drove them so far apart that they joined again on the other side of the world near the south pole. This again cracked into continents that drifted north and started roughly corresponding to those we know, though not in the order we know them at first. Some of the oceans between them widened, some narrowed or disappeared. The great plate of crust carrying India collided with Eurasia, elevating the Himalayas, our highest and youngest mountain range. The Alps are hardly middle-aged. The Wicklow Hills are all that remain of more ancient mountains.

When the Atlantic was a much narrower sea, the North American and Baltic landmasses had offshore islands with the same geology: granite, the world's oldest rock, and granite volcanically mixed with newer stuff, which is called *metamorphic*. The Eurasian landmass edged up from the south west, with offshore islands made of mainly sedimentary rock: chalk, clay and limestone. Slow convulsions jammed the north eastern islands together and rammed them onto a larger, more level coalition of the southern islands, creating an archipelago visited in the 4th century BC by Pytheas, a Greek explorer who gave it a Greek name. Nearly sixty years before Christ's birth it was invaded by Romans who learned most of their science from the Greeks and Latinised the name into Britannia. This happened because an unusual beast had appeared half a million years earlier.

Different thinkers have called *Homo Sapiens* a featherless biped, a tool-using animal, and "the glory, jest and riddle of the world". We are the only creature who drink when not thirsty, eat when not hungry, and take twelve years or more to become adult. One year old humans totter on unsteady legs when horses of that age walk, gallop and feed themselves in open fields. One year old birds have hatched, learned to fly, mated, built nests and begun feeding their own children because birds, bees, ponies etcetera mostly act instinctively; human instincts are so weakened that our actions have to be learned through imitation of adults (starting with mum and dad) who act differently from each other. This forces self-conscious choice called *learning* upon us, hence our prolonged immaturity. Adults are usually compensated for this by being ready for sexual intercourse all year round. Conscious choice has made us capable of new inventions – lighting fires, shaping sharp-edged tools, and sewing needles – so since homo sapiens learned to stand upright and use our hands in Africa we have kept a common body pattern by changing our minds, habits and societies. The Arctic ice cap once expanded south until most of Britain and adjacent lands were under a mile-thick layer of it. This thawed, retreated and returned, altering climates and sea levels. Other species were killed off or survived by evolving different bodies and instincts. Our kind survived by killing other creatures, roasting their flesh, turning their bones and skin into tools and clothing. As we spread around the globe some details of our physique changed a little. Hunters in the frozen north grew paler and plumper, those in the south leaner and darker. Where food was abundant the average human height grew to six feet or more. Poor food supplies made us dwarfish, led to immigration, warfare and murder, for we lacked the instinct that stops other beasts killing helpless members of their own species. Settled farmers on Chinese plains grew extra inches of gut to draw more nourishment from their rice, yet they too are of the same species as Inuits in Alaska, Pigmies in the Congo, Cleopatra, Robert Burns, Mahatma Ghandi and Condoleezza Rice. The big differences between races, nations and tribes come from folk learning to live in very different landscapes. A vast plain watered by three rivers explains why China is the largest, most peopled and most ancient nation. A smaller, equally self-centred nation was made by layers of limestone, chalk and clay forming a saucer of land with Paris in the middle. The Baltic sea explains

why such close neighbours as Norway, Sweden and Denmark
have different governments though a similar language.

Like all efficient imperialists Romans divided lands they invaded along natural borders. They called the south mainland Albion, the north mainland Caledonia, the western island Hibernia. Albion was very woody and marshy but had few natural barriers impeding the march of Roman legions. The tribes of Albion that joined to fight those were defeated, then the level parts of the south British mainland (all Albion except Wales) were planted over by Roman camps. These were connected by well-built roads to each and to *Londinium*, Britain's first big city. The camps were sited in fertile places and grew to be centres of still-thriving towns: Bath, York, Lincoln, Carlisle and other cities with names ending in *chester* or *caster*. The broad, fertile, generally level nature of Albion with its road network explains why it fell quickly to later invaders after Rome pulled out – first fell to Saxons and Angles who renamed it Angle-land or England, then to King Canute's Danish empire, then in 1066 to the Norman French. It explains why London-on-Thames became the capital of the English state, and why the the Bishop of Canterbury has been the High Priest of England since 598, and why England had only two universities in market towns near London until 1828.

Any map shows Scotland's difference from England what it originally was – several different islands jammed together. They are so narrowly joined that the Romans found it convenient to wall Caledonia off. Scotland's grotesquely irregular coastline shows the tip of the most southerly peninsula is only twelve miles from the Irish coast; the nearest neighbour on the European mainland is Norway, with the Orkney and Shetland islands like stepping stones between. Inside Scotland's ragged coastline the glens and plains are so separated by highland sea-lochs and mountain ranges, by lowland moors and firths, that cultivation produced very little surplus wealth before the mid 18th century. The natural barriers made conquest of the whole impossible for invaders, and a united Scotland almost impossible for the natives. It was four kingdoms, each an unstable union of fiercely independent clans, each with a capital city on the rock of an extinct volcano. Dumbarton (meaning *Fort of the Britons*) was capital of Strathclyde, a mainly Welsh-speaking kingdom that included Galloway and the west coast down to Barrow in Furness. Edinburgh was capital of a nation in east Scotland, south of the Firth of Forth and partly English-speaking, for it had been part of Northumbria before Duke William conquered all England up to the Tyne. Fife and the north west, with much of the Highlands, belonged to a people called Picts whose language is unknown and whose capital was on Craig Phadraig, Inverness. The Scottish king's nation, Dalriada, had its capital on Dunadd in Argyllshire, where the Scots tribes, Gaelic-speaking incomers, had arrived from Ireland. It is also pertinent that Shetland, Orkney, and Sutherland for centuries belonged to Norway and there were Scandinavian settlements all round the place, though that was also frequent in England.

This is the on;y complete chapter in a chaos of scribbled papers, news cuttings, copies of extracts from other people's work: raw materials of a book explaining Scotland in space and time from its part in the Crusades, its lack of an archbishop in Catholic times and Calvinism later; also its present place in the international financial war machine. A report on unused mineral beds

In days when kings were hardly anything but warlords, King Kenneth mac Alpin of Dalriada gave the Caledonian clanjamfrie the name of Scotland by conquest of some neighbours and alliances with others. That Scotland continued as a nation, however, is an English achievement, because ever since then the government of the bigger, richer nation tried and usually failed to make Scotland one of its counties – a kind of Cornwall or Yorkshire. Scotland's people have never been more than a tenth of England's, so why did England's far greater military power fail to incorporate us before Oliver Cromwell's brief success under the Commonwealth? Why did Scotland's three centuries of being Scotlandshire never quite destroy her independent culture? Why is she at last bound to win the same freedom as Portugal from Spain, Austria from Germany, Iceland from Denmark?

Robert Louis Stevenson gave the simplest answer when he noted that Gaelic-speaking Highlanders regard English-speaking Lowlanders with a suspicion the Lowlander is inclined to return unless both meet in English company where they at once feel like blood brothers. Why? There are many partial answers. One is the comparative poverty ensuring that for centuries the Scots gentry, whether Lowland lairds or Highland chiefs, did not speak wholly differently from their lowly employees, unlike England whose chief officials still speak a mandarin dialect learned in expensive private schools like Rugby, Marlborough etcetera. Around 1370 a French traveller visiting Scotland thought it remarkable that if a knight rode his horse over a Scot's grain field an angry peasant ran up and cursed him. No peasant dared do that in rich lands where the nobility had hundreds of workers so could have one flogged or hung without loss of income. Scots aristocrats were mostly too poor to damage crops on which they and their peasants depended. In the late 19th century Robert Louis Stevenson was dismayed by how completely his English friends behaved as if their servants and other low-class folk did not exist. Such national differences may be thought obsolete relics, and should be forgotten. This book will explain otherwise, not by inflaming anti-English sentiment, but by showing how local conditions have created a unique culture, so a separate government has always been required by those who share this land, these conditions.

The following chapters explain how Scottish people's *land*, rocks, soil distribution, mineral resources, waters and those great potential dynamos the sea lochs, ensure that all who live and work here come to feel part of it like the Irish who came to found Dalriada and later fled here from the potato famine – the Anglo-Saxons who escaped across the border from Duke William and Margaret Thatcher into the Lothians – Jews driven here by Czarist and Nazi pogroms – Italians by the phylloxera epidemic that destroyed their vineyards – Indians, Pakistanis, Chinese and other former subjects of the British empire, together with refugees from wars Britain has fought since then and are now wickedly labelled *asylum seekers*. I believe that all who stay to live, work and vote here will invigorate this nation that
has always been a colloquium of different people,
as every sane nation must be.

(chiefly coal) were mixed with prophecies that in 2020 or earlier, bankers will combat oil famine by hastily exploiting nuclear power and mutated crops. This will make everything catastrophically worse until folk see that their only hope is in small co-operative Socialist nations. The next diary extract explains why this huge work was abandoned.

Nineteen
Tunnock's Diary
2004

Highly perplexed. Around Saturday lunchtime yesterday life changed in a way that almost makes my entire past irrelevant, uninteresting. Shortly before noon I brought Niki her usual brunch in bed. She complained about amount of butter on toast. Told her she had a tenth part of what I put on my slice. She said that was why I was fat, then doorbell rang. Went down, opened it. Bustled in past me a person of my own height but sturdier, wearing a kind of battle dress with camouflage pattern designed for jungle warfare. She turned and facing me, hands on hips, said belligerently, "Where's that Is?"

"Who are you?" I said, astonished.

"Where is that Is?" she demanded, fiercer still. Beginning to recognize her I said, "I don't know! You led Isabel in here with two other girls three years ago. I had never seen them before and have never seen them since."

"Hm!" she said, frowning, and, "Are you telling me the truth?"

"Why should I tell lies?" I cried, exasperated. "Who are you? What do you want here?"

"Are you telling me there's no woman in this house?"

"Why should I tell you anything?" I demanded.

"I'm the woman in this house," said a voice and there was Niki on the stair landing, her coat slipped on over her nightgown and Moloch in her arms.

"Then clear out!" said this total stranger. Niki, obviously as astonished as I was, said faintly "Who are you?"

"Don't you know?"

Niki stood staring and shaking her head. She had been redder than usual but was now paler than usual. The invader said,

"If you don't know me, ask around. I know you Mrs Kate MacNulty! Your man knows me even better so go back hame and ask him who I am! You'll find him a lot nicer after his wee spell in jail, so put on your claes and get out of here because your arnae needed. John's had enough of you and that wean you carted here instead of chucking it in the Clyde. Amn't I right John?"

That question was flung at me like a stone, and because I was indeed tired of Niki and Moloch I could not say no. Niki yelled, "Don't worry! I'm sick of you John Tunnock and you're welcome to that bitch whoever she is! I was going to clear out soon anyway ye fat, stupid, mean, TV-less wee bastard!" Moloch started wailing.

When life grows too complicated for intelligent management, sit down till it simplifies. I did so in the dining-room, elbows on knees, head in hands. The invader stayed in the lobby until I heard Niki leave, muttering what were either ugly remarks to the stranger or soothing sounds to Mo. The front door slammed. The new presence entered the room and sat opposite me. Relief at departure of lodgers was blocked by dread of new burden. Without looking up I asked what she wanted. She said sullenly, "I wouldnae mind a whisky. A big one. No water. And I wouldnae mind chocolate biscuits or stuff like that, if you've got any."

I gave her what she asked and sat down again facing her, sipping a whisky I had poured for myself and wondering what to say. She said suddenly, "Put on some of that music."

"What kind?" I asked. She leaned toward me so that her hair fell forward and hid her face. She mumbled, "Something romantic."

I went, tingling a little, to the pianola and inserted the Siegfried Idyll with which Wagner greeted Cosima on the morning she gave birth to their son. I returned to where the intruder sat, her face still hidden behind her curtain of hair. I again sat opposite not knowing what to say until, "Are you Zoe?" occurred to me. She said, "Aye."

I said I had met her father a while ago. She said, "Where? How?"

*"In a pub," I said. She said, "Aye. Give me another whisky."
I poured it saying, "Exactly what do you want? Is it money?"
She said, "I don't need* money.*"*

"So what do you want?"

*"Is that not obvious?" she shouted, angrily glaring at me. I gaped
at her. She said, "Let's go to bed."*

"Not," I said firmly, "before I have another whisky."

*Sounding disappointed she said she hadn't known I was the kind
that needed it.*

*What followed was too quick to be perfectly satisfying, but the
relief was wonderful.*

All animals
are sad after
sexual
intercourse.

> *Post coitum omne animal triste est is attributed to Aristotle
who never said it, because it is Latin and he Greek. It is not
always true of me but is certainly true of every woman who has
lain with me, so I was not surprized when Zoe, after bringing me
to that rapid climax, started sobbing. Feeling happy and grateful
I asked what was wrong, knowing from experience nothing I said
would help. She said, "Now you'll think I'm just a hoor, nothing
but a hoor."*

*I pointed out that a whore was paid for being fucked; she had
fucked me rather than vice versa and had refused my offer of
money. She said, "I told you I don't want your money."*

*"Then you aren't a whore," I said. She said, "Aye, alright, but
I'm still a bad girl. I've done things, I do things that are utterly
wrong, completely rotten. You see I – "*

*Not wanting to be horrified I firmly interrupted saying, "Say no
more. I hold myself to be indifferent honest, but know such things
of me it were better my mother had never bore me."*

*She stopped sobbing and asked what the hell did that mean? I
said I was quoting Hamlet by William Shakespeare, and in
Shakespeare's time "indifferent" meant "ordinary", so Hamlet
meant he was as honest as most folk, but had still done things
that meant the world would be better if he had never existed. She
said, "Does that mean everybody is as bad as me?"*

"That's what Hamlet meant."

"Even you?"

*"Certainly," I said, though doubting it. I was a fair kind of school
teacher and never needed to use the belt in any class I had charge*

of, though until 1986 in Britain it was legal to do so. Even in primary schools a well-dressed, confident male teacher could torture the hand of a little girl in districts where working class parents thought that commonplace. When headmaster I told my staff not to use it, but to send troublemakers they could not handle to me, and every week four or five came to my door, usually the same four or five. Most were very active kids incapable of sitting still, or had bad manners learned at home which teachers had no time to correct. I am now ashamed of having belted these kids, but had I not done so my staff would have felt unsupported, insecure, so I tortured small children at least four times a week. Too disgusted to work out how many times a year, how often in a lifetime of teaching I said in a firmer voice, "Yes, perhaps even worse than you, though not as bad as Eichman."

Zoe, highly interested, said, "Tell me about it."

I said, "No. I will not tell you how rotten I have been if you don't tell me how bad you are. Let us please just be good to each other."

She said thoughtfully, "That's an idea. Do you want us to do the other thing again?"

I said yes, if we did it slowly this time. She said, "I thought men like it quick."

I said a lot of men learned about sex in ways that stopped them doing it slowly, but I was too old to be quick twice a night. We cuddled. She began weeping again in a different, less stormy way and at last I may or may not have ejaculated and we fell asleep with my male part comfortable inside her.

Which I hope often happens. This morning I awoke greatly refreshed, kissed her awake, said "Breakfast!" and rushed downstairs to make it, dressing as I went. She followed soon after, not realising I would have brought it to her in bed. Facing this bossy, confident woman across the kitchen table, drinking coffee with her and eating poached eggs on toast with grilled tomatoes felt familiar because the last time I had felt that way was with Aunt Nan before illness confined her to bed. Well, if Zoe stays long enough I'll die long before she does, hooray hooray. And it's wonderful that she doesn't expect me to serve her hand and foot. After the meal she said, "Mind if I smoke?" and rolled and smoked a thin cigarette, watching while I washed, dried and put away breakfast things. She said, "You're a very queer kind of man."

I told her it would be a bad world if men were all the same and now I must work. She said, "So will I as soon as the pub's open, but I thought you'd retired from teaching."

I told her I was a writer. She asked what stuff I wrote and could she get it from the library. I said I hadn't been published yet and my field was historical sociology. She said, obviously disappointed, "O very highbrow," but came into the sitting room and sat smoking, being careful not to scatter the cigarette ash while I scribbled in this notebook. She showed no interest in what I scribbled, probably thinking it was historical sociology. Perhaps it is, but I am also coming to terms with the new adventure my life has become. At intervals I put on rolls of – Bach, Joplin, Stravinsky, Souza, Verdi, varying the music as much as possible and asking after each piece if she liked it. She always said, "Just you carry on playing it."

Shortly before noon she stood up saying, "I'm for offski."

I gave her a key so she could return when she liked. That was ten minutes ago. This house feels like a home again.

The miracle of Zoe makes me astonishingly happy. I now know why bad sex is a big part of life and good sex a small part – it lets me enjoy so many other things. Each morning I waken refreshed for the adventure of a new day and our breakfast together tastes as good as breakfasts in childhood. I kiss her goodbye, scoot to the library, immerse myself in exciting new researches. Building a scientific Scottish history on its geological foundation is certainly essential to making us a nation again, but a chore good research students could finish if they continued on lines I have laid down. My masterpiece should draw readers into a real life as free and romantic as my own – need I first steep them in their present miseries by showing how these evolved? I am studying the historical vision of Goethe's Faust, Ibsen's Emperor and Galilean, Tolstoy's War and Peace, Hardy's Dynasts. Can I reconcile these while adding something of my own?

This morning a letter from —— commanded me to lunch with
her at the Hasta Mañana, because she had information the book
she thinks I am writing needs. The worst lunch of my life. She
began by asking what extraordinary rendition meant. I did not
know. She said, "It is American jargon for disappearing people
– the C.I.A. secretly kidnap them, usually on foreign soil, with
or without the secret connivance of the local police, because
they are suspected of being or knowing active terrorists. They
are then taken into U.S.A.-run jails in other countries like
Guantanamo in Cuba or Abu Ghraib in Iraq (there are plenty
of others), and there they are questioned – which means tortured
– and sometimes killed without a trial." She went on to say
that trials held in public according to U.S.A. and European
laws prove most folk arrested on mere suspicion are innocent,
and when Nazi or Russian dictatorships did these things U.S.A.
and British newspapers denounced them as evil. But though
Amnesty International and other decent organisations know
extraordinary rendition had disappeared hundreds, maybe
thousands since Bush announced his War on Terror, the fact
that R.A.F. bases in Scotland are being used in these illegal
abductions was not mentioned by British newspapers or
broadcasting – "which is why you must write about it!" I said
I would think about that and tried to leave, which stimulated
an even longer diatribe about what she called global money
and the international arms trade which she said was responsible
for World War 1, the 1930s Depression, the Nazi Party, World
War 2 and every war since. She said that after Britain started
the industrial arms-race in 1890 every leading politician from
Lloyd George to Thatcher and Blair have been secretly enriched
by policies whose result in human deaths they openly regret or
denounce. "So you believe world history is controlled by a
conspiracy?" I managed to interject: she replied, "Of course!
An obvious, undisguised conspiracy! Britain has now only seven
highly profitable industries and they all sell armaments! Every
prosperous bastard has investments in them!" Not me, I told
her, because my accountant had invested my savings ethically.
She cried, "That's what the Corporation of London and
Manchester and half the other local authorities say and they're

lying, deliberately or through ignorance. The universities, successful trade unions and so-called charities have all invested in them! So has Cancer Research, Care for the Handicapped, Co-operative Insurance, the Boys Brigade. The arms industries produce several things with peaceful uses so brokers and accountants fool folk like you into thinking your money only helps these, but they're lying. For over a century the names of politicians, newspaper owners, clergymen etcetera enriched by the arms trade have been recorded in stock exchange reports, but the only folk who try to publicise the fact are denounced as Loony Leftists by the media." She also said Britain's secret police force has been part of this open conspiracy since 1993 when its headquarters shifted from a drab, inconspicuous building off the Euston Road to a swaggeringly huge structure in the Postmodern or revived Art Deco style, which is now as conspicuous a part of 2004 London as Orwell's Ministry of Truth in 1984. When she was a student it was an open secret that the head of the Extra-mural department was Glasgow University's spy for the Ministry of Information. Everyone found that comic. That Ministry is now inviting staff in every British university department to apply for the job of spying for it. Those who apply successfully will not be made known: their extra source of income will not be taxed, and they will earn it by reporting on every student or colleague who questions the wisdom of what our increasingly right-wing government does. An American celebrity law professor is now arguing that the Geneva Conventions are out of date and the U.S.A. government should legalise torture and the assassination of its enemies, even if this causes the death of innocent people in the vicinity. Lawyers who want such things legalised know their government has already started doing them. I said, "How can I put all that into a book?" She said, "It's your job to find out – you're the historian." I told her I would think about it and rushed off leaving her to pay the bill, for she insists on doing that anyway. As a child I saw Viva Zapata in the Hillhead Salon, and since I left her something said in it has been echoing in my head: "Jesus Christ! I'm not the world's conscience."

*I love the twelfth floor of this library. It allows views across
Glasgow in every direction. Instead of reading today I strolled,
just looking, from one glass wall to another. Recent strong winds
had swept away clouds and haze so eastward I saw the Victorian
terraces of Park Circus and tops of 1960s tower-blocks. Between
a couple I saw the cathedral spire. The Cathkin Braes summit
above Rutherglen has a line of trees with sky visible between
the trunks – near there in 1820 Purly Wilson raised the red flag
to start the Great Scottish Insurrection – that never happened.
Further east was the dim Fuji Yama-like cone of Tinto, the
ancient volcanic centre of Scotland round which the Clyde flows
from the border country. I looked down on the Gothic-revival
pinnacles and quadrangles of the university, with the red
sandstone minarets of Kelvingrove museum and gallery beyond,
and beyond them, then grey tenements and the long white wall
of Yorkhill Hospital, and the tops of some big cranes to remind
me Glasgow is still a port. Through a gap between facades a
ship's funnel slid past. The slender pencil of the research tower
building reminded me how modern technology can get things
wrong. South of the river were the wooded hills of Queen's Park
and Bellahouston Park, with white farmhouses, fields and lines
of hedge on hills beyond rising to Neilston Padd, that queer,
steep-sided plateau beside Fenwick Moor. Further west were
the Gleniffer Braes of which poor Tannahill sang, and the dim
but distinct summit of Goat Fell on Arran. On a summer holiday
in my teens I climbed that mountain with Gordon MacLean.
Why not climb it again with Zoe? It is a Munro, but the gradient
is easy.*

*Yes, today I feel so happy that I no longer want to show how
Scotland, Britain and the world is being messed about, probably
destroyed by get-rich-quick financiers and corrupted
politicians. Scotland is now exactly where I want to be and I
refuse to worry about it.*

*Suddenly the story of Belovéd Henry James Prince dawned
on me like a holiday excursion. The information needed to write
it is in this library. Abandoning all other research notes crossed
to the office of the Special Collection with its view to the North
of the Campsie Fells, Kilpatrick Hills and Ben Lomond. Here I*

The funnel
was on The
Waverley,
the last
Clyde-built
passenger
steamer. The
research
tower is
currently the
tallest
structure in
Scotland
(127 metres)
and the only
one in the
world
designed to
revolve
round a
static pylon
to which it is
hinged,
allowing
visitors a
splendid 360
degree view
over the city.
It has been
static since
30 January
2005 when
10 people
were trapped
for 5 hours
half way up
in the lift.

ordered Br. Prince's Journal and volume one of Hepworth Dixon's Spiritual Wives. They were brought.

Having immersed myself again in these familiar pages I will now write Prince's tale as briskly as if singing love's old sweet song — tell how a terribly conscientious Christian so loathed his evil Self (which Freud calls the Ego) that he cast it out, becoming nothing but a mad imagination with a penis — a Super-ego and Id in such harmony that he created a New Jerusalem in England's Green and Pleasant Land where he was the only cock in a coop of crinolined hens, and enjoyed his Zoe for Ever and Ever Amen! I will enjoy writing this.

Upon surveying the texture of what has been wrote, it is necessary, that a good quantity of heterogeneous matter be inserted, to keep up that just balance between wisdom and folly, without which a book would not hold together for a single year, and swim down the gutter of time with the legation of Moses and *A Tale of a Tub*.

— *Tristam Shandy*
by Lawrence Sterne

BELOVÉD

20: THE YOUNG PRINCE

NEAR THE START OF THE 19TH CENTURY there was a brief truce in the commercial warfare that France and Britain had fought from the reign of Queen Anne to the Battle of Waterloo. Gilray, a popular artist, depicted two statesmen enjoying a little supper, their meal being the world laid out like a big plum pudding on a table between them. At one side small swarthy Napoleon enthusiastically sliced western Europe onto his plate with a sabre; on the other Britain's Prime Minister, tall, thin, pointy-nosed William Pitt, quietly helped himself to most of the rest of the globe. In 1815 Napoleon's empire ended at Waterloo but the British King George III still nominally ruled Ireland, Canada, the Caribbean, Australia, India, many Chinese and African ports: also Hanover, a German state that was his family's homeland. The British Empire was now the richest and biggest in the world, without a single competitor, but the British did not yet trust their monarchs enough to give them the title of Emperor. Poor George was now incurably mad so the Prince Regent performed the crown's few legaly required ceremonies. In 1816 Rossini's *The Barber of Seville* was first performed, and Jane Austen's *Emma* and Coleridge's *Kubla Khan* were published.

Widdicombe Crescent, Bath, was then a terrace of smart houses in that most aristocratic of British holiday resorts and here a little boy had a pain in his side. It brought tears to his eyes and sweat to a brow he pressed against the cool glass of a window. Behind him a doctor told his widowed mother that he could help the boy no further: cold compresses had brought no relief; purging and reduced diet had merely weakened the lad; so had bloodletting which must not continue, despite the temporary alleviation it induced.

"I will give drops to ensure he sleeps at night, Mrs Prince. I could give more tincture of opium to reduce his pains when wakeful, but more will stupefy him. I fear that, like older people, he should learn that pain must be lived with."

"I have told him so many times, Doctor, but he seems to want me to bear it for him. Two other sons, three daughters and a paying guest leave me no time for that," said his mother.

"There are physicians in Bath who charge higher fees, Mrs Prince, but none I can honestly recommend. In London you might find one who would prescribe opening him surgically –" (the boy whimpered; they glanced at him) "– I do not advize it. If he were female and older his pains might be due to hysteria, which is incurable. As things are I advize you to let nature take its course."

The doctor left. Without turning the boy said in a small voice, "Mamma, let me go to Miss Freeman."

"You spent most of yesterday with her, Henry."

"She helps me. She's nice to me."

"I would be nice to you too if I had nothing else to do all day, but we will go to her since you insist. And remember, she is a papist. You must pay no attention if she talks to you about the Pope, or confessors, or transmutation, or other foreign things."

They went upstairs and on the first floor landing tapped a door; it was opened by a plump, hectically flushed young woman wearing a black dress and thin gold necklace with small pendant cross.

"I dislike troubling you again Miss Freeman, but the doctor is helpless and Henry loves being with you – "

" – I love to have him – "

"But you too are an invalid Miss Freeman!"

"Which is why Henry and I understand each other. Come here Henry James."

She held out her arms. The boy ran into them and pressed his face to her stomach. She caressed the back of his neck, smiling fondly and saying, "Leave us Mrs Prince, we will refer our troubles to Jesus."

As the door closed she drew him to a chaise longue beside a small table on which lay an open box of chocolates, a Bible and a standing ebony crucifix. Fixed to the crucifix with gold-headed pins was a white ivory figure crowned with gold thorns. She sat down asking, "Where does it hurt Henry James?"
"Here," he said, kneeling at her feet, pressing his side with one hand and clasping her knee with the other.
"Yes! That is where the cruel Romans thrust their spear into the flesh of Lord Jesus on the cross – " (Her fingertip touched the side of the ivory figure.) " – do you see the wound? He must have felt as you do."
"Did he?" said the boy staring.
"Worse! See those nails through his hands and feet and the crown of cruel thorns. And Jesus was God's beloved son."
"But I'm not, why should I be hurt?"
"Because," Miss Freeman gently whispered, "you are an evil little sinner, Henry. But another sinner much worse than you, a wicked robber was crucified beside Jesus, and loved Him, and that night the robber sat in Heaven at God's right hand."
"I'm afraid of going to Hell, Miss Freeman."
"Where you *will* go Henry, if you don't love Jesus."
"How can I love anybody when I'm hurt?"
"That is how God tests our love, Henry. You must forget your wicked fleshly body Henry. You must think only of Christ, and how he desires you. Listen! This is what Christ is saying to you . . . and sit beside me, Henry."
He sat on the sofa, leaning against her side, staring at the chocolates.
"You may take one," she said, lifting and opening the Bible at a page marked by an embroidered ribbon, "Listen Henry, listen. *Thou hast ravished my heart, my sister, my spouse; thou hast ravished my heart with one of thine eyes, with one chain of thy neck.*"
"I'm not a sister Miss Freeman, I'm a brother," said the boy

indistinctly, for he was chewing.

"I know that, Henry, but when God – who is also Jesus – loves somebody he talks to them as if they are women, even when they aren't."

"Why?"

Miss Freeman, slightly puzzled, said, "Perhaps because women are . . . usually . . . more lovely than men. I'm not sure. So just listen Henry, and remember, Christ is really speaking to *you* in the words of Solomon, that great wise king. *How fair is thy love, my sister, my spouse! How much better is thy love than wine! Thy lips, O my spouse, drop as the honey comb: honey and milk are under thy tongue* . . . Is that not lovely Henry ? –" (she stroked his hair) "– *and the smell of thy garments is like the smell of Lebanon.* Leb . . . a . . . non. What a delicious word!"

She sighed happily. The boy said drowsily, "I'm feeling a lot better, Miss Freeman." She said, "So am I. *Awake, O north wind; and come, thou south; blow upon my garden that the spices thereof may flow out. Let my beloved come into his garden, and eat his pleasant fruits.*"

Nearly twenty years later the wallpaper in that room had been changed twice and Miss Freeman was white-haired and stouter. She lay on the chaise longue with closed eyes still smiling fondly, her head resting on a flowery big cushion, her feet on a smaller one. Henry James Prince, a pale young man with a careworn, patient face, sat on an easy chair nearby, one leg flung over the other to support the Bible. He was soberly dressed and reading out a favourite passage in a low, sweet but unemphatic voice that allowed full value to the beauty of each word.

"*Thy navel is like a round goblet that wanteth not liquor,*" he said. "*Thy belly is like an heap of wheat set about with lilies. Thy two breasts are like two roes that are twins. Thy neck is like a tower of ivory, thine eyes are like the fish-pools of Heshbon; the hair of thine head like purple; the King is held in the galleries. How fair and pleasant art thou O love for delights!*"

Miss Freeman sighed, opened her eyes, clipped to the bridge of her nose the pince nez she now needed to see things near her and said, "O Henry James, I'm *glad* your mother is letting you train for the church at last."

He closed the Bible and placed it on the table by the crucifix saying gravely, "She would not have done so were you not paying the fees. She thought that having one son a clergyman was sufficient."

"But everything about you speaks of God! Your voice, your manners, your . . . hands."

He smiled, clasping the hand she stretched out to him and saying, "You've forgotten my soul, Martha."

"No I haven't," she said tenderly, "and your new clothes suit you wonderfully."

21: LAMPETER

Hale Holy Love! Hale Holy Love!

S AID THE PRINCIPAL, "Welcome, gentlemen, to St David's College, Lampeter. We don't know each other yet, but when we separate four years from now I hope we shall be firm friends."

He was middle aged, robust, bland, ruddy and stood, teacup in hand, his back to a sideboard supporting an arrangement of silver plate. On the wall behind hung framed engravings of the Holy Family by Raphael and Michelangelo's Creation of Adam; before him was a room of new students. Some wore dark clothes and seemed uneasy with the teacups and saucers they held; a few wore more fashionably-cut clothes with notes of colour in the waistcoats, and these students held their tea things more nonchalantly. Henry James Prince, though most soberly dressed, handled cup and saucer with the ease of the more obviously fashionable.

"Ours is not a venerable institution, gentlemen," said the Principal, "and maybe some of you regret that your parents or guardians could not afford the fees demanded by Oxford. Speakin' as a former senior wrangler I can honestly say that you are better off here. Oxford is now infested by sophistical vipers who have turned against the mother who bore them – the Church of England – and degraded themselves to the worship of saints, angels, fumigations and all kinds of unmanly rot. You're well out of it.

"A dangerous age, gentlemen! Mad messiahs are springin' up like mushrooms. Meanwhile the leaders of the rabble are barkin' 'Reform! Reform!' like a lot of rabid dogs, as if unemployment, high prices and occasional starvation among the masses are things a government can cure. But I mustn't bore you with politics. You don't want that, hey?"

He cocked his head, smiling at the audience who mostly smiled back and murmured agreement.

"You'll find this excellent walkin' and climbin' country, gentlemen, and we have a very decent little trout-stream in the grounds. So study hard, and learn how to pray and preach and perhaps learn to *practise* what you preach, hey?" – (Another pause for smiles and amused murmurs) – "But gentlemen, don't neglect the body God gave you. *Mens sano incorpore sane.* A healthy mind and healthy body will help you avoid the pitfalls of papish superstition on one side and the blue devils of Methodist fanaticism on the other. And a word of warning. Many of you are Welsh so know how quickly gossip travels in rural areas. I do not want to hear of anyone drinkin' in a local pothouse before he has learned to carry his liquor like a gentleman."

Nothing in the Principal's speech had amused Henry James Prince and the widespread approving response left him feeling lonely. The first lectures and the communal evening meal left him lonelier still. He went despondently to his room. Though as small as a monk's cell it was plainly but sufficiently carpeted, wallpapered and furnished. A small fireplace had a grate with coals laid above sticks and papers. He knelt on the hearthrug, lit the fire and was about to continue kneeling in prayer when someone tapped the door. He opened it and saw a young man with a creased, leathery, solemn face who said, "Good evening. My name is Arthur Rees. My room is next door."

"Henry James Prince," said Prince, bowing slightly. "Would you care to take tea with me?"

"Yes thanks," said Rees entering, "but what I'd like most is a word with you. We seem the oldest of the new lot."

"I am twenty-six," said Prince closing the door. "I trained as a doctor before deciding to come here. Please sit down."

He placed a kettle of water on a hob attached to the grate and poked the fire. Rees said, "I was a seaman."

"Indeed?"

"A sailor in peril on the deep. Trivial danger of broken bones and drowning of course, but I encountered worse perils. Know what I mean?"

"I suppose you refer to sins. As a doctor I have encountered most forms of evil, Mr Rees, so know the sin most dangerous to seamen. Not drunkenness, eh?" asked Prince, smiling thinly.

"Not drunkenness, no. O no."

"Since you are obviously earnest about your soul's salvation I am very pleased to meet you."

Prince brought utensils from a corner cupboard and made tea. As they drank it Rees said, "If you will allow the question, Mr Prince, what brings you here?"

"Many things, Mr Rees. As a child I was taught to love God by an unusually sincere Christian. Then my medical work in London and Bath showed me how little can be done to help sick bodies, how much is *not* done to help sick souls. I also became very ill, nearly died last year and was advized to recuperate through rest and a change of air. I went north and lived for a while with my brother – he is a vicar at Shincliffe, near Durham. This experience shocked me more than my recent surgical operation! No doubt in London and Bath I had met many infidels, but the churches where I worshipped were always well attended. My brother's church was never more than a quarter full. The colliers in his parish openly despized it. They drank deep, swore loudly and fought hard. Their Sunday mornings were chiefly spent in brutal fisticuffs that continued quarrels begun in previous Sundays. Men loved their puppies more than their wives, who were regularly beaten as often as the men got drunk. Their employers were no better, for such gentry spent the Sabbath shooting, fishing or riding to hounds. I wish I could say that my brother's parishioners hated him for being a true Christian. Alas, I cannot say so. The Church, I saw, stood in dire need of sincere priests. Something I could not deny urged me to become one. That something – I hope and pray – was God's Holy Spirit. What brought you here, Mr

Rees?"

"My sins."

"O?"

There was a silence then Rees added, "I fear I am more naturally vicious than most men – certainly most of my appetites are vicious. By frequent prayer I hardly ever indulge them, but have known for years that my one chance of salvation is in coming closer to God. None of the ministers I have so far met have brought me closer. By saving every spare penny I can now pay the fees of this college which may teach me to come closer."

"May I shake your hand, Rees?" said Henry, and they shook hands warmly.

Then Rees asked diffidently, "What's your impression of the other students, Prince?"

"I am vexed by their levity, Rees. God forgive me if I'm wrong but some seem educating for the stage rather than the pulpit."

"Dry bones! Dry bones the lot of them!"

"God can give life to dry bones," said Prince, reprovingly.

"Yes, we must pray for that."

"Will we pray for it now?", said Prince, staring at him. Rees, nodding, smiled radiantly back. Prince chuckled and nodded also. They knelt facing each other on the hearthrug, half a yard apart, heads bowed, hands clasped on stomachs. In a low voice Prince asked, "Shall I begin? After The Lord's Prayer?"

"Yes, after The Lord's Prayer."

They said that prayer in unison and then, with Prince leading, spoke alternately as the spirit moved them, begging Almighty God to give special help to the moral state of the college, to its Principal, its lecturers, its students and, lastly, to themselves.

At first their prayers had no obvious effect. All students observed a decent gravity during communal prayers, services and lectures, but between these facetious levity was the most obvious mood. The tutor of Greek, despite a dry manner, did not discourage some levity in his classroom. He said,

"Thucydides now describes the sporting customs of the Spartans. Will you translate Mr Rees? Egoom-no-they-san tay protoy kai – ?"

With much hesitation Rees said, "They were the first also who . . . stripped themselves and . . . pulling off their clothes in public, anointed themselves with fat for, for, for athletic exercizes. Whereas . . . formerly . . . even in the Olympic Games the wrestlers used to fight wearing . . . exontes, exontes . . ."

"Skirts," said the tutor, "Girdles. Belts."

Hurriedly Rees muttered, " . . . used to fight with belts round their loins which shows that the primitive Greeks lived like the barbarians of the present day."

"Yes," said the tutor urbanely, "The custom of sporting nudity was started by Orsippus of Megara, who accidentally lost his girdle in the Olympic stadium and consequently won the race. Greek notions of barbarism you see, were in some matters the reverse of ours. You look as if you wish to say something, Mr Prince."

"Yes. Can you tell me sir how knowledge of Greek depravity will help our study to administer Christ's Gospels?"

"I can. You are here to learn the original *language* of the Gospels, Mr Prince, which was first written in Greek. But it was written by Jews whose Greek dialect, though adequate, was provincial, and to understand a language well it is always wise to start by studying those who wrote it best. You should therefore learn to construe Aristotle and Thucydides before giving your minds to the less definite subject of pastoral theology. Anything pernicious you acquire from these great writers and reasononers is your responsibility, not mine, and so Mr Prince please translate what Thucydides says about early cities, piracy and the foundations of capital."

After a pause Prince said in a low voice, "I will not."

"Oho! It goes against your conscience, sir?"

"Sir, it does."

"Well, being an *Anglican* Christian I have no wish to martyr anyone. Mr Thomas, since Mr Prince will not or cannot oblige me, will you?"

Mr Thomas did.

The discipline of St David's College was meant to be tighter than at the old English universities but the staff were tolerant former Oxford and Cambridge men who let through most students who paid their fees and subscribed to the thirty-nine articles ratified by the English Protestant parliament of 1571. Other students came to admire Prince and join him and Rees in private prayer meetings. This offended nobody at first.

One evening the Principal presided at a dinner where wine was served. Conversation grew louder, laughter more raucous, Prince and Rees remained the only students whose gravity was not impaired. At last the Principal rose to his feet and called for attention. Waiters deftly, assiduously topped up wine glasses in the silence and short speech that followed.

"The Epicureans among you may have noticed that our dinner this evening was perhaps more to their taste than usual, hey? A little more lavish, hey?" – (there were murmurs of "Yes yes", "Indeed", "Hear hear") – "I cannot pretend not to know that rumour has spread the reason for this festivity. Yes. This morning my wife presented me with a little daughter and I am pleased to inform you that the infant and her excellent mother are in the pink of condition. She is to be christened Maria Augusta Ollivant. Are your glasses fully primed? Then please be upstanding, gentlemen, to drink a health to Maria Augusta Ollivant."

Everyone but Prince stood up, glass in hand. Rees, staring open mouthed at Prince, slowly put his wine glass down. Others took longer to notice Prince, the Principal being last. He stared hard at the seated figure then said softly but distinctly, "Mr . . . Mr, er . . . Mr Prince, will you not drink my daughter's health sir?"

"Dr Ollivant," said Prince loudly, "I would rather pray for your daughter's soul. I will gladly go down on my knees to do so here and now! Yes, here and now!"

He pushed his chair back and knelt on the floor with hands clasped on table edge and chin resting on them, then jerked his head back and cried, "I call upon the rest of you to join me! I really think it will be best."

The company stared and buzzed at each other. Rees, torn between normal manners and Prince's example, compromized by sitting down. After an astonished moment the Principal again spoke quietly but distinctly.

"Mr Prince, we said grace at the start of our meal. It would be impious to mingle prayers with our wine."

"That was not Christ's opinion, Dr Ollivant."

There were murmurs and cries of "Shame!" and "O come now!" until the Principal said fiercely, "Stand up sir and tell me *why* you refuse to drink my daughter's health."

Prince stood and waited for silence before saying, "I have a low opinion of what the world calls good health, sir. As a doctor I have watched at the bedside of many dying sinners. In a few cases their last moments were their holiest. I have often been very ill, and have lost blood in a painful operation, and I know that nothing in this world is dependable except an abject faith in God. That is why I wish to be a clergyman. I find that as my health improves I grow proud, carnal, independent. The flesh becomes mighty in me, I feel I will never die. Tonight most of us here – perhaps you too Dr Ollivant – have forgotten you are going to die. You forget that the eye of an angry God is upon you, following you with a vengeance that you can never escape! Yet you are training to be priests or are priests already! Will you not join me in praying for the soul of a newborn child? Yes, and for the soul of every one of us?"

He knelt down as before – Rees also knelt down – while a murmur of protest that began near the end of his speech became an uproar. The Principal silenced it by announcing, "You are excused this company, Mr Prince, and so is anyone else who cannot reconcile Christianity with the friendly customs of English gentlemen."

Prince stood up, bowed to the Principal and walked out. Rees and four others followed. George Thomas, a dandy student who had hitherto been foremost in joking about Henry James Prince and his followers, caused most astonishment by muttering an inarticulate apology and hurrying out after. The

Principal said dryly, "There seems to be a little college inside our college."

But Anglican tolerance was such that the careers of students in Prince's meetings in no way suffered, for in due course those who attended were, like others at St David's College, free to promote their kind of Protestant Christianity among the lower classes around Lampeter where Methodism had a strong foothold and Roman Catholicism a feeble one.

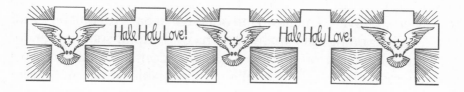

Bᴿ· PRINCE'S JOURNAL;*

OR,

AN ACCOUNT OF THE DESTRUCTION OF THE WORKS OF THE DEVIL IN THE HUMAN SOUL,

BY THE

LORD JESUS CHRIST,

THROUGH THE GOSPEL.

———

"For this purpose the Son of God was manifested, that He might destroy the works of the devil." – 1. Jᴏʜɴ iii. 8.

———

LONDON:

PUBLISHED FOR THE PROPRIETOR BY

ARTHUR HALL, VIRTUE, AND CO.,

25, PATERNOSTER ROW.

1859.

* Twelve of the following fifteen dated diary extracts are in words Prince published, but Tunnock shortened by removing many phrases about the beauty of Christ's love and Prince's evil nature and the sinfulness of the human soul. Three marginally noted entries are partly John Tunnock's invention, but use phrases from other entries.

May 7th – Glory be to Thee, O God! A day to be much remembered. The 7th May two years ago (1834) the Lord in Mercy delivered me from the bondage of Satan at half past four in the evening after many months of dreadful suffering under the conviction of sin and the temptations of Satan. When I deemed I had committed the unpardonable sin, in an hour of extreme agony Christ was revealed to me by faith, and my soul found peace in an instant.

Was enabled this day to declare my religious principles boldly before the college. The ———— had given wine to drink his infant's birth. Speeches were made. I called upon them all to unite *in prayer* for the child's spiritual happiness. Afterwards pride strove hard for establishment; a day of darkness, deep darkness. I am far from God and in deep misery. Was much helped in exposition to my little congregation.

The last three 1836 entries are partly fictional, the dates wholly so. Tunnock synthesized them from events and phrases found in Dec 17th 1837, May 24th, June 1st, 2nd and 3rd 1838, Feb 17th 1839 of the published journal.

June 14th – A strong east wind was blowing today which always exerts a pestilential influence upon my flesh, but I had to visit a poor woman half dead in body and wholly so in spirit. My appearance alarmed her at first and even the announcement of my name, which she had heard from Arthur Rees, failed to reassure her. Gasping for breath she said her husband was not at home and asked if I could not wait till evening. I examined the sputum in a bowl beside her chair, felt her pulse, asked her to breathe deep while listening to her chest. I then asked if she knew she was dying of consumption. Between coughs she nodded agreement. I asked if she was not afraid. She said no, she knew that Christ would save her. I asked how she knew that. She said, because she felt comfortable in *herself*. She knew she was a sinner but thought she was not a very bad one. The Reverend Mr Griffiths had spoken to her so she did not need me. I said, "Your priest has made you comfortable in your *self* and you think this the work of God?"

She said, "Yes I'm at peace sir. Thank you for calling but I don't need you."

I told her what the Scriptures say about false peace: From the prophet even unto the priest everyone dealeth falsely. For they

have healed the hurt of the daughter of my people *slightly* saying "Peace! Peace!" where there is no peace. I told her Jeremiah was speaking about clergy who lead their flocks to Hell by dealing *slightly* with their conscience. I said I had come to deal with her *hardly*. She stared at me and said, "*I* will not go to Hell sir! *I* am not afraid to die!"

I told her that many consumptives feel this sensation of comfort before their end but it is a fleshly delusion, and it is a fearful thing to fall in to the hands of an angry God. She said, "God be praised he will never abandon *me*!"

I told her that only the poor in spirit enter the Kingdom of Heaven, whereupon she declared her spiritual poverty with a vehemence only pride could inspire. I told her so. She screamed, "I am not proud. I am Humble! Humble! Humble!" which brought on such a violent fit of coughing that I had to support her back and hold the bowl while she retched into it. After this she lay down exhausted and I pointed out that God *would* save her if she loved him utterly, but she was in peril because she still loved herself. Weeping she said that, if she was wrong, surely God would show her? I said he was showing her through me.

June 18th – Tonight, by the grace of God, another addition to my little congregation, and I believe a firm one. Since my declaration at Dr Ollivant's banquet George Thomas has come to it twice only, praying almost inaudibly, otherwise maintaining a silence throughout our discussions that showed the spirit in him was still weak indeed. He came an hour late tonight and surveyed us with his back against the door and an expression I can only call sarcastic. We did not rise from our knees. He said, "The Lampeter Brethren! The Lampeter Brethren!" and chuckled. I asked if he was drunk. He said, "Not very. *In vino veritas* you know," and asked if he should leave. I said, not if he had something to say.

He said that in some ways he admired us. He didn't object to our Principal riding to hounds because there was nothing in Holy Writ against killing foxes, but Ollivant was too fond of money. He was Rector of two parishes, and angling for a third, and his work here meant he hardly visited any. Then he said, "But Prince, you are an abominable fellow. Abominable."

At this Rees told Thomas he had better leave. I said "No, stay Thomas," (standing up to face him) and, "Abominable, yes, carry on."

He then said I kept suggesting people were not humble enough and I had the pride of Lucifer. I thought only of myself – how could I help people if I didn't love them? I wanted fellow students in this prayer group because through prayer I could master them *without* liking them. That was also why I searched out poor dying men and women and plagued their last moments. It was not gentlemanly. It was not nice. He had no wish to be offensive but it was not nice.

I had difficulty silencing the protests of the others but they listened when I told them that Thomas was right about me. I am cold-hearted. My mother and sister have idolized me and given me all they can but I do not love them. They are the kind of church-goers who have never experienced God, and the fact that they will go to Hell does not dismay me as it should. The only human creature I much like is an elderly Catholic lady who taught me to pray from the heart, but I love her less than I love Jesus, and my love for Jesus is feeble indeed. *Sometimes* I feel close to him and swim serenely in an ocean of living, liquid love. But after an hour of this Holy Communion with the bridegroom of my soul I feel, not that God is good and glorious, but that *I* am good and glorious. And at once I am cast down and have to lie many weeks before the gate of Hell without one drop of Heavenly moisture to wet my tongue. Yes, my pride is like Lucifer's. I need honest friends to show me the detestable body of my wicked will. That was why Thomas had been sent here tonight by God. Could Thomas not see that? Would he not join us in a prayer for the salvation of my soul and the souls of my spiritual brothers here assembled? For the souls, if he wished, of all the college?

He said he could hardly refuse a request like that, and knelt and joined us, heart and soul, I verily believe.

June 20th – I returned today to my dying penitent. Her husband

opened the door and tried to deny me entrance. He said his wife was very ill and I had made her terribly unhappy. I told him she needed me. He said violently, "You will not cross this door sir!"

She heard his voice and screamed, "O David let him in! Let him in David."

He hesitated and I entered.

At once she began telling me she was a great sinner and much afraid of dying. She incessantly asked me, "Shall I die? Am I dying? Has God answered your prayers? Will he forgive my sins? Are you sure?"

The anguish of her mind became intolerable. Some perspiration appearing on the body she thought to be the forerunner of death, and jumping out of bed she dashed herself naked upon the floor, crying and shrieking in a most horrible manner. She called for leeches, blisters, bleeding to save her life, and then cried for prayer, Bible, sacraments to save her soul. And at last I dared to feel that it was indeed the hand of the living God who was shaking her soul and preparing it to receive his overwhelming grace. At last she lay still and exhausted in bed, her husband standing amazed at the door, biting his knuckles. As she stared into my eyes I asked if she recognized me? She nodded. I told her I thought she was now ready to meet God. Her mouth was moved by something like a smile. I asked if she loved him? She whispered, "I love God and I love you."

1837

Sept. 24th – The Spirit having moved me to fast for several days, I feel the power of the flesh very much in respect of appetite: I frequently prefer a piece of bread and cheese to God. I discern distinctly that I am a *beast* – earthly, sensual, devilish; also that the world, all that is seen, is *outside of God. The whole world lieth in the devil*, but I am of God. Lord deliver me from self, and let *my* will be so wholly swallowed up in Thine that *Thou* mayest become my *Self*. Amen, and Amen!

My health continues very precarious. Deemed it to be the will of God that I should not complete the College term; wrote for a certificate of exemption; the authorities readily consented. It is wonderful how God disposes the hearts of others toward me. Am to return to Bath on Wednesday with Mother who will take me up when her carriage passes through Lampeter: her plan to visit cousins (which would have made that impossible) is now put off. Truly, God is "wonderful in working". When the promptings of a man's heart affect the purposes of Jehovah, He makes a way for them. I have done with *plans, purposes, intentions,* I am a *mere instrument,* in the hands of The Divine Architect, for the *building of His spiritual temple.*

Oct. 5th – Have been shaken over the grave by an attack of dysentery attended with extreme pain, tendency to fainting, with a fluttering pulse above one hundred, and a clammy skin, that I thought it not improbable that I should die in a few minutes. Like one hovering between life and death I took a hasty review of my past – the whole appeared like one long, uninterrupted sin. How wonderful is the wisdom of God: had this taken place at Lampeter, I should have died without the diet and close attention that has barely kept life in me, even here. Save me, O Lord, from my most subtle, persevering, ever present and most deadly enemy, my *self*; blot out my sin with Thine most precious blood. Cleanse my polluted soul with Thine own indwelling holiness! Amen, and Amen.

Nov. 29th – The lord has been conducting my soul through clouds and darkness, and has convinced me of my entire *impotency,* to a degree I could scarcely conceive. My soul has been like a waste and howling wilderness, dark, barren, hard, and desolate; my Heaven was brass, and my Earth iron; and my soul seemed only fit to be the habitation of dragons, and a court for screech owls. Self was bound hand and foot in the midst of this unadulterated misery; corruption raged. I could see neither light, nor grace, nor God; could neither think, nor reflect, nor turn to God, nor recollect myself. My soul was driven to an extremity εu στευοχωρία: I could not turn to the right hand nor to the left. All *doing* was come to an end; it was a time of *pure suffering*: yet I was in perfect peace for my *spirit* was abiding in God, and dwelt in "a peaceable habitation", even while the hail came "down on the forest".

I visited poor Y. last week; he had been ill three weeks. The door of the house was locked, so that I was obliged to clamber in at the window. He was alone in his miserable hovel, sitting shivering over a small fire, with a few potatoes and his Bible. The poor fellow had just been passing through a fiery trial, during which he was sore pressed by Satan to destroy himself: Hell seemed open to him, Christ far away, prayer almost impossible: he wandered about in agony and terror for many days until comfort gradually returned. He was much in the Spirit when I saw him, and very changed in character – though haughty, proud and independent spirit had sunk into the gentleness and meekness of a little child; he could not open his mouth for shame; he prayed and so did I: it was a good time; I felt God to be in the room, and found much communion of spirit.

Y. was converted many years ago; his conversion was remarkable, and attended, at first, with great alarm, and subsequently, with full reconciliation, and much joy and love. Some years afterwards – about nine years ago – he was prevailed upon to take more liquor than he could bear, under the influence of which he was tempted by others, and actually committed fornication. The result was a total departure of his former peace, great anguish, fear of hell, and an accusing conscience. He has never known settled peace since, through he has sought it with many tears, but has been a mourner all his days. And not withstanding his outward diseases, which have been severe, he has scarcely ever known what it is to have the light of the Lord's countenance shine upon him since the days of his iniquity. Surely, sin is indeed an *evil*, and a *bitter* thing; or, as *he* says, "God will not let His people have sin *cheap*."

Dec 6th – This day my beloved Mother in Christ consented to become my wife.

"This is the Lord's doing; it is marvellous in our eyes." How peculiar has been our intercourse; how remote from everything that could have led me to anticipate such a result as this. God has been wonderfully preparing us for each other, without *our* entertaining the least suspicion of what He was about. As I walk upon the downs with my dear Martha I am happy to find that, though I love her dearly, she is not the supreme object of my affections for I love God and Jesus Christ infinitely better. He reminds us that the other is a creature, and I feel that if God were to make over the whole universe to my absolute control, there is an appetite for Jesus which only He could satisfy. He calls me to walk with Him and be perfect.

1838

Dec 10th – Yesterday I saw myself so exceedingly wicked that I felt I had done M. an injury in asking her to marry such a wretch, and ought to ask forgiveness for doing so. Then I suffered, for about two hours, intense agony from toothache, during which I was enabled, through grace, to cleave unto Jesus inwardly, and find enjoyment in Him. I could bless Him for my pain and thankful that He allowed me to *suffer* in anyway to His glory. O *self*, *thou* are my bitterest, most implacable and cruel enemy! Why does't thou pursue me so, even to the *very gate* of Heaven? For thou cans't not *enter* it.

Am returning to Lampeter. I do not go *here* or *there*; but God takes me up and puts me down just where He pleases. He gives me grace and strength to preach the Gospel from the sofa and armchair as effectually as from the pulpit.

---

*Tunnock has not given the date of this entry, nor have I found it in the turgid pages of Prince's published journal.

183? * – Yesterday I had arranged to walk with Rees and Thomas into Swansea. Today they came into my room when I was asking the Holy Spirit whether or not I should take an umbrella and had received no clear reply. I told them that perhaps God did not choose that I visit Swansea. Rees asked me if some matters were not too trivial to refer to Almighty God. None, I told him. He said he was quite sure God did not mind *him* visiting

Swansea. I bade him goodbye and he left. Brother Thomas chose to remain. I told him that my mother in God, my Catholic friend Miss Freeman, had written to tell me she is being baptized in to the Church of England. He agreed that as we are engaged to marry this is splendid news, then suggested that, since we were staying indoors this afternoon, we might construe Aristotle together. I told him God's spirit did not move me to study the classics. Christ did not choose scholars to spread his word, he chose ignorant fishermen. The Holy Spirit taught them what to do and say: will teach us also, so I would not prepare for the examination. He said, "I loath the classics too – they keep referring to beastly natural functions as if they were ordinary. But if we don't pass the exam we won't be ordained clergymen – we'll be as cut off from the Apostolic Succession as any Methodist or Quaker. How can you get over that?"
I told him that problem could be left in the hands of God.

But Hepworth Dixon refers to the umbrella incident, so I have no doubt it could be found.

1839

April 12th – The east wind usually makes me dreadfully ill. It has blown steadily for three weeks, but God gave me faith to believe it would not injure me, nor did it, though I went out in it daily. Yesterday my faith failed, and the wind being strong and the sun hot I expected to be laid up when Lo! the wind shifted to the North. I have no doubt that God gave me special faith and then took it away when it was no longer needed. Nor do I doubt that I, through faith, subdued the east wind to the glory of God.

June 7th – Today Dr Ollivant announced what he said would come as a relief to many. Queen Victoria's coronation will soon be upon us. With that in mind he had petitioned the Archbishop for a remission of the approaching examination. That remission had now been granted. All students are therefore to consider themselves as having passed. Many outside the circle of the Brethren burst into unseemly applause. Only those proud of their scholastic merit were disgruntled. Only Thomas, formerly a doubter, looked at me with full understanding of this miracle. I fear that Rees, like many others, thanks God for it but thinks *Ollivant* mainly responsible!

July 16th – On Tuesday, July 10 was married to my beloved M. Truly I may say of Thee, O my God, "*This* is the *Lord's* doing, it is *marvellous* in our eyes." I never discerned the Lord's hand so distinctly in any event of my life, than I do in my union with dear M. He has *abundantly confirmed* my trust in His wondrous condescension and tender regard for His dear, though undeserving, children. With respect to my health I may say I know not when I felt so well as I did on the morning of my marriage. God is allowing me rest and quietude, with some relaxation of the outer man to confirm my health with a view to more effective future duty, either in *doing* or *suffering*. As I walk and drive about the Downs with dear M., enjoying the fine air and *doing nothing*, I feel how utterly contemptible life would be if the object and end were nothing better than *enjoyment*, indeed had not the *Will of God* called me to this life I would feel it were *no life*. I seem no better than a vegetation. O how truly miserable must be those who *live to be happy*.

Aug 15th – I protest that I die daily. My inward life is undergoing a gradual destruction. I perceive *life* lies *substantially in the will*; and only Spirit of God can destroy the will, the iron-hearted will of man, keeping it in a state of continual crucifixion, cutting asunder *soul* and *spirit* like a two edged sword. O Love. Whose life is the Light of Thine unsullied truth, it is *Thou* art that "devouring fire" – *Thou* art those "everlasting burnings" of eternity. O, *who* shall dwell with *Thee*?

Oct 28th – I have had no permission from God to write this journal since I made my last entry. It would not be possible, if indeed it were *lawful* to describe the marvellous work God has been carrying on in my soul in the last seven weeks. *I have passed through the middle of self*, and now, at length, *come out at the other side into God.* God has answered my prayer and condescended to teach me Himself by His own Spirit. For the last two and a half years this journal has been penned under *the guidance and Spirit of God within me*, faithfully recording the long and toilsome journey from the *creature* up to God. Though the *expectations* behind my prayers were almost unbounded, yet God, in answering them, has done exceeding abundantly more than I could either ask or think. I, being *routed* and *grounded* in love, can comprehend the breadth, and depth, and length, and height of Christ's love and can say in all sobriety and seriousness "*I am filled with all the fullness of God.*" Unto Him in the church of Christ Jesus, throughout all ages, world without end Amen! Amen! and Amen!

Many mystics have described this "dying to the self". In Sartor Resartus Carlyle describes it as passing through "the everlasting No to the evelasting Yes".

– These Amens are the last words of Henry James Prince's published diary. In the three years it covers he had introduced his sister to Arthur Rees, at first his closest friend at Lampeter, and they had married. No entries refer to these events. When he gave his manuscript to the printers twenty years later his sister and Rees had no place in this spiritual autobiography.

23: CHARLINCH

BEFORE LEAVING ST DAVID'S COLLEGE as an ordained clergyman Henry James Prince visited the Principal for the customary exchange of farewell civilities. Dr Ollivant, though glad to be seeing this troublesome former student for the last time, offered Prince a glass of wine and no flicker of annoyance changed his bland, ruddy face when the offer was quietly refused. Standing aside his hearthrug he said, "I wish you joy of your curacy, Prince. Charlinch, eh?"

"Charlinch, near Bridgwater."

"Rural and secluded. I thought you would have preferred a busy parish in an infernal manufacturin' town where you would have had scope to evangelize. Agricultural congregations are brutish and dull rather than vicious and lost – Charlinch doesn't even have a public house. But the rectory is quite large, I believe. I hope Mrs Prince did not come to you empty-handed, I know you are not a rich man."

"Her fortune is sufficient for us," said Henry quietly.

"Good. Good. The Church of England is like the British Army: you can't go far in it without money or connections. Sam Starky, your rector, is well connected. Nephew of Lady Alicia Coventry, related through her to half the nobility of England. If not exactly a foot-hold it is a good toe-hold, if you know how to climb. I was impressed by how adroitly you set up your own little establishment here – The Lampeter Brethren, no less! Enthusiasm was thought a disease of the labourin' classes when I was young. Our aristocracy were nearly all

atheists, though it was bad form to say so – they knew the
Church of England was needed to hold the rabble down. French aristos were open atheists and look what happened to them! But times have changed, Prince. Yes, nerve and imagination can work wonders. However, Starky is a sickly fellow, a valetudinarian if not exactly a hypochondriac, always takin' the cure at waterin' places and south coast resorts. I doubt if you'll ever actually *see* him."

There was a brief silence in which Henry was about to take his leave when Ollivant said abruptly, "You are a good soul and mean well, Prince, so I am moved to offer advice. I hear that – apart from readin' a few heady mystics – you despize erudition."

"The disciples Jesus called were not erudite, Dr Ollivant."

"Quite so, but then Jesus instructed them, and He taught those ignorant fishermen so well that by their eloquence the whole Roman Empire was at last converted."

"And by the miracle of Pentecost, sir."

"O yes. Tongues of fire from Heaven givin' everyone the gift of tongues. Well, we must not look for that miracle nowadays, for if we do it will turn us into lunatics, charlatans, or dupes like poor Edward Irving. He prayed for the gift of tongues and got it with a vengeance! Hysterical women where he preached started babblin' nonsense until they and their supporters took Irving over and made a new religion of him – The Catholic Apostolic Pentecostal Church, no less! A church that rejects the doctrine of Original Sin. The Church of Scotland must be glad they excommunicated him before that happened. The Churches of England, Rome and every decent non-conformist sect would have done the same. Irving saw the error of his ways before he died but fools rich enough to know better still keep Catholic Apostolic churches goin' strong, not just in London and Edinburgh but France, Germany, Switzerland and the United States. They must think they're buyin' places in the Kingdom of Heaven. Any danger of you goin' Pentecostal, Prince?"

Henry slightly smiled and slightly shook his head.

"Good. Now, I have no wish to hurt your feelin's but I hear that compared with your impromptu prayers, your sermons are, shall I say – inadequate?"

"I have had little pulpit experience, sir."

"Most of us are shaky at the start. I certainly was. On preachin' my first sermon before a Bishop I tried to impress him by sayin' it all without notes. Result: young Ollivant dries up halfway through and stumbles as fast as he can into the blessin'. A disgustin' performance. I see you pull a wry face at the word *performance*. Is that because it suggests play actin'?"

Henry nodded.

"No matter. An honest intelligent clergyman can even learn to do better from the theatre. Well, the Bishop was a good old soul *and* a relative of mine. Over dinner afterward he said what I have never forgotten and will now pass on to you. *Every old rectory and vicarage in England*, said he, *has a shelf of sermons, the best of them written by great clerics who founded the Anglican church when English prose was at its best, as is proved by our prayer book and the King James authorized Bible. Read those sermons. Memorize passages whose truth and beauty strikes you. Of course, you have six days a week to write sermons of your own, but few vicars of Christ preached as mightily as Latimer, for example. When your pulpit eloquence falters you should find support in the words of men who were* (dare I say this to you Prince? Yes . . .) *men who were wiser and wittier than you will ever be.* I put that to you, Prince, and leave it with you."

"Thank you sir. Good day," said Prince. He stood, bowed slightly and turned to the door. Before reaching it he heard Ollivant chuckle and turned enquiringly.

"Forgive me Prince, but I've remembered somethin' funny. Know anythin' about Carlyle? Thomas Carlyle?"

"No sir."

"I'm glad. He's a Scotch Radical pamphleteer who's all for the French Revolution. London society tolerates him because his wife is both pretty and witty. In their younger days the Carlyles and Edward Irving were so close that the present Mrs Carlyle nearly became Mrs Irving. A pity she did not. She has since been heard to say, *If Irving had married me there would have been no gift of tongues.* Good, isn't it haha? *If Irving had married me there would have been no gift of tongues.* I am sure Mrs Prince is also a sensible woman."

Charlinch lay in a valley between dark green wooded hills, the fields on lower ground divided by thick hedges and narrow winding roads. The village, never large, had shrunk smaller around 1800 when the chief landowner enclosed the common, evicted smallholders and let their fields to richer farmers. It was now a cross-roads with cottages housing families of ploughmen, a shop that was also the Post Office, a dame's school and a small, dilapidated church on a hill. The dilapidation had happened because local gentry who owned carriages now attended larger churches further away. The churchyard had become a wilderness of overgrown plots with broken and sinking stones. There was a path through it to the adjacent rectory which was large and well-built, in a garden with high walls sheltered by trees. Here Brother Prince began his new life as a country priest under the guidance of the Holy Spirit, and here his forty-five year old wife spent the unhappiest months of her life.

The rectory was rent free, well furnished, well carpeted, with cupboards of fine linen and bedclothes. This was fortunate as the curate's stipend was small. Income from Martha's investments let them hire local women as cook, house-maid and laundry-maid, but they could not afford a housekeeper and Martha had no experience of household management. She saw rooms were not being thoroughly cleaned, that Henry's shirts were badly starched and clumsily folded, that under-cooked cutlets and over-boiled vegetables were served on stone-cold plates, but could not tell her servants how to do better – they seemed to understand her instructions as little as she understood their dialect. She might have resigned herself to these misfortunes had they not hurt Henry. The Spirit guiding him accepted badly-served food and badly-laundered linen as minor forms of crucifixion, but his wife knew how much better his mother managed a household so his almost inaudible sighs, sometimes with eyes closed in prayer, struck Martha like rebukes. Pains she had patiently suffered in Widdicombe Crescent worsened. One night after a dinner where both had eaten only a few mouthfuls she openly wept. He sat by her, patted her hand, said in the soft, remote voice habitual with him, "Perhaps you should send for mother."

Mrs Prince arrived in an irritable mood that she hid from her son but not from her daughter-in-law. She spoke severely to housemaid and laundry-maid, dismissed the cook, hired in her place another local woman and severely lectured her also before returning to Bath. For a while the house was managed a little better, though not much better. Martha still had cause for tears, Henry for sighs and silent prayers, and his sufferings had a more than domestic cause. Despite marriage he found Charlinch an even more miserable place than London where, a lonely medical student, his fastidious nature had excluded him from the rude conviviality of social equals. At Lampeter he had made friends and visited people who recognized his spiritual authority: Charlinch was a whole parish of souls to be saved, yet he could persuade none of their deadly peril.

The Anglican prayer book, printed by Royal Command, dictated the church services in words carefully composed to exclude radical politics and personal remarks. Only the sermon gave a chance of impressive speech, and Henry failed to impress. His pulpit overlooked a floor boxed into pews rented by the wealthiest and most respected local families, each box with its own little door. Labourers and servants sat on benches between or behind these. There was a gallery for singers and two parishioners who played a cornet and a bassoon. When Henry announced the sermon's text in his clear sweet voice he saw his listeners compose themselves for a state resembling slumber, even if they did not close their eyes. He could have wakened the nearest at once by talking straight down to them, but his words must reach everyone including many who were more haggard, worse dressed and (when their mouths opened

for responses and hymns) more gap-toothed than any
congregation he had seen. Words he uttered with passionate
conviction had no visible effect on anyone.

That Dr Ollivant had foreseen this was not consoling. The
rectory study had many bound sermons but, "I will *not* mouth
the words of dead men." Henry told himself, glaring at them.
He knelt and begged God to let him speak with the simplicity
of a little child, and the simple words came, but had no effect,
even when spoken in the parishioners' homes. Nobody in
Charlinch was of higher social standing than Henry so the
farmers' wives were at first delighted with his visits. They served
him afternoon tea and when asked about the state of their
souls assured him that these were quite all right. When he
told them this was unlikely and insisted on more heart-felt
answers they turned resentful or embarrassed. Most took it as
an insult that he wished to confer with their servants, and
when he said poorer folk also had souls to be saved the faces
of their employers indicated doubt. In Welsh Lampeter he had
enjoyed several passionate dialogues with sick or dying people
and, compared with them, the Somerset natives seemed pagan.
"If God don't want my soul after all he's put me through," said
an old labourer, crippled by arthritis and lying between
blankets stained by his bed sores, "He may do without it."
"Hell fire! Hell fire!" whispered Henry.
"Can't be worse than this," said the man, "but give me a sup
of gin or brandy and I'll gladly hear you tell me all about hell
fire till the cows come home."

The school children could chant the Lord's Prayer and parts
of the Shorter Catechism in unison, but no matter how intensely
he lectured and questioned them they answered with
monosyllables or giggles or dumb grins. At length, having
prayed to God for guidance and receiving assurance that God
wished this, Henry told the schoolteacher he was abandoning
her pupils until they asked for him. He visited two consumptive
little girls in their home until their mother told him to stop
frightening them. When he ignored her she fetched her

husband from a nearby field who expelled Henry with threats to fling him out. Henry told the man's employer, suggesting the labourer might allow Christ's ministry if threatened with dismissal. The farmer said, "I couldn't do that sir. He may be stiff-necked but he's an honest worker."

"I do not ask you to dismiss him but to *threaten* him with dismissal."

"Too risky, sir. He's so stiff-necked he might take offence and leave me, and bein' widely known as a honest good worker he'd have no trouble gettin' employment elsewhere."

Henry's only happiness now was in writing to his Lampeter Brethren, some still at college, some of them curates like himself. His letters asked searching questions about the state of their souls, discussed their replies in detail, contained prayers and exhortations applicable to their weakness and troubles. He mentioned the sad state of his parishioners but not his own unhappy state. One of the Brethren, inspired and consoled by his letters, suggested making a book of them. Henry borrowed back the best, copied them out with improvements, raised money by subscriptions from the Brethren and had them printed in Bristol. Copies posted to Church of England magazines were kindly reviewed. This modest fame did not lessen his grief at the state of Charlinch parish. Martha was increasingly troubled by backaches with hot and cold flushes, swollen limbs, and constipation alternating with diarrhoea. Henry prayed to God that these were not symptoms of incurable dropsy. A doctor summoned from Bridgwater comforted him slightly by diagnosing *sub-acute* dropsy, and prescribing a strict diet, laudanum drops and rest. Martha returned to stay with his mother in Widdicombe Crescent until her health improved, but it never improved. Henry remained in Charlinch to hope, pray, correspond with the Brethren and conduct services that seemed spiritually fruitless.

In the fourteenth month of his curacy came a letter postmarked Ventnor in the Isle of Wight. It said: *Dear Mr Henry James Prince, or if you will forgive this impertinence, Dear*

BROTHER Henry James Prince, I must see you as soon as

possible since no merely written language can express my
feelings, my gratitude. I, my wife and sister are coming with
all possible haste to visit you in the rectory, our old family
home. Expect us on the evening of the day after you receive
this epistle. Ever, My Very Dear Sir,

Yours in the Lord,

Sam Starky.

This, from the rector Henry had been told he would probably never see, was encouraging. He ordered fires lit in the four main bedrooms, three of which had stood empty since Martha left. He ordered sheets and blankets to be aired, beds to be made, the house thoroughly cleaned for the following day. Though he had never reproved the servants they were slightly in awe of him, even more in awe of the returning rector whose father they remembered and who was nephew of a Lord. By the following afternoon the rectory was in a cleaner, neater state than Henry had ever seen. He watched the maid set a tea table, suggested improvements, retired to his study. For a while he stood at a window allowing a view of the crossroads. After two or three carriages had passed he sat down and tried to concentrate on a vague but inspiring chapter by the German psalmist, Gerhard Tersteegen. Only on hearing approaching hoof beats did he go to the entrance hall and stand, hands folded meekly before him, waiting for the housemaid to open the front door. She did, and when three people entered he bowed, saying softly, "Welcome."

"Hello!" said the foremost visitor, removing his hat and extending a hand, "Sam Starky! Are you indeed –?"

Henry murmured, "Henry Prince," and shook the slightly moist hand of a man who seemed breathless and excited.

Starky was tall and not much older than Henry and wore dark expensive clothes of fashionable cut, only a white neck-cloth suggesting his clerical status. His handsome face had the nobility of a marble bust, perhaps because it was so pale. His manner was excited but oddly evasive. He clasped Henry's hand longer than usual without looking straight at his face.

Henry saw that here was one who knew he needed guidance. "This is my belovéd wife," said Starky gesturing to a woman who appeared to be all a prosperous and respected husband in those days could wish: pretty, well dressed, submissive and slightly alarmed at meeting someone new. Henry bowed to her.

"And here is my dear sister Julia," said Starky. "We find in her a tower of strength."

"I am reading your *Letters to the Lampeter Brethren*, Mr Prince," said Julia with emphasis suggesting approval. While the maid helped Mrs Starky remove her bonnet and shawl Julia removed her own in a way that showed she was thoroughly at home.

"I am honoured," said Henry. "I regret that my own wife is not here to receive you all. A liver ailment has taken her to recuperate at my mother's home in Bath. Shall there be tea after the maid has shown you to your rooms? Tea and something to eat after you have had time to wash and settle in?"

"Yes," said Julia, "that will be thoroughly welcome when my dear sister-in-law has had a little rest and I have supervized unpacking. But I know Sam cannot wait for a word with you." With the keen eyes of a natural housekeeper she watched a servant carry in a box and portmanteau. Henry said to Starky, "Let me take your hat."

Starky stared at the hat in his hand as if astonished to see it then cried, " O no no no no no!", and hurriedly placed it with his overcoat on the hallstand saying, "Julia is right. I must speak with you alone for a while."

"Certainly. Of course," murmured Henry and led him to the study.

With a gesture he invited Starky to take an armchair by the fire but, "No no no no no, you sit. I am overwrought. I must pace about a bit," said Starky. Henry settled down with elbows on armrests, watching his visitor across fingertips placed together in the shape of a tent.

"Pardon my agitation," said Starky abruptly, "You have been my curate here for fourteen months, and I am a stranger to you. But you are no stranger to me!"

"Yes?"

"Miracles still happen, do they not?"

"It is blasphemy to doubt it."

"*You* have performed a miracle. And another miracle is, that you do not know it."

"You will tell me of it," said Henry quietly.

"A fortnight ago I lay very ill at Ventnor, and in the morning the nurse told me I would not live until night. At noon the post brought me a letter from a clerical friend in Bath with a printed slip of paper which he prayed might be read to me before I died. The words described how a man may know he believes in Christ."

"Ah," said Henry.

"When the reading was done I asked the preacher's name and only then heard he was you, my curate. I thanked God he had sent such a pastor to my flock. I felt very happy in mind, said the last few words to my wife and sister, and lay back to depart in peace."

"But did not die," said Henry mildly.

"Yes! My pulse beat quicker, my tongue was loosened, strength returned to my limbs and – I am here."

He stood suddenly still and gazed open-mouthed at Henry who, smiling, rose to his feet and held out his arms. Starky stepped between them and hugged Henry passionately. Henry's embrace was more paternal. When he lowered his arms Starky moved away whispering, "It is wonderful!"

"May I call you *Brother* Starky?" asked Henry softly.

"Please!" said Starky with a vehement nod, "To be accepted as one of the Lampeter Brethren is an honour I hardly dared pray for."

"Then sit down Brother Starky," said Henry in a louder voice than Starky had yet heard from him, "It is now your turn to listen and mine to render up accounts of my service here."

"Eh?"

"Sit down, if you please."

Starky sat with mouth slightly open while Prince stood

before him, hands clasped behind back, saying grimly, "You thanked God for making me pastor of your flock. I confess to not dealing well with it. I am a bad pastor."

"How so?"

"For more than a year I have laboured in Charlinch Church, school and homes and found only a disobedient and gainsaying people. I have told them how much they need Christ's salvation; I have exhorted, I have begged those who see they need guidance to visit me here for instruction and prayer. Shall I tell you how many have answered that call?"

"Please do."

"Three."

"Horrible! Horrible!"

"And these three are from neighbouring parishes, *not* from Charlinch. But for these three I would have quit this place when my wife's illness forced her to leave a fortnight ago – the very time when you were miraculously cured by my words. God has preserved us both for this meeting. His Holy Spirit must have work for us here in Charlinch."

"What work can it be?"

"You are my rector," said Prince gently.

"But I have not conducted half a dozen services since I was ordained. This living is mine because my father had it. I fear I have been a poor, woefully formal Christian."

"Christ loves the poor in spirit, brother Starky, and did not a certain prayer convince you of His power?"

"Yes! I believe your prayer cured me in body and soul. Before it, the slightest unexpected chill induced pulmonary qualms, fever and coughing that kept me in bed for weeks at a time. You have made a new man of me . . . "

"Not I," said Henry. "The Spirit *through* me gave you a new and cleaner birth."

"And you say it has work for us here?"

"The Spirit has work in Charlinch for us both," said Henry, with complete conviction.

24: THE GROWTH OF THE SPIRIT

NEXT SUNDAY the young rector's return to his parish ensured a large church attendance. The rectory pew that had stood empty since Martha left held that morning Mrs Starky and Julia. Henry James Prince sat before the pulpit at a desk formerly used by a parish clerk who had announced hymns, psalms and led the singing. As usual Henry wore the black Doctor of Divinity gown with white neckbands, worn throughout the eighteenth century and still favoured at Lampeter; but Oxford divines were making Roman vestments fashionable again so Starky, though Cambridge educated, emerged from the vestry dressed as his congregation had never before seen, in a flowing white surplice over a dark ankle-length cassock, both of which suited his tall, fine figure and statuesque head. He chanted prayers and led responses in tones as gentlemanly as Prince had used but more monotonous. Unlike Prince he preached his sermon from notes, sometimes pausing to look down at the pew where his wife and sister gazed back with ardent, approving smiles and the desk where Henry sat staring hard at the floor between his boots. Before the final blessing he announced, "Our dearly belovéd brother in Christ, Henry James Prince, will on Tuesday evening hold his usual Bible study group in the rectory and on Friday evening his usual prayer meeting. I cannot too strongly exhort all who care for the welfare of their souls to attend these meetings."

Walking back to the rectory Starky said gloomily, "The service went well on the whole, but I am a poor preacher."

"You should not have used notes," said Henry mildly.

"I could not have spoken without them – I would have dried up."

"Spiritual *dryness* is a condition the Spirit recognizes. Such dryness invites the Spirit to water it. Preaching from notes shuts the Spirit out."

"You really think so?"

"I really do."

"Henry may be right about that, Sam," said Julia, "I think I see what he means."

"*Please* Henry," Starky pled, "let me use notes again at the evening service – I would fear to enter the pulpit without that prop."

"You must do as you will, my dear brother Starky," said Henry sadly. At the evening service Starky preached very haltingly, but the Tuesday evening study group was joined by a milkmaid, a road mender and a farmer who, with the three Starkys, trebled Henry's audience and the fervour of its mood. The farmer was the one who had refused to threaten the stiff-necked labourer with dismissal. He said, "I was wrong not to do as you bid sir. I see I was wrong, but it's too late now for me to do right. Brackley's daughters are dead and gone to Hell I suppose. He is mainly to blame but I too am damnable, I suppose. I should have tried to make a way for you, and I did not."

"But you are contrite! That is a blesséd thing, it means you are at last on the right path. You make me very happy," said Henry, warmly shaking his hand.

At the next Sunday morning service Starky announced the text for his sermon, stood chewing his lower lip for a while then said unhappily, "I confess to all here that I, Samuel Starky, am a sinner like yourselves, of the Earth, earthly. In this church you should hear nothing speak but God's Holy Spirit. Alas, alas, *Sam Starky's* words are not fit for your ears so I will now pray silently that the Holy Spirit descend and use my voice as its instrument. I know at least nine souls who will also pray for that, and I humbly beg the rest of you to pray for that also." He clasped hands and closed eyes. Those in the rectory pew and six others in the church did the same. A majority looked at each other in perplexity and as minutes passed started

whispering in voices that grew to a conversational hum. At
last Starky opened his eyes and said brokenly, "The Holy Ghost
has not accepted my petition. I will petition Him again at the
evening service."

After removing their robes in the vestry Starky and Prince joined
Mrs Starky and Julia and then went outside through a loudly
gossiping throng, some puzzled, some amused. Most fell silent
as the rector and his company emerged leaving the voice of
an old man with his back to them declaiming, "Boy and man
I have happily slept through a parcel of sermons so I don't like
this dumb parson who why is you nudgin' me? . . . Ah."

On entering the rectory Starky said, "O please, Brother Henry,
please conduct the evening service! I am not able, indeed I
am not."

"Dear Brother Starky, I will not conduct the evening service
because your inability to preach is more effective than anything
I could say."

"Impossible!"

"Not impossible – certain. Before you returned here my
sermons were heard without unease and without murmuring.
I spoke to them honestly, but The Spirit did not dictate my
words as it does when I speak to willing ears. I should have
publicly awaited The Spirit's coming as you are doing, but
now your silence in the pulpit is more effective than mine
will ever be."

"And tonight, Sam, you may have better luck," said Mrs Starky.

"O no dear! Luck is a *pagan* deity!" said Julia, "We must
continue to invoke God's help through prayer."

She looked to Henry who rewarded her with a smile and nod.

The evening service passed like the morning one, except
that Starky's distress was greater. But attendance at Prince's
Bible study group rose from nine (counting the Starkys) to
seventeen, and nineteen attended the Friday prayer meeting.
At the next Sunday service Starky, having announced the
sermon's text, sobbed aloud then begged concerned Christians
to follow him across to the rectory and help him pray that he

receive the power of the Holy Spirit. Over thirty of the congregation followed him there while Henry conducted the traditional service, minus sermon, to just before the final blessing, then paused and waited. Soon after Starky and his followers rejoined the congregation and Starky, in a stoical, monotonous voice, brought the service to the traditional end. "How *brave* you were dear," said Mrs Starky as they returned to the rectory.

"Heroic! That is the word," said Julia.

"The Lord chastens who He loveth," said Henry calmly, "He is chastening you, Sam! Be assured, dear Brother Samuel, that The Spirit cannot desert one as humbled as you have become. It is biding its time, which must now be very, very near."

A miserable smile was Starky's only reply.

Next Sunday the congregation was swelled by an influx of curious visitors from neighbouring parishes. Some were dissenters who had heard that a Church of England rector was about to turn Methodist, Baptist or Quaker, others wanted to enjoy the antics of a mad parson. In the morning service Starky's plea for the Holy Spirit to descend on him was a despairing yell answered from the back of the church by jeers, laughter and clapping, along with many indignant shushing sounds from elsewhere.

"I *cannot* conduct another service, Brother Prince! You *must* do it for me at Evensong," groaned Starky as they returned to the rectory, arm-in-arm with Henry on one side and his wife on the other.

"You can. You will. I know you will."

"Hear hear, well said Brother Henry! We *all* know you will," said his sister stoutly.

"You'll feel better after lunch, dear," said his wife.

The Evensong congregation was like the morning's at first, apart from Starky's conduct of the service being more lost and halting than ever. At sermon time he ascended the pulpit and stared out for almost half a minute, open-mouthed, wide-eyed and visibly sweating, then said with difficulty, "Belovéd . . .

dearly belovéd brothers . . . and sisters . . . I will read the fourteenth verse of the fifth chapter of Paul's Epistle to the Ephesians. If the Lord is pleased to speak by me . . . then He will. If He will not I must hold my tongue because I *will* not, I *cannot* speak for myself."

He then read out quietly but clearly, "*Awake, thou that sleepest; and arize from the dead; and Christ shall give thee light,*" and with no change of voice said, "Wise men tell us that this world of ours is a great globe hurtling round the Sun, spinning like a huge cannonball as it goes yet holding on its surface oceans, mountains, cities, you, me, all of us. What a *terrible* thought!" After a brief pause he added urgently, "Why are we all not sick with dizziness? What stops the bodies of you, me, everybody on this planet being flung out by this whirling wheel of a world into boundless space? Scientific men say our bodies are held here by a force called gravity, a force pulling everything down toward the Earth's centre, a centre where many imagine Hell to be. But Hell *cannot* be inside the Earth because the Earth is a mortal body that will die and pass away! When it does only Hell will remain here and it will be eternal. These bodies of ours also *must* and *will* die – as we all know – but they contain immortal souls that will *not* and *cannot* die, as most of you forget. O you poor, poor souls, think how frantically you will beg for death when death is no longer possible! When the last trump sounds, the sky rolls up like a scroll, the stars fall like ripe figs, the world vanishes yet ye are resurrected! Where will you stand when there is no ground to stand upon? I tell you, you *will* not stand, it will be impossible! Some of us, thank God, will be drawn up easily and gladly into the eternally happy companionship of Jesus Christ our Lord, in the Kingdom of Heaven for which he created you all, and into which he invites you all, and where all who gladly accept His loving invitation will certainly go. But the vast majority of you who are refusing that loving invitation will exist with no ground beneath your feet – exist in eternal torturing darkness, without light, without hope of light . . . without hope of anything, ever!

"Not many of you have been in one of Her Majesty's new

improved prisons where the inmates break stones with heavy hammers, trudge for hours on end over treadmills, stagger with big iron cannonballs round a yard from one heap to another whenever a warder blows a whistle. In return they are allowed just enough food and sleep to keep them alive for the duration of their sentence. How like most people's life on Earth that is! Has anyone here never been sickened by toil? And come to the end of the day's drudgery feeling exactly where they were at the start? And wakened next morning to a life they must lift and go on carrying like an almost unbearable burden? Such are the lives in Queen Victoria's new improved prisons, but he who protests against this punishing labour must endure worse. That man is taken down a dark tunnel through several thicknesses of wall and locked in a tiny cell without windows or light. Bread and water is passed to him through a tiny opening by someone he never sees. The silence here is so complete that only by muttering or yelling or scraping his heels on the floor may a man know he is not struck deaf, and he has *no* way of knowing he has not been struck blind. Five days of this punishment turns the strongest criminal into a gibbering lunatic, yet he has merely disobeyed a human, prison governor. How much more dreadful *must* be the imprisonment of we who disobey the governor of the universe! *Awake, thou that sleepest; and arise from the dead; and Christ will give thee light!* Do you not fear to disobey that call? Why will you not leave this earthly prison house by taking steps toward joining Christ in his Holy Kingdom? The punishment I described never lasts as long as a week! God's spell of solitary confinement will never end. The punishment I described is mental, but on the last day to your souls all-horrible alone-ness will be added a resurrected, undying body of flesh whose every inch, inside and out, will be gripped and crushed by a scorching mass of unendurable – but eternally to *be* endured – *agony."*

This start of Starky's sermon blended ideas he had heard from Henry with ideas from the notes he no longer used, but all were strongly combined and fluently uttered. The Spirit

possessing him did not rave or shout, it spoke of Heaven
solemnly yet joyfully, and spoke of Hell with such pity and
distress that men hearing him dropped their heads upon their
chests or gaped, amazed, at sobbing wives. Most women wept
and one or two shrieked. Children clung to each other. Starky's
wife and sister and all who attended the evening prayer groups
looked up to their rector with tears of joy while Henry, at the
pulpit foot, smiled with calm satisfaction. A deep silence
following the sermon was broken by a choirboy in the gallery
suddenly guffawing until the bassoonist clouted his ear. Starky
ended the service with a calm, firm authority he had never
before shown.

Rector and curate retired to the vestry and gazed at each
other for a moment before disrobing.
"You are now a mouthpiece of Almighty God, Brother Starky.
Your trumpet blast is the opening of a new spiritual era."
"You were right, master! You were right! The Spirit at last
descended," said Starky happily.
"You must not call me master, Brother Starky – only Christ is
our master."
"Yes but – please forgive me! – *brother* places us on an equal
footing. I am not, I cannot be on an equal footing with you. It
would be falsehood for me to pretend to it my dear, dear
master."
Henry brooded a little then smiled and said, "Call me Belovéd."
"O I will," whispered Starky, " I will."
A very happy group returned to the rectory through a crowd
of awe-struck gazers.
"Yes, we will *all* call you Belovéd, Brother Henry," said Julia,
"Won't we dear?"
Mrs Starky could only nod, being too happy to speak.

From now on Starky conducted Sunday services without
faltering. Those who had come from other parishes to mock
him no longer came, some who had come out of mere curiosity
remained to pray. His sermons never again caused such wild
reactions as that first and most inspired one, but his

congregation remained large, and interested with many who responded fervently to the services. On the following Sunday he announced that our Belovéd Brother Henry Prince had been directed by the Lord to say, that if any persons would send their children to the schoolroom later that evening, he would lecture to them. About fifty came. In a pamphlet published in 1842 – *The CHARLINCH REVIVAL or, an Account of the Remarkable Work of Grace which has lately taken place in Somersetshire* – Henry described what happened in the schoolroom:

The words spoken were at first very solemn, but in a few minutes the Holy Ghost came on the minister with the most tremendous power, so that the word of the Lord was really like fire. About twenty of the children were pierced to the heart, and appeared to be in great distress, but the bigger boys still continued unmoved, and some of them even seemed disposed to laugh. In a short time however the word reached them, too, and they were smitten to the hearts with the most dreadful conviction of their sin and danger: it appeared as if the arrows of the Almighty had pierced their very reins. In about ten minutes the spectacle presented by their schoolroom was truly awful: out of fifty children present there were not as many as ten could stand upright: boys and girls, great and small together, were either leaning against the wall quite overcome by their feelings of distress, or bowed down with their faces hidden in their hands and sobbing in the severest agony. For some time after the minister ceased to pray, they continued where they were, not weeping, but literally deeply wailing. They expressed their desire henceforth to forsake their sins and pleasures, and seek the Lord.

It would be impossible to express in words, the awful sense of God's presence and power felt by those who were in the schoolroom on that occasion. Four or five obtuse ploughboys were sobbing as though they had the hearts of women. Three of those most deeply smitten were hardened reckless boys, whom the minister had been obliged long before to turn out of the school, after which they used to come to the church and sit opposite the minister, and make faces at him as he was preaching the most solemn and affecting truths. Often he looked from his pulpit on these boys where they were grinning at him, and said in his heart, "What can God bring these boys here for? Surely he cannot intend to convert them." Now only one was altogether unaffected: this boy stood upright, with a vacant stare of stupid astonishment on his face, in the midst of the children who were weeping around him, as though God had permitted him to come there to contrast between one on whom the word did not take affect, and on those whom it did.

Henry's prayer meetings for adults in the rectory were often as passionate for he could be eloquent, with small, willing audiences.

After a sermon in December that year Starky made a peculiar announcement: "Christmas is nearly upon us – a joyful yet solemn time for all true Christians mindful of our Saviour's coming, and who are willing to receive him. Our Belovéd Brother Prince and I will conduct the Christmas Eve service with prayer, fasting, exhortation and psalms from six o'clock to midnight, and the Christmas Day service, along with Holy Communion, from nine in the morning till nine in the evening, or later, if the Spirit so wills. We realize this will not please a majority who regard the Christmas Holy-Days, alas alas alas!, as an opportunity to eat, drink and be merry, and the Yuletide services as pauses for digestion before again joining the revels. We do not wish those who view Christmas in that light way to attend our services. The time has come to make a separation between the concerned and the careless, the wheat and the chaff, sheep and goats. For three months God has been calling the faithful of this parish to him. A great many have answered that call and, though not yet converted, are struggling along the pathway *to* conversion. These will be heartily welcome. Our Christmas services can do the rest of you no possible good so please do not attend."

Before most of his hearers had grasped the sense of this announcement he resumed the words of the prayer book, praying that, "At Christ's second coming to judge the world, all present will be found an acceptable people, in the sight of Him who lives and reigns with the Father and the Holy Spirit, ever one God, world without end, Amen. O God, our Father in Heaven; have mercy upon us miserable sinners."

Roughly half the congregation repeated the response to that while a few started whispering and buzzing. Speaking louder to overcome their noise he cried, "O God the Son, Redeemer of the world; have mercy upon us miserable sinners."

The buzz became a clamour as many protesters stood up, looked round and spoke to each other. Starky shouted, "O God the Holy Ghost . . ." before his voice was drowned by uproar. The concerned part of his congregation stayed kneeling and responding so loudly that their voices almost overcame the tumult of the rest and certainly greatly increased it.

So in Charlinch Church in 1841 Christmas Day was celebrated exactly as the rector and his curate wished, and as Henry later described it: *The whole body of believers spent this day in fasting and prayer. It was a blesséd day: twenty-six believers, unaccompanied by any of the unconverted, met at the Lord's table, and truly, the Lord Himself was present with them. The King sat at His table, a soft and loving Spirit pervaded all the people, and the Spirit knit all their hearts together into one. Can anyone resist the conviction that this is **God's** work? If it be not **His**, **whose** work is it?*

By 1842 the Royal Mail penny postal service was running smoothly, and over breakfast one morning Henry received a letter from his mother in Widdicombe Crescent saying that Martha's health was much, much worse. He went at once to Bath leaving Starky to conduct the evening meetings and Sunday services, for he was now able to do both. A fortnight later Henry returned to the rectory in time for he and Starky to receive a messenger from the Bishop of Bath and Wells, who introduced himself as the Bishop's chaplain then said, "We are sorry to hear your wife has been very ill, Mr Prince."

"No longer, sir. It is true that she suffered terribly at the end, but that is no longer the case. Martha Prince is now perfectly well and happy, in a better world than ours."

"I am glad she is in a better world, but sorry that you are bereft of a helpmeet in these difficult times."

"Why do you think the times difficult, sir?"

"Because you and your rector are both making them difficult for your Right Reverend Father in God, George Henry Law. He is now a very old man. Letters of complaint from your Charlinch parishioners have alarmed him extremely. I arrived here two days ago to investigate these complaints and find good cause for them."

"What cause have you found?"

"Mr Starky, you have forbidden the Evensong service to many respectable Christians. Prominent farmers, dealers and artisans are now ordering their wives and servants not to attend *any* of the Sunday services. Women are threatening to leave husbands who will not go to Mr Prince's prayer meetings and enraged husbands are threatening to kill wives who *do* go to them. Children are quarrelling with parents, servants with masters while the ungodly look on, laughing and hooting because they find these scandals highly entertaining. This is not Christianity. Christ is the Prince of Peace."

Henry sighed and looked at Starky who murmured, "Christ said *I come not to send peace; but a sword, for I am come to set a man at variance against his father, and a daughter against her mother, and a daughter-in-law against her –* "

"Yes yes, we know that, but Christ was referring to the sword wielded by Roman persecutors. He never rejected any who came to hear Him. You must allow *all* in Charlinch to attend Evensong. Those who pay life rent for pews are entitled to them under the law of the land."

"Alas, our small church has no room for all who wish to hear God's word from Brother Starky's lips," said Henry.

"That is because you have been poaching – attracting people from other parishes."

Henry and Starky stared at each other but said nothing.

"I have a mandate from the Bishop to withdraw your licences to preach unless you, Mr Starky, stop excluding any of your own parishioners, and Mr Prince leaves Charlinch forthwith.

What do you say to that?"

"But!" pleaded Starky, "But! But does the Bishop not know the strength of Belovéd Brother Prince's following? The Lampeter Brethren are not a negligible body. If our Belovéd is excommunicated by the Church of England, others too may leave."

"Bishop Law threatens no one with excommunication. Mr Prince is free to seek more useful work in a different parish, if it is also in a different diocese. Will he do so?"

Henry said gloomily, "Does the Bishop really want Charlinch church to be a place where people once again come for a nap on Sundays?"

"I will not answer that question. I insist on you answering mine – will you leave Charlinch?"

Starky looked appealingly to Prince who said, "Before answering I must consult with The Spirit in prayer."

"Do so. I will call for the answer tomorrow. Good day."

Henry sat silent for a long time not responding to Starky's few, timidly spoken words: "The Church of England, I fear, is governed by very worldly men . . . If The Spirit wishes, of course, my family connections can easily place you in another parish . . . Or will it command us, Belovéd, to defy the Bishop and leave the Church of England? . . . If it does we will surely be able to continue in the rectory for a while because my father built it . . . Several Anglicans have left the Church recently by turning Catholic . . . Of course the incomes of me, my wife and sister will easily support us all, that is certainly a comfort and yet . . . Many Scottish ministers so detest the patronage of landlords that they threaten to break away and found a *Free Church* . . ."

"I must pray for guidance alone, Brother Starky," said Henry, and went to his room.

The Starkys had never doubted that Henry's amazingly unruffled composure came from God. He had told them his strange life story: that his mother in God had been a Catholic who taught him to love Jesus from the Bible; that she had persuaded his bodily mother of his priestly vocation; that four

years ago she had become Anglican and joined him in holy
wedlock before suffering at his side in this then faithless parish.
They knew Martha's death must have disturbed him more
deeply than he had shown, and when he joined them in the
drawing room later his air of wild distraction frightened them.

"My brother and sisters in Christ! O how I need your help,"
he cried, weeping, "Is it possible that I am the most selfish,
the most deluded of men? Can Satan – not the Holy Spirit –
have led me into troubling this peaceful English parish? Has
my inordinate pride deluded me and you and half a respectable
Christian congregation? O say it is not so! Or else say, say, say
that it is!"
He knelt down and raised clasped hands looking from Starky
to the women and back. They clustered round him with
soothing sounds from the women soon silenced by Starky's
ringing words: "Do not torment yourself, Belovéd! It is now
my turn to reprove *your* lack of faith. *By their fruits ye shall
know them*, declare the Scriptures. How can the fruits you
have borne through the Lampeter Brethren and through me
be Satan's work? Satan cannot bring infidels to God, or heal
the sick, or make active, experimental Christians out of worldly,
formal ones. Remember that you are a Branch of the Tree of
Life – that man called Branch whose fruit gives eternal life.
Has the death of your belovéd Martha made you doubt your
divine vocation? But she loved you and had faith in you, a
faith you must not betray. Please get up."
"I want to believe you dear, dear Sam," sobbed Henry, still
kneeling, "But The Spirit has commanded something so
unexpected and strange – so outrageous to what worldly
people think right – that I fear it cannot be obeyed."
His listeners stared at each other, bewildered. Starky said, "The
Spirit is surely not asking you to commit a crime!"
"Not a crime, no. What it commands breaks no human law
and it is surely not sinful in the eyes of God."
"Then who will it harm?"
"None, but a great many will be shocked."

"If what the Spirit commands is not sinful, the Spirit must be obeyed," said Starky, "What does it command?"

In a strangely timid voice Henry asked the women, "Do you agree with Brother Samuel?"

They agreed vehemently. Henry whispered, "Julia, the Spirit commands me to marry you."

Julia's mouth fell open. For several seconds, as the others gazed, the blood left her cheeks very pale, then returned in a blush that spread to her throat, ears and forehead. At last she nodded and said, "Since the Spirit commands us, yes, Henry. Yes my belovéd Henry. Yes, my belovéd Prince."

He sighed deeply, said, "You have removed a great burden from me," stood up and began drying his face with a handkerchief. Mrs Starky said faintly, "But I suppose the wedding need not take place very soon? Need it? There will be the usual year or so of mourning before it is solemnised."

Henry said, "Dear sister – dear all of you, I am tired. The Spirit has wrought mightily in a feeble body. For the past week I have hardly slept. Tomorrow morning we will talk of what should be done in light of the Bishop's mandate. It may be, indirectly, a message from God who requires me – having planted the seed of The Word in Charlinch – to sow it elsewhere. But now I must rest."

He was about to leave but something in Julia's face made him pause and raise her right hand to his mouth by the fingertips. He touched the back of it very slightly with his lips then said, "You realize that our marriage will not be of the flesh, but pure, and of The Spirit?"

Julia, blushing again, murmured, "Yes – O yes."

He went to bed.

25: STOKE, BRIGHTON, WEYMOUTH

Hale Holy Love!   Hale Holy Love!

HENRY AND JULIA'S WEDDING very soon after Martha's death shocked or amazed many and amused some (though Sam Starky conducted it). The couple bore these reactions meekly as they had married for the glory of God, not for earthly profit. One of Starky's relations gave Henry the parish of Stoke in Suffolk, where his Father in God was Dr Allen of Ely, a bishop friendlier than Law of Bath and Wells toward a new breed of evangelical clergy. Meanwhile Starky remained rector of Charlinch and obtained as his new curate George Thomas, one of the early Lampeter Brethren.

Two years later Henry, with Julia's support, had raised such a storm of annoyance in Stoke that Dr Allen summoned Henry to the episcopal palace and said, "What are we to do with you, Mr Prince?"

"Who does Your Lordship signify when he says *we?*", murmured Henry.

"By *we* I signify the Church of England by Law Established, the Church you have studied to join, and which has made me your unhappy Father in God."

He sighed. Henry waited. Dr Allen pointed to a desk saying, "That heap of letters contains more complaints than I can properly answer. Once again you are promoting domestic and social strife."

"May I remind Your Lordship of Christ's own words? He said *Think not that I come to send peace on earth: I come not to send peace; but a –* "

"Yes yes! May I remind you of Shakespeare's words? *The*

devil may cite the scriptures to his advantage."

"Is it devilish of me to prefer the words of Christ to Shakespeare's, Your Lordship?"

"No, but I assure you Christ's words nowhere entitle a priest to exclude Christians from his services."

"A Christian, Your Lordship, is someone who does more than chant words in unison. Services are a senseless mockery if not performed by hearts experiencing new birth through The Spirit, after which, says Jesus, the wheat must be divided from the chaff, the sheep from the goats."

"He was speaking of the last days of mankind – the time of the general resurrection. Do *you* believe we are living in these last days?"

Henry did not reply.

"Will you persist in excluding parishioners from your services?"

"I will do as the Holy Spirit commands, Your Lordship."

"Might it occur to you, Mr Prince, that in the Church of England the Holy Spirit commands you through me, your Bishop?"

Henry said nothing.

"If you do not concur I must withdraw your licence to preach in English Episcopal Churches."

"Your Lordship will do precisely what God allows you to do."

"If that is all you have to say, you may leave."

Henry bowed and left.

This interview and its outcome had been foreseen and had stimulated Julia's practical intelligence. She said, "The advowson of Stoke is still in our family's gift. My baronet uncle will appoint one of the Brethren in your place here also, no matter what Dr Allen wants, so the best of your followers in Stoke will not be lost to us. Who would you like to choose – O Belovéd forgive me! – Who would the Holy Spirit choose in your place here?"

"Lewis Price, I suppose."

"That will make him very happy. Shall we now discuss the

new situation with Sam, since he is similarly placed?"
Henry nodded agreement. He had come to believe a saying
of Thomas à Kempis, that silence is usually wiser than
speech.

Complaints to the Bishop of Bath and Wells had
continued after Henry and Julia left Charlinch because
Starky and his new curate, George Thomas, were ardent
Princeites as some of the Lampeter Brethren were now being
called. Most people in the Church of England thought their
appointed clergymen adequate, but Princeites believed
Henry – at first or second-hand – was essential. His
Charlinch followers flocked so closely around Starky and
Thomas that the rest, feeling excluded, at last persuaded
Bishop Law to withdraw Starky's licence. Thomas lasted
longer. His popular sermons so increased Prince's Charlinch
following that when the Bishop eventually expelled him
too nearly half his congregation also left. They now
worshipped God in a Princeite farmer's barn renamed the
Charlinch Free Church where Thomas and Starky conducted
services. A curate from a neighbouring parish led Sunday
services in the old Charlinch church. Starky retained the
rectory, so here he and Henry and their wives conferred.

"Things are working out wonderfully well, Belovéd!" said
Starky. "We who have left the Church of England for
conscience' sake must now be as many as the first few
Christians who separated from the Jews. With your following
in Stoke and elsewhere we may soon be as many as the
Children of Israel who followed Moses into the wilderness!"
"We have *not* left the Church of England Brother Starky,"
said Henry firmly, "The Church of England has left *us*, or
some of us. Our faith is unchanged. I have told the Lampeter
Brethren this by letter. It is an important distinction."
"Most of the Brethren are still Anglicans," said Julia, "We
should not needlessly estrange them."
"You are quite right – I stand rebuked," said Starky happily.
"Another wonderful thing is the better class of people

joining our free church – not just milkmaids, road-menders and inferior farming people but people with money and land and respectable professions. We have a civil engineer with the Bristol and Exeter Railway!"

"The men are mostly bachelors and the women spinsters or widows," said Mrs Starky. "I sometimes feel quite strange, being one of the few married people."

"The engineer is Brother William Cobbe," said Starky, "His sister, Miss Frances Cobbe, is the well known writer on social problems. He is so devoted to us that he has drawn plans for our very own church building and will pay for the construction! A site has been found for it only two or three miles away by Brother Hotham Mayber, a lovely spot at Spaxton Bottom where he owns land."

Henry said thoughtfully, "At Stoke there is also a better class of people among my faithful."

He was silent for a time. The rest waited patiently until The Spirit moved him to say, "I must meet Brothers Cobbe and Mayber at Spaxton. But it is time, Brother Sam, for us to spread the Word of God to fresh pastures in less rural places."

Which happened. Henry and Julia moved to Brighton where he rented a hall to preach in; Sam and wife went to Weymouth and did the same.

These pleasant seaside resorts contained many who had retired from cities like London where their money had been made, and where polluted air and water reduced life expectancy, even among the rich. Most of the retired were no longer young and often worried about the health of their bodies and souls. Those who overcame the first shock of attending Princeite meetings (which diverged more and more from traditional Anglican services) found great comfort in them. At least once a week Starky joined Henry in Adullam Hall, Brighton, or Henry joined Starky in a Weymouth tavern where they rented a room. Instead of the usual sermon they stood side by side making short speeches, turn and turn about. Their passionate duet first said all mankind was living under a dreadful impending catastrophe, then offered listeners a mysterious escape route.

Prince might begin by saying sadly, "What a beautiful thing was the human body when it came fresh from the hand of the Maker! Even now it is a noble thing, though it is but a temple in ruins! But in Eden it was bright with the beautiful image of God; it bore on its noble front the name of Him who made it, and man was the honoured link between Spirit and matter, Earth linked to Heaven by his living soul, united to Earth by his living body. His eye, his ear, his taste, his touch, his smell, his skin, his every sense was conscious only of good. Because Adam was a creature of *sense* rather than thought. Eve also. Their senses were alive in God, giving them the bright sun and the heaven in its clearness, the flowers in their sweetness, the streams in their gentleness. All these were mediums by which their Maker ministered to them as *flesh*."

Starky said, "Adam, Eve and we their children would be living in eternal happiness to this day, as God wished, but that subtle serpent Satan tempted them to doubt God, yes, doubt God who had told them they would die if they ate fruit giving knowledge of good and evil! For to *know* evil is to *become* evil. They *doubted* God's word, ate that fruit, were *ashamed* of their nakedness, and *thought* to hide themselves from God's eye. Yes, doubt and knowledge and thought brought us all to sin, shame and death. So at last God took another woman – a virgin in Nazareth, Judaea – and made in her flesh Jesus Christ through whom the *souls* of believers will be redeemed. But where does that leave our bodies?"

"Look on the human body now!" cried Prince, "Look at those shrivelled anatomies of once human men, women and children starved by the failure of the potato crops in Holland, Belgium and Ireland! But why look so far? London is now the largest, richest, most scientifically governed city in the world and capital of an empire ruling, in every continent, a full quarter of the world's people. Yet poisonous sewage has turned the Thames into the foulest river on earth. On its banks great lords and senators sitting in the Westminster Palace can hardly stand the stink, yet know not how to cure it. At night gas candelabra light up every London lane, street and public building but what does that light reveal? Filthy and turbulent mobs!"

"Look into any hospital," cried Starky, "Into any prison – workhouse – factory – sweatshop – gin palace – tenement – slum. Are not even the mansions of the wealthy repositories of misery and sin? Can you see among so many weak and unhealthy bodies, so many painful forms of torn humanity, the lines of beauty and the mark of God? What *do* you see in all this? *Death reigns. Death reigns.* Need it always reign?"

"It *shall* not always reign!" cried Henry, "We have been sent by The Spirit to offer you redemption of the body!"

Then with alternating quotations from the Old and New Testaments he and Starky showed that God would now destroy most mankind as he had done before in the deluge that drowned all but Noah and his family; but here in England another family of the faithful would be made immortal if they cleaved to someone sent by God to save them.

"That pure Vessel of the Holy Spirit stands among us!" cried Starky, "But it is not yet time to utter his name."

"Those who have ears to hear, let them await in readiness and soon they *shall* hear," said Henry, "And believing, they will receive eternal life. Amen, Amen and Amen."

In little more than a year Brighton and Weymouth, Charlinch and Stoke had each a hive buzzing with expectant Princeites. There was even a cluster of them in Swansea, where one of the Lampeter Brethren had let Henry and Starky preach to his congregation. Princeites who knew what they expected could not be counted because they discussed it in low voices and groups of two or three. In 1846 Henry was five years older than Jesus when He entered

Jerusalem. Henry's followers might have begun to doubt
his Heaven on Earth had he not started building it by first gathering the most devoted into one place. As Brighton was a notorious haven for weekend adulterers he and Julia joined Sam and Mrs Starky in Belfield Terrace, Weymouth. To an adjacent house came Harriet, Agnes and Clara Nottidge, daughters of a London merchant who had retired with his family to Stoke. There the three sisters became such ardent Princeites that they had followed Henry to Brighton. In Belfield Terrace they joined the Princes and Starkys for breakfast and morning prayers, also for evening prayers and supper. Henry now commanded enough spare rooms to house all his richest followers and occasionally those with businesses outside Weymouth, but who occasionally needed strengthening by close contact with him. Two of these were William Cobbe and Hotham Mayber.

"I call our Belfield houses *Agapemone*," he told them, "which is Greek for the dwelling place or abode of love. Here even we who are husbands and wives live in perfect spiritual harmony and happiness, quite free of fleshly sin because we are brothers and sisters whose only parent is Almighty God. But this little abode is the seed of something larger – a great estate with a mansion that can comfortably accommodate at least thirty gentry with as many servants. There must be gardens around the mansion and space for it to be made larger if that is needed, also an extensive home farm with cottages for labourers and other servants. You, Brothers Cobbe and Mayber, are of all men the most practical who have faith in me! Through you God has chosen the site of his New Jerusalem. Brother Mayber, that land you gave to our free church at Spaxton Bottom – can more be obtained?"

Mayber smiled and shrugged saying, "Apart from cathedrals, army barracks, royal palaces and dockyards there is no part of England that cannot be bought for ready money. The land at Spaxton is good agricultural land so cannot be bought cheap, but it has no mineral deposits and is far from any railway line, so will not be unusually dear."

"There is a house near the church?"

"Yes, and unoccupied, but it is not much larger than Charlinch Rectory."

"Brother Cobbe!" said Henry, "Survey the land round Spaxton Bottom, mapping buildings and farmlands needed by our estate. Consult with Brother Mayber in deciding its extent. The house near the church must be enlarged by adding wings. Design it beautifully. You are building God's final earthly home."

Stroking his beard thoughtfully Cobbe said, "We *can* do all that, Belovéd. I can ensure the mansion has gas lighting with every modern plumbing facility. But such building may cost almost as much as the land itself. Will Mayber and I offend the Holy Spirit if we ask – in all humility – for you to name purchase prices and construction costs we should not exceed?"

"The Holy Spirit is not offended by your question," said Henry, smiling, "because it does not hear it. The Spirit merely requires you to survey the ground, map the estate and design a house fit for the Lord of All the Earth and His followers. The Spirit asks Brother Mayber to begin negotiating the purchase. Do not doubt that the Spirit will provide what we need to complete God's Holy Work. Let us pray."

They knelt with him in prayer then, glad and determined, went to do as he said.

Then Henry sent letters inviting all the Lampeter Brethren to a special conference in the Weymouth Royal Hotel, to stop them losing contact with each other. The mood of this well-attended meeting was at first cordial because so many Brethren were glad to meet again. They found themselves among many they did not know: excited, fashionable ladies and gentlemen, and common people in their best Sunday clothes. The Reverend George Thomas started the business of the day by mounting a platform and proposing that Henry James Prince be elected chairman, since he had called the meeting. Nobody opposed that; the motion was carried by a great show of hands. Henry mounted the platform and sat gravely behind a table there. From the floor of the hall Lewis Price now moved that George Thomas be the minutes secretary, a motion also seconded and accepted without opposition. Thomas, producing a notebook, mounted the platform and sat beside Henry who called the meeting to order and asked Brother Starky to open it.

Starky began by saying it was an overpowering honour for him to speak first, because of all ordained Lampeter Brethren he was certainly the last and least, having studied divinity at Cambridge – not Lampeter. For most of his life he had been a sick man, a wholly formal Christian, and a completely useless priest. He described at great length how his Belovéd Brother Prince had miraculously restored him to health and the love of Jesus, then described at greater length the mighty works of The Spirit in creating Charlinch Free Church and other wonderful Christian congregations in Stoke, Brighton and Weymouth. It was plain (he said) that an even mightier Work of the Spirit impended, and he demonstrated this with biblical quotations from the start of *Genesis* to the book of *Revelations*. But this Work must be wrought through a human instrument and where would such a Vessel of The Pure Spirit appear? Surely not in the corrupted Catholic Church, mighty and widespread though Rome still was. Surely not in the Churches of Czarist Russia and Greece, or the fragmented Protestant sects of Europe and America; nor could this saviour stand high in the Church of England, which was ruled by very worldly men. This Vessel could only appear among the Lampeter Brethren. He ended by saying, "I, Samuel Starky, firmly believe – indeed, *I know* – that this Vessel, this Man we call Branch foretold in the Scriptures, is among us here now. I hereby move that this meeting call upon that Man to reveal himself! Who will second my motion?"

Starky's words excited all his listeners except Henry who

sat behind the table with folded hands and downcast eyes. A great number now gazed at him, their right arms straining above their heads and shouting, "Yes yes!" "I second that!" "Hear hear!", but most of the Lampeter Brethren present stared around as if lost or looked enquiringly at each other. The chairman raised his head, then his hand and there was silence. He said, "Does anyone oppose that motion?"

"May I say a few words?" said a voice from the floor.

"Certainly," said the chairman.

"Thankyou, Brother Henry. You will know that I am Laurence Deck, who attended our old college at Lampeter. You invited me here to discuss the present state of the Lampeter Brethren, and I am delighted to find us surrounded by so many from Brother Starky's south coast congregation and probably your own. You did not ask the rest of we Brethren to bring members of our congregations, probably because we live far from Weymouth and our congregations are mostly too poor to travel. My accent tells everyone here that I am Welsh, and we Welsh greatly admire England's love of fair play. I ask every honest English man and woman present, is it fair for them to help three or four priests outvote a larger number, simply because that larger number have brought no followers?"

Deck sat down. A murmuring that had started during his speech now broke out into cries of, "Nonsense!" "Pedantry!" "Turn him out!", yet whispering in the audience showed many quieter voices were discussing his words. On the platform Starky and Thomas looked appealingly to the chairman who again sat with downcast eyes until another voice from the floor said, "Brother Henry, I am Arthur Rees from Sunderland in Northumbria. May I speak?"

"Certainly," said Henry.

"When Brother Starky says a Vessel of the Holy Ghost may be among us, does he refer to Christ's second coming?"

"Eh . . . yes! I do! But in The Spirit!" cried Starky, then added hastily, "And in the body too . . . of course . . . also in the body."

"Thankyou for being so clear," said Rees. "True Christians

should always expect Christ's second coming at any
moment, for if we do not we may miss it, as the foolish virgins missed the bridegroom in the parable. That is why we Christians have been expecting Christ ever since His resurrection. But can we be sure His second coming is now so very near? Brother Starky says the world has grown as wicked as when God drowned nearly everyone in Noah's flood, but is not the world today, with its many admitted evils, better than it was in the days of the Emperor Nero? Or before the Protestant Reformation? I agree with him that many Church of England clergy are worldly men with worldly motives, but do *not* agree that there are no pure-hearted Christians outside the Lampeter Brethren. In other churches there are many pure believers. I myself am thinking of joining the Baptists . . ."

This caused a muffled commotion in which a woman screamed, "Shame!", then tried to look as if she had not. Rees cried, "Surely we should only do what Jesus commanded! Let us love the Lord our God with all our hearts and souls and minds and our neighbour as ourselves! Let us even love neighbours who ignore us, mock us or treat us as enemies! God still wants Christians to love and serve fallen humanity, especially if we are priests."

He sat down in a sudden, respectful silence which lasted some seconds before hands were raised by many eager to speak. The chairman suddenly looked up and in a strange sing-song that disconcerted everyone chanted, "Brother Deck again has the floor."

"I d-d-do not wish to suggest anything of-of-of-offensive to Brother Prince and his followers," said Deck, confused by the strange voice that singled him out but swiftly mastering his stammer, "I only suggest that Brother Starky's motion is prem – is premature. Let all the Lampeter Brethren and their congregations watch for signs that Christ is returning or has returned, because surely these signs will be miracles that none who see them can doubt, and that no show of hands, no counting of heads can set in train. I move that all in the Lampeter Brotherhood correspond with each other, perhaps using our minutes secretary, Brother Thomas, as a kind of central post office. If any of us encounter a miracle showing that Christ has returned, let him share that news, not confine it to one circle of ad-ad-ad-admirers."

"Let Brother Deck's commands be obeyed!" Henry almost screamed in his peculiar new voice, "This meeting is now at an end! Amen, Amen, and Amen!"

He swiftly left the platform and room, followed closely by Starky, Thomas, Julia, Mrs Starky and Rees. The remaining Lampeter Brethren and Princeites were so confused that they mutteringly left the hotel without more public discussion.

A fortnight after the Royal Hotel meeting Arthur Rees and Laurence Deck called on Prince at Belfield Terrace, Weymouth. He received them as he received all visitors nowadays, Julia seated on one side and Starky on the other. He arose as Rees and Deck entered – murmured a welcome – shook their hands warmly – sat calmly smiling as the visitors, on a sofa facing them, exchanged remarks about the weather with his followers. Suddenly Rees said wildly, "O Brother Prince, I do not know *how* to start saying what we are here to say!"

"Yet say it."

"This letter in my hand – Brother Deck has also received a copy – purports to be minutes of our last meeting of the Brethren. It is not! I doubt if Brother Thomas wrote a word of it!"

"He wrote every word of it," said Prince mildly, "I know this because he wrote down what The Spirit dictated to him through my lips. The voice was mine but the words were God's. Brother Thomas then made a copy in his own hand while Sisters Julia and Starky made other copies. The Spirit directed that Thomas's manuscript epistles be posted to you and Deck. The other copies went to the other former Brethren."

"Who are as shocked as we are! The only Lampeter Brethren it mentions as present are you, Starky, Thomas and Price!"

"Because we were the only Brethren present in heart and soul. You and the rest were not. You heard Brother Starky

knocking at the door of your hearts, begging you to open
and admit salvation through the Holy Spirit's love. You
preferred to shut it out."

"O Brother Prince! O my dear, dear Brother Henry!" cried
Rees, starting to weep.

"*Are* we brothers?" murmured Henry.

"Yes! Brothers in God from the moment we first confessed
and prayed together in your room at St David's College,
Lampeter, brothers-in-law since I married your sister!"

Henry said absently, "I regret that. There is still enough
fleshly inclination in my heart to regret that you are no
longer, in truth, my brother."

He closed his eyes and kept them shut until Rees and Deck
left the room.

"Brother Prince – for I insist on still calling you so – " said
Deck, "This letter lies when it says the meeting ended with
everyone present unanimously voting you to be the
Redeemer foretold in the Bible."

"That letter tells a truth you did not see, and cannot see
because you are blind."

"But it stands to reason! –"

"I am not reasonable, Deck," Henry interrupted smoothly,
"If I fell so low as to reason with you I would become the
old, selfish, fleshly Henry Prince you once knew. I would
have to agree with you. But that Henry Prince is dead. I am
now as a little child who says only what The Spirit wishes.
Sometimes I hardly understand what it says through me,
but I know it is eternal damnation not to obey."

Deck stood up saying, "Rees, we had better leave," but Rees
begged, "Let me try once more! Henry, on our way here
yesterday we stopped in Brighton where I questioned some
who have heard you preach . . ."

"You were spying, in fact," said Julia.

"I was enquiring. One said you and Starky claimed to be
the two witnesses of *Revelations*, another that you call
yourselves the Prophet Elijah and the Holy Ghost made
flesh. Is this true?"

Henry said, "I am not permitted to reply".

"We do not say we did, neither do we say we did not," Starky explained.

"O my poor Brother Henry!" sobbed Rees, standing up, "You were the best of us at Lampeter – the purest, bravest and most truly humble. O what has turned you into such a *dreadful*, such a *silly* creature?"

At this impiety Julia and Starky stared aghast at Henry. One of his eyes may have flickered open and shut, otherwise he did not move for two or three seconds then whispered, "Get thee behind me, Rees. Get thee behind me, Deck."

Julia stood up saying coldly, "I will show you out, *Mister* Rees, *Mister* Deck. Our Belovéd carries many heavy burdens. You have failed to add another."

Shortly after returning to his family in Sunderland Arthur Rees received a letter with a south coast postmark, addressed to him in an unfamiliar hand. As was then common the envelope was fastened with a circular blob of sealing wax, but remarkably big, and black instead of the usual red. He broke the seal and took out two sheets of thick, good-quality paper called mourning card, because printed with a black border for people sending news of a death or funeral. The first card had these words written large in the unknown hand:

JUDAS!
Guide to them that took
THE HOLY ONE
Go to thine own place!

The second said:

Let his days be few!
Let another take his Office.
Let his children be fatherless
and his wife a widow.
Let their names be blotted out.

Below the last sentence a row of names was made illegible

by ink blots, so Rees could not see if they were names of
him and his wife and children, or of him and other Lampeter
Brethren who doubted Henry's divinity. Rees groaned, knelt
on the carpet and begged God to cure
Henry of a blasphemous
delusion.

26: THE ABODE OF LOVE

Hale Holy Love!   Hale Holy Love!

HENRY CALLED THE FAITHFUL to a second meeting in the Weymouth Royal Hotel, a meeting so important that Lampeter Brethren who had not shown themselves unbelievers were ordered to come. Julia visited Swansea and explained the urgency of Henry's summons to the Princeite clergy there, but Rees and Deck's influence was such that only one of them attended beside Henry and Starky, Thomas and Price.

The platform at this meeting had an easy chair at the back with two upright chairs nearer the front, one on each side. Henry sat in the centre with the absent look he now always wore when not speaking; Starky sat to his left, Thomas to the right. They began the meeting by standing together with Henry behind them.

"Dearly belovéd brothers and sisters in God," said Thomas, "you are about to hear a sermon, but not an ordinary sermon from an ordinary preacher."

"We are sent to you from the courts of Heaven," said Starky, "From the bosom of eternity, to proclaim the second coming of Our Lord."

"His coming is nigh!" said Thomas.

"Very nigh!" said Starky.

"Very nigh indeed!" said Thomas, and together they cried, "Behold He cometh!", and moved apart, sitting down again as Henry stepped forward.

And quietly asked, "Who am I who stand before you? I am
Brother Prince. Who is Brother Prince? Is Brother Prince . . .
God? Only very foolish or very wicked people can ask such a
question. I'm a man like yourselves, a vessel of clay. But God,
for his own purpose, has emptied out this vessel and filled it
with mercy: mercy for all who will drink of it. Look well upon
me! In me you behold the *love* of Christ for fallen humanity.

"I am here to speak of the redemption of the body, by which
I mean, its deliverance from the power of Satan, who is the
author of all evil, whether it is sin in the soul, or disease and
death in the body. *All* evil, I say, including headache, stomach
ache and toothache. Jesus Christ came to destroy Satan in the
soul of man, but his blesséd Gospel made no provision for the
flesh, which is God's greatest enemy. But *you* are flesh! You are
of the earth, earthy! Behold, He is coming to judge the Earth!
Believe me, the bridegroom already stands outside the door!
O, how will you bear it when you behold Him?"
Suddenly he cried aloud, "I will tell you – You will not bear it!
You will burn, like chaff, in the fire of his unending love, which
you will feel as eternal torture if you now reject His mercy!"
He paused for a moment then said, quietly again, "But do not
the Scriptures say we shall be changed, those of us who are
alive and await the coming of the Lord? *Behold*, declares Isaiah,
the prophet, *Behold, I create new Heavens!*

"That prophesy is being fulfilled. The day of judgement
has come. God is creating the new Heaven through *me*:
Brother Prince. Be glad therefore, and join me in that which I
create, for behold, I build the New Jerusalem, rejoicing! At
Spaxton in Somerset an Abode is arising, an Abode where
those of you who leave their houses, wives, husbands, parents,
children and lands for My sake will enter and live for ever in
the Pure Enjoyment of the Love of Angels! But do not tarry.
God still sits in his Mercy Seat, but not even I – a Branch of
the Tree of Life whose fruit I bear for you – not even I know
how soon He will leave it, consigning to eternal darkness all
who linger outside the gates. When the world is burning into
ashes, and the sky is melting in the fervent heat, what use
then will be your flocks and herds? Rank and state? Property

and capital? Shares, dividends and financial securities? Do you hope to ride on horses to the throne of grace? Or drive in carriages to the judgement seat? *Sell what thou hast* is the Divine Injunction to the called. Will you stand on the edge of doom and dispute the Words of God? Or will you, at the end of the Christian era, do as did all who answered Christ's call at the start of it? – Join with those who, believing in Him, entered the Peace of God and His heavenly kingdom by giving up to Him everything they had?"

Henry retired to his seat, obviously exhausted by the passionate working of the Spirit in him. Nothing he had said was wholly unexpected – his audience had heard some of it before from Starky, Thomas, Price and the Belovéd himself – yet an intense murmuring arose and subsided as Starky and Thomas again came forward.
"Our Abode of Love," Starky announced, "Shall be known as *Agapemone.*"
"At the back of this hall," said Thomas, "Brother James Rouse, our attorney, has opened the Book of Mercy where he will register the names of those willing to enter the Agapemone by giving their All to it."
Said Starky, "Only your *intention* will be recorded today, as the legal transfer of property to our Abode will take a little longer. I and Brother Thomas will be foremost in setting our names there."
He and Thomas left the platform together and strode side by side to the back of the hall where Julia, Mrs Starky and Price waited to sign their names.

In Belfield Terrace that evening donations indicated in The Book of Mercy were compared with the estimated costs of the estate. Henry's seven most faithful followers discussed these while he, wearing quilted dressing gown, velvet smoking cap and slippers, lay back in an armchair and only spoke when a final decision was needed. The book registered the following: –
4 clergymen (not counting Henry) – Thomas, Starky, Price and the Swansea Curate

a civil engineer – William Cobbe
a landed proprietor – Hotham Mayber
a surgeon – Arthur Mayber, Hotham's brother
an attorney – James Rouse
7 fund-holders – 3 Nottidge sisters and Mayber's 4 sisters
2 annuitants – Julia and a widow called Paterson
3 farmers, 1 with five hundred acres employing thirty labourers
a twelve-year-old girl, the daughter of Mrs Paterson
9 house servants, one of them male
6 laundresses
2 dressmakers
3 helpers in stables
3 carpenters
a mason
a groom
a post-boy
a shoe-maker
a tailor

"An excellent beginning – really excellent," said Starky, "Though, alas, the All our brothers and sisters are willing to donate is less that the amount our greater Abode requires."
"Because some are *not* donating their All, like we in this room!" said Julia sharply, "Our lawyer James Rouse is withholding a very great deal. His income must be much larger than he admits – he says nothing about the savings or the value of his properties. Which of us should speak to him about that?" she asked Henry. He murmured, "Nobody, as yet."
"It would be unwise to estrange him," said Mayber, "while he is drawing up deeds of gift for signature by our Belovéd's other followers."
"Then what about the Nottidge girls?" demanded Julia, "Each offers the thousand a year interest on her capital, but not the capital itself."
They glanced toward Henry who said quietly, "Do not worry; the Lord will provide. Show me the plans again please."
Cobbe laid them on his knees saying, "The church at least is completed, apart from the spire."

"It needs no spire," said Henry, "It needs, however, a conservatory or at least a corridor joining it to the main residence."

"What a good idea!" cried Mrs Starky, "Because, you know, we can then go back and forth to divine service quite untroubled by the weather until . . . until . . . "

She frowned uncertainly. Thomas suggested, "Until time stops, eternity begins and the weather is as heavenly as God will make it?"

"Yes! That is exactly what I meant."

"I too look forward to that blesséd day," said Starky, "though I am sorry for the doomed multitude who will never enjoy it."

"You should not be sorry, they will have brought it on themselves," said Julia.

A few weeks later Starky told the Nottidge sisters that the Spirit required them to travel with him, Henry and their wives to view the work going forward at Spaxton. They went by coach into Somerset and stopped in Taunton where the Princes and Starkys rested at Giles' Hotel, the three spinster ladies at the nearby Castle Inn. Early next day Henry sent for Harriet. She put on her bonnet and crossed to the Giles' Hotel where he received her kindly but solemnly. In the presence of Julia and the Starkys he explained that it would be for the Glory of God if she married his young friend, the Reverend Lewis Price. Harriet blushed and agreed. Henry bade her return in peace to the Castle Inn and lock this secret closely in her heart. This she did.

Then Henry sent for Agnes, a less biddable woman. In a voice as kind as he had used with her sister but more solemnly he said, "Agnes, God is about to confer on you a special blessing; but ere I tell you what it is, you must give me your word to obey the Lord and accept His gift."

Agnes gave her word after the slightest of hesitations. Henry said, "In a few days you will be united in marriage to our Brother George Robinson Thomas."

Agnes, confused by the news, cried out, "In a *few days?*"

"Such is God's will."

"But – but – but I have relations to consult, legal settlements to make!"

"You need none of these things. You must not think of the world, but of God."

"But my mother must be told!" Agnes pleaded.

"God is your father and mother," said Prince.

"But lawyers take time . . ."

"Why do you want a lawyer, dear?" asked Mrs Starky, looking up from her knitting.

"Well . . . for the children's sake."

"You will have no children!" said Prince, patiently. "Your marriage with our Brother will be spiritual only; your love to your husband will be pure, according to the Will of God. And now," he added more warmly, "take tea with us, Agnes, and know that this blesséd moment is a happy one."

Later in the day the two sisters dined with the Princes and Starkys at the Giles' Hotel where they met their new fiancés, Thomas and Price. Two days later Clara was similarly engaged to William Cobbe. The three sisters now wished to return to their mother's home in Stoke for a while, but Henry said God forbade that and also forbade them to tell anyone by letter before the marriages. Meanwhile Harriet and Clara willingly signed their fortunes over to Henry. Agnes refused, but finally signed an agreement that her husband Thomas could invest her property in their joint names. All these details were arranged through communal prayers led by Henry. A fortnight later the three marriages were solemnized in Swansea by one of the Brethren, Starky giving the brides away and Henry looking on.

By these means eighteen thousand pounds of Nottidge money was added to the Agapemone fund. Continuous inflation during the twentieth century has made it almost impossible to convert such a sum into a modern equivalent – in those days servants who ate and lodged with a family were often paid a pound a year or less. Postal rates may give another clue. In Victoria's reign an early Socialist had organized the

Royal Mail to deliver any letter in Britain for the price of a
penny stamp. It was a first class service – there was no second
class. In 2006 a first class stamp costs 33 pence, but multiplying
the Nottidge £18,000 by 33 would still be too little, for in
Britain's pre-decimal days a pound contained 240 pence. By
a conservative estimate Henry acquired by these three
marriages more than a million modern pounds sterling, which
was a fraction of what he got from other followers when
income tax was so small and such a recent innovation that
important statesmen (Gladstone was one) proposed abolishing
it. The estate was now perfectly solvent.

Henry called Julia and the Starkys, Thomas and Price,
Mayber and Cobbe, "my seven-branched golden candlestick".
One evening, after calculating all the moneys transferred to
Henry's account, an awestruck silence befell them. Mrs Starky
broke it by saying, "Well, Belovéd, you must now certainly
have your own carriage and pair."
Henry had hitherto hired a carriage when he needed one.
Owning a one-horse carriage was then a mark of middle-class
prosperity: a carriage and pair signified a much higher social
standing.
"No!" cried Julia, "A carriage and *four*! With outriders! Your
dignity demands it, Belovéd."
The idea astonished and excited nearly everyone present – a
carriage drawn by four horses was seldom used except by
royalty and lords travelling in state processions. If it occurred
to the horsemen present that a carriage and four would need
unusually skilful management on the twisting roads of southern
England they did not say so. When, with a slight chuckle,
Henry asked, "What is the sentiment of this meeting toward
Sister Julia's somewhat audacious suggestion?" they all smiled,
delighted that the Spirit was allowing their Belovéd to unbend
in a joke.
"Yes, you *must* have a carriage and four Belovéd!", cried Starky,
"It is owed to the Spirit moving you!"
"Hear hear!" cried the others so Henry, amused yet resigned,
murmured, "If I must, I must."

Julia and Mrs Starky devized sober yet eye-catching suits of livery in two shades of grey for the Belovéd's coachman and footmen. These were cut by Samuel Tricksey, the Agapemone tailor, a small man who fancied himself as a jockey. To stop the harness tangling at sharp bends he gladly rode one of the foremost horses when Henry drove outside Weymouth. This splendid equipage astonished commoners who had seen nothing like it and annoyed gentry who thought it a vulgar display of ill-gotten wealth.

One day Henry urgently summoned George Thomas to the Weymouth Agapemone, and Thomas answered that he could not come at once as he and Agnes were going on holiday to his mother in Wales. Henry had not met such disobedience since his days as a Charlinch curate and had never before found it in Thomas, one of the earliest Lampeter Brethren and also the preacher on whom, after Starky, he most depended. Thomas was obviously now under his wife's bad influence. When the sinful couple came to Belfield Terrace on the way back from Wales they were put on trial before Henry and Julia, Sam and Mrs Starky. The main accusers were Agnes' sisters and their husbands. Thomas had never been rebuked by Henry before. He wept, knelt on the floor, confessed his sin and begged forgiveness. Agnes stared at him in astonishment tinged with contempt that struck the rest as open defiance. Thomas leapt to his feet and cried out in as terrible a voice as he could manage, "Agnes! I command you to obey henceforth the Spirit of God in me, made known to me through our Belovéd servant of the Lord!"
Agnes crept to her bedroom in a house that felt more like a Spanish inquisitor's jail than an abode of love.

Worse followed. Harriet, Agnes and Clara had a younger sister Louisa, a woman of forty who still lived with their widowed mother and was also heiress to a big slice of their father's fortune. In the next few days Agnes realized Louisa was being invited to join the Agapemone too, so began writing a letter advizing her not to come. In a commune privacy is almost impossible. Thomas found the letter and showed it to Henry. When Agnes went to her bedroom that night her husband stood in the doorway and said, "You are lost, Agnes. From now on any room where I am is locked against you, is an empty room as far as you are concerned. Go and beg for a sleeping space from one of the female servants in the basement or attic. You will not find her so easy to corrupt as you have corrupted me once, but never again! I have repented and have been forgiven. You have twice defied the Servant of the Lord and now can never be forgiven."

Next day Agnes was left in Belfield Terrace with two servants when Henry, Thomas and other chief Princeites went by carriage to Spaxton, where a row of cottages had been made habitable for them. A week after that a letter from a servant at Weymouth told Henry that Agnes was certainly pregnant. Thomas wrote to her at once, commanding her to go and live with his mother in Wales. Instead she returned to her own mother's house near Stoke where she gave birth to a son a few months later.

Louisa Nottidge, despite the sufferings of her sister Agnes, despite the opposition of her mother and other relatives, came to live in one of Henry's completed cottages at Spaxton. One evening a carriage arrived containing her brother, a clergyman-cousin and a stranger who turned out to be a police officer. They said they had come to take her home because her mother was ill. She refused to believe them so was forced into the carriage, fighting and screaming, and driven to a private hospital near London where she was locked up as a madwoman. Harriet, Clara and their husbands could get no news of Louisa's whereabouts from her mother. After eighteen months Louisa managed to send word of the madhouse address to William Cobbe, her brother-in-law. Cobbe applied to the Commissioners of Lunacy who investigated, found imprisonment was damaging Louisa's health, that she had religious delusions but was otherwise sane. When freed she legally transferred all her property to Henry and returned to the Abode.

The Spaxton Agapemone was then complete and the one
in Weymouth abandoned. There is no record of how Henry
finally entered the great new Abode but surely he did it
splendidly, going with Julia and the two Starkys in the carriage
and four down long lanes through woodlands, two liveried
footmen seated behind, and in front beside the coachman on
the box, a postillion blowing a long horn to herald the
Belovéd's approach. I imagine as outriders beside the carriage
all the Agapemone male gentry – three clergymen, two
Maybers, William Cobbe and the attorney Rouse. A groom
rides one of the foremost horses because the tailor – Samuel
Tricksey – is now the Agapemone gateman. At the sound of
the horn he appears from his gatehouse, above which is a
tower with flagpole and flag bearing the Agapemone emblem:
a lamb, lion and dove on a bed of roses with the motto *Oh,
Hail, Holy Love*. From now on this flag will be flown whenever
Henry is at home. As Tricksey and a servant open the gates for
the carriage please imagine the *Old Hundredth* struck up by a
mighty cathedral choir and organ: –

> *O enter in his gates with praise;*
> *Approach with joy His courts unto;*
> *Praise, laud, and bless His Name always,*
> *For it is seemly so to do.*

> *For why? the Lord our God is good;*
> *His mercy is for ever sure;*
> *His truth at all times firmly stood,*
> *And shall from age to age endure* – as carriage

and outriders canter up a drive to a front door where all the
servants are ranged on each side of the front steps, with the ladies
of leisure at the top. Henry and companions leave the carriage;
his entourage dismounts. Grooms lead carriage and horses away
to the stables as Henry leads everyone else into the house with a
radiant smile that seems to shine on all while focusing on none.

Maybe an hour or two later we see him in the Agapemone
church. It has no altar, lectern, pulpit or choir stalls. The only
religious symbols are the lamb, lion, dove and roses in the

stained glass windows. The interior is furnished like an opulent Victorian drawing room with a large red ottoman sofa in the chancel where the communion table normally stands. On this Henry comfortably sits, right leg cast over left knee, and addresses the gentlefolk standing before him.

"Dear Brothers and Sisters in Christ," he says sweetly, "today we have entered Jerusalem with psalms of praise and now the Day of Judgement is past. The Angel has left the Mercy Seat, and we, the Blesséd, are gathered into the bosom of God. From now onwards psalms, prayers, sermons and services are at an end, and we will live for ever surrounded by all that can delight the eye and satisfy the sense. Only one ceremony remains – that great manifestation of the Holy Spirit's love for the Body by which he redeems it from sin and death. And just as Satan started the fall of the old earth in Adam's flesh – that is, in Eve, who was living earth – so will God restore the earth by creating a new consciousness in the flesh of a woman once again. It behoves the virgins among you, therefore, to adorn yourself and await the coming of the bridegroom. The hour is nigh!"

"Very nigh indeed!", said Starky, smiling and nodding on Henry's right with Thomas on the left. Henry stands, places a hand on each of their shoulders and tells the rest, "My witnesses will summon you when the time is right."

He clasps his hands on his chest and leaves, the company parting to let him through. Most of those present, especially the ladies, are left in a state of whispering confusion.

Since Henry, as always, used the language of King James' authorized bible nobody is sure how far his speech is metaphorical. Though four of the women present are legally married and all but one are middle-aged, all are or claim to be virgins. This is too delicate a matter to discuss so Fanny Mayber says, "Sister Julia, what does Belovéd mean when he tells us to adorn ourselves? I have some jewellery, of course, but . . ."

She falls silent, confused. Three years before all Princeite women were told to sell their jewellery and give the money to Henry. Most did. Julia says kindly, "None of us, I am sure, should try to outshine the rest. Any personal adornment that has been accidentally retained should be shared equally with all of us,

but it will be easier if we wear nothing that is not ordered new
for the occasion. And whatever we wear, let it be white."
A kind of thrill goes through the ladies as Annie Mayber
murmurs, "Belovéd seemed to suggest His final manifestation
would be a kind of wedding."
"Brídal veils?", suggests someone.
"With chaplets of white roses?", breathes another.

Julia is the only one among them who can sometimes ask
Henry direct questions. She brings them word that bridal attire
will be appropriate for all and no expense need be spared.
White silks and satins, white velvets, laces and gauze are
ordered from London, also the latest pattern of bridal gown.
In less than a month the Agapemone dressmakers make nine
gowns for women of several ages, shapes and sizes. Mrs Starky
and Fanny Mayber have the finest dress sense and unselfishly
suggest adjustments that show their sisters' figures to the best
advantage. When all are satisfied with their bridal gowns Henry
announces the day of the final manifestation, which takes place
before the congregated faithful on the sofa in the Agapemone
church.

The ceremony is described in a pamphlet called *The Little
Book Open – The Testimony of Br. Prince concerning what
Jesus Christ has done by His Spirit to Redeem the Earth: In
Voices from Heaven*. Henry published it in 1856, five years
after the his Manifestation. A long preamble explains why God
required it, then says. "*Thus the Holy Ghost took flesh in the
presence of those whom He called as flesh. Out of this one
lump of clay – dust of the ground, living earth – flesh – He,
the Great Potter took one piece to make it new. He took flesh
– a woman – in their presence, and told them it was his
intention to make it one with him, even as a man is one flesh
with his wife. He consulted nobody's pleasure in doing this
but his own. He was not influenced by what others might
think or say. And he took it with power and authority as flesh
that belonged to God, and was at his absolute disposal. In*

taking it he left it no choice of its own. He did not take it because it loved him, for it did not – but because it pleased him to set his love upon it. Yet he took it in love; for having taken it his manner in it was such as flesh could know and appreciate as love. He kept it with him continually day and night. He took it openly with him wherever he went, not being ashamed of it. He made its life happy and agreeable by affording it the enjoyment of every simple and innocent gratification. Thus he made it one with him, and made it new flesh. He created it a new consciousness".

Which means he began by raping the youngest virgin in the presence of the others (including his legal wife) and the Agapemone gentlemen. She was the daughter of the widow Paterson, a girl of fifteen. Her mother, as devoted to Henry as any other Princeite, had died a few months earlier of what doctors called consumption but Henry called doubt. He told the others, "She erred, so God took her", which explained the matter. Female fashions in 1851 make his rape hard to imagine. Paris dominated these fashions more than nowadays, and French fashion was ruled by the wife of Napoleon's nephew. She was a handsome Spaniard who loved ballroom dancing so popularized the crinoline to hide her pregnancies, for it covered women's bodies from waist to feet in a circular whalebone cage a yard or more across at knee level, under a skirt descending to the ground. This fashion was denounced from pulpits, mocked by caricaturists and heartily complained of by most men, especially those who travelled in railway carriages and small horse-drawn buses, yet it triumphed for nearly two decades. Fashionable women liked it for the same reason as the French Empress; poorer women because, in days when Britain's overcrowded industrial cities had no public lavatories for women, it let them urinate in streets and parks without noticeably doing so. Unless the Agapemone bridal gowns were unfashionably designed only an expert in historic costume can perhaps explain how Henry got through Miss Paterson's crinoline. If his pamphlet is true he treated her afterwards with as much kindness and consideration as any devoted Victorian husband. There is now no way of knowing his wife Julia's feelings. Neither she, he or anyone left word of them.

Not doubting he had done as God commanded, Henry wrote a description of his Great Manifestation in the third person (like Caesar describing his Gallic Wars) and published it, and sent Starky and Thomas out to preach it in Bridgwater and London. He must have changed his mind about God finally closing the gates of the Abode to everyone else, and was ready to let in new believers and (if they came in sufficient numbers with sufficient money) perhaps greatly enlarge the Abode of Love. That did not happen. The Bridgwater meeting was a failure and the best account of the London meeting is in a September 1856 edition of *The Times*:

On Friday evening two members of the "Agapemone" near Bridgwater appeared at the Hanover Square rooms according to their advertizement. The large room was densely crowded. Two respectably dressed men spoke to the meeting, urging the claims of their leader, "Brother Prince." According to the speakers Brother Prince was "a child of wrath who had been made by grace into a vessel of mercy." Some eleven years ago the Holy Ghost had fulfilled in Brother Prince all that He meant to be and do. The audience evinced much disapprobation and disgust, and cried out that this was gross blasphemy, and worse than Mormonism. The speaker, who seemed quite imperturbable and who calmly surveyed the meeting though a single glass stuck jauntily in one eye proceeded to allude to a second spiritual manifestation which had, he said, occurred at the Agapemone about five years ago, in which the phenomenon was exhibited in the person of a woman – a prophetess – "Not privately, but in the presence of us all." Some of the expressions used in describing this transaction were perhaps misunderstood by many of his hearers, for they interrupted him indignantly, and at last stopped him with a general howl of execration. The two strangers then retired from the room; upon which Mr Newman, apparently a working man, arose and announced the doctrines of the Agapemone as impious. He moved as a resolution, "That the statements made by the two persons on the platform were contrary to common sense, degrading to humanity, and blasphemous toward God." The resolution was carried with acclamation amid vociferous cheers. A sergeant of police stepped forward and said good-humouredly, "Now gentlemen, the meeting is over."

After that only occasional newspaper reports brought the Agapemone to public notice. There was first the Rev. George Thomas' unsuccessful attempt to remove his small son from Agnes, his wife, which ended with her divorcing Thomas and gaining legal custody of the child. The Great Manifestation estranged Rouse the attorney who left the Agapemone and brought a legal action that recovered some of his money. Lewis Price also left but could not persuade Harriet to go with him, nor could he persuade the police that she was kept in the Abode against her will. He therefore invaded it with about twenty local men who thought he had a right to his own wife, but Harriet had fled with Mrs Starky to lodgings in Salisbury. When she returned he obtained a writ claiming she was retained against her will, but she declared this was not true before a judge who dismissed the case. Said *The Times*, "As may be expected, Mr Price has obtained the sympathy of all right-minded people in the neighbourhood." Then came the death of Mary Mayber, whose body was found in a sheep-dip pond. At the inquest Harriet Price (formerly Nottidge) declared that Mary had not been kept in the Agapemone against her will. Fanny Mayber declared that her sister Mary had been depressed for many months because she could not be as happy as others in the Agapemone, so felt Christ had abandoned her. A surgeon who conducted an autopsy on the deceased said she had died of drowning, not poisoning, and an adhesion of her brain to the skull indicated a tumour that explained her depression. The coroner's verdict was suicide while of unsound mind.

It would be depressing to chart how all the original members of the Abode left or died away leaving Henry who outlasted them all. It is pleasanter to end with an account of the Agapemone by a friendly but critical reporter who went there in 1866 when most of its troubles seemed overcome.

27: HEPWORTH DIXON'S REPORT

Hale Holy Love!   Hale Holy Love!

HEPWORTH DIXON was a journalist, novelist, editor and one of those busy, worldly, free-thinking yet discreet men who, in a phrase fashionable in late 19th century England, were said to have *gone everywhere and done everything*. In the Baltic provinces of East Prussia – in Salt Lake City and Oneida Creek, U.S.A. – in England at Spaxton Bottom he noticed communities who had scandalized public opinion by practising new kinds of marriage. He investigated these communities and, in a two volume study called *Spiritual Wives* showed how they differed from highly sensational accounts in the popular press. His book was published in 1867. Here is his description of a visit to the Agapemone:

"No stranger is admitted into the Agapemone," says Murray's Handbook.
"The Abode of Love," said Sir Frederick Thesiger, speaking as a prosecuting council, "is a family consisting of four apostate clergymen, an engineer, a medical man, an attorney, and two bloodhounds."
"The Agapemone", says Boyd Dawkins, the latest lay writer who has paid attention to this subject, "is surrounded by a wall from twelve to fifteen feet high."
These statements are untrue. The Saints who are gathered at Spaxton have audacities and heresies enough without being charged with these idle tales.

Dixon here
makes the
town-
dwellers'
usual
mistake of
thinking the
country as he
saw it had
always been
like that. In
1867 it had
been created
by acts of
parliament
about sixty
years earlier.
An England
where
cultivated
land was
separated by
commons
(wildernesses
where
anyone
could build a
shelter, snare
a rabbit, fish
a stream,
keep a
beehive,
graze a horse
or goat) had
been
replaced by
a countryside
of densely-
hedged fields
and landed
estates
guarded by
spring
mantraps and
signs saying
TRESPASSERS
WILL BE
PROSECUTED.

As your carriage rolls from the quaint old streets of Bridgwater into the green country lanes, you seem to pass from the age of Victoria into the age of King Alfred. Saxon Somerset was, I fancy, as green and bright, with corn-sheaves on these slopes; stone homesteads, snug with thatch, upon these knolls; with village towers and spires among the trees; and with a slow but sturdy population, like those of Spaxton and Charlinch. The road is bad, the mire is deep, the descents are sharp. The lanes are sunk below hedges of thorns and briars, so that an unfriendly invasion would find it no easy task to push their way from town to town. Pull up the horses on the brow of this hill. The scene is beautiful with the beauty of western England. In front springs a dome of corn-field, crowned with the picturesque nave and tower of Charlinch church. At the base of this hillock flows the soft wooded valley towards Over Stowy, a place renowned in the poetry of Wordsworth and Coleridge. But what, in this valley at our feet in the winding lane on our left, is that fanciful group of buildings; a church to which the spire has not yet been built; a garden, cooled by shrubs and trees; a greenhouse thronged with plants; an ample sward of grass cut through by winding walks; a row of picturesque cottages on the road, a second row in the garden; high gates by the church; a tangle of buildings in the front and rear; farms, granaries, stables, all of the crimson with creeping autumnal plants? That group of buildings is the Agapemone; the home of our male and female saints.

In a few seconds we alight in front of the Abode of Love. The large gates are closed, but a side door stands ajar. The man who drives me seems surprized – he too had been told that no one is admitted into the Abode of Love. Once in his life, however, he had been taken into the stables by a groom who was proud of his horses, as he might very well be, since they had come from the royal stud. My driver tells me with a shudder that the strange people in the Abode play billiards on a Sunday in their church. He does not mind a game of nine-pins in the ale-house yard with other poor fellows on Sunday afternoons; but that is very different from gentlefolks hitting ivory balls in a church. As I entered by the open door a gentleman in black came from the house and shook my

hand. This was the Rev. George Robinson Thomas, once a student
of St David's College, Lampeter, afterwards a curate at Charlinch,
then a witness for Brother Prince and now First of the Agapemone's
Two Anointed Ones. His figure was tall, spare and well made,
crowned with an intellectual head and pair of sharp blue eyes in a
face no longer youthful, but whose every line showed he had been
a scholar and preacher. Such was the gentleman known to me from
report as the husband of Agnes Nottidge, the hero of an ale-house
comedy, and defeated party in a scandalous court case.

Thomas led me into the chief room, which I saw at once was a
church. Three ladies were seated near a piano at which one of
them was playing. My name was mentioned to them; they curtseyed
and left, their own names not having been pronounced. One of
them, as I afterwards found by a lucky guess, had once been Julia
Starky, daughter of a clergyman with high standing in society and
of high repute in the English Church. She was now the second
wife of Brother Prince but not, then or afterwards, made known to
me by her married name.

After the usual remarks had been made about the fine morning
and pleasant drive, I mentioned that the Agapemone farm – or
farms? – were reputed to be the best managed in Somerset. Thomas
said, "Under the old dispensation some of our Brethren were
farmers. Would you like to visit Brother Prince's room?"
I said I should first like to ask him four or five questions. He bowed,
and bent himself to answer; but seemed ill at ease while we
remained alone. Our talk was now and then broken by the entrance
of some sister who slipped into the room, listened for a moment,
then went away. I began to see that it is not the habit of this place
to allow any brother or sister to hold private conversations with a
guest. Each Saint appears to keep watch upon his fellow. Prince
may dwell apart and hold himself accountable to none, but his
people only speak in each other's presence, moving in pairs, trios,
and septets. I was soon struck by the fact that I was never left
alone with either man or woman, a thing I never experienced in
the homes of either German or American Saints. If we lounged in
the lovely greenhouse, took a turn in the garden, idled about the

stables and offices, either Sister Ellen, Sister Annie, or some other lady would slip in quietly to our side, and take her share in any talk that might be going on. In short, some sister kept me in sight and hearing until I drove away from the Abode of Love.

I first asked the reason for the high wall that Professor Dawkins says surrounds the estate. Thomas said, "There is no such wall. Dawkins may have got the idea from an equally mistaken local guide book. Soon after coming here we had a short length of wall built on the road-ward side of this church, to stop neighbouring rustics gazing in at us through the windows. They used to do that."
"Why do you keep bloodhounds?"
"We have none now but once we needed their protection. On several occasions we were physically assaulted by neighbours. In public."
"Did you not seek redress through the courts?"
"Yes. We were awarded a farthing damages. It is now said that anyone can knock down four of us for a penny."
Thomas cut short my four or five questions by leaving the room. In a minute he returned to offer me food – a cup of coffee, a biscuit, a glass of wine. Being fresh from my early meal and cigar I was declining his offer with thanks when his way of pressing his little courtesies struck me as like the manner of an Arab sheik, who offers you bread and salt, not simply as food but as a sign of peace.
"Let it be a glass of wine."
A woman brought in a tray with biscuits and two decanters; one of good dry sherry, the other of a sweet new port. She laid them on a table, bid me help myself and left. For half an hour I was left alone with these two bottles in the church.

Yes; in the church; lounging on a red sofa, near a bright fire, in the coloured light of a high lancet window filled with rich stained glass; soft cushions beneath my feet; a billiards table on my right; oak panelling round the walls; and above my head the sacred symbol of the Lamb and Dove, flanked and supported by a rack of billiard cues. This room, I knew, was that in which the Great Manifestation had taken place; that mystic rite through which living flesh is said to have been reconciled to God. Lovely to the eye, calming to the heart, this chamber was, and is. A rich red Persian

carpet covered the floor, in contrast with the brown oaken roof.
Red curtains draped the windows, the glass in which was painted
a mystical device, a lamb, a lion and a dove – the lion standing on
a bed of roses, with a banner on which these words are inscribed,

OH, HAIL, HOLY LOVE!

The chimneypiece was a fine oak frame of Gothic work, let in
with mirrors. A harp stood in one corner of the room; a large
euterpean in another. A few books, not much used, lay on the tables
– Young's *Night Thoughts*, a *Turner Gallery*, Wordsworth's *Greece*
and a few more. Ivory balls lay on the green baize as if the Sisters
had been recently at play. The whole room had in it a hush and
splendour which affected the imagination with a kind of awe. How
could I help thinking of that mystic drama in which Brother Prince
had played the part of hero, "Madonna" Paterson the part of
heroine? I was suddenly surprized by the feeling of being closely
watched from very near. Yes! A face was pressed against the lowest
part of a window opposite, the face of a small child with large,
sad, questioning eyes. It disappeared as the First Anointed One
returned.

Euterpean –
a machine
with
revolving
cylinders that
played
symphonies
and opera
overtures.

"Do you work and play on Sundays?" I enquired.

"We have no Sundays," he replied; "all days with us are Sabbaths,
and everything we do is consecrated to the Lord. Will you now
come in to see Brother Prince?"

"Oh, yes," I answered softly; and the keeper of the Seven Stars
and the Seven Golden Candlesticks led the way.

"Good day sir; I am glad to see you; take this chair," said a
gentleman in black, with sweet, grave face, a broad white neckcloth,
and shining leather shoes. He had come to meet me at the door; he
led me quietly into a luxurious parlour, and seated me in an easy
chair beside the fire. The room was like a lady's boudoir; the
furniture was rich and good; the chairs were cosy; and the
ornaments were of the usual kind. I had come to Spaxton from a
country house; and nothing in the room appeared to be much unlike
what I had left behind, except the men and women.

Prince sat in a semicircle of his elect; one brother and two
sisters on either side, the Rev. Samuel Starky on the far left, the

Rev. George R. Thomas on the far right. Starky, eldest and whitest of my seven hosts was a tall, stout man of sixty-one years, with mild blue eyes, a little weak and wandering in expression. His name was well known in these Somerset dales and woods, among the gentry of which the Starkys had always held their heads very high. Next to Starky were Sister Ellen and Sister Zoe; next to Thomas were Sister Annie and Sister Sarah. Two of the four ladies would have been thought comely in any place and one was very lovely. Sister Annie was a fine model of female beauty in middle life; plump, rosy, ripe; with a pair of laughing eyes, a full red cheek, and ripples of curling dark brown hair. Some softness of the place lay on her as on all the rest; hush in her movement, waiting in her eyes, silence on her lips. She was the only woman I saw at Spaxton who seemed in perfect health.

The second lady, Sister Zoe, was one of those rare feminine creatures who lash poets into song, who drive artists to despair, and cause common mortals to risk their souls for love. You saw, in time, that the woman was young, and lithe, and dressed in the purest taste; but you could not see all this at once; for when you came into her presence you saw nothing save the whiteness of her brow, the marble-like composure of her face, the wondrous light of her big blue eyes. She sat there, nestling by the side of Prince; in a robe of white stuff, with violet tags and drops, the tiny streaks of colour throwing out into relief the creamy paleness of her cheek. But for the gleaming light in her eye, Guercino might have painted her as one of his rapt and mourning angels. I do not know that I have ever seen a face more full of high, serene, and happy thoughts; yet gazing on her folded hands and saintly brows, an instinct in my blood compelled me, much against my will, to think of her in connection with that scene which had taken place in the adjoining church; the strangest mystery, perhaps the darkest iniquity of these days; through which Prince asserts, and Thomas testifies, that God has reconciled living flesh unto Himself. Of the other two ladies I shall only say that Sister Sarah is young and tall, and Sister Ellen about fifty-five years old. I was not told what names these ladies had been called in the world outside.

Wishing to learn if Sister Zoe and "Madonna" Paterson were
one, I asked by what name I should speak to her.

"Zoe," she replied.

"But think," I urged; "I am a stranger; how can I use that sweet, familiar name?"

"Pray do so," answered Zoe; "it is very nice."

"No doubt; if I were here a month; meantime it would be easier for me to call you Miss – "

"Call me Zoe," she answered with a patient smile, "Zoe; nothing but Zoe."

Looking toward Prince I said, "Do your people take new names on coming into residence, like the monks and nuns of an Italian convent?"

"Not like monks and nuns," said Prince; "we do not put ourselves under the protection of our saints. We have no saints. We simply give ourselves to God, of whom this mansion is the seat. At yonder gates we leave the world behind; its words, its laws, its passions; all of which are things of the Devil's kingdom. Living in the Lord, we follow His leading light, even in the simple matter of our names. They call me Belovéd. I call this lady Zoe, because the sound pleases me. I call Thomas there Mossoo, because he speaks French so well."

I never got beyond this point with the Saints. When bidding them goodbye I said to Zoe, holding her hand in mine, "May I not hear some word to know you by when I am far away?"

"Yes; Zoe," she said, and smiled.

"Zoe . . . what else?"

Her thin lips parted as if to speak. Was the name that rose to her lips . . . Paterson? Who knows? With her fingers linked in mine she turned to Prince, and whispered in melting tones, "Belovéd!" Prince told me in a voice of playful softness; "She is Zoe; you must think of her as Zoe; nothing else."

The gentleman called Belovéd by his followers is fifty-six years old, spare in person with the traces of much pain and weariness on his pale cheek. His face is very sweet, his manner very smooth, his smile very soft and the key of his voice is low. He has about him something of a woman's grace and charm, and in his eyes which were apt to close, you seemed to see a light

Frock here
means Frock
coat, knee-
length and
thinner than
an overcoat,
worn instead
of what is
now usually
called a
jacket.

from some other sphere. As we sat before his warm and cheery fire he seemed at once rapt into his own dreams. When the sound of voices roused him he crossed his hands upon his black frock, put his shiny shoes on the rug and bore a luxurious part in a long, singular conversation.

"You hold," I asked him, " that the day of grace is past?"

"We know it is; the day of judgement is at hand."

"You expect the world to pass away?"

"The old world is no more. God has withdrawn us from it."

"How many are you in the Abode?", I asked.

"About sixty souls in all."

At this moment a manservant, dressed in sober black came into the room. I said, "You count the domestics in that number?"

"Yes. They are all members of our family and share its blessings."

"Do you take the service needed in the house, each in turn, like the Brethren and Sisters of Mount Lebanon?" (I saw a faint smile ripple on the servant's face.)

"Oh no," broke in upon us Sister Ellen; "we do nothing of that kind; our people serve us; but they do it for love."

"Do you mean that they serve you without being paid?"

The only reply to my question was a laugh from the lady and a grin from the domestic.

"Among these sixty inmates, how many are male and female? How many are young, how many grown up?"

"The sexes are nearly equal," answered Thomas, "there are no children."

"None at all?" I asked, thinking of the Great Manifestation, and what was said to have come of it.

"You do not understand the life we live here in the Lord. Those who married in the world aforetime now live as though they had not. We are as the angels in Heaven and have no craving after devil's love."

"What do you wish me to understand as devil's love?"

"Love that is of the flesh – all love not holy, spiritual, and of God."

"Have I not just seen a child through the church window? A little girl playing on the lawn?"

Prince seemed to be dreaming again. Thomas said with deep

emotion, "She is a child of shame – a broken link in our line of life
– Satan's offspring in the flesh."

A look of anguish clouded all their faces except Sister Zoe's, whose sweetly serene countenance was quite unmoved.

"The work of that time," put in Sister Ellen with a sigh, "was the saddest thing I have ever known. For a whole year we lay in the shadow of death, and near to hell; but God wrought out His purpose in us. It was a bitter time for all but most for our Belovéd."

Poor little girl!

"Your rule of life is now – a rule of abstinence?"

"It is the rule of angels," answered Prince. "we live in love, but not in sin; for sin is death and our life in the Lord is eternal."

"Yet surely all men die?"

"Yes," said Thomas, "they have mostly done so; but death is subject to the Lord in whom we live. We shall not die. We have no such thought."

"But some among you have passed away; Louisa Nottidge, for example?"

"Yes, some erred and the Lord took them; but many examples do not make a necessary rule. If I saw the valley outside our Abode choking with ten thousand corpses, the sight would not convince me that I too would one day die."

"Where do you put the departed ones?"

"Some are buried at the farm, some rest under the green lawn. We think that all bodies not saved eternally by Christ go back into the earth from which they sprang."

"But you are all growing older! As more of you drop away you will be forced to see that death will come."

"Not so," said Belovéd, "we will never expect death. Death is a word that belongs to time."

"But everyone lives in time."

"You live in time. We do not."

"You see the sun rise and set," I urged, "you know that yesterday was Friday, that tomorrow will be Sunday; that springtime passes and the harvest comes about."

"Well, yes," said Belovéd in a pitying tone, "we feel the flow you must take as your measure of time. It is no sign of change to us, who dwell for ever in the living God."

Such is the Abode of Love. A dozen ardent clergymen, smitten with a passion to save souls, possessing power to warn and softness to persuade, after various grapplings with the world have left their posts and shut themselves up in a garden where they muse and dream, surrounding themselves with lovely women, eating from rich tables, pretending that their passions are dead, and waiting, in the midst of luxury and idleness, for the whole world to be damned!

Is this all? No; not quite all: in the meantime the reverend gentlemen play a game of billiards in what was once their church.

28: TAILPIECE

Hale Holy Love!   Hale Holy Love!

TO THE END OF HIS LIFE the Reverend Henry James Prince kept a strangely ageless look that attracted new followers as the original ones died. In 1892 he converted to his faith another equally charismatic Anglican priest, John Hugh Smyth-Pigott, then aged thirty. In London Smyth-Pigott repeated the Prince story of fifty years earlier by gaining a large congregation with a core of professional men (stockbroker, chartered accountant, tax collector, civil engineer, architect, master baker) and several hundred ardent female admirers. Like Prince's early followers these combined to build for Smyth-Pigott and Prince a unique church, but much larger and more splendidly ornate, in what was then known as the "muscular Gothic" style. It was called The Ark of the Covenant, on Rookwood Road, Hackney. The cathedral-like spire is visible for miles around, and the beautiful stained-glass windows are designed by Walter Crane. This church opened with a service of dedication attended by Brother Prince in 1896. Every seat was crammed with eager followers, apart from some allocated to the press and public. After the dedication Prince finally retired for the last time to his Agapemone at Spaxton, Somerset.

In the last year of the 19th century the chief Agapemone housekeeper sent word that the impossible seemed to be happening: Brother Prince was dying. Smyth-Pigott hurried to the bedside and found Henry almost unable to speak, but according to the few people present his last word was spoken to this, the most powerful of all his disciples. The word was "Belovéd!"

*The Abode of
Love*: a
Memoir by
Kate Barlow,
issued by
Mainstream
Publishing
Company
(Edinburgh)
Ltd, 2006.

What follows is described by Kate Barlow, Smyth-Pigott's granddaughter, in her book about him and how he prolonged the Agapemone into the 20th century –
"Prince's followers were confused, appalled and frightened by his death. When others had died it had been easy to dismiss their parting as a failure on their part, but Brother Prince? Surely not. It took all my grandfather's considerable skill to soothe the confused faithful and at the same time get the old man laid to rest in the garden of the Somerset Abode of Love in what I was to know as Katie's corner."

Twenty-Nine
Tunnock's Diary
2006

I never listened consciously to popular songs but as a student heard them on juke boxes when every café and pub had them instead of television sets. Nowadays phrases from them come to mind for no apparent reason. I awoke this morning with the tune of these words in my head: Hey mister tambourine man sing a song for me, I'm lonely as can be, I'm lonely and I don't know where I'm goin'. I was not lonely. I was cuddling Zoe which always makes me feel thoroughly happy and good. I had made my arms and body like a basket holding her, keeping her warm and safe and both of us at peace. Yes indeed.

These lines of the Bob Dylan song are misquoted.

Having completed Victorian English tale will I resume Classical Greek? Or Renaissance Italian? Or Scottish history from big bang till now? Where will I get the knowledge, strength, enthusiasmos to continue one of these? As the second policeman says, this is a compound crux, an almost insoluble pancake. Until a solution is found this diary must contain my furor scribendi.

Greek: enthusiasm. The second policeman is a character in Flann O'Brien's The Third Policeman. Furor scribendi – Latin for writing fever.

But how can I stop her bringing terrible people to the house? Last night one of them, a big lad with a bright blue saltire tattooed on his ugly mug, brandished a switch blade when I told him "fucking" was not an adjective appropriate to every noun. I was terrified, may have gone pale but stared frigidly back. Zoe lost her temper and made him apologize. Why did he fear her more than he hated me? Why does she invite him here? That's the third time. I can't believe they are lovers. Should I ask her to come drinking with me? She would meet nobody like that in Tennants, but going public with her would be a step toward proposing marriage. Query: is that what she wants? O my God, of course that's what she wants. Well she won't get it. Should I accompany her to the Dumbarton

*Road pubs where she drinks? But that might not stop her inviting
ruffians back with us on leaving. Another insoluble pancake.*

*This has been an odd year that began with winter prolonged
through an extra month, not by frost and snow – for decades snow
starts to thaw as soon as it falls in Glasgow – but by occasional
sunlit days, each followed by two or three rainy ones. In Hillhead
gardens and parks the trees were bare branched far into May,
then suddenly in less than a week it seemed that buds unfurled,
exploded into dense varieties of lovely green, followed by a warm
bright season refreshed by a few cool moist days, a season that
has not stopped. Toward the 20th century's end I noticed a few
chairs and tables appearing on the pavement before some Byres
Road snack bars. I did not notice the increase of this practice (due
to global warming?) until recently, but Hillhead on fine evenings
and weekends has an astonishingly Parisian look. I believe a social
history of Glasgow – of Britain! – could appear in a short
description of how Hillhead shops have changed in the last sixty
years, if we count Byres Road and the adjacent part of Great
Western Road. Here goes!*

In my childhood and student days the main Hillhead streets
had all the small useful provision shops found in any British
country town or large village. They included a Woolworths,
two Post Offices (the biggest with a sorting and telegram office),
two bookshops (one of them second-hand), a cobbler or shoe
repair shop, and a clock mender. I do not remember who
mended defective radios, gramophones (as record players were
called), hoovers and other household appliances, but think it
was done by taking them to shops where we had bought them.
Hillhead had at least three restaurants of a sort called tea-
rooms, where genteel women like my aunts took afternoon
tea or sometimes a lunch they regarded as dinner. The many
university students lodging here ensured customers for many
pubs, cafés, fish-and-chip shops. There must have been an
estate agent's office somewhere but I cannot remember it.

A change began in the 1970s when two big, useful, well

supplied hardware shops closed, the owner of one telling me
he could no longer afford to pay the increased rates. It may
not be a coincidence that a mile away in Anniesland a huge
B&Q arrived selling every sort of household tool and appliance
but mending none. There is still a shop selling clocks and
jewellery, and twenty years ago I took in a very pretty little
clock presented to me by my staff when I left Molendinar
Primary. They had several of the same kind for sale, but
explained that mending it would cost me £7.50 but I could
buy a new one for £5.50. Then a big supermarket opened at
the top of Byres Road and soon the butchers and most small
provision shops vanished leaving only one shop I remember
from childhood, selling fish and game. The others have been
taken by several glossy estate agents' offices that can easily
pay the district councils high rates, and many second-hand or
foreign craft shops largely exempt from rates by being
registered charities, and which are mostly staffed by voluntary
workers. Other shops are chiefly staffed by young folk who
know nothing about the manufacture and quality of what they
sell, do not even need to know arithmetic because cash
machines do their addition, multiplication and subtraction.
Universal state education was made the law in 1870 Britain
because (as Napoleon said) Britain was a nation of
shopkeepers, highly productive ones, who could not have
lasted as long as they did without a big workforce able to
read, write and count. A Victorian statesman who had hitherto
opposed state education because it might lead to social
revolution of the French sort, now publically announced, "We
must now educate our new masters!" and became foremost
in committees that ensured state schools taught children:
1) to sit still in rows,
2) to never question a teacher,
3) to only talk when asked by a teacher,
4) to *learn*, not *think*.
This system was imperfect because it enlarged the middle class
with more teachers than could be drawn from its upper ranks.
Many of these liked thinking and encouraged it in some of the
state-funded schools, generally called Board Schools because

This was
Robert Lowe,
Liberal
chancellor of
the
Exchequer
and wholly
opposed to
democracy
in Britain

Britain is a Kingdom whose governments don't want to rule a state. But the increase of literate thinking people in Britain led to the founding of the old Labour Party, though the people who governed Britain still graduated from those ancient privatized English schools misleadingly called Public. These no longer care if or what the state schools now teach, since productive British industries are now reduced to banking and weapons manufacture. The owners of British shops and stores fill them with goods packaged in outsourced factories.

Outsourced is postmodern slang for run more cheaply in foreign lands.

The genteel Byres Road tea-rooms are long gone, but many more restaurants, cafes and pubs have opened there or in back lanes. The customers are partly the local middle class enriched by the privatisation of public wealth begun in Thatcher's reign, and partly Glasgow University students who have been more than doubled by a huge intake of students from abroad. They are taken because their fees make up for the lost student grants once paid by the government, so the entrance qualifications have been lowered and in some courses the standard of teaching. Students from poorer families support themselves with bank loans or by working locally as waiters and bar tenders or some other counter job. Their wages are often less than the minimum that European regulations are meant to impose. The two Post Offices are closed but packages can be posted from the back of a Pakistani general dealer.

Will think about other changes I have seen in Hillhead streets.

This festival, was started by local town councillors and business people acting unofficially, helped by Michael Dale, former Edinburgh Festival Fringe organiser.

After Zoe left on her mysterious businesses this morning I stayed in, brooding brooding brooding on which avenue of research to explore in the library, then grew aware of distant crowd susurrations punctuated by erratic music. The West End Festival had started. Don't know who organizes this which has happened for several years, closing upper Byres Road to motor traffic, replacing it with funfair stalls, a bouncy castle, musicians on platforms, and filling the street wall to wall with mobile citizens. Have avoided it hitherto but today was strangely attracted. Wandered there and among the huge undisciplined genial crowd,

bathing in it, enjoying I suppose the mild communal ecstasy Walt
Whitman enjoyed in 19th century Manhattan. I lunched at a table
outside the Antipasti, pondering the great changes in people's
clothing for the Byres Road history.

Before the 1970s I think nearly half of all women over thirty-five in Hillhead wore skirts or dresses. Now only a minority of young women do, mostly girls in the brown or green skirts that are the Notre Dame and Laurelbank school uniforms. I believe women's trouser suits became fashionable in the 1960s and miniskirts in the 1970s, and when I first saw each I was amused, thinking them not at all sexually attractive, but in a few days they started exciting me as I suppose any eye-catching women's fashion always will. I was glad when the Turkish bare midriff became fashionable before the 20th century ended. I have always liked women's stomachs, perhaps because as a child I believed sexual intercourse was through the navel. At the same time young folk, not all of them women, began sporting tattoos, also studs and rings through parts of their faces. Though used to earrings I hate seeing that. I cannot help thinking it painful. Hey ho. But the main fashion change is in pockets.

These were once only seen in army uniforms and workers' overalls. Professional folk and people at leisure wore trousers, jackets and blazers with pockets sewn within the linings to interrupt, as little as possible, the body's outline. A single breast pocket in jackets was sometimes made noticeable by a protruding fountain pen or, on formal occasions the triangular corner of a neatly folded white handkerchief. Women's dresses and skirts had no pockets, so they carried handbags. It is now not fashionable to look suave and neat in modern Britain so every garment I saw from my pavement table had external pockets of the workmen or military kind. On baggy jeans several looked as big as buckets. Some big pockets had small ones on top. There were jeans with four or five pairs of pockets, some at ankle level. Miniskirts also had them. They were fastened by a variety of buttons, buckles, studs and zips. Girls in slim jeans only had them on hip pockets where, seen in motion from behind, they pleasantly emphasized the changing balance of the buttocks, but baggier trousers were more frequent, often made tougher-looking by conspicuous seams. Some women's jeans have the oblique canvas strip at the side for tradesmen to sling their hammers, and I saw a skirt with that too. Nearly all clothing suggest the wearers are ready for hard work, while some were deliberately torn to suggest they had suffered rough treatment, why? Saw one slim, attractive girl with huge ragged holes through which were visible expensive stockings with a delicate openwork pattern of leaves and fruit. And amidst the brightly coloured stalls, bouncy castle, balloons and candyfloss most clothes were black, khaki or blue-grey.

But police clothing has changed most between 20 or 30 years ago and now. The police uniform of Victorian days were intended to be quite unlike police on the European continent, most of whom wore a military style of uniform, and carried visble weapons. The dark uniform of the London Bobby did not attract the eye; his helmet was comic rather than martial; his weapon was a wooden baton carried out of sight within his uniform, unless violence erupted. This was the policy of governments who thought threatening displays would make British policemen unpopular. Nowadays our police have been re-styled on the American cop pattern with highly visible jackets in fluorescent colour and waist belts from which dangle handcuffs, radios and blunt instruments that can probably gas or stun people. While worn thus to be more rapidly used if needed, they have the effect of being flaunted. We know some carry guns but not how many, as these are probably worn out of sight, like the old batons.

After 2 p.m. the centre of Byres Road was cleared for a colourful parade emerging from the Botanic Garden gates. It was led by a band of carnival drummers and musicians followed by groups of children from local schools dressed like butterflies or wearing elephant masks or equally droll disguizes; then came   gyrating belly-dancers and bicycles

supporting fantastic frames resembling dragons, the Loch Ness
Monster, King Kong and Marilyn Monroe; also stilt-stalking
tall Mexican-Day-of-the-Dead skeletons with wreaths on their
skulls and flowers in their ribcages. I was so enraptured by
this procession that I was tempted to join in behind some ten-
year-olds in the costume of a martial arts club who marched
along striking martial postures, but eventually joined some
older people carrying the banners of the Green Movement.
We all processed down to Dumbarton Road then turned left
past the old Andersonian College to finally enter Kelvingrove
Park behind the Art Galleries. Here we mingled with the Mela
Festival, a big gathering of Glasgow Asians that had been
running all day. Wearing the brightest dresses and costumes
of their original homelands they were cooking, serving and
eating their national foodstuffs to the music of their own bands
and singers. Almost intoxicated by this abundance of new
colour I wandered back home. No wonder those who bathe
daily in sensual experience are incapable of historical thinking.
End of modern social history lesson.

---

*I am weary of unending news about British political corruption. It
has been steadily increasing along with crime at street level and
accidental shooting of innocent folk by armed police. In the 1960s*

As editor I
have been
obliged to
omit several
of Tunnock's
remarks that
I have been
advised
would make
me
actionable at
law.

*Several Tories were delighted and declared this was such a
splendidly 18ᵗʰ century response to criticism*

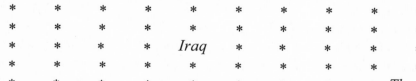

*in the 90s Blair's New Labour Party promised "an end of sleaze"
– a friendly word for corruption. I hear today that*   *   *

*   *   *   *   *   *   *   *   *   *
*   *   *   *   *   *   *   *   *   *
*   *   *   *   *   *   *   *   *   *The*

Tory Party has always been funded by rich businessmen because it exists to represent them. The Labour Party was founded to represent the common workers, so funded by the trade unions. Since New Labour has rejected the unions and courted the rich, where else can poor Blair get all the money he needs?

Sick of these thoughts I tried to change my mind yesterday (which was Sunday and warm), by wandering around Whitmanizing as I had done in the West End Festival last year. How time flies. The old Kelvinside and Botanic Gardens Free Church of Scotland is now a pub with restaurants, theatre and concert hall. In the yard between pavement and front door I joined drinkers at tables under parasols. Bought half pint, edged towards empty table in far corner, noticed ——— crouched over cup of coffee, talking rapidly as usual into mobile phone. Hoped she had not seen me but had hardly settled down when she sat opposite saying, "For three years you've not answered my postcards and never phoned me, why?"

Explained I had been inspired to write a different book from the one we had discussed, but I had worked hard and recently finished it. She said, "Has another woman got hold of you?"

"Yes!" I said sternly, "And I will not say one word to you about her because she is an essential part of my private life."

After staring hard at me ——— said, "And your public life? Have you abandoned writing about modern Scotland? Have you gone ostrich again?"

I told her that I was now a Pepys, a Boswell recording everyday life for the benefit of posterity. She said, "Then you should tell posterity the state of our refugees because the fucking Scots today don't want to know," and spoke of a Chinaman she was defending whose ancestors had cultivated a piece of land for centuries, even under the rule of Chairman Mao. But that government now deals with global capitalism so the Party sold his land, despite his protests, to a U.S.A. company that did not want him. He was promised a sum of money in compensation, but on going to collect was offered a third of that by a Party official who said legal

Since 2003 this building has been called the Oran Mor Arts and Leisure Centre.

expenses had consumed the rest. He therefore knocked the official
down with a mattock, fled from China and was briefly harboured
in Scotland as an asylum seeker. Said ———, "We called them
refugees when they were escaping from Fascist or old Communist
regimes, but now they're called asylum seekers, so no matter how
long they live here their case can be reviewed and a legal loophole
found to again shunt them out into homelessness, hopelessness,
perhaps prison and death. Did you know that an Asiatic family of
four was recently arrested here by the police at four o'clock in the
morning? The Soviet police also arrested people at that hour to
stop folk seeing their neighbours deported. This family were driven
in a windowless van to London and questioned by immigration
officials who discovered what had been officially recorded years
ago: the parents had entered Scotland as subjects of The British
Empire and the children had been born here! Well, they were
returned to Glasgow but others born and taught in schools here,
knowing no language but English, have been suddenly extradited
with their parents on a small legal technicality without right of
appeal! What do you think of that?"

Instead of answering I asked what became of the Chinaman. She
said a legal tribunal had ruled that he had no right to political
asylum here since he was obnoxious to the Chinese government
over a matter of land owning, and that was not political! She spoke
the last two words so intensely that folk nearby turned to look then
said, "Ownership of land, theft of land, depriving folk of their
birthplace is the world's first and worst political crime! I appealed
against that decision, and since my house is big enough I told a
senior judge I would give him a residence in Scotland but no!
Back to China he must go and be punished, perhaps executed for
fighting injustice because Lord Kingarth says the Chinese
Communist and American Capitalist theft of his land is not a
political matter."

At that moment I saw across the wall at my elbow Zoe passing
along Great Western Road. As usual outside home we exchanged
the slightest of glances so I was shocked when ——— said, "Is
she your new woman?"

I got up and said, "I'm leaving if you say another word about her."

"Calm down ostrich," said ———, "I'm going to get another

coffee. Another lager?" I offered to get both if she would change the subject when I returned. I came back and she talked about Glasgow's drug trade. The chiefs who invest in it and collect the profits are businessmen and property developers known to the police, but in no danger of arrest because they mix socially with local politicians who they also bribe, and never themselves handle smack, crack or other opium derivatives. Tougher criminals, also known to the police, control the source of the drug and also keep out of the public eye. The stuff is handled at street level by three classes of underling, the lowest and largest being ordinary users, many of them unemployed youngsters who often rob and mug people for money to buy it. From these the most desperate addicts are recruited to sell it in homes, pubs and lavatories. The careful and efficient among these distributors are also the least addicted, so can graduate to dealing with top suppliers and the police. The public and the press want frequent news of successful drug raids and arrests, so every week or two these smart distributors tell the drug squad where they can arrest their least useful underlings, after which they recruit others. "So Glasgow is like every other place where drugs are criminalized. Rich, secure bastards cream off the trade's profits while exploiting and buggering the poorest. If drugs were freely sold as they were before the 1960s a third of British crime would stop, our jails be half emptied, a few addicts would continue to die annually of overdoses, a lot of fat cats would be poorer and the police free to concentrate on arresting thieves, frauds and other murderers. So in Britain and the U.S.A. the use of all drugs but alcohol and nicotine will be kept criminal despite Baroness Wooton's government committee in the 1960s announcing that marijuana is safer."

This was more than I could stand. I am going to avoid ————— because she is trying to start a drug rehabilitation unit and wants me to help her! I hurried away under pretext of needing to pee and came home, terribly depressed.

Tonight there erupted into Tennants the historian Angus Calder who hailed the Mastermind, sat down and talked enthusiastically. He had come from a Glasgow meeting of Independence First group who want a referendum to find how many Scots want a truly independent parliament. Public opinion polls show a high likelihood of the Scot Nats having a majority at the Scottish Parliamentary Election next month. He said, *"Next year is the 300th anniversary of the Anglo-Scottish Union of Parliaments and a major chance to show we do not want it – that we are sick of Scotland being used as a NATO military and nuclear missile base by the English government, and deprived of every industry that the Scots pioneered, and once made Scotland famous."*

Said Mastermind, *"You seem in pursuit of an old-fashioned Scotland running on Owenite New Lanark lines, in fact a Scottish Socialist Co-operative Wholesale Republic. But Alex Salmond and others in that party are promising better investment opportunities to businessmen, and at least one is urging total privatisation of hospitals."*

"Every good government must encourage productive business, and have a right-wing and left-wing party. When a separate Scottish Parliament has signed a new, fairer peace treaty with England than the 1707 Treaty the Scottish National Party will vanish and I believe the new Scotland will make Norway its example, not the Channel Islands."

"What if the London government refuses to sign a new treaty allowing an independent Scottish one?"

"With a majority of voters on our side we can appeal to the European Parliament."

I was amused to hear this English Socialist from Edinburgh discussing Scotland's future with an English Tory in Glasgow. Calder does not know me by sight so kindly old Mastermind interrupted his torrent of speech by bringing me into the conversation. When he mentioned my name Calder murmured, *"Tunnock? John Tunnock?"* and stared hard at me before asking sharply, *"How's your work going?"*

"What work?"

"Your great historical triptych or trilogy about love, sex, money, art, politics and everything. It starts in Athens. I read several chapters in Chapman a few months ago."

"A few years", I told him.

"How's it going?"

"Nowhere. You wrote a letter that destroyed my ambitions in that direction."

"How can I possibly have done that?" he cried, astonished.

"You persuaded me that the historical fiction I planned was escapist fantasy. You urged me to write about Scotland instead. I tried that and failed."

"I remember writing what I meant to be an encouraging letter because I liked the start of your novel. Most historical fiction is trash of course, because most of every kind of fiction is trash, but I am second to none in my admiration for Walter Scott at his best. He created, single-handed, a new kind of novel and a new school of social historians. Read what Carlyle, Thiers, Michelet and Ranke say about him as well as Pushkin, Balzac and Manzoni. I refuse to be found guilty of a crime I never committed. Those chapters you wrote about Periclean Athens were damned good."

I explained the impossibility of describing The Clouds performance.

"Leave it out."

I told him there was a worse problem: my story had to end with the trial of Socrates. Plato's account showed a wholly good, wise man being condemned to death by a democratic court merely because he was too good for it. I too believed Socrates was wise and good. I also believed the democracy had a strong case against him that Plato had not acknowledged. I could only show the strength of the democracy's case by bringing in witnesses who were dead or in exile at the time of the trial. How could I possibly do that? Calder said, "Do what Walter Scott did in Quentin Durward. Tell a historical story as well as you can and put notes at the end saying where you departed from the record but don't blame me for your difficulties."

He downed his drink, jumped up and rushed off.

"A precipitate fellow, but not unwise," rumbled Mastermind.

It was far from closing time but I left Tennants soon after, excited and buoyant. Leave out The Clouds chapter? What other chapters could I omit before tackling The Trial of Socrates, for which the others were mainly introductory? At home I emptied pigeonholes of my research notes for The Plague, Death of Pericles, The Sicilian Expedition, Victorious Sparta, The Tyranny of The Nine and laid them out in chronological order on desktop, sideboard, sofa and

armchairs and mantelpiece. If Zoe brought people home tonight
she would have to entertain them in the dining room downstairs. I
was awed by the idea of condensing all these preparatory notes
into a few sentences of The Trial. Was pleased when Zoe returned
without horrible company and stood staring, never having seen
me so enthusiastically at work before. She said, "Why are you
buzzing about like a bee in a bottle?"

I explained why and pointed to the sideboard, suggesting we drink
to celebrate the birth of a grand new idea that would let my original
masterpiece – my life task! – be completed in two or three months
instead of years. She poured me a big whisky and herself a small
one, "You need a holiday."

I denied that because from now on I would be working hard every
day and evening. She said she was not suggesting a long holiday –
just a night or weekend away. I said fine, where did she want us to
go? She said it was me who needed the holiday, not her. I said,
"I'm not taking a holiday by myself!"

She said, "Of course not. I'll get somebody to go with you, what
about Is? You're keen on Is. She introduced us."

That was gibberish. I told her Isobel had never introduced us
because she (Zoe) had introduced herself. She said, "Aye, alright,
but I can get you someone else you'll like, someone younger than
me – I'm ancient."

I told her I didn't want anyone but her. She sighed and spoke slowly
like a schoolmistress to a stupid but not hopeless pupil. She said
something like this:

"I've an important job coming up. It will look like a party but it's
really a business meeting. A lot of folk you wouldnae like will be
here and they wouldnae like you so take the night off. I'll book you
into the Buchanan Arms Hotel near Drymen with Is or Mish or
anybody else you want. I think I could even get Niki back for a
night without Mo, if you're keen. I know all kinds of lassies who'll
let you do anything you want with them without you having to pay
a penny."

I sat down because this speech made me feel crippled in every
limb. At last I said I loved her.

"Same back," she said, "but I really do need this place for a night
without you around. I'll tell you why. It's like this –"

I interrupted, saying I wanted to know NOTHING about her business because it was obviously a business no respectable householder would ever want to know. My house had once been the manse of Hillhead Parish Church. My mother and aunts and I had spent most of our lives here and I would not let her (Zoe) turn it into a den of thieves. I don't know why that biblical phrase popped out of me but it impressed Zoe. She went pale, said I could stay at home if I just locked myself in our bedroom for five or six hours and pretended nothing was happening outside it. I said, "Meet your strange pals in one of their own houses."
She said, "I wouldnae be safe if I did."
"Then you should get rid of them," I said firmly, "they must not come here," and busied myself again with my papers. She said, "But that could get me into a lot of trouble – you too."
In coarse demotic Glaswegian I told her I wasnae feart, and heard her leave the room, then the front door slam as she left the house. This was our first quarrel, but if my experience of Niki, Yvonne etcetera is anything to go by it will not be the last. She did not come home last night but I am certain she will return soon. This waiting would drive me mad if Who Paid for all This? was not occupying nine-tenths of my acting intelligence.

That title, however, will no longer suit a trilogy that contains my Belovéd Prince Henry, no no no, I will call it Money at Play, and to Hell with the muscles of worn-out workmen, the broken hearts and crazed brains of defeated women and children and what is happening now in Scotland. Concentrate on the trial of Socrates.

Professor Moignard teaches classics in the University of Glasgow, does not drink in Tennants, but was Tunnock's neighbour in Hillhead.

I once thought it was held on a hillside west of the Acropolis where the Athenian parliament met, but Elizabeth Moignard says the likeliest place was the council house on the marketplace. The entrance lobby before the trial started would be thronged by folk wanting jury service as trade would not have recovered from the Athenian empire's collapse three years earlier, so a juror's wage was desirable. The selection process must have been lengthy, being designed to ensure parity between three main voting districts: the high ground where farmers and tradesmen lived; the plain with its owners of rich estates; the coast where lived merchants, dockers and seamen. There must have been many arguments between court officials chosen by lot and citizens who felt unfairly excluded. It

would be afternoon before all 899 jurors were admitted: a number
ensuring votes for and against the accused were never even. Since the president was chosen by lot I will make him the farmer who did most of the talking in my first chapter. There was no Athenian legal profession so trials were run like the Athenian parliament. Any citizen could denounce another in court, then the accused spoke in their own defence, then innocence or guilt was decided by a majority vote.

Plato says Socrates was accused by someone put up to the job by Anytus, a dealer in leather who had recently fought to depose the tyrants installed by Sparta. But the reasons for the trial will be clearer if Anytus is on stage instead of a front man. I imagine him tall, gaunt and tense, standing to one side of the president's chair, talking to a group of supporters as the jurors settle into their places. Socrates, of course, stands on the other side of the chair chatting cheerfully to friends. The siege of Potidia is now twenty years ago. Socrates is seventy with bald, wrinkled brow above alert eyes, piggy nose, bushy white moustache and beard. His hands are clasped on a stout walking stick over which he sometimes leans to hear someone talking quietly to him. His friends would not be noticed in isolation, but their characters and manners are so different that together they look distinctly odd.

I will follow the example of Plato in writing out the trial like a play of speeches between accuser and accused, but my courtroom drama will have four witnesses Plato never refers to, also a noisier jury.

30: THE TRIAL OF SOCRATES

THE JURORS' HUBBUB is interrupted by an official striking a gong, ringing a bell or smiting a board with a mallet. Silence begins to fall as our old friend the farmer, looking like any other venerable citizen, stands up in front of the presidential chair while Anytus and Socrates settle into chairs on each side of him, Socrates sitting comfortably with hands folded on top of the stick between his legs.

PRESIDENT: Men of Athens, the trial is starting! Will that gaggle at the back please shut up? Worse than women some of you. Alright Anytus. State the charge and give your reasons. (*He sits.*)

Anytus, standing up, speaks calmly, clearly.

ANYTUS: Socrates is a criminal, firstly by not believing in the Gods of our nation; secondly, by preaching a false God of his own; thirdly, by corrupting our young men. If you agree with me then you must also agree that the proper punishment is death.

Men of Athens, we all know Socrates. He's a charming old fellow, an eccentric, knows the richest men in Athens and dresses like a scarecrow. He's seventy, a widower remarried with a grownup son and two infants, yet the people he loves most are attractive young men. Most of us were children when he gave up his business and became an expert. He stood about the public places like the others; he talked enthusiastically like the others; he acquired followers just like the others; but he never gave public lectures and nobody knew what he was expert at. The other experts were wise about something – politics, medicine, arithmetic, the stars. Socrates mentioned these but didn't seem specially keen on any. Most of us thought him an ambitious simpleton, a fool who wanted to be wise but didn't know how to do it. There was a joke at the time: "What is Socrates wise about?" Answer: "He's wise about wisdom." Then one day a disciple of his asked the oracle of Apollo at Delphi who was the wisest man in Greece and the oracle said "Socrates" –

Socrates starts shaking his head from side to side.

ANYTUS: – The joke stopped being funny then, it had become the truth. Why are you shaking your head Socrates, don't you agree with the oracle?

SOCRATES: The oracle did not say that. A friend of mine asked if anyone in Greece was wiser than me. She said "No."

ANYTUS: But you agree some people are wiser than others?

SOCRATES: Yes.

ANYTUS: So you must agree that a few must be wiser than the rest?

SOCRATES: Mm . . . Yes!

ANYTUS: Of that few two or three will be wisest of all?

SOCRATES: (*gravely*) I'm afraid you're right.

ANYTUS: Have you ever been in the company of two or three equally wise men, Socrates? Wasn't one always wiser than the others? And wasn't he always you?
Some laughter in court.

SOCRATES: (*clapping his hands cheerfully*) Well done Anytus!

ANYTUS: (*smiling thinly*) Charming isn't he? I agree with the oracle. Socrates is the wisest man. And where does he get his wisdom? His followers say he hears a demon, a voice within his brain or heart or belly – exactly where do you hear it, Socrates?

SOCRATES: I don't know Anytus, I'm not hot on anatomy.

ANYTUS: (*fiercely*) Never mind! That demon, that voice is your god, Socrates and beside it the eternal Father of Heaven and lesser gods of our nation are – not your enemies for a man takes his enemies seriously – they're toys; our gods are toys to you, aren't they? Aren't they?

SOCRATES: Well –

PRESIDENT: Wait a minute! Anytus, is that question rhetorical or do you want it answered now?

ANYTUS: Let him answer it in his defence speech.

PRESIDENT: If you direct rhetorical questions to the jury in future you'll make my job a lot easier.

Anytus nods and addresses the jury, starting quietly.

ANYTUS: If a man lives among us with an extra, perhaps divine source of wisdom how should he use it? I say he should use it to instruct and help people. All the people. If he sees our laws are wrong he should seek to change them by speaking in parliament. If he has friends – and Socrates has many – he can be made a magistrate or ambassador because our democracy has always been able to use superior intelligences. But Socrates prefers to teach *special* people. Look at his disciples over there! Yes, there's a ragged coat or two among them but most are rich and half are very young. And what does the Socratic demon teach these rich young men? It teaches them about goodness. Goodness fascinates Socrates like a beautiful child fascinates a pederast. He can't leave it alone. Mention love, justice, courage and he's on to you at once. "What is love? What is justice? Are they good? Is goodness not sometimes a badness? Are the things we call bad not sometimes very good indeed?"

Well, I'm no expert, I'm an Athenian citizen who loves his city, so I'll remind you of the effects of this teaching on rich young men who heard it. Not long ago we lost a great war and a great empire by the treachery of that man's *darling* pupil. The Spartans destroyed our democracy and set up a bloody dictatorship of our richest citizens. Three pupils of Socrates were among them and the richest of all was head of it! Never mind! Democracy has been restored and that man is continuing to spread his evil wisdom. Let us hear how he does it. Can I call a witness Mr President?

PRESIDENT: (*looking at a paper in his hand*) Yes, but I must ask the court to refrain from demonstrations of disapproval. We'll never get at the truth without some intelligent self-restraint. You're all Athenians, so show it.

ANYTUS: (*loudly*) Alcibiades!

Murmurs from the crowd as Alcibiades strolls on stage. Forty, still strikingly handsome in semi-military dress, he stands at ease with fists on hips, facing the jurors and looking slightly amused. He does not look at Anytus who is a little way behind him and equally ignores Socrates, who watches him wistfully.

ANYTUS: I want to summarize your political career.

ALCIBIADES: Why? Evwybody knows it.

ANYTUS: A few have short memories. We used to call you the Darling of Athens. You were the nephew of the great Pericles, and a rich playboy, and a popular war leader.

ALCIBIADES: (*ruefully*) Long, long ago.

ANYTUS: At the height of the war, when Athens and Sparta were about to sign a peace treaty, you got it rejected by telling both sides a pack of lies.

ALCIBIADES: (*sighing*) I was ambitious.

ANYTUS: Ambitious, yes. You tricked us into invading Sicily. You led a gigantic army out there which ought to have been defending our empire at home.

ALCIBIADES: Yes, it was a gamble. (*smiling*) Think how *wich* we'd have been if we'd won!

ANYTUS: How *could* we win? You turned traitor and deserted to the Spartans before we even engaged them! Our army was . . . (*shakes head and shrugs, helplessly*) . . . destroyed. Massacred. Except for the few who were allowed to surrender and become slaves. A few still trickle back to us sometimes. Cripples, with brands on their brows. From the quarries of Syracuse.

Silence in court has almost the pressure of an explosive uproar.

ALCIBIADES: (*coolly*) I wish I had led that army. It could have won.

ANYTUS: You deserted to the enemy!

ALCIBIADES: Nowhere else to go, old boy. Your lot – the majority party – were sending the police to awest me.

ANYTUS: (*loudly*) On a charge of heresy! We had proof that you and a parcel of rich young degenerates had been acting obscene parodies of the most sacred ceremony in our religion. The ceremony . . . (*suddenly, in a low voice*) . . . the ceremony of the mothers.

Over-loud murmurs and cries of disapproval from many jurors the president shouts:

ALCIBIADES: (*out-yelling everyone*) Yes it was all twemendous fun!

Shocked silence ensues. Alcibiades turns and looks at Anytus.

ALCIBIADES: What has this to do with Socwates?

PRESIDENT: Tell him, Anytus.

ANYTUS: Socrates was your teacher.

ALCIBIADES: (*shrugging*) He did his best.

ANYTUS: He was your lover?

ALCIBIADES: If you mean, did he love me? (*sighs*) Yes, he was like most people in Athens then.

ANYTUS: I think he corrupted you.

ALCIBIADES: (*with a pleased grin*) Are you talking about sodomy?

ANYTUS: Partly.

ALCIBIADES: (*enjoying himself*) I see! Well, speaking as a part-time sodomite I'm afwaid I found Socwates disappointing. You may wemember that my good looks in those days were . . . wemarkable. (*sighs*) Never mind. Late one evening I invited him home for a meal. We ate, I sent the slaves away and he talked about beauty, love, wisdom. I was beautiful, he was wise and loved me, so I pwetended to be dwunker than I was. I undwessed and thwew my wobe over both of us. (*histrionically*) "Do what you like with me!" (*matter of factly*) You know the sort of thing. But he went on talking about beauty, love and wisdom until I fell asleep. When I woke next morning I might have been sleeping with my father. Yet he loved me, I knew that.

SOCRATES: (*who has become cheerful while listening*) I still do, Alcibiades!

ALCIBIADES: (*still ignoring him*) Doesn't help.

ANYTUS: Did he corrupt you in another way?

ALCIBIADES: (*too quickly*) Not intentionally.

ANYTUS: Explain that.

ALCIBIADES: (*after frowning thoughtfully then smiling suddenly*) No.

PRESIDENT: Explain it, Alcibiades! That's a court order.

Alcibiades, chuckles, shakes head. Socrates raises a hand.

SOCRATES: Can I say something, Mr President?

PRESIDENT: If it's to the point.

SOCRATES: Forget this trial, Alcibiades. If I've hurt you I want to know how. Please tell me about it.

ALCIBIADES: (*looking at him for the first time*) Here?

SOCRATES: (*smiling*) This may be the last time you ever see me. Did I once really harm you?

ALCIBIADES: (*not bitterly*) Yes, vewy much. Before meeting you I thought I was going to be a gweat man. I had vewy foolish confused ideas about how to do it but they were common ideas – most young men have them – and if I'd stuck

to them I'd have become an ordinawy politician and militawy
leader doing the usual amount of damage and being highly wespected for it. But you made me despise what other people think. When you were talking I felt above all that. You were like wine to me! I *knew* myself when we were together. When we were apart I was sure of nothing. Well, I've often been dwunk but never been alcoholic. I've often been in love but never dependent. That's why I stopped seeing you. It hurt both of us, I suppose –

Socrates smiles and nods.

ALCIBIADES: – I think it hurt me most. After that I knew the only uncommon thing about me is my . . . (*he makes an effort*) . . . courrrage. Nobody has ever doubted that. I've astounded the world with it. Yes, I've given people something to talk about. Otherwise I've been completely useless.

ANYTUS: And now you're a common pirate.

ALCIBIADES: (*amused*) Not common at all. I wun a pwivate shipping concern under the pwotection of the Persian Empewor. He's a close fwiend of mine. For the time being. (*to Socrates, softly, but with an effort*) I'm sorry.

SOCRATES: (*earnestly*) You should have seen more of me, Alcibiades.

ANYTUS: Alcibiades has just made it clear that he would have been happier and a better man if he'd never seen you at all.

ALCIBIADES: (*to Socrates, tenderly smiling*) I'm afwaid he's wight.
SOCRATES: (*smiling and sitting down*) You should have seen more of me.

ANYTUS: You can go, Alcibiades.

Alcibiades leaves the stage and sits where he can see what follows.

ANYTUS: (*to the president*) There could be a lot more trouble with the next witness.

PRESIDENT: (*consulting his paper*) Yes, I see. (*loudly to the whole court*) Listen you lot, listen everyone. We are trying Socrates today. Socrates. Nobody else. Our feelings about the witnesses are irrelevant and should be kept in check, so I am going to ask a favour from each one of you, especially ones with brains in their heads. If a neighbour interrupts proceedings with violent expressions of vocal disgust, gently remind him of his dignity as an Athenian juryman by punching him in the throat, will you?

Laughter in court and some cries of "Yes!" "Alright!"

PRESIDENT: Say it a bit louder, I'm hard of hearing – (*Louder cries of agreement*) – Good! Otherwise I have to stop the trial. I mean that. Come on Critias, come on.

In dead silence Critias takes the floor, an urbane big whitehaired business and military man.

ANYTUS: (*pointing at Socrates*) You were a follower of that man?

CRITIAS: I learned a lot from him, if that's what you mean.

ANYTUS: (*nodding*) About politics?

CRITIAS: (*nodding*) It was my business. It is supposed to be every Athenians business, God knows why.

ANYTUS: What did Socrates teach you? We all know what you went on to do, so don't try to hide what you believed.

CRITIAS: I certainly won't. Socrates demonstrated, again and

again, that we can trust a builder to build, a tradesman to
trade and a doctor to heal, but we cannot trust a parliament to
govern.

ANYTUS: Why not?

CRITIAS: Because parliamentary skill is all in the mouth.
Socrates wanted nations ruled by the best people for the job.

ANYTUS: We all want that, Critias. The problem is choosing
them. So Socrates was opposed to democracy?

CRITIAS: He was opposed to slackness, evasion, incompetence
and passing the buck. Of course he was opposed to democracy.

*Socrates scratches his head. From the jurors comes a rising
murmur of disapproval.*

ANYTUS: Thank you for being frank. Besides being an
aristocrat, a general and a tyrant, you once wrote a play. In it
a character said that even if gods did not exist, wise politicians
would prop them up like scarecrows, to frighten people into
obedience. Did you get that from Socrates?

CRITIAS: Of course not. Politicians have always known that,
which is why you are charging Socrates with heresy. You are
propping up the gods of the state in order to stay in power and
silence your critics . . . the clever ones, not most people.

ANYTUS: (*vehemently*) I believe in the gods! I love the people!

CRITIAS: (*amused*) And probably most people *believe* you
believe, Anytus. They may even believe you love them. I have
fallen from power, I don't need to pretend.

PRESIDENT: (*roughly*) Less of the clever stuff, Critias.

ANYTUS: (*shouting*) Didn't you write that the Spartan system of government is the best in Greece? And isn't that the opinion of your master Socrates?

CRITIAS: No. I praised it as the most stable government in Greece. It has lasted two centuries without change so it must be. They also breed the bravest soldiers, one reason why they defeated us. Every Greek knows that.

ANYTUS: No wonder they turned you into our dictator!

CRITIAS: Nonsense, the Spartans are practical men, they wouldn't trust someone because he'd written something. An agreement with a parliament isn't worth the paper it's written on so they signed a treaty with people from the best Athenian families, having made *them* the government. I became leader because I was the best manager of men among them. Don't blame Socrates for that. Blame my ancestors. They made me what I am.

ANYTUS: We know how you managed men! Thirty of your best people put fifteen hundred of our people to death without trial.

An uproar of boos, yells and hisses. Critias glances humorously at Socrates as if to say "We understand the mob, don't we?" Socrates ignores him, frowning thoughtfully. The President stands up.

PRESIDENT: (*bellowing*) If you don't! . . . Stop this din! . . . I will end! . . . The trial! . . . Now! . . . And nobody will get paid!

Many start making "shush" sounds. Uproar lessens, stops.
PRESIDENT: Thanks for your support citizens. The man's a bastard but we need him to get at the truth. (*he sits*) Socrates, have you any questions for your . . . pupil?

SOCRATES: Critias, you and I often talked about politics so tell the court the truth. I criticized the democracy for pursuing a war we could never win. I also praised the Spartans for the care they took to educate their young. Did I ever praise a government that killed and robbed its own people?

CRITIAS: (*grimly*) No, I had to learn the practical details for myself.

SOCRATES: Mm! (*he sighs*) Do you remember ordering the arrest of Theramines? It was six years ago, in this council chamber.

CRITIAS: Yes. (*sarcastically*) Would it help you if I reminded the court of what happened?

SOCRATES: It might.

CRITIAS: You and a couple of friends got between the condemned man and the police, shouting that Athenians should not kill one another and asking the crowd to help you stop that arrest. Of course the chicken-livered majority stayed clear. If I had been longer in power I would have had to get you killed, too. You criticized my regime, you disobeyed it and that was illogical! You obeyed the orders of a democracy you despised, why inconvenience a friend who was doing the best possible thing?

SOCRATES: What does *best* mean, Critias?

CRITIAS: Preventing civil war. Everyone wants to forget the conditions in which my party took power. We were managing a conquered and bankrupt state. In other cities the working classes would have starved or emigrated or sold themselves into slavery, but not the free men of Athens! They had been spoiled by two generation of cheap food, full employment, pensions for the disabled and free theatre tickets. Pericles was to blame. He paid for all that out of the Empire. We *had* no Empire and our workmen had forgotten how to suffer. To prevent rebellion our dictatorship needed money, and fast.

We sold the new harbour at a tenth of the building cost. We confiscated the wealth of rich foreigners, then the wealth of rich tradesmen, then the wealth of our critics. Who squealed, or course. So we executed them. Nasty! Very nasty! But we restored the economy and kept Athens intact.

ANYTUS: You kept your fortunes intact! And enlarged them! And you were already our richest citizens!

CRITIAS: Your crowd profited! When you saw our brutal, necessary, unpopular work had stabilized the economy you started a civil war with us, won it and grabbed the credit and the benefits.

SOCRATES: Has this argument anything to do with me?

CRITIAS: Not much. Your notions led me into politics but they were no good once I arrived there.

SOCRATES: (*placidly*) Thank you, Critias.

ANYTUS: Yes, thank you, Critias! The jury will note that Socrates led you into politics but stayed firmly outside them.

SOCRATES: (*placidly*) Bravo, Anytus.

Critias retires.

ANYTUS: I thank God that Alcibiades and Critias – the traitor and the dictator – are figures from the dead past. Which doesn't mean they won't come back – if we aren't very careful. Meanwhile, since most of us have sons, let us see his effect on a young fellow of today. (*yelling*) Come here Phoebus!

From the edge of the group of Socrates' friends a thin, dishevelled figure detaches himself and slouches onto the stage. He bows mockingly once or twice to the jury then hunches his shoulders, folds his arms and looks up sideways at his father with a mixture of fear and obstinacy.

ANYTUS: Tell the jury what you feel about me.

PHOEBUS: (*gently*) I . . . I hate you, Dad.

ANYTUS: (*nodding*) Tell the jury why.

PHOEBUS: You're a rich man, Dad. You could afford to give me a horse. Why should I work in your stinking tannery handling their hides?

ANYTUS: I did that when I was your age. Tell them why you hate honest toil.

PHOEBUS: I'd rather . . . learn, yes learn about . . . things.

ANYTUS: (*glaring at Socrates*) What things?

PHOEBUS: Reasons, mainly. Why make shoe leather if I haven't exactly found what feet are for? Walking, of course, everybody knows that but walking where? Nobody really knows where they're going or what *living* is for. I want to see more life before I make a living. The sons of rich men usually do. Beauty, geometry, tragedy, racehorses, you can afford to give me some, why don't you?

ANYTUS: (*harshly*) And Socrates?

PHOEBUS: I love him as much, almost, as I hate you. (*he laughs uneasily*) He doesn't jeer when I say things but I mostly just listen. Anybody can do that, nobody has to pay. He's very like me. He knows you dads and bosses and bullies are a lot of shams. That's why you're afraid of us. He thinks a lot, but he doesn't take thinking seriously, he listens to his demon, like I do. Though he's luckier than me. My demon says some very nasty things. (*he shivers*) He drinks too, does Socrates, wine by the bucket and never gets drunk, they say. Just like me. None of you have noticed I'm drunk. Have you? Couldn't have. Come here. Otherwise (*to Socrates, quietly*) would you ask him to let me go home?

Socrates makes a small gesture of appeal to Anytus, who continues glaring at him stonily. Phoebus looks pleadingly to his father, then the president, then the jury who he addresses wildly and feebly.

PHOEBUS: Men of Athens, what is matter? Why is there pressure? Single uniform unchanging solid concentric whirlpools of energy, Socrates is calm about that because *nothing* matters, money, clothes, work, people, politics, Gods are all *filth* to him that's why he's calm, no? (*he looks at Socrates*) – Not now. Now he's looking calm but I can see he's not. Why have you stopped being calm, Socrates? (*aghast*) Are you starting to think I'm dreadful too?

ANYTUS: (*desperately yelling*) Do you want to ask the witness any questions?

Socrates looks with deep pity on father and son who both now look gaunt and dishevelled.

SOCRATES: (*gently*) Let him go home Anytus.

Anytus waves his hand and Phoebus stumbles off. With an effort, Anytus brings his emotions under control and addresses the jury.

ANYTUS: I have one thing in common with my son. My appearance here is unattractive. I am asking for the death of a cheerful, vigorous, charming, *charming* old man but you know I'm not bloodthirsty. I drew up the act of oblivion by which nobody in Athens is punished for his political past and that act is still in force. I called Alcibiades and Critias to remind you of the sickness Socrates is spreading around him even now. It is doubt – doubt of the great simple truths our mothers and fathers

taught us – respect for God and respect for law. If this doubt is
wisdom; it is evil wisdom which *cannot* come from God because it destroys ordinary people's understanding. Those who have heard him argue know what I mean. By steps which seem so sensible you can't remember them afterwards he brings you to admit that nothing you're sure of is right. A paralysis creeps over your brain. Mature citizens know what to do, they leave him and don't come back. But if you're young you're in danger. Young men attract him and he attracts them! This numbing of the thinking process, this rational destruction of reason releases the demon in them, the demon which is normally held down by the laws of God and the laws of our state. So, as you have seen, the brave young soldier becomes a reckless traitor. And the practical businessman becomes a ruthless tyrant. And weaklings become selfish, shameless parasites and spongers. As for his *intellectual* disciples, once again, look at them! Look at that . . . crowd! (*he points*) Our great comic playwright described them – "They disagree with each other but have one thing in common – they fit in with nobody else." Socrates is now going to speak to you. Don't let his *charm* distract you from what you know already. Don't let his eloquence make you forget what you have seen here, just now! (*he points at Socrates, who stares back in astonishment*) I fear that man, because I honour God and love civilization! I ask you to defend Athens, her religion and her sons by silencing him.

Loud, civilized applause. The president has been greatly impressed by Anytus' peroration.

PRESIDENT: Your turn Socrates. Defend yourself.

Socrates stands, leans sideways on his stick and scratches his head.
SOCRATES: I don't know, men of Athens, how that speech struck you but it convinced me, before I remembered the chap Anytus was supposed to be denouncing is me. He didn't. He warned you against my eloquence, I've got none, that's why I hardly ever pipe up in parliament. This is my first speech to such a huge number, and please don't worry about my famous

charm. Perhaps I could charm you all if I had more time but Athenian trials are rapid affairs. In Sparta, now, a trial on a capital charge takes two or three days –

Some disapproving murmurs and one cry of "Boo!" from the jurors.

SOCRATES: (*snapping fingers*) Blast! I shouldn't have said that! Mr President, you see what a child I am in legal matters: please tell the jury to forget I said something good about Sparta!

PRESIDENT: (*rolling up his eyes and sighing*) Just defend yourself, Socrates.

SOCRATES: (*humbly*) I'll try. I was pleased to hear Anytus say some true things about the days when I was a young fellow of forty and regarded, quite correctly, as a simpleton who wanted to be wise but didn't know how. What turned a tongue-tied stupid stonemason into the famous, extraordinary *me*? How did a National Service private with a habit of sleeping on his feet become the money-grubbing pederast you've seen caricatured on the stage by my pal Aristophanes: the menace to civilization who terrifies Anytus; the buffoon of Athens, as some folk call me; the wise man of Greece – if you'd rather believe Apollo, God of sunlight and harmony? That isn't a rhetorical question. Shall I answer it?

Someone yells "Get to the point!" Socrates nods, sits on the edge of the stage with his legs dangling and says in an ordinary voice:

SOCRATES: Alcibiades made me a philosopher. I met him in the army at the start of the war and I loved that beautiful man. I wanted to fascinate him, delight him, give him something great to remember me ever afterwards by. And I had nothing to give. Nothing at all. (*he stares at the palms of his hands*) A stonemason. Ugly. Shy. Until I spoke to him. And then I was inspired. (*he looks at the jury*) Love inspires us all, of course.

It gives some people the strength to support a husband, a wife, a family for years and years and years. Love never made me as strong as that – I support my wife and children on handouts from friends – but the love which makes others strong made me see things clearly, yes it did. Anytus says my wisdom is evil, that's daft. If I do evil then what Anytus calls my wisdom is only cleverness – there are many clever men in Athens but I'm not one. Only love could have taught me the wise trick I played on Alcibiades. I had nothing of my own to attract him so I gave him back the lovely thing he was giving me: the vision of his own true splendid self.

ANYTUS: (*loudly and coldly*) Toady! Sycophant! Arselicker!

Disapproving cries of "Yes!" "That's right Anytus!" "Boo!" from the jurors, during which Socrates rises and stumps cheerfully up and down before the stage.

PRESIDENT: You're out of order, Anytus!

SOCRATES: No he isn't, I like a bit of friendly badinage. But he's missed the point, as usual. I couldn't make Alcibiades love me *for ever* by flattering him – (*he points to Alcibiades with his stick*) – by the way, you still love me, don't you?

ALCIBIADES: (*laughing with appreciation at the show*) Yes!

SOCRATES: (*laughing and smiling*) Yes! (*to the jury*) You see, arselicking or flattery, as some people call it, is praising a man for something he's proud of. It can never please for very long because we all know, in our hearts, that we are only proud of the rubbishy bits of ourselves – the parts we would be better off wothout. A short while ago Alcibiades stood on that very spot – (*points with stick*) – and very solemnly told us his uncommon courage had astounded the world. And nobody laughed! I was so amazed that I couldn't. (*points stick*) Him? Alcibiades? Courageous? Because he gambled with an army and lost it? A gambler can't be brave! If he wins people are fascinated. If he loses people are fascinated. Either way he gets what he wants, which is people saying, Oo aren't you wonderful, oo aren't you wicked! Alcibiades the daring gambler is rubbish! Just rubbish! The true Alcibiades I love knows it – when he listens to me. I love him because he's lonely and desperately humble. The men of Athens praised him because he was wild and glamorous. Who flattered him, you or me? Fancy putting a child of twenty-five in charge of an army then blaming him when he runs away!

ANYTUS: He was not a child! We followed him because he tricked us! He made us think his allies were rich by showing treasure chests full of broken pottery with a layer of gold on top!

SOCRATES: You must have been very keen to be fooled if you were fooled by a schoolboy prank like that. I honestly thought a democratic majority would have more sense, but when my darling stood up in parliament and announced his grandiose cheeky, world-conquering scheme most of you acted like a Persian Emperor gone gaga. Instead of laughing at him you *idiots* voted for him!

Loud cries of annoyance from jurors. Socrates climbs on stage again, raises a hand, and shouts at them: –

SOCRATES: Men of Athens, were you blind? Did you not see where Alcibiades' talent lay? He gave me a new kind of wisdom which I have given to the world. Throughout Greece clever professors are calling me the father of moral philosophy – Alcibiades was father. I'm the *mother* of moral philosophy. Of course like many fathers he refused to acknowledge the child, but I blame you idiots for that –
Protesting cries become uproar. Socrates climbs up on his chair and points with his stick.

SOCRATES: (*yelling*) Men of Athens, I accuse you of seducing, corrupting and perverting my darling! If you'd left him with me he would have become a philosopher, which is what

everyone should be, because . . .

The jurors' vocal reactions drown his words. Many boo and shout, many are laughing, many argue vehemently with neighbours. Socrates stands on the chair, both hands folded patiently on the stick-handle, waiting to continue. The president has left his chair and stands conferring with Anytus. Anytus turns to the jury and raises his hands for silence. It gradually happens.

ANYTUS: (*sternly*) Yes, men of Athens, we are all disgusted by the cynical, facetious abuse that man has heaped on us. But we are here to judge him, and judges should be calm.

PRESIDENT: (*huffily*) A man *must* be heard before we condemn him. That's the law. (*he goes back to his seat*)

ANYTUS: (*reasonably*) Outcries only make the trial last longer. Save your anger till it's time to vote and *then* show what you think. It's your vote that matters. (*he sits*)

SOCRATES: Thank you for that friendly speech, Anytus. (*climbs down and wipes his brow*) Phew! (*to the jury*) You had me quite excited there. I could never be a politician – too emotional. (*he sits on chair*) Well, when Alcibiades left me – for you lot – O, I was depressed. I didn't realize I'd become a philosopher. Love for him had untied my tongue and let me think aloud. I thought all that would stop now. It didn't! I discovered I could talk to anyone – pretty young boys, ugly old men – anyone! I'd acquired a gift. But I swear by the great God of Heaven that I did not know I was being wise, I thought I was just finding out what people thought. Those I spoke to kept coming up with astonishing ideas, and saying they had learned them from me. (*he chuckles*) I've never had an original idea in my life! They wrote books, too, and the critics blamed me for those as well. Anytus mentioned Critias' attack on democracy; he should have mentioned Kairafon's defence.

Kairafon said he learned that from me and the dictators banished him. Anyway, one morning as Homer puts it "A thunderbolt descended from the blue Aegean sky." (*spreading his arms wide*) "News from Delphi! Oracle's Astounding Revelation! Nobody in Greece is wiser than Socrates!" (*drops hands, suddenly really puzzled and worried*) Nobody wiser than me? But friends, I am like other people! When love and friendship inspire me I have glimpses of beauty and goodness; otherwise there is *nothing* in here – (*taps chest*) – nothing but a little voice which sometimes says "No. Don't do that."

Socrates ends the following long speech from the centre of the floor.

SOCRATES: Of course in the middle of a crowd like this I enjoy feeling as good as anyone else: but alone I am sometimes . . . terrified by the thought that there is nobody in the world superior to me. I wanted to prove that oracle wrong so went straight to the top. I visited a great and noble statesman whose name – I shall not disclose. He was twice divorced, lived with a foreign prostitute and had a bald head which came to a point like the dome of the new music-hall. His head embarrassed him, so you see him in public statues wearing a helmet like Agamemnon and Achilles wore when the Greeks fought the Trojans, and why should he not? In warfare he was a better general than Agamemnon who, by Homer's account, antagonized his bravest officer, and better than Achilles who spent most of the war sulking behind the lines . . .

PRESIDENT: (*exasperated*) You're supposed to be defending *yourself* man, not praising Pericles.

SOCRATES: (*as if puzzled*) Is that what I'm doing? I'm sorry. This statesman ruled Athens for thirty years because the majority party thought he was defending them from the greed of the rich, and the *best* people thought he protected them from the many. He kept both sides happy by plundering our allies under the pretext of defending them from Persia, and many folk still think that the goodness and beauty of Athens was all his doing.

But when I asked him how men could learn to be good his answer – when I stripped away the trimmings – was "Vote for me". About virtue that great man was as stupid as I am – in fact stupider, because he thought he was wise *and* virtuous. I tried to explain his curious mistake and he got very cross. So did his friends. They stopped inviting me to their houses.

Now a great scientist lived in Athens at that time, a foreigner from Ionia who we nicknamed "Heavenly Reason". (*points forefinger*) You condemned him to death for heresy, didn't you? You shouldn't have. He really did worship God, but where a peasant sees the maker of the universe as a mysteriously angry old man chucking lightning around, Anaxagoras saw him as a heavenly energy driving streams of atoms to resolve their friction by electrical discharges of an occasionally lethal nature. That made no sense to me, but when this old chap spoke about it his eyes opened wide and stopped focusing – he was as full of reverence and wonder as a priestess on a tripod. I said "Master! Teach me wisdom please". He showed me his big new map of the heavens. Very pretty it was, hundreds of circles with the sun in the middle instead of the world. He said "Believe this. It is true." "All right", I said, "But I live in Athens. How can Athenians become better men?" He said "Study the stars. When men appreciate the vastness of the heavenly harmony, they will forget their petty differences and harmonize with each other." He thought that answered my question. I disagreed.

For the last twenty years I have used my little bit of genius to examine men who were thought to be geniuses all the way through, and all I've found are people clever at their job. In everyday life they are as ignorant as shopkeepers, labourers and slaves. Apollo is right! We're complicated, we Athenians – kind to animals at home and killing innocent families in lands which want nothing to do with us. I believe God likes me to spread uncertainty, I won't stop doing it. And of course, a lot of rich young idlers follow me around because they like seeing their elders looking uncomfortable.

They imitate me too, and anyone who's exposed as a bit muddle-headed and inconsistent – (and who isn't? I know I am) – blames me instead of himself. And any politician who starts losing votes blames me instead of himself. And any father whose son doesn't love him blames me instead of himself. (*he is near Anytus and looks at him*) Tell me, Anytus. If I am a danger to the youth of this city, what men are good for them? Who teaches them virtue?

ANYTUS: All of them. Except you.

SOCRATES: All of them? (*he glances, puzzled, at the jury*) Will you explain that?

ANYTUS: I will. Other teachers talk to the people in crowds: you speak to them in small private parties. You say this is because you lack eloquence – a lie. The jury have heard you now and know you lied. You deal with us in ones and twos because we are weaker that way. When a useful citizen is separated from others and examined on his wisdom of course he does badly. Taken separately we are ignorant and selfish, as you easily prove. But when we co-operate our small bits of knowledge become a wisdom surrounding and supporting everyone – even you, who are too vain to notice it. Through democracy we feed, love and defend each other, we stand up, look at the stars and salute the Gods, that isn't ignorance. Joined in society we teach our children to serve themselves by serving others. Some teaching comes from experts but the best teaching is the example of ordinary citizens. The only man who teaches nothing but wrong is the one who stands outside society and beckons.

Cries of approval from some jurors.
SOCRATES: Anytus, I am the most sociable man in the state! The streets are my clubrooms. I talk to anyone.

ANYTUS: It's easy for the parasite to stump up and down, gather an audience of two or three and teach it to sneer at the majority he depends upon. Your questions split us up. When we doubt our small store of traditional wisdom we cannot act together. Society lives by actions, not by puzzling over demoralising questions. You are a criminal because you are a demoralizer!

SOCRATES: (*staring at him*) The only one?

ANYTUS: The main one! (*he points at the disciples*) If society shuts your mouth these people will close theirs.

Louder cries of approval.

PRESIDENT: (*loudly*) Now then, a little patience please, we're getting to the end.

SOCRATES: (*thoughtfully*) Anytus, before you spoke of shutting my mouth you were almost talking intelligently. I like the idea of this great wise giant called society. Can he instruct me? Where can I hear his voice? It surely wasn't that braying sound I heard a moment ago . . .

Loud boos and hisses from jurors, silenced when Anytus raises his hand, shaking his head.

SOCRATES: (*smiling*) . . . was it?

ANYTUS: The voice of a society is in our laws. Laws made and voted for in parliament by the people.

SOCRATES: I don't contradict that voice, Anytus. I've never broken that law. No law forbids a man saying what he thinks.

ANYTUS: Another voice of society is public opinion revealed through a legal action – this legal action. I tell you that Athens is sick of you.

SOCRATES: So you are the voice of Athens?

ANYTUS: The vote will tell us. If the majority are for you I must pay a very large fine.

SOCRATES: That hardly seems right when you've only said what you sincerely believe. (*loudly*) Mr President, let's have the voting. (*stumps over to his disciples waving stick at the jury and shouting*) I hope there are philosophers among you lot.

The jurors engage in arguments and conversations. The president consults the paper in his hand. Two court officials mount the stage and stand, one on each side of him.

PRESIDENT: Will three friends of the accuser and three of the accused kindly join the tellers?

The official on Socrates' side is joined by Plato, a handsome young aristocrat; by Crito, who is a fat, bald, comfortable-looking person; by Aeschines, a haggard working-class intellectual. The three who join Anytus are all middle-class. The president, paper in hand, comes to the front of the stage where he can most closely dominate the assembly. A gong, bell or board is struck loudly. The crowd falls silent.

PRESIDENT: Attention. I'm going to read the charge again. Socrates opposes the Gods of the Athenian state, sets up a false god of his own and uses it to corrupt young men, right? You've all seen enough today to make up your minds about this so I want no swithering. When I give the word all free men who agree with that charge will raise their hands and keep them up till I say so. No half lifting a hand and looking round to see if you're in the majority. If you've doubts, give the accused the benefit of them. We're doing a parliamentary job today so there must be no idiotic don't knows. Citizens who think Socrates guilty will now raise their right hands.

Many jurors at once raise their hands and then a great many. Anytus paces restlessly back and forth beside his chair.

Socrates sits back in his with thoughtfully pursed lips. A few
of his disciples glumly imitate his calm, the rest are frankly
worried. Court officials, after counting hands and conferring
with assistants, confer with each other. One writes figures on
a card, gives it to the President.

PRESIDENT: Hands down. Four hundred and seventy eight of
you support the charge. That means four hundred and twenty
one disagree and Socrates is guilty by a fifty eight majority.
The guilt of the accused having thus been proved, we must
now vote for an appropriate punishment. What do you
propose, Anytus?

ANYTUS: *(facing the jury)* You know what I want. Socrates
must be silenced and death is the one sure way of doing it.
But if he proposes banishment instead, and you vote for that,
I will be satisfied. Either way Athens will be rid of him. You
have seen him treat this trial as a joke! He has treated you, a
jury representing the whole Athenian state, as a joke. This
moral philosopher thinks the legal process of a democratic
state is a laughing matter. So if he suggests it, and you prefer
it, let him leave here for his beloved Sparta, or even Persia
where most of the enemies we banish find a home. He's a
famous man! Every city which hates ours will welcome him.
But not for long, I think. Only the democracy of Athens could
have borne such a man as long as you have. I propose the
hemlock. (*He sits down*)

PRESIDENT: Your turn, Socrates.

Socrates has sat smiling and shaking his head while the three
disciples who helped the teller have tried to persuade him of
something. He stands and moves to centre stage saying: –
SOCRATES: Banishment. Banishment. No you won't get rid
of me that way. (*faces jury with hands folded on stick*) Anytus
is right: only a democracy could have put up with me. I am a
democratic growth and at my age I refuse to be transplanted.
I profited by our laws so I will die by them, if that is what you

want. But the law requires me to propose an alternative to capital punishment so by rejecting banishment I will have to propose a fine. I can't possibly pay more than I have here. Here it is in my pocket – one minae – not a coin of great value. Will it do? (*holds it out in palm of hand*)

Jeers and catcalls from jurors. The President covers his eyes with his hands. Plato from the side of the stage starts desperately waving his hands and shouting.

PLATO: Socrates! . . . Men of Athens, I propose –

SOCRATES: (*loudly over Plato's voice*) Men of Athens, my young friend here wants to tell you that he and other rich pals of mine will pay the state a large fine on my behalf. I won't tell you how much because it might tempt you into perverting the course of justice. But for me to propose a fine of even one small coin is an admission of guilt so I withdraw that offer, and before I make another let me say something about Anytus, who I have heard with more sympathy and respect than he will ever believe.

Anytus regards our country, doesn't he? as a giant man whose strength is the strength of everyone in it and whose wisdom is as great as all our intelligences put together. And it could be that. If we truly loved each other it would be that. But we don't work together, we compete – the rich with the poor, businesses with businesses, trades with trades, sex with sex. We have only truly co-operated when at war: at war with Persia or Sparta or small states sick of us taxing them. When not at war our peace is more like the fixity of wrestlers with holds on each other too tight to be broken. So instead of Athens being a vigorous intelligent giant MAN it is like a huge fat horse with rheumatic joints which likes lying all day on the hillside listening to its stomach rumble. Anytus called me a parasite, I agree. I am a very special kind of blood-sucker, a gadfly sent by God the Father – who loves you – to sting your fatty complacency and goad you into healthy mental exercize. You need me. I need you. While I live I will not be silenced,

so I propose the following punishment. For the rest of my life
let me dine in the council refectory next door to this chamber, eating free of charge. Olympic athletes have that privilege – give it to me. My job is more important. That is my final offer.

He goes back to his seat and sits down with folded arms. A storm of hissing and jeers has arisen from most parts of the council chamber. The president stands up, says loudly, –

PRESIDENT: Will the tellers please go to their places . . .

The hissing continues.

PRESIDENT: (*distressed*) Please shut up. I've got something to say that may be out of order but I've got to say it . . . listen here!

Silence falls.

PRESIDENT: Isn't there an explanation for Socrates' very peculiar attitude? Isn't there something lacking in him (*taps brow*) up here? That's what I think. He seems to have no sense of self preservation. Might that be a reason for . . . preserving him?

Socrates is highly amused. Several jurors shout "Out of order!"

PRESIDENT: (*shrugging*) Just an idea I had. Alright. Those who want the death penalty raise their right hands.

A forest of hands are immediately raised. The counting process is carried out as formerly, though there can no be no doubt of the verdict. Socrates looks absent- mindedly out over the jurors' heads, his mouth open as when we first saw him on the hilltop. The President, sighing, addresses the court.

PRESIDENT: Anytus wins by a hundred and forty nine majority. That means five hundred and twenty four of you want him poisoned with hemlock, three hundred and seventy five would rather see him fed at public expense. Is there anything you want to say, Socrates, before we have you jailed? (*louder, noticing Socrates still seems absent minded*) Socrates! Have you any last words for the Athenian public?

SOCRATES: (*rousing himself*) Yes, quite a few.

He sits up and talks placidly at first, later becoming animated in a very ordinary way. He is now the only perfectly happy man in the court.

SOCRATES: Do you remember what the old physicist Anaxagoras said when the Athenian people condemned him to death for heresy? He said, "Nature has done that already – and them too." (*he chuckles*) But a third of you don't want me dead so I'd like to cheer those good friends up a bit. Dying won't hurt me. A man is only badly hurt by his own bad actions and death now may do me good. I'm seventy and still intelligent, but in a few years I might have gone stupid and started setting bad examples, like many old people do. Remember too that mine will be a civilized execution. Instead of being left to rot in a dungeon or nailed to a cross I will die among friends, drinking painless poison while at rest in a clean bed. As for after death, nobody alive knows anything about it and it's stupid to fear what we don't know. Death is either endless, dreamless sleep – a remarkably good thing as all people who can't sleep know – or something different that is equally good. If our souls are immortal and live after our body dies they must have lived before it was born, so we have all lived many lives, died many deaths and will continue doing it. May I remind you that Hell is not part of every religion? Greeks only started imagining it when we began working slaves to death in our silver mines. I haven't exploited anyone so I'm not worried.

Now some words of comfort to you who want me dead. One day most of you will be sorry you voted for it, and when that time comes please don't think you were very

wicked or unusually stupid. Folk who think that are as mistaken as those who think they're very wise and good. Just remember that when you thought you were freeing Athens from a dangerous enemy you were really losing a useful friend. And smile, rather sadly, at how ignorant you were but don't get upset! You will only have "enthroned me" – as Homer says – "in death's impregnable castle." I think that's all I want to say.

He turns round, sees two officials waiting to arrest him, turns back to the jury with raised arm.

SOCRATES: Stop! I've remembered something. Come here Aeschines. (*Aeschines, notebook in hand, approaches*) This worthy fellow has for years been trying to write down everything he hears me say – that young fellow Plato has started doing it too. They think they can become philosophers by studying my words, but they can't. We can only be philosophers by studying ourselves. No great cleverness is needed, I proved that. What you do is look carefully into yourself and think hard about what you see there. The only help you need is the good-humoured conversation of friends who don't want to flatter you. Men of Athens! Men of Greece! Men of the World, don't let philosophy become a thing experts lecture on – if that happens it will lose all value, become just another tool people use to get money or social promotion. The only true philosopher is the honest lover. Remember that. No, DON'T remember it, discover it together with others. Goodbye. No! Stop a minute! (*scratches his head*) Jail is a bit like hospital and a whole month will elapse before my big operation. I will be delighted to receive visitors with a taste for dialectical conversations about truth, beauty and goodness. Handsome young men will be specially welcome of course, but I don't need more than one in a company of five or six. Nobody will be turned away on grounds of age, appearance or low income. And as usual, there will be no charge. Thank you.

He turns and walks off stage between the officials followed by Aeschines, Plato and other disciples who surround and obscure his cheerful, animated person. The President mingles with the jurors who start drifting towards an anteroom where they will be paid. Anytus, having been congratulated by friends on the success of his action, sits for a while, brooding on how the issue of the trial will affect forthcoming elections.

Thirty-One
Tunnock's Diary
2007

Life with Zoe has been much nicer since I forbade her to bring dangerous people home. Nothing much is open in Glasgow after Hogmanay so yesterday, feeling we ought to be more companionable, I taught her after a late breakfast to play cribbage. This day must be Monday 1st or Tuesday 2nd of January. *We played all afternoon and evening without once stopping to eat, though shortly before ten she insisted on going out and bringing back fish and chips from McPhee's. When at last we went to bed she had beaten me several times and asked if more than two could play. Four, I told her. She suggested that later in the month she might bring back some pals for a game with us. I asked what kind of pals. She laughed and said, "Don't worry – none that will pull knives on you."*
Is our life together entering a jolly new domestic phase?

---

*An ominous start to unsatisfactory day. Wakened from dream of a Scottish Pope being Fascist President-Prime Minister of Anglo-America and making torture on television a popular entertainment. Every politician and cardinal in his government was a Scottish thug who spoke with a posh English accent. On way to library this morning saw on pavement at corner of Byres and Observatory Road a fat eight-foot high pillar topped by a black cupola, like a dirty big fungus with too thick a stalk. The sides were plastered with concert adverts under a narrow notice with these words which I copied down: **THIS SITE IS MANAGED BY CITY CENTRE POSTERS WORKING IN PARTNERSHIP WITH GLASGOW CITY COUNCIL FOR A CLEANER, MORE ATTRACTIVE CITY. TO ADVERTISE CONTACT** – I omit email address. This structure cannot make*

*Glasgow cleaner, only makes it more attractive to lovers of
adverts who don't get enough from billboards, sides of taxicabs,
buses, commercial vehicles, from newspapers, magazines, sound
and television broadcasting and film shows. Paris has had
similar pillars for over a century but her avenues have wide
pavements, her posters were once masterpieces by Mucha and
Toulouse-Lautrec, and Paris has no other displays of street
posters. The French loved their architecture too much to disfigure
it with billboards. I later saw more of these toadstools sprouting
on Byres and Great Western Road, a new way to make money
out of Glasgow while doing it no good at all.*

    *For lunch today went to café in Creswell Lane, once a big
sky-lit room built as sorting room of Hillhead post office, then
an auction room, then the Metropolitan Café, a pleasant self-
service restaurant in revived art deco style. It is now Bar
Buddha, made mysteriously dark by blocking the skylight
windows and having low table lights, intimate corners and
waiters. One greeted me by saying, "How you doin'?" I asked
for soup and a salad and he said, "No problem." On placing
them before me he said, "There you go. Enjoy." A large
television screen was showing a glamorous woman talking to a
seemingly normal young man to the sound of laughter and
clapping. I stopped looking by reading a cheap newspaper left
on a nearby chair. Since British jails have more prisoners than
they can decently hold (it said) the Home Secretary (a Scot)
proposes to make a former RAF camp a jail, and use two naval
vessels as prison ships, so Britain will get a concentration camp
for civilians – as was first used by Britain in the South African
Boer War and hugely emulated in Nazi Germany and USSR
Russia – while locking up other civilians in off-shore hulks, as
in pre-Victorian days. He also suggests police and judges do
not press charges or jail people for crimes they think slight,
thus contradicting New Labour's past policy of tougher
penalties for all crimes except fraud by businessmen and
politicians. I recoiled from the newspaper to the television
screen and found the ordinary young man is famous throughout
Britain for surviving longer than anyone else in a reality show.
Mastermind tells me all networks broadcast them, showing*

ordinary folk in a house from which they are one at a time,

steadily, humiliatingly evicted by a popular voting system until
only one is left. My nightmare about Britain was contemporary,
not prophetic. Even so, I looked forward to a pleasant evening
card-party with Zoe and pals.

At half past five she brought home Is, who I had not seen for
five years, a girl called Mish, an Indian meal from the Ashoka
and six bottles of wine. I thought that number excessive as I
have not seen Zoe drink much alcohol since three years ago
when she came here to seduce me, nor did she drink any tonight.
Our guests drank it all with the meal and while playing cards
afterwards, which did not improve their manners. To teach them
the game Zoe partnered Is, I partnered Mish who became so
flirtatious and come-hither that I could not treat it as a joke.
She and Is gave the game so little serious attention that I was
soon disgusted and went to bed. Zoe joined me much later, said
I had been rude to Mish, refused to be cuddled. Today she stayed
in bed all morning and afternoon, not touching meals I brought,
snorting at suggestions that I call a doctor. Saw half bottle of
vodka under her pillow – this is unusual. Assumed she was
sulking. It is 7.35 p.m. and half an hour ago, heard the front
door slam. She has gone out without a word. Everybody I love
at last becomes a pain.

This morning she sat silently glooming over the breakfast table,
refusing to touch the omelette I served, then suddenly said, "Well
it's tonight."
"What is?" I asked. She said, "The meeting here, with those
folk you don't want to see. But you neednae see them. Lie low
in the bedroom like I suggested if you won't spend the night in
a hotel. Everything should go fairly quietly."
I said I would not let such strangers into my house and would
call the police if she tried to bring them. She said, "How? You
havenae a phone."
I told her that today I would buy a mobile phone. On a shrill
note she asked did I want her to get her throat cut? Or worse?
I stared at her, speechless, and saw she was panic-stricken,

with facial twitches and trembling I have never seen before and want never to see again. If she had started weeping I could not have borne it. I said alright, her visitors could come, but I would certainly not hide from them as if I was a criminal and they were police. I would meet them at the front door, offer them sandwiches and drinks in the living room, then withdraw to the study, leaving her to discuss business without my presence. In a smaller voice than I have heard her use before she whispered, "Thanks," and went out, not seeming much cheered up. But that is what I have decided, what I will certainly do.

Despite which surprisingly happy day re-reading, re-planning book as originally intended, but named Money at Play. It only needs now a short end note for Socratic part, and enlarged Renaissance part showing workings of Medici capitalism, fall of Constantinople, French invasion. From Filippo Lippi's standpoint these will appear like a brilliant landscape above which looms a huge storm cloud he does not notice – the coming Protestant Reformation and Catholic Counter-Reformation that will change most of Europe for the worse. That may take months but the end is certainly in sight.

An almost incredibly great idea seizes me. Can I also complete for this book my panoptic vision of Scotland from the Genesis of the universe to the near future? If I did, would it not become the Bible of a new and independent Scotland? Perhaps. I will now throw together the Athenian end notes then pop down to Buchanan Street, buy a mobile phone and see if it can be activated before Zoe brings her visitors. Best be on the safe side.

32: SOCRATIC END NOTES

WITNESSES WERE NOT CALLED at Athenian trials and none of the important witnesses I have described could have attended the trial of Socrates in 399 BC. Alcibiades had died five years earlier, murdered by enemies after betraying so many people that nobody knows who hired the assassins. It may have been Critias who died a year later, in battle against the restoration of Athenian democracy. The name of Anytus' son is not recorded but was almost certainly not Phoebus. He is said to have liked Socrates more than his own father, but may not have been the neurotic wretch I invented to show the bad effect of a strong, original thinker upon a weak one.

It is a pleasant fact that the restored Athenian democracy prospered without its empire for centuries after the trial of Socrates. It lived up to Pericles' boast of being a school for other nations, though soon after Pericles died the Athens of his day was thought a golden age. Romans who made Greece part of their empire studied Greek poetry, philosophy, art and science in Athens which seemed their strongest source. Many schools of philosophy flourished there, Idealist and Cynic, Academic and Realist, Stoic and Epicurean. All claimed Socrates as their founder. Statues of him were erected in public places.

If I knew Greek well enough to understand the plays of Aristophanes he would have had a bigger part in my story, being as great an original genius in drama as Socrates in philosophy. His plays are great poetry, like Shakespeare's, and satirize every aspect of life in his day: Olympian gods, the mighty dead, the Athenian state, its politicians and celebrities. He understood the democracy so completely – it understood him so well – that he successfully caricatured it in *The Wasps* as a daft old man who has to be locked up by his son because he prefers parliamentary politics to minding his own business. When Cleon, a tanner like Anytus, became popular by a vulgar display of bad parliamentary manners, Aristophanes showed him being pushed out of office by a sausage-seller whose manners were even worse. No good actor could be found brave enough to perform as Cleon on stage so Aristophanes acted the part himself. During the war with Sparta his comedies constantly, wittily denounced it. No government, democratic or monarchic, has since allowed such freedom to a great satirist.

The Greek empire Alcibiades dreamed of leading was made real by Alexander, young king of Macedonia, the Greek state closest to barbarism. He conquered all Greece, Palestine, Babylon, Egypt, Persia and part of India. He died at the age of thirty-three and his generals dismembered his empire. The Romans later reconquered much of it, adding on Italy, Spain, France, the Balkans and south Britain. Then the Roman empire split in two, the eastern and richest part being ruled by emperors with a bureaucracy speaking Greek. In the 1322nd year of the Christian era that part was conquered by an Islamic empire that renamed the capital city Istanbul. It ruled what is now called Turkey, Greece and most of the Balkans until 1864 when Greece got independence under a constitutional monarchy whose capital was Athens. In World War 2 it was conquered by the Third Reich, a German empire that held it for three or four years, after which the constitutional monarchy was restored. In 1967 a left-wing government was overthrown by a military coup aided by the United States. This dictatorship lasted until 1974 when Greece got back a form of parliamentary democracy with Athens still the capital.

Nowadays the securest nations have elected assemblies acting as their governments. None would have appeared democratic to Athenians who believed democracy was impossible in big nations, since in a vast population the influence of a single individual hardly exists, if he is not very rich. Plato said the ideal state should have 5,040 citizens, a number divisible by all numbers up to 13 except 11, thus making subdivisions of populace easy. Aristotle preferred solid things to ideal numbers and said the best size of nation was one with borders visible from a high point in the centre. The quarter-million people in the Icelandic Republic would have seemed unmanageably vast to democrats before the days of radio, telephone and cheap swift transport. But in small democracies (Denmark, Sweden, Norway, Iceland, Holland, New Zealand) goods are still shared best. I hear the Irish Republic is a better place to live since a hierarchy's hold on it loosened. Even before then hardly anyone in the Irish Republic wanted to be ruled again by the London parliament, hence Brendan Behan's words:

The sea, the sea, the blesséd sea!
Long may it flow between England and me.
God help the Scots, they'll never be free.

These words are mis-quotations from a song in Behan's play, *The Hostage.*

He may turn out to be wrong. The Scottish general election next week will show us. Surely at last some of Scotland's faithful Labour party voters will see Blair, Brown and his crew had become Thatcherite Tories when they came to power? That is why the English money market let them come to power.

33: HERALD OBITUARY, 2 MAY 2007

Schoolteacher, writer.
born 1940
died 2007

JOHN SIM TUNNOCK died on 28th April as the result of a fall in his Hillhead home. He was for many years a well-known figure around Glasgow's Byres Road, having lived in Hillhead all his life. After attending Glasgow University and Jordanhill Training College he was first a teacher, then headmaster in Molendinar Primary School, Robroyston accepting early retirement for family reasons in 1977. A life-long bachelor, his literary hobbies made him a contributor to Chapman, the Edinburgh-based literary magazine. His funeral service at the Linn Crematorium was attended by a few close friends, among them Dr Francis Lambert and the lawyer, Angela Mullane. His only surviving relative is in the U.S.A.

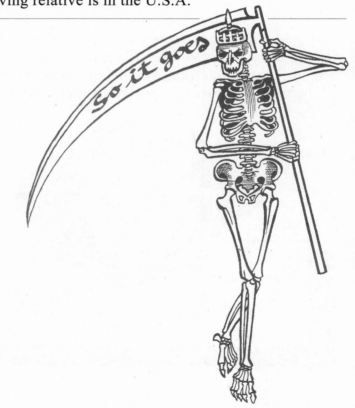

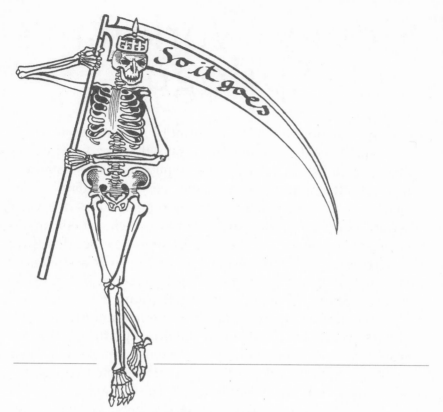

JOHN TUNNOCK'S
CROSSWORD TESTAMENT

Dirty stuff, dust, turmoil in Scots is stoor,
stofzuiger Dutch for hoover. Love, desire,
lust are English, lust Deutsche, désir Francais
so spirits, sprites, geists, ghosts inspire esprit.
Great Yeats creates, sweet Keats repeats, eager
Edgar Poe try poetry games until
dog shout, tree skin, water car meet in one word,
a curtailed world. See saw so we embark,
go out into nothing like candle flames.

Sidney Workman's Epilogue

In his introduction to the 2007 reprint by Canongate of Gray's first book, *Lanark*, William Boyd says that years before the publication in 1981 it had a Scottish reputation as "a vast novel, decades in the writing, still to see the light of day . . . an impossibly gargantuan, time-consuming labour of love, a thousand pages long, Glasgow's *Ulysses* – such were the myths swirling about the book at the time, as far as I can recall." Boyd is referring to the early seventies when he was a student at Glasgow University. I was then a young lecturer in English at the Adam Smith Teachers' Training Institute, Kirkcaldy, and had encountered *Lanark* through the publication of two early chapters in a short-lived but influential quarterly, *Scottish International*. Finding some of my students impressed by what they thought "the novelty" of that sample I wrote to the editor, Robert Tait, pointing out how much these chapters owed to Màrquez's *One Hundred Years of Solitude*, published three years before, and the first magic realist novel to be noticed internationally. *Scottish International* did not print my letter but Gray certainly read it. Shortly before *Lanark* was published in 1981 he sent me a proof copy and letter begging me to return it with any critical remarks I wished to make. "The severer the better!" he wrote. "I promise to take account of them, and acknowledge your contribution."

This request seemed honest so I honestly replied, saying (among other things) that the only apparent reason for combining two very different narratives in *Lanark* was the author's assumption that a heavier book would make a bigger splash. I also noted several misleading and unjustified ploys in a so-called "epilogue" between chapters 40 and 41. On receiving a final copy of the book I found my criticisms had moved Gray to change his book in one way only: he had separated my strictures and added them as footnotes to his "epilogue". But he certainly acknowledged me as their author! The novel's success in Scotland led to smiling colleagues congratulating me on my part in it. Lecturers from other colleges began greeting me with surprise because they had thought me a figment of Gray's imagination – thought the footnotes a device to deflect criticism, not voice it. Gray had lured me into a trap. That I really exist has led those who know this to see me as Gray's dupe or stooge, thus irrevocably damaging my career. Since the mid 1980s it has been obvious that my Cambridge First will never lead to a more important teaching post, and that only retirement will let me escape from Fife. This has left me with a strong but unenchanted interest in Gray's work.

In February 2007 I received a parcel through the post and, opening it, had a déjà vu experience that almost set my hair on end. It was a proof copy of *Old Men in Love* and letter from Gray profusely apologising for the bad effect of *Lanark* upon my career, which had been the opposite of his intention. *Old Men in Love* (he wrote) was a chance for us both "to set the record straight". He invited me to review it, at any length I liked, with any other of his books. He promised to publish this review as an epilogue to *Old Men in Love* without comment or alteration, and since this novel would be his last (for he is seventy-two and in poor health) I could be sure of having the last word. This smooth invitation was obviously Gray's way of obtaining another critic-deflecting device. I have accepted it with open eyes, believing that a cool statement of facts will let me at last indeed "set the record straight".

The attention that Gray's first novel *Lanark* received in Scotland is not surprising. A small country of about five million souls will make the most of what literature it has, and *Lanark* appeared in 1981 when northern universities urgently needed such a book. For nearly two centuries Scots literature had been taught as a branch of English. The post-war increase in Scottish national feeling finally made it a separate university course with only some twentieth-century poetry worth lecturing upon, and hardly any fiction. England had H.G. Wells, D.H. Lawrence, Virginia Woolf, Forster, Greene and Orwell, but the only well-known Scottish author was a thriller writer, John Buchan. From Chaucer's *Canterbury Tales* to D.H. Lawrence's *The Rainbow* England has had a great tradition of invigorating novels showing its social breadth. The nearest Scots equivalent, if we ignore Sir Walter Scott, has been a line of dour working-class novels set in depressed local communities. Brown's *House with the Green Shutters* (1901), Grassic Gibbon's *Scots Quair* (1934) were the best and William McIlvanney's *Docherty* (1975) the most recent. When *Docherty* received the Whitbread award Scots critics hoped McIlvanney would go on to produce something new and surprising, but McIlvanney, tired of high critical attention and low royalty cheques, turned to crime thrillers and left a gap in modern Scots literary courses that *Lanark* filled perfectly.

In the first place it was very big, combining three different genres in two main halves with a short linking story. One half was in the Scottish depressed working-class tradition, enlivened by elements from Joyce's *Portrait of the Artist as a Young Man*. The other half was a Kafka-esque pilgrimage mingled with science fiction. They were linked by a Borges type of story, a fantasia on memory, and the whole was welded together by devices that began to be labelled Postmodern in the 1980s, most of these being in the so-called "epilogue". Here, like Fowles in *The French Lieutenant's Woman*, Gray described himself inside his book, writing it. He put in a large index of authors he had plagiarised, except for Fowles, and named many friends and acquaintances in a west of Scotland literary clique that east coast critics had begun to call "the Glasgow literary mafia". He disarmed criticism yet further by enlisting me, as I have described.

In 1981 senior academics had just started lecturing on popular culture, so by ostentatiously blending fairy tale, science fiction and horror film elements with liftings from twentieth century authors most fashionable with academics, Gray boiled them into that 560 page postmodern stew, *Lanark*. The epilogue

with my edited footnotes persuaded critics that the author was
as smart as themselves. Favourably reviewed by the London
press, *Lanark* was short-listed for the Booker prize, and two
years after publication was on the curriculum of Scottish
literature courses. Since then most studies of contemporary
Scots literature suggest *Lanark* began a new Scottish
Renaissance, without exactly dating the old one.

Between *Lanark* and *Old Men in Love* Gray has published
eighteen books, none more than normal length. They consist of:
Two realistic novels involving sadomasochistic fantasies,
Four books of short stories (one shared with his friends Agnes
Owens, James Kelman),
Two satirical novellas about young Scotsmen in the London media
world,
Two science-fiction fantasies, one set in nineteenth-century
Glasgow, one in a war-games future,
Three pamphlets urging Scots home rule, the last written with
Professor Adam Tomkins,
Two histories of literature,
Two collections of verse,
One autobiographical pamphlet published by the Saltire Society,
One play script.

The novels and stories above are mostly prose versions
of forgotten plays written between 1967 and 1977 for early
television, radio and small stage companies. He admits this in
epilogues usually headed Critic Fuel which, like the one in
Lanark, defuse criticism by anticipating it. Since *Lanark* he
has frequently given interviews suggesting his latest work of
fiction will be the last since he has "no ideas for more". These
efforts to hold public attention have succeeded in Scotland,
though most critics at home and abroad agree that his most
pornographic novel, *Something Leather*, should be forgotten.
Even so he has received a more than fair share of critical
attention in two Festschrifts.

The Arts of Alasdair Gray (Edinburgh University Press,

1992), and *Alasdair Gray: Critical Appreciations* (British
Library, 2002). The second is not a Scottish production, but like
the first nearly every critic in it is Scottish and about half are friends
of Gray, some of them close friends. Both books have a multitude
of Gray's illustrations, which proves Gray had access to the proofs,
so must have overseen the texts. A cool, serious appraisal of Gray's
work cannot be found in them or, I believe, anywhere in Scotland,
but they show why he has a following among bibliophiles – those
who enjoy books for visual and typographical reasons quite separate
from their literary value. Before appearing as a novelist at the age
of forty-five Gray had not only failed as a dramatist, but as a
commercial artist, portrait painter and mural painter. By bringing
visual showmanship to book production he has contrived, with
illustrations and jingling rhymes, to make the jackets, blurbs,
boards, typography, layouts and even errata slips in his publications
more entertaining than the main texts. Not since William Morris's
News from Nowhere and Rudyard Kipling's *Just So Stories* has an
author so controlled the appearance of his books, often varying
them from one edition to the next, allowing collectors to always
find something new. The two festschrifts are no doubt useful guides
to these parasites on the tree of literature.

But outside academia and bibliomania Gray's reputation
is fading. Younger folk find more up-to-date working-class
realism in Irvine Welsh, better science-fiction fantasy in Iain
Banks. The minority interested in brazen Postmodern
obscurantism find Gray's *Lanark* far surpassed by James
Kelman's *Translated Accounts* (published 2001). Of all his
works only *Lanark* has never been out of print, but here – and
finally, claims Gray – we have over a hundred thousand words
of his final novel.

Henry James said H.G. Wells made novels by tipping his
mind up like a cart and pouring in the contents. At first *Old
Men in Love* seems to have been made in the same haphazard
way, but some research in the National Library of Scotland
shows it is stuffed with extracts from Gray's earlier writings.
The two big historical narratives are from television plays

commissioned by Granada in the 1970s. The Greek one was
broadcast in a series called *For Conscience's Sake*, with
Christopher Logue in the part of Socrates. It extensively
plagiarised Plato's *Symposium* and passages in *Plutarch*. For a
Queen Victoria's Scandals series Gray then plagiarised Henry
James Prince's published diaries and Hepworth Dixon's
Spiritual Wives. He refused to let his name be attached to the
broadcast because a producer or director had changed the script
in ways he disliked, after which British television had no use
for Alasdair Gray. The archive has three typed dialogues for a
TV play about Filippo Lippi that was never commissioned, so
Old Men in Love has only three Florentine chapters. These rags
of forgotten historical plays fill nineteen chapters.

The rest are stuffed with a great deal of half-baked
popular science tipped in from Gray's 2000 anthology *The Book
of Prefaces*, also political diatribes from pamphlets published
before three general elections that were victories for New
Labour. These diatribes were and are protests against the
dismantling of peaceful British industries and the welfare state,
a process that has made Gray and many other professional
people richer. The description of an anti-war march was written
for *The Herald* in February 2003, then added inappropriately
to *The Ends of Our Tethers*, a collection of tales printed in 2004.
(It may be no coincidence that Will Self describes a similar
protest march in *The Book of Dave*, published 2006.) Like most
Scotsmen Gray thinks himself an authority on Burns, so we
find an essay about Burns mostly published in volume 30 of
the 1998 *Studies in Scottish Literature*, edited by Professor Ross
Roy. The most shameless padding is in chapter 17 which reprints
verbatim a section from chapter 8. The marginal note
signposting this obviously invites readers to think it a
charmingly eccentric *Shandyan* device, but Laurence Sterne's
typographical stunts in *Tristam Shandy* are never more than a
page long. This repetition is beyond a joke.

Three literary ploys try to unify the whole rag-bag. The
Introduction uses the text-as-found-manuscript invented by

Scott for his *Tales of My Landlord* novels and afterwards
plagiarised by Hogg, Pushkin, Kierkegaard, Dostoevsky and
Gray in two earlier novels. From Scott also comes the printing
of portentous quotations as epigraphs, some genuine and some
pseudonymous, a device run to death by Pushkin, Poe, George
Eliot and Rudyard Kipling. All but the introduction are cynically
sandwiched between references to the 2001 Trade Center
atrocity and May 2007 Scottish election in order to give the
whole thing spurious contemporary relevance. When all the
above is discounted we are left with the dreary tale of a failed
writer and dirty old man, who comes to a well-deserved end
through an affair with a drug-dealing procuress. This story is
neither tragic nor funny.

The best criticism of Gray is to quote his own and believe
it. In an 1990s epilogue to *Something Leather* he says all his
stories were about *men who found life a task they never doubted
until an unexpected collision opened their eyes and changed
their habits. The collision was usually with a woman, and the
transformation often ended in death.* He adds that knowing how
his talent works shows it is defunct because *imagination will
not employ whom it cannot surprise.* After that Gray published
nine more fictions with this hackneyed plot, *Old Men in Love*
being the last. The four old men are all versions of Gray in
fancy dress, with the Socratic collision homosexual, and though
this novel may indeed be his last I cannot simply dismiss it (as
Allan Massie dismissed Gray's 2004 *The Ends of Our Tethers*)
by calling it a collection of scraps from a tired writer's bottom
drawer. Neither the jacket into which Gray has lured Will Self
nor the egoism of the text will repel empty-headed fans of these
egregious authors. Many may fall under the influence of its
sinister propaganda for Scottish Nationalism and Socialism.

Far too many have forgotten or never known that the
German acronym for National Socialism is Nazi. Yeats' play
The Countess Kathleen, first performed in Dublin 1902, was a
bad poetic play that annoyed orthodox Catholics but
scandalously excited Irish Nationalists. After the 1916 Easter

Rising Yeats wondered if his play had stimulated rebellion among "certain men the English shot". From their comfortable studies plausible authors often give murderous lunatics high-minded excuses for atrocities. *Old Men in Love* cunningly avoids Hugh MacDiarmid's rabid Anglophobia; but as Billy Connolly, the New Labour Party and all respectable defenders of the 1707 Union point out, racist hatred of the English is what the Scottish lust for an impossible independence feeds upon. This book should therefore not be read, or if read, swiftly forgotten.

Hello and Goodbye, Mr Gray.

Sidney Workman
17 Linoleum Terrace
Kirkcaldy, June 2007

ADVANCED ELECTRONIC COMMUNICATIONS SYSTEMS

ADVANCED ELECTRONIC COMMUNICATIONS SYSTEMS

SECOND EDITION

WAYNE TOMASI
Mesa Community College

PRENTICE HALL, Englewood Cliffs, N.J. 07632

Tomasi, Wayne.
    Advanced electronic communications systems / Wayne Tomasi.—2nd ed.
        p.   cm.
    Includes index.
    ISBN 0-13-005901-3
    1. Digital communications.   I. Title.
TK5103.7.T65   1992
621.382—dc20

91-33809
CIP

Editorial/production supervision and
    interior design: Eileen M. O'Sullivan
Cover design: Bruce Kenselaar
Prepress buyer: Ilene Levy
Manufacturing buyer: Ed O'Dougherty

© 1992, 1987, by Prentice-Hall, Inc.
A Simon & Schuster Company
Englewood Cliffs, New Jersey 07632

Printed in the United States of America
10 9 8 7 6 5 4 3 2 1

ISBN 0-13-005901-3

Prentice-Hall International (UK) Limited, *London*
Prentice-Hall of Australia Pty. Limited, *Sydney*
Prentice-Hall Canada Inc., *Toronto*
Prentice-Hall Hispanoamericana, S.A., *Mexico*
Prentice-Hall of India Private Limited, *New Delhi*
Prentice-Hall of Japan, Inc., *Tokyo*
Simon & Schuster Asia Pte. Ltd., *Singapore*
Editora Prentice-Hall do Brasil, Ltda., *Rio de Janeiro*

In loving memory of my father,
Harry Tomasi

AH THATS NICE

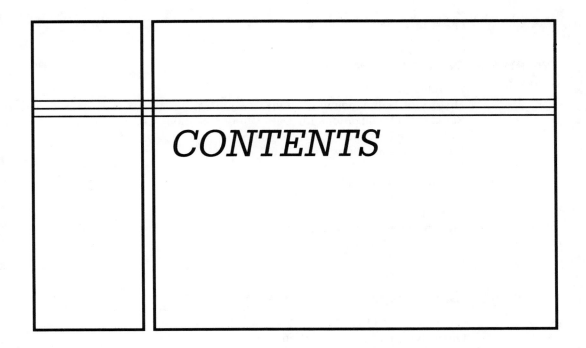

CONTENTS

PREFACE   **xi**

CHAPTER 1   DIGITAL COMMUNICATIONS   **1**

Introduction   1
Digital Communications   2
Shannon Limit for Information Capacity   2
Digital Radio   4
Frequency Shift Keying   4
Phase Shift Keying   11
Binary Phase Shift Keying   11
Quarternary Phase Shift Keying   17
Eight-Phase PSK   28
Sixteen-Phase PSK   32
Quadrature Amplitude Modulation   32
Eight QAM   33
Sixteen QAM   36
Bandwidth Efficiency   41
PSK and QAM Summary   42
Carrier Recovery   42
Differential Phase Shift Keying   45
Differential BPSK   45
Clock Recovery   47
Probability of Error and Bit Error Rate   47
Applications for Digtial Modulation   57

Questions 57
Problems 59

CHAPTER 2   DATA COMMUNICATIONS   61

Introduction 61
History of Data Communications 61
Standards Organizations for Data Communications 62
Data Communications Circuits 63
Data Communications Codes 68
Error Control 75
Synchronization 84
Data Communications Hardware 86
Serial Interfaces 94
Transmission Media and Data Modems 104
Modem Synchronization 109
Questions 114
Problems 115

CHAPTER 3   DATA COMMUNICATIONS PROTOCOLS   116

Introduction 116
Open Systems Interconnection 117
Asynchronous Protocols 119
Synchronous Protocols 122
Public Data Network 143
CCITT X.25 User-to-Network Interface Protocol 146
Local Area Networks 151
Ethernet 154
Questions 158
Problems 160

CHAPTER 4   DIGITAL TRANSMISSION   161

Introduction 161
Pulse Modulation 162
Pulse Code Modulation 163
PCM Codes 168
Delta Modulation PCM 191
Adaptive Delta Modulation PCM 193
Differential Pulse Code Modulation 194
Pulse Transmission 195
Questions 200
Problems 201

CHAPTER 5   DIGITAL MULTIPLEXING   203

Introduction 203
Time-Division Multiplexing 203

T1 Digital Carrier System   204
CCITT Time-Division-Multiplexed Carrier System   211
CODECS   212
2913/14 Combo Chip   212
North American Digital Hierarchy   227
Line Encoding   231
T Carriers   235
Frame Synchronization   238
Bit Interleaving versus Word Interleaving   240
Questions   241
Problems   242

CHAPTER 6   FREQUENCY-DIVISION MULTIPLEXING   **243**

Introduction   243
AT&T'S FDM Hierarchy   244
Composite Baseband Signal   246
L Carriers   257
Carrier Synchronization   257
Hybrid Data   261
Questions   264
Problems   266

CHAPTER 7   MICROWAVE RADIO COMMUNICATIONS AND
              SYSTEM GAIN   **267**

Introduction   267
Frequency versus Amplitude Modulation   267
Simplified FM Microwave Radio System   268
FM Microwave Radio Repeaters   270
Diversity   272
Protection Switching   274
FM Microwave Radio Stations   277
Path Characteristics   283
System Gain   286
Questions   296
Problems   297

CHAPTER 8   SATELLITE COMMUNICATIONS   **298**

Introduction   298
History of Satellites   299
Orbital Satellites   300
Geostationary Satellites   301
Orbital Patterns   302
Summary   303
Look Angles   304

Orbital Classifications, Spacing, and Frequency
Allocation   308
Radiation Patterns: Footprints   311
Satellite System Link Models   313
Satellite System Parameters   315
Satellite System Link Equations   327
Link Equations   327
Link Budget   328
Nonideal System Parameters   334
Questions   335
Problems   335

**CHAPTER 9   SATELLITE MULTIPLE-ACCESS
ARRANGEMENTS**   **338**

Introduction   338
FDM/FM Satellite Systems   338
ANIK-D Communications Satellite   340
Multiple Accessing   340
Frequency Hopping   353
Channel Capacity   353
Questions   355
Problems   356

CHAPTER 10   FIBER OPTIC COMMUNICATIONS   **357**

Introduction   357
History of Fiber Optics   358
Optical Fibers versus Metallic Cable Facilities   359
Electromagnetic Spectrum   360
Optical Fiber Communications System   362
Optical Fibers   363
Light Propagation   365
Propagation of Light through an Optical Fiber   371
Optical Fiber Configurations   372
Comparison of the Three Types of Optical Fibers   375
Acceptance Angle and Acceptance Cone   376
Losses in Optical Fiber Cables   379
Light Sources   387
Light Detectors   392
Lasers   395
Questions   397
Problems   398

SOLUTIONS TO ODD-NUMBERED PROBLEMS   **399**

INDEX   **403**

PREFACE

The second edition of *Advanced Electronic Communications Systems* provides a modern, comprehensive coverage of the field of electronic communications. The book extends and updates the coverage of digital and data communications, satellite communications, and fiber optics communications that was presented in the first edition. The major new topics and extended coverage of existing topics in this edition are:

1. Bit-error-rate and probability of error
2. Standards organizations for data communications
3. Open Systems Interconnection (OSI)
4. Ethernet system
5. Pulse transmission and eye patterns
6. Radio-wave path characteristics
7. *ANIK-D* communications satellite system
8. Introduction to laser technology

This book was written so that a reader with previous knowledge in basic electronic communications theory, basic digital theory, a basic knowledge of filter concepts, and an understanding of mathematics through trigonometry will have little trouble grasping the concepts presented. Also, the order in which the chapter topics are covered does not need to be followed strictly. Digital, data, and analog communications techniques are separated in such a way that almost any chapter sequence can be used. Within the text, there are numerous examples that emphasize the important concepts, and questions and problems are included at the end of each chapter. Also, answers to the odd-numbered problems are given at the end of the book.

Chapter 1 introduces the concepts of digital transmission and digital modulation. In this chapter, the most common modulation schemes used in modern digital radio systems (FSK, PSK, and QAM) are described. The concepts of information capacity and bandwidth efficiency are explained. An extended coverage of probability of error and bit-error-rate has been added to the end of this chapter. Chapter 2 introduces the field of data communications. Detailed explanations are given for numerous data communications concepts, including transmission methods, circuit configurations, topologies, character codes, error control mechanisms, data formats, and data modems. A description of standards organizations for data communications has been added to this chapter. Chapter 3 describes data communications protocols. Synchronous and asynchronous data protocols are first defined, then explicit examples are given for each. The most popular character and bit-oriented protocols are described. A section on Open Systems Interconnections (OSI) and Ethernet has been added to this chapter. Chapter 4 introduces digital transmission techniques. This includes a detailed explanation of pulse code modulation. The concepts of sampling, encoding, and companding are explained. Chapter 4 also includes descriptions of adaptive delta modulation pulse code modulation and differential pulse code modulation. A section on pulse transmission and eye patterns has been added to this chapter. Chapter 5 explains the multiplexing of digital signals. Time-division multiplexing is discussed in detail and the operation of a modern LSI combo chip is explained. The North American Digital Hierarchy for digital transmission is outlined, including explanations of line encoding schemes, error detection/correction methods, and synchronization techniques. In Chapter 6 analog multiplexing is explained and AT&T's North American frequency-division multiplexing hierarchy is described. Several methods are explained in which digital information can be transmitted with analog signals over the same communications medium. Chapter 7 introduces microwave radio communications and the concept of system gain. A block diagram approach to the operation of a microwave radio system is presented and numerous examples are included. A section on radio-wave path characteristics has been added to this chapter. In Chapter 8 satellite communications is introduced and the basic concepts of orbital patterns, radiation patterns, geosynchronous, and nonsynchronous systems are covered. System parameters and link equations are discussed and a detailed explanation of a satellite link budget is given. Chapter 9 extends the coverage of satellite systems to methods of multiple accessing. The three predominant methods for multiple accessing— frequency-division, time-division, and code-division multiple accessing—are explained. A section describing the *ANIK-D* communications satellite system has been added to this chapter. Chapter 10 covers the basic concepts of a fiber optic communications system. A detailed explanation is given for light-wave propagation through a guided fiber. Also several light sources and detectors are discussed, contrasting their advantages and disadvantages. A section on lasers has been added to this chapter.

ACKNOWLEDGMENTS

I would like to acknowledge the following individuals for their contributions to this book: Kathryn Pavelec, production editor for the first edition; Eileen O'Sullivan, production editor for this edition; the three reviewers of the original manuscript—John Browne, SUNY—Farmingdale; Robert E. Greenwood, Ryerson Polytechnical Institute; and James W. Stewart, DeVry, Woodbridge; and the three reviewers of the manuscript for this edition, Larry A. Welles, ITT Technical Institute Indianapolis; James W. Stewart, DeVry, Woodbridge; and Susan A.R. Garrod, Purdue University, Indiana.

Wayne F. Tomasi

ADVANCED ELECTRONIC COMMUNICATIONS SYSTEMS

1

DIGITAL COMMUNICATIONS

INTRODUCTION

During the past several years, the *electronic communications* industry has undergone some remarkable technological changes. Traditional electronic communications systems that use conventional analog modulation techniques, such as *amplitude modulation* (AM), *frequency modulation* (FM), and *phase modulation* (PM), are gradually being replaced with more modern *digital communications systems*. Digital communications systems offer several outstanding advantages over traditional analog systems: ease of processing, ease of multiplexing, and noise immunity.

In essence, electronic communications is the transmission, reception, and processing of *information* with the use of electronic circuits. Information is defined as knowledge or intelligence communicated or received. Figure 1-1 shows a simplified block diagram of an electronic communications system, which comprise three primary sections: a *source*, a *destination*, and a *transmission medium*. Information is propagated through a communications system in the form of symbols which can be *analog* (proportional), such as the human voice, video picture information, or music, or *digital* (discrete), such as binary-coded numbers, alpha/numeric codes, graphic symbols, microprocessor op codes, or data base information. However, very often the source information is unsuitable for transmission in its original form and must be converted to a more suitable form prior to transmission. For example, with digital communications systems, analog information is converted to digital form prior to transmission, and with analog

1

Figure 1-1 Simplified block diagram for an electronic communications system.

communications systems, digital data are converted to analog signals prior to transmission.

DIGITAL COMMUNICATIONS

The term *digital communications* covers a broad area of communications techniques, including *digital transmission* and *digital radio*. Digital transmission is the transmittal of digital pulses between two or more points in a communications system. Digital radio is the transmittal of digitally modulated analog carriers between two or more points in a communications system. Digital transmission systems require a physical facility between the transmitter and receiver, such as a metallic wire pair, a coaxial cable, or an optical fiber cable. In digital radio systems, the transmission medium is free space or the earth's atmosphere.

Figure 1-2 shows simplified block diagrams of both a digital transmission system and a digital radio system. In a digital transmission system, the original source information may be in digital or analog form. If it is in analog form, it must be converted to digital pulses prior to transmission and converted back to analog form at the receive end. In a digital radio system, the modulating input signal and the demodulated output signal are digital pulses. The digital pulses could originate from a digital transmission system, from a digital source such as a mainframe computer, or from the binary encoding of an analog signal.

SHANNON LIMIT FOR INFORMATION CAPACITY

The *information capacity* of a communications system represents the number of independent symbols that can be carried through the system in a given unit of time. The most basic symbol is the *binary digit* (bit). Therefore, it is often convenient to express the information capacity of a system in *bits per second* (bps). In 1928, R. Hartley of Bell Telephone Laboratories developed a useful relationship among bandwidth, transmission time, and information capacity. Simply stated, *Hartley's law* is

$$C \propto B \times T \tag{1-1}$$

where

C = information capacity
B = bandwidth
T = transmission time

From Equation 1-1 it can be seen that the information capacity is a linear function of bandwidth and transmission time and is directly proportional to both. If either the bandwidth or the transmission time is changed, a directly proportional change in information capacity will occur.

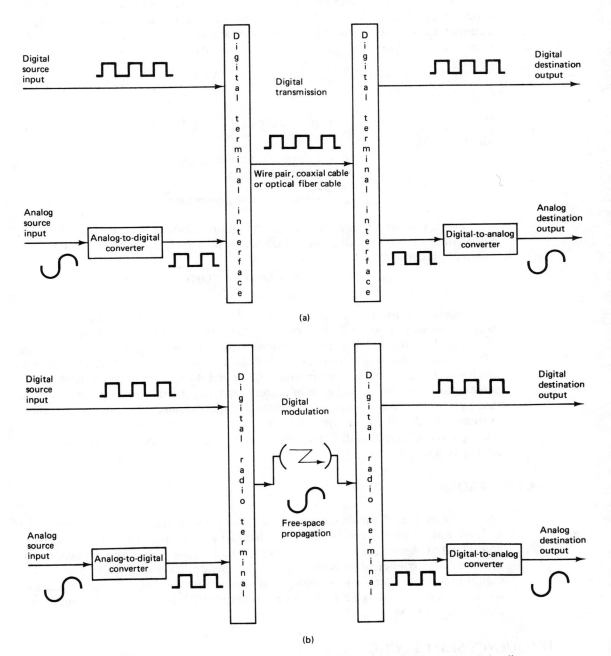

Figure 1-2 Digital communications systems: (a) digital transmission; (b) digital radio.

Shannon Limit for Information Capacity

3

In 1948, C. E. Shannon (also of Bell Telephone Laboratories) published a paper in the *Bell System Technical Journal* relating the information capacity of a communications channel to bandwidth and signal-to-noise ratio. Mathematically stated, the *Shannon limit for information capacity* is

$$C = B \log_2 \left(1 + \frac{S}{N} \right)$$
(1-2a)

or

$$C = 3.32 \, B \log_{10} \left(1 + \frac{S}{N} \right)$$
(1-2b)

where

C = information capacity (bps)
B = bandwidth
$\frac{S}{N}$ = signal-to-noise power ratio

For a standard voice band communications channel with a signal-to-noise power ratio of 1000 (30 dB) and a bandwidth of 2.7 kHz, the Shannon limit for information capacity is

$$C = 2700 \log_2 (1 + 1000)$$
$$= 26.9 \, \text{kbps}$$

Shannon's formula is often misunderstood. The results of the preceding example indicate that 26.9 kbps can be transferred through a 2.7-kHz channel. This may be true, but it cannot be done with a binary system. To achieve an information transmission rate of 26.9 kbps through a 2.7-kHz channel, each symbol transmitted must contain more than one bit of information. Therefore, to achieve the Shannon limit for information capacity, digital transmission systems that have more than two output conditions (symbols) must be used. Several such systems are described in the following chapters. These systems include both analog and digital modulation techniques and the transmission of both digital and analog signals.

DIGITAL RADIO

The property that distinguishes a digital radio system from a conventional AM, FM, or PM radio system is that in a digital radio system the modulating and demodulated signals are digital pulses rather than analog waveforms. Digital radio uses analog carriers just as conventional systems do. Essentially, there are three digital modulation techniques that are commonly used in digital radio systems: *frequency shift keying* (FSK), *phase shift keying* (PSK), and *quadrature amplitude modulation* (QAM).

FREQUENCY SHIFT KEYING

Frequency shift keying (FSK) is a relatively simple, low-performance form of digital modulation. Binary FSK is a form of constant-envelope angle modulation similar to conventional frequency modulation except that the modulating signal is a binary pulse stream that varies between two discrete voltage levels rather than a continuously changing analog waveform. The general expression for a binary FSK signal is

$$v(t) = V_c \cos \left[\left(\omega_c + \frac{f_m(t)\, \Delta\omega}{2} \right) t \right]$$
(1-3)

where

$v(t)$ = binary FSK waveform
V_c = peak unmodulated carrier amplitude
ω_c = radian carrier frequency
$f_m(t)$ = binary digital modulating signal frequency
$\Delta\omega$ = radian difference in output frequency

From Equation 1-3 it can be seen that with binary FSK the carrier amplitude V_c remains constant with modulation. However, the output carrier radian frequency (ω_c) shifts by an amount equal to $\pm \Delta\omega/2$. The frequency shift ($\Delta\omega/2$) is proportional to the amplitude and polarity of the binary input signal. For example, a binary one could be $+1$ volt and a binary zero -1 volt producing frequency shifts of $+\Delta\omega/2$ and $-\Delta\omega/2$, respectively. In addition, the rate at which the carrier frequency shifts is equal to the rate of change of the binary input signal $f_m(t)$ (i.e., the input bit rate). Thus the output carrier frequency deviates (shifts) between $\omega_c + \Delta\omega/2$ and $\omega_c - \Delta\omega/2$ at a rate equal to f_m.

FSK Transmitter

With binary FSK, the center or carrier frequency is shifted (deviated) by the binary input data. Consequently, the output of a binary FSK modulator is a step function in the frequency domain. As the binary input signal changes from a logic 0 to a logic 1, and vice versa, the FSK output shifts between two frequencies: a *mark* or *logic 1 frequency* and a *space* or *logic 0 frequency*. With binary FSK, there is a change in the output frequency each time the logic condition of the binary input signal changes. Consequently, the output rate of change is equal to the input rate of change. In digital modulation, the rate of change at the input to the modulator is called the *bit rate* and has the units of bits per second (bps). The rate of change at the output of the modulator is called *baud* or *baud rate* and is equal to the reciprocal of the time of one output signaling element. In essence, baud is the line speed in symbols per second. In binary FSK, the input and output rates of change are equal; therefore, the bit rate and baud rate are equal. A simple binary FSK transmitter is shown in Figure 1-3.

Bandwidth Considerations of FSK

As with all electronic communications systems, bandwidth is one of the primary considerations when designing a binary FSK transmitter. FSK is similar to conventional frequency modulation and so can be described in a similar manner.

Frequency Shift Keying   5

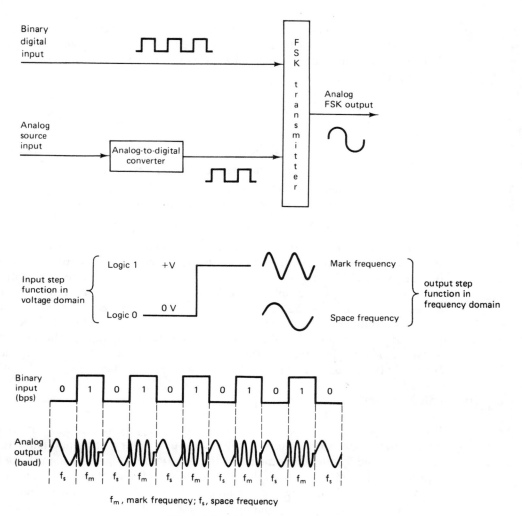

Figure 1-3 Binary FSK transmitter.

Figure 1-4 shows a binary FSK modulator. FSK modulators are very similar to conventional FM modulators and are very often *voltage-controlled oscillators* (VCOs). The fastest input rate of change occurs when the binary input is a series of alternating 1's and 0's: namely, a square wave. Consequently, if only the *fundamental frequency* of the input is considered, the *highest modulating frequency* is equal to one-half of the input bit rate.

The rest frequency of the VCO is chosen such that it falls halfway between the mark and space frequencies. A logic 1 condition at the input shifts the VCO from its rest frequency to the mark frequency, and a logic 0 condition at the input shifts the VCO from its rest frequency to the space frequency. Consequently, as the input binary signal changes from a logic 1 to a logic 0, and vice versa, the

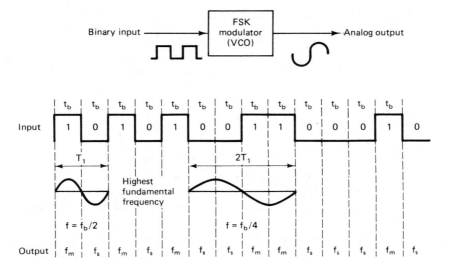

Figure 1-4 FSK modulator, t_b, Time of one bit = 1/bps; f_m, mark frequency; f_s, space frequency; T1, period of shortest cycle; 1/T1, fundamental frequency of binary square wave; f_b, input bit rate (bps).

VCO output frequency *shifts* or *deviates* back and forth between the mark and space frequencies. Because binary FSK is a form of frequency modulation, the formula for *modulation index* used in FM is also valid for binary FSK. Modulation index is given as

$$\text{MI} = \frac{\Delta f}{f_a} \tag{1-4}$$

where

$$\text{MI} = \text{modulation index}$$
$$\Delta f = \text{frequency deviation (Hz)}$$
$$f_a = \text{modulating frequency (Hz)}$$

The worst-case modulation index is the modulation index that yields the widest output bandwidth, called the *deviation ratio*. The worst-case or widest bandwidth occurs when both the frequency deviation and the modulating frequencies are at their maximum values.

In a binary FSK modulator, Δf is the peak frequency deviation of the carrier and is equal to the difference between the rest frequency and either the mark or space frequency (or half the difference between the mark and space frequencies). The peak frequency deviation depends on the amplitude of the modulating signal. In a binary digital signal, all logic 1's have the same voltage and all logic 0's have the same voltage; consequently, the frequency deviation is constant and always at its maximum value. f_a is equal to the fundamental frequency of the binary input which under the worst-case condition (alternating 1's and 0's) is equal to

Frequency Shift Keying   **7**

one-half of the bit rate (f_b). Consequently, for binary FSK,

$$\text{MI} = \frac{\left|\dfrac{f_m - f_s}{2}\right|}{\dfrac{f_b}{2}} = \frac{|f_m - f_s|}{f_b} \tag{1-5}$$

where

$$\frac{|f_m - f_s|}{2} = \text{peak frequency deviation}$$

$$f_b = \text{input bit rate}$$

$$\frac{f_b}{2} = \text{fundamental frequency of the binary input signal}$$

With conventional FM, the bandwidth is directly proportional to the modulation index. Consequently, in binary FSK the modulation index is generally kept below 1.0, thus producing a relatively narrow band FM output spectrum. The minimum bandwidth required to propagate a signal is called the *minimum Nyquist bandwidth* (f_n). When modulation is used and a double-sided output spectrum is generated, the minimum bandwidth is called the *minimum double-sided Nyquist bandwidth* or the *minimum IF bandwidth*.

Example 1-1

For a binary FSK modulator with space, rest, and mark frequencies of 60, 70, and 80 MHz, respectively and an input bit rate of 20 Mbps, determine the output baud and the minimum required bandwidth.

Solution   Substituting into Equation 1-5, we have

$$\text{MI} = \frac{|f_m - f_s|}{f_b} = \frac{|80\,\text{MHz} - 60\,\text{MHz}|}{20\,\text{Mbps}}$$

$$= \frac{20\,\text{MHz}}{20\,\text{Mbps}} = 1.0$$

From the Bessel chart (Table 1-1), a modulation index of 1.0 yields three sets of significant side frequencies. Each side frequency is separated from the center frequency or an adjacent side frequency by a value equal to the modulating frequency,

TABLE 1-1   BESSEL FUNCTION CHART

MI	J_0	J_1	J_2	J_3	J_4
0.0	1.00				
0.25	0.98	0.12			
0.5	0.94	0.24	0.03		
1.0	0.77	0.44	0.11	0.02	
1.5	0.51	0.56	0.23	0.06	0.01
2.0	0.22	0.58	0.35	0.13	0.03

which in this example is 10 MHz (f_b/2). The output spectrum for this modulator is shown in Figure 1-5. It can be seen that the minimum double-sided Nyquist bandwidth is 60 MHz and the baud rate is 20 megabaud, the same as the bit rate.

Because binary FSK is a form of narrowband frequency modulation, the minimum bandwidth is dependent on the modulation index. For a modulation index between 0.5 and 1, either two or three sets of significant side frequencies are generated. Thus the minimum bandwidth is two to three times the input bit rate.

FSK Receiver

The most common circuit used for demodulating binary FSK signals is the *phase-locked loop* (PLL), which is shown in block diagram form in Figure 1-6. A PLL-FSK demodulator works very much like a PLL-FM demodulator. As the input to the PLL shifts between the mark and space frequencies, the *dc error voltage* at the output of the phase comparator follows the frequency shift. Because there are only two input frequencies (mark and space), there are also only two output error voltages. One represents a logic 1 and the other a logic 0. Therefore, the output is a two-level (binary) representation of the FSK input. Generally, the natural frequency of the PLL is made equal to the center frequency of the FSK modulator. As a result, the changes in the dc error voltage follow the changes in the analog input frequency and are symmetrical around 0 Vdc.

Binary FSK has a poorer error performance than PSK or QAM and, consequently, is seldom used for high-performance digital radio systems. Its use is restricted to low-performance, low-cost, asynchronous data modems that are used for data communications over analog, voice band telephone lines (see Chapter 2).

Minimum Shift-Keying FSK

Minimum shift-keying FSK (MSK) is a form of *continuous-phase* frequency shift keying (CPFSK). Essentially, MSK is binary FSK except that the mark and space frequencies are *synchronized* with the input binary bit rate. Synchronous

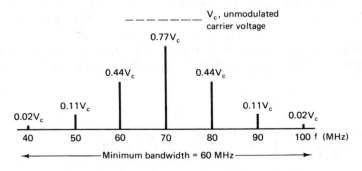

Figure 1-5 FSK output spectrum for Example 1-1.

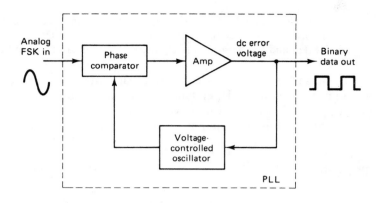

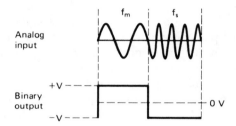

Figure 1-6 PLL-FSK demodulator.

simply means that there is a precise time relationship between the two; it does not mean they are equal. With MSK, the mark and space frequencies are selected such that they are separated from the center frequency by an exact odd multiple of one-half of the bit rate [f_m and $f_s = n(f_b/2)$, where n = any odd integer]. This ensures that there is a smooth phase transition in the analog output signal when it changes from a mark to a space frequency, or vice versa. Figure 1-7 shows a *noncontinuous* FSK waveform. It can be seen that when the input changes from a logic 1 to a logic 0, and vice versa, there is an abrupt phase discontinuity in the analog output signal. When this occurs, the demodulator has trouble following the frequency shift; consequently, an error may occur.

Figure 1-8 shows a continuous phase MSK waveform. Notice that when the output frequency changes, it is a smooth, continuous transition. Consequently, there are no phase discontinuities. MSK has a better bit-error performance than conventional binary FSK for a given signal-to-noise ratio. The disadvantage of

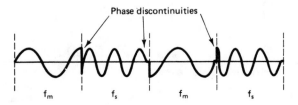

Figure 1-7 Noncontinuous FSK waveform.

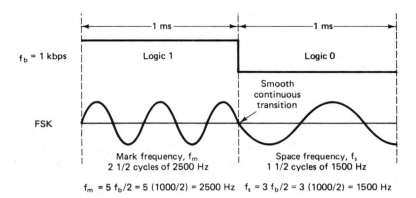

$$f_m = 5\, f_b/2 = 5\, (1000/2) = 2500\ \text{Hz} \quad f_s = 3\, f_b/2 = 3\, (1000/2) = 1500\ \text{Hz}$$

Figure 1-8 Continuous-phase MSK waveform.

MSK is that it requires synchronizing circuits and is therefore more expensive to implement.

PHASE SHIFT KEYING

Phase shift keying (PSK) is another form of angle-modulated, constant-envelope digital modulation. PSK is similar to conventional phase modulation except that with PSK the input signal is a binary digital signal and a limited number of output phases are possible.

BINARY PHASE SHIFT KEYING

With *binary phase shift keying* (BPSK), two output phases are possible for a single carrier frequency ("binary" meaning "2"). One output phase represents a logic 1 and the other a logic 0. As the input digital signal changes state, the phase of the output carrier shifts between two angles that are 180° out of phase. Other names for BPSK are *phase reversal keying* (PRK) and *biphase modulation*. BPSK is a form of suppressed carrier, square-wave modulation of a continuous wave (CW) signal.

BPSK Transmitter

Figure 1-9 shows a simplified block diagram of a BPSK modulator. The balanced modulator acts like a phase reversing switch. Depending on the logic condition of the digital input, the carrier is transferred to the output either in phase or 180° out of phase with the reference carrier oscillator.

Figure 1-10a shows the schematic diagram of a balanced ring modulator. The balanced modulator has two inputs: a carrier that is in phase with the reference oscillator and the binary digital data. For the balanced modulator to operate properly, the digital input voltage must be much greater than the peak

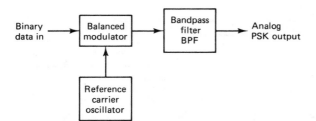

Figure 1-9   BPSK modulator.

carrier voltage. This ensures that the digital input controls the on/off state of diodes D1–D4. If the binary input is a logic 1 (positive voltage), diodes D1 and D2 are forward biased and "on," while diodes D3 and D4 are reverse biased and "off" (Figure 1-10b). With the polarities shown, the carrier voltage is developed across transformer T2 in phase with the carrier voltage across T1. Consequently, the output signal is in phase with the reference oscillator.

If the binary input is a logic 0 (negative voltage), diodes D1 and D2 are reverse biased and "off," while diodes D3 and D4 are forward biased and "on" (Figure 1-10c). As a result, the carrier voltage is developed across transformer T2 180° out of phase with the carrier voltage across T1. Consequently, the output signal is 180° out of phase with the reference oscillator. Figure 1-11 shows the truth table, phasor diagram, and constellation diagram for a BPSK modulator. A *constellation diagram,* which is sometimes called a *signal state-space diagram,* is similar to a phasor diagram except that the entire phasor is not drawn. In a constellation diagram, only the relative positions of the peaks of the phasors are shown.

Bandwidth Considerations of BPSK

A balanced modulator is a *product modulator;* the output signal is the product of the two input signals. In a BPSK modulator, the carrier input signal is multiplied by the binary data. If $+1$ V is assigned to a logic 1 and -1 V is assigned to a logic 0, the input carrier ($\sin \omega_c t$) is multiplied by either a $+$ or $-$ 1. Consequently, the output signal is either $+1 \sin \omega_c t$ or $-1 \sin \omega_c t$; the first represents a signal that is *in phase* with the reference oscillator, the latter a signal that is 180° out of phase with the reference oscillator. Each time the input logic condition changes, the output phase changes. Consequently, for BPSK, the output rate of change (baud) is equal to the input rate of change (bps), and the widest output bandwidth occurs when the input binary data are an alternating 1/0 sequence. The fundamental frequency (f_a) of an alternating 1/0 bit sequence is equal to one-half of the bit rate ($f_b/2$). Mathematically, the output phase of a BPSK modulator is

$$\text{output} = \underbrace{(\sin \omega_a t)}_{\substack{\text{fundamental frequency} \\ \text{of the binary} \\ \text{modulating signal}}} \times \underbrace{(\sin \omega_c t)}_{\substack{\text{unmodulated} \\ \text{carrier}}} \qquad (1\text{-}6)$$

or

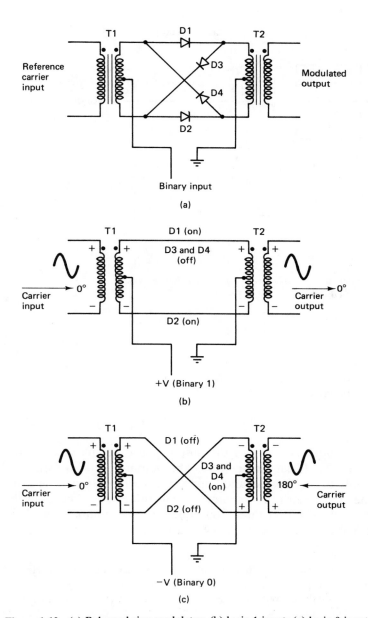

Figure 1-10 (a) Balanced ring modulator; (b) logic 1 input; (c) logic 0 input.

$$\tfrac{1}{2} \cos (\omega_c - \omega_a)t - \tfrac{1}{2} \cos (\omega_c + \omega_a)t$$

Consequently, the minimum double-sided Nyquist bandwidth (f_n) is

$$\begin{array}{ccc} \omega_c + \omega_a & & \omega_c + \omega_a \\ - (\omega_c - \omega_a) & \text{or} & - \omega_c + \omega_a \\ \hline & & 2\omega_a \end{array}$$

Binary Phase Shift Keying   **13**

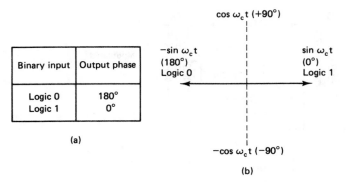

Binary input	Output phase
Logic 0	180°
Logic 1	0°

(a)

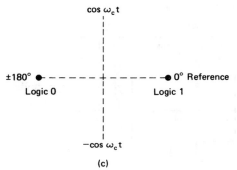

(b)

(c)

Figure 1-11 BPSK modulator: (a) truth table; (b) phasor diagram; (c) constellation diagram.

and because $\omega_a = f_b/2$,

$$f_n = 2\left(\frac{f_b}{2}\right) = f_b$$

Figure 1-12 shows the output phase versus time relationship for a BPSK waveform. It can be seen that the output spectrum from a BPSK modulator is simply a double-sideband suppressed carrier signal where the upper and lower side frequencies are separated from the carrier frequency by a value equal to one-half of the bit rate. Consequently, the minimum bandwidth (f_n) required to pass the worst-case BPSK output signal is equal to the input bit rate.

Example 1-2

For a BPSK modulator with a carrier frequency of 70 MHz and an input bit rate of 10 Mbps, determine the maximum and minimum upper and lower side frequencies, draw the output spectrum, determine the minimum Nyquist bandwidth, and calculate the baud.

Solution Substituting into Equation 1-6 yields

$$\text{output} = (\sin \omega_a t)\,(\sin \omega_c t)$$
$$= [\sin 2\pi(5\text{ MHz})t][\sin 2\pi(70\text{ MHz})t]$$
$$= \tfrac{1}{2}\cos 2\pi\underbrace{(70\text{ MHz} - 5\text{ MHz})t}_{\text{lower side frequency}} - \tfrac{1}{2}\cos 2\pi\underbrace{(70\text{ MHz} + 5\text{ MHz})t}_{\text{upper side frequency}}$$

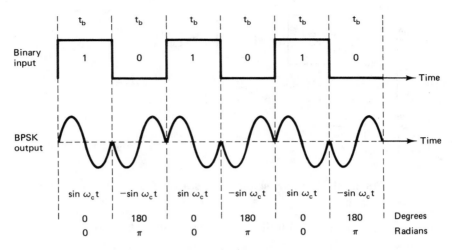

Figure 1-12 Output phase versus time relationship for a BPSK modulator.

Minimum lower side frequency (LSF):

$$\text{LSF} = 70 \text{ MHz} - 5 \text{ MHz} = 65 \text{ MHz}$$

Maximum upper side frequency (USF):

$$\text{USF} = 70 \text{ MHz} + 5 \text{ MHz} = 75 \text{ MHz}$$

Therefore, the output spectrum for the worst-case binary input conditions is as follows:

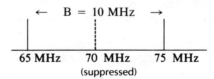

The minimum Nyquist bandwidth (f_n) is

$$f_n = 75 \text{ MHz} - 65 \text{ MHz} = 10 \text{ MHz}$$

and the baud $= f_b$ or 10 megabaud.

BPSK Receiver

Figure 1-13 shows the block diagram of a BPSK receiver. The input signal may be $+\sin \omega_c t$ or $-\sin \omega_c t$. The coherent carrier recovery circuit detects and regenerates a carrier signal that is both frequency and phase coherent with the original transmit carrier. The balanced modulator is a product detector; the output is the product of the two inputs (the BPSK signal and the recovered carrier). The low-pass filter (LPF) separates the recovered binary data from the complex demodulated spectrum. Mathematically, the demodulation process is as follows.

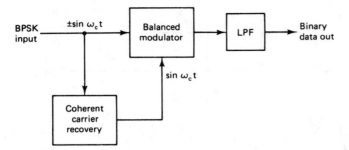

Figure 1-13 PSK receiver.

For a BPSK input signal of $+\sin \omega_c t$ (logic 1), the output of the balanced modulator is

$$\text{output} = (\sin \omega_c t)(\sin \omega_c t) = \sin^2 \omega_c t \qquad (1\text{-}7)$$

or

$$\sin^2 \omega_c t = \tfrac{1}{2}(1 - \cos 2\omega_c t) = \tfrac{1}{2} - \tfrac{1}{2}\cos 2\omega_c t \nearrow \text{(filtered out)}$$

leaving
$$\text{output} = +\tfrac{1}{2}\text{V dc} = \text{logic } 1$$

It can be seen that the output of the balanced modulator contains a positive dc voltage $(+\tfrac{1}{2}\text{ V})$ and a cosine wave at twice the carrier frequency $(2\omega_c)$. The LPF has a cutoff frequency much lower than $2\omega_c$ and thus blocks the second harmonic of the carrier and passes only the positive dc component. A positive dc voltage represents a demodulated logic 1.

For a BPSK input signal of $-\sin \omega_c t$ (logic 0), the output of the balanced modulator is

$$\text{output} = (-\sin \omega_c t)(\sin \omega_c t) = -\sin^2 \omega_c t \qquad (1\text{-}8)$$

or

$$-\sin^2 \omega_c t = -\tfrac{1}{2}(1 - \cos 2\omega_c t) = -\tfrac{1}{2} + \tfrac{1}{2}\cos 2\omega_c t \nearrow \text{(filtered out)}$$

leaving
$$\text{output} = -\tfrac{1}{2}\text{V dc} = \text{logic } 0$$

The output of the balanced modulator contains a negative dc voltage $(-\tfrac{1}{2}\text{ v})$ and a cosine wave at twice the carrier frequency $(2\omega_c)$. Again, the LPF blocks the second harmonic of the carrier and passes only the negative dc component. A negative dc voltage represents a demodulated logic 0.

M-ary Encoding

M-ary is a term derived from the word "binary." *M* is simply a digit that represents the number of conditions possible. The two digital modulation tech-

16   **Digital Communications**   **Chap. 1**

niques discussed thus far (binary FSK and BPSK) are binary systems; there are only two possible output conditions. One represents a logic 1 and the other a logic 0; thus they are M-ary systems where $M = 2$. With digital modulation, very often it is advantageous to encode at a level higher than binary. For example, a PSK system with four possible output phases is an M-ary system where $M = 4$. If there were eight possible output phases, $M = 8$, and so on. Mathematically,

$$N = \log_2 M \qquad (1\text{-}9)$$

where

N = number of bits
M = number of output conditions possible with N bits

For example, if 2 bits were allowed to enter a modulator before the output were allowed to change,

$$2 = \log_2 M \quad \text{and} \quad 2^2 = M \qquad \text{thus } M = 4$$

An $M = 4$ indicates that with 2 bits, four different output conditions are possible. For $N = 3$, $M = 2^3$ or 8, and so on.

QUATERNARY PHASE SHIFT KEYING

Quaternary phase shift keying (QPSK), or *quadrature PSK* as it is sometimes called, is another form of angle-modulated, constant-envelope digital modulation. QPSK is an M-ary encoding technique where $M = 4$ (hence the name "quaternary," meaning "4"). With QPSK four output phases are possible for a single carrier frequency. Because there are four different output phases, there must be four different input conditions. Because the digital input to a QPSK modulator is a binary (base 2) signal, to produce four different input conditions it takes more than a single input bit. With 2 bits, there are four possible conditions: 00, 01, 10, and 11. Therefore, with QPSK, the binary input data are combined into groups of 2 bits called *dibits*. Each dibit code generates one of the four possible output phases. Therefore, for each 2-bit dibit clocked into the modulator, a single output change occurs. Therefore, the rate of change at the output (baud rate) is one-half of the input bit rate.

QPSK Transmitter

A block diagram of a QPSK modulator is shown in Figure 1-14. Two bits (a dibit) are clocked into the bit spliter. After both bits have been serially inputted, they are simultaneously parallel outputted. One bit is directed to the I channel and the other to the Q channel. The I bit modulates a carrier that is in phase with the reference oscillator (hence the name "I" for "in phase" channel), and the Q bit modulates a carrier that is 90° out of phase or in quadrature with the reference carrier (hence the name "Q" for "quadrature" channel).

It can be seen that once a dibit has been split into the I and Q channels.

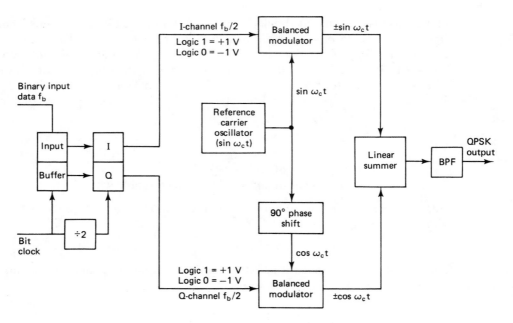

Figure 1-14 QPSK modulator.

the operation is the same as in a BPSK modulator. Essentially, a QPSK modulator is two BPSK modulators combined in parallel. Again, for a logic 1 = +1 V and a logic 0 = −1 V, two phases are possible at the output of the I balanced modulator (+sin $\omega_c t$ and −sin $\omega_c t$), and two phases are possible at the output of the Q balanced modulator (+cos $\omega_c t$ and −cos $\omega_c t$). When the linear summer combines the two quadrature (90° out of phase) signals, there are four possible resultant phases: +sin $\omega_c t$ + cos $\omega_c t$, +sin $\omega_c t$ − cos $\omega_c t$, −sin $\omega_c t$ + cos $\omega_c t$, and −sin $\omega_c t$ − cos $\omega_c t$.

Example 1-3

For the QPSK modulator shown in Figure 1-14, construct the truth table, phasor diagram, and constellation diagram.

Solution For a binary data input of Q = 0 and I = 0, the two inputs to the I balanced modulator are −1 and sin $\omega_c t$, and the two inputs to the Q balanced modulator are −1 and cos $\omega_c t$. Consequently, the outputs are

$$\text{I balanced modulator} = (-1)\,(\sin \omega_c t) = -1 \sin \omega_c t$$

$$\text{Q balanced modulator} = (-1)\,(\cos \omega_c t) = -1 \cos \omega_c t$$

and the output of the linear summer is

$$-1 \cos \omega_c t - 1 \sin \omega_c t = 1.414 \sin \omega_c t - 135°$$

For the remaining dibit codes (01, 10, and 11), the procedure is the same. The results are shown in Figure 1-15.   •

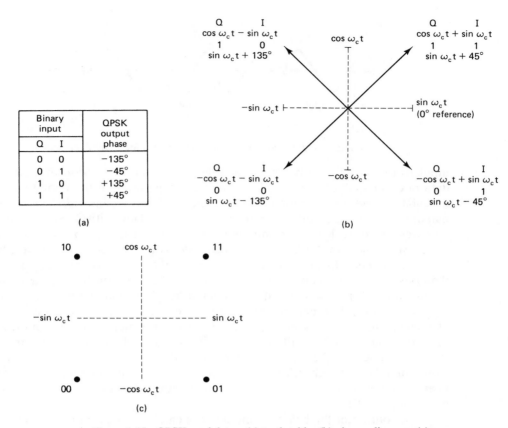

Binary input		QPSK output phase
Q	I	
0	0	−135°
0	1	−45°
1	0	+135°
1	1	+45°

(a)

(b)

(c)

Figure 1-15 QPSK modulator: (a) truth table; (b) phasor diagram; (c) constellation diagram.

In Figure 1-15b it can be seen that with QPSK each of the four possible output phasors has exactly the same amplitude. Therefore, the binary information must be encoded entirely in the phase of the output signal. This is the most important characteristic of PSK that distinguishes it from QAM, which is explained later in this chapter. Also, from Figure 1-15b it can be seen that the angular separation between any two adjacent phasors in QPSK is 90°. Therefore, a QPSK signal can undergo almost a +45° or −45° shift in phase during transmission and still retain the correct encoded information when demodulated at the receiver. Figure 1-16 shows the output phase versus time relationship for a QPSK modulator.

Bandwidth Considerations of QPSK

With QPSK, since the input data are divided into two channels, the bit rate in either the I or the Q channel is equal to one-half of the input data rate $(f_b/2)$. (Essentially, the bit splitter stretches the I and Q bits to twice their input bit length.) Consequently, the highest fundamental frequency present at the data

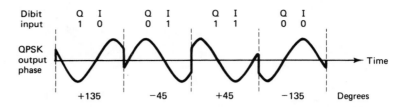

Figure 1-16 Output phase versus time relationship for a QPSK modulator.

input to the I or the Q balanced modulator is equal to one-fourth of the input data rate (one-half of $f_b/2 = f_b/4$). As a result, the output of the I and Q balanced modulators requires a minimum double-sided Nyquist bandwidth equal to one-half of the incoming bit rate ($f_n =$ twice $f_b/4 = f_b/2$). Thus with QPSK, a bandwidth compression is realized (the minimum bandwidth is less than the incoming bit rate). Also, since the QPSK output signal does not change phase until 2 bits (a dibit) have been clocked into the bit splitter, the fastest output rate of change (baud) is also equal to one-half of the input bit rate. As with BPSK, the minimum bandwidth and the baud are equal. This relationship is shown in Figure 1-17.

In Figure 1-17 it can be seen that the worst-case input condition to the I or Q balanced modulator is an alternating 1/0 pattern, which occurs when the binary input data has a 1100 repetitive pattern. One cycle of the fastest binary transition (a 1/0 sequence) in the I or Q channel takes the same time as 4 input data bits. Consequently, the highest fundamental frequency at the input and fastest rate of change at the output of the balanced modulators is equal to one-fourth of the binary input bit rate.

The output of the balanced modulators can be expressed mathematically as

$$\theta = (\sin \omega_a t)(\sin \omega_c t)$$

where

$$\underbrace{\omega_a t = 2\pi \frac{f_b}{4} t}_{\substack{\text{modulating} \\ \text{signal}}} \quad \text{and} \quad \underbrace{\omega_c t = 2\pi f_c t}_{\substack{\text{unmodulated} \\ \text{carrier}}}$$

Thus

$$\theta = \left(\sin 2\pi \frac{f_b}{4} t \right) (\sin 2\pi f_c t)$$

$$\frac{1}{2} \cos 2\pi \left(f_c - \frac{f_b}{4} \right) t - \frac{1}{2} \cos 2\pi \left(f_c + \frac{f_b}{4} \right) t$$

The output frequency spectrum extends from $f_c + f_b/4$ to $f_c - f_b/4$ and the minimum bandwidth (f_N) is

$$\left(f_c + \frac{f_b}{4} \right) - \left(f_c - \frac{f_b}{4} \right) = \frac{2f_b}{4} = \frac{f_b}{2}$$

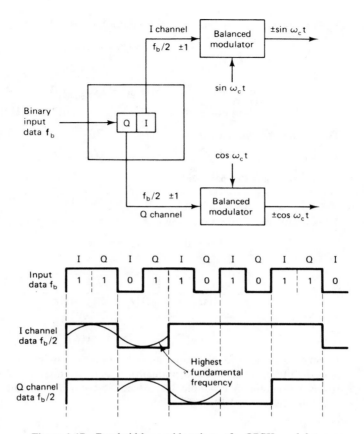

Figure 1-17 Bandwidth considerations of a QPSK modulator.

Example 1-4

For a QPSK modulator with an input data rate (f_b) equal to 10 Mbps and a carrier frequency of 70 MHz, determine the minimum double-sided Nyquist bandwidth (f_N) and the baud. Also, compare the results with those achieved with the BPSK modulator in Example 1-2. Use the QPSK block diagram shown in Figure 1-14 as the modulator model.

Solution The bit rate in both the I and Q channels is equal to one-half of the transmission bit rate or

$$f_{bQ} = f_{bI} = \frac{f_b}{2} = \frac{10\,\text{Mbps}}{2} = 5\,\text{Mbps}$$

The highest fundamental frequency presented to either balanced modulator is

$$f_a = \frac{f_{bQ}}{2} \quad \text{or} \quad \frac{f_{bI}}{2} = \frac{5\,\text{Mbps}}{2} = 2.5\,\text{MHz}$$

Quaternary Phase Shift Keying

The output wave from each balanced modulator is

$$(\sin 2\pi f_a t)(\sin 2\pi f_c t)$$

$$\tfrac{1}{2}\cos 2\pi(f_c - f_a)t - \tfrac{1}{2}\cos 2\pi(f_c + f_a)t$$

$$\tfrac{1}{2}\cos 2\pi[(70 - 2.5)\ \text{MHz}]t - \tfrac{1}{2}\cos 2\pi[(70 + 2.4)\ \text{MHz}]t$$

$$\tfrac{1}{2}\cos 2\pi(67.5\ \text{MHz})t - \tfrac{1}{2}\cos 2\pi(72.5\ \text{MHz})t$$

The minimum Nyquist bandwidth is

$$f_N = (72.5 - 67.5)\ \text{MHz} = 5\ \text{MHz}$$

The baud equals the bandwidth; thus

$$\text{baud} = 5\ \text{megabaud}$$

The output spectrum is as follows:

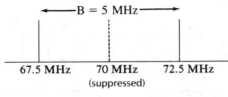

$$f_N = 5\ \text{MHz}$$

It can be seen that for the same input bit rate the minimum bandwidth required to pass the output of the QPSK modulator is equal to one-half of that required for the BPSK modulator in Example 1-2. Also, the baud rate for the QPSK modulator is one-half that of the BPSK modulator.

QPSK Receiver

The block diagram of a QPSK receiver is shown in Figure 1-18. The power splitter directs the input QPSK signal to the I and Q product detectors and the carrier recovery circuit. The carrier recovery circuit reproduces the original transmit carrier oscillator signal. The recovered carrier must be frequency and phase coherent with the transmit reference carrier. The QPSK signal is demodulated in the I and Q product detectors, which generate the original I and Q data bits. The outputs of the product detectors are fed to the bit combining circuit, where they are converted from parallel I and Q data channels to a single binary output data stream.

The incoming QPSK signal may be any one of the four possible output phases shown in Figure 1-15. To illustrate the demodulation process, let the incoming QPSK signal be $-\sin \omega_c t + \cos \omega_c t$. Mathematically, the demodulation process is as follows.

The receive QPSK signal $(-\sin \omega_c t + \cos \omega_c t)$ is one of the inputs to the I product detector. The other input is the recovered carrier $(\sin \omega_c t)$. The output

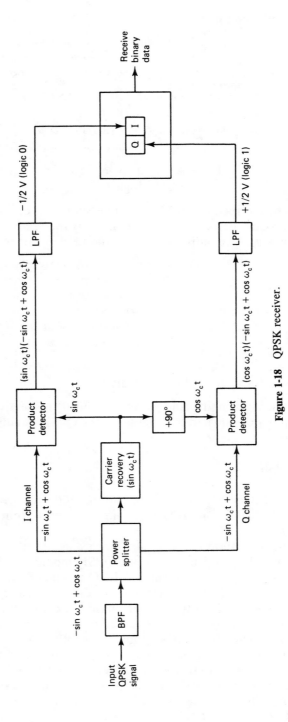

Figure 1-18 QPSK receiver.

of the I product detector is

$$I = (-\sin \omega_c t + \cos \omega_c t)(\sin \omega_c t)$$

$$\underbrace{\qquad\qquad\qquad\qquad}_{\text{QPSK input signal}} \underbrace{\qquad\quad}_{\text{carrier}}$$

$$= (-\sin \omega_c t)(\sin \omega_c t) + (\cos \omega_c t)(\sin \omega_c t)$$
$$= -\sin^2 \omega_c t + (\cos \omega_c t)(\sin \omega_c t)$$
$$= -\tfrac{1}{2}(1 - \cos 2\omega_c t) + \tfrac{1}{2}\sin(\omega_c + \omega_c)t + \tfrac{1}{2}\sin(\omega_c - \omega_c)t$$

$$\qquad\qquad\qquad\qquad \overset{\text{(filtered out)}}{\nearrow} \quad \overset{\text{(equals 0)}}{\nearrow}$$

$$I = -\tfrac{1}{2} + \tfrac{1}{2}\cos 2\omega_c t + \tfrac{1}{2}\sin 2\omega_c t + \tfrac{1}{2}\sin 0$$
$$= -\tfrac{1}{2}\,\text{V dc (logic 0)}$$

Again, the receive QPSK signal $(-\sin \omega_c t + \cos \omega_c t)$ is one of the inputs to the Q product detector. The other input is the recovered carrier shifted 90° in phase $(\cos \omega_c t)$. The output of the Q product detector is

$$Q = (-\sin \omega_c t + \cos \omega_c t)(\cos \omega_c t)$$

$$\underbrace{\qquad\qquad\qquad\qquad}_{\text{QPSK input signal}} \underbrace{\qquad\quad}_{\text{carrier}}$$

$$= \cos^2 \omega_c t - (\sin \omega_c t)(\cos \omega_c t)$$
$$= \tfrac{1}{2}(1 + \cos 2\omega_c t) - \tfrac{1}{2}\sin(\omega_c + \omega_c)t - \tfrac{1}{2}\sin(\omega_c - \omega_c)t$$

$$\qquad\qquad\qquad\qquad \overset{\text{(filtered out)}}{\nearrow} \quad \overset{\text{(equals 0)}}{\nearrow}$$

$$Q = \tfrac{1}{2} + \tfrac{1}{2}\cos 2\omega_c t - \tfrac{1}{2}\sin 2\omega_c t - \tfrac{1}{2}\sin 0$$
$$= {}^1\!/_2\,\text{V dc (logic 1)}$$

The demodulated I and Q bits (1 and 0, respectively) correspond to the constellation diagram and truth table for the QPSK modulator shown in Figure 1-15.

Offset QPSK

Offset QPSK (OQPSK) is a modified form of QPSK where the bit waveforms on the I and Q channels are offset or shifted in phase from each other by one-half of a bit time.

Figure 1-19 shows a simplified block diagram, the bit sequence alignment, and the constellation diagram for a OQPSK modulator. Because changes in the I channel occur at the midpoints of the Q-channel bits, and vice versa, there is never more than a single bit change in the dibit code, and therefore there is never more than a 90° shift in the output phase. In conventional QPSK, a change in the input dibit from 00 to 11 or 01 to 10 causes a corresponding 180° shift in the output phase. Therefore, an advantage of OQPSK is the limited phase shift that must be imparted during modulation. A disadvantage of OQPSK is that changes in the output phase occur at twice the data rate in either the I or Q channels. Consequently, with OQPSK the baud and minimum bandwidth are twice that of conventional QPSK for a given transmission bit rate. OQPSK is sometimes called OKQPSK (*offset-keyed PSK*).

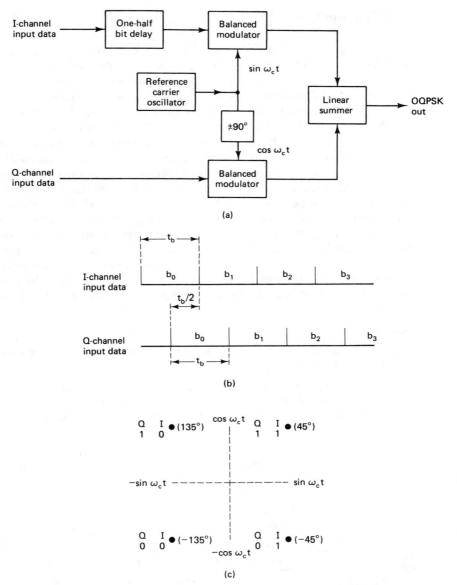

Figure 1-19 Offset keyed PSK (OQPSK): (a) block diagram; (b) bit alignment; (c) constellation diagram.

EIGHT-PHASE PSK

Eight-phase PSK (8-PSK) is an *M*-ary encoding technique where $M = 8$. With an 8-PSK modulator, there are eight possible output phases. To encode eight different phases, the incoming bits are considered in groups of 3 bits, called *tribits* ($2^3 = 8$).

Eight-Phase PSK   **25**

8-PSK Transmitter

A block diagram of an 8-PSK modulator is shown in Figure 1-20. The incoming serial bit stream enters the bit splitter, where it is converted to a parallel, three-channel output (the I or in-phase channel, the Q or in-quadrature channel, and the C or control channel). Consequently, the bit rate in each of the three channels is $f_b/3$. The bits in the I and C channels enter the I-channel 2-to-4 level converter, and the bits in the Q and $\overline{C}$ channels enter the Q-channel 2-to-4-level converter. Essentially, the 2-to-4-level converters are parallel-input *digital-to-analog converters* (DACs). With 2 input bits, four output voltages are possible. The algorithm for the DACs is quite simple. The I or Q bit determines the polarity of the output analog signal (logic 1 = $+V$ and logic 0 = $-V$) while the C or $\overline{C}$ bit determines the magnitude (logic 1 = 1.307 V and logic 0 = 0.541 V). Consequently, with two magnitudes and two polarities, four different output conditions are possible.

Figure 1-21 shows the truth table and corresponding output conditions for the 2-to-4-level converters. Because the C and $\overline{C}$ bits can never be the same logic state, the outputs from the I and Q 2-to-4-level converters can never have the same magnitude, although they can have the same polarity. The output of a 2-to-4-level converter is an *M*-ary, *pulse-amplitude-modulated* (PAM) signal where $M = 4$.

Example 1-5

For a tribit input of Q = 0, I = 0, and C = 0 (000), determine the output phase for the 8-PSK modulator shown in Figure 1-20.

Solution The inputs to the I-channel 2-to-4-level converter are I = 0 and C = 0. From Figure 1-21 the output is -0.541 V. The inputs to the Q-channel 2-to-4-level converter are Q = 0 and $\overline{C}$ = 1. Again from Figure 1-21, the output is -1.307 V.

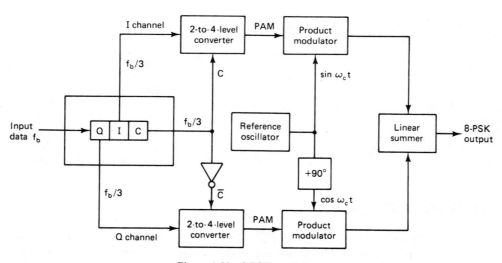

Figure 1-20 8-PSK modulator.

Digital Communications   Chap. 1

I	C	Output
0	0	−0.541 V
0	1	−1.307 V
1	0	+0.541 V
1	1	+1.307 V

Q	C̄	Output
0	1	−1.307 V
0	0	−0.541 V
1	1	+1.307 V
1	0	+0.541 V

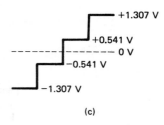

    (a)   (b)   (c)

Figure 1-21 I- and Q-channel 2-to-4-level converters: (a) I-channel truth table; (b) Q-channel truth table; (c) PAM levels.

Thus the two inputs to the I-channel product modulators are -0.541 and $\sin \omega_c t$. The output is

$$I = (-0.541)(\sin \omega_c t) = -0.541 \sin \omega_c t$$

The two inputs to the Q-channel product modulator are -1.307 V and $\cos \omega_c t$. The output is

$$Q = (-1.307)(\cos \omega_c t) = -1.307 \cos \omega_c t$$

The outputs of the I- and Q-channel product modulators are combined in the linear summer and produce a modulated output of

$$\text{summer output} = -0.541 \sin \omega_c t - 1.307 \cos \omega_c t$$
$$= 1.41 \sin \omega_c t - 112.5°$$

For the remaining tribit codes (001, 010, 011, 100, 101, 110, and 111), the procedure is the same. The results are shown in Figure 1-22.

From Figure 1-22 it can be seen that the angular separation between any two adjacent phasors is 45°, half what it is with QPSK. Therefore, an 8-PSK signal can undergo almost a ±22.5° phase shift during transmission and still retain its integrity. Also, each phasor is of equal magnitude; the tribit condition (actual information) is again contained only in the phase of the signal. The PAM levels of 1.307 and 0.541 are relative values. Any levels may be used as long as their ratio is 0.541/1.307 and their arc tangent is equal to 22.5°. For example, if their values were doubled to 2.614 and 1.082, the resulting phase angles would not change, although the magnitude of the phasor would increase proportionally.

It should also be noted that the tribit code between any two adjacent phases changes by only one bit. This type of code is called the *Gray code* or, sometimes, the *maximum distance code*. This code is used to reduce the number of transmission errors. If a signal were to undergo a phase shift during transmission, it would most likely be shifted to an adjacent phasor. Using the Gray code results in only a single bit being received in error.

Figure 1-23 shows the output phase-versus-time relationship of an 8-PSK modulator.

Eight-Phase PSK

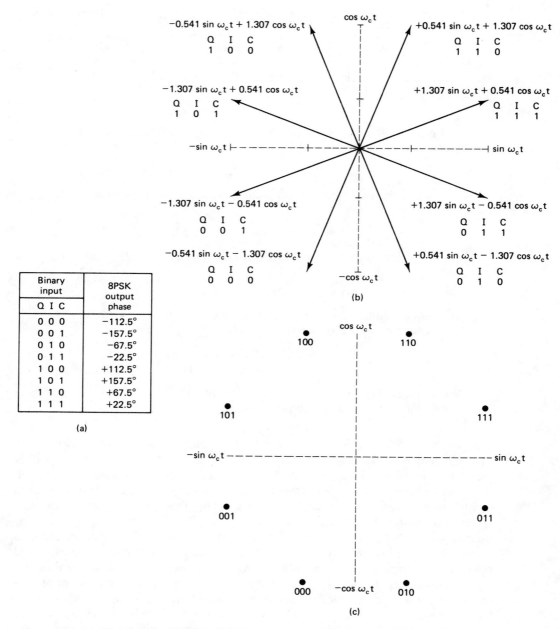

Binary input	8PSK output phase
Q I C	
0 0 0	−112.5°
0 0 1	−157.5°
0 1 0	−67.5°
0 1 1	−22.5°
1 0 0	+112.5°
1 0 1	+157.5°
1 1 0	+67.5°
1 1 1	+22.5°

(a)

Figure 1-22 8-PSK modulator: (a) truth table; (b) phasor diagram; (c) constellation diagram.

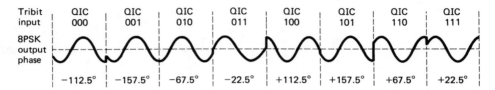

Tribit input	QIC 000	QIC 001	QIC 010	QIC 011	QIC 100	QIC 101	QIC 110	QIC 111

| | −112.5° | −157.5° | −67.5° | −22.5° | +112.5° | +157.5° | +67.5° | +22.5° |

Figure 1-23 Output phase versus time relationship for an 8-PSK modulator.

Bandwidth Considerations of 8-PSK

With 8-PSK, since the data are divided into three channels, the bit rate in the I, Q, or C channel is equal to one-third of the binary input data rate ($f_b/3$). (The bit splitter stretches the I, Q, and C bits to three times their input bit length.) Because the I, Q, and C bits are outputted simultaneously and in parallel, the 2-to-4-level converters also see a change in their inputs (and consequently their outputs) at a rate equal to $f_b/3$.

Figure 1-24 shows the bit timing relationship between the binary input data; the I-, Q-, and C-channel data; and the I and Q PAM signals. It can be seen that the highest fundamental frequency in the I, Q or C channel is equal to one-sixth of the bit rate of the binary input (one cycle in the I, Q, or C channel takes the same amount of time as six input bits). Also, the highest fundamental frequency in either PAM signal is equal to one-sixth of the binary input bit rate.

With an 8-PSK modulator, there is one change in phase at the output for every 3 data input bits. Consequently, the baud for 8-PSK equals $f_b/3$, the same as the minimum bandwidth. Again, the balanced modulators are product modulators; their outputs are the product of the carrier and the PAM signal. Mathematically, the output of the balanced modulators is

$$\theta = (X \sin \omega_a t)(\sin \omega_c t) \tag{1-10}$$

where

$$\underbrace{\omega_a t = 2\pi \frac{f_b}{6} t}_{\text{modulating signal}} \quad \text{and} \quad \underbrace{\omega_c t = 2\pi f_c t}_{\text{carrier}}$$

and

$$X = \pm 1.307 \quad \text{or} \quad \pm 0.541$$

Thus

$$\theta = \left(X \sin 2\pi \frac{f_b}{6} t \right)(\sin 2\pi f_c t)$$
$$= \frac{X}{2} \cos 2\pi \left(f_c - \frac{f_b}{6} \right) t - \frac{X}{2} \cos 2\pi \left(f_c + \frac{f_b}{6} \right) t$$

Eight-Phase PSK   **29**

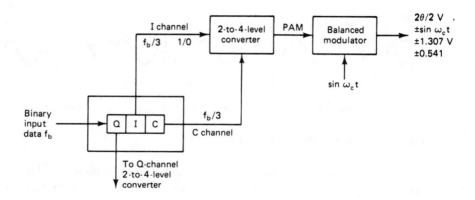

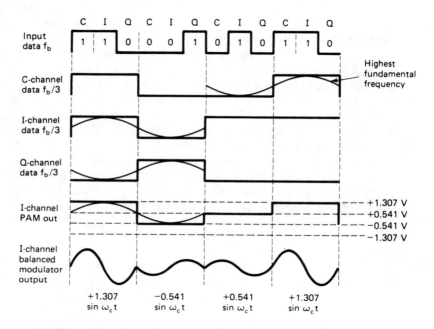

Figure 1-24 Bandwidth considerations of an 8-PSK modulator.

The output frequency spectrum extends from $f_c + f_b/6$ to $f_c - f_b/6$ and the minimum bandwidth (f_N) is

$$\left(f_c + \frac{f_b}{6}\right) - \left(f_c - \frac{f_b}{6}\right) = \frac{2f_b}{6} = \frac{f_b}{3}$$

Example 1-6

For an 8-PSK modulator with an input data rate (f_b) equal to 10 Mbps and a carrier frequency of 70 MHz, determine the minimum double-sided Nyquist bandwidth (f_N) and the baud. Also, compare the results with those achieved with the BPSK and

QPSK modulators in Examples 1-2 and 1-4. Use the 8-PSK block diagram shown in Figure 1-20 as the modulator model.

Solution The bit rate in the I, Q, and C channels is equal to one-third of the input bit rate, or

$$f_{bC} = f_{bQ} = f_{bI} = \frac{10 \text{ Mbps}}{3} = 3.33 \text{ Mbps}$$

Therefore, the fastest rate of change and highest fundamental frequency presented to either balanced modulator is

$$f_a = \frac{f_{bC}}{2} \text{ or } \frac{f_{bQ}}{2} \text{ or } \frac{f_{bI}}{2} = \frac{3.33 \text{ Mbps}}{2} = 1.667 \text{ Mbps}$$

The output wave from the balance modulators is

$$(\sin 2\pi f_a t)(\sin 2\pi f_c t)$$

$$\tfrac{1}{2} \cos 2\pi (f_c - f_a)t - \tfrac{1}{2} \cos 2\pi (f_c + f_a)t$$

$$\tfrac{1}{2} \cos 2\pi [(70 - 1.667) \text{ MHz}]t - \tfrac{1}{2} \cos 2\pi [(70 + 1.667) \text{ MHz}]t$$

$$\tfrac{1}{2} \cos 2\pi (68.333 \text{ MHz})t - \tfrac{1}{2} \cos 2\pi (71.667 \text{ MHz})t$$

The minimum Nyquist bandwidth is

$$f_N = (71.667 - 68.333) \text{ MHz} = 3.333 \text{ MHz}$$

Again, the baud equals the bandwidth; thus

$$\text{baud} = 3.333 \text{ megabaud}$$

The output spectrum is as follows:

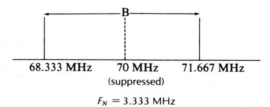

It can be seen that for the same input bit rate the minimum bandwidth required to pass the output of an 8-PSK modulator is equal to one-third that of the BPSK modulator in Example 1-2 and 50% less than that required for the QPSK modulator in Example 1-4. Also, in each case the baud has been reduced by the same proportions.

8-PSK Receiver

Figure 1-25 shows a block diagram of an 8-PSK receiver. The power splitter directs the input 8-PSK signal to the I and Q product detectors and the carrier recovery circuit. The carrier recovery circuit reproduces the original reference

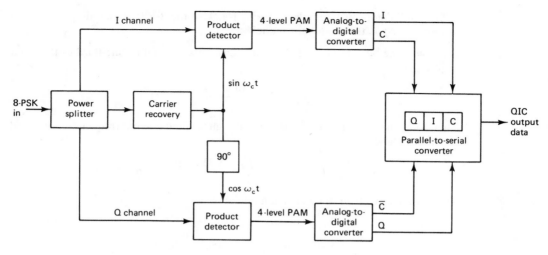

Figure 1-25 8-PSK receiver.

oscillator signal. The incoming 8-PSK signal is mixed with the recovered carrier in the I product detector and with a quadrature carrier in the Q product detector. The outputs of the product detectors are 4-level PAM signals that are fed to the 4-to-2-level *analog-to-digital converters* (ADCs). The outputs from the I-channel 4-to-2-level converter and the I and C bits, while the outputs from the Q-channel 4-to-2-level converter are the Q and $\overline{C}$ bits. The parrallel-to-serial logic circuit converts the I/C and Q/$\overline{C}$ bit pairs to serial I, Q, and C output data streams.

SIXTEEN-PHASE PSK

Sixteen-phase PSK (16-PSK) is an *M*-ary encoding technique where $M = 16$; there are 16 different output phases possible. A 16-PSK modulator acts on the incoming data in groups of 4 bits ($2^4 = 16$), called *quadbits*. The output phase does not change until 4 bits have been inputted into the modulator. Therefore, the output rate of change (baud) and the minimum bandwidth are equal to one-fourth of the incoming bit rate ($f_b/4$). The truth table and constellation diagram for a 16-PSK transmitter are shown in Figure 1-26.

With 16-PSK, the angular separation between adjacent output phases is only 22.5°. Therefore, a 16-PSK signal can undergo almost a ±11.25° phase shift during transmission and still retain its integrity. Because of this, 16-PSK is highly susceptible to phase impairments introduced in the transmission medium and is therefore seldom used.

QUADRATURE AMPLITUDE MODULATION

Quadrature amplitude modulation (QAM) is a form of digital modulation where the digital information is contained in both the amplitude and phase of the transmitted carrier.

Bit code	Phase	Bit code	Phase
0000	11.25°	1000	191.25°
0001	33.75°	1001	213.75°
0010	56.25°	1010	236.25°
0011	78.75°	1011	258.75°
0100	101.25°	1100	281.25°
0101	123.75°	1101	303.75°
0110	146.25°	1110	326.25°
0111	168.75°	1111	348.75°

(a)

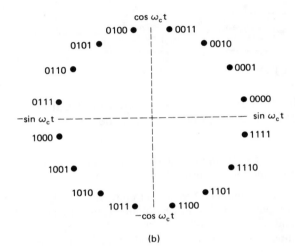

(b)

Figure 1-26 16-PSK: (a) truth table; (b) constellation diagram.

EIGHT QAM

Eight QAM (8-QAM is an *M*-ary encoding technique where $M = 8$. Unlike 8-PSK, the output signal from an 8-QAM modulator is not a constant-amplitude signal.

8-QAM Transmitter

Figure 1-27 shows the block diagram of an 8-QAM transmitter. As you can see, the only difference between the 8-QAM transmitter and the 8-PSK transmitter shown in Figure 1-19 is the omission of the inverter between the C channel and the Q product modulator. As with 8-PSK, the incoming data are divided into groups of three (tribits): the I, Q, and C channels, each with a bit rate equal to one-third of the incoming data rate. Again, the I and Q bits determine the polarity of the PAM signal at the output of the 2-to-4-level converters, and the C channel determines the magnitude. Because the C bit is fed uninverted to both the I- and Q-channel 2-to-4-level converters, the magnitudes of the I and Q PAM signals are always equal. Their polarities depend on the logic condition of the I and Q

Eight QAM

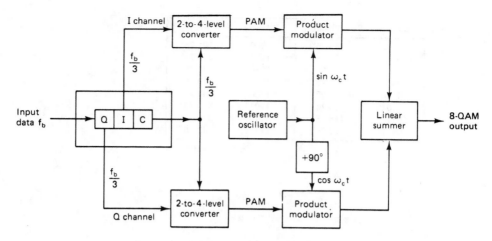

Figure 1-27 8-QAM transmitter block diagram.

bits and therefore may be different. Figure 1-28 shows the truth table for the I- and Q-channel 2-to-4-level converters; they are the same.

Example 1-7

For a tribit input of Q = 0, I = 0, and C = 0 (000), determine the output amplitude and phase for the 8-QAM modulator shown in Figure 1-27.

Solution The inputs to the I-channel 2-to-4-level converter are I = 0 and C = 0. From Figure 1-28 the output is −0.541 V. The inputs to the Q-channel 2-to-4-level converter are Q = 0 and C = 0. Again from Figure 1-28, the output is −0.541 V.

Thus the two inputs to the I-channel product modulator are −0.541 and $\sin \omega_c t$. The output is

$$I = (-0.541)(\sin \omega_c t) = -0.541 \sin \omega_c t$$

The two inputs to the Q-channel product modulator are −0.541 and $\cos \omega_c t$. The output is

$$Q = (-0.541)(\cos \omega_c t) = -0.541 \cos \omega_c t$$

The outputs from the I- and Q-channel product modulators are combined in the linear summer and produce a modulated output of

$$\text{summer output} = -0.541 \sin \omega_c t - 0.541 \cos \omega_c t$$
$$= 0.765 \sin \omega_c t - 135°$$

For the remaining tribit codes (001, 010, 011, 100, 101, 110, and 111), the procedure is the same. The results are shown in Figure 1-29.

I/Q	C	Output
0	0	−0.541
0	1	−1.307 V
1	0	+0.541
1	1	+1.307 V

Figure 1-28 Truth table for the I- and Q-channel 2-to-4-level converters.

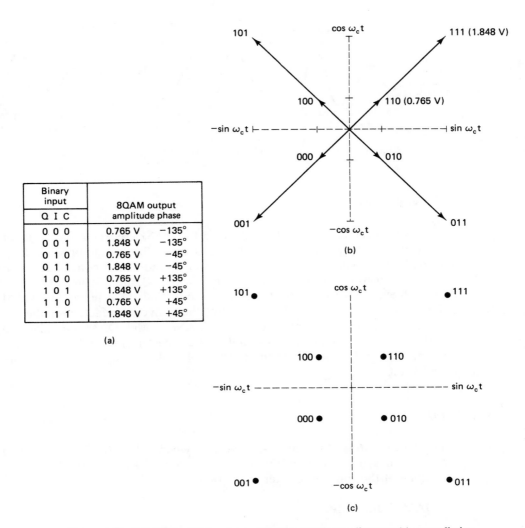

Binary input			8QAM output	
Q	I	C	amplitude	phase
0	0	0	0.765 V	−135°
0	0	1	1.848 V	−135°
0	1	0	0.765 V	−45°
0	1	1	1.848 V	−45°
1	0	0	0.765 V	+135°
1	0	1	1.848 V	+135°
1	1	0	0.765 V	+45°
1	1	1	1.848 V	+45°

(a)

(b)

(c)

Figure 1-29   8-QAM modulator: (a) truth table; (b) phasor diagram; (c) constellation diagram.

Figure 1-30 shows the output phase versus time relationship for an 8-QAM modulator. Note that there are two output amplitudes and only four phases are possible.

Bandwidth Considerations of 8-QAM

In 8-QAM, the bit rate in the I and Q channels is one-third of the input binary rate, the same as in 8-PSK. As a result, the highest fundamental modulating frequency and fastest output rate of change in 8-QAM are the same as with 8-PSK. Therefore, the minimum bandwidth required for 8-QAM is $f_b/3$, the same as in 8-PSK.

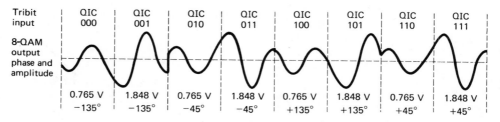

Tribit input	QIC 000	QIC 001	QIC 010	QIC 011	QIC 100	QIC 101	QIC 110	QIC 111
8-QAM output phase and amplitude								
	0.765 V −135°	1.848 V −135°	0.765 V −45°	1.848 V −45°	0.765 V +135°	1.848 V +135°	0.765 V +45°	1.848 V +45°

Figure 1-30 Output phase and amplitude versus time relationship for 8-QAM.

8-QAM Receiver

An 8-QAM receiver is almost identical to the 8-PSK receiver shown in Figure 1-25. The differences are the PAM levels at the output of the product detectors and the binary signals at the output of the analog-to-digital converters. Because there are two transmit amplitudes possible with 8-QAM that are different from those achievable with 8-PSK, the four demodulated PAM levels in 8-QAM are different from those in 8-PSK. Therefore, the conversion factor for the analog-to-digital converters must also be different. Also, with 8-QAM the binary output signals from the I-channel analog-to-digital converter are the I and C bits, and the binary output signals from the Q-channel analog-to-digital converter are the Q and C bits.

SIXTEEN QAM

Like 16-PSK, 16-QAM is an *M*-ary system where *M* = 16. The input data are acted on in groups of four (2^4 = 16). As with 8-QAM, both the phase and amplitude of the transmit carrier are varied.

16-QAM Transmitter

The block diagram for a 16-QAM transmitter is shown in Figure 1-31. The input binary data are divided into four channels: The I, I′, Q, and Q′. The bit rate in each channel is equal to one-fourth of the input bit rate ($f_b/4$). Four bits are serially clocked into the bit splitter; then they are outputted simultaneously and in parallel with the I, I′, Q, and Q′ channels. The I and Q bits determine the polarity at the output of the 2-to-4-level converters (a logic 1 = positive and a logic 0 = negative). The I′ and Q′ bits determine the magnitude (a logic 1 = 0.821 V and a logic 0 = 0.22 V). Consequently, the 2-to-4-level converters generate a 4-level PAM signal. Two polarities and two magnitudes are possible at the output of each 2-to-4-level converter. They are ±0.22 V and ±0.821 V. The PAM signals modulate the inphase and quadrature carriers in the product modulators. Four outputs are possible for each product modulator. For the I product modulator

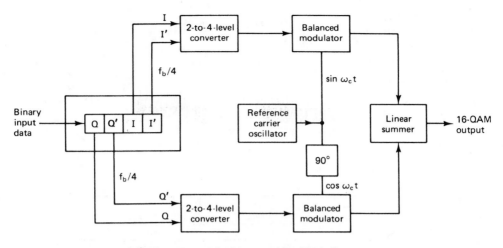

Figure 1-31 16-QAM transmitter block diagram.

they are $+0.821 \sin \omega_c t$, $-0.821 \sin \omega_c t$, $+0.22 \sin \omega_c t$, and $-0.22 \sin \omega_c t$. For the Q product modulator they are $+0.821 \cos \omega_c t$, $+0.22 \cos \omega_c t$, $-0.821 \cos \omega_c t$, and $-0.22 \cos \omega_c t$. The linear summer combines the outputs from the I- and Q-channel product modulators and produces the 16 output conditions necessary for 16-QAM. Figure 1-32 shows the truth table for the I- and Q-channel 2-to-4-level converters.

Example 1-8

For a quadbit input of $I = 0$, $I' = 0$, $Q = 0$, and $Q' = 0$ (0000), determine the output amplitude and phase for the 16-QAM modulator shown in Figure 1-31.

Solution The inputs to the I-channel 2-to-4-level converter are $I = 0$ and $I' = 0$. From Figure 1-32 the output is -0.22 V. The inputs to the Q-channel 2-to-4-level converter are $Q = 0$ and $Q' = 0$. Again from Figure 1-32, the output is -0.22 V.

Thus the two inputs to the I-channel product modulator are -0.22 V and $\sin \omega_c t$. The output is

$$I = (-0.22)(\sin \omega_c t) = -0.22 \sin \omega_c t$$

The two inputs to the Q-channel product modulator are -0.22 V and $\cos \omega_c t$. The output is

$$Q = (-0.22)(\cos \omega_c t) = -0.22 \cos \omega_c t$$

The outputs from the I- and Q-channel product modulators are combined in the linear summer and produce a modulated output of

$$\text{summer output} = -0.22 \sin \omega_c t - 0.22 \cos \omega_c t$$
$$= 0.311 \sin \omega_c t - 135°$$

For the remaining quadbit codes the procedure is the same. The results are shown in Figure 1-33.

Sixteen QAM 37

I	I'	Output
0	0	−0.22 V
0	1	−0.821 V
1	0	+0.22 V
1	1	+0.821 V

(a)

Q	Q'	Output
0	0	−0.22 V
0	1	−0.821 V
1	0	+0.22 V
1	1	+0.821 V

(b)

Figure 1-32 Truth tables for the I- and Q-channel 2-to-4 level converters: (a) I channel; (b) Q channel.

Binary input				16QAM output	
Q	Q'	I	I'		
0	0	0	0	0.311 V	−135°
0	0	0	1	0.850 V	−165°
0	0	1	0	0.311 V	−45°
0	0	1	1	0.850 V	−15°
0	1	0	0	0.850 V	−105°
0	1	0	1	1.161 V	−135°
0	1	1	0	0.850 V	−75°
0	1	1	1	1.161 V	−45°
1	0	0	0	0.311 V	135°
1	0	0	1	0.850 V	175°
1	0	1	0	0.850 V	45°
1	0	1	1	0.850 V	15°
1	1	0	0	0.850 V	105°
1	1	0	1	1.161 V	135°
1	1	1	0	0.850 V	75°
1	1	1	1	1.161 V	45°

(a)

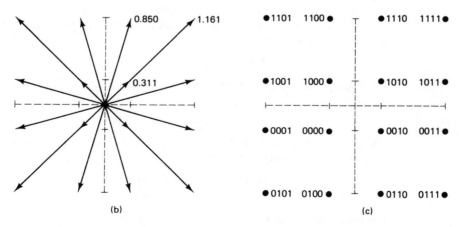

(b)

(c)

Figure 1-33 16-QAM modulator: (a) truth table; (b) phasor diagram; (c) constellation diagram.

Bandwidth Considerations of 16-QAM

With 16-QAM, since the input data are divided into four channels, the bit rate in the I, I', Q, or Q' channel is equal to one-fourth of the binary input data rate ($f_b/4$). (The bit splitter stretches the I, I', Q, and Q' bits to four times their input bit length.) Also, because the I, I', Q, and Q' bits are outputted simultaneously and in parallel, the 2-to-4-level converters see a change in their inputs and outputs at a rate equal to one-fourth of the input data rate.

   Figure 1-34 shows the bit timing relationship between the binary input data; the I, I', Q, and Q' channel data; and the I PAM signal. It can be seen that the highest fundamental frequency in the I, I', Q, or Q' channel is equal to one-

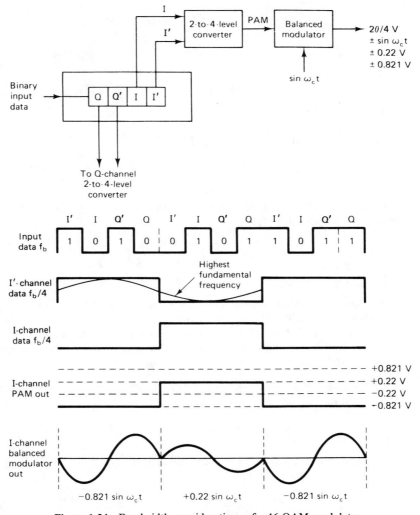

Figure 1-34 Bandwidth considerations of a 16-QAM modulator.

Sixteen QAM

eighth of the bit rate of the binary input data (one cycle in the I, I', Q, or Q' channel takes the same amount of time as 8 input bits). Also, the highest fundamental frequency of either PAM signal is equal to one-eighth of the binary input bit rate.

With a 16-QAM modulator, there is one change in the output signal (either its phase, amplitude, or both) for every 4 input data bits. Consequently, the baud equals $f_b/4$, the same as the minimum bandwidth.

Again, the balanced modulators are product modulators and their outputs can be represented mathematically as

$$\theta = (X \sin \omega_a t)(\sin \omega_c t) \qquad (1\text{-}11)$$

where

$$\underbrace{\omega_a t = 2\pi \frac{f_b}{8} t}_{\text{modulating signal}} \qquad \text{and} \qquad \underbrace{\omega_c t = 2\pi f_c t}_{\text{carrier}}$$

and

$$X = \pm 0.22 \quad \text{or} \quad \pm 0.821$$

Thus

$$\theta = \left(X \sin 2\pi \frac{f_b}{8} t \right) (\sin 2\pi f_c t)$$

$$= \frac{X}{2} \cos 2\pi \left(f_c - \frac{f_b}{8} \right) t - \frac{X}{2} \cos 2\pi \left(f_c + \frac{f_b}{8} \right) t$$

The output frequency spectrum extends from $f_c + f_b/8$ to $f_c - f_b/8$ and the minimum bandwidth (f_N) is

$$\left(f_c + \frac{f_b}{8} \right) - \left(f_c - \frac{f_b}{8} \right) = \frac{2f_b}{8} = \frac{f_b}{4}$$

Example 1-9

For a 16-QAM modulator with an input data rate (f_b) equal to 10 Mbps and a carrier frequency of 70 MHz, determine the minimum double-sided Nyquist frequency (f_N) and the baud. Also, compare the results with those achieved with the BPSK, QPSK, and 8-PSK modulators in Examples 1-2, 1-4, and 1-6. Use the 16-QAM block diagram shown in Figure 1-27 as the modulator model.

Solution The bit rate in the I, I', Q, and Q' channels is equal to one-fourth of the input bit rate or

$$f_{bI} = f_{bI'} = f_{bQ} = f_{bQ'} = \frac{f_b}{4} = \frac{10 \text{ Mbps}}{4} = 2.5 \text{ Mbps}$$

Therefore, the fastest rate of change and highest fundamental frequency presented to either balanced modulator is

$$f_a = \frac{f_{bI}}{2} \quad \text{or} \quad \frac{f_{bI'}}{2} \quad \text{or} \quad \frac{f_{bQ}}{2} \quad \text{or} \quad \frac{f_{bQ'}}{2} = \frac{2.5 \text{ Mbps}}{2} = 1.25 \text{ Mhz}$$

The output wave from the balanced modulator is

$$(\sin 2\pi f_a t)(\sin 2\pi f_c t)$$

$$\tfrac{1}{2} \cos 2\pi (f_c - f_a)t - \tfrac{1}{2} \cos 2\pi (f_c + f_a)t$$

$$\tfrac{1}{2} \cos 2\pi [(70 - 1.25) \text{ MHz}]t - \tfrac{1}{2} \cos 2\pi [(70 + 1.25) \text{ MHz}]t$$

$$\tfrac{1}{2} \cos 2\pi (68.75 \text{ MHz})t - \tfrac{1}{2} \cos 2\pi (71.25 \text{ MHz})t$$

The minimum Nyquist bandwidth is

$$f_N = (71.25 - 68.75) \text{ MHz} = 2.5 \text{ MHz}$$

The baud equals the bandwidth; thus

$$\text{baud} = 2.5 \text{ megabaud}$$

The output spectrum is as follows:

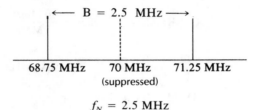

$$f_N = 2.5 \text{ MHz}$$

For the same input bit rate, the minimum bandwidth required to pass the output of a 16-QAM modulator is equal to one-fourth that of the BPSK modulator, one-half that of QPSK, and 25% less than with 8-PSK. For each modulation technique, the baud is also reduced by the same proportions.

BANDWIDTH EFFICIENCY

Bandwidth efficiency (or *information density* as it is sometimes called) is often used to compare the performance of one digital modulation technique to another. In essence, it is the ratio of the transmission bit rate to the minimum bandwidth required for a particular modulation scheme. Bandwidth efficiency is generally normalized to a 1-Hz bandwidth and thus indicates the number of bits that can be propagated through a medium for each hertz of bandwidth. Mathematically, bandwidth efficiency is

$$\text{BW efficiency} = \frac{\text{transmission rate (bps)}}{\text{minimum bandwidth (Hz)}} \tag{1-12}$$

$$= \frac{\text{bits/second}}{\text{hertz}} = \frac{\text{bits/second}}{\text{cycles/second}} = \frac{\text{bits}}{\text{cycle}}$$

Example 1-10

Determine the bandwidth efficiencies for the following modulation schemes: BPSK, QPSK, 8-PSK, and 16-QAM.

Solution Recall from Examples 1-2, 1-4, 1-6, and 1-9 the minimum bandwidths required to propagate a 10-Mbps transmission rate with the following modulation schemes:

Modulation scheme	Minimum bandwidth (MHz)
BPSK	10
QPSK	5
8-PSK	3.33
16-QAM	2.5

Substituting into Equation 1-12, the bandwidth efficiencies are determined as follows:

$$\text{BPSK:}\quad \text{BW efficiency} = \frac{10\,\text{Mbps}}{10\,\text{MHz}} = \frac{1\,\text{bps}}{\text{Hz}} = \frac{1\,\text{bit}}{\text{cycle}}$$

$$\text{QPSK:}\quad \text{BW efficiency} = \frac{10\,\text{Mbps}}{5\,\text{MHz}} = \frac{2\,\text{bps}}{\text{Hz}} = \frac{2\,\text{bits}}{\text{cycle}}$$

$$\text{8-PSK:}\quad \text{BW efficiency} = \frac{10\,\text{Mbps}}{3.33\,\text{MHz}} = \frac{3\,\text{bps}}{\text{Hz}} = \frac{3\,\text{bits}}{\text{cycle}}$$

$$\text{16-QAM:}\quad \text{BW efficiency} = \frac{10\,\text{Mbps}}{2.5\,\text{MHz}} = \frac{4\,\text{bps}}{\text{Hz}} = \frac{4\,\text{bits}}{\text{cycle}}$$

The results indicate that BPSK is the least efficient and 16-QAM is the most efficient. 16-QAM requires one-fourth as much bandwidth as BPSK for the same bit rate.

PSK AND QAM SUMMARY

The various forms of FSK, PSK, and QAM are summarized in Table 1-2.

CARRIER RECOVERY

Carrier recovery is the process of extracting a phase-coherent reference carrier from a received carrier waveform. This is sometimes called *phase referencing*.

TABLE 1-2   DIGITAL MODULATION SUMMARY

Modulation	Encoding	Bandwidth (Hz)	Baud	Bandwidth efficiency (bps/Hz)
FSK	Single bit	$\geq f_b$	f_b	≤ 1
BPSK	Single bit	f_b	f_b	1
QPSK	Dibit	$f_b/2$	$f_b/2$	2
8-PSK	Tribit	$f_b/3$	$f_b/3$	3
8-QAM	Tribit	$f_b/3$	$f_b/3$	3
16-PSK	Quadbit	$f_b/4$	$f_b/4$	4
16-QAM	Quadbit	$f_b/4$	$f_b/4$	4

In the phase modulation techniques described thus far, the binary data were encoded as a precise phase of the transmitted carrier. (This is referred to as *absolute phase encoding*.) Depending on the encoding method, the angular separation between adjacent phasors varied between 15 and 180°. To correctly demodulate the data, a phase-coherent carrier was recovered and compared with the received carrier in a product detector. To determine the absolute phase of the received carrier, it is necessary to produce a carrier at the receiver that is phase coherent with the transmit reference oscillator. This is the function of the carrier recovery circuit.

With PSK and QAM, the carrier is suppressed in the balanced modulators and is therefore not transmitted. Consequently, at the receiver the carrier cannot simply be tracked with a standard phase-locked loop. With suppressed carrier systems, such as PSK and QAM, sophisticated methods of carrier recovery are required such as a *squaring loop,* a *Costas loop,* or a *remodulator.*

Squaring Loop

A common method of achieving carrier recovery for BPSK is the *squaring loop.* Figure 1-35 shows the block diagram of a squaring loop. The received BPSK waveform is filtered and then squared. The filtering reduces the spectral width of the received noise. The squaring circuit removes the modulation and generates the second harmonic of the carrier frequency. This harmonic is phase tracked by the PLL. The VCO output frequency from the PLL is then divided by 2 and used as the phase reference for the product detectors.

With BPSK, only two output phases are possible: $+\sin \omega_c t$ and $-\sin \omega_c t$. Mathematically, the operation of the squaring circuit can be described as follows. For a receive signal of $+\sin \omega_c t$ the output of the squaring circuit is

$$\text{output} = (+\sin \omega_c t)(+\sin \omega_c t) = +\sin^2 \omega_c t$$

$$= \tfrac{1}{2}(1 - \cos 2\omega_c t) = \overset{\text{(filtered out)}}{\tfrac{1}{2}} - \tfrac{1}{2}\cos 2\omega_c t$$

For a received signal of $-\sin \omega_c t$ the output of the squaring circuit is

$$\text{output} = (-\sin \omega_c t)(-\sin \omega_c t) = +\sin^2 \omega_c t$$

$$= \tfrac{1}{2}(1 - \cos 2\omega_c t) = \overset{\text{(filtered out)}}{\tfrac{1}{2}} - \tfrac{1}{2}\cos 2\omega_c t$$

It can be seen that in both cases the output from the squaring circuit contained a dc voltage ($+\tfrac{1}{2}$ V) and a signal at twice the carrier frequency (cos $2\omega_c t$). The dc voltage is removed by filtering, leaving only cos $2\omega_c t$.

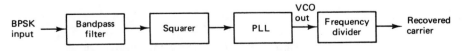

Figure 1-35   Squaring loop carrier recovery circuit for a BPSK receiver.

Costas Loop

A second method of carrier recovery is the Costas, or quadrature, loop shown in Figure 1-36. The Costas loop performs identical to a squaring circuit followed by an ordinary PLL in place of the BPF. This recovery scheme uses two parallel tracking loops (I and Q) simultaneously to derive the product of the I and Q components of the signal that drives the VCO. The in-phase (I) loop uses the VCO as in a PLL, and the quadrature (Q) loop uses a 90° shifted VCO signal. Once the frequency of the VCO is equal to the suppressed carrier frequency, the product of the I and Q signals will produce an error voltage proportional to any phase error in the VCO. The error voltage controls the phase and thus the frequency of the VCO.

Remodulator

A third method of achieving recover of a phase and frequency coherent carrier is the remodulator, shown in Figure 1-37. The remodulator produces a loop error voltage that is proportional to twice the phase error between the incoming signal and the VCO signal. The remodulator has a faster acquisition time than either the squaring or the Costas loops.

Carrier recovery circuits for higher-than-binary encoding techniques are similar to BPSK except that circuits which raise the receive signal to the fourth, eighth, and higher powers are used.

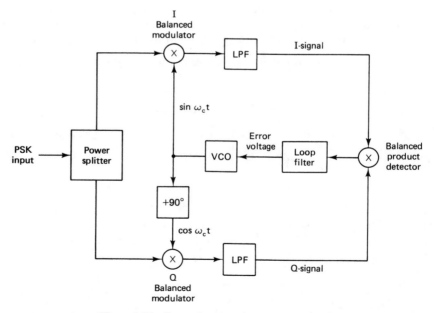

Figure 1-36 Costas loop carrier recovery circuit.

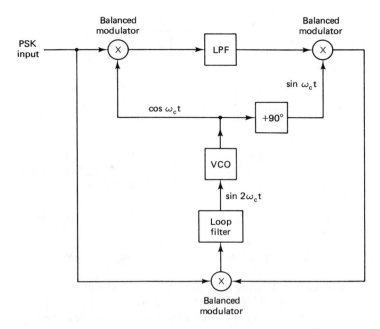

Figure 1-37 Remodulator loop carrier recovery circuit.

DIFFERENTIAL PHASE SHIFT KEYING

Differential phase shift keying (DPSK) is an alternative form of digital modulation where the binary input information is contained in the difference between two successive signaling elements rather than the absolute phase. With DPSK it is not necessary to recover a phase-coherent carrier. Instead, a received signaling element is delayed by one signaling element time slot and then compared to the next received signaling element. The difference in the phase of the two signaling elements determines the logic condition of the data.

DIFFERENTIAL BPSK

DBPSK Transmitter

Figure 1-38a shows a simplified block diagram of a *differential binary phase shift keying* (DBPSK) transmitter. An incoming information bit is XNORed with the preceding bit prior to entering the BPSK modulator (balanced modulator). For the first data bit, there is no preceding bit with which to compare it. Therefore, an initial reference bit is assumed. Figure 1-38b shows the relationship between the input data, the XNOR output data, and the phase at the output of the balanced modulator. If the initial reference bit is assumed a logic 1, the output from the XNOR circuit is simply the complement of that shown.

Differential BPSK **45**

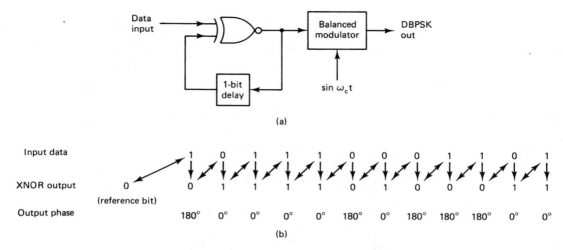

(a)

Input data

XNOR output

Output phase

(b)

Figure 1-38 DBPSK demodulator: (a) block diagram; (b) timing diagram.

In Figure 1-38b the first data bit is XNORed with the reference bit. If they are the same, the XNOR output is a logic 1; if they are different, the XNOR output is a logic 0. The balanced modulator operates the same as a conventional BPSK modulator; a logic 1 produces $+\sin \omega_c t$ at the output and a logic 0 produces $-\sin \omega_c t$ at the output.

DBPSK Receiver

Figure 1-39 shows the block diagram and timing sequence for a DBPSK receiver. The received signal is delayed by one bit time, then compared with the next

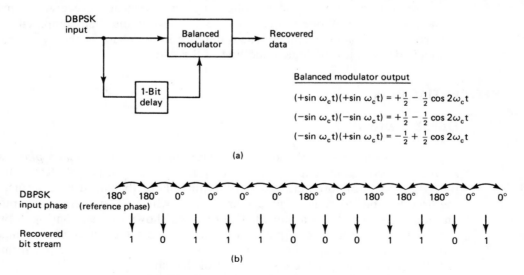

(a)

(b)

Figure 1-39 DBPSK demodulator: (a) block diagram; (b) timing sequence.

Digital Communications   Chap. 1

signaling element in the balanced modulator. If they are the same, a logic 1 (+ voltage) is generated. If they are different, a logic 0 (− voltage) is generated. If the reference phase is incorrectly assumed, only the first demodulated bit is in error. Differential encoding can be implemented with higher-than-binary digital modulation schemes, although the differential algorithms are much more complicated than for DBPSK.

The primary advantage of DPSK is the simplicity with which it can be implemented. With DPSK, no carrier recovery circuit is needed. A disadvantage of DPSK is that it requires between 1 and 3 dB more signal-to-noise ratio to achieve the same bit error rate as that of absolute PSK.

CLOCK RECOVERY

As with any digital system, digital radio requires precise timing or clock synchronization between the transmit and the receive circuitry. Because of this, it is necessary to regenerate clocks at the receiver that are synchronous with those at the transmitter.

Figure 1-40a shows a simple circuit that is commonly used to recover clocking information from the received data. The recovered data are delayed by one-half a bit time and then compared with the original data in an XOR circuit. The frequency of the clock that is recovered with this method is equal to the received data rate (f_b). Figure 1-40b shows the relationship between the data and the recovered clock timing. From Figure 1-40b it can be seen that as long as the receive data contains a substantial number of transitions (1/0 sequences), the recovered clock is maintained. If the receive data were to undergo an extended period of successive 1's or 0's, the recovered clock would be lost. To prevent this from occurring, the data are scrambled at the transmit end and descrambled at the receive end.

PROBABILITY OF ERROR AND BIT ERROR RATE

Probability of error P(e) and *bit error rate* (BER) are often used interchangeably, although in practice they do have slightly different meanings. *P(e)* is a theoretical (mathematical) expectation of the bit error rate for a given system. BER is an empirical (historical) record of a system's actual bit error performance. For example, if a system has a *P(e)* of 10^{-5}, this means that mathematically, you can expect one bit error in every 100,000 bits transmitted ($1/10^5 = 1/100,000$). If a system has a BER of 10^5, this means that in the past there was one bit error for every 100,000 bits transmitted. A bit error rate is measured, then compared to the expected probability of error to evaluate a system's performance.

Probability of error is a function of the *carrier-to-noise power ratio* (or more specifically, the average *energy per bit-to-noise power density ratio*) and the number of possible encoding conditions used (*M*-ary). Carrier-to-noise power

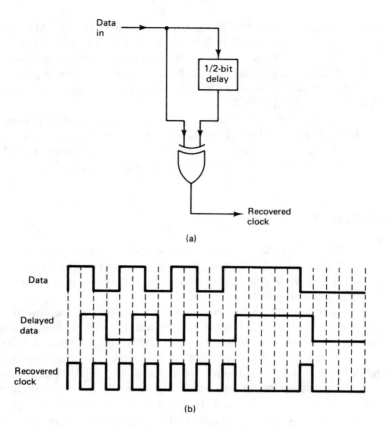

Figure 1-40 (a) Clock recovery circuit; (b) timing diagram.

ratio is the ratio of the average carrier power (the combined power of the carrier and its associated sidebands) to the *thermal noise power*. Carrier power can be stated in watts or dBm, where

$$C \text{ (dBm)} = 10 \log \frac{C \text{ watts}}{0.001} \qquad (1\text{-}13)$$

Thermal noise power is expressed mathematically as

$$N = KTB \qquad \text{(watts)} \qquad (1\text{-}14a)$$

where

N = thermal noise power (W)
K = Boltzmann's proportionality constant (1.38×10^{-23} J/K)
T = temperature (kelvin: 0 kelvin = -273 degrees Celsius, room temperature = 290 K)
B = bandwidth (Hz)

Stated in dBm,

$$N\,(\text{dBm}) = 10 \log \frac{KTB}{0.001} \tag{1-14b}$$

Mathematically, the carrier-to-noise power ratio is

$$\frac{C}{N} = \frac{C}{KTB} \quad (unitless\ ratio) \tag{1-15a}$$

where

$$C = \text{carrier power (W)}$$
$$N = \text{noise power (W)}$$

Stated in dB,

$$\frac{C}{N}\,(\text{dB}) = 10 \log \frac{C}{N} \tag{1-15b}$$
$$= C\,(\text{dBm}) - N\,(\text{dBm})$$

Energy per bit is simply the energy of a single bit of information. Mathematically, energy per bit is

$$E_b = CT_b \quad (\text{J/bit}) \tag{1-16a}$$

where

$$E_b = \text{energy of a single bit (J/bit)}$$
$$T_b = \text{time of a single bit (s)}$$
$$C = \text{carrier power (W)}$$

Stated in dBJ,

$$E_b\,(\text{dBJ}) = 10 \log E_b \tag{1-16b}$$

and because $T_b = 1/f_b$, where f_b is the bit rate in bits per second, E_b can be rewritten as

$$E_b = \frac{C}{f_b} \quad (\text{J/bit}) \tag{1-16c}$$

Stated in dBJ,

$$E_b\,(\text{dBJ}) = 10 \log \frac{C}{f_b} \tag{1-16d}$$
$$= 10 \log C - 10 \log f_b \tag{1-16e}$$

Noise power density is the thermal noise power normalized to a 1-Hz bandwidth (i.e., the noise power present in a 1-Hz bandwidth). Mathematically, noise power density is

$$N_0 = \frac{N}{B} \quad (\text{W/Hz}) \tag{1-17a}$$

Probability of Error and Bit Error Rate   **49**

where

$$N_0 = \text{noise power density (W/Hz)}$$
$$N = \text{thermal noise power (W)}$$
$$B = \text{bandwidth (Hz)}$$

Stated in dBm,

$$N_0 \text{(dBm)} = 10 \log \frac{N}{0.001} - 10 \log B \qquad (1\text{-}17\text{b})$$

$$= N \text{(dBm)} - 10 \log B \qquad (1\text{-}17\text{c})$$

Combining Equations 1-14a and 1-17a yields

$$N_0 = \frac{KT}{B} \qquad \text{(W/Hz)} \qquad (1\text{-}17\text{d})$$

Stated in dBm,

$$N_0 \text{(dBm)} = 10 \log \frac{K}{0.001} + 10 \log T - 10 \log B \qquad (1\text{-}17\text{e})$$

   Energy per bit-to-noise power density ratio is used to compare two or more digital modulation systems that use different transmission rates (bit rates), modulation schemes (FSK, PSK, QAM), or encoding techniques (*M*-ary). The energy per bit-to-noise power density ratio is simply the ratio of the energy of a single bit to the noise power present in 1 Hz of bandwidth. Thus E_b/N_0 normalizes all multiphase modulation schemes to a common noise bandwidth allowing for a simpler and more accurate comparison of their error performance. Mathematically, E_b/N_0 is

$$\frac{E_b}{N_0} = \frac{C/f_b}{N/B} = \frac{CB}{Nf_b} \qquad (1\text{-}18\text{a})$$

where E_b/N_0 is the energy per bit-to-noise power density ratio. Rearranging Equation 1-18a yields the following expression:

$$\frac{E_b}{N_0} = \frac{C}{N} \times \frac{B}{f_b} \qquad (1\text{-}18\text{b})$$

where

$$\frac{E_b}{N_0} = \text{energy per bit-to-noise power density ratio}$$

$$\frac{C}{N} = \text{carrier-to-noise power ratio}$$

$$\frac{B}{f_b} = \text{noise bandwidth-to-bit ratio}$$

Stated in dB,

$$\frac{E_b}{N_0} \text{(dB)} = 10 \log \frac{C}{N} + 10 \log \frac{B}{f_b} \qquad (1\text{-}18\text{c})$$

or

$$= 10 \log E_b - 10 \log N_0 \qquad (1\text{-}18\text{d})$$

From Equation 1-18b it can be seen that the E_b/N_0 ratio is simply the product of the carrier-to-noise power ratio and the noise bandwidth-to-bit ratio. Also, from Equation 1-18b, it can be seen that when the bandwidth equals the bit rate, $E_b/N_0 = C/N$.

In general, the minimum carrier-to-noise power ratio required for QAM systems is less than that required for comparable PSK systems. Also, the higher the level of encoding used (the higher the value of M), the higher the minimum carrier-to-noise power ratio. In Chapter 8, several examples are shown for determining the minimum carrier-to-noise power and energy per bit-to-noise power density ratios for a given M-ary system and desired $P(e)$.

Example 1-11

For a QPSK system and the given parameters, determine (a) the carrier power in dBm, (b) the noise power in dBm, (c) the noise power density in dBm, (d) the energy per bit in dBJ, (e) the carrier-to-noise power ratio in dB, and (f) the E_b/N_0 ratio.

$$C = 10^{-12}\,\text{W} \qquad f_b = 60\,\text{kbps}$$
$$N = 1.2 \times 10^{-14}\,\text{W} \qquad B = 120\,\text{kHz}$$

Solution (a) The carrier power in dBm is determined by substituting into Equation 1-13.

$$C = 10 \log \frac{10^{-12}}{0.001} = -90\,\text{dBm}$$

(b) The noise power in dBm is determined by substituting into Equation 1-14b.

$$N = 10 \log \frac{1.2 \times 10^{-14}}{0.001} = -109.2\,\text{dBm}$$

(c) The noise power density is determined by substituting into Equation 1-17c.

$$N_0 = -109.2\,\text{dBm} - 10 \log 120\,\text{kHz} = -160\,\text{dBm}$$

(d) The energy per bit is determined by substituting into Equation 1-16d.

$$E_b = 10 \log \frac{10^{-12}}{60\,\text{kbps}} = -167.8\,\text{dBJ}$$

(e) The carrier-to-noise power ratio is determined by substituting into Equation 1-15b.

$$\frac{C}{N} = 10 \log \frac{10^{-12}}{1.2 \times 10^{-14}} = 19.2\,\text{dB}$$

(f) The energy per bit-to-noise density ratio is determined by substituting into Equation 1-18c.

$$\frac{E_b}{N_0} = 19.2 + 10 \log \frac{120\,\text{kHz}}{60\,\text{kbps}} = 22.2\,\text{dB}$$

Probability of Error and Bit Error Rate

PSK Error Performance

The bit error performance for the various multiphase digital modulation systems is directly related to the distance between points on a signal state-space diagram. For example, on the signal state-space diagram for BPSK shown in Figure 1-41a, it can be seen that the two signal points (logic 1 and logic 0) have maximum separation (d) for a given power level (D). In essence, one BPSK signal state is the exact negative of the other. As the figure shows, a noise vector (V_N), when combined with the signal vector (V_S), effectively shifts the phase of the signaling

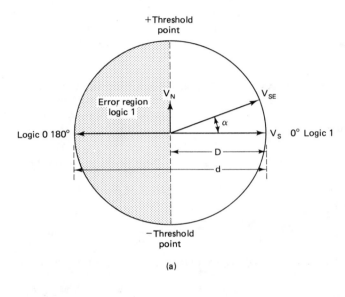

(a)

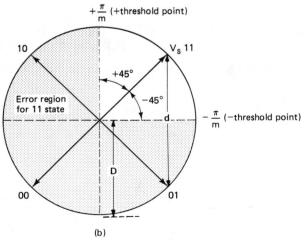

(b)

Figure 1-41 PSK error region: (a) BPSK; (b) QPSK.

element (V_{SE}) alpha degrees. If the phase shift exceeds $\pm 90°$, the signal element is shifted beyond the threshold points into the error region. For BPSK, it would require a noise vector of sufficient amplitude and phase to produce more than a $\pm 90°$ phase shift in the signaling element to produce an error. For PSK systems, the general formula for the threshold points is

$$\text{TP} = \pm \frac{\pi}{M} \tag{1-19}$$

where M is the number of signal states.

The phase relationship between signaling elements for BPSK (i.e., 180° out-of-phase) is the optimum signaling format, referred to as *antipodal signaling,* and occurs only when two signal levels are allowed and when one signal is the exact negative of the other. Because no other bit-by-bit signaling scheme is any better, antipodal performance is often used as a reference for comparison.

The error performance of the other multiphase PSK systems can be compared to that of BPSK simply by determining the relative decrease in error distance between points on a single state-space diagram. For PSK, the general formular for the maximum distance between signaling points is given by

$$\sin \theta = \sin \frac{360°}{2M} = \frac{d/2}{D} \tag{1-20}$$

where

$$d = \text{error distance}$$
$$M = \text{number of phases}$$
$$D = \text{peak signal amplitude}$$

Rearranging Equation 1-20 and solving for d yields

$$d = \left(2 \sin \frac{180°}{M} \right) \times D \tag{1-21}$$

Figure 1-41b shows the signal state-space diagram for QPSK. From Figure 1-41b and Equation 1-21, it can be seen that QPSK can tolerate only a $\pm 45°$ phase shift. From Equation 1-19, the maximum phase shift for 8-PSK and 16-PSK is $\pm 22.5°$ and $\pm 11.25°$, respectively. Consequently, the higher levels of modulation (i.e., the greater the value of M) require a greater energy per bit-to-noise power density ratio to reduce the effect of noise interference. Hence the higher the level of modulation, the smaller the angular separation between signal points and the smaller the error distance.

The general expression for the bit-error probability of an M-phase PSK system is

$$P(e) = \frac{1}{\log_2 M} \text{erf} (z) \tag{1-22}$$

where

$$\text{erf} = \text{error function}$$
$$z = \sin \frac{\pi}{M} \left(\sqrt{\log_2 M} \right) \left(\sqrt{E_b/N_0} \right)$$

Probability of Error and Bit Error Rate

By substituting into Equation 1-22, it can be shown that QPSK provides the same error performance as BPSK. This is because the 3-dB reduction in error distance for QPSK is offset by the 3-dB decrease in its bandwidth (in addition to the error distance, the relative widths of the noise bandwidths must also be considered). Thus both systems provide optimum performance. Figure 1-42 shows the error performance for 2-, 4-, 8-, 16-, and 32-PSK systems as a function of E_b/N_0.

Example 1-12

Determine the minimum bandwidth required to achieve a $P(e)$ of 10^{-7} for an 8-PSK system operating at 10 Mbps with a carrier-to-noise power ratio of 11.7 dB.

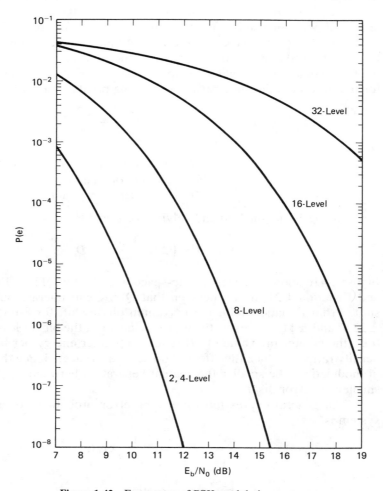

Figure 1-42 Error rates of PSK modulation systems.

Solution   From Figure 1-42, the minimum E_b/N_0 ratio to achieve a $P(e)$ of 10^{-7} for an 8-PSK system is 14.7 dB. The minimum bandwidth is found by rearranging Equation 1-18b.

$$\frac{B}{F_b} = \frac{E_b}{N_0} - \frac{C}{N}$$
$$= 14.7\,\mathrm{dB} - 11.7\,\mathrm{dB} = 3\,\mathrm{dB}$$
$$\frac{B}{F_b} = \text{antilog } 3 = 2$$
$$B = 2 \times 10\,\mathrm{Mbps} = 20\,\mathrm{MHz}$$

QAM Error Performance

For a large numbers of signal points (i.e., M-ary systems greater than 4), QAM outperforms PSK. This is because the distance between signaling points in a PSK system is smaller than the distance between points in a comparable QAM system. The general expression for the distance between adjacent signaling points for a QAM system with L levels on each axis is

$$d = \frac{2}{L-1} \times D \tag{1-23}$$

where

$$d = \text{error distance}$$
$$L = \text{number of levels on each axis}$$
$$D = \text{peak signal amplitude}$$

In comparing Equation 1-21 to Equation 1-23, it can be seen that QAM systems have an advantage over PSK systems with the same peak signal power level.

The general expression for the bit error probability of an L-level QAM system is

$$P(e) = \frac{1}{\log_2 L}\left(\frac{L-1}{L}\right)\text{erfc}(z) \tag{1-24}$$

where $\text{erfc}(z)$ = complementary error function

$$z = \frac{\sqrt{\log_2 L}}{L-1}\sqrt{\frac{E_b}{N_0}}$$

Figure 1-43 shows the error performance for 4-, 16-, 32-, and 64-QAM systems as a function of E_b/N_0.

Table 1-3 lists the minimum carrier-to-noise power ratios and energy per bit-to-noise power density ratios required for a probability of error of 10^{-6} for several PSK and QAM modulation schemes.

Probability of Error and Bit Error Rate   **55**

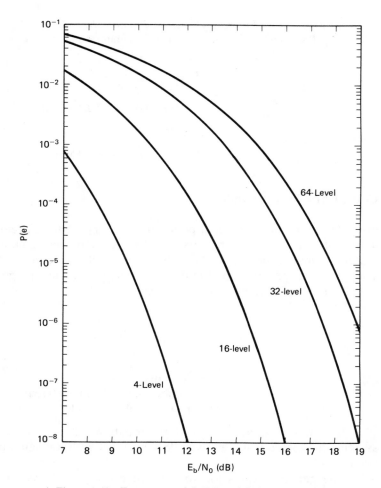

Figure 1-43 Error rates of QAM modulation systems.

Example 1-13

Which system requires the highest E_b/N_0 ratio for a probability of error of 10^{-6}, a four-level QAM system or an 8-PSK system?

Solution From Figure 1-43, the minimum E_b/N_0 ratio required for a four-level QAM system is 10.6 dB. From Figure 1-42, the minimum E_b/N_0 ratio required for an 8-PSK system is 14 dB. Therefore, to achieve a $P(e)$ of 10^{-6}, a four-level QAM system would require 3.4-dB less E_b/N_0 ratio.

FSK Error Performance

The error probability for FSK systems is evaluated in a somewhat different manner than PSK and QAM. There are essentially only two types of FSK systems: noncoherent (asynchronous) and coherent (synchronous). With non-

TABLE 1-3 PERFORMANCE COMPARISON OF VARIOUS DIGITAL MODULATION SCHEMES (BER = 10^{-6})

Modulation technique	C/N ratio (dB)	E_b/N_0 ratio (dB)
BPSK	13.6	10.6
QPSK	13.6	10.6
4-QAM	13.6	10.6
8-QAM	13.6	10.6
8-PSK	18.8	14
16-PSK	24.3	18.3
16-QAM	20.5	14.5
32-QAM	24.4	17.4
64-QAM	26.6	18.8

coherent FSK, the transmitter and receiver are not frequency or phase sychronized. With coherent FSK, local receiver reference frequencies are in frequency and phase lock with the transmitted reference frequencies. The probability of error for noncoherent FSK is

$$P(e) = \frac{1}{2} \exp\left(-\frac{E_b}{2N_0}\right) \tag{1-25}$$

The probability of error for coherent FSK is

$$P(e) = \text{erfc} \sqrt{\frac{E_b}{N_0}} \tag{1-26}$$

From Equations 1-25 and 1-26 it can be seen that the probability of error for noncoherent FSK is greater than that of coherent FSK for equal energy per bit-to-noise power density ratios. Figure 1-44 shows probability of error curves for both coherent and noncoherent FSK for several values of E_b/N_0.

APPLICATIONS FOR DIGITAL MODULATION

A digitally modulated transceiver (*trans*mitter-re*ceiver*) that uses FSK, PSK, or QAM has many applications. They are used in digitally modulated microwave radio and satellite systems (Chapter 8) with carrier frequencies from tens of megahertz to several gigahertz, and they are also used for voice band data modems (Chapter 2) with carrier frequencies between 300 and 3000 Hz.

QUESTIONS

1-1. Explain *digital transmission* and *digital radio*.

1-2. Define *information capacity*.

1-3. What are the three most predominant modulation schemes used in digital radio systems?

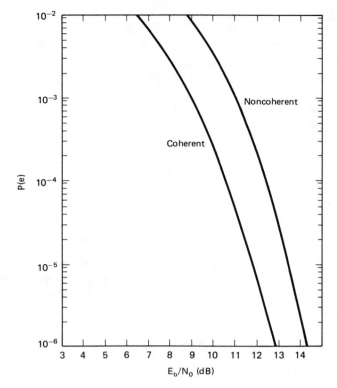

Figure 1-44 Error rates for FSK modulation systems.

1-4. Explain the relationship between bits per second and baud for an FSK system.

1-5. Define the following terms for FSK modulation: frequency deviation, modulation index, and deviation ratio.

1-6. Explain the relationship between (a) the minimum bandwidth required for an FSK system and the bit rate, and (b) the mark and space frequencies.

1-7. What is the difference between standard FSK and MSK? What is the advantage of MSK?

1-8. Define *PSK*.

1-9. Explain the relationship between bits per second and baud for a BPSK system.

1-10. What is a constellation diagram, and how is it used with PSK?

1-11. Explain the relationship between the minimum bandwidth required for a BPSK system and the bit rate.

1-12. Explain *M-ary*.

1-13. Explain the relationship between bits per second and baud for a QPSK system.

1-14. Explain the significance of the I and Q channels in a QPSK modulator.

1-15. Define *dibit*.

1-16. Explain the relationship between the minimum bandwidth required for a QPSK system and the bit rate.

1-17. What is a coherent demodulator?

1-18. What advantage does OQPSK have over conventional QPSK? What is a disadvantage of OQPSK?

1-19. Explain the relationship between bits per second and baud for an 8-PSK system.

1-20. Define *tribit*.

1-21. Explain the relationship between the minimum bandwidth required for an 8-PSK system and the bit rate.

1-22. Explain the relationship between bits per second and baud for a 16-PSK system.

1-23. Define *quadbit*.

1-24. Define *QAM*.

1-25. Explain the relationship between the minimum bandwidth required for a 16-QAM system and the bit rate.

1-26. What is the difference between PSK and QAM?

1-27. Define *bandwidth efficiency*.

1-28. Define *carrier recovery*.

1-29. Explain the differences between absolute PSK and differential PSK.

1-30. What is the purpose of a clock recovery circuit? When is it used?

1-31. What is the difference between probability of error and bit error rate?

PROBLEMS

1-1. For an FSK modulator with space, rest, and mark frequencies of 40, 50, and 60 MHz, respectively, and an input bit rate of 10 Mbps, determine the output baud and minimum bandwidth. Sketch the output spectrum.

1-2. Determine the minimum bandwidth and baud for a BPSK modulator with a carrier frequency of 40 MHz and an input bit rate of 500 kbps. Sketch the output spectrum.

1-3. For the QPSK modulator shown in Figure 1-14, change the $+90°$ phase-shift network to $-90°$ and sketch the new constellation diagram.

1-4. For the QPSK demodulator shown in Figure 1-18, determine the I and Q bits for an input signal of $\sin \omega_c t - \cos \omega_c t$.

1-5. For an 8-PSK modulator with an input data rate (f_b) equal to 20 Mbps and a carrier frequency of 100 MHz, determine the minimum double-sided Nyquist bandwidth (f_N) and the baud. Sketch the output spectrum.

1-6. For the 8-PSK modulator shown in Figure 1-20, change the reference oscillator to $\cos \omega_c t$ and sketch the new constellation diagram.

1-7. For a 16-QAM modulator with an input bit rate (f_b) equal to 20 Mbps and a carrier frequency of 100 MHz, determine the minimum double-sided Nyquist bandwidth (f_N) and the baud. Sketch the output spectrum.

1-8. For the 16-QAM modulator shown in Figure 1-31, change the reference oscillator to $\cos \omega_c t$ and determine the output expressions for the following I, I', Q, and Q' input conditions: 0000, 1111, 1010, and 0101.

1-9. Determine the bandwidth efficiency for the following modulators.
  (a) QPSK, $f_b = 10$ Mbps
  (b) 8-PSK, $f_b = 21$ Mbps
  (c) 16-QAM, $f_b = 20$ Mbps

1-10. For the DBPSK modulator shown in Figure 1-38, determine the output phase sequence for the following input bit sequence: 00110011010101 (assume that the reference bit = 1).

1-11. For a QPSK system and the given parameters, determine (a) the carrier power in dBm, (b) the noise power in dBm, (c) the noise power density in dBm, (d) the energy per bit in dBj, (e) the carrier-to-noise power ratio, and (f) the E_b/N_0 ratio.

$$C = 10^{-13}\,\text{W} \qquad f_b = 30\,\text{kbps}$$
$$N = 0.06 \times 10^{-15}\,\text{W} \quad B = 60\,\text{kHz}$$

1-12. Determine the minimum bandwidth required to achieve a $P(e)$ of 10^{-6} for an 8-PSK system operating at 20 Mbps with a carrier-to-noise power ratio of 11 dB.

2

DATA COMMUNICATIONS

INTRODUCTION

Data communications is the process of transferring digital *information* (usually in binary form) between two or more points. Information is defined as knowledge or intelligence. Information that has been processed and organized is called *data*. Data can be any alphabetical, numeric, or symbolic information, including binary-coded alpha/numeric symbols, microprocessor op-codes, control codes, user addresses, program data, or data base information. At both the source and the destination, data are in digital form. However, during transmission, data may be in digital or analog form.

A data communications network can be as simple as two personal computers connected together through the public telephone network, or it can comprise a complex network of one or more mainframe computers and hundreds of remote terminals. Data communications networks are used to connect automatic teller machines (ATMs) to bank computers or they can be used to interface computer terminals (CTs) or keyboard displays (KDs) directly to application programs in mainframe computers. Data communications networks are used for airline and hotel reservation systems and for mass media and news networks such as the Associated Press (AP) or United Press International (UPI). The list of applications for data communications networks goes on almost indefinitely.

HISTORY OF DATA COMMUNICATIONS

It is highly likely that data communications began long before recorded time in the form of smoke signals or tom-tom drums, although it is improbable that these signals were binary coded. If we limit the scope of data communications to methods that use electrical signals to transmit binary-coded information, then data communications began in 1837 with the invention of the *telegraph* and the development of the *Morse code* by Samuel F. B. Morse. With telegraph, dots and dashes (analogous to binary 1's and 0's) are transmitted across a wire using electromechanical induction. Various combinations of these dots and dashes were used to represent binary codes for letters, numbers, and punctuation. Actually, the first telegraph was invented in England by Sir Charles Wheatstone and Sir William Cooke, but their contraption required six different wires for a single telegraph line. In 1840, Morse secured an American patent for the telegraph and in 1844 the first telegraph line was established between Baltimore and Washington, D.C. In 1849, the first slow-speed telegraph printer was invented, but it was not until 1860 that high-speed (15 bps) printers were available. In 1850, the Western Union Telegraph Company was formed in Rochester, New York, for the purpose of carrying coded messages from one person to another.

In 1874, Emile Baudot invented a telegraph *multiplexer,* which allowed signals from up to six different telegraph machines to be transmitted simultaneously over a single wire. The telephone was invented in 1876 by Alexander Graham Bell and, consequently, very little new evolved in telegraph until 1899, when Marconi succeeded in sending radio telegraph messages. Telegraph was the only means of sending information across large spans of water until 1920, when the first commercial radio stations were installed.

Bell Laboratories developed the first special-purpose computer in 1940 using electromechanical relays. The first general-purpose computer was an automatic sequence-controlled calculator developed jointly by Harvard University and International Business Machines Corporation (IBM). The UNIVAC computer, built in 1951 by Remington Rand Corporation (now Sperry Rand), was the first mass-produced electronic computer. Since 1951, the number of mainframe computers, small business computers, personal computers, and computer terminals has increased exponentially, creating a situation where more and more people have the need to exchange digital information with each other. Consequently, the need for data communications has also increased exponentially.

Until 1968, the AT&T operating tariff allowed only equipment furnished by AT&T to be connected to AT&T lines. In 1968, a landmark Supreme Court decision, the Carterfone decision, allowed non-Bell companies to interconnect to the vast AT&T communications network. This decision started the *interconnect industry,* which has led to competitive data communications offerings by a large number of independent companies.

STANDARDS ORGANIZATIONS FOR DATA COMMUNICATIONS

During the past decade, the data communications industry has grown at an astronomical rate. Consequently, the need to provide communications between dissimilar computer systems has also increased. Thus, to ensure an orderly transfer of information between two or more data communications systems using different equipment with different needs, a consortium of organizations, manufacturers, and users meet on a regular basis to establish guidelines and standards. It is the intent that all data communications users comply with these standards. Several of the organizations are described below.

International Standards Organization (ISO): The ISO is the international organization for standardization. The ISO creates the sets of rules and standards for graphics, document exchange, and related technologies. The ISO is responsible for endorsing and coordinating the work of the other standards organizations.

Consultative Committee for International Telephony and Telegraphy (CCITT): The membership of the CCITT consists of government authorities and representatives from many countries. The CCITT is now the standards organization for the United Nations and develops the recommended sets of rules and standards for telephone and telegraph communications. The CCITT has developed three sets of specifications: the V series for modem interfacing, the X series for data communications, and the I and Q series for Integrated Services Digital Network (ISDN).

American National Standards Institute (ANSI): ANSI is the official standards agency for the United States and the U.S. voting representative for ISO.

Institute of Electrical and Electronic Engineers (IEEE): The IEEE is a U.S. professional organization of electronics, computer, and communications engineers.

Electronic Industries Association (EIA): The EIA is a U.S. organization that establishes and recommends industrial standards. The EIA is responsible for developing the RS (recommended standard) series of standards for data and telecommunications.

Standards Council of Canada (SCC): The SCC is the official standards agency for Canada with similar responsibilities to those of ANSI.

DATA COMMUNICATIONS CIRCUITS

Figure 2-1 shows a simplified block diagram of a data communications network. As the figure shows, there is a source of digital information (primary station), a transmission medium (facility), and a destination (*secondary* station). The *primary* (or host) location is very often a mainframe computer with its own set of local terminals and peripheral equipment. For simplicity, there is only one secondary (or remote) station shown on the figure. The secondary stations are the users of the network. How many secondary stations there are and how they are interconnected to each other and the host station vary considerably depending on the system and its applications. There are many different types of transmission media, including free-space radio transmission (microwave and satellite), metallic cable facilities (both digital and analog systems), and optical fiber cables (light wave propagation).

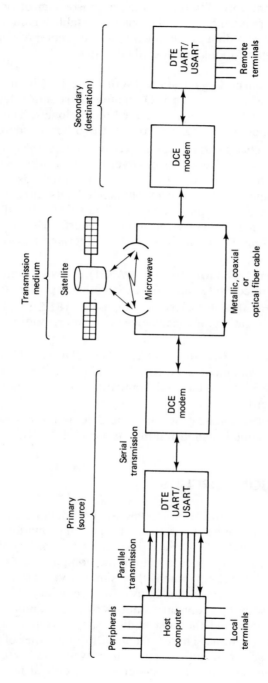

Figure 2-1 Simplified block diagram of a data communications network.

Data terminal equipment (DTE) is a general term that describes the interface equipment used at the stations to adapt the digital signals from the computers and terminals to a form more suitable for transmission. Essentially, any piece of equipment between the mainframe computer and the modem or the station equipment and its modem is classified as data terminal equipment. *Data communications equipment* (DCE) is a general term that describes the equipment that converts digital signals to analog signals and interfaces the data terminal equipment to the transmission medium. In essence, a DCE is a *modem* (*mod*ulator/*dem*odulator). A modem converts binary digital signals to analog signals such as FSK, PSK, and QAM, and vice versa.

Serial and Parallel Data Transmission

Binary information can be transmitted either in parallel or serially. Figure 2-2a shows how the binary code 0110 is transmitted from location A to location B in parallel. As the figure shows, each bit position (A0 to A3) has its own transmission line. Consequently, all 4 bits can be transmitted simultaneously during the time of a single clock pulse (*T*). This type of transmission is called *parallel-by-bit* or *serial-by-character*.

Figure 2-2b shows how the same binary code is transmitted serially. As the figure shows, there is a single transmission line, and thus only one bit can be

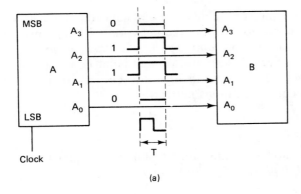

(a)

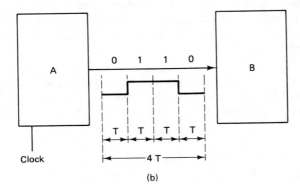

(b)

Figure 2-2 Data transmission: (a) parallel; (b) serial.

Data Communications Circuits

transmitted at a time. Consequently, it requires four clock pulses (4*T*) to transmit the entire word. This type of transmission is often called *serial-by-bit*.

Obviously, the principal trade-off between parallel and serial transmission is speed versus simplicity. Data transmission can be accomplished much more quickly using parallel transmission. However, parallel transmission requires more lines between the source and destination. As a general rule, parallel transmission is used for short distances, and within a computer, and serial transmission is used for long-distance communications.

Data Communications Circuit Configurations and Topologies

Configurations. Data communications circuits can be generally categorized as either two-point or multipoint. A *two-point* configuration involves only two locations or stations, whereas a *multipoint* configuration involves three or more stations. A two-point circuit can involve the transfer of information between a mainframe computer and a remote computer terminal, two mainframe computers, or two remote computer terminals. A multipoint circuit is generally used to interconnect a single mainframe computer (*host*) to many remote computer terminals, although any combination of three or more computers or computer terminals constitutes a multipoint circuit.

Topologies. The topology or architecture of a data communications circuit identifies how the various locations within the network are interconnected. The most common topologies used are the *point to point*, the *star*, the *bus* or *multidrop*, the *ring* or *loop*, and the *mesh*. These are all multipoint configurations except the point to point. Figure 2-3 shows the various circuit configurations and topologies used for data communications networks.

Transmission Modes

Essentially, there are four modes of transmission for data communications circuits: *simplex, half duplex, full duplex,* and *full/full duplex*.

Simplex. With simplex operation, data transmission is unidirectional; information can be sent only in one direction. Simplex lines are also called *receive-only, transmit-only,* or *one-way-only* lines. Commercial television and radio systems are examples of simplex transmission.

Half duplex (HDX). In the half-duplex mode, data transmission is possible in both directions, but not at the same time. Half-duplex lines are also called two-way alternate or either way lines. Citizens band (CB) radio is an example of half-duplex transmission.

Full duplex (FDX). In the full-duplex mode, transmissions are possible in both directions simultaneously, but they must be between the same two stations.

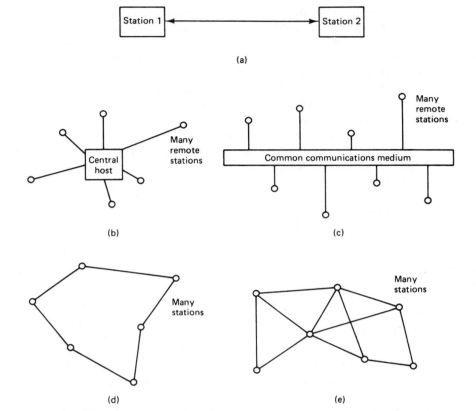

Figure 2-3 Data network topologies: (a) point to point; (b) star; (c) bus or multidrop; (d) ring or loop; (e) mesh.

Full-duplex lines are also called two-way-simultaneous, *duplex,* or both way lines. A standard telephone system is an example of full-duplex transmission.

Full/full duplex (F/FDX). In the F/FDX mode, transmission is possible in both directions at the same time but not between the same two stations (i.e., one station is transmitting to a second station and receiving from a third station at the same time). F/FDX is possible only on multipoint circuits. The U.S. postal system is an example of full/full duplex transmission.

Two-Wire versus Four-Wire Operation

Two-wire, as the name implies, involves a transmission medium that either uses two wires (a signal and a reference lead) or a configuration that is equivalent to having only two wires. With two-wire operation, simplex, half-, or full-duplex transmission is possible. For full-duplex operation, the signals propagating in opposite directions must occupy different bandwidths; otherwise, they will mix linearly and interfere with each other.

Data Communications Circuits 67

Four-wire, as the name implies, involves a transmission medium that uses four wires (two are used for signals that are propagating in opposite directions and two are used for reference leads) or a configuration that is equivalent to having four wires. With four-wire operation, the signals propagating in opposite directions are physically separated and therefore can occupy the same bandwidths without interfering with each other. Four-wire operation provides more isolation and is preferred over two-wire, although four-wire requires twice as many wires and, consequently, twice the cost.

A transmitter and its associated receiver are equivalent to a two-wire circuit. A transmitter and a receiver for both directions of propagation is equivalent to a four-wire circuit. With full-duplex transmission over a two-wire line, the available bandwidth must be divided in half, thus reducing the information capacity in either direction to one-half of the half-duplex value. Consequently, full-duplex operation over two-wire lines requires twice as much time to transfer the same amount of information.

DATA COMMUNICATIONS CODES

Data communications codes are prescribed bit sequences used for encoding characters and symbols. Consequently, data communications codes are often called *character sets, character codes, symbol codes,* or *character languages.* In essence, there are only three types of characters used in data communications codes: *data link control characters,* which are used to facilitate the orderly flow of data from a source to a destination; *graphic control characters,* which involve the syntax or presentation of the data at the receive terminal; and *alpha/numeric* characters, which are used to represent the various symbols used for letters, numbers, and punctuation in the English language.

The first data communications code that saw widespread usage was the Morse code. The Morse code used three unequal-length symbols (dot, dash, and space) to encode alpha/numeric characters, punctuation marks, and an interrogation word.

The Morse code is inadequate for use in modern digital computer equipment because all characters do not have the same number of symbols or take the same length of time to send, and each Morse code operator transmits code at a different rate. Also, with Morse code, there is an insufficient selection of graphic and data link control characters to facilitate the transmission and presentation of the data typically used in contemporary computer applications.

The three most common character sets presently used for character encoding are the Baudot code, the American Standard Code for Information Interchange (ASCII), and the Extended Binary-Coded Decimal Interchange Code (EBCDIC).

Baudot Code

The *Baudot code* (sometimes called the *Telex code* was the first fixed-length character code. The Baudot code was developed by a French postal engineer,

Thomas Murray, in 1875 and named after Emile Baudot, an early pioneer in telegraph printing. The Baudot code is a 5-bit character code that is used primarily for low-speed teletype equipment such as the TWX/Telex system. With a 5-bit code there are only 2^5 or 32 codes possible, which is insufficient to represent the 26 letters of the alphabet, the 10 digits, and the various punctuation marks and control characters. Therefore, the Baudot code uses *figure* shift and *letter* shift characters to expand its capabilities to 58 characters. The latest version of the Baudot code is recommended by the CCITT as the International Alphabet No. 2. The Baudot code is still used by Western Union Company for the TWX and Telex teletype systems. The AP and UPI news services for years used the Baudot code for sending news information around the world. The most recent version of the Baudot code is shown in Table 2-1.

TABLE 2-1   BAUDOT CODE

Character shift		Binary code					
Letter	*Figure*	*Bit:*	*4*	*3*	*2*	*1*	*0*
A	—		1	1	0	0	0
B	?		1	0	0	1	1
C	:		0	1	1	1	0
D	$		1	0	0	1	0
E	3		1	0	0	0	0
F	!		1	0	1	1	0
G	&		0	1	0	1	1
H	#		0	0	1	0	1
I	8		0	1	1	0	0
J	'		1	1	0	1	0
K	(		1	1	1	1	0
L	)		0	1	0	0	1
M	.		0	0	1	1	1
N	,		0	0	1	1	0
O	9		0	0	0	1	1
P	0		0	1	1	0	1
Q	1		1	1	1	0	1
R	4		0	1	0	1	0
S	bel		1	0	1	0	0
T	5		0	0	0	0	1
U	7		1	1	1	0	0
V	;		0	1	1	1	1
W	2		1	1	0	0	1
X	/		1	0	1	1	1
Y	6		1	0	1	0	1
Z	"		1	0	0	0	1
Figure shift			1	1	1	1	1
Letter shift			1	1	0	1	1
Space			0	0	1	0	0
Line feed (LF)			0	1	0	0	0
Blank (null)			0	0	0	0	0

ASCII Code

In 1963, in an effort to standardize data communications codes, the United States adopted the Bell System model 33 teletype code as the United States of America Standard Code for Information Interchange (USASCII), better known simply as ASCII-63. Since its adoption, ASCII has generically progressed through the 1965, 1967, and 1977 versions, with the 1977 version being recommended by the CCITT as the International Alphabet No. 5. ASCII is a 7-bit character set which has 2^7 or 128 codes. With ASCII, the least significant bit (LSB) is designated b_0 and the most significant bit (MSB) is designated b_6. b_7 is not part of the ASCII code but is generally reserved for the parity bit, which is explained later in this chapter. Actually, with any character set, all bits are equally significant because the code does not represent a weighted binary number. It is common with character codes to refer to bits by their order; b_0 is the zero-order bit, b_1 is the first-order bit, b_7 is the seventh-order bit, and so on. With serial transmission, the bit transmitted first is called the LSB. With ASCII, the low-order bit (b_0) is the LSB and is transmitted first. ASCII is probably the code most often used today. The 1977 version of the ASCII code is shown in Table 2-2.

TABLE 2-2   ASCII-77 CODE—ODD PARITY

			Bin	ary	cod	e								Bin	ary	cod	e				
Bit:	7	6	5	4	3	2	1	0	Hex	Bit:	7	6	5	4	3	2	1	0	Hex
NUL	1	0	0	0	0	0	0	0	00	@	0	1	0	0	0	0	0	0	40
SOH	0	0	0	0	0	0	0	1	01	A	1	1	0	0	0	0	0	1	41
STX	0	0	0	0	0	0	1	0	02	B	1	1	0	0	0	0	1	0	42
ETX	1	0	0	0	0	0	1	1	03	C	0	1	0	0	0	0	1	1	43
EOT	0	0	0	0	0	1	0	0	04	D	1	1	0	0	0	1	0	0	44
ENQ	1	0	0	0	0	1	0	1	05	E	0	1	0	0	0	1	0	1	45
ACK	1	0	0	0	0	1	1	0	06	F	0	1	0	0	0	1	1	0	46
BEL	0	0	0	0	0	1	1	1	07	G	1	1	0	0	0	1	1	1	47
BS	0	0	0	0	1	0	0	0	08	H	1	1	0	0	1	0	0	0	48
HT	1	0	0	0	1	0	0	1	09	I	0	1	0	0	1	0	0	1	49
NL	1	0	0	0	1	0	1	0	0A	J	0	1	0	0	1	0	1	0	4A
VT	0	0	0	0	1	0	1	1	0B	K	1	1	0	0	1	0	1	1	4B
FF	1	0	0	0	1	1	0	0	0C	L	0	1	0	0	1	1	0	0	4C
CR	0	0	0	0	1	1	0	1	0D	M	1	1	0	0	1	1	0	1	4D
SO	0	0	0	0	1	1	1	0	0E	N	1	1	0	0	1	1	1	0	4E
SI	1	0	0	0	1	1	1	1	0F	O	0	1	0	0	1	1	1	1	4F
DLE	0	0	0	1	0	0	0	0	10	P	1	1	0	1	0	0	0	0	50
DC1	0	0	0	1	0	0	0	1	11	Q	0	1	0	1	0	0	0	1	51
DC2	1	0	0	1	0	0	1	0	12	R	0	1	0	1	0	0	1	0	52
DC3	0	0	0	1	0	0	1	1	13	S	1	1	0	1	0	0	1	1	53
DC4	1	0	0	1	0	1	0	0	14	T	0	1	0	1	0	1	0	0	54
NAK	0	0	0	1	0	1	0	1	15	U	1	1	0	1	0	1	0	1	55
SYN	0	0	0	1	0	1	1	0	16	V	1	1	0	1	0	1	1	0	56
ETB	1	0	0	1	0	1	1	1	17	W	0	1	0	1	0	1	1	1	57
CAN	1	0	0	1	1	0	0	0	18	X	0	1	0	1	1	0	0	0	58
EM	0	0	0	1	1	0	0	1	19	Y	1	1	0	1	1	0	0	1	59
SUB	0	0	0	1	1	0	1	0	1A	Z	1	1	0	1	1	0	1	0	5A

TABLE 2-2   ASCII-77 CODE—ODD PARITY (Continued)

	Binary code								Hex		Binary code								Hex
Bit:	7	6	5	4	3	2	1	0		Bit:	7	6	5	4	3	2	1	0	
ESC	1	0	0	1	1	0	1	1	1B	[	0	1	0	1	1	0	1	1	5B
FS	0	0	0	1	1	1	0	0	1C	\	1	1	0	1	1	1	0	0	5C
GS	1	0	0	1	1	1	0	1	1D	]	0	1	0	1	1	1	0	1	5D
RS	1	0	0	1	1	1	1	0	1E	∧	0	1	0	1	1	1	1	0	5E
US	0	0	0	1	1	1	1	1	1F	—	1	1	0	1	1	1	1	1	5F
SP	0	0	1	0	0	0	0	0	20	`	1	1	1	0	0	0	0	0	60
!	1	0	1	0	0	0	0	1	21	a	0	1	1	0	0	0	0	1	61
"	1	0	1	0	0	0	1	0	22	b	0	1	1	0	0	0	1	0	62
#	0	0	1	0	0	0	1	1	23	c	1	1	1	0	0	0	1	1	63
$	1	0	1	0	0	1	0	0	24	d	0	1	1	0	0	1	0	0	64
%	0	0	1	0	0	1	0	1	25	e	1	1	1	0	0	1	0	1	65
&	0	0	1	0	0	1	1	0	26	f	1	1	1	0	0	1	1	0	66
'	1	0	1	0	0	1	1	1	27	g	0	1	1	0	0	1	1	1	67
(	1	0	1	0	1	0	0	0	28	h	0	1	1	0	1	0	0	0	68
)	0	0	1	0	1	0	0	1	29	i	1	1	1	0	1	0	0	1	69
*	0	0	1	0	1	0	1	0	2A	j	1	1	1	0	1	0	1	0	6A
+	1	0	1	0	1	0	1	1	2B	k	0	1	1	0	1	0	1	1	6B
,	0	0	1	0	1	1	0	0	2C	l	1	1	1	0	1	1	0	0	6C
-	1	0	1	0	1	1	0	1	2D	m	0	1	1	0	1	1	0	1	6d
.	1	0	1	0	1	1	1	0	2E	n	0	1	1	0	1	1	1	0	6E
/	0	0	1	0	1	1	1	1	2F	o	1	1	1	0	1	1	1	1	6F
0	1	0	1	1	0	0	0	0	30	p	0	1	1	1	0	0	0	0	70
1	0	0	1	1	0	0	0	1	31	q	1	1	1	1	0	0	0	1	71
2	0	0	1	1	0	0	1	0	32	r	1	1	1	1	0	0	1	0	72
3	1	0	1	1	0	0	1	1	33	s	0	1	1	1	0	0	1	1	73
4	0	0	1	1	0	1	0	0	34	t	1	1	1	1	0	1	0	0	74
5	1	0	1	1	0	1	0	1	35	u	0	1	1	1	0	1	0	1	75
6	1	0	1	1	0	1	1	0	36	v	0	1	1	1	0	1	1	0	76
7	0	0	1	1	0	1	1	1	37	w	1	1	1	1	0	1	1	1	77
8	0	0	1	1	1	0	0	0	38	x	1	1	1	1	1	0	0	0	78
9	1	0	1	1	1	0	0	1	39	y	0	1	1	1	1	0	0	1	79
:	1	0	1	1	1	0	1	0	3A	z	0	1	1	1	1	0	1	0	7A
;	0	0	1	1	1	0	1	1	3B	{	1	1	1	1	1	0	1	1	7B
<	1	0	1	1	1	1	0	0	3C	|	0	1	1	1	1	1	0	0	7C
=	0	0	1	1	1	1	0	1	3D	}	1	1	1	1	1	1	0	1	7D
>	0	0	1	1	1	1	1	0	3E	~	1	1	1	1	1	1	1	0	7E
?	1	0	1	1	1	1	1	1	3F	DEL	0	1	1	1	1	1	1	1	7F

NUL = null
SOH = start of heading
STX = start of text
ETX = end of text
EOT = end of transmission
ENQ = enquiry
ACK = acknowledge
BEL = bell
BS = back space
HT = horizontal tab
NL = new line
VT = vertical tab

FF = form feed
CR = carriage return
SO = shift-out
SI = shift-in
DLE = data link escape
DC1 = device control 1
DC2 = device control 2
DC3 = device control 3
DC4 = device control 4
NAK = negative acknowledge
SYN = synchronous

ETB = end of transmission
    block
CAN = cancel
SUB = substitute
ESC = escape
FS = field separator
GS = group separator
RS = record separator
US = unit separator
SP = space
DEL = delete

Data Communications Codes   71

EBCDIC Code

EBCDIC is an 8-bit character code developed by IBM and used extensively in IBM and IBM-compatible equipment. With 8 bits, 2^8 or 256 codes are possible, making EBCDIC the most powerful character set. Note that with EBCDIC the LSB is designated b_7 and the MSB is designated b_0. Therefore, with EBCDIC, the high-order bit (b_7) is transmitted first and the low-order bit (b_0) is transmitted last. The EBCDIC code does not facilitate the use of a parity bit. The EBCDIC code is shown in Table 2-3.

TABLE 2-3 EBCDIC CODE

	Binary code								Hex		Binary code								Hex
Bit:	0	1	2	3	4	5	6	7		Bit:	0	1	2	3	4	5	6	7	
NUL	0	0	0	0	0	0	0	0	00		1	0	0	0	0	0	0	0	80
SOH	0	0	0	0	0	0	0	1	01	a	1	0	0	0	0	0	0	1	81
STX	0	0	0	0	0	0	1	0	02	b	1	0	0	0	0	0	1	0	82
ETX	0	0	0	0	0	0	1	1	03	c	1	0	0	0	0	0	1	1	83
	0	0	0	0	0	1	0	0	04	d	1	0	0	0	0	1	0	0	84
PT	0	0	0	0	0	1	0	1	05	e	1	0	0	0	0	1	0	1	85
	0	0	0	0	0	1	1	0	06	f	1	0	0	0	0	1	1	0	86
	0	0	0	0	0	1	1	1	07	g	1	0	0	0	0	1	1	1	87
	0	0	0	0	1	0	0	0	08	h	1	0	0	0	1	0	0	0	88
	0	0	0	0	1	0	0	1	09	i	1	0	0	0	1	0	0	1	89
	0	0	0	0	1	0	1	0	0A		1	0	0	0	1	0	1	0	8A
	0	0	0	0	1	0	1	1	0B		1	0	0	0	1	0	1	1	8B
FF	0	0	0	0	1	1	0	0	0C		1	0	0	0	1	1	0	0	8C
	0	0	0	0	1	1	0	1	0D		1	0	0	0	1	1	0	1	8D
	0	0	0	0	1	1	1	0	0E		1	0	0	0	1	1	1	0	8E
	0	0	0	0	1	1	1	1	0F		1	0	0	0	1	1	1	1	8F
DLE	0	0	0	1	0	0	0	0	10		1	0	0	1	0	0	0	0	90
SBA	0	0	0	1	0	0	0	1	11	j	1	0	0	1	0	0	0	1	91
EUA	0	0	0	1	0	0	1	0	12	k	1	0	0	1	0	0	1	0	92
IC	0	0	0	1	0	0	1	1	13	l	1	0	0	1	0	0	1	1	93
	0	0	0	1	0	1	0	0	14	m	1	0	0	1	0	1	0	0	94
NL	0	0	0	1	0	1	0	1	15	n	1	0	0	1	0	1	0	1	95
	0	0	0	1	0	1	1	0	16	o	1	0	0	1	0	1	1	0	96
	0	0	0	1	0	1	1	1	17	p	1	0	0	1	0	1	1	1	97
	0	0	0	1	1	0	0	0	18	q	1	0	0	1	1	0	0	0	98
EM	0	0	0	1	1	0	0	1	19	r	1	0	0	1	1	0	0	1	99
	0	0	0	1	1	0	1	0	1A		1	0	0	1	1	0	1	0	9A
	0	0	0	1	1	0	1	1	1B		1	0	0	1	1	0	1	1	9B
DUP	0	0	0	1	1	1	0	0	1C		1	0	0	1	1	1	0	0	9C
SF	0	0	0	1	1	1	0	1	1D		1	0	0	1	1	1	0	1	9D
FM	0	0	0	1	1	1	1	0	1E		1	0	0	1	1	1	1	0	9E
ITB	0	0	0	1	1	1	1	1	1F		1	0	0	1	1	1	1	1	9F
	0	0	1	0	0	0	0	0	20		1	0	1	0	0	0	0	0	A0
	0	0	1	0	0	0	0	1	21	~	1	0	1	0	0	0	0	1	A1
	0	0	1	0	0	0	1	0	22	s	1	0	1	0	0	0	1	0	A2
	0	0	1	0	0	0	1	1	23	t	1	0	1	0	0	0	1	1	A3
	0	0	1	0	0	1	0	0	24	u	1	0	1	0	0	1	0	0	A4
	0	0	1	0	0	1	0	1	25	v	1	0	1	0	0	1	0	1	A5

TABLE 2-3   EBCDIC CODE (Continued)

Bit:	0	1	2	3	4	5	6	7	Hex	Bit:	0	1	2	3	4	5	6	7	Hex
ETB	0	0	1	0	0	1	1	0	26	w	1	0	1	0	0	1	1	0	A6
ESC	0	0	1	0	0	1	1	1	27	x	1	0	1	0	0	1	1	1	A7
	0	0	1	0	1	0	0	0	28	y	1	0	1	0	1	0	0	0	A8
	0	0	1	0	1	0	0	1	29	z	1	0	1	0	1	0	0	1	A9
	0	0	1	0	1	0	1	0	2A		1	0	1	0	1	0	1	0	AA
	0	0	1	0	1	0	1	1	2B		1	0	1	0	1	0	1	1	AB
	0	0	1	0	1	1	0	0	2C		1	0	1	0	1	1	0	0	AC
ENQ	0	0	1	0	1	1	0	1	2D		1	0	1	0	1	1	0	1	AD
	0	0	1	0	1	1	1	0	2E		1	0	1	0	1	1	1	0	AE
	0	0	1	0	1	1	1	1	2F		1	0	1	0	1	1	1	1	AF
	0	0	1	1	0	0	0	0	30		1	0	1	1	0	0	0	0	B0
	0	0	1	1	0	0	0	1	31		1	0	1	1	0	0	0	1	B1
SYN	0	0	1	1	0	0	1	0	32		1	0	1	1	0	0	1	0	B2
	0	0	1	1	0	0	1	1	33		1	0	1	1	0	0	1	1	B3
	0	0	1	1	0	1	0	0	34		1	0	1	1	0	1	0	0	B4
	0	0	1	1	0	1	0	1	35		1	0	1	1	0	1	0	1	B5
	0	0	1	1	0	1	1	0	36		1	0	1	1	0	1	1	0	B6
EOT	0	0	1	1	0	1	1	1	37		1	0	1	1	0	1	1	1	B7
	0	0	1	1	1	0	0	0	38		1	0	1	1	1	0	0	0	B8
	0	0	1	1	1	0	0	1	39		1	0	1	1	1	0	0	1	B9
	0	0	1	1	1	0	1	0	3A		1	0	1	1	1	0	1	0	BA
	0	0	1	1	1	0	1	1	3B		1	0	1	1	1	0	1	1	BB
RA	0	0	1	1	1	1	0	0	3C		1	0	1	1	1	1	0	0	BC
NAK	0	0	1	1	1	1	0	1	3D		1	0	1	1	1	1	0	1	BD
	0	0	1	1	1	1	1	0	3E		1	0	1	1	1	1	1	0	BE
SUB	0	0	1	1	1	1	1	1	3F		1	0	1	1	1	1	1	1	BF
SP	0	1	0	0	0	0	0	0	40	{	1	1	0	0	0	0	0	0	C0
	0	1	0	0	0	0	0	1	41	A	1	1	0	0	0	0	0	1	C1
	0	1	0	0	0	0	1	0	42	B	1	1	0	0	0	0	1	0	C2
	0	1	0	0	0	0	1	1	43	C	1	1	0	0	0	0	1	1	C3
	0	1	0	0	0	1	0	0	44	D	1	1	0	0	0	1	0	0	C4
	0	1	0	0	0	1	0	1	45	E	1	1	0	0	0	1	0	1	C5
	0	1	0	0	0	1	1	0	46	F	1	1	0	0	0	1	1	0	C6
	0	1	0	0	0	1	1	1	47	G	1	1	0	0	0	1	1	1	C7
	0	1	0	0	1	0	0	0	48	H	1	1	0	0	1	0	0	0	C8
	0	1	0	0	1	0	0	1	49	I	1	1	0	0	1	0	0	1	C9
¢	0	1	0	0	1	0	1	0	4A		1	1	0	0	1	0	1	0	CA
.	0	1	0	0	1	0	1	1	4B		1	1	0	0	1	0	1	1	CB
<	0	1	0	0	1	1	0	0	4C		1	1	0	0	1	1	0	0	CC
(	0	1	0	0	1	1	0	1	4D		1	1	0	0	1	1	0	1	CD
+	0	1	0	0	1	1	1	0	4E		1	1	0	0	1	1	1	0	CE
¦	0	1	0	0	1	1	1	1	4F		1	1	0	0	1	1	1	1	CF
&	0	1	0	1	0	0	0	0	50	}	1	1	0	1	0	0	0	0	D0
	0	1	0	1	0	0	0	1	51	J	1	1	0	1	0	0	0	1	D1
	0	1	0	1	0	0	1	0	52	K	1	1	0	1	0	0	1	0	D2
	0	1	0	1	0	0	1	1	53	L	1	1	0	1	0	0	1	1	D3
	0	1	0	1	0	1	0	0	54	M	1	1	0	1	0	1	0	0	D4
	0	1	0	1	0	1	0	1	55	N	1	1	0	1	0	1	0	1	D5
	0	1	0	1	0	1	1	0	56	O	1	1	0	1	0	1	1	0	D6

Continued

Data Communications Codes

TABLE 2-3   EBCDIC CODE (Continued)

	Binary code								Hex		Binary code								Hex
Bit:	0	1	2	3	4	5	6	7		Bit:	0	1	2	3	4	5	6	7	
	0	1	0	1	0	1	1	1	57	P	1	1	0	1	0	1	1	1	D7
	0	1	0	1	1	0	0	0	58	Q	1	1	0	1	1	0	0	0	D8
	0	1	0	1	1	0	0	1	59	R	1	1	0	1	1	0	0	1	D9
!	0	1	0	1	1	0	1	0	5A		1	1	0	1	1	0	1	0	DA
$	0	1	0	1	1	0	1	1	5B		1	1	0	1	1	0	1	1	DB
*	0	1	0	1	1	1	0	0	5C		1	1	0	1	1	1	0	0	DC
)	0	1	0	1	1	1	0	1	5D		1	1	0	1	1	1	0	1	DD
;	0	1	0	1	1	1	1	0	5E		1	1	0	1	1	1	1	0	DE
¬	0	1	0	1	1	1	1	1	5F		1	1	0	1	1	1	1	1	DF
-	0	1	1	0	0	0	0	0	60	\	1	1	1	0	0	0	0	0	E0
/	0	1	1	0	0	0	0	1	61		1	1	1	0	0	0	0	1	E1
	0	1	1	0	0	0	1	0	62	S	1	1	1	0	0	0	1	0	E2
	0	1	1	0	0	0	1	1	63	T	1	1	1	0	0	0	1	1	E3
	0	1	1	0	0	1	0	0	64	U	1	1	1	0	0	1	0	0	E4
	0	1	1	0	0	1	0	1	65	V	1	1	1	0	0	1	0	1	E5
	0	1	1	0	0	1	1	0	66	W	1	1	1	0	0	1	1	0	E6
	0	1	1	0	0	1	1	1	67	X	1	1	1	0	0	1	1	1	E7
	0	1	1	0	1	0	0	0	68	Y	1	1	1	0	1	0	0	0	E8
	0	1	1	0	1	0	0	1	69	Z	1	1	1	0	1	0	0	1	E9
	0	1	1	0	1	0	1	0	6A		1	1	1	0	1	0	1	0	EA
,	0	1	1	0	1	0	1	1	6B		1	1	1	0	1	0	1	1	EB
%	0	1	1	0	1	1	0	0	6C		1	1	1	0	1	1	0	0	EC
	0	1	1	0	1	1	0	1	6D		1	1	1	0	1	1	0	1	ED
>	0	1	1	0	1	1	1	0	6E		1	1	1	0	1	1	1	0	EE
?	0	1	1	0	1	1	1	1	6F		1	1	1	0	1	1	1	1	EF
	0	1	1	1	0	0	0	0	70	0	1	1	1	1	0	0	0	0	F0
	0	1	1	1	0	0	0	1	71	1	1	1	1	1	0	0	0	1	F1
	0	1	1	1	0	0	1	0	72	2	1	1	1	1	0	0	1	0	F2
	0	1	1	1	0	0	1	1	73	3	1	1	1	1	0	0	1	1	F3
	0	1	1	1	0	1	0	0	74	4	1	1	1	1	0	1	0	0	F4
	0	1	1	1	0	1	0	1	75	5	1	1	1	1	0	1	0	1	F5
	0	1	1	1	0	1	1	0	76	6	1	1	1	1	0	1	1	0	F6
	0	1	1	1	0	1	1	1	77	7	1	1	1	1	0	1	1	1	F7
	0	1	1	1	1	0	0	0	78	8	1	1	1	1	1	0	0	0	F8
▲	0	1	1	1	1	0	0	1	79	9	1	1	1	1	1	0	0	1	F9
:	0	1	1	1	1	0	1	0	7A		1	1	1	1	1	0	1	0	FA
#	0	1	1	1	1	0	1	1	7B		1	1	1	1	1	0	1	1	FB
@	0	1	1	1	1	1	0	0	7C		1	1	1	1	1	1	0	0	FC
'	0	1	1	1	1	1	0	1	7D		1	1	1	1	1	1	0	1	FD
=	0	1	1	1	1	1	1	0	7E		1	1	1	1	1	1	1	0	FE
"	0	1	1	1	1	1	1	1	7F		1	1	1	1	1	1	1	1	FF

DLE = data link escape
DUP = duplicate
EM = end of medium
ENQ = enquiry
EOT = end of transmission
ESC = escape
ETB = end of transmission block
ETX = end of text

EUA = erase unprotected to address
FF = form feed
FM = field mark
IC = insert cursor
ITB = end of intermediate transmission block
NUL = null
PT = program tab

RA = repeat to address
SBA = set buffer address
SF = start field
SOH = start of heading
SP = space
STX = start of text
SUB = substitute
SYN = synchronous
NAK = negative acknowledge

ERROR CONTROL

A data communications circuit can be as short as a few feet or as long as several thousand miles, and the transmission medium can be as simple as a piece of wire or as complex as a microwave, satellite, or optical fiber system. Therefore, due to the nonideal transmission characteristics that are associated with any communications system, it is inevitable that errors will occur and that it is necessary to develop and implement procedures for error control. Error control can be divided into two general categories: error detection and error correction.

Error Detection

Error detection is simply the process of monitoring the received data and determining when a transmission error has occurred. Error detection techniques do not identify which bit (or bits) is in error, only that an error has occurred. The purpose of error detection is not to prevent errors from occurring but to prevent undetected errors from occurring. How a system reacts to transmission errors is system dependent and varies considerably. The most common error detection techniques used for data communications circuits are: redundancy, exact-count encoding, parity, vertical and longitudinal redundancy checking, and cyclic redundancy checking.

Redundancy. *Redundancy* involves transmitting each character twice. If the same character is not received twice in succession, a transmission error has occurred. The same concept can be used for messages. If the same sequence of characters is not received twice in succession, in exactly the same order, a transmission error has occurred.

Exact-count encoding. With *exact-count encoding,* the number of 1's in each character is the same. An example of an exact-count encoding scheme is the ARQ code shown in Table 2-4. With the ARQ code, each character has three 1's in it, and therefore a simple count of the number of 1's received in each character can determine if a transmission error has occurred.

Parity. *Parity* is probably the simplest error detection scheme used for data communications systems and is used with both vertical and horizontal redundancy checking. With parity, a single bit (called a *parity bit*) is added to each character to force the total number of 1's in the character, including the parity bit, to be either an odd number (odd parity) or an even number (even parity). For example, the ASCII code for the letter "C" is 43 hex or P1000011 binary, with the P bit representing the parity bit. There are three 1's in the code, not counting the parity bit. If odd parity is used, the P bit is made a 0, keeping the total number of 1's at three, an odd number. If even parity is used, the P bit is made a 1 and the total number of 1's is four, an even number.

Taking a closer look at parity, it can be seen that the parity bit is independent of the number of 0's in the code and unaffected by pairs of 1's. For the letter

TABLE 2-4   ARQ EXACT-COUNT CODE

	Binary code							Character	
Bit:	1	2	3	4	5	6	7	Letter	Figure
	0	0	0	1	1	1	0	Letter shift	
	0	1	0	0	1	1	0	Figure shift	
	0	0	1	1	0	1	0	A	—
	0	0	1	1	0	0	1	B	?
	1	0	0	1	1	0	0	C	:
	0	0	1	1	1	0	0	D	(WRU)
	0	1	1	1	0	0	0	E	3
	0	0	1	0	0	1	1	F	%
	1	1	0	0	0	0	1	G	@
	1	0	1	0	0	1	0	H	£
	1	1	1	0	0	0	0	I	8
	0	1	0	0	0	1	1	J	(bell)
	0	0	0	1	0	1	1	K	(
	1	1	0	0	0	1	0	L	)
	1	0	1	0	0	0	1	M	.
	1	0	1	0	1	0	0	N	,
	1	0	0	0	1	1	0	O	9
	1	0	0	1	0	1	0	P	0
	0	0	0	1	1	0	1	Q	1
	1	1	0	0	1	0	0	R	4
	0	1	0	1	0	1	0	S	'
	1	0	0	0	1	0	1	T	5
	0	1	1	0	0	1	0	U	7
	1	0	0	1	0	0	1	V	=
	0	1	0	0	1	0	1	W	2
	0	0	1	0	1	1	0	X	/
	0	0	1	0	1	0	1	Y	6
	0	1	1	0	0	0	1	Z	+
	0	0	0	0	1	1	1		(blank)
	1	1	0	1	0	0	0		(space)
	1	0	1	1	0	0	0		(line feed)
	1	0	0	0	0	1	1		(carriage return)

"C," if all the 0 bits are dropped, the code is P1———11. For odd parity, the P bit is still a 0 and for even parity, the P bit is still a 1. If pairs of 1's are also excluded, the code is either P1———, P———1, or P———1—. Again, for odd parity the P bit is a 0, and for even parity the P bit is a 1.

The definition of parity is *equivalence of equality*. A logic gate that will determine when all its inputs are equal is the XOR gate. With an XOR gate, if all the inputs are equal (either all 0's or all 1's), the output is a 0. If all inputs are not equal, the output is a 1. Figure 2-4 shows two circuits that are commonly used to generate a parity bit. Essentially, both circuits go through a comparison process eliminating 0's and pairs of 1's. The circuit shown in Figure 2-4a uses *sequential (serial)* comparison, while the circuit shown in Figure 2-4 uses *combinational (parallel)* comparison. With the sequential parity generator b_0 is XORed with b_1, the result is XORed with b_2, and so on. The result of the last XOR operation is compared with a *bias* bit. If even parity is desired, the bias bit

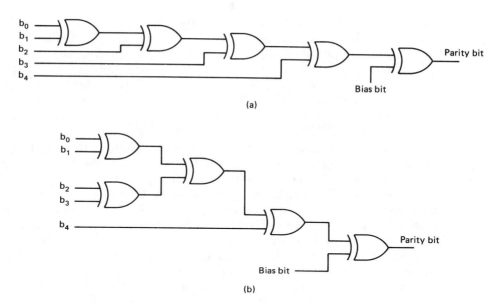

Figure 2-4 Parity generators: (a) serial; (b) parallel. 1, Odd parity; 2, even parity.

is made a logic 0. If odd parity is desired, the bias bit is made a logic 1. The output of the circuit is the parity bit, which is appended to the character code. With the parallel parity generator, comparisons are made in layers or levels. Pairs of bits (b_0 and b_1, b_2 and b_3, etc.) are XORed. The results of the first-level XOR gates are then XORed together. The process continues until only one bit is left, which is XORed with the bias bit. Again, if even parity is desired, the bias bit is made a logic 0 and if odd parity is desired, the bias bit is made a logic 1.

The circuits shown in Figure 2-4 can also be used for the parity checker in the receiver. A parity checker uses the same procedure as a parity generator except that the logic condition of the final comparison is used to determine if a parity violation has occurred (for odd parity a 1 indicates an error and a 0 indicates no error; for even parity, a 1 indicates an error and a 0 indicates no error).

The primary advantage of parity is its simplicity. The disadvantage is that when an even number of bits are received in error, the parity checker will not detect it (i.e., if the logic conditions of 2 bits are changed, the parity remains the same). Consequently, parity, over a long period of time, will detect only 50% of the transmission errors (this assumes an equal probability that an even or an odd number of bits could be in error).

Vertical and horizontal redundancy checking. *Vertical redundancy checking* (VRC) is an error detection scheme that uses parity to determine if a transmission error has occurred within a character. Therefore, VRC is sometimes called *character parity*. With VRC, each character has a parity bit added to it prior to transmission. It may use even or odd parity. The example shown under the topic "parity" involving the ASCII character "C" is an example of how VRC is used.

Horizontal or longitudinal redundancy checking (HRC or LRC) is an error detection scheme that uses parity to determine if a transmission error has occurred in a message and is therefore sometimes called *message parity*. With LRC, each bit position has a parity bit. In other words, b_0 from each character in the message is XORed with b_0 from all of the other characters in the message. Similarly, b_1, b_2, and so on, are XORed with their respective bits from all the other characters in the message. Essentially, LRC is the result of XORing the "characters" that make up a message, whereas VRC is the XORing of the bits within a single character. With LRC, only even parity is used.

The LRC bit sequence is computed in the transmitter prior to sending the data, then transmitted as though it were the last character of the message. At the receiver, the LRC is recomputed from the data and the recomputed LRC is compared with the LRC transmitted with the message. If they are the same, it is assumed that no transmission errors have occurred. If they are different, a transmission error must have occurred.

Example 2-1 shows how VRC and LRC are determined.

Example 2-1

Determine the VRC and LRC for the following ASCII-encoded message: THE CAT. Use odd parity for VRC and even parity for LRC.

Solution

Character		T	H	E	sp	C	A	T	LRC
Hex		*54*	*48*	*45*	*20*	*43*	*41*	*54*	*2F*
LSB	b_0	0	0	1	0	1	1	0	1
	b_1	0	0	0	0	1	0	0	1
ASCII	b_2	1	0	1	0	0	0	1	1
code	b_3	0	1	0	0	0	0	0	1
	b_4	1	0	0	0	0	0	1	0
	b_5	0	0	0	1	0	0	0	1
MSB	b_6	1	1	1	0	1	1	1	0
VRC	b_7	0	1	0	0	0	1	0	0

The LRC is 2FH or 00101111 binary. In ASCII, this is the character /.

The VRC bit for each character is computed in the vertical direction, and the LRC bits are computed in the horizontal direction. This is the same scheme that was used with early teletype paper tapes and keypunch cards and has subsequently been carried over to present-day data communications applications.

The group of characters that make up the message (i.e., THE CAT) is often called a *block* of data. Therefore, the bit sequence for the LRC is often called a *block check character* (BCC) or a *block check sequence* (BCS). BCS is more appropriate because the LRC has no function as a character (i.e., it is not an alpha/numeric, graphic, or data link control character); the LRC is simply a *sequence of bits* used for error detection.

Historically, LRC detects between 95 and 98% of all transmission errors. LRC will not detect transmission errors when an even number of characters have an error in the same bit position. For example, if b_4 in two different characters is in error, the LRC is still valid even though multiple transmission errors have occurred.

If VRC and LRC are used simultaneously, the only time an error would go undetected is when an even number of bits in an even number of characters were in error and the same bit positions in each character are in error, which is highly unlikely to happen. VRC does not identify which bit is in error in a character, and LRC does not identify which character has an error in it. However, for single bit errors, VRC used together with LRC will identify which bit is in error. Otherwise, VRC and LRC only identify that an error has occurred.

Cyclic redundancy checking. Probably the most reliable scheme for error detection is *cyclic redundancy checking* (CRC). With CRC, approximately 99.95% of all transmission errors are detected. CRC is generally used with 8-bit codes such as EBCDIC or 7-bit codes when parity is not used.

In the United States, the most common CRC code is CRC-16, which is identical to the international standard, CCITT V.41. With CRC-16, 16 bits are used for the BCS. Essentially, the CRC character is the remainder of a division process. A data message polynomial $G(x)$ is divided by a generator polynomial function $P(x)$, the quotient is discarded, and the remainder is truncated to 16 bits and added to the message as the BCS. With CRC generation, the division is not accomplished with a standard arithmetic division process. Instead of using straight subtraction, the remainder is derived from an XOR operation. At the receiver, the data stream and the BCS are divided by the same generating function $P(x)$. If no transmission errors have occurred, the remainder will be zero.

The generating polynomial for CRC-16 is

$$P(x) = x^{16} + x^{12} + x^5 + x^0$$

where

$$x^0 = 1.$$

The number of bits in the CRC code is equal to the highest exponent of the generating polynomial. The exponents identify the bit positions that contain a 1. Therefore, b_{16}, b_{12}, b_5, and b_0 are 1's and all of the other bit positions are 0's.

Figure 2-5 shows the block diagram for a circuit that will generate a CRC-16 BCS for the CCITT V.41 standard. Note that for each bit position of the generating polynomial that is a 1 there is an XOR gate.

Example 2-2

Determine the BSC for the following data and CRC generating polynomials:

$$\text{data } G(x) = x^7 + x^5 + x^4 + x^2 + x^1 + x^0 \quad \text{or} \quad 10110111$$
$$\text{CRC } P(x) = x^5 + x^4 + x^1 + x^0 \quad \text{or} \quad 110011$$

Error Control

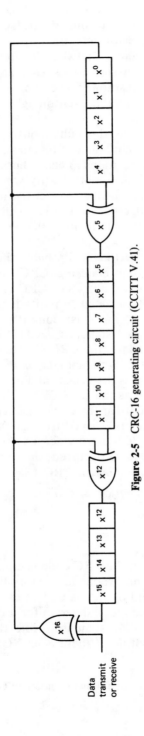

Figure 2-5 CRC-16 generating circuit (CCITT V.41).

Solution   First $G(x)$ is multiplied by the number of bits in the CRC code, 5.

$$x^5 (x^7 + x^5 + x^4 + x^2 + x^1 + x^0) = x^{12} + x^{10} + x^9 + x^7 + x^6 + x^5$$
$$= 1011011100000$$

```
                       11010111
              110011|1011011100000
                     110011
                      111101
                      110011
                       111010
                       110011
                        100100
                        110011
                         101110
                         110011
                          111010
                          110011
                           01001  = CRC
```

The CRC is appended to the data to give the following transmitted data stream:

```
         G(x)         CRC
       10110111     01001
```

At the receiver, the transmitted data are again divided by $P(x)$.

```
                      11010111
             110011|1011011101001
                    110011
                     111101
                     110011
                      111010
                      110011
                       100110
                       110011
                        101010
                        110011
                         110011
                         110011
                          000000  remainder = 0
                                  no error occurred
```

Error Correction

Essentially, there are three methods of error correction: symbol substitution, retransmission, and forward error correction.

   Symbol substitution.   *Symbol substitution* was designed to be used in a human environment: when there is a human being at the receive terminal to analyze the received data and make decisions on its integrity. With symbol substitution, if a character is received in error, rather than revert to a higher level of error correction or display the incorrect character, a unique character that is undefined by the character code, such as a reverse question mark (⸮), is substituted for the bad character. If the character in error cannot be discerned by the operator, retransmission is called for (i.e., symbol substitution is a form of selective retransmission). For example, if the message "Name" had an error in the first character, it would be displayed as "⸮ame." An operator can discern the correct message by inspection and retransmission is unnecessary. However, if the message "$⸮,000.00" were received, an operator could not determine the correct character, and retransmission is required.

Retransmission. *Retransmission,* as the name implies, is when a message is received in error and the receive terminal automatically calls for retransmission of the entire message. Retransmission is often called ARQ, which is an old radio communications term that means *automatic request for retransmission.* ARQ is probably the most reliable method of error correction, although it is not always the most efficient. Impairments on transmission media occur in bursts. If short messages are used, the likelihood that an impairment will occur during a transmission is small. However, short messages require more acknowledgments and line turnarounds than do long messages. Acknowledgments and line turnarounds for error control are forms of *overhead* (characters other than data that must be transmitted). With long messages, less turnaround time is needed, although the likelihood that a transmission error will occur is higher than for short messages. It can be shown statistically that message blocks between 256 and 512 characters are of optimum size when using ARQ for error correction.

Forward error correction. *Forward error correction* (FEC) is the only error correction scheme that actually detects and corrects transmission errors at the receive end without calling for retransmission.

With FEC, bits are added to the message prior to transmission. A popular error-correcting code is the *Hamming code,* developed by R. W. Hamming at Bell Laboratories. The number of bits in the Hamming code is dependent on the number of bits in the data character. The number of Hamming bits that must be added to a character is determined from the following expression:

$$2^n \geq m + n + 1 \tag{2-1}$$

where

n = number of Hamming bits
m = number of bits in the data character

Example 2-3

For a 12-bit data string of 101100010010, determine the number of Hamming bits required, arbitrarily place the Hamming bits into the data string, determine the condition of each Hamming bit, assume an arbitrary single-bit transmission error, and prove that the Hamming code will detect the error.

Solution Substituting into Equation 2-1, the number of Hamming bits is

$$2^n \geq m + n + 1$$

for $n = 4$:

$$2^4 = 16 \geq m + n + 1 = 12 + 4 + 1 = 17$$

$16 < 17$; therefore, 4 Hamming bits are insufficient.
For $n = 5$:

$$2^5 = 32 \geq m + n + 1 = 12 + 5 + 1 = 18$$

$32 > 18$; therefore, 5 Hamming bits are sufficient to meet the criterion of Equation 2-1. Therefore, a total of $12 + 5 = 17$ bits make up the data stream.

Arbitrarily place 5 Hamming bits into the data stream:

```
17 16 15 14 13 12 11 10 9 8 7 6 5 4 3 2 1
 H  1  0  1  H  1  0  0 H H 0 1 0 H 0 1 0
```

To determine the logic condition of the Hamming bits, express all bit positions that contain a 1 as a 5-bit binary number and XOR them together.

Bit position	Binary number
2	00010
6	00110
XOR	00100
12	01100
XOR	01000
14	01110
XOR	00110
16	10000
XOR	10110 = Hamming code

$$b_{17} = 1, \quad b_{13} = 0, \quad b_9 = 1, \quad b_8 = 1, \quad b_4 = 0$$

The 17-bit encoded data stream becomes

```
H       H       H H       H
1 1 0 1 0 1 0 0 1 1 0 1 0 0 0 1 0
```

Assume that during transmission, an error occurs in bit position 14. The received data stream is

```
1 1 0 0 0 1 0 0 1 1 0 1 0 0 0 1 0
```

At the receiver to determine the bit position in error, extract the Hamming bits and XOR them with the binary code for each data bit position that contains a 1.

Bit position	Binary number
Hamming code	10110
2	00010
XOR	10100
6	00110
XOR	10010
12	01100
XOR	11110
16	10000
XOR	01110 = binary 14

Bit position 14 was received in error. To fix the error, simply complement bit 14.

The Hamming code described here will detect only single-bit errors. It cannot be used to identify multiple-bit errors or errors in the Hamming bits themselves. The Hamming code, like all FEC codes, requires the addition of bits to the data, consequently lengthening the transmitted message. The purpose of FEC codes is to reduce or eliminate the wasted time of retransmissions. However, the addition of the FEC bits to each message wastes transmission time in itself. Obviously, a trade-off is made between ARQ and FEC and system requirements determine which method is best suited to a particular system. FEC is often used for simplex transmissions to many receivers when acknowledgements are impractical.

SYNCHRONIZATION

Synchronize means to coincide or agree in time. In data communications, there are four types of synchronization that must be achieved: bit or clock synchronization, modem or carrier synchronization, character synchronization, and message synchronization. The clock and carrier recovery circuits discussed in Chapter 1 accomplish bit and carrier synchronization, and message synchronization is discussed in Chapter 3.

Character Synchronization

Clock synchronization ensures that the transmitter and receiver agree on a precise time slot for the occurrence of a bit. When a continuous string of data is received, it is necessary to identify which bits belong to which characters and which bit is the least significant data bit, the parity bit, and the stop bit. In essence, this is character synchronization: identifying the beginning and the end of a character code. In data communications circuits, there are two formats used to achieve character synchronization: asynchronous and synchronous.

Asynchronous data format. With *asynchronous data,* each character is framed between a *start* and a *stop* bit. Figure 2-6 shows the format used to frame a character for asynchronous data transmission. The first bit transmitted is the start bit and is always a logic 0. The character code bits are transmitted next beginning with the LSB and continuing through the MSB. The parity bit (if used) is transmitted directly after the MSB of the character. The last bit transmitted is the stop bit, which is always a logic 1. There can be either 1, 1.5, or 2 stop bits.

A logic 0 is used for the start bit because an idle condition (no data transmission) on a data communications circuit is identified by the transmission of continuous 1's (these are often called *idle line 1's*). Therefore, the start bit of the first character is identified by a high-to-low transition in the received data, and the bit that immediately follows the start bit is the LSB of the character code. All stop bits are logic 1's, which guarantees a high-to-low transition at the beginning of each character. After the start bit is detected, the data and parity bits are clocked into the receiver. If data are transmitted in real time (i.e., as an

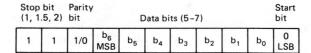

Stop bit (1, 1.5, 2)	Parity bit	Data bits (5–7)							Start bit
1	1	1/0	b_6 MSB	b_5	b_4	b_3	b_2	b_1	b_0	0 LSB

Figure 2-6 Asynchronous data format.

operator types data into their computer terminal), the number of idle line 1's between each character will vary. During this *dead time,* the receiver will simply wait for the occurrence of another start bit before clocking in the next character.

Example 2-4

For the following string of asynchronous ASCII-encoded data, identify each character (assume even parity and 2 stop bits).

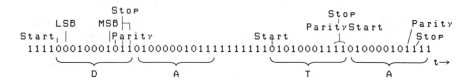

Synchronous data format.   With *synchronous data,* rather than frame each character independently with start and stop bits, a unique synchronizing character called a SYN character is transmitted at the beginning of each message. For example with ASCII code, the SYN character is 16H. The receiver disregards incoming data until it receives the SYN character, then it clocks in the next 7 bits and interprets them as a character. The character that is used to signify the end of a transmission varies with the type of protocol used and what kind of transmission it is. Message-terminating characters are discussed in Chapter 3.

With asynchronous data, it is not necessary that the transmit and receive clocks be continuously synchronized. It is only necessary that they operate at approximately the same rate and be synchronized at the beginning of each character. This was the purpose of the start bit, to establish a time reference for character synchronization. With synchronous data, the transmit and receive clocks must be synchronized because character synchronization occurs only once at the beginning of the message.

Example 2-5

For the following string of synchronous ASCII-encoded data, identity each character (assume odd parity).

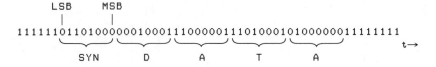

With asynchronous data, each character has 2 or 3 bits added to each character (1 start and 1 or 2 stop bits). These bits are additional overhead and thus reduce the efficiency of the transmission (i.e., the ratio of information bits

Synchronization   **85**

to total transmitted bits). Synchronous data have two SYN characters (16 bits of overhead) added to each message. Therefore, asynchronous data are more efficient for short messages, and synchronous data are more efficient for long messages.

DATA COMMUNICATIONS HARDWARE

Figure 2-7 shows the block diagram of a multipoint data communications circuit that uses a bus topology. This arrangement is one of the most common configurations used for data communications circuits. At one station there is a mainframe computer and at each of the other two stations there is a *cluster* of computer terminals. The hardware and associated circuitry that connect the host computer to the remote computer terminals is called a *data communications link*. The station with the mainframe is called the *host* or *primary* and the other stations are called *secondaries* or simply *remotes*. An arrangement such as this is called a *centralized network;* there is one centrally located station (the host) with the responsibility of ensuring an orderly flow of data between the remote stations and itself. Data flow is controlled by an applications program which is stored at the primary station.

At the primary station there is a mainframe computer, a *line control unit* (LCU), and a *data modem* (a data modem is commonly referred to simply as a

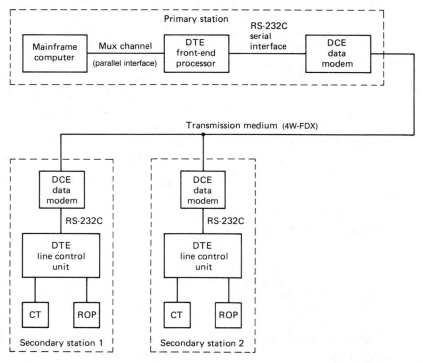

Figure 2-7 Multipoint data communications circuit block diagram.

modem). At each secondary station there is a modem, an LCU, and terminal equipment, such as computer terminals, printers, and so on. The mainframe is the host of the network and is where the applications program is stored for each circuit it serves. For simplicity, Figure 2-7 shows only one circuit served by the primary, although there can be many different circuits served by one mainframe computer. The primary station has the capability of storing, processing, or retransmitting the data it receives from the secondary stations. The primary also stores software for data base management.

The LCU at the primary station is more complicated than the LCUs at the secondary stations. The LCU at the primary station directs data traffic to and from many different circuits, which could all have different characteristics (i.e., different bit rates, character codes, data formats, etc.). The LCU at a secondary station directs data traffic between one data link and a few terminal devices which all operate at the same speed and use the same character code. Generally speaking, if the LCU has software associated with it, it is called a *front-end processor* (FEP). The LCU at the primary station is usually an FEP.

Line Control Unit

The LCU has several important functions. The LCU at the primary station serves as an interface between the host computer and the circuits that it serves. Each circuit served is connected to a different port on the LCU. The LCU directs the flow of input and output data between the different data communications links and their respective applications program. The LCU performs parallel-to-serial and serial-to-parallel conversion of data. The mux interface channel between the mainframe computer and the LCU transfers data in parallel. Data transfers between the modem and the LCU is done serially. The LCU also houses the circuitry that performs error detection and correction. Also, data link control (DLC) characters are inserted and deleted in the LCU. Data link control characters are explained in Chapter 3.

The LCU operates on the data when it is in digital form and is therefore called *data terminal equipment* (DTE). Within the LCU, there is a single integrated circuit that performs several of the LCU's functions. This circuit is called a UART when asynchronous transmission is used and a USRT when synchronous transmission is used.

Universal asynchronous receiver/transmitter (UART). The UART is used for asynchronous transmission of data between the DTE and the DCE. Asynchronous transmission means that an asynchronous data format is used and there is no clocking information transferred between the DTE and the DCE. The primary functions of the UART are:

1. To perform serial-to-parallel and parallel-to-serial conversion of data
2. To perform error detection by inserting and checking parity bits
3. To insert and detect start and stop bits

Functionally, the UART is divided into two sections: the transmitter and the receiver. Figure 2-8a shows a simplified block diagram of a UART transmitter.

Prior to transferring data in either direction, a *control* word must be programmed into the UART control register to indicate the nature of the data, such as the number of data bits; if parity is used, and if so, whether it is even or odd; and the number of stop bits. Essentially, the start bit is the only bit that is not optional; there is always only one start bit and it must be a logic 0. Figure 2-8b shows how to program the control word for the various functions. In the UART, the control word is used to set up the data-, parity-, and stop-bit steering logic circuit.

UART transmitter. The operation of the UART transmitter section is really quite simple. The UART sends a transmit buffer empty (TBMT) signal to the DTE to indicate that it is ready to receive data. When the DTE senses an active condition on TBMT, it sends a parallel data character to the transmit data lines (TD0–TD7) and strobes them into the transmit buffer register with the transmit data strobe signal ($\overline{\text{TDS}}$). The contents of the transmit buffer register are transferred to the transit shift register when the transmit-end-of-character (TEOC) signal goes active (the TEOC signal simply tells the buffer register when the shift register is empty and available to receive data). The data pass through the steering logic circuit, where they pick up the appropriate start, stop, and parity bits. After data have been loaded into the transmit shift register, they are serially outputted on the transmit serial output (TSO) pin with a bit rate equal to the transmit clock (TCP) frequency. While the data in the transmit shift register are sequentially clocked out, the DTE loads the next character into the buffer register. The process continues until the DTE has transferred all its data. The preceding sequence is shown in Figure 2-9.

UART receiver. A simplified block diagram of a UART receiver is shown in Figure 2-10. The number of stop bits, data bits, and the parity-bit information for the UART receiver are determined by the same control word that is used by the transmitter (i.e., the type of parity, the number of stop bits, and the number of data bits used for the UART receiver must be the same as that used for the UART transmitter).

The UART receiver ignores idle line 1's. When a valid start bit is detected by the start bit verification circuit, the data character is serially clocked into the receive shift register. If parity is used, the parity bit is checked in the parity check circuit. After one complete data character is loaded into the shift register, the character is transferred in parallel into the buffer register and the receive data available (RDA) flag is set in the status word register. To read the status register, the DTE activates status word enable ($\overline{\text{SWE}}$) and if it is active, reads the character from the buffer register by placing an active condition on the receive data enable (RDE) pin. After reading the data, the DTE places an active signal on the receive data available reset ($\overline{\text{RDAR}}$) pin, which resets the RDA pin. Meanwhile, the next character is received and clocked into the receive shift register and the process repeats itself until all the data have been received. The preceding sequence is shown in Figure 2-11.

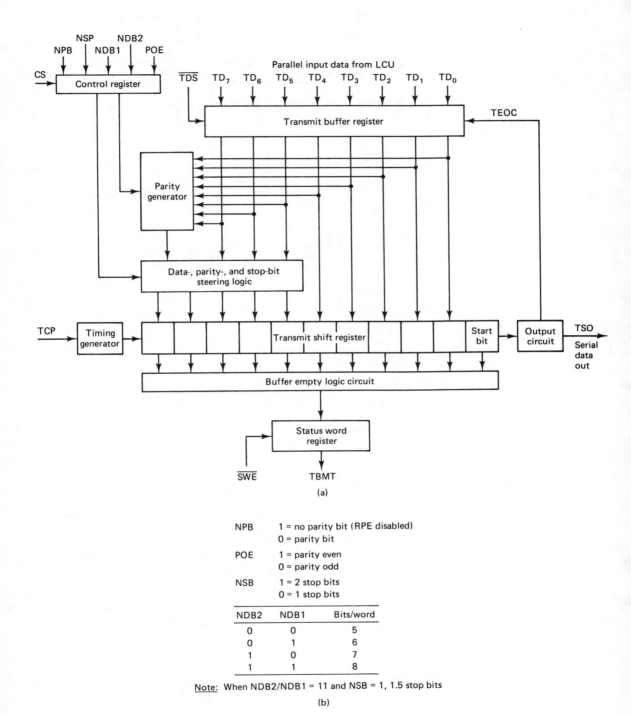

NPB   1 = no parity bit (RPE disabled)
               0 = parity bit

POE   1 = parity even
               0 = parity odd

NSB   1 = 2 stop bits
               0 = 1 stop bits

NDB2	NDB1	Bits/word
0	0	5
0	1	6
1	0	7
1	1	8

Note: When NDB2/NDB1 = 11 and NSB = 1, 1.5 stop bits

(b)

Figure 2-8   UART transmitter: (a) simplified block diagram; (b) control word.

Data Communications Hardware

89

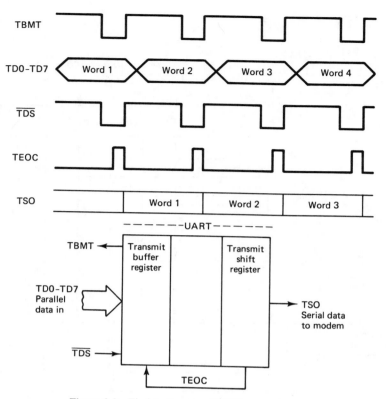

Figure 2-9 Timing diagram: UART transmitter.

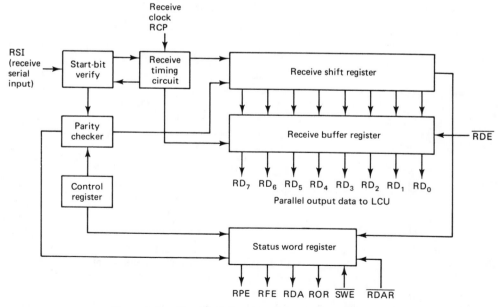

Figure 2-10 Simplified block diagram of a UART receiver.

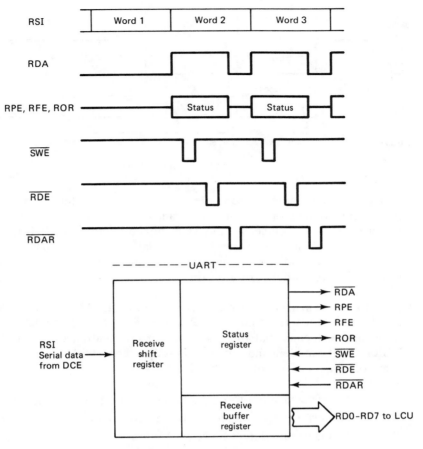

Figure 2-11 Timing diagram: UART receiver.

The status word register is also used for diagnostic information. The receive parity error (RPE) flag is set when a received character has a parity error in it. The receive framing error (RFE) flag is set when a character is received without any or an improper number of stop bits. The receive overrun (ROR) flag is set when a character in the buffer register is written over with another character (i.e., the DTE failed to service an active condition on RDA before the next character was received by the shift register).

The receive clock for the UART (RCP) is 16 times higher than the receive data rate. This allows the start-bit verification circuit to determine if a high-to-low transition in the received data is actually a valid start bit and not simply a negative-going noise spike. Figure 2-12 shows how this is accomplished. The incoming idle line 1's (continuous high condition) are sampled at a rate 16 times the actual bit rate. This assures that a high-to-low transition is detected within $\frac{1}{16}$ of a bit time after it occurs. Once a low is detected, the verification circuit counts off seven clock pulses, then resamples the data. If it is still low, it is assumed

Data Communications Hardware   91

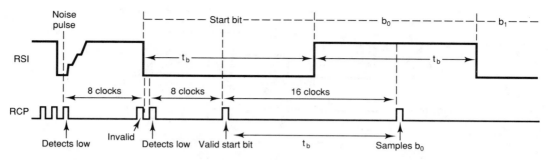

Figure 2-12 Start-bit verification.

that a valid start bit has been detected. If it has reverted to the high condition, it is assumed that the high-to-low transition was simply a noise pulse and is therefore ignored. Once a valid start bit has been detected and verified, the verification circuit samples the incoming data once every 16 clock cycles, which is equal to the data rate. Sampling at 16 times the bit rate also establishes the sample time to within $\frac{1}{16}$ of a bit time from the center of a bit.

Universal synchronous receiver/transmitter (USRT). The USRT is used for synchronous data transmission between the DTE and the DCE. Synchronous transmission means that there is clocking information transferred between the USRT and the modem and each transmission begins with a unique SYN character. The primary functions of the USRT are:

1. To perform serial-to-parallel and parallel-to-serial conversion of data
2. To perform error detection by inserting and checking parity bits
3. To insert and detect SYN characters

The block diagram of the USRT is shown in Figure 2-13a. The USRT operates very similarly to the UART, and therefore only the differences are explained. With the USRT, start and stop bits are not allowed. Instead, unique SYN characters are loaded into the transmit and receive SYN registers prior to transferring data. The programming information for the control word is shown in Figure 2-13.

USRT transmitter. The transmit clock signal (TCP) is set at the desired bit rate and the desired SYN character is loaded from the parallel input pins (DB1–DB8) into the transmit SYN register by pulsing transmit SYN strobe (TSS). Data are loaded into the transmit data register from DB1–DB8 by pulsing the transmit data strobe (TDS). The next character transmitted is extracted from the transmit data register provided that the TDS pulse occurs during the presently transmitted character. If TDS is not pulsed, the next transmitted character is extracted from the transmit SYN register and the SYN character transmitted (SCT) signal is set. The transmit buffer empty (TBMT) signal is used to request the next character

Data Communications   Chap. 2

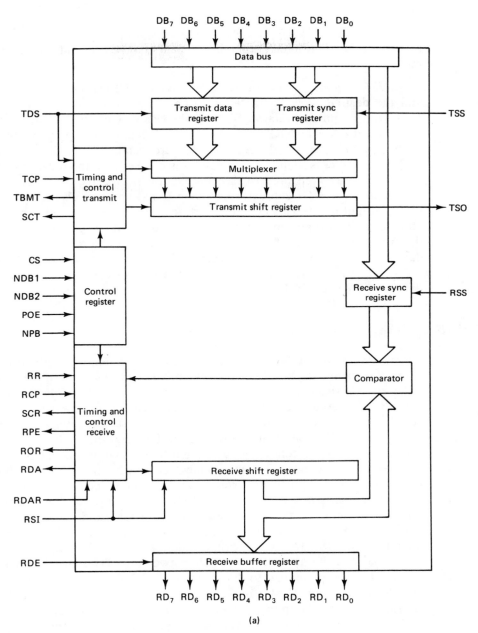

DB_7 DB_6 DB_5 DB_4 DB_3 DB_2 DB_1 DB_0

Data bus

TDS

Transmit data register

Transmit sync register

TSS

TCP

Timing and control transmit

Multiplexer

TBMT

Transmit shift register

TSO

SCT

CS

NDB1

NDB2

Control register

POE

NPB

Receive sync register

RSS

RR

RCP

Comparator

SCR

Timing and control receive

RPE

ROR

RDA

Receive shift register

RDAR

RSI

RDE

Receive buffer register

RD_7 RD_6 RD_5 RD_4 RD_3 RD_2 RD_1 RD_0

(a)

NPB   1 = no parity bit (RPE disabled)
      0 = parity bit

POE   1 = parity even
      0 = parity odd

NDB2	NDB1	Bits/word
0	0	5
0	1	6
1	0	7
1	1	8

Figure 2-13 USRT transceiver:
(a) block diagram; (b) control word.

(b)

93

from the DTE. The serial output data appears on the transmit serial output (TSO) pin.

USRT receiver. The receive clock signal (RCP) is set at the desired bit rate and the desired SYN character is loaded into the receive SYN register from DB1–DB8 by pulsing receive SYN strobe (RSS). On a high-to-low transition of the receiver rest input (RR), the receiver is placed in the search (bit phase) mode. In the search mode, serially received data are examined on a bit-by-bit basis until a SYN character is found. After each bit is clocked into the receive shift register, its contents are compared to the contents of the receive SYN register. If they are identical, a SYN character has been found and the SYN character receive (SCR) output is set. This character is transferred into the receive buffer register and the receiver is placed into the character mode. In the character mode, receive data are examined on a character-by-character basis and receiver flags for receive data available (RDA), receiver overrun (ROR), receive parity error (RPE), and SYN character received are provided to the status word register. Parallel receive data are outputted to the DTE on RB1–RB8.

SERIAL INTERFACES

To ensure an orderly flow of data between the line control unit and the modem, a *serial interface* is placed between them. This interface coordinates the flow of data, control signals, and timing information between the DTE and the DCE.

Before serial interfaces were standardized, every company that manufactured data communications equipment used a different interface configuration. More specifically, the cabling arrangement between the DTE and the DCE, the type and size of the connectors used, and the voltage levels varied considerably from vender to vender. To interconnect equipment manufactured by different companies, special level converters, cables, and connectors had to be built. The Electronic Industries Association (EIA), in an effort to standardize interface equipment between the data terminal equipment and data communications equipment, agreed on a set of standards which are called the RS-232C specifications. The RS-232C specifications identify the mechanical, electrical, and functional description for the interface between the DTE and the DCE. The RS-232C interface is similar to the combined CCITT standards V.28 (electrical specifications) and V.24 (functional description) and is designed for serial transmission of data up to 20,000 bps for a distance of approximately 50 ft. The EIA has recently adopted a new set of standards called the RS-449A, which when used in conjunction with the RS-422A or RS-423A standard, can operate at data rates up to 10 Mbps and span distances up to 1200 m.

RS-232C Interface

The RS-232C interface specifies a 25-wire cable with a DB25P/DB25S-compatible connector. Figure 2-14 shows the electrical characteristics of the RS-232C interface. The terminal load capacitance of the cable is specified as 2500 pF,

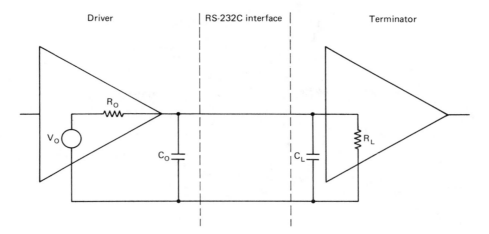

Figure 2-14 RS-232C electrical specifications.

which includes cable capacitance. The impedance at the terminating end must be between 3000 and 7000 Ω, and the output impedance is specified as greater than 300 Ω. With these electrical specifications and for a maximum bit rate of 20,000 bps, the nominal maximum length of the RS-232C interface is approximately 50 ft.

Although the RS-232C interface is simply a cable and two connectors, the standard also specifies limitations on the voltage levels that the DTE and DCE can output onto or receive from the cable. In both the DTE and DCE, there are circuits that convert the internal logic level to RS-232C values. For example, a DTE uses TTL logic and is interfaced to a DCE which uses ECL logic; they are not compatible. Voltage-leveling circuits convert the internal voltage values of the DTE and DCE to RS-232C values. If both the DCE and DCE output and input RS-232C levels, they are electrically compatible regardless of which logic family they use internally. A leveler is called a *driver* if it outputs a signal voltage to the cable and a *terminator* if it accepts a signal voltage from the cable. Table 2-5 lists the voltage limits for both drivers and terminators. Note that the data lines use negative logic and the control lines use positive logic.

From Table 2-5 it can be seen that the limits for a driver are more inclusive than those for a terminator. The driver can output any voltage between $+5$ and $+15$ or -5 and -15 V dc, and a terminator will accept any voltage between $+3$ and $+25$ and -3 and -25 V dc. The difference in the voltage levels between a driver and a terminator is called *noise margin*. The noise margin reduces the susceptibility of the interface to noise transients on the cable. Typical voltages used for data and control signals are ±7 V dc and ±10 V dc.

The pins on the RS-232C interface cable are functionally categorized as either ground, data, control (handshaking), or timing pins. All the pins are unidirectional (signals are propagated only from the DTE to the DCE, or vice versa). Table 2-6 lists the 25 pins of the RS-232C interface, their designations, and the direction of signal propagation (i.e., either toward the DTE or toward

Serial Interfaces   **95**

TABLE 2-5   RS232C VOLTAGE SPECIFICATIONS (V DC)

	Data pins	
	Logic 1	*Logic 0*
Driver	−5 to −15	+5 to +15
Terminator	−3 + −25	+3 to +25

	Control pins	
	Enable "on"	*Disable "off"*
Driver	+5 to +15	−5 to −15
Terminator	+3 to +25	−3 to −25

the DCE). The RS-232C specifications designate the ground, data, control, and timing pins as A, B, C, and D, respectively. These are nondescriptive designations. It is more practical and useful to use acronyms to designate the pins that reflect the pin functions. Table 2-6 lists the CCITT and EIA designations and the nomenclature more commonly used by industry in the United States.

EIA RS-232C pin functions.   Twenty of the 25 pins of the RS-232C interface are designated for specific purposes or functions. Pins 9, 10, 11, 18, and 25 are unassigned; pins 1 and 7 are grounds; pins 2, 3, 14 and 16 are data pins; pins 15, 17, and 24 are timing pins; and all the other assigned pins are reserved for control or handshaking signals. There are two full-duplex data channels available with the RS-232C interface; one channel is for primary data (actual information) and the second channel is for secondary data (diagnostic information and handshaking signals). The functions of the 20 assigned pins are summarized below.

Pin 1—protective ground. This pin is frame ground and is used for protection against electrical shock. Pin 1 should be connected to the third-wire ground of the ac electrical system at one end of the cable (either at the DTE or the DCE, but not at both ends).

Pin 2—transmit data (TD). Serial data on the primary channel from the DTE to the DCE are transmitted on this pin. TD is enabled by an active condition on the CS pin.

Pin 3—received data (RD). Serial data on the primary channel are transferred from the DCE to the DTE on this pin. RD is enabled by an active condition on the RLSD pin.

Pin 4—request to send (RS). The DTE bids for the primary communications channel from the DCE on this pin. An active condition on RS turns on the modem's analog carrier. The analog carrier is modulated by a unique bit pattern called a training sequence which is used to initialize the communications channel and synchronize the receive modem. RS cannot go active unless pin 6 (DSR) is active.

TABLE 2-6   EIA RS-232C PIN DESIGNATIONS

Pin Number	EIA nomenclature	Common acronym	Direction
1	Protective ground (AA)	GWG	None
2	Transmitted data (BA)	TD, SD	DTE to DCE
3	Received data (BB)	RD	DCE to DTE
4	Request to send (CA)	RS, RTS	DTE to DCE
5	Clear to send (CB)	CS, CTS	DCE to DTE
6	Data set ready (CC)	DSR, MR	DCE to DTE
7	Signal ground (AB)	GND	None
8	Received line signal detect (CF)	RLSD, CD	DCE to DTE
9	Unassigned		
10	Unassigned		
11	Unassigned		
12	Secondary received line signal detect (SCF)	SRLSD	DCE to DTE
13	Secondary clear to send (SCB)	SCS	DCE to DTE
14	Secondary transmitted data (SBA)	STD	DTE to DCE
15	Transmission signal element timing (DB)	SCT	DCE to DTE
16	Secondary received data (SBB)	SRD	DCE to DTE
17	Receiver signal element timing (DD)	SCR	DCE to DTE
18	Unassigned		
19	Secondary request to send (SCA)	SRS	DTE to DCE
20	Data terminal ready (CD)	DTR	DTE to DCE
21	Signal quality detector (CG)	SQD	DCE to DTE
22	Ring indicator (CE)	RI	DCE to DTE
23	Data signal rate selector (CH)	DSRS	DTE to DCE
24	Transmit signal element timing (DA)	SCTE	DTE to DCE
25	Unassigned		

Pin 5—clear to send (CS). This signal is a handshake from the DCE to the DTE in response to an active condition on request to send. CS enables the TD pin.

Pin 6—data set ready (DSR). On this pin the DCE indicates the availability of the communications channel. DSR is active as long as the DCE is connected to the communications channel (i.e., the modem or the communications channel is not being tested or is not in the voice mode).

Serial Interfaces   **97**

Pin 7—signal ground. This pin is the signal reference for all the data, control, and timing pins. Usually, this pin is strapped to frame ground (pin 1).

Pin 8—receive line signal detect (RLSD). The DCE uses this pin to signal the DTE when the DCE is receiving an analog carrier on the primary data channel. RSLD enables the RD pin.

Pin 9. Unassigned.

Pin 10. Unassigned.

Pin 11. Unassigned.

Pin 12—secondary receive line signal detect (SRLSD). This pin is active when the DCE is receiving an analog carrier on the secondary channel. SRLSD enables the SRD pin.

Pin 13—secondary clear to send (SCS). This pin is used by the DCE to send a handshake to the DTE in response to an active condition on the secondary request to send pin. SCS enables the STD pin.

Pin 14—secondary transmit data (STD). Diagnostic data are transferred from the DTE to the DCE on this pin. STD is enabled by an active condition on the SCS pin.

Pin 15—transmission signal element timing (SCT). Transmit clocking signals are sent from the DCE to the DTE on this pin.

Pin 16—secondary received data (SRD). Diagnostic data are transferred from the DCE to the DTE on this pin. SRD is enabled by an active condition on the SCS pin.

Pin 17—receive signal element timing (SCR). Receive clocking signals are sent from the DCE to the DTE on this pin. The clock frequency is equal to the bit rate of the primary data channel.

Pin 18. Unassigned.

Pin 19—secondary request to send (SRS). The DTE bids for the secondary communications channel from the DCE on this pin.

Pin 20—data terminal ready (DTR). The DTE sends information to the DCE on this pin concerning the availability of the data terminal equipment (i.e., access to the mainframe at the primary station or status of the computer terminal at the secondary station). DTR is used primarily with dial-up data communications circuits to handshake with RI.

Pin 21—signal quality detector (SQD). The DCE sends signals to the DTE on this pin that reflect the quality of the received analog carrier.

Pin 22—ring indicator (RI). This pin is used with dial-up lines for the DCE to signal the DTE that there is an incoming call.

Pin 23—data signal rate selector (DSRS). The DTE uses this pin to select the transmission bit rate (clock frequency) of the DCE.

Pin 24—transmit signal element timing (SCTE). Transmit clocking signals are sent from the DTE to the DCE on this pin when the master clock oscillator is located in the DTE.

Pin 25. Unassigned.

Pins 1 through 8 are used with both asynchronous and synchronous modems. Pins 15, 17, and 24 are used for only synchronous modems. Pins 12, 13, 14, 16, and 19 are used only when the DCE is equipped with a secondary channel. Pins 19 and 22 are used exclusively for dial-up telephone connections.

The basic operation of the RS-232C interface is shown in Figure 2-15 and described as follows. When the DTE has primary data to send, it enables request to send ($t = 0$ ms). After a predetermined time delay (50 ms), CS goes active. During the RS/CS delay the modem is outputting an analog carrier that is modulated by a unique bit pattern called a *training sequence*. The training sequence is used to initialize the communications line and synchronize the carrier and clock recovery circuits in the receive modem. After the RS/CS delay, TD is enabled and the DTE begins to transmit data. After the receive DTE detects an

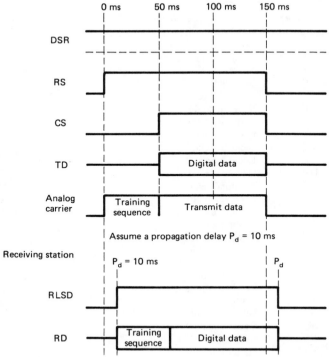

Figure 2-15   Timing diagram: basic operation of the RS-232C interface.

analog carrier, RD is enabled. When the transmission is complete ($t = 150$ ms), RS goes low turning off the analog carrier and shutting off CS. For a more detailed explanation, timing diagrams, and illustrative examples, see V. Alisouskas and W. Tomasi, *Digital and Data Communications* (Englewood Cliffs, N.J.: Prentice Hall, 1985).

RS-449A Interface

Contemporary data rates have exceeded the capabilities of the RS-232C interface. Therefore, it was necessary to adopt and implement a new standard that allows higher bit rates to be transmitted for longer distances. The RS-232C has a maximum bit rate of 20,000 bps and a maximum distance of approximately 50 ft. Consequently, the EIA has adopted a new standard: the RS-449A interface. The RS-449A is essentially an updated version of the RS-232C except that the RS-449A outlines only the mechanical and functional specifications of the cable and connectors.

The RS-449A specifies two cables: one with 37 wires that is used for serial data transmission and one with 9 wires that is used for secondary diagnostic information. Table 2-7 lists the 37 pins of the RS-449A primary cable and their

TABLE 2-7 EIA RS-449A PRIMARY CHANNEL PIN DESIGNATIONS

Pin number	Mneumonic	Circuit name
1	None	Shield
2	SI	Signaling rate indicator
3,21	None	Spare
4,22	SD	Send data
5,23	ST	Send timing
6,24	RD	Receive data
7,25	RS	Request to send
8,26	RT	Receive timing
9,27	CS	Clear to send
10	LL	Local loopback
11,29	DM	Data mode
12,30	TR	Terminal ready
13,31	RR	Receiver ready
14	RL	Remote loopback
15	IC	Incoming call
16	SF/SR	Select frequency/signaling rate
17,23	TT	Terminal timing
18	TM	Test mode
19	SG	Signal ground
20	RC	Receive common
28	IS	Terminal in service
32	SS	Select standby
33	SQ	Signal quality
34	NS	New signal
36	SB	Standby indicator
37	SC	Send common

designations, and Table 2-8 lists the 9 pins of the diagnostic cable and their designations. Note that the acronyms used with the RS-449A are more descriptive than those recommended by the EIA for the RS-232C. The functions specified by the RS-449A are very similar to the RS-232C. The major difference between the two standards is the separation of the primary data and secondary diagnostic channels onto two cables.

The RS-232C and RS-449A standards provide specifications for answering calls, but not for dialing. The EIA has a different standard, RS-366, for automatic calling units. The principal use of RS-366 is for dial backup of private-line data circuits and for automatic dialing of remote terminals.

The electrical specifications used with the RS-449A are specified by either the RS-422A or the RS-423A standard. The RS-422A standard specifies a balanced interface cable that will operate at bit rates up to 10 Mbps and span distances up to 1200 m. This does not mean that 10 Mbps can be transmitted 1200 m. At 10 Mbps the maximum distance is 15 m, and 90 kbps is the maximum bit rate that can be transmitted 1200 m. The RS-423A standard specifies an unbalanced interface cable that will operate at a maximum line speed of 100 kbps and span a maximum distance of 90 m.

Figure 2-16 shows the *balanced* digital interface circuit for the RS-422A, and Figure 2-17 shows the *unbalanced* digital interface circuit for the RS-423A.

A balanced interface, such as the RS 422A, transfers information to a *balanced transmission line*. With a balanced transmission line, both conductors carry current and the current in each wire is 180° out of phase with the current in the other wire. With a bidirectional *unbalanced* line, one wire is at ground potential while the other wire carries signal currents in both directions. The two signal currents are equal in magnitude with respect to electrical ground but travel in opposite directions. Currents that flow in opposite directions in a balanced wire pair are called *metallic circuit* currents. Currents that flow in the same direction are called *longitudinal* currents. A balanced pair has the advantage that most noise interference is induced equally in both wires, producing longitudinal currents that cancel in the load. Figure 2-18 shows the results of metallic and longitudinal currents on a balanced transmission line. It can be seen that

TABLE 2-8 EIA RS-449A SECONDARY DIAGNOSTIC CHANNEL PIN DESIGNATIONS

Pin number	Mneumonic	Circuit name
1	None	Shield
2	SRR	Secondary receiver ready
3	SSD	Secondary send data
4	SRD	Secondary receive data
5	SG	Signal ground
6	RC	Receive common
7	SRS	Secondary request to send
8	SCS	Secondary clear to send
9	SC	Send common

Serial Interfaces

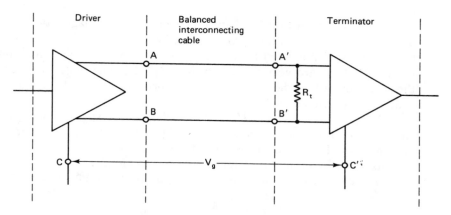

Figure 2-16 RS-422A interface circult. R_t, optional cable termination resistance; V_g, ground potential difference; A, B, driver interface points; A', B', terminator interface points; C, driver circuit ground; C', terminator circuit ground; A-B, balanced driver output; A'-B', balanced terminator input.

longitudinal currents (generally produced by static interference) cancel in the load. Balanced transmission lines can be connected to unbalanced loads and vice versa, with special transformers called *baluns* (*balanced* to *unbalanced*).

CCITT X.21

In 1976, the CCITT introduced the X.21 recommendation, which includes the specifications for placing and receiving calls and for sending and receiving data using full-duplex synchronous transmission. The X.21 recommendation presumes a direct digital connection to a digital telephone network. Thus all data transmissions must be synchronous, and the data communications equipment will need to provide both bit and character synchronization. The minimum data rate for

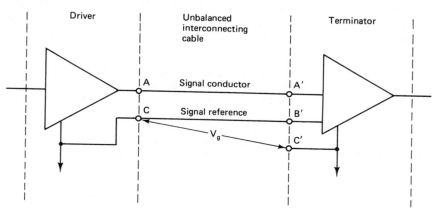

Figure 2-17 RS-423A interface circuit. A, C, driver interface; A', B', terminator interface; V_g, ground potential difference; C, driver circuit ground; C', terminator circuit ground.

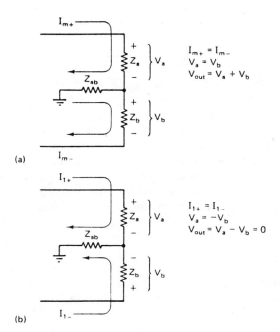

$$I_{m+} = I_{m-}$$
$$V_a = V_b$$
$$V_{out} = V_a + V_b$$

$$I_{1+} = I_{1-}$$
$$V_a = -V_b$$
$$V_{out} = V_a - V_b = 0$$

Figure 2-18 Results of metallic and longitudinal currents on a balanced transmission line: (a) metallic currents due to signal voltages; (b) longitudinal currents due to noise voltages.

X.21 will probably be 64 kbps because this is the bit rate currently used to encode voice in digital form on the telephone network.

The X.21 specifies only six signals, which are listed in Table 2-9. Data are transmitted toward the modem on the Transmit line, and the modem returns data on the Receive line. The Control and Indication lines are control channels for the two transmission directions. The Signal Element Timing line carries the bit timing signal (clock) and the Byte Timing line carries the character synchronization information. The electrical specifications for X.21 are listed either in recommendation X.26 (balanced) or recommendation X.27 (unbalanced).

The major advantage of the X.21 standard over the RS-232C and RS-449A standards is that X.21 signals are encoded in serial digital form, which sets the stage for providing special new services in computer communications.

TABLE 2-9   CCITT X.21 PIN DESIGNATIONS

Interchange circuit	Name	Direction
G	Signal ground	*a*
GA	DTE common return	DTE to DCE
T	Transmit	DTE to DCE
R	Receive	DCE to DTE
C	Control	DTE to DCE
I	Indication	DCE to DTE
S	Signal element timing	DCE to DTE
B	Byte timing	DCE to DTE

*a*See X.24 Recommendations

TRANSMISSION MEDIA AND DATA MODEMS

In its simplest form, data communication is the transmittal of digital information between two DTEs. The DTEs may be separated by a few feet or several thousand miles. At the present time, there is an insufficient number of transmission media to carry digital information from source to destination in digital form. Therefore, the most convenient alternative is to use the existing public telephone network (PTN) as the transmission media for data communications circuits. Unfortunately, the PTN was designed (and most of it constructed) long before the advent of large-scale data communications. The PTN was intended to be used for transferring voice telephone communications signals, not digital data. Therefore, to use the PTN for data communications, the data must be converted to a form more suitable for transmission over analog carrier systems.

Transmission Media

As stated previously, the public telephone network is a convenient alternative to constructing alternate digital facilities (at a tremendous cost) for carrying only digital data. The public telephone network comprises over 2000 local telephone companies and several long-distance common carriers such as Microwave Communications Incorporated (MCI), GTE Sprint, and the American Telephone and Telegraph Company (AT&T). Local telephone companies provide voice and data services for relatively small geographic areas, whereas long-distance common carriers provide voice and data services for relatively large geographic areas.

Essentially, there are two types of circuits available from the public telephone network: *direct distance dialing* (DDD) and *private line*. The DDD network is commonly called the *dial-up network*. Anyone who has a telephone number subscribes to the DDD network. With the DDD network, data links are established and disconnected in the same manner as normal voice calls are established and disconnected—with a standard telephone or some kind of an automatic dial/answer machine. Data links that are established through the DDD network use *common usage* equipment and facilities. Common usage means that a subscriber uses the equipment and transmission medium for the duration of the call, then they are relinquished to the network for other subscribers to use. With private-line circuits, a subscriber has a permanent dedicated communications link 24 hours a day.

Figure 2-19 shows a simplified block diagram of a telephone communications link. Each subscriber has a dedicated cable facility between his station and the nearest telephone office called a *local loop*. The local loop is used by the subscriber to access the PTN. The facilities used to interconnect telephone offices are called *trunk* circuits and can be a metallic cable, a digital carrier system, a microwave radio, an optical fiber link, or a satellite radio system, depending on the distance between the two offices. For temporary connections using the DDD network, telephone offices are interconnected through sophisticated electronic switching systems (ESS) and use intricate switching arrangements. With private-line circuits, data links are permanently hardwired through telephone offices

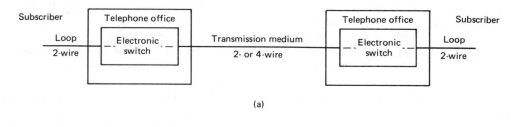

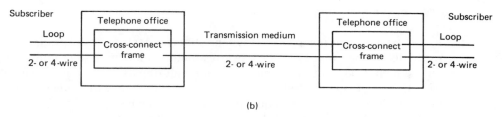

Figure 2-19 Telephone communications link: (a) direct distance dialing; (b) dedicated private line.

without going through a switch. Dial-up data links are preferred when there are a large number of subscribers in a network or if there is a small volume of data traffic. Private-line circuits are preferred for limited-access networks when there is a large volume of data throughput.

The quality of a dial-up circuit is guaranteed to meet the minimum requirements for a *voice band* (VB) communications circuit. With a private-line circuit, the communications link can be improved by adding amplifiers and equalizers to the circuit. This is called *conditioning* the line. A voice-grade circuit using the PTN has an ideal passband from 0 to 4 kHz, although the usable passband is limited to approximately 300 to 3000 Hz. The minimum-quality circuit available using the PTN is called a basic voice grade (VG) circuit. The quality of a dial-up circuit is guaranteed to meet basic requirements and can be as good as a private-line circuit. However, with the DDD network, the transmission characteristics of the data link vary from call to call, while in a private line circuit they remain relatively constant. With the DDD network, *contention* can be a problem; each subscriber must contend for a connection through the network with every other subscriber in the network. With private-line circuits, there is no contention because each circuit has only one subscriber. Consequently, there are several advantages that private-line circuits have over dial-up networks: increased availability, more consistent performance, greater reliability, and lower costs for moderate to high volumes of data. Dial-up circuits are limited to two-wire operation, whereas private-line circuits can operate either two- or four-wire.

Data Modems

The primary purpose of the data modem is to interface the digital terminal equipment to an analog communications channel. The data modem is also called a DCE, a *dataset,* a *dataphone,* or simply a *modem.* At the transmit end, the modem converts digital pulses from the serial interface to analog signals, and at the receive end, the modem converts analog signals to digital pulses.

Modems are generally classified as either asynchronous or synchronous and use either FSK, PSK, or QAM modulation. With synchronous modems, clocking information is recovered in the receive modem; with asynchronous modems, it is not. Asynchronous modems use FSK modulation and are restricted to low-speed applications (below 2000 bps). Synchronous modems use PSK and QAM modulation and are used for medium-speed (2400 to 4800 bps) and high-speed (9600 bps) applications.

Asynchronous modems.   Asynchronous modems are used primarily for low-speed dial-up circuits. There are several standard modem designs commonly used for asynchronous data transmission. For half-duplex operation using the two-wire DDD network or full-duplex operation with four-wire private line circuit, the Bell System 202T/S or equivalent is a popular modem. The 202T is a four-wire full-duplex modem and the 202S is a two-wire, half-duplex modem.

The 202T modem is an asynchronous transceiver utilizing frequency shift keying. It uses a 1700-Hz carrier that can be shifted at a maximum rate of 1200 times a second. When a logic 1 (mark) is applied to the modulator, the carrier is shifted down 500 Hz, to 1200 Hz. When a logic 0 (space) is applied, the carrier is shifted up 500 Hz, to 2200 Hz. Consequently, as the data input signal alternates between 1 and 0, the carrier is shifted back and forth between 1200 and 2200 Hz, respectively. This process can be related to conventional frequency modulation. The difference between the mark and space frequencies (1200 to 2200 Hz) is the peak-to-peak frequency deviation, and the rate of change of the digital input signal (bit rate) is equal to twice the frequency of the modulating signal. Therefore, for the worst-case situation, the 1700-Hz carrier is frequency modulated by a 1200-Hz square wave.

A figure of merit often used to express the degree of modulation achieved in an FSK modulator is the *h factor,* which is defined as

$$h = \frac{|f_m - f_s|}{\text{bps}} \tag{2-2}$$

where

$$f_m = \text{mark (logic 1) frequency (Hz)}$$
$$f_s = \text{space (logic 0) frequency (Hz)}$$
$$\text{bps} = \text{input bit rate (bps)}$$

For the 202T modem,

$$h = \frac{|1200 - 2200|}{1200} = \frac{1000}{1200} = 0.83$$

As a general rule and for best performance, the *h* factor is limited to a value less than 1. The *h* factor is equivalent to the modulation index for conventional FM. Consequently, with FSK the number of side frequencies generated is directly

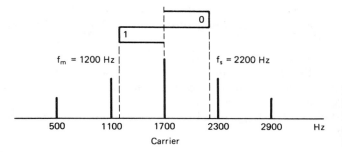

Figure 2-20 Output spectrum for a 202T/S modem. Carrier frequency = 1700 Hz, input data = 1200 bps alternating 1/0 pattern, modulation index = 0.83.

related to the *h* factor. The separation between adjacent side frequencies is equal to one-half the input bit rate. The frequency spectrum for the 202T modem is shown in Figure 2-20. As the figure shows, for an *h* factor of 0.83, only two sets of significant side frequencies are generated, resulting in a worst-case bandwidth of 2400 Hz.

To operate full duplex with a two-wire dial-up circuit, it is necessary to divide the usable bandwidth of a voice band circuit in half, creating two equal-capacity data channels. A popular modem that does this is the Bell System 103 or equivalent. The 103 modem is capable of full-duplex operation over a two-wire line at bit rates up to 300 bps. With the 103 modem, there are two data channels each with separate mark and space frequencies. One channel is the *low-band channel* and occupies a passband from 300 to 1650 Hz. The second channel is the *high-band channel* and occupies a passband from 1650 to 3000 Hz. The mark and space frequencies for the low-band channel are 1270 and 1070 Hz, respectively. The mark and space frequencies for the high-band channel are 2225 and 2025 Hz, respectively. For a bit rate of 300 bps, the modulation index for the 103 modem is 0.67. The output spectrum for the 103 modem is shown in Figure 2-21. The high- and low-band data channels occupy different frequency

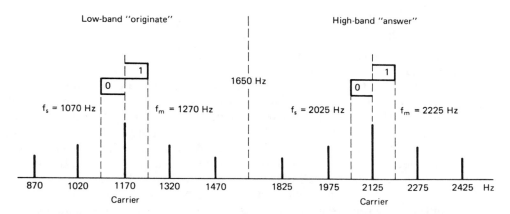

Figure 2-21 Output spectrum for a 103 modem. Carrier frequency: low band = 1170, high band = 2125; input data = 300 bps alternating 1/0 sequence; modulation index = 0.67.

Transmission Media and Data Modems

bands and can therefore use the same two-wire facility without interfering with each other. This is called *frequency-division multiplexing* and is explained in detail in Chapter 6.

The low-band channel is commonly called the *originate channel* and the high-band channel is called the *answer channel*. It is standard procedure on a dial-up circuit for the station that originates the call to transmit on the low-band frequencies and receive on the high-band frequencies, and the station that answers the call to transmit on the high-band frequencies and receive on the low-band frequencies.

Synchronous modems. Synchronomous modems are used for medium- and high-speed data transmission and use either PSK or QAM modulation. With synchronous modems the transmit clock, together with the data, digitally modulate an analog carrier. The modulated carrier is transmitted to the receive modem, where a coherent carrier is recovered and used to demodulate the data. The transmit clock is recovered from the data and used to clock the received data into the DTE. Because of the clock and carrier recovery circuits, a synchronous modem is more complicated and thus more expensive than its asynchronous counterpart.

PSK modulation is used for medium-speed (2400 to 4800 bps) synchronous modems. More specifically, QPSK is used with 2400-bps modems and 8-PSK is used with 4800-bps modems. QPSK has a bandwidth efficiency of 2 bps/Hz; therefore, the baud rate and minimum bandwidth for a 2400-bps synchronous modem are 1200 baud and 1200 Hz. The standard 2400-bps synchronous modem is the Bell System 201C or equivalent. The 201C uses a 1600-Hz carrier and has an output spectrum that extends from 1000 to 2200 Hz. 8-PSK has a bandwidth efficiency of 3 bps/Hz; therefore, the baud rate and minimum bandwidth for 4800-bps synchronous modems are 1600 baud and 1600 Hz. The standard 4800-bps synchronous modem is the Bell System 208A or equivalent. The 208A also uses a 1600-Hz carrier but has an output spectrum that extends from 800 to 2400 Hz. Both the 201C and 208A are full-duplex modems designed to be used with four-wire private line circuits. The 201C and 208A can operate over two-wire dial-up circuits but only in the simplex mode. There are half-duplex two-wire versions of both models: the 201B and 208B.

High-speed synchronous modems operate at 9600 bps and use 16-QAM modulation. 16-QAM has a bandwidth efficiency of 4 bps/Hz; therefore, the baud rate and minimum bandwidth for 9600-bps synchronous modems are 2400 baud and 2400 Hz. The standard 9600-bps modem is the Bell System 209A or equivalent. The 209A uses a 1650-Hz carrier and has an output spectrum that extends from 450 to 2850 Hz. The Bell System 209A is a four-wire synchronous modem designed to be used on full-duplex private-line circuits. The 209B is the two-wire version designed for half-duplex dial-up circuits.

Normally, an asynchronous data format is used with asynchronous modems and a synchronous data format is used with synchronous modems. However, asynchronous data are occasionally used with synchronous modems; this is called *isochronous transmission.* Synchronous data are never used with asynchronous modems.

Table 2-10 summarizes the standard Bell System modems.

MODEM SYNCHRONIZATION

During the RTS/CTS delay, the transmit modem outputs a special, internally generated bit pattern called the *training sequence*. This bit pattern is used to synchronize (train) the receive modem. Depending on the type of modulation, transmission bit rate, and the complexity of the modem, the training sequence accomplishes one or more of the following functions in the receive modem:

1. Verify continuity (activate RLSD).
2. Initialize the descrambler circuits. (These circuits are used for clock recovery—explained later in this chapter.)
3. Initialize the automatic equalizer. (These circuits compensate for telephone line impairments—explained later in this chapter.)
4. Synchronize the transmitter and receiver carrier oscillators.
5. Synchronize the transmitter and receiver clock oscillators.
6. Disable any echo suppressors in the circuit.
7. Establish the gain of any AGC amplifiers in the circuit.

Low-Speed Modems

Since these modems are generally asynchronous and use noncoherent FSK, the transmit carrier and clock frequencies need not be recovered by the receive modem. Therefore, scrambler and descrambler circuits are unnecessary. The

TABLE 2-10   MODEM SUMMARY

Bell designation	Line facility	Operating mode	Synchronization	Type of modulation	Maximum data rate (bps)
103	Dial-up	FDX	Asynchronous	FSK	300
113A	Dial-up	Simplex	Asynchronous	FSK	300
113B	Dial-up	Simplex	Asynchronous	FSK	300
201B	Dial-up	HDX	Synchronous	QPSK	2400
201C	Private	HDX/FDX	Synchronous	QPSK	2400
202S	Dial-up	HDX	Asynchronous	FSK	1200
202T	Private	HDX/FDX	Asynchronous	FSK	1200 (basic)
					1800 (CI conditioning)
208A	Private	HDX/FDX	Synchronous	8-PSK	4800
208B	Dial-up	HDX	Synchronous	8-PSK	4800
209A	Private	HDX/FDX	Synchronous	16-QAM	9600 (DI conditioning)
209B	Dial-up	HDX	Synchronous	16-QAM	9600

pre- and post-equalization circuits, if used, are generally manual and do not require initialization. The special bit pattern transmitted during the RTS/CTS delay is usually a constant string of 1's (idle line 1's) and is used to verify continuity, set the gain of the AGC amplifiers, and disable any echo suppressors in dial-up applications.

Medium- and High-Speed Modems

These modems are used where transmission rates of 2400 bps or more are required. In order to transmit at these higher bit rates, PSK or QAM modulation is used which requires the receive carrier oscillators to be at least frequency coherent (and possibly phase coherent). Since these modems are synchronous, clock timing recovery by the receive modem must be achieved. These modems contain *scrambler* and *descrambler circuits* and *adaptive* (*automatic*) *equalizers.*

Training. The type of modulation and encoding technique used determines the number of bits required and therefore the duration of the training sequence. The Bell System 208 modem is a synchronous, 4800-bps modem which uses 8-DPSK. The training sequence for this modem is shown in Figure 2-22. Each symbol represents 3 bits (1 tribit) and is 0.625 ms in duration. The four-phase idle code sequences through four of the eight possible phase shifts. This allows the receiver to recover the carrier and the clock timing information rapidly. The four-phase test word allows the adaptive equalizer in the receive modem to adjust to its final setting. The eight-phase initialization period prepares the descrambler circuits for eight-phase operation. The entire training sequence (234 bits) requires 48.75 ms for transmission.

Clock recovery. Although timing (clock) synchronization is first established during the training sequence, it must be maintained for the duration of the transmission. The clocking information can be extracted from either the I or the Q channel, or from the output of the bit combiner. If an alternating 1/0 pattern is assumed at the output of the LPF (Figure 2-23) a clock frequency at the bit rate of the I (or Q) channel can be recovered. The waveforms associated with Figure 2-23 are shown in Figure 2-24.

This clocking information is used to phase-lock loop the receive clock oscillator onto the transmitter clock frequency. To recover clocking information

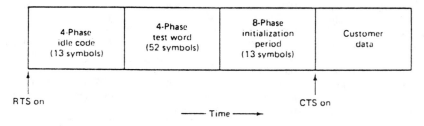

Figure 2-22 Training sequence for a 208 modem.

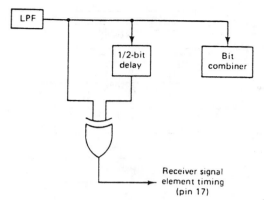

Figure 2-23 Clock recovery circuit for QPSK demodulator.

by this method successfully, there must be sufficient transitions in the received data stream. That these transitions will automatically occur cannot be assumed. In a QPSK system, an alternating I/O pattern applied to the transmit modulator produces a sequence of all 1's in the I or Q channel, and a sequence of all 0's in the opposite channel. A prolonged sequence of all 1's or all 0's applied to the transmit modulator would not provide any transitions in either the I, Q, or the composite received data stream. Restrictions could be placed on the customer's protocol and message format to prevent an undesirable bit sequence from occurring, but this is a poor solution to the problem.

Scramblers and descramblers. A better method is to scramble the customer's data before it modulates the carrier. The receiver circuitry must contain the corresponding descrambling algorithm to recover the original bit sequence before data are sent to the DTE. The purpose of a scrambler is not simply to randomize the transmitted bit sequence, but to detect the occurrence of an undesirable bit sequence and convert it to a more acceptable pattern.

A block diagram of a scrambler and descrambler circuit is shown in Figure 2-25. These circuits are incomplete since an additional gate would be required to

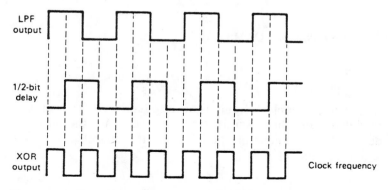

Figure 2-24 Clock recovery from I (or Q) channel of a QPSK demodulator.

Modem Synchronization

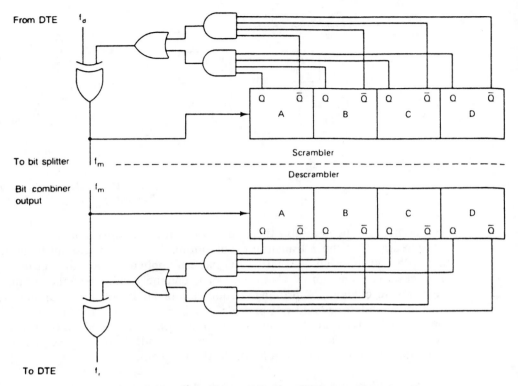

Figure 2-25 Scrambler and descrambler circuits.

detect a varying sequence that would create an all 1 or all 0 sequence in a modulator channel after the bits were split.

Example 2-6

For QPSK or 4-QAM:

```
0 1 0 1 0 1 0 1 0 1 0 1
I Q I Q I Q I Q I Q I Q
```

For 8-PSK or 8-QAM:

```
0 1 1 0 1 0 0 1 1 0 1 1
I Q   I Q   I Q   I Q
```

The scrambler circuit is inserted prior to the bit splitter of the QPSK modulator and the descrambler is inserted after the bit combiner of the QPSK demodulator. In general, the output of the scrambler or descrambler OR gate is
A B C D + A′ B′ C′ D′.

$$f_m = f_d \oplus (A\,B\,C\,D + A'\,B'\,C'\,D') \quad \text{top XOR gate}$$
$$f_r = f_m \oplus (A\,B\,C\,D + A'\,B'\,C'\,D') \quad \text{bottom XOR gate}$$

112   **Data Communications   Chap. 2**

Substituting for f_m in the second equation, we have

$$f_r = f_d \oplus (\text{A B C D} + \text{A}' \, \text{B}' \, \text{C}' \, \text{D}') \oplus (\text{A B C D} + \text{A}' \, \text{B}' \, \text{C}' \, \text{D}')$$

Since any identity XORed with itself yields 0,

$$f_r = f_d \oplus 0$$
$$f_r = f_d$$

This simply shows that the original transmitted data (f_d) will be fully recovered by the receiver.

The output of either OR gate will be a 1 if the 4-bit register contains either all 1's or all 0's. Neither of these is a desirable sequence. If the OR gate output is a 1, f_m will be the complement (opposite) of f_d, or f_r will be complement of f_m. The intent is to create transitions in a prolonged bit stream of either all 1's or all 0's. If the output of the OR gate is a 0, neither of these undesired conditions exists and $f_m = f_d$ or $f_r = f_m$: the data pass through the XOR gate unchanged. If the other logic gates (AND, OR, NAND, NOR) were used either alone or in combination in place of the XOR gates, the necessary transitions could be created in the scrambler circuit, but the original data could not be recovered in the descrambler circuit. If a long string of all 1's or all 0's is applied to the scrambler circuit, this circuit will introduce transitions. However, there may be times when the scrambler creates an undesired sequence. The XOR output is always either a 1 or a 0. No matter what the output of the OR gate, a value of f_d may be found to produce a 1 or a 0 at the XOR output. If either value for f_d was equiprobable, the scrambler circuit would be unnecessary. If the 4-bit register contains all 1's, if $f_d = 1$, we would like to see it inverted. However, if $f_d = 0$, we'd prefer to pass it through the XOR gate unchanged. The scrambler circuit for this situation inverts the 0 and extends the output string of 1's. It is beyond the intended scope of this book to delve deeply into all parameters involved in scrambler design. Let it be enough to say that scramblers will cure more problems than they create.

Equalizers. *Equalization* is the compensation for the phase delay distortion and amplitude distortion of a telephone line. One form of equalization is C-type conditioning. Additional equalization may be performed by the modems. *Compromise equalizers* are contained in the transmit section of the modem and they provide *pre-equalization*. They shape the transmitted signal by altering its delay and gain characteristics before it reaches the telephone line. It is an attempt to compensate for impairments anticipated in the bandwidth parameters of the line. When a modem is installed, the compromise equalizers is manually adjusted to provide the best *bit error rate* (BER). Typically, compromise equalizer settings affect:

1. Amplitude only
2. Delay only
3. Amplitude and delay
4. Neither amplitude nor delay

The setting above may be applied to either the high or low voice band frequencies or symmetrically to both at the same time. Once a compromise equalizer setting has been selected, it can only be changed manually. The setting that achieves the best BER is dependent on the electrical length of the circuit and the type of facilities that make it up. *Adaptive equalizers* are located in the receiver section of the modem and provide *post-equalization* to the received analog signal. Adaptive equalizers automatically adjust their gain and delay characteristics to compensate for telephone-line impairments. An adaptive equalizer may determine the quality of the received signal within its own circuitry or it may acquire this information from the demodulator or descrambler circuits. Whichever the case, the adaptive equalizer may continuously vary its settings to achieve the best overall bandwidth characteristics for the circuit.

QUESTIONS

2-1. Define *data communications*.

2-2. What was the significance of the Carterfone decision?

2-3. Explain the difference between a two-point and a multipoint circuit.

2-4. What is a data communications topology?

2-5. Define the four transmission modes for data communications circuits.

2-6. Which of the four transmission modes can be used only with multipoint circuits?

2-7. Explain the differences between two-wire and four-wire circuits.

2-8. What is a data communications code? What are some of the other names for data communications codes?

2-9. What are the three types of characters used in data communications codes?

2-10. Which data communications code is the most powerful? Why?

2-11. What are the two general categories of error control? What is the difference between them?

2-12. Explain the following error detection techniques: redundancy, exact-count encoding, parity, vertical redundancy checking, longitudinal redundancy checking, and cyclic redundancy checking.

2-13. Which error detection technique is the simplest?

2-14. Which error detection technique is the most reliable?

2-15. Explain the following error correction techniques: symbol substitution, retransmission, and forward error correction.

2-16. Which error correction technique is designed to be used in a human environment?

2-17. Which error correction technique is the most reliable?

2-18. Define *character synchronization*.

2-19. Describe the asynchronous data format.

2-20. Describe the synchronous data format.

2-21. Which data format is best suited to long messages? Why?

2-22. What is a cluster?

2-23. Describe the functions of a control unit.

2-24. What is the purpose of the data modem?

2-25. What are the primary functions of the UART?

2-26. What is the maximum number of bits that can make up a single character with a UART?

2-27. What do the status signals RPE, RFE, and ROR indicate?

2-28. Why does the receive clock for a UART operate 16 times faster than the receive bit rate?

2-29. What are the major differences between a UART and a USRT?

2-30. What is the purpose of the serial interface?

2-31. What is the most prominent serial interface in the United States?

2-32. Why did the EIA establish the RS-232C interface?

2-33. What is the nominal maximum length for the RS-232C interface?

2-34. What are the four general classifications of pins on the RS-232C interface?

2-35. What is the maximum positive voltage that a driver will output?

2-36. Which classification of pins uses negative logic?

2-37. What is the primary difference between the RS-449A interface and the RS-232C interface?

2-38. Higher bit rates are possible with a (balanced, unbalanced) interface cable.

2-39. Who provides the most commonly used transmission medium for data communications circuits? Why?

2-40. Explain the differences between DDD circuits and private line circuits.

2-41. Define the following terms: local loop, trunk, common usage, and dial switch.

2-42. What is a DCE?

2-43. What is the primary difference between a synchronous and an asynchronous modem?

2-44. What is necessary for full-duplex operation using a two-wire circuit?

2-45. What do *originate* and *answer mode* mean?

2-46. What modulation scheme is used for low-speed applications? For medium-speed applications? For high-speed applications?

2-47. Why are synchronous modems required for medium- and high-speed applications?

PROBLEMS

2-1. Determine the LRC and VRC for the following message (use even parity for LRC and odd parity for VRC).

DATA sp COMMUNICATIONS

2-2. Determine the BCS for the following data- and CRC-generating polynomials.

$$G(x) = x^7 + x^4 + x^2 + x^0 = 1\,0\,0\,1\,0\,1\,0\,1$$
$$P(x) = x^5 + x^4 + x^1 + x^0 = 1\,1\,0\,0\,1\,1$$

2-3. How many Hamming bits are required for a single ASCII character?

2-4. Determine the Hamming bits for the ASCII character "B." Insert the Hamming bits into every other location starting at the left.

3

DATA COMMUNICATIONS PROTOCOLS

INTRODUCTION

The primary goal of *network architecture* is to give the users of the network the tools necessary for setting up the network and for performing flow control. A network architecture outlines the way in which a data communications network is arranged or structured and generally includes the concept of *levels* or *layers* within the architecture. Each layer within the network consists of specific *protocols* or rules for communicating that perform a given set of functions.

Protocols are agreements between people or processes. In essence, a protocol is a set of customs or regulations dealing with formality or precedence, such as diplomatic or military protocol. A *data communications network protocol* is a set of rules governing the orderly exchange of data.

As stated previously, the function of a line control unit is to control the flow of data between the applications program and the remote terminals. Therefore, there must be a set of rules that govern how an LCU reacts to or initiates different types of transmissions. This set of rules is called a *data link protocol*. Essentially, a data link protocol is a set of procedures, including precise character sequences, that ensure an orderly exchange of data between two LCUs.

In a data communications circuit, the station that is presently transmitting is called the *master* and the receiving station is called the *slave*. In a centralized network, the primary station controls when each secondary station can transmit. When a secondary station is transmitting, it is the master and the primary station is now the slave. The role of master is temporary and which station is master is delegated by the primary. Initially, the primary is master. The primary station

116

solicits each secondary station, in turn, by *polling* it. A poll is an invitation from the primary to a secondary to transmit a message. Secondaries cannot poll a primary. When a primary polls a secondary, the primary is initiating a *line turnaround;* the polled secondary has been designated the master and must respond. If the primary *selects* a secondary, the secondary is identified as a receiver. A selection is an interrogation by the primary of a secondary to determine the secondary's status (i.e., ready to receive or not ready to receive a message). Secondary stations cannot select the primary. Transmissions from the primary go to all the secondaries; it is up to the secondary stations to individually decode each transmission and determine if it is intended for them. When a secondary transmits, it sends only to the primary.

Data link protocols are generally categorized as either asynchronous or synchronous. As a rule, asynchronous protocols use an asynchronous data format and asynchronous modems, whereas synchronous protocols use a synchronous data format and synchronous modems.

OPEN SYSTEMS INTERCONNECTION

The term *open systems interconnection* (OSI) is the name for the set of standards for communications among computers. The primary purpose of OSI standards is to serve as a structural guideline for exchanging information between computers, terminals, and networks. The OSI is endorsed by both the ISO and CCITT, which have worked together to establish a set of ISO standards and CCITT recommendations that are essentially identical. In 1983, the ISO and CCITT adapted a seven-layer communication architecture reference model. Each layer consists of specific protocols for communicating.

The ISO Protocol Hierarchy

The ISO–Open Systems Interconnection Seven-Layer Model is shown in Figure 3-1. This hierarchy was developed to facilitate the intercommunications of data processing equipment by separating network responsibilities into seven distinct layers. The basic concept of layering responsibilities is that each layer adds value to services provided by the sets of lower layers. In this way, the highest level is offered the full set of services needed to run a distributed data application.

There are several advantages to using a layered architecture for the OSI model. The different layers allow different computers to communicate at different levels. In addition, as technological advances occur, it is easier to modify one layer's protocol without having to modify all of the other layers. Each layer is essentially independent of every other layer. Therefore, many of the functions found in the lower layers have been removed entirely from software tasks and replaced with hardware. The primary disadvantage of the seven-layer architecture is the tremendous amount of overhead required in adding headers to the information being transmitted through the various layers. In fact, if all seven levels are addressed, less than 15% of the transmitted message is source information; the rest is overhead.

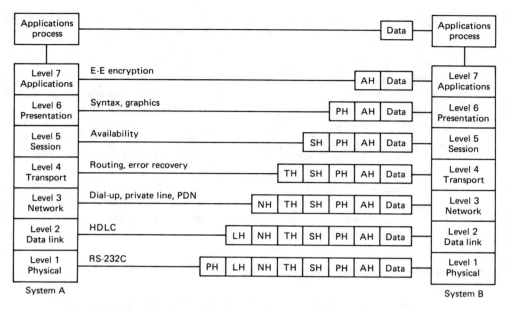

Figure 3-1 ISO international protocol hierarchy. AH, applications header; PH, presentation header; SH, session header; TH, transport header; NH, network header; LH, link header; PH, physical header.

Levels 4, 5, 6, and 7 allow for two host computers to communicate directly. The three bottom layers are concerned with the actual mechanics of moving data (at the bit level) from one machine to another. The basic services provided by each layer of the hierarchy are summarized below.

1. Physical layer. The physical layer is the lowest level of the hierarchy and specifies the physical, electrical, functional, and procedural standards for accessing the data communications network. Definitions such as maximum and minimum voltage levels and circuit impedances are made at the physical layer. The specifications outlined by the physical layer are similar to those specified by the EIA RS-232C serial interface standard.

2. Data link layer. The data link layer is responsible for communications between primary and secondary nodes within the network. The data link layer provides a means to activate, maintain, and deactivate the data link. The data link layer provides the final framing of the information envelope, facilitates the orderly flow of data between nodes, and allows for error detection and correction. Examples of data link protocols are IBM's bisynchronous communications (Bisync) and synchronous data link communications (SDLC).

3. Network layer. The network layer determines which network configuration (dial-up, leased, or packet) is most appropriate for the function provided by the network. The network layer also defines the mechanism in which messages are broken into data packets and routed from a sending node to a receiving node within a communications network.

4. *Transport layer*. The transport layer controls the end-to-end integrity of the message, which includes message routing, segmenting, and error recovery. The transport layer is the highest layer in terms of communications. Layers above the transport layer are not concerned with technological aspects of the network. The upper three layers address the software aspects of the network, where the lower three layers address the hardware. Thus the transport layer acts as the interface between the network and the session layers.

5. *Session layer*. The session layer is responsible for network availability (i.e., buffer storage and processor capacity). Session responsibilities include network log-on and log-off procedures and user authentication. A session is a temporary condition that exists when data are actually in the process of being transferred and does not include procedures such as call establishment, setup, or disconnect procedures. The session layer determines the type of dialogue available (i.e., simplex, half-duplex, or full duplex).

6. *Presentation layer*. The presentation layer addresses any code or syntax conversion necessary to present the data to the network in a common format for communications. Presentation functions include data file formatting, encoding (ASCII, EBCDIC, etc.), encryption and decryption of messages, dialogue procedures, data compression, synchronization, interruption, and termination. The presentation layer performs code and character set translation and determines the display mechanism for messages.

7. *Applications layer*. The application layer is the highest layer in the hierarchy and is analogous to the general manager of the network. The application layer controls the sequence of activities within an application and also the sequence of events between the computer application and the user of another application. The application layer communicates directly with the user's application program.

ASYNCHRONOUS PROTOCOLS

Two of the most commonly used asynchronous data protocols are the Bell System's *selective calling system* (8A1/8B1) and IBM's *asynchronous data link protocol* (83B). In essence, these two protocols are the same set of procedures.

Asynchronous protocols are *character oriented*. That is, unique data link control characters such as end of transmission (EOT) and start of text (STX), no matter where they occur in a transmission, warrant the same action or perform the same function. For example, the end-of-transmission character used with ASCII is 04H. No matter when 04H is received by a secondary, the LCU is cleared and placed in the line monitor mode. Consequently, care must be taken to ensure that the bit sequences for data link control characters do not occur within a message unless they are intended to perform their designated data link functions. Vertical redundancy checking (parity) is the only type of error detection used with asynchronous protocols, and symbol substitution and ARQ (retransmission) are used for error correction. With asynchronous protocols, each secondary station is generally limited to a single terminal/printer pair. This station arrangement is called a *stand alone*. With the stand-alone configuration, all messages transmitted from or received on the terminal CRT are also written on the printer. Thus the printer simply generates a hard copy of all transmissions.

In addition to the line monitoring mode, a remote station can be in any one of three operating modes: *transmit, receive,* and *local.* A secondary station is in the transmit mode whenever it has been designated master. In the transmit mode, the secondary can send formatted messages or acknowledgments. A secondary is in the receive mode whenever it has been selected by the primary. In the receive mode, the secondary can receive formatted messages from the primary. For a terminal operator to enter information into his or her computer terminal, the terminal must be in the local mode. A terminal can be placed in the local mode through software sent from the primary or the operator can do it manually from the keyboard.

The polling sequence for most asynchronous protocols is quite simple and usually encompasses sending one or two data link control characters, then a *station polling address.* A typical polling sequence is

```
E   D
O   C   A
T   3
```

The EOT character is the *clearing* character and always precedes the polling sequence. EOT places all the secondaries in the line monitor mode. When in the line monitor mode, a secondary station listens to the line for its polling or selection address. When DC3 immediately follows EOT, it indicates that the next character is a station polling address. For this example, the station polling address is the single ASCII character "A." Station "A" has been designated the master and must respond with either a formatted message or an acknowledgment. There are two acknowledgment sequences that may be transmitted in response to a poll. They are listed below together with their functions.

Acknowledgment	Function
A \ C K	No message to transmit, ready to receive
\\	No message to transmit, not ready to receive

The selection sequence, which is very similar to the polling sequence, is

```
E
O   X   Y
T
```

Again, the EOT character is transmitted first to ensure that all the secondary stations are in the line monitor mode. Following the EOT is a two-character

Data Communications Protocols   Chap. 3

selection address "XY." Station XY has been selected by the primary and designated as a receiver. Once selected, a secondary station must respond with one of three acknowledgment sequences indicating its status. They are listed below together with their functions.

Acknowledgment	Function
A \ C K	Ready to receive
\\	Not ready to receive, terminal in local, or printer out of paper
**	Not ready to receive, have a formatted message to transmit

More than one station can be selected simultaneously with *group* or *broadcast* addresses. Group addresses are used when the primary desires to select more than one but not all of the remote stations. There is a single broadcast address that is used to select simultaneously all the remote stations. With asynchronous protocols, acknowledgment procedures for group and broadcast selections are somewhat involved and for this reason are seldom used.

Messages transmitted from the primary and secondary use exactly the same data format. The format is as follows:

```
S                E
T message data   O
X                T
```

The preceding format is used by the secondary to transmit data to the primary in response to a poll. The STX and EOT characters frame the message. STX precedes the data and indicates that the message begins with the character that immediately follows it. The EOT character signals the end of the message and relinquishes the role of master to the primary. The same format is used when the primary transmits a message except that the STX and EOT characters have an additional function. The STX is a *blinding* character. Upon receipt of the STX character, all previously unselected stations are "blinded," which means that they ignore all transmissions except EOT. Consequently, the subsequent message transmitted by the primary is received only by the previously selected station. The unselected secondaries remain blinded until they receive an EOT character, at which time they will return to the line monitor mode and again listen to the line for their polling or selection addresses. STX and EOT are not part of the message; they are data link control characters and are inserted and deleted by the LCU.

Sometimes it is necessary or desirable to transmit coded data in addition to the message that are used only for data link management, such as date, time of message, message number, message priority, routing information, and so on. This bookkeeping information is not part of the message; it is overhead and is

Asynchronous Protocols   121

transmitted as *heading* information. To identify the heading, the message begins with a start-of-heading character (SOH). SOH is transmitted first, followed by the heading information, STX, then the message. The entire sequence is terminated with an EOT character. When a heading is included, STX terminates the heading and also indicates the beginning of the message. The format for transmitting heading information together with message data is

```
S              S                    E
O  heading     T  message data      O
H              X                    T
```

SYNCHRONOUS PROTOCOLS

With synchronous protocols, a secondary station can have more than a single terminal/printer pair. The group of devices is commonly called a *cluster*. A single LCU can serve a cluster with as many as 50 devices (terminals and printers). Synchronous protocols can be either character or bit oriented. The most commonly used character-oriented synchronous protocol is IBM's 3270 binary synchronous communications (BSC or bisync), and the most popular bit-oriented protocol (BOP) is IBM's synchronous data link communications (SDLC).

IBM's Bisync Protocol

With bisync, each transmission is preceded by a unique SYN character: 16H for ASCII and 32H for EBCDIC. The SYN character places the receive USRT in the character or byte mode and prepares it to receive data in 8-bit groupings. With bisync, SYN characters are always transmitted in pairs (hence the name "bisync"). Therefore, if 8 successive bits are received in the middle of a message that are equivalent to a SYN character, they are ignored. For example, the characters "A" and "b" have the following hex and binary codes:

```
A = 41H = 0 1 0 0 0 0 0 1
b = 62H = 0 1 1 0 0 0 1 0
```

If the ASCII characters A and b occur successively during a message or heading, the following bit sequence occurs:

```
       A (41H)              b (62H)
  0 1 0 0 0 0 0 1 0 1 1 0 0 0 1 0
            SYN (16H)
```

As you can see, it appears that a SYN character has been transmitted when actually it has not. To avoid this situation, SYN characters are always transmitted in pairs, and consequently, if only one is received, it is ignored. The likelihood of two false SYN characters occurring one immediately after the other is remote.

With synchronous protocols, the concepts of polling, selecting, and acknowledging are identical to those used with asynchronous protocols except, with bisync, group, and broadcast selections are not allowed. There are two polling formats used with bisync: general and specific. The format for a general poll is

```
P S S E P S S S     E P
A Y Y O A Y Y P P " " N A
D N N T D N N A A     Q D
```

The PAD character at the beginning of the sequence is called a *leading* pad and is either a 55H or an AAH (01010101 or 10101010 binary). As you can see, a leading pad is simply a string of alternating 1's and 0's. The purpose of the leading pad is to ensure that transitions occur in the data prior to the actual message. The transitions are needed for clock recovery in the receive modem to maintain bit synchronization. Next, there are two SYN characters to establish character synchronization. The EOT character is again used as a clearing character and places all the secondary stations into the line monitor mode. The PAD character immediately following the second SYN character is simply a string of successive logic 1's that is used for a time fill, giving each of the secondary stations time to clear. The number of 1's transmitted during this time fill may not be a multiple of 8 bits. Consequently, the two SYN characters are repeated to reestablish character synchronization. The SPA is not an ASCII or EBCDIC character. The letters SPA stand for *station polling address*. Each secondary station has a unique SPA. Two SPAs are transmitted for the purpose of error detection (redundancy). A secondary will not respond to a poll unless its SPA appears twice. The two quotation marks signify that the poll is for any device at that station that is in the send mode. If two or more devices are in the send mode when a general poll is received, the LCU determines which device's message is transmitted. The enquiry (ENQ) character is sometimes called a *format* or *line turnaround character* because it completes the polling format and initiates a line turnaround (i.e., the secondary station identified by the SPA is designated master and must respond).

The PAD character at the end of the polling sequence is called a *trailing* pad and is simply a 7FH (DEL or delete character). The purpose of the trailing pad is to ensure that the RLSD signal in the receive modem is held active long enough for the entire received message to be demodulated. If the carrier were shut off immediately at the end of the message, RLSD would go inactive and disable the receive data pin. If the last character of the message were not completely demodulated, the end of it would be cut off.

The format for a specific poll is

```
P S S E P S S S     E P
A Y Y O A Y Y P P D D N A
D N N T D N N A A A A Q D
```

The character sequence for a specific poll is similar to that of a general poll except that the two DAs (*device addresses*) are substituted for the two quotation marks. With a specific poll, both the station and device addresses are included. Therefore, a specific poll is an invitation to transmit to a specific device at a given station. Again, two DAs are transmitted for redundancy error detection.

The character sequence for a selection is

```
P S S E P S S S       E P
A Y Y D A Y Y S S D D N A
D N N T D N N A A A A Q D
```

The sequence for a selection is similar to that of a specific poll except that two SSA characters are substituted for the two SPAs. SSA stands for "station select address." All selections are specific; they are for a specific device (device DA). Table 3-1 lists the SPAs, SSAs, and DAs for a network that can have a maximum of 32 stations and the LCU at each station can serve a 32-device cluster.

Example 3-1

Determine the character sequences for (a) a general poll for station 8, (b) a specific poll for device 6 at station 8, and (c) a selection of device 6 at station 8.

Solution   (a) From Table 3-1 the SPA for station 8 is H; therefore the sequence for a general poll is

```
P S S E P S S              E P
A Y Y D A Y Y H H " " N A
D N N T D N N              Q D
```

TABLE 3-1   STATION AND DEVICE ADDRESSES

Station or device number	SPA	SSA	DA	Station or device number	SPA	SSA	DA
0	sp	-	sp	16	&	Ø	&
1	A	/	A	17	J	1	J
2	B	S	B	18	K	2	K
3	C	T	C	19	L	3	L
4	D	U	D	20	M	4	M
5	E	V	E	21	N	5	N
6	F	W	F	22	O	6	O
7	G	X	G	23	P	7	P
8	H	Y	H	24	Q	8	Q
9	I	Z	I	25	R	9	R
10	[	¦	[	26	]	:	]
11	.	,	.	27	$	#	$
12	<	%	<	28	*	@	*
13	(	—	(	29	)	'	)
14	+	>	+	30	;	=	;
15	!	?	!	31	∧	"	∧

(b) From Table 3-1 the DA for device 6 is F; therefore, the sequence for a specific poll is

```
P S S E P S S           E P
A Y Y D A Y Y H H F F N A
D N N T D N N           Q D
```

(c) From Table 3-1 the SSA for station 8 is Y; therefore, the sequence for a selection is

```
P S S E P S S           E P
A Y Y D A Y Y Y Y F F N A
D N N T D N N           Q D
```

With bisync, there are only two ways in which a secondary can respond to a poll: with a formatted message or with a *handshake*. A handshake is simply a response from the secondary that indicates it has no formatted messages to transmit (i.e., a handshake is a negative acknowledgment to a poll). The character sequence for a handshake is

```
P S S E P
A Y Y D A
D N N T D
```

A secondary can respond to a selection with either a positive or a negative acknowledgment. A positive acknowledgment to a selection indicates that the device selected is ready to receive. The character sequence for a positive acknowledgment is

```
P S S D 0 P
A Y Y L 0 A
D N N E   D
```

A negative acknowledgment to a selection indicates that the device selected is not ready to receive. A negative acknowledgment is called a *reverse interrupt* (RVI). The character sequence for an RVI is

```
P S S D     P
A Y Y L < A
D N N E     D
```

With bisync, formatted messages are sent from a secondary to the primary in response to a poll and sent from the primary to a secondary after the secondary has been selected. Formatted messages use the following format:

```
P S S S             S           E B P
A Y Y D heading T message T C A
D N N H             X           X C D
```

Note: If CRC-16 is used for error detection, there are two block check characters.

Longitudinal redundancy checking (LRC) is used for error detection with ASCII-coded messages, and cyclic redundancy checking (CRC) is used for EBCDIC. The BCC is computed beginning with the first character after SOH and continues through and includes ETX. (If there is no heading, the BCC is computed beginning with the first character after STX.) With synchronous protocols, data are transmitted in blocks. Blocks of data are generally limited to 256 characters. ETX is used to terminate the last block of a message. ETB is used for multiple block messages to terminate all message blocks except the last one. The last block of a message is always terminated with ETX. All BCCs must be acknowledged by the receiving station. A positive acknowledgment indicates that the BCC was good and a negative acknowledgment means that the BCC was bad. A negative acknowledgment is an automatic request for retransmission. The character sequences for positive and negative acknowledgments are as follows:

Positive acknowledgment:

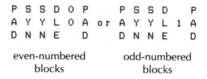

```
P S S D 0 P     P S S D   P
A Y Y L 0 A  or A Y Y L 1 A
D N N E   D     D N N E   D

   even-numbered   odd-numbered
      blocks          blocks
```

Negative acknowledgment:

```
P S S N P
A Y Y A A
D N N K D
```

Examples of dialogue using bisync protocol.

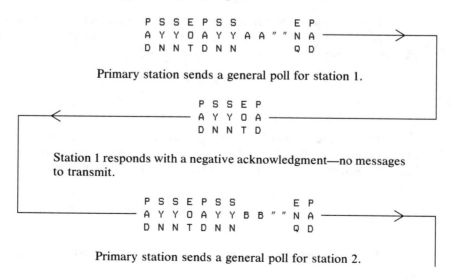

```
P S S E P S S       E P
A Y Y 0 A Y Y A A " " N A ────────────→
D N N T D N N       Q D
```

Primary station sends a general poll for station 1.

```
        P S S E P
 ──────  A Y Y 0 A  ──────
        D N N T D
```

Station 1 responds with a negative acknowledgment—no messages to transmit.

```
P S S E P S S       E P
A Y Y 0 A Y Y B B " " N A ────────────→
D N N T D N N       Q D
```

Primary station sends a general poll for station 2.

```
P S S     S           E B P
A Y Y O heading T message T C A
D Y Y H         X block 1 B C D
```

Station 2 responds with the first block of a multiblock message.

```
P S S D   P
A Y Y L 1 A
D N N E   D
```

Primary sends a positive acknowledgment indicating that block 1 was received without any errors—because block 1 is an odd-numbered block, DLE 1 is used.

```
P S S S         E B P
A Y Y T message T C A
D N N X block 2 X C D
```

Station 2 sends the second and final block of the message—note that there is no heading at the beginning of the second block—a heading is transmitted only with the first block of a message.

```
P S S N P
A Y Y A A
D N N K D
```

Primary sends a negative acknowledgment to station 2 indicating that block 2 was received with an error and must be transmitted.

```
P S S S         E B P
A Y Y T message T C A
D N N X block 2 X C D
```

Station 2 resends block 2.

```
P S S D O P
A Y Y L O A
D N N E   D
```

Primary sends a positive acknowledgment to station 2 indicating that block 2 was received without any errors—because block 2 is an even-numbered block, DLE 0 is used.

```
P S S E P
A Y Y O A
D N N T D
```

Secondary responds with a handshake—a secondary sends a handshake whenever it is its turn to transmit but it has nothing to say.

Synchronous Protocols

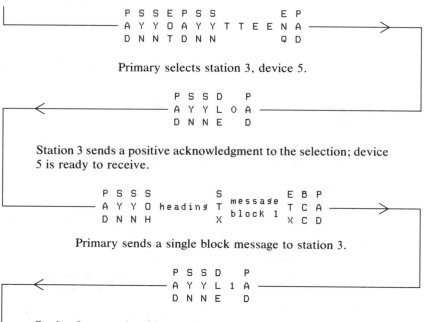

```
                    P S S E P S S         E P
        ───────── A Y Y D A Y Y T T E E N A ──────────────────→
                    D N N T D N N         Q D
```

Primary selects station 3, device 5.

```
                        P S S D   P
        ←───────────── A Y Y L O A ───────────────
                        D N N E   D
```

Station 3 sends a positive acknowledgment to the selection; device
5 is ready to receive.

```
              P S S S         S  message  E B P
        ───── A Y Y O heading T  block 1  T C A ──────────→
              D N N H         X           X C D
```

Primary sends a single block message to station 3.

```
                        P S S D   P
        ←───────────── A Y Y L 1 A ───────────────
                        D N N E   D
```

Station 3 responds with a positive acknowledgment indicating the
block of data was received without any errors.

Transparency. It is possible that a device that is attached to one of the
ports of a station LCU is not a computer terminal or a printer. For example, a
microprocessor-controlled monitor system that is used to monitor environmental
conditions (temperature, humidity, etc.) or a security alarm system. If so, the
data transferred between it and the applications program are not ASCII- or
EBCDIC-encoded characters; they are microprocessor op-codes or binary-
encoded data. Consequently, it is possible that an 8-bit sequence could occur in
the message that is equivalent to a data link control character. For example, if
the binary code 00000011 (03H) occurred in a message, the LCU would misinterpret
it as the ASCII code for ETX. Consequently, the receive LCU would prematurely
terminate the message and interpret the next 8-bit sequence as a BCC. To prevent
this from occurring, the LCU is made *transparent* to the data. With bisync, a
data link escape character (DLE) is used to achieve transparency. To place an
LCU in the transparent mode, STX is preceded by a DLE (i.e., the LCU simply
transfers the data to the selected device without searching through the message
for data link control characters). To come out of the transparent mode, DLE
ETX is transmitted. To transmit a DLE as part of the text, it must be preceded
by DLE (i.e., DLE DLE). Actually, there are only five characters that it is
necessary to precede with DLE:

1. *DLE STX:* places the receive LCU into the transparent mode.
2. *DLE ETX:* used to terminate the last block of transparent text and take
   the LCU out of the transparent mode.

3. *DLE ETB:* used to terminate blocks of transparent text other than the final block.

4. *DLE ITB:* used to terminate blocks of transparent text other than the final block when ITB is used for a block terminating character.

5. *DLE SYN:* used only with transparent messages that are more than 1 s long. With bisync, two SYN characters are inserted in the text every 1 s to ensure that the receive LCU does not lose character synchronization. In a multipoint circuit with a polling environment, it is highly unlikely that any blocks of data would exceed 1 s in duration. SYN character insertion is used almost exclusively for two-point circuits.

Synchronous Data Link Communications

Synchronous data link communications (SDLC) is a synchronous *bit-oriented* protocol developed by IBM. A bit-oriented protocol (BOP) is a discipline for serial-by-bit information transfer over a data communication channel. With a BOP, data link control information is transferred and interpreted on a bit-by-bit basis rather than with unique data link control characters. SDLC can transfer data either simplex, half-duplex, or full duplex. With a BOP, there is a single control field that performs essentially all the data link control functions. The character language used with SDLC is EBCDIC and data are transferred in groups called *frames*. Frames are generally limited to 256 characters in length. There are two types of stations in SDLC: primary stations and secondary stations. The *primary station* controls data exchange on the communications channel and issues *commands*. The *secondary station* receives commands and returns *responses* to the primary.

There are three transmission states with SDLC: transient, idle, and active. The *transient state* exists before and after the initial transmission and after each line turnaround. An *idle state* is presumed after 15 or more consecutive 1's have been received. The *active state* exists whenever either the primary or a secondary station is transmitting information or control signals.

Figure 3-2 shows the frame format used with SDLC. The frames sent from the primary and the frames sent from a secondary use exactly the same format. There are five fields used with SDLC: the flag field, the address field, the control field, the text or information field, and the frame check field.

Information field.   All information transmitted in an SDLC frame must be in the information field (I field), and the number of bits in the I field must be a multiple of 8. An I field is not allowed with all SDLC frames. The types of frames that allow an I field are discussed later.

Flag field.   There are two flag fields per frame: the beginning flag and the ending flag. The flags are used for the *delimiting sequence* and to achieve character synchronization. The delimiting sequence sets the limits of the frame (i.e., when the frame begins and when it ends). The flag is used with SDLC in the same manner that SYN characters are used with bisync, to achieve character synchro-

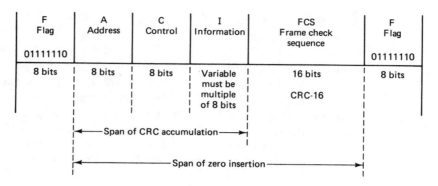

Figure 3-2 SDLC frame format.

nization. The sequence for a flag is 7EH, 01111110 binary, or the EBCDIC character "=." There are several variations of how flags are used. They are:

1. One beginning and one ending flag for each frame.

```
   beginning flag                              ending flag
. . . 01111110 address control text FCC 01111110 . . .
```

2. The ending flag from one frame can be used for the beginning flag for the next frame.

```
                                    ←————————————————— frame N + 1—————————→
————————————frame N————————————→
. . . text FCC 01111110 address control text FCC 01111110 . . .
                     /        \
              ending flag  beginning flag
              frame N      frame N+1
```

3. The last zero of an ending flag is also the first zero of the beginning flag of the next frame.

```
                          ←————————————————— frame N+1 —————————
                    shared 0
              frame N————→ /
. . . text FCC 0111111101111110 address control FCC . . .
                  /        \
           ending flag  beginning flag
           frame N      frame N+1
```

4. Flags are transmitted in lieu of idle line 1's.

```
01111110111111101111110101111110 address control text . . .
   /       /       /     _____/
idle line flags      beginning flag
```

Address field. The address field has 8 bits; thus 256 addresses are possible with SDLC. The address 00H (00000000) is called the *null* or *void address* and is never assigned to a secondary. The null address is used for network testing. The address FFH (11111111) is the *broadcast address* and is common to all secondaries. The remaining 254 addresses can be used as *unique* station addresses or as *group* addresses. In frames sent from the primary, the address field contains the address of the destination station (a secondary). In frames sent from a secondary, the address field contains the address of that secondary. Therefore, the address is always that of a secondary. The primary station has no address because all transmissions from secondary stations go to the primary.

Control field. The control field is an 8-bit field that identifies the type of frame it is. The control field is used for polling, confirming previously received information frames, and several other data link management functions. There are three frame formats used with SDLC: *information*, *supervisory*, and *unnumbered*.

Information frame. With an information frame there must be an information field. Information frames are used for transmitting sequenced information. The bit pattern for the control field of an information frame is

Bit:	b_0	b_1	b_2	b_3	b_4	b_5	b_6	b_7
Function:	$\leftarrow$	nr	$\rightarrow$	P or F $\overline{\text{P or F}}$	$\leftarrow$	ns	$\rightarrow$	0

An information frame is identified by a 0 in the least significant bit position (b_7 with EBCDIC code). Bits b_4, b_5, and b_6 are used for numbering transmitted frames (ns = number sent). With 3 bits, the binary numbers 000 through 111 ($0-7$) can be represented. The first frame transmitted is designated frame 000, the second frame 001, and so on up to frame 111 (the eighth frame); then the count cycles back to 000 and repeats.

Bits b_0, b_1, and b_2 are used to confirm correctly received information frames (nr = number received) and to automatically request retransmission of incorrectly received information frames. The nr is the number of the next frame that the transmitting station expects to receive, or the number of the next frame that the receiving station will transmit. The nr confirms received frames through nr-1. Frame nr-1 is the last frame received without a transmission error. Any transmitted I frame not confirmed must be retransmitted. Together, the ns and nr bits are used for error correction (ARQ). The primary must keep track of an ns and nr for each secondary. Each secondary must keep track of only its ns and nr. After all frames have been confirmed, the primary's ns must agree with the secondary's nr, and vice versa. For the example shown next, the primary and secondary stations begin with their ns and nr counters reset to 000. The primary sends three numbered information frames (ns = 0, 1, and 2). At the same time the primary sends nr = 0 because the next frame it expects to receive is frame 0, which is the secondary's present ns. The secondary responds with two information frames (ns = 0 and 1). The secondary received all three frames from the primary without any errors, so the nr transmitted in the secondary's control field is 3 (which is the number of the next frame that the primary will send). The primary now sends information frames 3 and 4 with an nr = 2. The nr = 2 confirms the correct

Synchronous Protocols

reception of frames 0 and 1. The secondary responds with frames ns = 2, 3, and 4 with an nr = 4. The nr = 4 confirms reception of only frame 3 from the primary (nr-1). Consequently, the primary must retransmit frame 4. Frame 4 is retransmitted together with four additional frames (ns = 5, 6, 7, and 0). The primary's nr = 5, which confirms frames 2, 3, and 4 from the secondary. Finally, the secondary sends information frame 5 with an nr = 1. The nr = 1 confirms frames 4, 5, 6, 7 and 0 from the primary. At this point, all the frames transmitted have been confirmed except frame 5 from the secondary.

| Primary's ns: | 0 1 2 | 3 4 | 4 5 6 7 0 |
| Primary's nr: | 0 0 0 | 2 2 | 5 5 5 5 5 |

| Secondary's ns: | | 0 1 | 2 3 4 | | 5 |
| Secondary's nr: | | 3 3 | 4 4 4 | | 1 |

With SDLC, a station can never send more than seven numbered frames without receiving a confirmation. For example, if the primary sent eight frames (ns = 0, 1, 2, 3, 4, 5, 6, and 7) and the secondary responded with an nr = 0, it is ambiguous which frames are being confirmed. Does nr = 0 mean that all eight frames were received correctly, or that frame 0 had an error in it and all eight frames must be retransmitted? (With SDLC, all previously transmitted frames beginning with frame nr-1 must be retransmitted.)

Bit b_3 is the *poll* (P) or *not-a-poll* ($\overline{P}$) bit when sent from the primary and the *final* (F) or *not-a-final* ($\overline{F}$) bit when sent by a secondary. In a frame sent by the primary, if the primary desires to poll the secondary, the P bit is set (1). If the primary does not wish to poll the secondary, the P bit is reset (0). A secondary cannot transmit unless it receives a frame addressed to it with the P bit set. In a frame sent from a secondary, if it is the last (final) frame of the message, the F bit is set (1). If it is not the final frame, the F bit is reset (0). With I frames, the primary can select a secondary station, send formatted information, confirm previously received I frames, and poll with a single transmission.

Example 3-2

Determine the bit pattern for the control field of a frame sent from the primary to a secondary station for the following conditions: primary is sending information frame 3, it is a poll, and the primary is confirming the correct reception of frames 2, 3, and 4 from the secondary.

Solution

$b_7 = 0$ because it is an information frame.

b_4, b_5, and b_6 are 011 (binary 3 for ns = 3).

$b_3 = 1$, it is a polling frame.

b_0, b_1, and b_2 are 101 (binary 5 for nr = 5).

control field = B6H.

b_0	b_1	b_2	b_3	b_4	b_5	b_6	b_7
1	0	1	1	0	1	1	0

Supervisory frame.   An information field is now allowed with a supervisory frame. Consequently, supervisory frames cannot be used to transfer information; they are used to assist in the transfer of information. Supervisory frames are used to confirm previously received information frames, convey ready or busy conditions, and to report frame numbering errors. The bit pattern for the control field of a supervisory frame is

Bit: b_0 b_1 b_2 b_3 b_4 b_5 b_6 b_7
Function: $\leftarrow$ nr $\rightarrow$ P or F   X   X   0   1
                              $\overline{\text{P}}$ or $\overline{\text{F}}$

A supervisory frame is identified by a 01 in bit positions b_6 and b_7, respectively, of the control field. With the supervisory format, bit b_3 is again the poll/not-a-poll or final/not-a-final bit and b_0, b_1, and b_2 are the nr bits. However, with a supervisory format, b_5 and b_6 are used to indicate either the receive status of the station transmitting the frame or to request transmission or retransmission of sequenced information frames. With two bits, there are four combinations possible. The four combinations and their functions are as follows:

b_4	b_5	Receiver status
0	0	Ready to receive (RR)
0	1	Ready not to receive (RNR)
1	0	Reject (REJ)
1	1	Not used with SDLC

When the primary sends a supervisory frame with the P bit set and a status of ready to receive, it is equivalent to a general poll with bisync. Supervisory frames are used by the primary for polling and for confirming previously received information frames when there is no information to send. A secondary uses the supervisory format for confirming previously received information frames and for reporting its receive status to the primary. If a secondary sends a supervisory frame with RNR status, the primary cannot send it numbered information frames until that status is cleared. RNR is cleared when a secondary sends an information frame with the F bit = 1 or a RR or REJ frame with the F bit = 0. The REJ command/response is used to confirm information frames through nr-1 and to request retransmission of numbered information frames beginning with the frame number identified in the REJ frame. An information field is prohibited with a supervisory frame and the REJ command/response is used only with full-duplex operation.

Example 3-3

Determine the bit pattern for the control field of a frame sent from a secondary station to the primary for the following conditions: the secondary is ready to receive, it is the final frame, and the secondary station is confirming frames 3, 4, and 5.

Synchronous Protocols   133

Solution

b_6 and $b_7 = 01$ because it is a supervisory frame.

b_4 and $b_5 = 00$ (ready to receive).

$b_3 = 1$ (it is the final frame).

b_0, b_1, and $b_2 = 110$ (binary 6 for nr = 6).

control field = D1H

b_0	b_1	b_2	b_3	b_4	b_5	b_6	b_7
1	1	0	1	0	0	0	1

Unnumbered frame. An unnumbered frame is identified by making bits b_6 and b_7 in the control field 11. The bit pattern for the control field of an unnumbered frame is

Bit:	b_0	b_1	b_2	b_3	b_4	b_5	b_6	b_7
Function:	X	X	X	P or F $\overline{\text{P}}$ or $\overline{\text{F}}$	X	X	1	1

With an unnumbered frame, bit b_3 is again either the $P/\overline{P}$ or $F/\overline{F}$ bit. Bits b_0, b_1, b_2, b_4, and b_5 are used for various unnumbered commands and responses. With 5 bits available, 32 unnumbered commands/responses are possible. The control field in an unnumbered frame sent by the primary is a command. The control field in an unnumbered frame sent by a secondary is a response. With unnumbered frames, there are no ns or nr bits. Therefore, numbered information frames cannot be sent or confirmed with the unnumbered format. Unnumbered frames are used to send network control and status information. Two examples of control functions are (1) placing secondary stations on-line and off-line and (2) LCU initialization. Table 3-2 lists several of the more commonly used unnumbered commands and responses. An information field is prohibited with all the unnumbered commands/responses except UI, FRMR, CFGR, TEST and XID.

A secondary station must be in one of three modes: the initialization mode, the normal response mode, or the normal disconnect mode. The procedures for the *initialization mode* are system specified and vary considerably. A secondary in the *normal response mode* cannot initiate unsolicited transmissions; it can transmit only in response to a frame received with the P bit set. When in the *normal disconnect mode,* a secondary is off-line. In this mode, a secondary can receive only a TEST, XID, CFGR, SNRM, or SIM command from the primary and can respond only if the P bit is set.

The unnumbered commands and responses are summarized below.

Unnumbered information (UI). UI is a command/response that is used to send unnumbered information. Unnumbered information transmitted in the I field is not confirmed.

Set initialization mode (SIM). SIM is a command that places the secondary station into the initialization mode. The initialization procedure is system specified and varies from a simple self-test of the station controller to executing a complete

TABLE 3-2 UNNUMBERED COMMANDS AND RESPONSES

Binary configuration			Acronym	Command	Response	1 field prohibited	Resets ns and nr
b_0		b_7					
000	P/F	0011	UI	Yes	Yes	No	No
000	F	0111	RIM	No	Yes	Yes	No
000	P	0111	SIM	Yes	No	Yes	Yes
100	P	0011	SNRM	Yes	No	Yes	Yes
000	F	1111	DM	No	Yes	Yes	No
010	P	0011	DISC	Yes	No	Yes	No
011	F	0011	UA	No	Yes	Yes	No
100	F	0111	FRMR	No	Yes	No	No
111	F	1111	BCN	No	Yes	Yes	No
110	P/F	0111	CFGR	Yes	Yes	No	No
010	F	0011	RD	No	Yes	Yes	No
101	P/F	1111	XID	Yes	Yes	No	No
001	P	0011	UP	Yes	No	Yes	No
111	P/F	0011	TEST	Yes	Yes	No	No

IPL (initial program logic) program. SIM resets the ns and nr counters at the primary and secondary stations. A secondary is expected to respond to a SIM command with a UA response.

Request initialization mode (RIM). RIM is a response sent by a secondary station to request the primary to send an SIM command.

Set normal response mode (SNRM). SNRM is a command that places a secondary station in the normal response mode (NRM). A secondary station cannot send or receive numbered information frames unless it is in the normal response mode. Essentially, SNRM places a secondary station on-line. SNRM resets the ns and nr counters at the primary and secondary stations. UA is the normal response to an SNRM command. Unsolicited responses are not allowed when the secondary is in the NRM. A secondary remains in the NRM until it receives a DISC or SIM command.

Disconnect mode (DM). DM is a response that is sent from a secondary station if the primary attempts to send numbered information frames to it when the secondary is in the normal disconnect mode.

Request disconnect (RD). RD is a response sent when a secondary wishes to be placed in the disconnect mode.

Disconnect (DISC). DISC is a command that places a secondary station in the normal disconnect mode (NDM). A secondary cannot send or receive numbered information frames when it is in the normal disconnect mode. When in the normal disconnect mode, a secondary can receive only an SIM or SNRM

Synchronous Protocols 135

command and can transmit only a DM response. The expected response to a DISC command is UA.

Unnumbered acknowledgment (UA). UA is an affirmative response that indicates compliance to a SIM, SNRM, or DISC command. UA is also used to acknowledge unnumbered information frames.

Frame reject (FRMR). FRMR is for reporting procedural errors. The FRMR sequence is a response transmitted when the secondary has received an invalid frame from the primary. A received frame may be invalid for any one of the following reasons:

1. The control field contains an invalid or unassigned command.
2. The amount of data in the information field exceeds the buffer space at the secondary.
3. An information field is received in a frame that does not allow information.
4. The nr received is incongruous with the secondary's ns. For example, if the secondary transmitted ns frames 2, 3, and 4 and then the primary responded with an nr of 7.

A secondary cannot release itself from the FRMR condition, nor does it act on the frame that caused the condition. The secondary repeats the FRMR response until it receives one of the following *mode-setting* commands: SNRM, DISC, or SIM. The information field for a FRMR response always contains three bytes (24 bits) and has the following format:

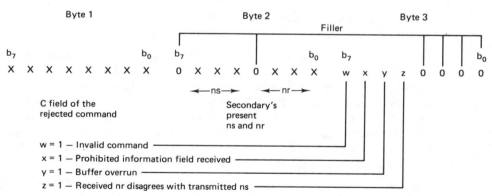

TEST. Test is a command that can be sent in any mode to solicit a TEST response. If an information field is included with the command, the secondary returns it with the response. The TEST command/response is exchanged for link testing purposes.

Exchange station identification (XID). As a command, XID solicits the identification of the secondary station. An information field can be included in the frame to convey the identification data of either the primary or secondary station. For dial-up circuits, it is often necessary that the secondary station identify itself before the primary will exchange information frames with it, although XID is not restricted to only dial-up data circuits.

Frame check sequence field.　　The FCS field contains the error detection mechanism for SDLC. The FCS is equivalent to the BCC used with bisync. SDLC uses CRC-16 and the following generating polynomial: $x^{16} + x^{12} + x^5 + x^1$.

SDLC Loop Oeration

An SDLC *loop* is operated in the half-duplex mode. The primary difference between the loop and bus configurations is that in a loop, all transmissions travel in the same direction on the communications channel. In a loop configuration, only one station transmits at a time. The primary transmits first, then each secondary station responds sequentially. In an SDLC loop, the transmit port of the primary station controller is connected to one or more secondary stations in a serial fashion; then the loop is terminated back at the receive port of the primary. Figure 3-3 shows an SDLC loop configuration.

In an SDLC loop, the primary transmits frames that are addressed to any or all of the secondary stations. Each frame transmitted by the primary contains an address of the secondary station to which that frame is directed. Each secondary station, in turn, decodes the address field of every frame, then serves as a repeater for all stations that are down-loop from it. If a secondary detects a frame with its address, it accepts the frame, then passes it on to the next down-loop station. All frames transmitted by the primary are returned to the primary. When the primary has completed transmitting, it follows the last flag with eight consecutive 0's. A flag followed by eight consecutive 0's is called a *turnaround* sequence which signals the end of the primary's transmission. Immediately following the turnaround sequence, the primary transmits continuous 1's, which generates a *go-ahead* sequence (01111111). A secondary cannot transmit until it has received a frame addressed to it with the P bit set, a turnaround sequence, and then a go-ahead sequence. Once the primary has begun transmitting 1's, it goes into the receive mode.

The first down-loop secondary station that has received a frame addressed to it with the P bit set, changes the seventh 1 bit in the go-ahead sequence to a 0, thus creating a flag. That flag becomes the beginning flag of the secondary's response frame or frames. After the secondary has transmitted its last frame, it again becomes a repeater for the idle line 1's from the primary. These idle line 1's again become the go-ahead sequence for the next secondary station. The next down-loop station that has received a frame addressed to it with the P bit set detects the turnaround sequence, any frames transmitted from up-loop secondaries, and then the go-ahead sequence. Each secondary station inserts its response frames immediately after the last repeated frame. The cycle is completed when the primary receives its own turnaround sequence, a series of response frames, and then the go-ahead sequence.

Synchronous Protocols　　　　　　　　　　　　　　　　　　　　　**137**

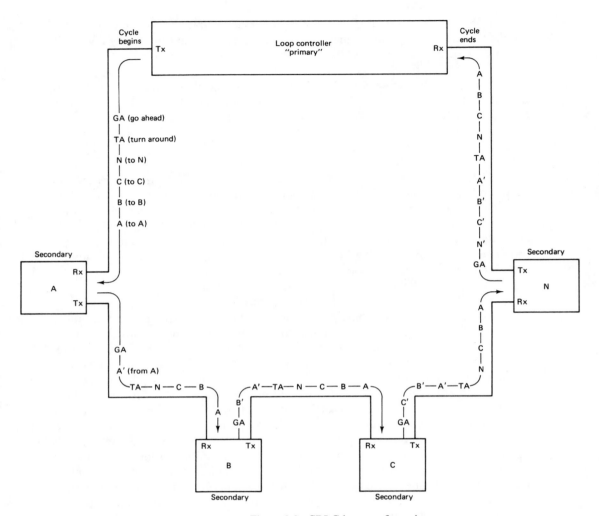

Figure 3-3 SDLC loop configuration.

Configure command/response. The configure command/response (CFGR) is an unnumbered command/response that is used only in a loop configuration. CFGR contains a one-byte *function descriptor* (essentially a subcommand) in the information field. A CFGR command is acknowledged with a CFGR response. If the low-order bit of the function descriptor is set, a specified function is initiated. If it is reset, the specified function is cleared. There are six subcommands that can appear in the configure command's function field.

1. *Clear—00000000.* A clear subcommand causes all previously set functions to be cleared by the secondary. The secondary's response to a clear subcommand is another clear subcommand, 00000000.

2. *Beacon test (BCN)—0000000X*. The beacon test causes the secondary receiving it to turn on or turn off its carrier. If the X bit is set, the secondary suppresses transmission of the carrier. If the X bit is reset, the secondary resumes transmission of the carrier. The beacon test is used to isolate an open-loop problem. Also, whenever a secondary detects the loss of a receive carrier, it automatically begins to transmit its beacon response. The secondary will continue transmitting the beacon until the loop resumes normal status.

3. *Monitor mode—0000010X*. The monitor command causes the addressed secondary to place itself into a monitor (receive only) mode. Once in the monitor mode, a secondary cannot transmit until it receives a monitor mode clear (00000100) or a clear (00000000) subcommand.

4. *Wrap—0000100X*. The wrap command causes the secondary station to loop its transmissions directly to its receiver input. The wrap command places the secondary effectively off-line for the duration of the test. A secondary station does not send the results of a wrap test to the primary.

5. *Self-test—0000101X*. The self-test subcommand causes the addressed secondary to initiate a series of internal diagnostic tests. When the tests are completed, the secondary will respond. If the P bit in the configure command is set, the secondary will respond following completion of the self-test at its earliest opportunity. If the P bit is reset, the secondary will respond following completion of the test to the next poll-type frame it receives. All other transmissions are ignored by the secondary while it is performing the self-tests. The secondary indicates the results of the self-test by setting or resetting the low-order bit (X) of its self-test response. A 1 indicates that the tests were unsuccessful, and a 0 indicates that they were successful.

6. *Modified link test—0000110X*. If the modified link test function is set (X bit set), the secondary station will respond to a TEST command with a TEST response that has an information field containing the first byte of the TEST command information field repeated *n* times. The number *n* is system implementation dependent. If the X bit is reset, the secondary station will respond to a TEST command, with or without an information field, with a TEST response with a zero-length information field. The modified link test is an optional subcommand and is only used to provide an alternative form of link test to that previously described for the TEST command.

Transparency

The transparency mechanism used with SDLC is called *zero-bit insertion* or *zero stuffing*. The flag bit sequence (01111110) can occur in a frame where this pattern is not intended to be a flag. For example, any time that 7EH occurs in the address, control, information, or FCS field it would be interpreted as a flag and disrupt character synchronization. Therefore, 7EH must be prohibited from occurring except when it is intended to be a flag. To prevent a 7EH sequence from occurring, a zero is automatically inserted after any occurrence of five consecutive 1's except in a designated flag sequence (i.e., flags are not zero inserted). When five consecutive 1's are received and the next bit is a 0, the 0 is deleted or removed. If the next bit is a 1, it must be a valid flag. An example of zero insertion/deletion is shown below.

Original frame bits at the transmit station:

```
01111110   01101111   11010011   1110001100110101   01111110
  flag      address    control          FCS             flag
```

After zero insertion but prior to transmission:

```
01111110   01101111   101010011   11100001100110101   01111110
  flag      address    control            FCS             flag
                     inserted zeros
```

After zero deletion at the receive end:

```
01111110   01101111   11010011   1110001100110101   01111110
  flag      address    control          FCS             flag
```

Message Abort

Message abort is used to prematurely terminate a frame. Generally, this is only done to accommodate high-priority messages such as emergency link recovery procedures, and so on. A message abort is any occurrence of 7 to 14 consecutive 1's. Zeros are not inserted in an abort sequence. A message abort terminates an existing frame and immediately begins the higher-priority frame. If more than 14 consecutive 1's occur in succession, it is considered an idle line condition. Therefore, 15 or more successive 1's place the circuit into the idle state.

Invert-on-Zero Encoding

A binary synchronous transmission such as SDLC is time synchronized to enable identification of sequential binary digits. Synchronous data communications assumes that bit or clock synchronization is provided by either the DCE or the DTE. With synchronous transmissions, a receiver samples incoming data at the same rate that they were transmitted. Although minor variations in timing can exist, synchronous modems provide received data clock recovery and dynamically adjusted sample timing to keep sample times midway between bits. For a DTE or a DCE to recover the clock, it is necessary that transitions occur in the data. *Invert-on-zero coding* is an encoding scheme that guarantees at least one transition in the data for every 7 bits transmitted. Invert-on-zero coding is also called NRZI (*nonreturn-to-zero inverted*).

With NRZI encoding, the data are encoded in the transmitter, then decoded in the receiver. Figure 3-4 shows an example of NRZI encoding. 1's are unaffected

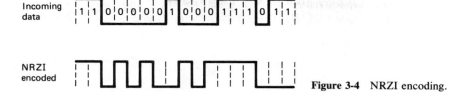

Figure 3-4 NRZI encoding.

by the NRZI encoder. However, 0's invert the encoded transmission level. Consequently, consecutive 0's generate an alternating high/low sequence. With SDLC, there can never be more than six 1's in succession (a flag). Therefore, a high-to-low transition is guaranteed to occur at least once for every 7 bits transmitted except during a message abort or an idle line condition. In a NRZI decoder, whenever a high/low transition occurs in the received data, a 0 is generated. The absence of a transition simply generates a 1. In Figure 3-4, a high level is assumed prior to encoding the incoming data.

NRZI encoding was intended to be used with asynchronous modems which do not have clock recovery capabilities. Consequently, the DTE must provide time synchronization which is aided by using NRZI-encoded data. Synchronous modems have built in scramblers and descramblers which ensure that transitions occur in the data, and thus NRZI encoding is unnecessary. The NRZI encoder/decoder is placed between the DTE and the DCE.

High-Level Data Link Control

In 1975, the International Standards Organization (ISO) defined several sets of substandards that, when combined, are called *high-level data link control* (HDLC). Since HDLC is a superset of SDLC, only the added capabilities are explained.

HDLC comprises three standards (subdivisions) that, when combined, outline the frame structure, control standards, and class of operation for a bit-oriented data link control (DLC).

ISO 3309–1976(E). This standard defines the frame structure, delimiting, sequence, and transparency mechanism used with HDLC. These are essentially the same as with SDLC except that HDLC has extended addressing capabilities and checks the FCS in a slightly different manner. The delimiting sequence used with HDLC is identical to SDLC: a 01111110 sequence.

HDLC can use either the *basic* 8-bit address field or an *extended* addressing format. With extended addressing the address field may be extended recursively. If b_0 in the address byte is a logic 1, the 7 remaining bits are the secondary's address (the ISO defines the low-order bit as b_0, whereas SDLC designates the high-order bit as b_0). If b_0 is a logic 0, the next byte is also part of the address. If b_0 of the second byte is a 0, a third address byte follows, and so on, until an address byte with a logic 1 for the low-order bit is encountered. Essentially, there are 7 bits available in each address byte for address encoding. An example of a three-byte extended addressing scheme is shown below, b_0 in the first two bytes

Synchronous Protocols

of the address field are 0's, indicating that additional address bytes follow and b_0 in the third address byte is a logic 1, which terminates the address field.

```
      b₀ = 0         b₀ = 0         b₀ = 1
      |              |              |
01111110  0XXXXXXX  0XXXXXXX  1XXXXXXX  . . .

flag          three-byte address field      control field, etc.
```

HDLC uses CRC-16 with a generating polynomial specified by CCITT V.41 as the FCS. At the transmit station, the CRC is computed such that if it is included in the FCS computation at the receive end, the remainder for an errorless transmission is always F0BBH.

ISO 4335–1979(E). This standard defines the elements of procedure for HDLC. The control field, information field, and supervisory format have increased capabilities over SDLC.

Control field. With HDLC, the control field can be extended to 16 bits. Seven bits are for the ns and 7 bits are for the nr. Therefore, with the extended control format, there can be a maximum of 127 outstanding (unconfirmed) frames at any give time.

Information field. HDLC permits any number of bits in the information field of an information command or response (SDLC is limited to 8-bit bytes). With HDLC any number of bits may be used for a character in the I field as long as all characters have the same number of bits.

Supervisory format. With HDLC, the supervisory format includes a fourth status condition: selective reject (SREJ). SREJ is identified by a 11 in bit position b_4 and b_5 of a supervisory control field. With a SREJ, a single frame can be rejected. A SREJ calls for the retransmission of only the frame identified by nr, whereas a REJ calls for the retransmission of all frames beginning with nr. For example, the primary sends I frames ns = 2, 3, 4, and 5. Frame 3 was received in error. A REJ would call for a retransmission of frames 3, 4, and 5; a SREJ would call for the transmission of only frame 3. SREJ can be used to call for the retransmission of any number of frames except that only one is identified at a time.

Operational modes. HDLC has two operational modes not specified in SDLC: asynchronous response mode and asynchronous disconnect mode.

1. *Asynchronous response mode (ARM).* With the ARM, secondary stations are allowed to send unsolicited responses. To transmit, a secondary does not need to have received a frame from the primary with the P bit set. However, if a secondary receives a frame with the P bit set, it must respond with a frame with the F bit set.

2. *Asynchronous disconnect mode (ADM).* An ADM is identical to the normal disconnect mode except that the secondary can initiate a DM or RIM response at any time.

ISO 7809–1985(E). This standard combines previous standards 6159(E) (unbalanced) and 6256(E) (balanced) and outlines the class of operation necessary to establish the link-level protocol.

Unbalanced operation. This class of operation is logically equivalent to a multi-point private line circuit with a polling environment. There is a single primary station responsible for central control of the network. Data transmission may be either half- or full-duplex.

Balanced operation. This class of operation is logically equivalent to a two-point private line circuit. Each station has equal data link responsibilities, and channel access is through contention using the asynchronous response mode. Data transmission may be half- or full-duplex.

PUBLIC DATA NETWORK

A *public data network* (PDN) is a switched data communications network similar to the public telephone network except that a PDN is designed for transferring data only. Public data networks combine the concepts of both *value-added networks* (VANs) and *packet-switching networks*.

Value-Added Network

A value-added network "*adds value*" to the services or facilities provided by a common carrier to provide new types of communication services. Examples of added values are error control, enhanced connection reliability, dynamic routing, failure protection, logical multiplexing, and data format conversions. A VAN comprises an organization that leases communications lines from common carriers such as AT&T and MCI and adds new types of communications services to those lines. Examples of value-added networks are GTE Telnet, DATAPAC, TRANSPAC, and Tymnet Inc.

Packet-Switching Network

Packet switching involves dividing data messages into small bundles of information and transmitting them through communications networks to their intended destinations using computer-controlled switches. Three common switching techniques are used with public data networks: *circuit switching, message switching,* and *packet switching.*

Circuit switching. Circuit switching is used for making a standard telephone call on the public telephone network. The call is established, information is transferred, and then the call is disconnected. The time required to establish the call is called the *setup* time. Once the call has been established, the circuits interconnected by the network switches are allocated to a single user for the duration of the call. After a call has been established, information is transferred in *real time*. When a call is terminated, the circuits and switches are once again available for another user. Because there are a limited number of circuits and switching paths available, *blocking* can occur. Blocking is when a call cannot be completed because there are no facilities or switching paths available between the source and destination locations. When circuit switching is used for data transfer, the terminal equipment at the source and destination must be compatible; they must use compatible modems and the same bit rate, character set, and protocol.

A circuit switch is a *transparent* switch. The switch is transparent to the data; it does nothing more than interconnect the source and destination terminal equipment. A circuit switch adds no value to the circuit.

Message switching. Message switching is a form of *store-and-forward* network. Data, including source and destination identification codes, are transmitted into the network and stored in a switch. Each switch within the network has message storage capabilities. The network transfers the data from switch to switch when it is convenient to do so. Consequently, data are not transferred in real time; there can be a delay at each switch. With message switching, blocking cannot occur. However, the delay time from message transmission to reception varies from call to call and can be quite long (possibly as long as 24 hours). With message switching, once the information has entered the network, it is converted to a more suitable format for transmission through the network. At the receive end, the data are converted to a format compatible with the receiving data terminal equipment. Therefore, with message switching, the source and destination data terminal equipment do not need to be compatible. Message switching is more efficient than circuit switching because data that enter the network during busy times can be held and transmitted later when the load has decreased.

A message switch is a *transactional* switch because it does more than simply transfer the data from the source to the destination. A message switch can store data or change its format and bit rate, then convert the data back to their original form or an entirely different form at the receive end. Message switching multiplexes data from different sources onto a common facility.

Packet switching. With packet switching, data are divided into smaller segments called *packets* prior to transmission through the network. Because a packet can be held in memory at a switch for a short period of time, packet switching is sometimes called a *hold-and-forward* network. With packet switching, a message is divided into packets and each packet can take a different path through the network. Consequently, all packets do not necessarily arrive at the receive end at the same time or in the same order in which they were transmitted. Because packets are small, the hold time is generally quite short and message transfer is near real time and blocking cannot occur. However, packet-switching networks require complex and expensive switching arrangements and complicated protocols. A packet switch is also a transactional switch. Circuit, message, and packet switching techniques are summarized in Table 3-3.

TABLE 3-3 SWITCHING TECHNIQUE SUMMARY

Circuit switching	Message switching	Packet switching
Dedicated transmission path	No dedicated transmission path	No dedicated transmission path
Continuous transmission of data	Transmission of messages	Transmission of packets
Operates in real time	Not real time	Near real time
Messages not stored	Messages stored	Messages held for short time
Path established for entire message	Route established for each message	Route established for each packet
Call setup delay	Message transmission delay	Packet transmission delay
Busy signal if called party busy	No busy signal	No busy signal
Blocking may occur	Blocking cannot occur	Blocking cannot occur
User responsible for message-loss protection	Network responsible for lost messages	Network may be responsible for each packet but not for entire message
No speed or code conversion	Speed and code conversion	Speed and code conversion
Fixed bandwidth transmission (i.e., fixed information capacity)	Dynamic use of bandwidth	Dynamic use of bandwidth
No overhead bits after initial setup delay	Overhead bits in each message	Overhead bits in each packet

CCITT X.1 International User Class of Service

The CCITT X.1 standard divides the various classes of service into three basic modes of transmission for a public data network. The three modes are: *start/stop, synchronous,* and *packet.*

Start/stop mode.   With the start/stop mode, data are transferred from the source to the network and from the network to the destination in an asynchronous data format (i.e., each character is framed within a start and stop bit). Call control signaling is done in International Alphabet No. 5 (ASCII-77). Two common protocols used for start/stop transmission are IBM's 83B protocol and AT&T's 8A1/B1 selective calling arrangement.

Synchronous mode.   With the synchronous mode, data are transferred from the source to the network and from the network to the destination in a synchronous data format (i.e., each message is preceded by a unique synchronizing character). Call control signaling is identical to that used with private line data circuits and common protocols used for synchronous transmission are IBM's 3270 bisync, Burrough's BASIC, and UNIVAC's UNISCOPE.

Public Data Network   **145**

Packet mode. With the packet mode, data are transferred from the source to the network and from the network to the destination in a frame format. The ISO HDLC frame format is the standard data link protocol used with the packet mode. Within the network, data are divided into smaller packets and transferred in accordance with the CCITT X.25 user to network interface protocol.

Figure 3-5 illustrates a typical layout for a public data network showing each of the three modes of operation. The packet assembler/disassembler (PAD) interfaces user data to X.25 format when the user's data are in either the asynchronous or synchronous mode of operation. A PAD is unnecessary when the user is operating in the packet mode. X.75 is recommended by the CCITT for the gateway protocol. A gateway is used to interface two public data networks.

CCITT X.25 USER-TO-NETWORK INTERFACE PROTOCOL

In 1976, the CCITT designated the X.25 user interface as the international standard for packet network access. Keep in mind that X.25 is strictly a *user-to-network* interface and addresses only the physical, data link, and network layers in the ISO seven layer model. X.25 uses existing standards whenever possible. For example, X.25 specifies X.21, X.26, and X.27 standards as the physical interface, which correspond to EIA RS-232C, RS-423A, and RS-422A standards, respectively. X.25 defines HDLC as the international standard for the data link layer and the American National Standards Institute (ANSI) 3.66 *advanced data communications control procedures* (ADCCP) as the U.S. standard. ANSI 3.66 and ISO HDLC specify exactly the same set of data link control procedures. However, ANSI 3.66 and HDLC were designed for private line data circuits with a polling environment. Consequently, the addressing and control procedures outlined by them are not appropriate for packet data networks. ANSI 3.66 and

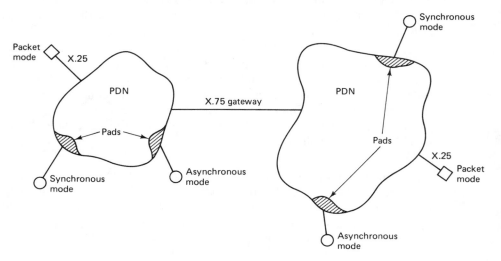

Figure 3-5 Public data network.

HDLC were selected for the data link layer because of their frame format, delimiting sequence, transparency mechanism, and error detection method.

At the link level, the protocol specified by X.25 is a subset of HDLC, referred to as *Link Access Procedure Balanced* (LAPB). LAPB provides for two-way, full-duplex communications between DTE and DCE at the packet network gateway. Only the address of the DTE or DCE may appear in the address field of a LAPB frame. The address field refers to a link address, not a network address. The network address of the destination terminal is embedded in the packet header, which is part of the information field.

Tables 3-4 and 3-5 show the commands and responses, respectively, for an LAPB frame. During LAPB operation, most frames are commands. A response frame is compelled only when a command frame is received containing a poll (P-bit) = 1. SABM/UA is a command/response pair used to initialize all counters and timers at the beginning of a session. Similarly, DISC/DM is a command/response pair used at the end of a session. FRMR is a response to any illegal command for which there is no indication of transmission errors according to the frame check sequence field.

Information (I) commands are used to transmit packets. Packets are never sent as responses. Packets are acknowledged using ns and nr just as they were in SDLC. RR is sent by a station when it needs to respond (acknowledge)

TABLE 3-4   LAPB COMMANDS

Command name	Bit number			
	8 7 6	*5*	*4 3 2*	*1*
I (information)	nr	P	ns	0
RR (receiver ready)	nr	P	0 0 0	1
RNR (receiver not ready)	nr	P	0 1 0	1
REJ (reject)	nr	P	1 0 0	1
SABM (set asynchronous balanced mode)	0 0 1	P	1 1 1	1
DISC (disconnect)	0 1 0	P	0 0 1	1

TABLE 3-5   LAPB RESPONSES

Command name	Bit number			
	8 7 6	*5*	*4 3 2*	*1*
RR (receiver ready)	nr	F	0 0 0	1
RNR (receiver not ready)	nr	F	0 1 0	1
REJ (reject)	nr	F	1 0 0	1
UA (unnumbered acknowledgment)	0 1 1	F	0 0 1	1
DM (disconnect mode)	0 0 0	F	1 1 1	1
FRMR (frame rejected)	1 0 0	F	0 1 1	1

CCITT X.25 User-To-Network Interface Protocol

something, but has no information packets to send. A response to an information command could be RR with $F = 1$. This procedure is called *checkpointing*.

REJ is another way of requesting transmission of frames. RNR is used for the flow control to indicate a busy condition and prevents further transmissions until cleared with an RR.

The network layer of X.25 specifies three switching services offered in a switched data network: permanent virtual circuit, virtual call, and datagram.

Permanent Virtual Circuit

A *permanent virtual circuit* (PVC) is logically equivalent to a two-point dedicated private line circuit except slower. A PVC is slower because a hardwired connection is not provided. Each time a connection is requested, the appropriate switches and circuits must be established through the network to provide the interconnection. A PVC establishes a connection between two predetermined subscribers of the network on demand, but not permanently. With a PVC, a source and destination address are unnecessary because the two users are fixed.

Virtual Call

A *virtual call* (VC) is logically equivalent to making a telephone call through the DDD network. A VC is a one-to-many arrangement. Any VC subscriber can access any other VC subscriber through a network of switches and communication channels. Virtual calls are temporary connections that use common usage equipment and circuits. The source must provide its address and the address of the destination before a VC can be completed.

Datagram

A *datagram* (DG) is, at best, vaguely defined by X.25 and, until it is completely outlined, has very limited usefulness. With a DG, users send small packets of data into the network. The network does not acknowledge packets nor does it guarantee successful transmission. However, if a message will fit into a single packet, a DG is somewhat reliable. This is called a *single-packet-per-segment* protocol.

X.25 Packet Format

A virtual call is the most efficient service offered for a packet network. There are two packet formats used with virtual calls: a call request packet and a data transfer packet.

Call request packet.   Figure 3-6 shows the field format for a call request packet. The delimiting sequence is 01111110 (an HDLC flag), and the error detection/correction mechanism is CRC-16 with ARQ. The link address field and the control field have little use and are therefore seldom used with packet networks. The rest of the fields are defined in sequence.

Flag	Link address field	Link control field	Format identifier	Logical channel identifier	Packet type	Calling address length	Called address length	Called address	Calling address	0	Facilities field length	Facilities field	Protocol ID	User data	Frame check sequence	Flag
Bits: 8	8	8	4	12	8	4	4	To 60	To 60	2	6	To 512	32	To 96	16	8

Figure 3-6 Call request packet format.

149

Format identifier. The format identifier identifies whether the packet is a new call request or a previously established call. The format identifier also identifies the packet numbering sequence (either 0–7 or 0–127).

Logical channel identifier (LCI). The LCI is a 12-bit binary number that identifies the source and destination users for a given virtual call. After a source user has gained access to the network and has identified the destination user, they are assigned an LCI. In subsequent packets, the source and destination addresses are unnecessary; only the LCI is needed. When two users disconnect, the LCI is relinquished and can be reassigned two new users. There are 4096 LCIs available. Therefore, there may be as many as 4096 virtual calls established at any given time.

Packet type. This field is used to identify the function and the content of the packet (i.e., new request, call clear, call reset, etc.).

Calling address length. This 4-bit field gives the number of digits (in binary) that appear in the calling address field. With 4 bits, up to 15 digits can be specified.

Called address length. This field is the same as the calling address field except that it identifies the number of digits that appear in the called address field.

Called address. This field contains the destination address. Up to 15 BCD digits (60 bits) can be assigned to a destination user.

Calling address. This field is the same as the called address field except that it contains up to 15 BCD digits that can be assigned to a source user.

Facilities length field. This field identifies (in binary) the number of 8-bit octets present in the facilities field.

Facilities field. This field contains up to 512 bits of optional network facility information, such as reverse billing information, closed user groups, and whether it is a simplex transmit or simplex receive connection.

Protocol identifier. This 32-bit field is reserved for the subscriber to insert user-level protocol functions such as long-on procedures and user identification practices.

User data field. Up to 96 bits of user data can be transmitted with a call request packet. These are unnumbered data which are not confirmed. This field is generally used for user passwords.

Data transfer packet. Figure 3-7 shows the field format for a data transfer packet. A data transfer packet is similar to a call request packet except that a data transfer packet has considerably less overhead and can accommodate a much larger user data field. The data transfer packet contains a send and receive packet sequence field that were not included with the call request format.

The flag, link address, link control, format identifier, LCI, and FCS fields

Flag	Link address field	Link control field	Format identifier	Logical channel identifier	Send packet sequence number P(s)	0	Receive packet sequence number P(r)	0	User data	Frame check sequence	Flag
Bits: 8	8	8	4	12	3/7	5/1	3/7	5/1	To 1024	16	8

Figure 3-7 Data transfer packet format.

are identical to those used with the call request packet. The send and receive packet sequence fields are described as follows.

Send packet sequence field. This field is used in the same manner that the ns and nr sequences are used with SDLC and HDLC. P(s) is analogous to ns, and P(r) is analogous to nr. Each successive data transfer packet is assigned the next P(s) number in sequence. The P(s) can be a 3- or a 7-bit binary number and thus number packets from either 0–7 or 0–127. The numbering sequence is identified in the format identifier. The send packet field always contains 8 bits and the unused bits are reset.

Receive packet sequence field. P(r) is used to confirm received packets and call for retransmission of packets received in error (ARQ). The I field in a data transfer packet can have considerably more source information than an I field in a call request packet.

The X Series of Recommended Standards

X.25 is part of the X series of CCITT-recommended standards for public data networks. The X series is classified into two categories: X.1 through X.39, which deal with services and facilities, terminals, and interfaces; and X.40 through X.199, which deal with network architecture, transmission, signaling, switching, maintenance, and administrative arrangements. Table 3-6 lists the most important X standards with their titles and descriptions.

LOCAL AREA NETWORKS

A *local area network* (LAN) is a data communications network that is designed to provide two-way communications between a large variety of data communications terminal equipment within a relatively small geographic area. LANs are privately owned and operated and are used to interconnect data terminal equipment in the same building, building complex, or geographical area.

Local Area Network System Considerations

Topology. The topology or physical architecture of a LAN identifies how the stations are interconnected. The most common configurations used with LANs are the star, bus, ring, and mesh topologies.

Local Area Networks 151

TABLE 3-6 CCITT X SERIES STANDARDS

X.1	International user classes of service in public data networks. Assigns numerical class designations to different terminal speeds and types.
X.2	International user services and facilities in public data networks. Specifies essential and additional services and facilities.
X.3	Packet assembly/disassembly facility (PAD) in a public data network. Describes the packet assembler/dissasembler, which normally is used at a network gateway to allow connection of a start/stop terminal to a packet network.
X.20-bis	Use on public data networks of DTE designed for interfacing to asynchronous full-duplex V-series modems. Allows use of V.24/V.28 (essentially the same as EIA RS-232C).
X.21-bis	Use on public data networks of DTE designed for interfacing to synchronous full-duplex V-series modems. Allows use of V.24/V.28 (essentially the same as EIA RS-232C) or V.35.
X.25	Interface between DTE and DCE for terminals operating in the packet mode on public data networks. Defines the architecture of three levels of protocols existing in the serial interface cable between a packet-mode terminal and a gateway to a packet network.
X.28	DTE/DCE interface for a start/stop mode DTE accessing the PAD in a public data network situated in the same country. Defines the architecture of protocols existing in a serial interface cable between a start/stop terminal and an X.3 PAD.
X.29	Procedures for the exchange of control information and user data between a PAD and a packet mode DTE or another PAD. Defines the architecture of protocols behind the X.3 PAD, either between two PADs or between a PAD and a packet-mode terminal on the other side of the network.
X.75	Terminal and transit call control procedures and data transfer system on international circuits between packet-switched data networks. Defines the architecture of protocols between two public packet networks.
X.121	International numbering plan for public data networks. Defines a numbering plan including code assignments for each nation.

Connecting medium. Presently, most LANs use coaxial cable as the transmission medium, although in the near future it is likely that optical fiber cables will predominate. Fiber cables can operate at higher bit rates and, consequently, have a larger capacity to transfer information than coaxial cables. LANs that use a coaxial cable are limited to an overall length of approximately 1500 m. Fiber links are expected to far exceed this distance.

Transmission format. There are two basic approaches to transmission format for LANs: *baseband* and *broadband*. Baseband transmission uses the connecting medium as a single-channel device. Only one station can transmit at a time and all stations must transmit and receive the same types of signals (encoding schemes and bit rates). Essentially, a baseband format time division multiplexes signals onto the transmission medium. Broadband transmission uses the connecting medium as a multi-channel device. Each channel occupies a different frequency band (i.e., frequency-division multiplexing). Consequently, each channel can contain different encoding schemes and operate at different bit rates. A broadband network permits voice, digital data, and video to be transmitted simultaneously over the same transmission medium. However, broadband systems require RF modems, amplifiers, and more complicated transceivers than baseband systems. For this reason, baseband systems are more prevalent. Table 3-7 summarizes baseband and broadband transmission techniques.

Channel Accessing

Channel accessing describes the mechanism used by a station to gain access to a local area network. There are essentially two methods used for channel accessing with LANs: carrier sense, multiple access with collision detection (CSMA/CD) and token passing.

Carrier sense, multiple access with collision detection. With CSMA/CD, a station monitors (listens to) the line to determine if the line is busy. If a station has a message to transmit but the line is busy, it waits for an idle condition before it transmits its message. If two stations begin transmitting at the same time, a *collision* occurs. When this happens, both stations cease transmitting (*back off*) and each station waits a random period of time before attempting a retransmission. The random delay time for each station is different and therefore allows for prioritizing the stations on the network. With CSMA/CD, stations must contend

TABLE 3-7 TRANSMISSION FORMAT SUMMARY

Baseband	Broadband
Characteristics	
Digital signaling	Analog signaling (requires RF modem)
Entire bandwidth used by signal	FDM possible (i.e., multiple data channels)
Bidirectional	Unidirectional
Bus topology	Bus topology
Maximum length approximately 1500 meters	Maximum length up to tens of kilometers
Advantages	
Less expensive	High capacity
Simpler technology	Multiple traffic types
Easy and quick to install	More flexible circuit configurations
	Larger area covered
Disadvantages	
Single channel	Modem required
Limited capacity	Complex installation and maintenance
Grounding problems	Double propagation delay
Limited distance	

for the network. A station is not guaranteed access to the network. To detect the occurrence of a collision, a station must be capable of transmitting and receiving simultaneously. CSMA/CD is used by most baseband LANs in the bus configuration. Ethernet is a popular local area network that uses baseband transmission with CSMA/CD. The transmission rate with Ethernet is 10 Mbps over a coaxial cable. Collision detection is accomplished by monitoring the line for phase violations in a Manchester-encoded (biphase) digital encoding scheme.

Token passing. Token passing is a channel-accessing arrangement that is best suited for a ring topology with either a baseband or a broadband network. With token passing, an electrical *token* (*code*) is circulated around the ring from station to station. Each station, in turn, acquires the token. In order to transmit, a station must first possess the token; then the station removes the token and places its message on the line. After a station transmits, it passes the token on to the next sequential station. With token passing, each station has equal access to the transmission medium. The Cambridge is a popular local area network that uses baseband transmission with token passing. The transmission rate with a Cambridge ring is 10 Mbps. Table 3-8 lists several local area networks and some of their characteristics.

In 1980, the IEEE local area network committee was established to standardize the means of connecting digital computer equipment and peripherals with the local area network environment. In 1983, the committee established IEEE standards 802.3 (CSMA/CD) and 802.4 (token passing) for a bus topology. In 1987, IEEE standard 802.5 (token passing) with a ring topology and Fiber Distributed Data Interface (FDDI) were adopted.

ETHERNET

Ethernet is a baseband system which uses a bus topology and is designed for use in a local area network. Since there are many computer manufacturers, the problem is to design a system in which different types of computers can communicate with each other. In a demonstration in 1982, the computers of 10 major companies were linked on a 1500-ft Ethernet cable for electronic mail, word processing, and so on.

Before explaining the operation of Ethernet, a description of this system's hardware and software is provided.

TABLE 3-8   LOCAL AREA NETWORK SUMMARY

Ethernet	Developed by Xerox Corporation in conjunction with Digital Equipment Corporation and Intel Corporation; baseband system using CSMA/CD; 10 Mbps
Wangnet	Developed by Wang Computer Corporation; broadband system using CSMA/CD
Localnet	Developed by Sytek Corporation; broadband system using CSMA/CD
Domain	Developed by Apollo Computer Corporation; broadband network using token passing
Cambridge ring	Developed by the University of Cambridge; baseband system using CSMA/CD; 10 Mbps

Preamble	Destination address	Source address	Type field	Data field	CRC

| Bytes: | 8 | 6 | 6 | 2 | 46-1500 | 4 |

Figure 3-8 Packet format for Ethernet.

Software

Information is transmitted from one station (computer) to another in the form of packets. The format for a packet is shown in Figure 3-8. The preamble is used for bit synchronization. The source and destination addresses and the field type make up the header information. The CRC is computed on the header information and the data field. The packet information is converted to Manchester code and transmitted at a 10-Mbps rate. In the Manchester encoding, each bit cell is divided into two parts. The first half contains the complement of the bit value and the second contains the actual bit value. This is illustrated in Figure 3-9. This code ensures that a signal transition exists in every bit.

The destination of a packet may be a single station or a group of stations. A *physical address* is a unique address of a single station and is denoted by a 0 as the first bit (LSB) of the destination address. A *multicast address* has two forms. If only a partial group of the total stations is addressed, the first bit is a 1. The destination address is all 1's if all of the stations in the network are to receive the transmitted packet. A delay of 9.6 μs is required between the transmission of packets.

Hardware

Coaxial cable is the transmission medium for Ethernet. A cable segment may have a maximum distance of 500 m (1640 ft). Each segment may have up to 100 transceivers attached by way of pressure taps. Since these taps do not require cable cutting for installation, additional stations may be added without interfering with normal system operations. Interlan has developed the NT10 transceiver, in which the taps consist of two probes. One probe contacts the center conductor while the other contacts the shield. Color bands on the segment cable identify

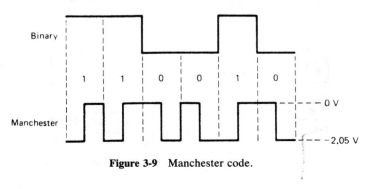

Figure 3-9 Manchester code.

Ethernet   155

where the taps may be placed. A maximum of three segments may be connected end to end by way of repeaters to extend the system length to 1500 m (4921 ft). In Figure 3-10, this is the path between A and C. Remote repeater may be used with a maximum distance of 1000 m between them. If these are used, the maximum end-to-end distance would be extended to 2.5 km (8202 ft). In Figure 3-10, if the center and right segments were interchanged, there would be a 2.5-km separation between A and B. There must always be only one signal path between any two stations. A station is connected to a controller, which is then interfaced with the transceiver to the transmission system. This is shown in Figure 3-11.

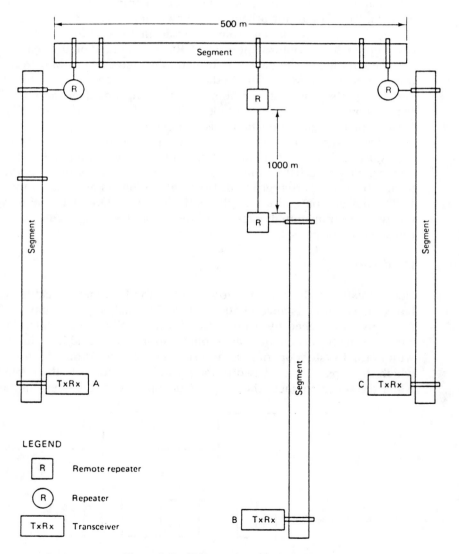

Figure 3-10 Ethernet transmission system.

Data Communications Protocols   Chap. 3

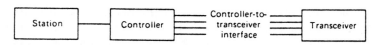

Figure 3-11 Ethernet station connection to the transmission system.

System Operation

Transmission. The data link control for Ethernet is CSMA/CD. Stations acquire access to the transmission system through contention. They are not polled, nor do they have specific time slots for transmission. A station wishing to transmit first determines if another station is currently using the transmission system. The controller accomplishes this through the transceiver by sensing the presence of a carrier on the line. The controller may be a hardware or a software function, depending on the complexity of the station. In 1983, Xerox Corporation, in conjunction with Digital Equipment Corporation and Intel Corporation, developed and introduced a single-chip controller for Ethernet. Later, Mostek Corporation, working with Digital Equipment Corporation and Advanced Micro Devices, announced a two-chip set for this purpose. One chip is the local area network controller for Ethernet (LANCE) and the second is a Serial Interface Adapter.

The presence of a carrier is denoted by the signal transitions on the line produced by the Manchester code. If a carrier is detected, the station defers transmission until the line is quiet. After the required delay, the station sends digital data to the controller. The controller converts these data to Manchester code, inserts the CRC, adds the preamble, and places the packet on-line. The transmission of the entire packet is not yet assured. A different station may also have detected the quiet line and started to transmit its own packet. The first station monitors the line for a period called the *collision window* or the *collision interval*. This interval is a function of the end-to-end propagation delay of the line. This delay, including the delay caused by any repeaters, measured in distance, cannot exceed 2.5 km. If a data collision has not occurred in this interval, the station is said to have line acquisition and will continue to transmit the entire packet. Should a collision be detected, both of the transmitting stations will immediately abort the transmission for a random period of time and then will attempt to retransmit. A data collision may be detected by the transceiver by comparing the received signal with the transmitted signal. To make this comparison, a station must still be transmitting its packet while a previously transmitted signal has propagated to the end of the line and back. This dictates that a packet be of some minimum size. If a collision is detected, it is the controller that must take the necessary action. The controller-transceiver interface contains a line for notification of Collision Presence (10-MHz square wave). The remaining three lines of this interface are the Transmit Data, Receive Data, and power for the transceiver. Since a collision is manifested in some form of phase violation, the controller alone may detect a collision. In Ethernet, data collision is detected mainly by the transceiver. When feasible, this is supplemented by a collision detection facility in the controller. To ensure that all stations are aware

Ethernet 157

of the collision, a *collision enforcement consensus procedure* is invoked. When the controller detects a collision, it transmits four to six bytes of random data. These bytes are called the *jam sequence.* If a collision has occurred, the station's random waiting time before retransmission is determined from a *binary exponential back-off algorithm.* The transmission time slot is usually set to be slightly longer than the round-trip time of the channel. The delay time is randomly selected from this interval.

Example 3-4

Transmission time slot = time of 512 bits

$$\text{Maximum time of the interval} = \frac{512 \text{ bits}}{10 \text{ Mbps}} = 51.2 \ \mu\text{s}$$

$$\text{Time interval} = 0 \text{ to } 51.2 \ \mu\text{s}$$

For each succeeding collision encountered by the same packet, the time interval is doubled until a maximum interval is reached. The maximum interval is given as $2^{10} \times$ transmission time slot. After 15 unsuccessful attempts at transmitting a packet have been made, no further attempts are made and the error is reported to the station. This is the major drawback of Ethernet—it cannot guarantee packet delivery at a time of heavy transmission load.

Reception. The line is monitored until the station's address is detected. The controller strips the preamble, checks the CRC, and converts the Manchester code back to digital format. If the packet contains any errors, it is discarded. The end of the packet is recognized by the absence of a carrier on the transmission line. This means that no transitions were detected for the period of 75 to 125 ns since the center of the last bit cell. The decoding is accomplished through a phase-locked loop. The phase-locked loop is initialized by the known pattern of the preamble.

QUESTIONS

3-1. Define *data communications protocol.*

3-2. What is a master station? A slave station?

3-3. Define *polling* and *selecting.*

3-4. What is the difference between a synchronous and an asynchronous protocol?

3-5. What is the difference between a character-oriented protocol and a bit-oriented protocol?

3-6. Define the three operating modes used with data communications circuits.

3-7. What is the function of the clearing character?

3-8. What is a unique address? A group address? A broadcast address?

3-9. What does a negative acknowledgment to a poll indicate?

3-10. What is the purpose of a heading?

3-11. Why is IBM's 3270 synchronous protocol called bisync?

3-12. Why are SYN characters always transmitted in pairs?

3-13. What is an SPA? An SSA? A DA?

3-14. What is the purpose of a leading pad? A trailing pad?

3-15. What is the difference between a general poll and a specific poll?

3-16. What is a handshake?

3-17. (Primary, secondary) stations transmit polls.

3-18. What does a negative acknowledgment to a poll indicate?

3-19. What is a positive acknowledgment to a poll?

3-20. What is the difference between ETX, ETB, and ITB?

3-21. What character is used to terminate a heading and begin a block of text?

3-22. What is transparency? When is it necessary? Why?

3-23. What is the difference between a command and a response with SDLC?

3-24. What are the three transmission states used with SDLC? Explain them.

3-25. What are the five fields used with an SDLC frame? Briefly explain each.

3-26. What is the delimiting sequence used with SDLC?

3-27. What is the null address in SDLC? When is it used?

3-28. What are the three frame formats used with SDLC? Explain what each format is used for.

3-29. How is an information frame identified in SDLC? A supervisory frame? An unnumbered frame?

3-30. What are the purposes of the nr and ns sequences in SDLC?

3-31. With SDLC, when is the P bit set? The F bit?

3-32. What is the maximum number of unconfirmed frames that can be outstanding at any one time with SDLC? Why?

3-33. With SDLC, which frame formats can have an information field?

3-34. With SLDC, which frame formats can be used to confirm previously received frames?

3-35. What command/response is used for reporting procedural errors with SDLC?

3-36. Explain the three modes in SDLC that a secondary station can be in.

3-37. When is the configure command/response used with SDLC?

3-38. What is a go-ahead sequence? A turnaround sequence?

3-39. What is the transparency mechanism used with SDLC?

3-40. What is a message abort? When is it transmitted?

3-41. Explain invert-on-zero encoding. Why is it used?

3-42. What supervisory condition exists with HDLC that is not included with SDLC?

3-43. What is the delimiting sequence used with HDLC? The transparency mechanism?

3-44. Explain extended addressing as it is used with HDLC.

3-45. What is the difference between the basic control format and the extended control format with HDLC?

3-46. What is the difference in the information fields used with SDLC and HDLC?

3-47. What operational modes are included with HDLC that are not included with SDLC?

3-48. What is a public data network?

3-49. Describe a value-added network.

3-50. Explain the differences in circuit-, message-, and packet-switching techniques.

3-51. What is blocking? With which switching techniques is blocking possible?

3-52. What is a transparent switch? A transactional switch?

3-53. What is a packet?

3-54. What is the difference between a store-and-forward and a hold-and-forward network?

3-55. Explain the three modes of transmission for public data networks.

3-56. What is the user-to-network protocol designated by CCITT?

3-57. What is the user-to-network protocol designated by ANSI?

3-58. Which layers of the ISO protocol hierarchy are addressed by X.25?

3-59. Explain the following terms: permanent virtual circuit, virtual call, and datagram.

3-60. Why was HDLC selected as the link-level protocol for X.25?

3-61. Briefly explain the fields that make up an X.25 call request packet.

3-62. Describe a local area network.

3-63. What is the connecting medium used with local area networks?

3-64. Explain the two transmission formats used with local area networks.

3-65. Explain CSMA/CD.

3-66. Explain token passing.

PROBLEMS

3-1. Determine the hex code for the control field in an SDLC frame for the following conditions: information frame, poll, transmitting frame 4, and confirming reception of frames 2, 3, and 4.

3-2. Determine the hex code for the control field in an SDLC frame for the following conditions: supervisory frame, ready to receive, final, confirming reception of frames 6, 7, and 0.

3-3. Insert 0's into the following SDLC data stream.

111 001 000 011 111 111 100 111 110 100 111 101 011 111 111 111 001 011

3-4. Delete 0's from the following SDLC data stream.

010 111 110 100 011 011 111 011 101 110 101 111 101 011 100 011 111 00

3-5. Sketch the NRZI levels for the following data stream (start with a high condition).

1 0 0   1 1 1   0 0 1   0 1 0

4

DIGITAL TRANSMISSION

INTRODUCTION

As stated previously, digital transmission is the transmittal of digital pulses between two points in a communications system. The original source information may already be in digital form or it may be analog signals that must be converted to digital pulses prior to transmission and converted back to analog form at the receive end. With digital transmission systems, a physical facility such as a metallic wire pair, a coaxial cable, or an optical fiber link is required to interconnect the two points in the system. The pulses are contained and propagate down the facility.

Advantages of Digital Transmission

1. The primary advantage of digital transmission is noise immunity. Analog signals are more susceptible than digital pulses to undesired amplitude, frequency, and phase variations. This is because with digital transmission, it is not necessary to evaluate these parameters as precisely as with analog transmission. Instead, the received pulses are evaluated during a sample interval, and a simple determination is made whether the pulse is above or below a certain threshold.

2. Digital pulses are better suited to processing and multiplexing than analog signals. Digital pulses can be stored easily, whereas analog signals cannot. Also, the transmission rate of a digital system can easily be changed to adapt to different environments and to interface with different types of equipment. Multiplexing is explained in detail in Chapter 5.

161

3. Digital systems use signal regeneration rather than signal amplification, thus producing a more noise resistant system than their analog counterpart.

4. Digital signals are simpler to measure and evaluate. Therefore, it is easier to compare the performance of digital systems with different signaling and information capacities than it is with comparable analog systems.

5. Digital systems are better suited to evaluate error performance (i.e., error detection and correction) than analog systems.

Disadvantages of Digital Transmission

1. The transmission of digitally encoded analog signals requires more bandwidth than simply transmitting the analog signal.

2. Analog signals must be converted to digital codes prior to transmission and converted back to analog at the receiver.

3. Digital transmission requires precise time synchronization between transmitter and receiver clocks.

4. Digital transmission systems are incompatible with existing analog facilities.

PULSE MODULATION

Pulse modulation includes many different methods of transferring pulses from a source to a destination. The four predominant methods are *pulse width modulation* (PWM), *pulse position modulation* (PPM), *pulse amplitude modulation* (PAM), and *pulse code modulation* (PCM). The four most common methods of pulse modulation are summarized below and shown in Figure 4-1.

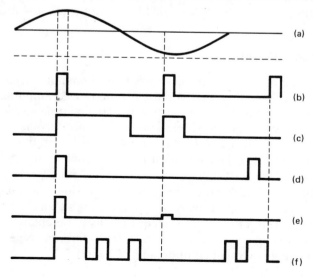

Figure 4-1 Pulse modulation: (a) analog signal; (b) sample pulse; (c) PWM; (d) PPM; (e) PAM; (f) PCM.

Digital Transmission   **Chap. 4**

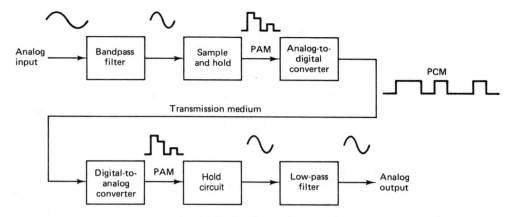

Figure 4-2 Simplified PCM system block diagram.

1. *PWM*. This method is sometimes called pulse duration modulation (PDM) or pulse length modulation (PLM). The pulse width (active portion of the duty cycle) is proportional to the amplitude of the analog signal.
2. *PPM*. The position of a constant-width pulse within a prescribed time slot is varied according to the amplitude of the analog signal.
3. *PAM*. The amplitude of a constant-width, constant-position pulse is varied according to the amplitude of the analog signal.
4. *PCM*. The analog signal is sampled and converted to a fixed-length, serial binary number for transmission. The binary number varies according to the amplitude of the analog signal.

PAM is used as an intermediate form of modulation with PSK, QAM, and PCM, although it is seldom used by itself. PWM and PPM are used in special-purpose communications systems (usually for the military) but are seldom used for commercial systems. PCM is by far the most prevalent method of pulse transmission and consequently, will be the topic of discussion for the remainder of this chapter.

PULSE CODE MODULATION

Pulse code modulation (PCM) is the only one of the pulse modulation techniques previously mentioned that is a digital transmission system. With PCM, the pulses are of fixed length and fixed amplitude. PCM is a binary system; a pulse or lack of a pulse within a prescribed time slot represents either a logic 1 or a logic 0 condition. With PWM, PPM, or PAM, a single pulse does not represent a single binary digit (bit).

Figure 4-2 shows a simplified block diagram of a single-channel, *simplex* (*one-way-only*) PCM system. The bandpass filter limits the input analog signal to the standard voice band frequency range 300 to 3000 Hz. The *sample-and-hold* circuit periodically samples the analog input and converts those samples to a multilevel PAM signal. The *analog-to-digital converter* (ADC) converts the PAM samples to a serial binary data stream for transmission. The transmission medium is generally a metallic wire pair.

At the receive end, the *digital-to-analog converter* (DAC) converts the serial binary data stream to a multilevel PAM signal. The hold circuit and low-pass filter convert the PAM signal back to its original analog form. An integrated circuit that performs the PCM encoding and decoding is called a *codec* (*co*der/*dec*oder). The codec is explained in detail in Chapter 5.

Sample-and-Hold Circuit

The purpose of the sample-and-hold circuit is to sample periodically the continually changing analog input signal and convert the samples to a series of constant-amplitude PAM levels. For the ADC to accurately convert a signal to a digital code, the signal must be relatively constant. If not, before the ADC can complete the conversion, the input would change. Therefore, the ADC would continually be attempting to following the analog changes and never stabilize on any PCM code.

Figure 4-3 shows the schematic diagram of a sample-and-hold circuit. The FET acts like a simple switch. When turned "on," it provides a low-impedance path to deposit the analog sample across the capacitor C1. The time that Q1 is "on" is called the *aperture* or *acquisition time*. Essentially, C1 is the hold circuit. When Q1 is "off," the capacitor does not have a complete path to discharge through and therefore stores the sampled voltage. The *storage time* of the capacitor is also called the A/D *conversion time* because it is during this time that the ADC converts the sample voltage to a digital code. The acquisition time should be very short. This assures that a minimum change occurs in the analog signal while it is being deposited across C1. If the input to the ADC is changing while it is performing the conversion, distortion results. This distortion is called *aperture distortion*. Thus, by having a short aperture time and keeping the input to the ADC relatively constant, the sample-and-hold circuit reduces aperture distortion. If the analog signal is sampled for a short period of time and the sample voltage is held at a constant amplitude during the A/D conversion time,

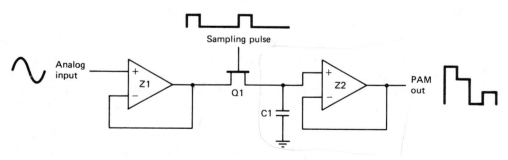

Figure 4-3 Sample-and-hold circuit.

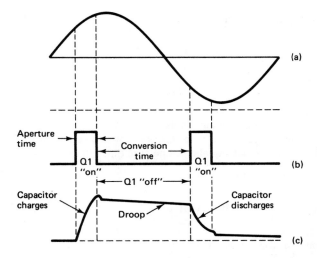

Figure 4-4 Sample-and-hold waveforms: (a) analog in; (b) sample pulse; (c) capacitor voltage.

this is called *flat-top sampling*. If the sample time is made longer and the analog-to-digital conversion takes place with a changing analog signal, this is called *natural sampling*. Natural sampling introduces more aperture distortion than flat-top sampling and requires a faster A/D converter.

Figure 4-4 shows the input analog signal, the sampling pulse, and the waveform developed across C1. It is important that the output impedance of voltage follower Z1 and the "on" resistance of Q1 be as small as possible. This assures that the *RC* charging time constant of the capacitor is kept very short, allowing the capacitor to charge or discharge rapidly during the short acquisition time. The rapid drop in the capacitor voltage immediately following each sample pulse is due to the redistribution of the charge across C1. The interelectrode capacitance between the gate and drain of the FET is placed in series with C1 when the FET is "off," thus acting like a capacitive voltage-divider network. Also, note the gradual discharge across the capacitor during the conversion time. This is called *droop* and is caused by the capacitor discharging through its own leakage resistance and the input impedance of voltage follower Z2. Therefore, it is important that the input impedance of Z2 and the leakage resistance of C1 be as high as possible. Essentially, voltage followers Z1 and Z2 isolate the sample-and-hold circuit (Q1 and C1) from the input and output circuitry.

Example 4-1

For the sample-and-hold circuit shown in Figure 4-3, determine the largest-value capacitor that can be used. Use an output impedance for Z1 of 10 Ω, an "on" resistance for Q1 of 10 Ω, an acquisition time of 10 µs, a maximum peak-to-peak input voltage of 10 V, a maximum output current from Z1 of 10 mA, and an accuracy of 1%.

Solution The expression for the current through a capacitor is

$$i = C\frac{dv}{dt}$$

Rearranging and solving for C yields

$$C = i\frac{dt}{dv}$$

where

C = maximum capacitance
i = maximum output current from Z1, 10 mA
dv = maximum change in voltage across C1, which equals 10 V
dt = charge time, which equals the aperture time, 10 μs

Therefore,

$$C_{max} = \frac{(10\,\text{mA})(10\,\mu\text{s})}{10\,\text{V}} = 10\,\text{nF}$$

The charge time constant for C when Q1 is "on" is

$$\tau = RC$$

where

τ = one charge time constant
R = output impedance of Z1 plus the "on" resistance of Q1
C = capacitance value of C1

Rearranging and solving for C gives us

$$C_{max} = \frac{\tau}{R}$$

The charge time of capacitor C1 is also dependent on the accuracy desired from the device. The percent accuracy and its required RC time constant are summarized as follows:

Accuracy (%)	Charge time
10	3τ
1	4τ
0.1	7τ
0.01	9τ

For an accuracy of 1%,

$$C = \frac{10\,\mu\text{s}}{4(20)} = 125\,\text{nF}$$

To satisfy the output current limitations of Z1, a maximum capacitance of 10 nF was required. To satisfy the accuracy requirements, 125 nF was required. To satisfy both requirements, the smaller-value capacitor must be used. Therefore, C1 can be no larger than 10 nF.

Sampling Rate

The Nyquist sampling theorem establishes the *minimum sampling rate* (f_s) that can be used for a given PCM system. For a sample to be reproduced accurately at the receiver, each cycle of the analog input signal (f_a) must be sampled at least twice. Consequently, the minimum sampling rate is equal to twice the highest audio input frequency. If f_s is less than two times f_a, distortion will result. This distortion is called *aliasing* or *foldover distortion*. Mathematically, the minimum Nyquist sample rate is

$$f_s \geq 2f_a \qquad (4\text{-}1)$$

where

$$f_s = \text{minimum Nyquist sample rate}$$
$$f_a = \text{highest frequency to be sampled}$$

   Essentially, a sample-and-hold circuit is an AM modulator. The switch is a nonlinear device that has two inputs: the sampling pulse and the input analog signal. Consequently, *nonlinear mixing (heterodyning)* occurs between these two signals. Figure 4-5a shows the frequency-domain representation of the output spectrum from a sample-and-hold circuit. The output includes the two original inputs (the audio and the fundamental frequency of the sampling pulse), their sum and difference frequencies ($f_s \pm f_a$), all the harmonics of f_s and f_a ($2f_s$, $2f_a$, $3f_s$, $3f_a$, etc.), and their associated cross products ($2f_s \pm f_a$, $3f_s \pm f_a$, etc.).

   Because the sampling pulse is a repetitive waveform, it is made up of a series of harmonically related sine waves. Each of these sine waves is amplitude modulated by the analog signal and produces sum and difference frequencies symmetrical around each of the harmonics of f_s. Each sum and difference frequency generated is separated from its respective center frequency by f_a. As

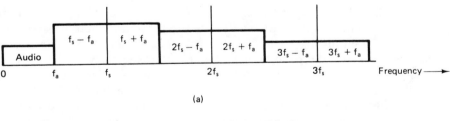

(a)

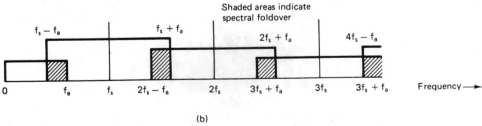

(b)

Figure 4-5 Output spectrum for a sample-and-hold circuit: (a) no aliasing; (b) aliasing distortion.

Pulse Code Modulation   **167**

long as f_s is at least twice f_a, none of the side frequencies from one harmonic will spill into the sidebands of another harmonic and aliasing does not occur. Figure 4-5b shows the results when an analog input frequency greater than $f_s/2$ modulates f_s. The side frequencies from one harmonic foldover into the sideband of another harmonic. The frequency that folds over is an alias of the input signal (hence the names "aliasing" or "foldover distortion"). If an alias side frequency from the first harmonic folds over into the input audio spectrum, it cannot be removed through filtering or any other technique.

Example 4-2

For a PCM system with a maximum audio input frequency of 4 kHz, determine the minimum sample rate and the alias frequency produced if a 5-kHz audio signal were allowed to enter the sample-and-hold circuit.

Solution Using Nyquist's sampling theorem (Equation 4-1), we have

$$f_s \geq 2f_a \qquad \text{therefore, } f_s \geq 8 \text{ kHz}$$

If a 5-kHz audio frequency entered the sample-and-hold circuit, the output spectrum shown in Figure 4-6 is produced. It can be seen that the 5-kHz signal produces an alias frequency of 3 kHz that folds over into the original audio spectrum.

The input bandpass filter shown in Figure 4-2 is called an *antialiasing* or *antifoldover filter*. Its upper cutoff frequency is chosen such that no frequency greater than one-half of the sampling rate is allowed to enter the sample-and-hold circuit, thus eliminating the possibility of foldover distortion occurring.

PCM CODES

With PCM, the analog input signal is sampled, then converted to a serial binary code. The binary code is transmitted to the receiver, where it is converted back to the original analog signal. The binary codes used for PCM are *n*-bit codes, where *n* may be any positive whole number greater than 1. The codes currently used for PCM are *sign-magnitude codes,* where the *most significant bit* (MSB) is the sign bit and the remaining bits are used for magnitude. Table 4-1 shows an *n*-bit PCM code where *n* equals 3. The most significant bit is used to represent the sign of the sample (logic 1 = positive and logic 0 = negative). The two remaining bits represent the magnitude. With 2 magnitude bits, there are four

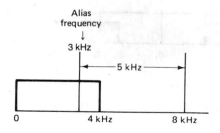

Figure 4-6 Output spectrum for Example 4-2.

TABLE 4-1 3-BIT PCM CODE

Sign	Magnitude		Level	Decimal
1	1	1		+3
1	1	0		+2
1	0	1		+1
1	0	0		+0
0	0	0		−0
0	0	1		−1
0	1	0		−2
0	1	1		−3

codes possible for positive numbers and four possible for negative numbers. Consequently, there is a total of eight possible codes ($2^3 = 8$).

Folded Binary Code

The PCM code shown in Table 4-1 is called a *folded binary code*. Except for the sign bit, the codes on the bottom half of the table are a mirror image of the codes on the top half. (If the negative codes were folded over on top of the positive codes, they would match perfectly.) Also, with folded binary there are two codes assigned to zero volts: 100 ($+0$) and 000 (-0). For this example, the magnitude of the minimum step size is 1 V. Therefore, the maximum voltage that may be encoded with this scheme is $+3$ V (111) or -3 V (011). If the magnitude of a sample exceeds the highest quantization interval, *overload distortion* (also called *peak limiting*) occurs. Assigning PCM codes to absolute magnitudes is called *quantizing*. The magnitude of the minimum step size is called *resolution,* which is equal in magnitude to the voltage of the least significant bit (V_{lsb} or the magnitude of the minimum step size of the DAC). The resolution is the minimum voltage other than 0 V that can be decoded by the DAC at the receiver. The smaller the magnitude of the minimum step size, the better (smaller) the resolution and the more accurately the quantization interval will resemble the actual analog sample.

In Table 4-1, each 3-bit code has a range of input voltages that will be converted to that code. For example, any voltage between $+0.5$ and $+1.5$ will be converted to the code 101. Any voltage between $+1.5$ and $+2.5$ will be encoded as 110. Each code has a *quantization range* equal to $+$ or $-$ one-half the resolution except the codes for $+0$ V and -0 V. The 0-V codes each have an input range equal to only one-half the resolution, but because there are two 0-V codes, the range for 0 V is also $+$ or $-$ one-half the resolution. Consequently, the maximum input voltage to the system is equal to the voltage of the highest magnitude code plus one-half of the voltage of the least significant bit.

Figure 4-7 shows an analog input signal, the sampling pulse, the corresponding PAM signal, and the PCM code. The analog signal is sampled three times. The first sample occurs at time t_1 when the analog voltage is $+2$ V. The PCM

PCM Codes 169

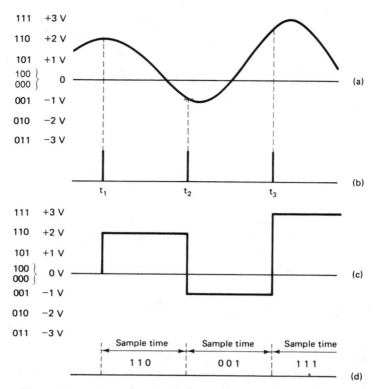

Figure 4-7 (a) Analog input signal; (b) sample pulse; (c) PAM signal; (d) PCM code.

code that corresponds to sample 1 is 110. Sample 2 occurs at time t_2 when the analog voltage is -1 V. The corresponding PCM code is 001. To determine the PCM code for a particular sample, simply divide the voltage of the sample by the resolution, convert it to an n-bit binary code, and add the sign bit to it. For sample 1, the sign bit is 1, indicating a positive voltage. The magnitude code (10) corresponds to a binary 2. Two times 1 V equals 2 V, the magnitude of the sample.

Sample 3 occurs at time t_3. The voltage at this time is $+2.6$ V. The folded PCM code for $+2.6$ V is $2.6/1 = 2.6$. There is no code for this magnitude. If successive approximation ADCs are used, the magnitude of the sample is rounded off to the nearest valid code (111 or $+3$ V for this example). This results in an error when the code is converted back to analog by the DAC at the receive end. This error is called *quantization error* (Qe). The quantization error is equivalent to additive noise (it alters the signal amplitude). Like noise, the quantization error may add to or subtract from the actual signal. Consequently, quantization error is also called *quantization noise* (Qn) and its maximum magnitude is one-half the voltage of the minimum step size ($V_{lsb}/2$). For this example, Qe = 1 V/ 2 or 0.5 V.

Figure 4-8 shows the input-versus-output transfer function for a linear analog-to-digital converter (sometimes called a linear quantizer). As the figure

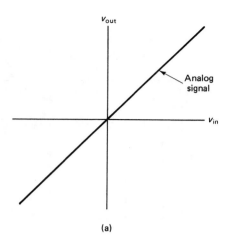

(a)

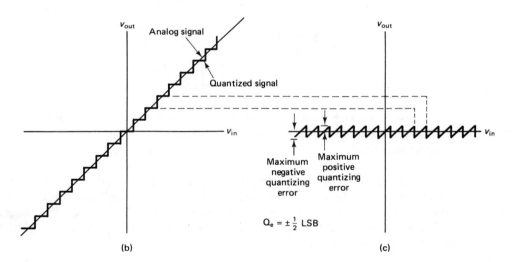

(b)   (c)

Figure 4-8 Linear input-versus-output transfer curve: (a) linear transfer function; (b) quantization; (c) Q_e.

shows for a linear analog input signal (i.e., a ramp), the quantized signal is a staircase. Thus, as shown in Figure 4-8c, the maximum quantization error is the same for any magnitude input signal.

Figure 4-9 shows the same analog input signal used in Figure 4-7 being sampled at a faster rate. As the figure shows, reducing the time between samples (i.e., increasing the sample rate) produces a PAM signal that more closely resembles the original analog input signal. However, it should also be noted that increasing the sample rate does not reduce the quantization error of the samples.

PCM Codes   **171**

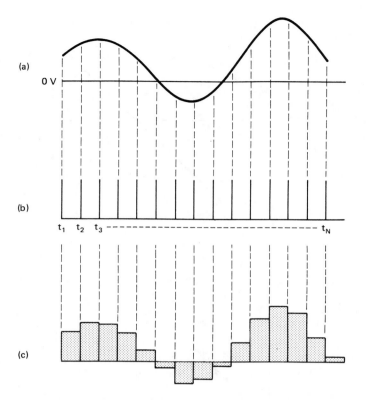

Figure 4-9 PAM: (a) input signal; (b) sample pulse; (c) PAM signal.

Dynamic Range

The number of PCM bits transmitted per sample is determined by several variables, which include maximum allowable input amplitude, resolution, and dynamic range. *Dynamic range* (DR) is the ratio of the largest possible magnitude to the smallest possible magnitude that can be decoded by the DAC. Mathematically, dynamic range is

$$DR = \frac{V_{max}}{V_{min}} \qquad (4\text{-}2a)$$

where V_{min} is equal to the resolution and V_{max} is the maximum voltage magnitude that can be decoded by the DACs. Thus

$$DR = \frac{V_{max}}{\text{resolution}}$$

For the system shown in Table 4-1,

$$DR = \frac{3 \text{ V}}{1 \text{ V}} = 3$$

It is common to represent dynamic range in decibels; therefore,

$$DR = 20 \log \frac{V_{max}}{V_{min}} = 20 \log \frac{3}{1} = 9.54 \text{ dB} \qquad (4\text{-}2b)$$

A dynamic range of 3 indicates that the ratio of the largest to the smallest decoded receive signal is 3.

If a smaller resolution is desired, such as 0.5 V, to maintain a dynamic range of 3, the maximum allowable input voltage must be reduced by the same factor, one-half.

$$DR = \frac{1.5}{0.5} = 3$$

Therefore, V_{max} is reduced by a factor of 2 and the dynamic range is independent of resolution. If the resolution were reduced by a factor of 2 (0.25 V), to maintain the same maximum input amplitude, the dynamic range must double:

$$DR = \frac{1.5}{0.25} = 6$$

The number of bits used for a PCM code depends on the dynamic range. With a 2-bit PCM code, the minimum decodable magnitude has a binary code of 01. The maximum magnitude is 11. The ratio of the maximum binary code to the minimum binary code is 3, the same as the dynamic range. Because the minimum binary code is always 1, DR is simply the maximum binary number for a system. Consequently, to determine the number of bits required for a PCM code the following mathematical relationship is used:

$$2^n - 1 \geq DR$$

and for a minimum value of n,

$$2^n - 1 = DR \qquad (4\text{-}3a)$$

where

$$n = \text{number of PCM bits, excluding sign bit}$$
$$DR = \text{absolute value of Dynamic Range}$$

Why $2^n - 1$? One PCM code is used for 0 V, which is not considered for dynamic range. Therefore,

$$2^n = DR + 1 \qquad (4\text{-}3b)$$

To solve for n, convert to logs:

$$\log 2^n = \log (DR + 1) \qquad (4\text{-}3c)$$
$$n \log 2 = \log (DR + 1)$$
$$n = \frac{\log (3 + 1)}{\log 2} = \frac{0.602}{0.301} = 2$$

For a dynamic range of 3, a PCM code with 2 bits is required.

PCM Codes

Example 4-3

A PCM system has the following parameters: a maximum analog input frequency of 4 kHz, a maximum decoded voltage at the receiver of $\pm 2.55 V_p$, and a minimum dynamic range of 46 dB. Determine the following: minimum sample rate, minimum number of bits used in the PCM code, resolution, and quantization error.

Solution Substituting into Equation 4-1, the minimum sample rate is

$$f_s = 2f_a = 2 \ (4 \text{ kHz}) = 8 \text{ kHz}$$

To determine the absolute value of the dynamic range, substitute into Equation 4-2b:

$$46 \text{ dB} = 20 \log \frac{V_{max}}{V_{min}}$$

$$2.3 = \log \frac{V_{max}}{V_{min}}$$

$$10^{2.3} = \frac{V_{max}}{V_{min}} = \text{DR}$$

$$199.5 = \text{DR}$$

Substitute into Equation 4-3b and solve for n:

$$n = \frac{\log (199.5 + 1)}{\log 2} = 7.63$$

The closest whole number greater than 7.63 is 8; therefore, 8 bits must be used for the magnitude.

Because the input amplitude range is $\pm 2.55 V_p$, one additional bit, the sign bit, is required. Therefore, the total number of PCM bits is 9 and the total number of PCM codes is 2^9 or 512. (There are 255 positive codes, 255 negative codes, and 2 zero codes.)

To determine the actual dynamic range, substitute into Equation 4-3c:

$$\text{DR} = 20 \log 255 = 48.13 \text{ dB}$$

To determine the resolution, divide the maximum + or − magnitude by the number of positive or negative nonzero PCM codes.

$$\text{resolution} = \frac{V_{max}}{2^n - 1}$$

$$= \frac{2.55}{2^8 - 1} = \frac{2.55}{256 - 1} = 0.01 \text{ V}$$

The maximum quantization error is

$$\text{Qe} = \frac{\text{resolution}}{2} = \frac{0.01}{2} = 0.005 \text{ V}$$

Coding Efficiency

Coding efficiency is a numerical indication of how efficiently a PCM code is utilized. Coding efficiency is the ratio of the minimum number of bits required to achieve a certain dynamic range to the actual number of PCM bits used. Mathematically, coding efficiency is

$$\text{coding efficiency} = \frac{\text{minimum number of bits}}{\substack{\text{actual number of bits} \\ \text{(including sign bit)}}} \times 100 \qquad (4\text{-}4)$$

The coding efficiency for Example 4-3 is

$$\text{coding efficiency} = \frac{8.63}{9} \times 100 = 95.89\%$$

Signal-to-Quantization Noise Ratio

The 3-bit PCM coding scheme described in the preceding section is a linear code. That is, the magnitude change between any two successive codes is uniform. Consequently, the magnitude of their quantization error is also equal. The maximum quantization noise is the voltage of the least significant bit divided by 2. Therefore, the worst possible *signal-to-quantization noise ratio* (SQR) occurs when the input signal is at its minimum amplitude (101 or 001). Mathematically, the worst-case SQR is

$$\text{SQR} = \frac{\text{minimum voltage}}{\text{quantization noise}} = \frac{V_{\text{lsb}}}{V_{\text{lsb}}/2} = 2$$

For a maximum amplitude input signal of 3 V (either 111 or 011), the maximum quantization noise is also the voltage of the least significant bit divided by 2. Therefore, the SQR for a maximum input signal condition is

$$\text{SQR} = \frac{\text{maximum voltage}}{\text{quantization noise}} = \frac{V_{\text{max}}}{V_{\text{lsb}}/2} = \frac{3}{0.5} = 6$$

From the preceding example it can be seen that even though the magnitude of error remains constant throughout the entire PCM code, the percentage of error does not; it decreases as the magnitude or the input signal increases. As a result, the SQR is not constant.

The preceding expression for SQR is for voltage and presumes the maximum quantization error and a constant-amplitude analog signal; therefore, it is of little practical use and is shown only for comparison purposes. In reality and as shown in Figure 4-7, the difference between the PAM waveform and the analog input waveform varies in magnitude. Therefore, the signal-to-quantization noise ratio is not constant. Generally, the quantization error or distortion caused by digitizing an analog sample is expressed as an average signal power-to-average noise power ratio. For linear PCM codes (all quantization intervals have equal magnitudes), the signal-to-quantizing noise ratio (also called *signal-to-distortion ratio* or *signal-to-noise ratio*) is determined as follows:

$$\text{SQR (dB)} = 10 \log \frac{v^2/R}{(q^2/12)/R}$$

where

$$R = \text{resistance}$$
$$v = \text{rms signal voltage}$$
$$q = \text{quantization interval}$$
$$\frac{v^2}{R} = \text{rms signal power}$$
$$\frac{q^2/12}{R} = \text{average RMS quantization noise power}$$

If the resistances are assumed to be equal,

$$\text{SQR (dB)} = 10 \log \frac{v^2}{q^2/12} \qquad (4\text{-}5a)$$

$$= 10.8 + 20 \log \frac{v}{q} \qquad (4\text{-}5b)$$

Linear versus Nonlinear PCM Codes

Early PCM systems used *linear codes* (i.e., the magnitude change between any two successive steps is uniform). With linear encoding, the accuracy (resolution) for the higher-amplitude analog signals is the same as for the lower-amplitude signals, and the SQR for the lower-amplitude signals is less than for the higher-amplitude signals. With voice transmission, low-amplitude signals are more likely to occur than large-amplitude signals. Therefore, if there were more codes for the lower amplitudes, it would increase the accuracy where the accuracy is needed. As a result, there would be fewer codes available for the higher amplitudes, which would increase the quantization error for the larger-amplitude signals (thus decreasing the SQR). Such a coding technique is called *nonlinear* or *nonuniform encoding*. With nonlinear encoding, the step size increases with the amplitude of the input signal. Figure 4-10 shows the step outputs from a linear and a nonlinear ADC.

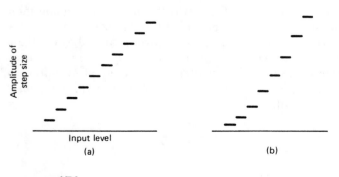

Figure 4-10 (a) Linear versus (b) nonlinear encoding.

Digital Transmission **Chap. 4**

Note, with nonlinear encoding, there are more codes at the bottom of the scale than there are at the top, thus increasing the accuracy for the smaller signals. Also note that the distance between successive codes is greater for the higher-amplitude signals, thus increasing the quantization error and reducing the SQR. Also, because the ratio of V_{max} to V_{min} is increased with nonlinear encoding, the dynamic range is larger than with a uniform code. It is evident that nonlinear encoding is a compromise; SQR is sacrificed for the high-amplitude signals to achieve more accuracy for the low-amplitude signals and to achieve a larger dynamic range.

It is difficult to fabricate nonlinear ADCs; consequently, alternative methods of achieving the same results have been devised.

Idle Channel Noise

During times when there is no analog input signal, the only input to the PAM sampler is random, thermal noise. This noise is called *idle channel noise* and is converted to a PAM sample just as if it were a signal. Consequently, even input noise is quantized by the ADC. Figure 4-11 shows a way to reduce idle channel noise by a method called *midtread quantization*. With midtread quantizing, the first quantization interval is made larger in amplitude than the rest of the steps. Consequently, input noise can be quite large and still be quantized as a positive or negative zero code. As a result, the noise is suppressed during the encoding process.

In the PCM codes described thus far, the lowest-magnitude positive and negative codes have the same voltage range as all the other codes (+ or − one-half the resolution). This is called *midrise quantization*. Figure 4-11 contrasts the idle channel noise transmitted with a midrise PCM code to the idle channel noise transmitted when midtread quantization is used. The advantage of midtread quantization is less idle channel noise. The disadvantage is a larger possible magnitude for Qe in the lowest quantization interval.

With a folded binary PCM code, residual noise that fluctuates slightly above and below 0 V is converted to either a + or − zero PCM code and is consequently

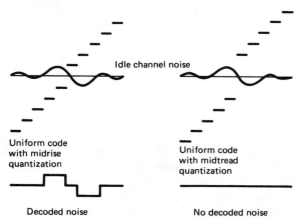

Idle channel noise

Uniform code
with midrise
quantization

Decoded noise

Uniform code
with midtread
quantization

No decoded noise

Figure 4-11   Idle channel noise.

eliminated. In systems that do not use the two 0-V assignments, the residual noise could cause the PCM encoder to alternate between the zero code and the minimum + or − code. Consequently, the decoder would reproduce the encoded noise. With a folded binary code, most of the residual noise is inherently eliminated by the encoder.

Coding Methods

There are several coding methods used to quantize PAM signals into 2^n levels. These methods are classified according to whether the coding operation proceeds a level at a time, a digit at a time, or a word at a time.

Level-at-a-time coding. This type of coding compares the PAM signal to a ramp waveform while a binary counter is being advanced at a uniform rate. When the ramp waveform equals or exceeds the PAM sample, the counter contains the PCM code. This type of coding requires a very fast clock if the number of bits in the PCM code is large. Level-at-a-time coding also requires that 2^n sequential decisions be made for each PCM code generated. Therefore, level-at-a-time coding is generally limited to low-speed applications. Nonuniform coding is achieved by using a nonlinear function as the reference ramp.

Digit-at-a-time coding. This type of coding determines each digit of the PCM code sequentially. Digit-at-a-time coding is analogous to a balance where known reference weights are used to determine an unknown weight. Digit-at-a-time coders provide a compromise between speed and complexity. One common kind of digit-at-a-time coder, called a *feedback coder,* uses a successive approximation register (SAR). With this type of coder, the entire PCM code word is determined simultaneously.

Word-at-a-time coding. Word-at-a-time coders are flash encoders and are more complex; however, they are more suitable for high-speed applications. One common type of word-at-a-time coder uses multiple threshold circuits. Logic circuits sense the highest threshold circuit sensed by the PAM input signal and produce the approximate PCM code. This method is again impractical for large values of n.

Companding

Companding is the process of *compressing,* then *expanding*. With companded systems, the higher-amplitude analog signals are compressed (amplified less than the lower-amplitude signals) prior to transmission, then expanded (amplified more than the smaller-amplitude signals) at the receiver.

Figure 4-12 illustrates the process of companding. An input signal with a dynamic range of 120 dB is compressed to 60 dB for transmission, then expanded

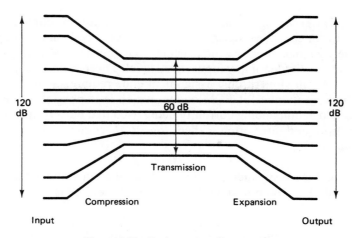

Figure 4-12 Basic companding process.

to 120 dB at the receiver. With PCM, companding may be accomplished through analog or digital techniques. Early PCM systems used analog companding, whereas more modern systems use digital companding.

Analog Companding

Historically, analog compression was implemented using specially designed diodes inserted in the analog signal path in the PCM transmitter prior to the sample-and-hold circuit. Analog expansion was also implemented with diodes that were placed just after the receive low-pass filter. Figure 4-13 shows the basic process of analog companding. In the transmitter, the analog signal is compressed, sampled, then converted to a linear PCM code. In the receiver, the PCM code is converted to a PAM signal, filtered, then expanded back to its original input amplitude characteristics.

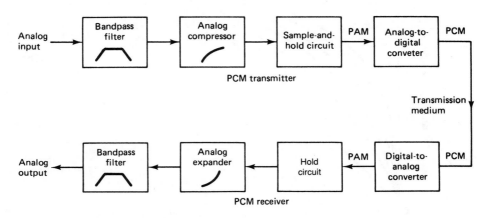

Figure 4-13 PCM system with analog companding.

Different signal distributions require different companding characteristics. For instance, voice signals require relatively constant SQR performance over a wide dynamic range, which means that the distortion must be proportional to signal amplitude for any input signal level. This requires a logarithmic compression ratio. A truly logarithmic assignment code requires an infinite dynamic range and an infinite number of PCM codes, which is impossible. There are two methods of analog companding currently being used that closely approximate a logarithmic function and are often called *log-PCM* codes. They are μ-*law* and *A-law* companding.

μ-Law companding. In the United States and Japan, μ-law companding is used. The compression characteristic for μ-law is

$$V_{out} = \frac{V_{max} \times \ln(1 + \mu V_{in}/V_{max})}{\ln(1 + \mu)} \tag{4-6}$$

where

$$V_{max} = \text{maximum uncompressed analog input amplitude}$$
$$V_{in} = \text{amplitude of the input signal at a particular instant of time}$$
$$\mu = \text{parameter used to define the amount of compression}$$
$$V_{out} = \text{compressed output amplitude}$$

Figure 4-14 shows the compression for several values of μ. Note that the higher the μ, the more compression. Also note that for a $\mu = 0$, the curve is linear (no compression).

The parameter μ determines the range of signal power in which the SQR is relatively constant. Voice transmission requires a minimum dynamic range of 40 dB and a 7-bit PCM code. For a relatively constant SQR and a 40-dB dynamic range, $\mu = 100$ or larger is required. The early Bell System digital transmission

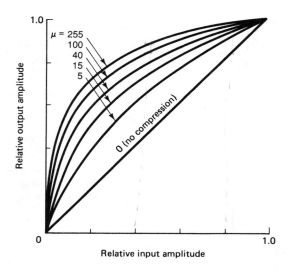

Figure 4-14 μ-Law compression characteristics.

Digital Transmission   Chap. 4

systems used a 7-bit PCM code with $\mu = 100$. The most recent digital transmission systems use 8-bit PCM codes and $\mu = 255$.

Example 4-4

For a compressor with $\mu = 255$, determine the gain for the following values of V_{in}: V_{max}, $0.75\ V_{max}$, $0.5\ V_{max}$, and $0.25\ V_{max}$.

Solution Substituting into Equation 4-6, the following gains are achieved for various input magnitudes:

V_{in}	Gain
V_{max}	1
$0.75V_{max}$	1.26
$0.5V_{max}$	1.75
$0.25V_{max}$	3

It can be seen that as the input signal amplitude increases, the gain decreases or is compressed.

A-Law companding. In Europe, the CCITT has established A-law companding to be used to approximate true logarithmic companding. For an intended dynamic range, A-law companding has a slightly flatter SQR than μ-law. A-law companding, however, is inferior to μ-law in terms of small-signal quality (idle channel noise). The compression characteristic for A-law companding is

$$V_{out} = V_{max}\frac{AV_{in}/V_{max}}{1 + \ln A} \qquad 0 \le \frac{V_{in}}{V_{max}} \le \frac{1}{A} \qquad (4\text{-}7a)$$

$$= V_{max}\frac{1 + \ln(AV_{in}/V_{max})}{1 + \ln A} \qquad \frac{1}{A} \le \frac{V_{in}}{V_{max}} \le 1 \qquad (4\text{-}7b)$$

Digital Companding

Digital companding involves compression at the transmit end after the input sample has been converted to a linear PCM code and expansion at the receive end prior to PCM decoding. Figure 4-15 shows the block diagram of a digitally companded PCM system.

With digital companding, the analog signal is first sampled and converted to a linear code, then the linear code is digitally compressed. At the receive end, the compressed PCM code is received, expanded, then decoded. The most recent digitally compressed PCM systems use a 12-bit linear code and an 8-bit compressed code. This companding process closely resembles a $\mu = 255$ analog compression curve by approximating the curve with a set of eight straight line *segments* (segments 0 through 7). The slope of each successive segment is exactly one-half that of the previous segment. Figure 4-16 shows the 12-bit-to-8-bit digital compression curve for positive values only. The curve for negative values is identical except the inverse. Although there are 16 segments (eight positive and eight negative) this scheme is often called *13-segment compression*. This is

PCM Codes   **181**

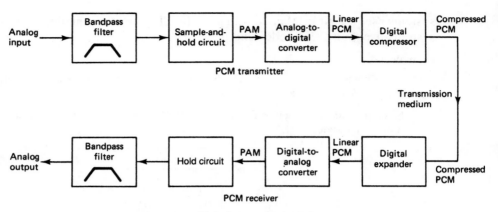

Figure 4-15 Digitally companded PCM system.

because the curve for segments $+0$, $+1$, -0, and -1 is a straight line with a constant slope and is often considered as one segment.

The digital companding algorithm for a 12-bit-linear-to-8-bit-compressed code is actually quite simple. The 8-bit compressed code is comprised of a sign bit, a 3-bit segment identifier, and a 4-bit magnitude code which identifies the *quantization interval* within the specified segment (see Figure 4-17a).

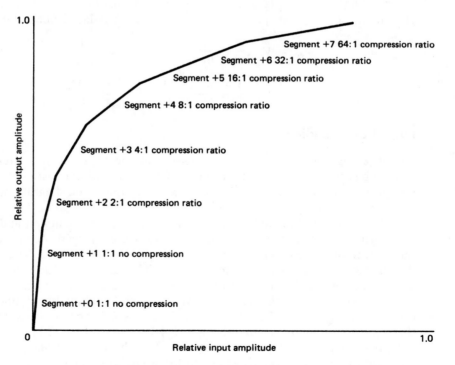

Figure 4-16 $\mu 255$ compression characteristics (positive values only).

Sign bit 1 = + 0 = −	3-Bit segment identifier	4-Bit quantization interval A B C D
	000 to 111	0000 to 1111

(a)

Segment	12-Bit linear code	8-Bit compressed code	8-Bit compressed code	12-Bit recovered code	Segment
0	s0000000ABCD	s000ABCD	s000ABCD	s0000000ABCD	0
1	s0000001ABCD	s001ABCD	s001ABCD	s0000001ABCD	1
2	s000001ABCDX	s010ABCD	s010ABCD	s000001ABCD1	2
3	s00001ABCDXX	s011ABCD	s011ABCD	s00001ABCD10	3
4	s0001ABCDXXX	s100ABCD	s100ABCD	s0001ABCD100	4
5	s001ABCDXXXX	s101ABCD	s101ABCD	s001ABCD1000	5
6	s01ABCDXXXXX	s110ABCD	s110ABCD	s01ABCD10000	6
7	s1ABCDXXXXXX	s111ABCD	s111ABCD	s1ABCD100000	7

(b)   (c)

Figure 4-17 12-bit to 8-bit digital companding: (a) 8-bit μ255 compressed code format; (b) μ255 encoding table; (c) μ255 decoding table.

In the μ255 encoding table shown in Figure 4-17b, the bit positions designated with an X are truncated during compression and are consequently lost. Bits designated A, B, C, and D are transmitted as is. The sign bit (s) is also transmitted as is. Note that for segments 0 and 1, the original 12 bits are duplicated exactly at the output of the decoder (Figure 4-17c), whereas for segment 7, only the most significant 6 bits are recovered. With 11 magnitude bits, there are 2048 possible codes. There are 16 codes in segment 0 and in segment 1. In segment 2, there are 32 codes; segment 3 has 64. Each successive segment beginning with segment 3 has twice as many codes as the previous segment. In each of the eight segments, only sixteen 12-bit codes can be recovered. Consequently, in segments 0 and 1, there is no compression (of the 16 possible codes, all 16 can be recovered). In segment 2, there is a compression ratio of 2:1 (32 possible transmit codes and 16 possible recovered codes). In segment 3, there is a 4:1 compression ratio (64 possible transmit codes and 16 possible recovered codes). The compression ratio doubles with each successive segment. The compression ratio in segment 7 is 2048/16 or 128:1.

The compression process is as follows. The analog signal is sampled and converted to a linear 12-bit sign-magnitude code. The sign bit is transferred directly to the 8-bit code. The segment is determined by counting the number of leading 0's in the 11-bit magnitude portion of the code beginning with the MSB. Subtract the number of leading 0's (not to exceed 7) from 7. The result is the segment number, which is converted to a 3-bit binary number and substituted into the 8-bit code as the segment identifier. The four magnitude bits (A, B, C, and D) are the quantization interval and are substituted into the least significant 4 bits of the 8-bit compressed code.

Segment	12-Bit linear code		12-Bit expanded code	Subsegment
7	s11111111111 .... s11111000000 } 64:1		s11111100000	15
7	s11110111111 .... s11110000000 } 64:1		s11110100000	14
7	s11101111111 .... s11101000000 } 64:1		s11101100000	13
7	s11100111111 .... s11100000000 } 64:1		s11100100000	12
7	s11011111111 .... s11011000000 } 64:1		s11011100000	11
7	s11010111111 .... s11010000000 } 64:1		s11010100000	10
7	s11001111111 .... s11001000000 } 64:1		s11001100000	9
7	s11000111111 .... s11000000000 } 64:1		s11000100000	8
7	s10111111111 .... s10111000000 } 64:1		s10111100000	7
7	s10110111111 .... s10110000000 } 64:1		s10110100000	6
7	s10101111111 .... s10101000000 } 64:1		s10101100000	5
7	s10100111111 .... s10100000000 } 64:1		s10100100000	4
7	s10011111111 .... s10011000000 } 64:1		s10011100000	3
7	s10010111111 .... s10010000000 } 64:1		s10010100000	2
7	s10001111111 .... s10001000000 } 64:1		s10001100000	1
7	s10000111111 .... s10000000000 } 64:1		s10000100000	0
	s1ABCD------			

(a)

Figure 4-18 12-bit segments divided into subsegments: (a) segment 7;

Essentially, segments 2 through 7 are subdivided into smaller subsegments. Each segment has 16 subsegments, which correspond to the 16 conditions possible for the bits A, B, C, and D (0000 – 1111). In segment 2 there are two codes per subsegment. In segment 3 there are four. The number of codes per subsegment doubles with each subsequent segment. Consequently, in segment 7, each subsegment has 64 codes. Figure 4-18 shows the breakdown of segments versus subsegments for segments 2, 5, and 7. Note that in each subsegment, all 12-bit

Segment	12-Bit linear code		12-Bit expanded code	Subsegment
5	s00111111111 .... s00111110000	} 16:1	s00111111000	15
5	s00111101111 .... s00111100000	} 16:1	s00111101000	14
5	s00111011111 .... s00111010000	} 16:1	s00111011000	13
5	s00111001111 .... s00111000000	} 16:1	s00111001000	12
5	s00110111111 .... s00110110000	} 16:1	s00110111000	11
5	s00110101111 .... s00110100000	} 16:1	s00110101000	10
5	s00110011111 .... s00110010000	} 16:1	s00110011000	9
5	s00110001111 .... s00110000000	} 16:1	s00110001000	8
5	s00101111111 .... s00101110000	} 16:1	s00101111000	7
5	s00101101111 .... s00101100000	} 16:1	s00101101000	6
5	s00101011111 .... s00101010000	} 16:1	s00101011000	5
5	s00101001111 .... s00101000000	} 16:1	s00101001000	4
5	s00100111111 .... s00100110000	} 16:1	s00100111000	3
5	s00100101111 .... s00100100000	} 16:1	s00100101000	2
5	s00100011111 .... s00100010000	} 16:1	s00100011000	1
5	s00100001111 .... s00100000000	} 16:1	s00100001000	0
	s001ABCD----			

(b)

(b) segment 5

codes, once compressed and expanded, yield a single 12-bit code. This is shown in Figure 4-18.

From Figures 4-17 and 4-18, it can be seen that the most significant of the truncated bits is reinserted at the decoder as a 1. The remaining truncated bits are reinserted as 0's. This ensures that the maximum magnitude of error introduced by the compression and expansion process is minimized. Essentially, the decoder guesses what the truncated bits were prior to encoding. The most logical guess

Segment	12-Bit linear code			12-Bit expanded code	Subsegment
2	s00000111111 .... s00000111110	}	2:1	s00000111111	15
2	s00000111101 .... s00000111100	}	2:1	s00000111101	14
2	s00000111011 .... s00000111010	}	2:1	s00000111011	13
2	s00000111001 .... s00000111000	}	2:1	s00000111001	12
2	s00000110111 .... s00000110110	}	2:1	s00000110111	11
2	s00000110101 .... s00000110100	}	2:1	s00000110101	10
2	s00000110011 .... s00000110010	}	2:1	s00000110011	9
2	s00000110001 .... s00000110000	}	2:1	s00000110001	8
2	s00000101111 .... s00000101110	}	2:1	s00000101111	7
2	s00000101101 .... s00000101100	}	2:1	s00000101101	6
2	s00000101011 .... s00000101010	}	2:1	s00000101011	5
2	s00000101001 .... s00000101000	}	2:1	s00000101001	4
2	s00000100111 .... s00000100110	}	2:1	s00000100111	3
2	s00000100101 .... s00000100100	}	2:1	s00000100101	2
2	s00000100011 .... s00000100010	}	2:1	s00000100011	1
2	s00000100001 .... s00000100000	}	2:1	s00000100001	0
	s000001ABCD-				

(c)

(c) segment 2.

is halfway between the minimum- and maximum-magnitude codes. For example, in segment 5, the 5 least significant bits are truncated during compression. At the receiver, the decoder must determine what those bits were. The possibilities are any code between 00000 and 11111. The logical guess is 10000, approximately half the maximum magnitude. Consequently, the maximum compression error is slightly more than one-half the magnitude of that segment.

Digital Transmission   Chap. 4

Example 4-5

For a resolution of 0.01 V and analog sample voltages of (a) 0.05 V, (b) 0.32 V, and (c) 10.23 V, determine the 12-bit linear code, the 8-bit compressed code, and the recovered 12-bit code.

Solution (a) To determine the 12-bit linear code for 0.05 V, Simply divide the sample voltage by the resolution and convert the result to a 12-bit sign-magnitude binary number.

12-bit linear code:

$$\frac{0.05\ V}{0.01\ V} = 5 = \begin{matrix} 1\ 0\ 0\ 0\ 0\ 0\ 0\ 0\ 0\ 1\ 0\ 1 \\ s\ \text{------magnitude-----} \end{matrix}$$

$$(11\text{-bit binary number})$$

8-bit compressed code:

```
 1   0   0  0  0  0  0  0  0   1   0   1
 s        (7 - 7 = 0 or 000)  A   B   C   D
 1          0  0  0           0   1   0   1
 ↑
sign bit          unit          quanti-
 (+)            identifier      zation
              (segment 0)       interval
```

12-bit recovered code:

```
 1                   0  0  0           0   1   0   1
 s       (7 - 0 = 7 leading 0's)       A   B   C   D
 1    0    0  0  0  0  0       0        0   1   0   1
 ↑
sign bit      segment identifier       quantization
              determines the             interval
              number of leading
                    0's
```

As you can see, the recovered 12-bit code is exactly the same as the original 12-bit linear code. This is true for all codes in segment 0 and 1. Consequently, there is no compression error in these two segments.

(b) For the 0.32-V sample:

12-bit linear code:

$$\frac{0.32\ V}{0.01\ V} = 32 = \begin{matrix} 1\ 0\ 0\ 0\ 0\ 0\ 1\ 0\ 0\ 0\ 0\ 0 \\ s\ \text{------magnitude-----} \end{matrix}$$

8-bit compressed code:

```
 1   0  0  0  0  0  1   0  0  0  0  0
 s       (7 - 5 = 2 or 010)  A  B  C  D  X
 1         0  1  0           0  0  0  0  ↑
 (+)       (segment 2)              truncated
```

12-bit recovered code:

```
1              0  1  0      0  0  0  0
s  (7 - 2 = 5 leading 0's)  A  B  C  D  X
1  0  0  0  0  0  1         0  0  0  0  1
                 ↑                       ↑
              inserted              inserted
```

Note the two inserted 1's in the decoded 12-bit code. The least significant bit is determined from the decoding table in Figure 4-17. The stuffed 1 in bit position 6 was dropped during the 12-bit-to-8-bit conversion. Transmission of this bit is redundant because if it were not a 1, the sample would not be in segment 3. Consequently, in all segments except 0, a 1 is automatically inserted after the reinserted zeros. For this sample, there is an error in the received voltage equal to the resolution, 0.01 V. In segment 2, for every two 12-bit codes possible, there is only one recovered 12-bit code. Thus a coding compression of 2:1 is realized.

(c) To determine the codes for 10.23 V, the process is the same:

12-bit linear code:

```
1   1 1111    111111
↑
s   ABCD      truncated
```

8-bit compressed code:

```
1     111     1111
↑
s   segment   ABCD
```

12-bit recovered code:

```
1   1   1111    100000
↑   ↑
s   |   ABCD    inserted
  inserted
```

The difference in the original 12-bit linear code and the recovered 12-bit code is

```
  111111111111
- 111111100000
  000000011111  = 31 (0.01 V) = 0.31 V
```

Percentage Error

For comparison purposes, the following formula is used for computing the *percentage of error* introduced by digital compression:

$$\% \text{ error} = \frac{|\text{Tx voltage} - \text{Rx voltage}|}{\text{Rx voltage}} \times 100 \qquad (4\text{-}8)$$

Example 4-6

The maximum percentage of error will occur for the smallest number in the lowest subsegment within any given segment. Because there is no compression error in segments 0 and 1, for segment 3 the maximum % error is computed as follows:

```
Transmit 12-bit code:   s00001000000
Receive 12-bit code:    s00001000010
Magnitude of error:      00000000010
```

$$\% \text{ error } \frac{|1000000 - 1000010|}{1000010} \times 100$$

$$= \frac{|64 - 66|}{66} \times 100 = 3.03\%$$

For segment 7:

```
Transmit 12-bit code:   s10000000000
Receive 12-bit code:    s10000100000
Magnitude of error:      00000100000
```

$$\% \text{ error } = \frac{|10000000000 - 10000100000|}{10000100000} \times 100$$

$$= \frac{|1024 - 1056|}{1056} \times 100 = 3.03\%$$

Although the magnitude of error is higher for segment 7, the percentage of error is the same. The maximum percentage of error is the same for segments 3 through 7, and consequently, the SQR degradation is the same for each segment.

Although there are several ways in which the 12-bit-to-8-bit compression and the 8-bit-to-12-bit expansion can be accomplished with hardware, the simplest and most economical method is with a look-up table in ROM (read-only memory).

Essentially every function performed by a PCM encoder and decoder is now accomplished with a single integrated-circuit chip called a *codec*. Most of the more recently developed codecs include an antialiasing (bandpass) filter, a sample-and-hold circuit, and an analog-to-digital converter in the transmit section and a digital-to-analog converter, a sample-and-hold circuit, and a bandpass filter in the receive section. The operation of a codec is explained in detail in Chapter 5.

Vocoders

The PCM coding and decoding processes described in the preceding sections were concerned primarily with reproducing waveforms as accurately as possible. The precise nature of the waveform was unimportant as long as it occupied the voice band frequency range. When digitizing speech signals only, special voice encoders/decoders called *vocoders* are often used. To achieve acceptable speech communications, the short-term power spectrum of the speech information is all that must be preserved. The human ear is relatively insensitive to the phase relationship between individual frequency components within a voice waveform. Therefore, vocoders are designed to reproduce only the short-term power spectrum, and the decoded time waveforms often only vaguely resemble the original input signal. Vocoders cannot be used in applications where analog signals other than voice are present, such as output signals from voice band data modems. Vocoders typically produce *unnatural* sounding speech and are therefore generally used for recorded information such as "wrong number" messages, encrypted voice for transmission over analog telephone circuits, computer output signals, and educational games.

The purpose of a vocoder is to encode the minimum amount of speech information necessary to reproduce a perceptible message with fewer bits than those needed by a conventional encoder/decoders. Vocoders are used primarily in limited bandwidth applications. Essentially, there are three vocoding techniques available: the *channel vocodor,* the *formant vocoder,* and the *linear predictive coder.*

Channel vocoders.   The first channel vocoder was developed by Homer Dudley in 1928. Dudley's vocoder compressed conventional speech waveforms into an analog signal with a total bandwidth of approximately 300 Hz. Present-day digital vocoders operate at less than 2 kbps. Digital channel vocoders use bandpass filters to separate the speech waveform into narrower *subbands*. Each subband is full-wave rectified, filtered, then digitally encoded. The encoded signal is transmitted to the destination receiver, where it is decoded. Generally speaking, the quality of the signal at the output of a vocoder is quite poor. However, some of the more advanced channel vocoders operate at 2400 bps and can produce a highly intelligible, although slightly synthetic sounding speech.

Formant vocoders.   A formant vocoder takes advantage of the fact that the short-term spectral density of typical speech signals seldom distributes uniformly across the entire voice band spectrum (300 to 3000 Hz). Instead, the spectral power of most speech energy concentrates at three or four peak frequencies called *formants*. A formant vocoder simply determines the location of these peaks and encodes and transmits only the information with the most significant short-term components. Therefore, formant vocoders can operate at lower bit rates and thus require narrower bandwidths. Formant vocoders sometimes have trouble tracking changes in the formants. However, once the formants have been identified, a formant vocoder can transfer intelligible speech at less than 1000 bps.

Linear predictive coders.   A linear predictive coder extracts the most significant portions of speech information directly from the time waveform rather than from the frequency spectra as with the channel and formant vocoders. A linear predictive coder produces a time-varying model of the *vocal tract excitation* and transfer function directly from the speech waveform. At the receive end, a *synthesizer* reproduces the speech by passing the specified excitation through a mathematical model of the vocal tract. Linear predictive coders provide more-natural-sounding speech than does either the channel or formant vocoder. Linear predictive coders typically encode and transmit speech at between 1.2 and 2.4 kbps.

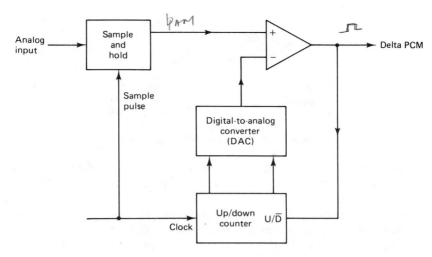

Figure 4-19 Delta modulation transmitter.

DELTA MODULATION PCM

Delta modulation uses a single-bit PCM code to achieve digital transmission of analog signals. With conventional PCM, each code is a binary representation of both the sign and magnitude of a particular sample. Therefore, multiple-bit codes are required to represent the many values that the sample can be. With delta modulation, rather than transmit a coded representation of the sample, only a single bit is transmitted which simply indicates whether that sample is larger or smaller than the previous sample. The algorithm for a delta modulation system is quite simple. If the current sample is smaller than the previous sample, a logic 0 is transmitted. If the current sample is larger than the previous sample, a logic 1 is transmitted.

Delta Modulation Transmitter

Figure 4-19 shows a block diagram of a delta modulation transmitter. The input analog is sampled and converted to a PAM signal which is compared to the output of the DAC. The output of the DAC is a voltage equal to the magnitude of the previous sample, which was stored in the up-down counter as a binary number. The up-down counter is incremented or decremented depending on whether the previous sample is larger or smaller than the current sample. The up-down counter is clocked at a rate equal to the sample rate. Therefore, the up-down counter is updated after each comparison.

Figure 4-20 shows the ideal operation of a delta modulation encoder. Initially, the up-down counter is zeroed and the DAC is outputting 0 V. The first sample is taken, converted to a PAM signal, and compared to zero volts. The output of the comparator is a logic 1 condition ($+$V), indicating that the current sample is larger in amplitude than the previous sample. On the next clock pulse, the up-down counter is incremented to a count of 1. The DAC now outputs a

Delta Modulation PCM   191

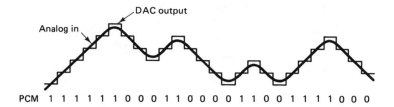

Figure 4-20 Ideal operation of a delta modulation encoder.

voltage equal to the magnitude of the minimum step size (resolution). The steps change value at a rate equal to the clock frequency (sample rate). Consequently, with the input signal shown, the up-down counter follows the input analog signal up until the output of the DAC exceeds the analog sample; then the up-down counter will begin counting down until the output of the DAC drops below the sample amplitude. In the idealized situation (shown in Figure 4-20), the DAC output follows the input signal. Each time the up-down counter is incremented, a logic 1 is transmitted, and each time the up-down counter is decremented, a logic 0 is transmitted.

Delta Modulation Receiver

Figure 4-21 shows the block diagram of a delta modulation receiver. As you can see, the receiver is almost identical to the transmitter except for the comparator. As the logic 1's and 0's are received, the up-down counter is incremented or decremented accordingly. Consequently, the output of the DAC in the decoder is identical to the output of the DAC in the transmitter.

With delta modulation, each sample requires the transmission of only one bit; therefore, the bit rates associated with delta modulation are lower than conventional PCM systems. However, there are two problems associated with delta modulation that do not occur with conventional PCM: slope overload and granular noise.

Slope overload.   Figure 4-22 shows what happens when the analog input signal changes at a faster rate than the DAC can keep up with. The slope of the

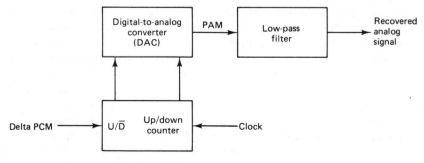

Figure 4-21   Delta modulation receiver.

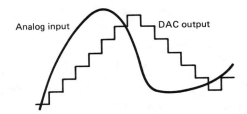

Figure 4-22 Slope overload distortion.

analog signal is greater than the delta modulator can maintain. This is called *slope overload*. Increasing the clock frequency reduces the probability of slope overload occurring. Another way is to increase the magnitude of the minimum step size.

   Granular noise.   Figure 4-23 contrasts the original and reconstructed signals associated with a delta modulation system. It can be seen that when the original analog input signal has a relatively constant amplitude, the reconstructed signal has variations that were not present in the original signal. This is called *granular noise*. Granular noise in delta modulation is analogous to quantization noise in conventional PCM.

   Granular noise can be reduced by decreasing the step size. Therefore, to reduce the granular noise, a small resolution is needed, and to reduce the possibility of slope overload occurring, a large resolution is required. Obviously, a compromise is necessary.

   Granular noise is more prevalent in analog signals that have gradual slopes and whose amplitudes vary only a small amount. Slope overload is more prevalent in analog signals that have steep slopes or whose amplitudes vary rapidly.

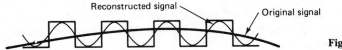

Figure 4-23 Granular noise.

ADAPTIVE DELTA MODULATION PCM

Adaptive delta modulation is a delta modulation system where the step size of the DAC is automatically varied depending on the amplitude characteristics of the analog input signal. Figure 4-24 shows how an adaptive delta modulator works. When the output of the transmitter is a string of consecutive 1's or 0's, this indicates that the slope of the DAC output is less than the slope of the analog signal in either the positive or negative direction. Essentially, the DAC has lost track of exactly where the analog samples are and the possibility of slope overload occurring is high. With an adaptive delta modulator, after a predetermined number of consecutive 1's or 0's, the step size is automatically increased. After the next sample, if the DAC output amplitude is still below the sample amplitude, the

Adaptive Delta Modulation PCM   **193**

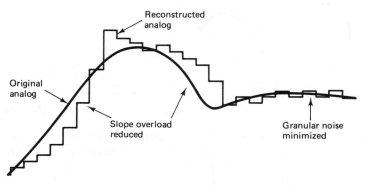

Figure 4-24 Adaptive delta modulation.

next step is increased even further until eventually the DAC catches up with the analog signal. When an alternating sequence of 1's and 0's is occurring, this indicates that the possibility of granular noise occurring is high. Consequently, the DAC will automatically revert to its minimum step size and thus reduce the magnitude of the noise error.

A common algorithm for an adaptive delta modulator is when three consecutive 1's or 0's occur, the step size of the DAC is increased or decreased by a factor of 1.5. Various other algorithms may be used for adaptive delta modulators, depending on particular system requirements.

DIFFERENTIAL PULSE CODE MODULATION

In a typical PCM-encoded speech waveform, there are often successive samples taken in which there is little difference between the amplitudes of the two samples. This facilitates transmitting several identical PCM codes, which is redundant. Differential pulse code modulation (DPCM) is designed specifically to take advantage of the sample-to-sample redundancies in typical speech waveforms. With DPCM, the difference in the amplitude of two successive samples is transmitted rather than the actual sample. Since the range of sample differences is typically less than the range of individual samples, fewer bits are required for DPCM than conventional PCM.

Figure 4-25 shows a simplified block diagram of a DPCM transmitter. The analog input signal is bandlimited to one-half of the sample rate, then compared to the preceding DPCM signal in the differentiator. The output of the differentiator is the difference between the two signals. The difference is PCM encoded and transmitted. The A/D converter operates the same as in a conventional PCM system except that it typically uses fewer bits per sample.

Figure 4-26 shows a simplified block diagram of a DPCM receiver. Each received sample is converted back to analog, stored, and then summed with the next sample received. In the receiver shown in Figure 4-26 the integration is performed on the analog signals, although it could also be performed digitally.

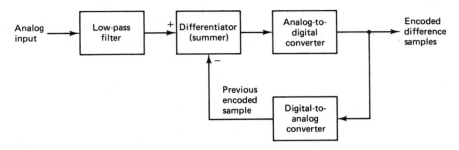

Figure 4-25 DPCM transmitter.

PULSE TRANSMISSION

All digital carrier systems involve the transmission of pulses through a medium with a finite bandwidth. A minimum-bandwidth system would require an infinite number of filter sections, which is impossible. Therefore, practical digital systems generally utilize filters with bandwidths that are approximately 30% or more in excess of the ideal Nyquist bandwidth. Figure 4-27a shows the typical output spectrum from a *bandlimited* communications channel when a narrow pulse is applied to its input. The figure shows that bandlimiting a pulse causes the energy from the pulse to be spread over a significantly wider bandwidth in the form of *secondary lobes*. The secondary lobes are called *ringing tails*. The output frequency spectrum corresponding to a rectangular pulse is referred to as a (sin x)/x response and is given as

$$f(\omega) = (T)\frac{\sin(\omega T/2)}{\omega T/2} \tag{4-9}$$

Figure 4-27b shows the approximate percentage of the total spectrum power at various bandwidths. It can be seen that approximately 90% of the signal energy is contained within the first *spectral null* (i.e., $f = 1/T$). Therefore, the signal can be confined to a bandwidth $B = 1/T$ and still pass most of the energy from the original waveform. In theory, only the amplitude at the middle of each pulse interval needs to be preserved. Therefore, if the bandwidth is confined to $B = 1/2T$, the maximum signaling rate achievable through a low-pass filter with a specified bandwidth without causing excessive distortion is given as the Nyquist rate and is equal to twice the bandwidth. Mathematically, the Nyquist rate is

$$R = 2B \tag{4-10}$$

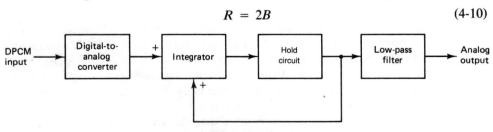

Figure 4-26 DPCM receiver.

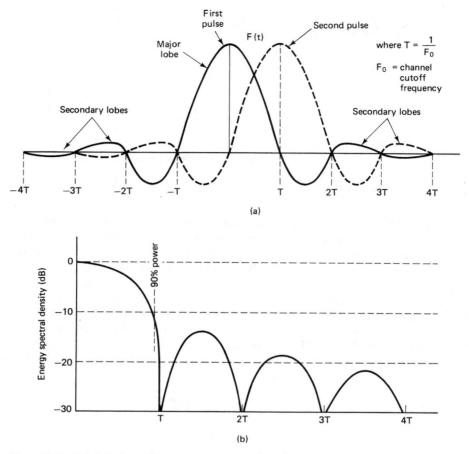

Figure 4-27 Pulse response: (a) typical pulse response of a bandlimited filter; (b) spectrum of square pulse with duration T.

where

$$R = \text{signaling rate} = 1/T$$
$$B = \text{specified bandwidth}$$

Intersymbol Interference

Figure 4-28 shows the input signal to an ideal minimum bandwidth lowpass filter. The input signal is a random, binary non-return-to-zero (NRZ) sequence. Figure 4-28b shows the output of a perfect filter (i.e., a filter that does not introduce any phase or amplitude distortion). Note that the output signal reaches its full value for each transmitted pulse at precisely the center of each sampling interval. However, if the lowpass filter is imperfect (which in reality it will be), the output response will more closely resemble that shown in Figure 4-28c. At the sampling instants (i.e., the center of the pulses), the signal does not always attain the maximum value. The ringing tails of several pulses have *overlapped,* thus interfering with the *major pulse lobe.* Assuming no time delays through the system, energy in the form of spurious responses from the third and fourth impulses from one pulse appears during the sampling instant ($T = 0$) of another pulse. This interference is commonly called *intersymbol interference* or simply *ISI.* ISI is an important consideration in the transmission of pulses over circuits with a limited bandwidth and a nonlinear phase response. Simply stated, rectangular pulses will not remain rectangular in less than an infinite bandwidth. The narrower the bandwidth, the more rounded the pulses. If the phase distortion is excessive, the pulse will *tilt* and, consequently, affect the next pulse. When pulses from more than one source are multiplexed together, the amplitude, frequency, and phase responses become even more critical. ISI causes *crosstalk* between channels that occupy adjacent time slots in a time-division-multiplexed carrier system. Special filters called *equalizers* are inserted in the transmission path to "*equalize*" the distortion for all frequencies, creating a uniform trans-

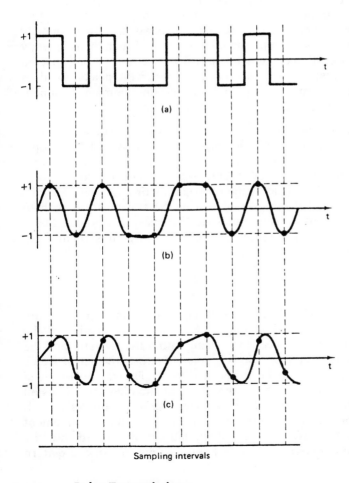

Figure 4-28 Pulse response: (a) NRZ input signal; (b) output from a perfect filter; (c) output from an imperfect filter.

Pulse Transmission 197

mission medium and reducing transmission impairments. The four primary causes of ISI are:

1. *Timing inaccuracies.* In digital transmission systems, transmitter timing inaccuracies cause intersymbol interference if the rate of transmission does not conform to the *ringing frequency* designed into the communications channel. Generally, timing inaccuracies of this type are insignificant. Since receiver clocking information is derived from the received signals, which are contaminated with noise, inaccurate sample timing is more likely to occur in receivers than in transmitters.

2. *Insufficient bandwidth.* Timing errors are less likely to occur if the transmission rate is well below the channel bandwidth (i.e., the Nyquist bandwidth is significantly below the channel bandwidth). As the bandwidth of a communications channel is reduced, the ringing frequency is reduced and intersymbol interference is more likely to occur.

3. *Amplitude distortion.* Filters are placed in a communications channel to bandlimit signals and reduce or eliminate predicted noise and interference. Filters are also used to produce a specific pulse response. However, the frequency response of a channel cannot always be predicted absolutely. When the frequency characteristics of a communications channel depart from the normal or expected values, *pulse distortion* results. Pulse distortion occurs when the peaks of pulses are reduced, causing improper ringing frequencies in the time domain. Compensation for such impairments is called amplitude equalization.

4. *Phase distortion.* A pulse is simply the superposition of a series of harmonically related sine waves with specific amplitude and phase relationships. Therefore, if the relative phase relations of the individual sine waves are altered, phase distortion occurs. Phase distortion occurs when frequency components undergo different amounts of time delay while propagating through the transmission medium. Special delay equalizers are placed in the transmission path to compensate for the varying delays, thus reducing the phase distortion. Phase equalizers can be manually adjusted or designed to automatically adjust themselves to varying transmission characteristics.

Eye Patterns

The performance of a digital transmission system depends, in part, on the ability of a repeater to regenerate the original pulses. Similarly, the quality of the regeneration process depends on the decision circuit within the repeater and the quality of the signal at the input to the decision circuit. Therefore, the performance of a digital transmission system can be measured by displaying the received signal on an oscilloscope and triggering the time base at the data rate. Thus all waveform combinations are superimposed over adjacent signaling intervals. Such a display is called an *eye pattern* or *eye diagram*. An eye pattern is a convenient technique for determining the effects of the degradations introduced into the pulses as they travel to the regenerator. The test setup to display an eye pattern

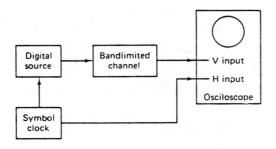

Figure 4-29 Eye diagram measurement setup.

is shown in Figure 4-29. The received pulse stream is fed to the vertical input of the oscilloscope, and the symbol clock is fed to the external trigger input, while the horizontal time base is set approximately equal to the symbol rate.

Figure 4-30 shows an eye pattern generated by a symmetrical waveform for *ternary* signals in which the individual pulses at the input to the regenerator have a cosine-squared shape. In an *m*-level system, there will be *m* − 1 separate eyes. The horizontal lines labeled +1, 0, and −1 correspond to the ideal received amplitudes. The vertical lines, separated by the signaling interval, *T*, correspond to the ideal *decision times*. The decision levels for the regenerator are represented by *crosshairs*. The vertical hair represents the decision time, while the horizontal hair represents the decision level. The eye pattern shows the quality of shaping and timing and discloses any noise and errors that might be present in the line equalization. The eye opening (the area in the middle of the eye pattern) defines a boundary within which no waveform *trajectories* can exist under any code-

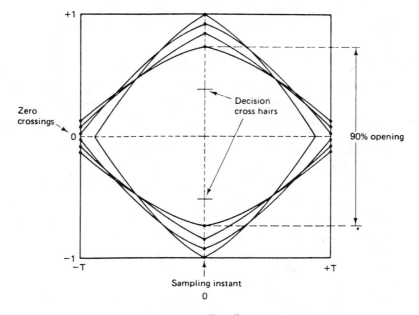

Figure 4-30 Eye diagram.

Pulse Transmission

pattern condition. The eye opening is a function of the number of code levels and the intersymbol interference caused by the ringing tails of any preceding or succeeding pulses. To regenerate the pulse sequence without error, the eye must be open (i.e., a decision area must exist), and the decision crosshairs must be within the open area. The effect of pulse degradation is a reduction in the size of the ideal eye. In Figure 4-30 it can be seen that at the center of the eye (i.e., the sampling instant) the opening is about 90%, indicating only minor ISI degradation due to filtering imperfections. The small degradation is due to the nonideal Nyquist amplitude and phase characteristics of the transmission system. Mathematically, the ISI degradation is

$$20 \log \frac{h}{H} \qquad (4\text{-}11)$$

where

$$H = \text{ideal vertical opening}$$
$$h = \text{degraded vertical opening}$$

For the eye diagram shown in Figure 4-30,

$$20 \log \frac{90}{100} = 0.915 \text{ dB ISI degradation}$$

In Figure 4-30 it can also be seen that the overlapping signal pattern does not cross the horizontal zero line at exact integer multiples of the symbol clock. This is an impairment known as data transition jitter. This jitter has an effect on the symbol timing (clock) recovery circuit and, if excessive, may significantly degrade the performance of cascaded regenerative sections.

QUESTIONS

4-1. Contrast the advantages and disadvantages of digital transmission.

4-2. What are the four most common methods of pulse modulation?

4-3. Which method listed in Question 4-2 is the only form of pulse modulation that is a digital transmission system? Explain.

4-4. What is the purpose of the sample-and-hold circuit?

4-5. Define *aperture* and *acquisition time*.

4-6. What is the difference between natural and flat-top sampling?

4-7. Define *droop*. What causes it?

4-8. What is the Nyquist sampling rate?

4-9. Define and state the causes of foldover distortion.

4-10. Explain the difference between a magnitude-only code and a sign-magnitude code.

4-11. Explain overload distortion.

4-12. Explain quantizing.

4-13. What is quantization range? Quantization error?

4-14. Define *dynamic range*.

4-15. Explain the relationship between dynamic range, resolution, and the number of bits in a PCM code.

4-16. Explain coding efficiency.

4-17. What is SQR? What is the relationship between SQR, resolution, dynamic range, and the number of bits in a PCM code?

4-18. Contrast linear and nonlinear PCM codes.

4-19. Explain idle channel noise.

4-20. Contrast midtread and midrise quantization.

4-21. Define *companding*.

4-22. What does the parameter μ determine?

4-23. Briefly explain the process of digital companding.

4-24. What is the effect of digital compression on SQR, resolution, quantization interval, and quantization noise?

4-25. Contrast delta modulation PCM and standard PCM.

4-26. Define *slope overload* and *granular noise*.

4-27. What is the difference between adaptive delta modulation and conventional delta modulation?

4-28. Contrast differential and conventional PCM.

PROBLEMS

4-1. Determine the Nyquist sample rate for a maximum analog input frequency of (a) 4 kHz, and (b) 10 kHz.

4-2. For the sample-and-hold circuit shown in Figure 4-3, determine the largest-value capacitor that can be used. Use the following parameters: an output impedance for Z1 = 20 Ω, an "on" resistance of Q1 of 20 Ω, an acquisition time of 10 μs, a maximum output current from Z1 of 20 mA, and an accuracy of 1%.

4-3. For a sample rate of 20 kHz, determine the maximum analog input frequency.

4-4. Determine the alias frequency for a 4-kHz sample rate and an analog input frequency of 1.5 kHz.

4-5. Determine the dynamic range for a 10-bit sign-magnitude PCM code.

4-6. Determine the minimum number of bits required in a PCM code for a dynamic range of 80 dB. What is the coding efficiency?

4-7. For a resolution of 0.04 V, determine the voltages for the following linear 7-bit sign-magnitude PCM codes.
  (a) 0110101
  (b) 0000011
  (c) 1000001
  (d) 0111111
  (e) 1000000

4-8. Determine the SQR for a 2-V rms signal and a quantization interval of 0.2 V.

4-9. Determine the resolution and quantization noise for an 8-bit linear sign-magnitude PCM code for a maximum decoded voltage of $1.27V_p$.

4-10. A 12 bit linear PCM code is digitally compressed into 8 bits. The resolution = 0.03 V. Determine the following for an analog input voltage of 1.465 V.

(a) 12-Bit linear PCM code

(b) 8-Bit compressed code

(c) Decoded 12-bit code

(d) Decoded voltage

(e) Percentage error

4-11. For a 12-bit linear PCM code with a resolution of 0.02 V, determine the voltage range that would be converted to the following PCM codes.

(a) 1 0 0 0 0 0 0 0 0 0 0 1

(b) 0 0 0 0 0 0 0 0 0 0 0 0

(c) 1 1 0 0 0 0 0 0 0 0 0 0

(d) 0 1 0 0 0 0 0 0 0 0 0 0

(e) 1 0 0 1 0 0 0 0 0 0 0 1

(f) 1 0 1 0 1 0 1 0 1 0 1 0

4-12. For each of the following 12-bit linear PCM codes, determine the 8-bit compressed code to which they would be converted.

(a) 1 0 0 0 0 0 0 0 1 0 0 0

(b) 1 0 0 0 0 0 0 0 1 0 0 1

(c) 1 0 0 0 0 0 0 1 0 0 0 0

(d) 0 0 0 0 0 0 1 0 0 0 0 0

(e) 0 1 0 0 0 0 0 0 0 0 0 0

(f) 0 1 0 0 0 0 1 0 0 0 0 0

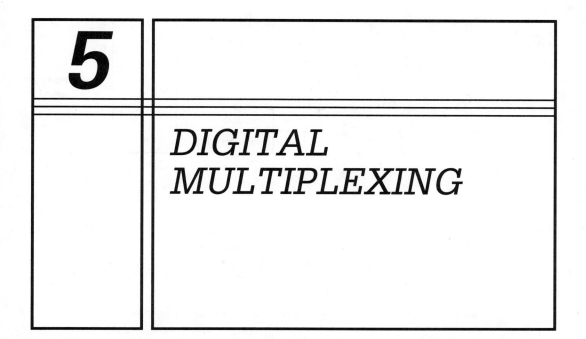

DIGITAL MULTIPLEXING

INTRODUCTION

Multiplexing is the transmission of information (either voice or data) from more than one source to more than one destination on the same transmission medium (*facility*). Transmissions occur on the same facility but not necessarily at the same time. The transmission medium may be a metallic wire pair, a coaxial cable, a microwave radio, a satellite radio, or an optical fiber cable. There are several ways in which multiplexing can be achieved, although the two most common methods are *frequency-division multiplexing* (FDM) and *time-division multiplexing* (TDM). Frequency-division multiplexing is discussed in Chapter 6.

TIME-DIVISION MULTIPLEXING

With TDM, transmissions from multiple sources occur on the same facility but not at the same time. Transmissions from various sources are *interleaved* in the time domain. The most common type of modulation used with TDM systems is PCM. With a PCM-TDM system, two or more voice band channels are sampled, converted to PCM codes, then time-division multiplexed onto a single metallic cable pair or an optical fiber cable.

Figure 5-1a shows a simplified block diagram of a two-channel PCM-TDM carrier system. Each channel is alternately sampled and converted to a PCM code. While the PCM code for channel 1 is being transmitted, channel 2 is sampled and converted to a PCM code. While the PCM code from channel 2 is being transmitted, the next sample is taken from channel 1 and converted to a

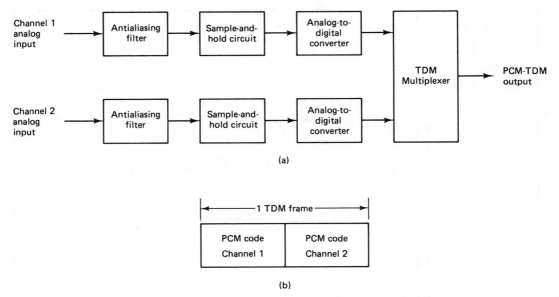

Figure 5-1 Two-channel PCM-TDM system: (a) block diagram; (b) TDM frame.

PCM code. This process continues and samples are taken alternately from each channel, converted to PCM codes, and transmitted. The multiplexer is simply an electronic switch with two inputs and one output. Channel 1 and channel 2 are alternately selected and connected to the multiplexer output. The time is takes to transmit one sample from each channel is called the *frame time*.

The PCM code for each channel occupies a fixed time slot (epoch) within the total TDM frame. With a two-channel system, the time allocated for each channel is equal to one-half of the total frame time. A sample from each channel is taken once during each frame. Therefore, the total frame time is equal to the reciprocal of the sample rate ($1/f_s$). Figure 5-1b shows the TDM frame allocation for a two-channel system.

T1 DIGITAL CARRIER SYSTEM

Figure 5-2 shows the block diagram of the Bell System T1 digital carrier system. This system is the North American telephone standard. A T1 carrier time-division multiplexes 24 PCM encoded samples for transmission over a single metallic wire pair. Again, the multiplexer is simply a switch except that now it has 24 inputs and one output. The 24 voice band channels are sequentially selected and connected to the multiplexer output. Each voice band channel occupies a 300- to 3000-Hz bandwidth.

Simply time-division multiplexing 24 voice band channels does not in itself constitute a T1 carrier. At this point, the output of the multiplexer is simply a multiplexed digital signal (DS-1). It does not actually become a T1 carrier until it is line encoded and placed on special conditioned wire pairs called *T1 lines*.

This is explained in more detail later in this chapter under the heading "North American Digital Hierarchy."

With the Bell System T1 carrier system, D-type (digital) channel banks perform the sampling, encoding, and multiplexing of 24 voice band channels. Each channel contains an 8-bit PCM code and is sampled 8000 times per second. (Each channel is sampled at the same rate but not at the same time; see Figure 5-3.) Therefore, a 64-kbps PCM encoded sample is transmitted for each voice band channel during each frame.

$$\frac{8 \text{ bits}}{\text{sample}} \times \frac{8000 \text{ samples}}{\text{second}} = 64 \text{ kbps}$$

Within each frame an additional bit called a *framing bit* is added. The framing bit occurs at an 8000-bps rate and is recovered in the receiver circuitry and used to maintain frame and sample synchronization between the TDM transmitter and receiver. As a result, each TDM frame contains 193 bits.

$$\frac{8 \text{ bits}}{\text{channel}} \times \frac{24 \text{ channels}}{\text{frame}} = \frac{192 \text{ bits}}{\text{frame}} + \frac{1 \text{ framing bit}}{\text{frame}} = \frac{193 \text{ bits}}{\text{frame}}$$

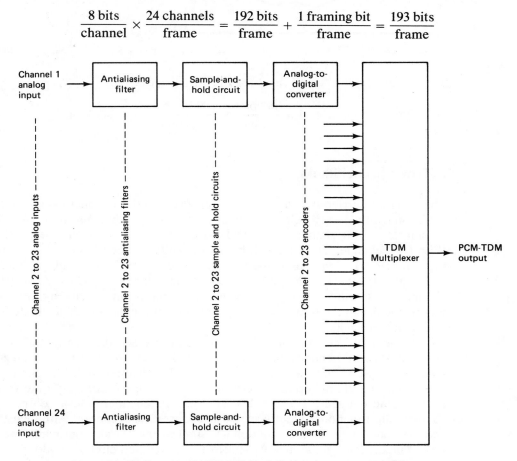

Figure 5-2 Bell system T1 PCM-TDM digital carrier system block diagram.

T1 Digital Carrier System

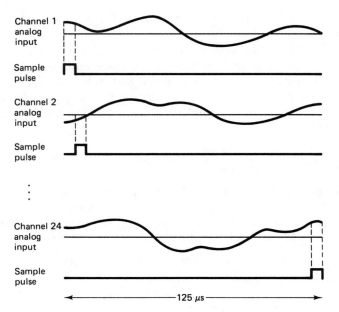

Figure 5-3 T1 sampling sequence.

As a result, the line speed (bps) for the T1 carrier is

$$\text{line speed} = \frac{193\ \text{bits}}{\text{frame}} \times \frac{8000\ \text{frames}}{\text{second}} = 1.544\ \text{Mbps}$$

D-Type Channel Banks

The early T1 carrier systems were equipped with D1A channel banks which use a 7-bit magnitude-only PCM code with analog companding and $\mu = 100$. A later version of the D1 channel bank (D1D) used an 8-bit sign-magnitude PCM code. With D1A channel banks an eighth bit (the s bit) is added to each PCM code for the purpose of *signaling* (supervision: on-hook, off-hook, dial pulsing, etc.) Consequently, the signaling rate for D1 channel banks is 8 kbps. Also, with D1 channel banks, the framing bit sequence is simply an alternating 1/0 pattern. Figure 5-4 shows the frame and sample alignment for the T1 carrier system using D1A channel banks.

Generically, the T1 carrier system has progressed through the D2, D3, D4, and D5. D4 and D5 channel banks use a digitally companded, 8-bit sign-magnitude compressed PCM code with $\mu = 255$. In the D1 channel bank, the compression and expansion characteristics were implemented in circuitry separate from the encoder and decoder. The D2, D3, D4, and D5 channel banks incorporate the companding functions directly in the encoders and decoders. Although the D2 and D3 channel banks are functionally similar, the D3 channel banks were the first to incorporate separate customized LSI integrated circuits (codecs) for each voice band channel. With D1, D2, and D3 channel banks, common equipment

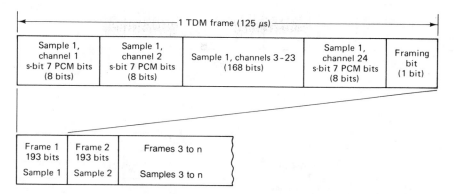

Figure 5-4 T1 carrier system frame and sample alignment using D1 channel banks.

performs the encoding and decoding functions. Consequently, a single equipment malfunction constitutes a total system failure.

D1A channel banks use a magnitude-only code; consequently, an error in the most significant bit (MSB) of a channel sample always produces a decoded error equal to one-half the total quantization range (V_{max}). Because D1D, D2, D3, D4, and D5 channel banks use a sign-magnitude code, an error in the MSB (sign bit) causes a decoded error equal to twice the sample magnitude (from $+V$ to $-V$, or vice versa). The worst-case error is equal to twice the total quantization range. However, maximum amplitude samples occur rarely and most errors with D1D, D2, D3, D4, and D5 coding are less than one-half the coding range. On the average, the error performance with a sign-magnitude code is better than with a magnitude-only code.

Superframe Format

The 8-kbps signaling rate used with D1 channel banks is excessive for voice transmission. Therefore, with D2 and D3 channel banks, a signaling bit is substituted only into the least significant bit (LSB) of every sixth frame. Therefore, five out of every six frames have 8-bit resolution, while one out of every six frames (the signaling frame) has only 7-bit resolution. Consequently, the signaling rate on each channel is 1.333 kbps (8000 bps/6) and the effective number of bits per sample is actually $7\frac{5}{6}$ bits and not 8.

Because only every sixth frame includes a signaling bit, it is necessary that all the frames are numbered so that the receiver knows when to extract the signaling information. Also, because the signaling is accomplished with a 2-bit binary word, it is necessary to identify the MSB and LSB of the signaling word. Consequently, the *superframe* format shown in Figure 5-5 was devised. Within each superframe, there are 12 consecutively numbered frames (1–12). The signaling bits are substituted in frames 6 and 12; the MSB into frame 6 and the LSB into frame 12. Frames 1–6 are called the A-highway with frame 6 designated as the A-channel signaling frame. Frames 7–12 are called the B-highway with frame 12

T1 Digital Carrier System   **207**

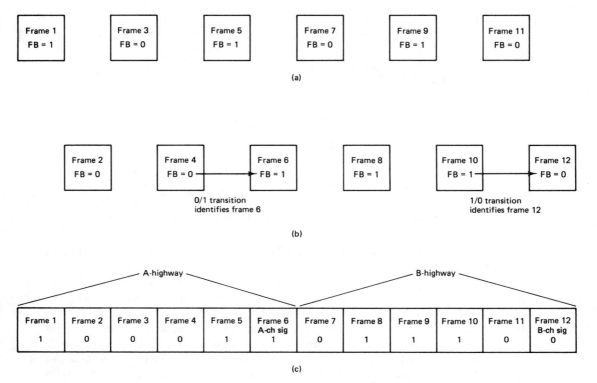

Figure 5-5 Framing bit sequence for the T1 superframe format using D2 or D3 channel banks: (a) frame synchronizing bits (odd-numbered frames); (b) signaling frame alignment bits (even-numbered frames); (c) composite frame alignment.

designated as the B-channel signaling frame. Therefore, in addition to identifying the signaling frames, the sixth and twelfth frames must be positively identified.

To identify frames 6 and 12, a different framing bit sequence is used for the odd- and even-numbered frames. The odd frames (frames 1, 3, 5, 7, 9, and 11) have an alternating 1/0 pattern, and the even frames (frames 2, 4, 6, 8, 10, and 12) have a 0 0 1 1 1 0 repetitive pattern. As a result, the combined bit pattern for the framing bits is a 1 0 0 0 1 1 0 1 1 1 0 0 repetitive pattern. The odd-numbered frames are used for frame and sample synchronization, while the even-numbered frames are used to identify the A and B channel signaling frames (6 and 12). Frame 6 is identified by a 0/1 transition in the framing bit between frames 4 and 6. Frame 12 is identified by a 1/0 transition in the framing bit between frames 10 and 12.

Figure 5-6 shows the frame, sample, and signaling alignment for the T1 carrier system using D2 or D3 channel banks.

In addition to *multiframe alignment* bits and PCM sample bits, certain time slots are used to indicate alarm conditions. For example, in the case of a transmit power supply failure, a common equipment failure, or loss of multiframe alignment; the second bit in each channel is made a 0 until the alarm condition has cleared. Also, the framing bit in frame 12 is complemented whenever multiframe alignment

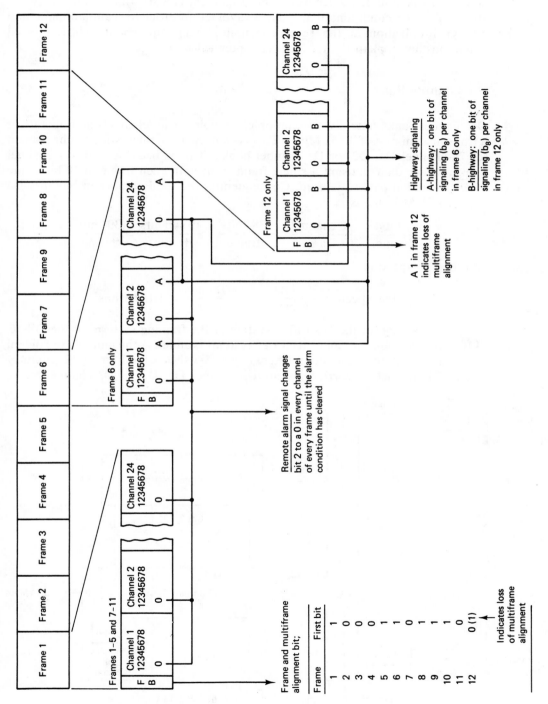

Figure 5-6 T1 carrier frame, sample, and signaling alignment for D2 and D3 channel banks.

is lost (this is assumed whenever frame alignment is lost). In addition, there are special framing conditions that must be avoided in order to maintain clock and bit synchronization at the receive demultiplexing equipment. These special conditions are explained later in this chapter.

D4 Channel Bank

D4 channel banks time-division multiplex 48 voice band channels and operate at a transmission rate of 3.152 Mbps. This is slightly more than twice the line speed for 24-channel D1, D2, or D3 channel banks. This is because with D4 channel banks, rather than transmit a single framing bit with each frame, a 10-bit frame synchronization pattern is used. Consequently, the total number of bits in a D4 (DS-1C) TDM frame is

$$\frac{8 \text{ bits}}{\text{channel}} \times \frac{48 \text{ channels}}{\text{frame}} = \frac{384 \text{ bits}}{\text{frame}} + \frac{10 \text{ syn bits}}{\text{frame}} = \frac{394 \text{ bits}}{\text{frame}}$$

and the line speed is

$$\text{line speed} = \frac{394 \text{ bits}}{\text{frame}} \times \frac{8000 \text{ frames}}{\text{second}} = 3.152 \text{ Mbps}$$

The framing for the DS-1 (T1) system or the framing pattern for the DS-1C (T1C) time-division-multiplexed carrier systems is added to the multiplexed digital signal at the output of the multiplexer. Figure 5-7 shows the framing bit circuitry for the 24-channel T1 carrier system using either D1, D2, or D3 channel banks

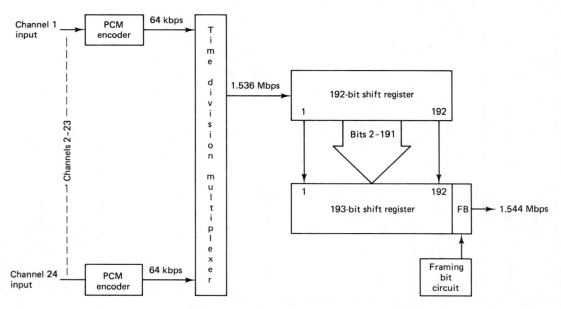

Figure 5-7 Framing bit circuitry for the DS-1 T1 carrier system.

(DS-1). Note that the bit rate at the output of the TDM multiplexer is 1.536 Mbps and the bit rate at the output of the 193-bit shift register is 1.544 Mbps. The difference (8 kbps) is due to the addition of the framing bit in the shift register.

CCITT TIME-DIVISION-MULTIPLEXED CARRIER SYSTEM

Figure 5-8 shows the frame alignment for the CCITT (Comité Consultatif International Téléphonique et Télégraphique) European standard PCM-TDM system. With the CCITT system, an 125-μs frame is divided into 32 equal time slots. Time slot 0 is used for a frame alignment pattern and for an alarm channel. Time slot 17 is used for a common signaling channel. The signaling for all the voice band channels is accomplished on the common signaling channel. Consequently, there are 30 voice band channels time-division multiplexed into each CCITT frame.

Time slot 0	Time slot 1	Time slots 2–16	Time slot 17	Time slots 18–30	Time slot 31
Framing and alarm channel	Voice channel 1	Voice channels 2–15	Common signaling channel	Voice channels 16–29	Voice channel 30
8 bits	8 bits	112 bits	8 bits	112 bits	8 bits

(a)

Time slot 17

	Bits	
Frame	1234	5678
0	0000	xyxx
1	ch 1	ch 16
2	ch 2	ch 17
3	ch 3	ch 18
4	ch 4	ch 19
5	ch 5	ch 20
6	ch 6	ch 21
7	ch 7	ch 22
8	ch 8	ch 23
9	ch 9	ch 24
10	ch 10	ch 25
11	ch 11	ch 26
12	ch 12	ch 27
13	ch 13	ch 28
14	ch 14	ch 29
15	ch 15	ch 30

16 frames equal one multiframe; 500 multiframes are transmitted each second

x = spare
y = loss of multiframe alignment if a 1

4 bits per channel are transmitted once every 16 frames, resulting in a 500-bps signaling rate for each channel

(b)

Figure 5-8 CCITT TDM frame alignment and common signaling channel alignment: (a) CCITT TDM frame (125 μs, 256 bits, 2.048 Mbps); (b) common signaling channel.

With the CCITT standard, each time slot has 8 bits. Consequently, the total number of bits per frame is

$$\frac{8 \text{ bits}}{\text{time slot}} \times \frac{32 \text{ time slots}}{\text{frame}} = \frac{256 \text{ bits}}{\text{frame}}$$

and the line speed is

$$\text{line speed} = \frac{256 \text{ bits}}{\text{frame}} \times \frac{8000 \text{ frames}}{\text{second}} = 2.048 \text{ Mbps}$$

CODECS

A *codec* is a large-scale-integration (LSI) chip designed for use in the telecommunications industry for *p*rivate *b*ranch e*x*changes (PBXs), central office switches, digital handsets, voice store-and-forward systems, and digital echo suppressors. Essentially, the codec is applicable for any purpose that requires the digitizing of analog signals, such as in a PCM-TDM carrier system.

"Codec" is a generic term that refers to the *co*ding functions performed by a device that converts analog signals to digital codes and digital codes to analog signals. Recently developed codecs are called *combo* chips because they combine codec and filter functions in the same LSI package. The input/output filter performs the following functions: bandlimiting, noise rejection, antialiasing, and reconstruction of analog audio waveforms after decoding. The codec performs the following functions: analog sampling, encoding/decoding (analog-to-digital and digital-to-analog conversions), and digital companding.

2913/14 COMBO CHIP

The 2913/14 is a combo chip manufactured by Intel Corp. that can provide the analog-to-digital and the digital-to-analog conversions and the transmit and receive filtering necessary to interface a full-duplex (four-wire) voice telephone circuit to the PCM highway of a TDM carrier system. Essentially, the 2913/14 combo chip replaces the older 2910A/11A codec and 2912A filter chip. The 2913 (20-pin package)/2914 (24-pin package) combo chip is manufactured with HMOS technology. There is a newer CHMOS version (29C13/14) that is functionally identical to the HMOS version except that it comes in a 28-pin package and has three low-power modes of operation. In addition, the 2916/17 and 29C16/17 are 16-pin limited-feature versions of the 2913/14 and 29C13/14. The following discussion is limited to the 2914 combo chip, although extrapolation to the other versions is quite simple.

Table 5-1 lists several of the combo chips available and their prominent features. Table 5-2 lists the pin names for the 2914 and gives a brief description of each of their functions. Figure 5-9 shows the block diagram of a 2914 combo chip.

TABLE 5-1   FEATURES OF SEVERAL CODEC/FILTER COMBO CHIPS

2916 (16-pin)	2917 (16-pin)	2913 (20-pin)	2914 (24-pin)
μ-law companding only	A-law companding only	μ/A-law companding	μ/A-law companding
Master clock 2.048 MHz only	Master clock 2.048 MHz only	Master clock 1.536 MHz, 1.544 MHz, or 2.048 MHz	Master clock 1.536 MHz, 1.544 MHz, or 2.048 MHz
Fixed data rate	Fixed data rate	Fixed data rate	Fixed data rate
Variable data rate 64 kbps–2.048 Mbps	Variable data rate 64 kbps–4.096 Mbps	Variable data rate 64 kbps–4.096 Mbps	Variable data rate 64 kbps–4.096 Mbps
78-dB dynamic	78-dB dynamic range	78-dB dynamic range	78-dB dynamic range
ATT D3/4 compatible	ATT D3/4 compatible	ATT D3/4 compatible	ATT D3/4 compatible.
Single-ended input	Single-ended input	Differential input	Differential input
Single-ended output	Single-ended output	Differential output	Differential output
Gain adjust transmit only	Gain adjust transmit only	Gain adjust transmit and receive	Gain adjust transmit and receive
Synchronous clocks	Synchronous clocks	Synchronous clocks	Synchronous clocks
			Asynchronous clocks
			Analog loopback
			Signaling

General Operation

The following major functions are provided by the 2914 combo chip:

1. Bandpass filtering of the analog signals prior to encoding and after decoding
2. Encoding and decoding of voice and call progress signals
3. Encoding and decoding of signaling and supervision information
4. Digital companding

System Reliability Features

The 2914 combo chip is powered up by pulsing the *transmit frame synchronization input* (FSX) and/or the *receive frame synchronization input* (FSR), while a TTL high (inactive condition) is applied to the *power down select pin* ($\overline{\text{PDN}}$) and all clocks and power supplies are connected. The 2914 has an internal reset on all power-ups (when VBB or VCC are applied or temporarily interrupted). This ensures the validity of the digital output and thereby maintains the integrity of the PCM highway.

On the transmit channel, PCM *data output* (DX) and *transmit timeslot strobe* ($\overline{\text{TSX}}$) are held in a high-impedance state for approximately four frames (500 μs) after power-up. After this delay DX, $\overline{\text{TSX}}$, and signaling are functional

2913/14 Combo Chip   **213**

TABLE 5-2 2914 COMBO CHIP

Symbol	Name	Function
VBB	Power (−5 V)	Negative supply voltage.
PWRO+	Receive power amplifier output	Noninverting output of the receive power amplifier. This output can drive transformer hybrids or high-impedance loads directly in either a differential or single-ended mode.
PWRO−	Receive power amplifier output	Inverting output of the receive power amplifier. Functionally, PWRO− is identical and complementary to PWRO+.
GSR	Receive gain control	Input to the gain-setting network on the receive power amplifier. Transmission level can be adjusted over a 12-dB range depending on the voltage at GSR.
$\overline{\text{PDN}}$	Power-down select	When $\overline{\text{PDN}}$ is a TTL high, the 2914 is active. When PDN is low, the 2914 is powered down.
CLKSEL	Master clock frequency select	Input that must be pinstrapped to reflect the master clock frequency at CLKX, CLKR. CLKSEL = VBB ....2.048 MHz CLKSEL = GRDD ....1.544 MHz CLKSEL = VCC ....1.536 MHz
LOOP	Analog loopback	When this pin is a TTL high, the analog output (PWRO+) is internally connected to the analog input (VFXI+), GSR is internally connected to PWRO−, and VFXI− is internally connected to GSX.
SIGR	Receive signaling bit output	Signaling bit output from the receiver. In the fixed data rate mode only, SIGR outputs the logic state of the eighth bit of the PCM word in the most recent signaling frame.
DCLKR	Receive variable data rate	Selects either the fixed or variable data rate mode of operation. When DCLKR is tied to VBB, the fixed data rate mode is selected. When DCLKR is not connected to VBB, the 2914 operates in the variable data rate mode and will accept TTL input levels from 64 kHz to 4.096 MHz.
DR	Receive PCM highway input	PCM data are clocked in on this lead on eight consecutive negative transitions of the receive data rate clock; CLKR in the fixed data rate mode and DCLKR in the variable data rate mode.
FSR	Receive frame synchronization clock	8-kHz frame synchronization clock input/time slot enable for the receive channel. Also in the fixed data rate mode, this lead designates the signaling and nonsignaling frames. In the variable data rate mode this signal must remain active high for the entire length of the PCM word (8 PCM bits). The receive channel goes into the standby mode whenever this input is TTL low for 300 ms.

GRDD	Digital ground	Digital ground for all internal logic circuits. This pin is not internally tied to GRDA.
CLKR	Receive master clock	Receive master clock and data rate clock in the fixed data rate mode, master clock only in the variable data rate mode.
CLKX	Transmit master clock	Transmit master clock and data rate clock in the fixed data rate mode, master clock only in the variable data rate mode.
FSX	Transmit frame synchronization clock	8-kHz frame synchronization clock input/time slot enable for the transmit channel. Operates independently but in an analogous manner to FSR.
DX	Transmit PCM output	PCM data are clocked out on this lead on eight consecutive positive transitions of the transmit data rate clock; CLKX in the fixed data rate mode and DCLKX in the variable data rate mode.
$\overline{\text{TSX}}$/ DCLKX	Times-slot strobe/ buffer enable Transmit variable data rate	Transmit channel timeslot strobe (output) or data rate clock (input) for the transmit channel. In the fixed data rate mode, this pin is an open drain output designed to be used as an enable signal for a three-state buffer. In variable data rate mode, this pin is the transmit data rate clock input which can operate at data rates between 64 kbps and 4096 kbps.
SIGX/ ASEL	Transmit signaling input μ- or A-law select	A dual-purpose pin. When connected to VBB, A-law companding is selected. When it is not connected to VBL, this pin is a TTL-level input for signaling bits. This input is substituted into the least significant bit position of the PCM word during every signaling frame.
GRDA	Analog ground	Analog ground return for all internal voice circuits. Not internally connected to GRDD.
VFXI+	Noninverting analog input	Noninverting analog input to uncommitted transmit operational amplifier.
VFXI−	Inverting analog input	Inverting analog input to uncommitted transmit operational amplifier.
GSX	Transmit gain control	Output terminal of on-chip uncommitted operational amplifier. Internally, this is the voice signal input to the transmit BPF.
VCC	Power (+5 V)	Positive supply voltage.

and will occur in the proper time slots. Due to the auto-zeroing circuit on the transmit channel, the analog circuit requires approximately 60 ms to reach equilibrium. Therefore, signaling information such as on/off hook detection is available almost immediately while analog input signals are not available until after the 60-ms delay.

On the receive channel, the *signaling bit output pin* SIGR is also held low (inactive) for approximately 500 μs after power-up and remains inactive until updated by reception of a signaling frame.

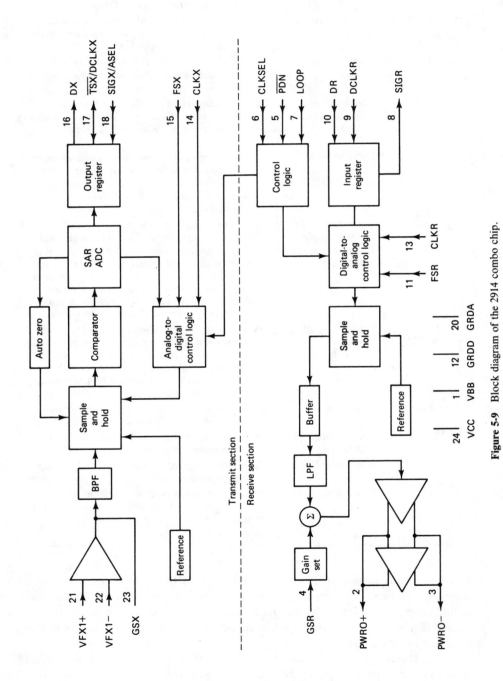

Figure 5-9 Block diagram of the 2914 combo chip.

216

$\overline{\text{TSX}}$ and DX are placed in the high-impedance state and SIGR is held low for approximately 20 μs after an interruption of the *master clock* (CLKX). Such an interruption could be caused by some kind of fault condition.

Power-Down and Standby Modes

To minimize power consumption, two power-down modes are provided in which most 2914 functions are disabled. Only the power-down, clock, and frame synchronization buffers are enabled in these modes.

The power-down is enabled by placing an external TTL low signal on $\overline{\text{PDN}}$. In this mode power consumption is reduced to an average of 5 mW.

The standby mode for the transmit and receive channels is separately controlled by removing FSX and/or FSR.

Fixed-Data-Rate Mode

In the *fixed-data-rate mode,* the master *transmit* and *receive clocks* (CLKX and CLKR) perform the following functions:

1. Provide the master clock for the on-board switched capacitor filter
2. Provide the clock for the analog-to-digital and digital-to-analog converters
3. Determine the input and output data rates between the codec and the PCM highway

Therefore, in the fixed-data-rate mode, the transmit and receive data rates must be either 1.536, 1.544, or 2.048 Mbps, the same as the master clock rate.

Transmit and receive frame synchronizing pulses (FSX and FSR) are 8-kHz inputs which set the transmit and receive sampling rates and distinguish between *signaling* and *nonsignaling* frames. $\overline{\text{TSX}}$ is a *time-slot strobe buffer enable* output which is used to gate the PCM word onto the PCM highway when an external buffer is used to drive the line. $\overline{\text{TSX}}$ is also used as an external gating pulse for a time-division multiplexer (see Figure 5-10).

Data are transmitted to the PCM highway from DX on the first eight positive transitions of CLKX following the rising edge of FSX. On the receive channel, data are received from the PCM highway from DR on the first eight falling edges of CLKR after the occurrence of FSR. Therefore, the occurrence of FSX and FSR must be synchronized between codecs in a multiple-channel system to ensure that only one codec is transmitting to or receiving from the PCM highway at any given time.

Figure 5-10 shows the block diagram and timing sequence for a single-channel PCM system using the 2914 combo chip in the fixed-data-rate mode and operating with a master clock frequency of 1.536 MHz. In the fixed-data-rate mode, data are inputted and outputted in short bursts. (This mode of operation is sometimes called the *burst mode.*) With only a single channel, the PCM highway is active only 1/24 of the total frame time. Additional channels can be

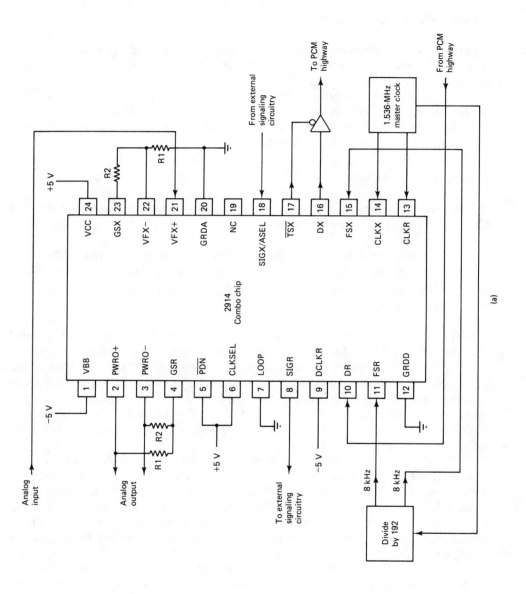

Digital Multiplexing   Chap. 5

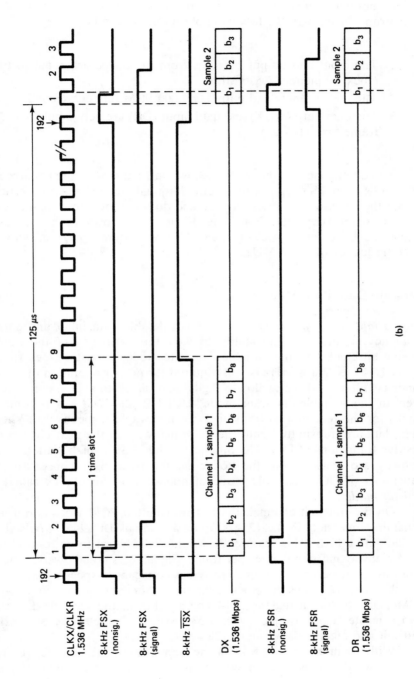

Figure 5-10 Single-channel PCM system using the 2914 combo chip in the fixed-data-rate mode: (a) block diagram; (b) timing sequence.

(b)

2913/14 Combo Chip

219

added to the system provided that their transmissions are synchronized so that they do not occur at the same time as transmissions from any other channel.

From Figure 5-10 the following observations can be made:

1. The input and output bit rates from the codec are equal to the master clock frequency, 1.536 Mbps.
2. The codec inputs and outputs 64,000 PCM bits per second.
3. The data output (DX) and data input (DR) are active only $\frac{1}{24}$ of the total frame time (125 μs).

To add channels to the system shown in Figure 5-10, the occurrence of the FSX, FSR, and $\overline{TSX}$ signals for each additional channel must be synchronized so that they follow a timely sequence and do not allow more than one codec to transmit or receive at the same time. Figure 5-11 shows the block diagram and timing sequence for a 24-channel PCM-TDM system operating with a master clock frequency of 1.536 MHz.

Variable-Data-Rate Mode

The *variable-data-rate mode* allows for a flexible data input and output clock frequency. It provides the ability to vary the frequency of the transmit and receive bit clocks. In the variable data rate mode, a master clock frequency of 1.536, 1.544, or 2.048 MHz is still required for proper operation of the on-board bandpass filters and the analog-to-digital and digital-to-analog converters. However, in the variable-data-rate mode, DCLKR and DCLKX become the data clocks for the receive and transmit PCM highways, respectively. When FSX is high, data are transmitted onto the PCM highway on the next eight consecutive positive transitions of DCLKX. Similarly, while FSR is high, data from the PCM highway are clocked into the codec on the next eight consecutive negative transitions of DCLKR. This mode of operation is sometimes called the *shift register mode*.

On the transmit channel, the last transmitted PCM word is repeated in all remaining time slots in the 125-μs frame as long as DCLKX is pulsed and FSX is held active high. This feature allows the PCM word to be transmitted to the PCM highway more than once per frame. Signaling is not allowed in the variable-data-rate mode because this mode provides no means to specify a signaling frame.

Figure 5-12 shows the block diagram and timing sequence for a two-channel PCM-TDM system using the 2914 combo chip in the variable-data-rate mode with a master clock frequency of 1.536 MHz, a sample rate of 8 kHz, and a transmit and receive data rate of 128 kbps.

With a sample rate of 8 kHz, the frame time is 125 μs. Therefore, one 8-bit PCM word from each channel is transmitted and/or received during each 125-

μs frame. For 16 bits to occur in 125 μs, a 128-kHz transmit and receive data clock is required.

$$\frac{1 \text{ channel}}{8 \text{ bits}} \times \frac{1 \text{ frame}}{2 \text{ channels}} \times \frac{125 \text{ μs}}{\text{frame}} = \frac{125 \text{ μs}}{16 \text{ bits}} = \frac{7.8125 \text{ μs}}{\text{bit}}$$

$$\text{bit rate} = \frac{1}{t_b} = \frac{1}{7.8125 \text{ μs}} = 128 \text{ kbps}$$

The transmit and receive enable signals (FSX and FSR) for each codec are active for one-half of the total frame time. Consequently, 8-kHz, 50% duty cycle transmit and receive data enable signals (FSX and FXR) are fed directly to one codec and fed to the other codec 180° out of phase (inverted), thereby enabling only one codec at a time.

To expand to a four-channel system, simply increase the transmit and receive data clock rates to 256 kHz and change the enable signals to an 8-kHz, 25% duty cycle pulse.

Supervisory Signaling

With the 2914 combo chip, *supervisory signaling* can be used only in the fixed-data-rate mode. A transmit signaling frame is identified by making the FSX and FSR pulses twice their normal width. During a transmit signaling frame, the signal present on input SIGX is substituted into the least significant bit position (b_1) of the encoded PCM word. At the receive end, the signaling bit is extracted from the PCM word prior to decoding and placed on output SIGR until updated by reception of another signaling frame.

Asynchronous operation is when the master transmit and receive clocks are derived from separate independent sources. The 2914 combo chip can be operated in either the synchronous or asynchronous mode. The 2914 has separate digital-to-analog converters and voltage references in the transmit and receive channels, which allows them to be operated completely independent of each other. With either synchronous or asynchronous operation, the master clock, data clock, and time-slot strobe must be synchronized at the beginning of each frame. In the variable data rate mode, CLKX and DCLKX must be synchronized once per frame but may be different frequencies.

Transmit Filter Gain

The analog input to the transmit section of the 2914 is equipped with an uncommitted operational amplifier that can operate in the single-ended or differential mode. Figure 5-13 shows a circuit configuration commonly used to provide input gain. To operate with unity gain, simply strap VFXI− to GSX and apply the analog input to VFXI+.

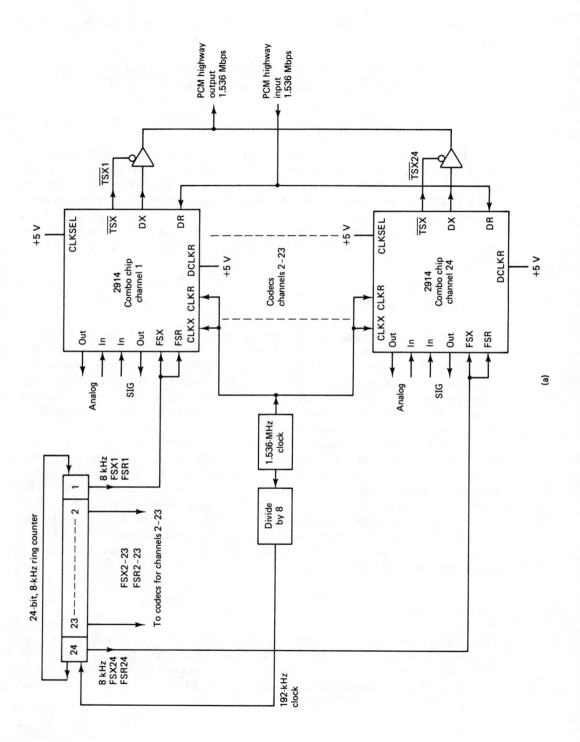

(a)

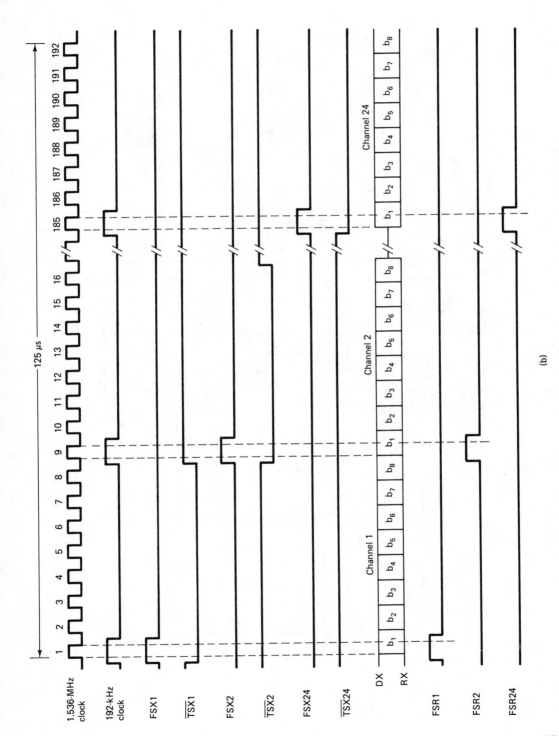

Figure 5-11 24-channel PCM-TDM system using the 2914 combo chip in the fixed-data-rate mode and operating with a master clock frequency of 1.536 MHz: (a) block diagram; (b) timing diagram.

(b)

223

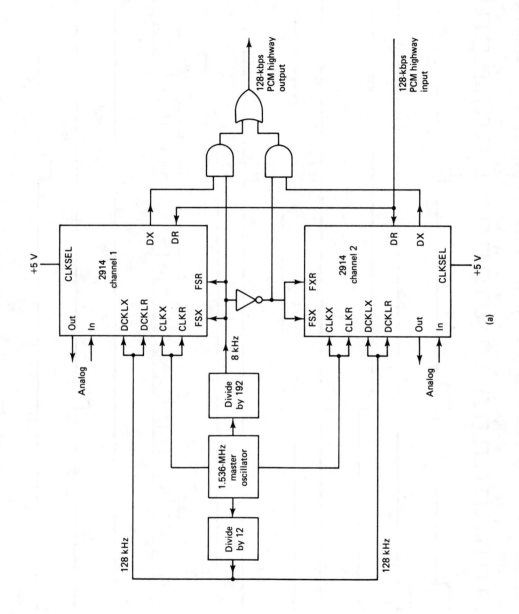

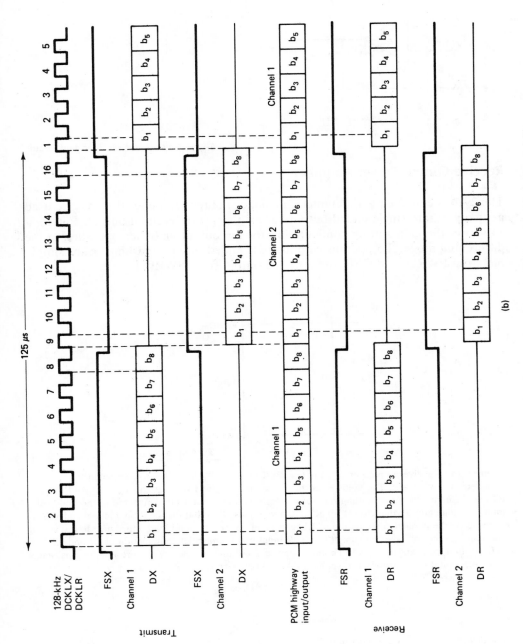

Figure 5-12 Two-channel PCM-TDM system using the 2914 combo chip in the variable-data-rate mode with a master clock frequency of 1.536 MHz: (a) block diagram; (b) timing diagram.

225

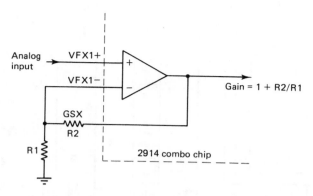

Figure 5-13 Transmit filter gain circuit.

Receive Output Power Amplifier

The 2914 is equipped with an internal balanced output amplifier that may be used as two separate single ended outputs or as a single differential output. Figure 5-14 shows the gain setting configuration for the output amplifier operating in the differential mode. To operate with a single ended output and unity gain, simply pin strap PWRO − to GSR and take the output from PWRO + .

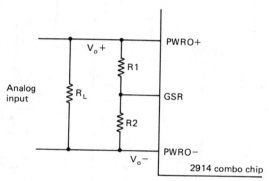

Figure 5-14 Receive output power amplifier. PWRO + and PWRO − are low-impedance complementary outputs. The voltages at the nodes are V_o + at PWRO+ and V_o − at PWRO−. R1 and R2 comprise a gain-setting resistor network with the center tap connected to the GSR input. A value greater than 10 kΩ for R1 and a value less than 100 kΩ for R2 is recommended because (1) the parallel combination of R1 + R2 and RL set the total load impedance to the analog sink, and (2) the total capacitance at the GSR input and the parallel combination of R1 and R2 define a time constant that has to be minimized to avoid inaccuracies. VA represents the maximum available digital miliwatt output response (VA = 3.006 V rms).

$$V_o = -A(VA)$$

where

$$A = \frac{1 + R1/R2}{4 + R1/R2}$$

For design purposes, a useful form is R1/R2 as a function of A.

$$R1/R2 = \frac{4A - 1}{1 - A}$$

Multiplexing signals in digital form lends itself easily to interconnecting digital transmission facilities with different transmission bit rates. Figure 5-15 shows the American Telephone and Telegraph Company's (AT&T) North American Digital Hierarchy for multiplexing digital signals with the same bit rates into a single pulse stream suitable for transmission on the next higher level of the hierarchy. To upgrade from one level in the hierarchy to the next higher level, special devices called *muldems* (*mul*tiplexers/*dem*ultiplexers) are used. Muldems can handle bit-rate conversions in both directions. The muldem designations (M12, M23, etc.) identify the input and output digital signals associated with that muldem. For instance, an M12 muldem is a multiplexer/demultiplexer that interfaces DS-1 and DS-2 *digital signals*. An M23 muldem interfaces DS-2 and DS-3 signals. DS-1 signals may be further multiplexed or line encoded and placed on specially conditioned lines called T1 lines. DS-2, DS-3, DS-4 and DS-5 signals may be placed on T2, T3, T4M, and T5 lines, respectively.

Digital signals are routed at central locations called *digital cross-connects*. A digital cross-connect (DSX) provides a convenient place to make patchable interconnects and to perform routine maintenance and troubleshooting. Each type of digital signal (DS-1, DS-2, etc.) has its own digital switch (DSX-1, DSX-2, etc.). The output from a digital switch may be upgraded to the next higher level or line encoded and placed on its respective T lines (T1, T2, etc.).

Table 5-3 lists the digital signals, their bit rates, channel capacities, and services offered for the line types included in the North American Digital Hierarchy.

When the bandwidth of the signals to be transmitted is such that after digital conversion it occupies the entire capacity of a digital transmission line, a single-channel terminal is provided. Examples of such single-channel terminals are picturephone, mastergroup, and commercial television terminals.

Mastergroup and Commercial Television Terminals

Figure 5-16 shows the block diagram of a mastergroup and commercial television terminal. The mastergroup terminal receives voice band channels that have already been frequency-division multiplexed (a topic covered in Chapter 6) without requiring that each voice band channel be demultiplexed to voice frequencies. The signal processor provides frequency shifting for the mastergroup signal (shifts it from a 564- to 3084-kHz bandwidth to a 0- to 2520-kHz bandwidth) and dc restoration for the television signal. By shifting the mastergroup band, it is possible to sample at a 5.1-MHz rate. Sampling of the commercial television signal is at twice that rate or 10.2 MHz.

To meet the transmission requirements, a 9-bit PCM code is used to digitize each sample of the mastergroup or television signal. The digital output from the terminal is therefore approximately 46 Mbps for the mastergroup and twice that much (92 Mbps) for the television signal.

The digital terminal shown in Figure 5-16 has three specific functions: it

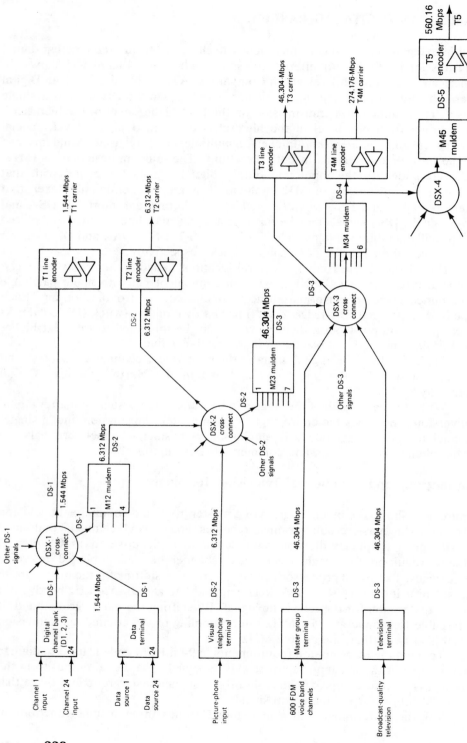

Figure 5-15 North American Digital Hierarchy.

TABLE 5-3 SUMMARY OF THE NORTH AMERICAN DIGITAL HIERARCHY

Line type	Digital signal	Bit rate (Mbps)	Channel capacities	Services offered
T1	DS-1	1.544	24	Voice band telephone
T1C	DS-1C	3.152	48	Voice band telephone
T2	DS-2	6.312	96	Voice band telephone and picturephone
T3	DS-3	46.304	672	Voice band telephone, picturephone, and broadcast-quality television
T4M	DS-4	274.176	4032	Same as T3 except more capacity
T5	DS-5	560.160	8064	Same as T4 except more capacity

converts the parallel data from the output of the encoder to serial data, it inserts frame synchronizing bits, and it converts the serial binary signal to a form more suitable for transmission. In addition, for the commercial television terminal, the 92-Mbps digital signal must be split into two 46-Mbps digital signals because there is no 92-Mbps line speed in the digital hierarchy.

Picturephone Terminal

Essentially, *picturephone* is a low-quality video transmission for use between nondedicated subscribers. For economic reasons it is desirable to encode a picturephone signal into the T2 capacity of 6.312 Mbps, which is substantially less than that for commercial network broadcast signals. This substantially reduces the cost and makes the service affordable. At the same time, this permits the transmission of adequate detail and contrast resolution to satisfy the average

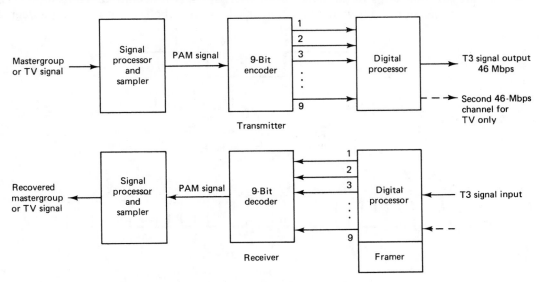

Figure 5-16 Block diagram of a mastergroup or commercial television digital terminal.

picturephone subscriber. Picturephone service is ideally suited to a differential PCM code. Differential PCM is similar to conventional PCM except that the exact magnitude of a sample is not transmitted. Instead, only the difference between that sample and the previous sample is encoded and transmitted. To encode the difference between samples requires substantially fewer bits than encoding the actual sample.

Data Terminal

The portion of communications traffic that involves data (signals other than voice) is increasing exponentially. Also, in most cases, the data rates generated by each individual subscriber are substantially less than the data rate capacities of digital lines. Therefore, it seems only logical that terminals be designed that transmit data signals from several sources over the same digital line.

Data signals could be sampled directly; however this would require excessively high sample rates resulting in excessively high transmission bit rates, especially for sequences of data with few or no transitions. A more efficient method is one that codes the transition times. Such a method is shown in Figure 5-17. With the coding format shown, a 3-bit code is used to identify when transitions occur in the data and whether that transition is from a 1 to a 0, or vice versa. The first bit of the code is called the address bit. When this bit is a logic 1 this indicates that no transition occurred, a logic 0 indicates that a transition did occur. The second bit indicates whether the transition occurred during the first half (0) or during the second half (1) of the sample interval. The third bit indicates the sign or direction of the transition; a 1 for this bit indicates a 0-to-1 transition and a 0 indicates a 1-to-0 transition. Consequently, when there are no transitions in the data, a signal of all 1's is transmitted. Transmission of only the address bit would be sufficient; however, the sign bit provides a degree

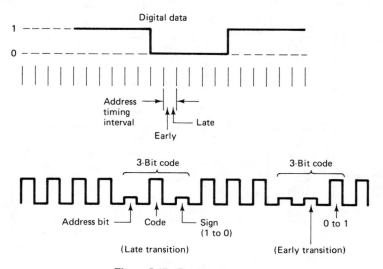

Figure 5-17 Data coding format.

of error protection and limits error propagation (when one error leads to a second error, etc.). The efficiency of this format is approximately 33%; there are 3 code bits for each data bit. The advantage of using a coded format rather than the original data is that coded data are more efficiently substituted for voice in analog systems. To transmit a 250-kbps data signal, the same bandwidth is required to transmit 60 voice channels with analog multiplexing. With this coded format, a 50-kbps data signal displaces three 64-kbps PCM encoded channels, and a 250-kbps data stream displaces only 12 voice band channels.

LINE ENCODING

Line encoding involves converting standard logic levels (TTL, CMOS, etc.) to a form more suitable to telephone line transmission. Essentially, there are four primary factors that must be considered when selecting a line-encoding format:

1. Transmission voltages and dc component
2. Timing (clock) recovery
3. Transmission bandwidth
4. Ease of detection and decoding
5. Error detection

Transmission Voltages and DC Component

Transmission voltages or levels can be categorized as either *unipolar* (UP) or *bipolar* (BP). Unipolar transmission of binary data involves the transmission of only a single nonzero voltage level (e.g., $+V$ for a logic 1 and 0 V or ground for a logic 0). In bipolar transmission, two nonzero voltage levels are involved (e.g., $+V$ for a logic 1 and $-V$ for a logic 0).

Over a digital transmission line, it is more power efficient to encode binary data with voltages that are equal in magnitude but opposite in polarity and symmetrically balanced about 0 V. For example, assuming a 1-Ω resistance and a logic 1 level of $+5$ V and a logic 0 level of 0 V, the average power required is 12.5 W (assuming an equal probability of the occurrence of a 1 or a 0). With a logic 1 level of $+2.5$ V and a logic 0 level of -2.5 V, the average power is only 6.25 W. Thus, by using bipolar symmetrical voltages, the average power is reduced by a factor of 50%.

Duty Cycle

The *duty cycle* of a binary pulse can also be used to categorize the type of transmission. If the binary pulse is maintained for the entire bit time, this is called *nonreturn-to-zero* (NRZ). If the active time of the binary pulse is less than 100% of the bit time, this is called *return-to-zero* (RZ).

Unipolar and bipolar transmission voltages and return-to-zero and nonreturn-to-zero encoding can be combined in several ways to achieve a particular line encoding scheme. Figure 5-18 shows five line-encoding possibilities.

In Figure 5-18a, there is only one nonzero voltage level ($+V$ = logic 1); a zero voltage simply implies a binary 0. Also, each logic 1 maintains the positive voltage for the entire bit time (100% duty cycle). Consequently, Figure 5-18a represents a unipolar nonreturn-to-zero signal (UPNRZ). In Figure 5-18b, there are two nonzero voltages ($+V$ = logic 1 and $-V$ = logic 0) and a 100% duty cycle is used. Figure 5-18b represents a bipolar nonreturn-to-zero signal (BPNRZ). In Figure 5-18c, only one nonzero voltage is used but each pulse is active for only 50% of the bit time. Consequently, Figure 5-18c represents a unipolar return-to-zero signal (UPRZ). In Figure 5-18d, there are two nonzero voltages ($+V$ = logic 1 and $-V$ = logic 0). Also, each pulse is active only 50% of the total bit time. Consequently, Figure 5-18d represents a bipolar return-to-zero (BPRZ) signal. In Figure 5-18e, there are again two nonzero voltage levels ($-V$ and $+V$),

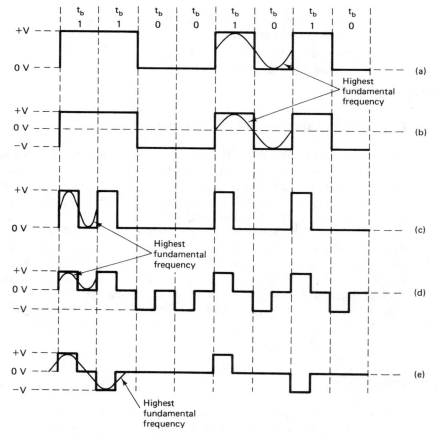

Figure 5-18 Line-encoding formats: (a) UPNRZ; (b) BPNRZ; (c) UPRZ; (d) BPRZ; (e) BPRZ-AMI.

Digital Multiplexing   Chap. 5

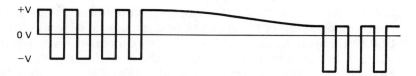

Figure 5-19 Dc wandering.

but here both polarities represent a logic 1 and 0 V represents a logic 0. This method of encoding is called *alternate mark inversion* (AMI). With AMI transmissions, each successive logic 1 is inverted in polarity from the previous logic 1. Because return-to-zero is used, this encoding technique is called *bipolar-return-to-zero alternate mark inversion* (BPRZ-AMI).

With NRZ encoding, a long string of either 1's or 0's produces a condition where a receiver may lose its amplitude reference for optimum discrimination between received 1's and 0's. This condition is called *dc wandering*. The problem may also arise when there is a significant imbalance in the number of ones and zeros transmitted. Figure 5-19 shows how dc wandering is produced by a long string of successive logic 1's. From the figure it can be seen that after a long string of 1's, 1-to-0 errors are more likely than 0-to-1 errors. Similarly, long strings of 0's increase the probability of a 0-to-1 error.

The method of line encoding used determines the minimum bandwidth required for transmission, how easily a clock may be extracted from it, how easily it may be decoded, the average dc level, and whether it offers a convenient means of detecting errors.

Bandwidth Considerations

To determine the minimum bandwidth required to propagate a line-encoded signal, you must determine the highest fundamental frequency associated with it (see Figure 5-18). The highest fundamental frequency is determined from the worst-case (fastest transition) binary bit sequence. With UPNRZ, the worst-case condition is an alternating 1/0 sequence; the highest fundamental frequency takes the time of 2 bits and is therefore equal to one-half the bit rate. With BPNRZ, again the worst-case condition is an alternating 1/0 sequence and the highest fundamental frequency is one-half of the bit rate. With UPRZ, the worst-case condition is two successive 1's. The minimum bandwidth is therefore equal to the bit rate. With BPRZ, the worst-case condition is either successive 1's or 0's and the minimum bandwidth is again equal to the bit rate. With BPRZ-AMI, the worst-case condition is two or more consecutive 1's, and the minimum bandwidth is equal to one-half of the bit rate.

Clock Recovery

To recover and maintain clocking information from received data, there must be a sufficient number of transitions in the data signal. With UPNRZ and BPNRZ, a long string of consecutive 1's or 0's generates a data signal void of transitions and is therefore inadequate for clock synchronization. With UPRZ and BPRZ-AMI, a long string of 0's also generates a data signal void of transitions. With BPRZ, a transition occurs in each bit position regardless of whether the bit is a 1 or a 0. In the clock recovery circuit, the data are simply full-wave rectified to produce a data-independent clock equal to the receive bit rate. Therefore, BPRZ encoding is best suited for clock recovery. If long sequences of 0's are prevented from occurring, BPRZ-AMI encoding is sufficient to ensure clock synchronization.

Error Detection

With UPNRZ, BPNRZ, UPRZ, and BPRZ transmissions, there is no way to determine if the received data have errors. With BPRZ-AMI transmissions, an error in any bit will cause a bipolar violation (the reception of two or more consecutive 1's with the same polarity). Therefore, BPRZ-AMI has a built-in error detection mechanism.

Ease of Detection and Decoding

Because unipolar transmission involves the transmission of only one polarity voltage, there is an average dc voltage associated with the signal equal to $+V/2$. Assuming an equal probability of 1's and 0's occurring, bipolar transmissions have an average dc component of 0 V. A dc component is undesirable because it biases the input to a conventional threshold detector (a biased comparator) and could cause a misinterpretation of the logic condition of the received pulses. Therefore, bipolar transmission is better suited to data detection.

Table 5-4 summarizes the minimum bandwidth, average dc voltage, clock recovery, and error detection capabilities of the line-encoding formats shown in Figure 5-18. From Table 5-4 it can be seen that BPRZ-AMI encoding has the best overall characteristics and is therefore the most commonly used method.

Digital Biphase

Digital *biphase* (sometimes called the *Manchester code* or *diphase*) is a popular type of line encoding that produces a strong timing component for clock recovery and does not cause dc wandering. Biphase is a form of BPRZ transmission that

TABLE 5-4 LINE-ENCODING SUMMARY

Encoding format	Minimum BW	Average DC	Clock recovery	Error detection
UPNRZ	$f_b/2$[a]	$+V/2$	Poor	No
BPNRZ	$f_b/2$[a]	0 V[a]	Poor	No
UPRZ	f_b	$+V/2$	Good	No
BPRZ	f_b	0 V[a]	Best[a]	No
BPRZ-AMI	$f_b/2$[a]	0 V[a]	Good	Yes[a]

[a] Denotes best performance or quality.

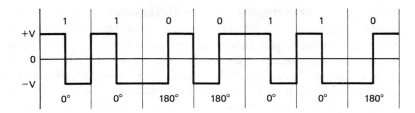

Figure 5-20 Digital biphase.

uses one cycle of a square wave at 0° phase to represent a logic 1 and one cycle of a square wave at 180° phase to represent a logic 0. Digital biphase encoding is shown in Figure 5-20. Notice that a transition occurs in the center of every signaling element, regardless of its phase. Thus biphase produces a strong timing component for clock recovery. In addition, assuming an equal probability of 1's and 0's, the average dc voltage is 0 V and there is no dc wandering. A disadvantage of biphase is that it contains no means of error detection.

T CARRIERS

T carriers involve the transmission of PCM-encoded time-division-multiplexed digital signals. In addition, T carriers utilize special line-encoded signals and metallic cables that have been conditioned to meet the relatively high bandwidths required for high-speed digital transmissions. Digital signals deteriorate as they propagate along a cable due to power loss in the metallic conductors and the low-pass filtering inherent in parallel wire transmission lines. Consequently, *regenerative repeaters* must be placed at periodic intervals. The distance between repeaters is dependent on the transmission bit rate and the line-encoding technique used.

Figure 5-21 shows the block diagram of a regenerative repeater. Essentially, there are three functional blocks: an amplifier-equalizer, a timing circuit, and the regenerator. The amplifier-equalizer shapes the incoming digital signal and raises

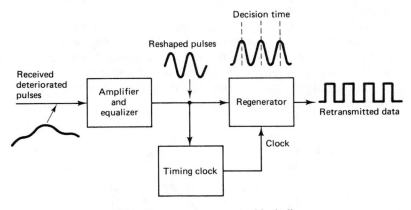

Figure 5-21 Regenerative repeater block diagram.

their power level so that a pulse/no pulse decision can be made by the regenerator circuit. The timing circuit recovers the clocking information from the received data and provides the proper timing information to the regenerator so that decisions can be made at the optimum time which minimizes the chance of an error occurring. Spacing of the repeaters is designed to maintain an adequate signal-to-noise ratio for error-free performance. The signal-to-noise ratio (S/N) at the output of a regenerator is exactly what it was at the output of the transmit terminal or at the output of the previous regenerator (i.e., the S/N does not deteriorate as a digital signal propagates through a regenerator; in fact, a regenerator reconstructs the original pulses and produces the original S/N ratio).

T1 and T1C Carrier Systems

The T1 carrier system utilizes PCM and TDM techniques to provide short-haul transmission of 24 voice band signals. The lengths of T1 carrier systems range from about 5 to 50 miles. T1 carriers use BPRZ-AMI encoding with regenerative repeaters placed every 6000 ft; 6000 ft was chosen because telephone company manholes are located at approximately 6000-ft intervals and these same manholes are used for placement of the repeaters, facilitating convenient installation, maintenance, and repair. The transmission medium for T1 carriers is either a 19- or 22-gauge wire pair.

Because T1 carriers use BPRZ-AMI encoding, they are susceptible to losing synchronization on a long string of consecutive 0's. With a folded binary PCM code, the possibility of generating a long string of consecutive 0's is high (whenever a channel is idle it generates a ±0-V code which is either seven or eight consecutive 0's). If two or more adjacent voice channels are idle, there is a high probability that a long string of consecutive 0's will be transmitted. To reduce this possibility, the PCM code is inverted prior to transmission and inverted again at the receiver prior to decoding. Consequently, the only time a long string of consecutive 0's is transmitted is when two or more adjacent voice band channels each encode the maximum possible positive sample voltage, which is unlikely to happen.

With T1 and T1C carrier systems, provisions are taken to prevent more than 14 consecutive 0's from occurring. The transmissions from each frame are monitored for the presence of either 15 consecutive 0's or any one PCM sample (8 bits) without at least one nonzero bit. If either of these conditions occurs, a 1 is substituted into the appropriate bit position. The worst-case conditions are as follows:

```
                     MSB      LSB MSB      LSB
     Original        1000 0000    0000 0001    14 consecutive 0's
     DS-1 signal                               (no substitution)

                     MSB      LSB MSB      LSB
     Original        1000 0000    0000 0000    15 consecutive 0's
     DS-1 signal
```

```
Substituted      1000 0000    0000 0010
DS-1 signal                        ↑
                              Substituted
                                  bit
```

A 1 is substituted into the second least significant bit. This introduces an encoding error equal to twice the amplitude resolution. This bit is selected rather than the least significance bit because, with the superframe format, during every sixth frame the LSB is the signaling bit and to alter it would alter the signaling word.

```
                 MSB      LSB MSB      LSB MSB      LSB
Original         1010 1000    0000 0000    0000 0001
DS-1 signal

Substituted      1010 1000    0000 0010    0000 0001
DS-1 signal                        ↑
                              Substituted
                                  bit
```

The process shown is used for T1 and T1C carrier systems. Also, if at any time 32 consecutive 0's are received, it is assumed that the system is not generating pulses and is therefore out of service; this is because the occurrence of 32 consecutive 0's is prohibited.

T2 Carrier System

The T2 carrier utilizes PCM to time-division multiplex 96 voice band channels into a single 6.312-Mbps data signal for transmission up to 500 miles over a special LOCAP (low capacitance) cable. A T2 carrier is also used to carry a single picturephone signal. T2 carriers also use BPRZ-AMI encoding. However, because of the higher transmission rate, clock synchronization becomes more critical. A sequence of six consecutive 0's could be sufficient to cause loss of clock synchronization. Therefore, T2 carrier systems use an alternative method of ensuring that ample transitions occur in the data. This method is called *binary six zero substitution* (B6ZS).

With B6ZS, whenever six consecutives 0's occur, one of the following codes is substituted in its place: $0 - + 0 + -$ or $0 + - 0 - +$. The $+$ and $-$ represent positive and negative logic 1's. A zero simply indicates a logic 0 condition. The 6-bit code substituted for the six 0's is selected to purposely cause a bipolar violation. If the violation is caught at the receiver and the B6ZS code is detected, the original six 0's can be substituted back into the data signal. The substituted patterns cause a bipolar violation in the second and fifth bits of the substituted pattern. If DS-2 signals are multiplexed to form DS-3 signals, the B6ZS code must be detected and stripped from the DS-2 signal prior to DS-3 multiplexing. An example of B6ZS is as follows:

```
                 MSB       LSB MSB       LSB MSB
Original         +000  −0+0    000−  0000    000+ ⋯
data signal
                                   └──────────┘
                                      6 0's
```

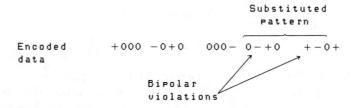

T3 Carrier System

A T3 carrier time-division multiplexes 672, PCM-encoded voice channels for transmission over a single metallic cable. The transmission rate for T3 signals is 44.736 Mbps. The encoding technique used with T3 carriers is *binary three zero substitution* (B3ZS). Substitutions are made for any occurrence of three consecutive 0's. There are four substitution patterns used: $00-$, $-0-$, $00+$, and $+0+$. The pattern chosen should cause a bipolar error in the third substitute bit. An example is as follows:

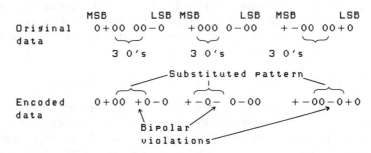

T4M Carrier System

A T4M carrier time-division multiplexes 4032 PCM-encoded voice band channels for transmission over a single coaxial cable up to 500 miles. The transmission rate is sufficiently high that substitute patterns are impractical. Instead, T4M-carriers transmit scrambled unipolar NRZ digital signals where the scrambling and descrambling functions are performed in the subscriber's terminal equipment.

T5 Carrier System

A T5 carrier system time-division multiplexes 8064 PCM-encoded voice band channels and transmits them at a 560.16-Mbps rate over a single coaxial cable.

FRAME SYNCHRONIZATION

With TDM systems it is imperative that a frame is identified and that individual time slots (samples) within the frame are also identified. To acquire frame synchronization, there is a certain amount of overhead that must be added to the

Digital Multiplexing   Chap. 5

transmission. There are five methods commonly used to establish frame synchronization: added digit framing, robbed digit framing, added channel framing, statistical framing, and unique line signal framing.

Added Digit Framing

T1 carriers using D1 or D2, or D3 channel banks use *added digit framing*. There is a special *framing digit* (Framing pulse) added to each frame. Consequently, for an 8-kHz sample rate (125-μs frame), there are 8000 digits added per second. With T1 carriers, an alternating 1/0 frame synchronizing pattern is used.

To acquire frame synchronization, the receive terminal searches through the incoming data until it finds the alternating 1/0 sequence used for the framing bit pattern. This encompasses testing a bit, counting off 193 bits, then testing again for the opposite condition. This process continues until an alternating 1/0 sequence is found. Initial frame synchronization is dependent on the total frame time, the number of bits per frame, and the period of each bit. Searching through all possible bit positions requires N tests, where N is the number of bit positions in the frame. On the average, the receiving terminal dwells at a false framing position for two frame periods during a search; therefore, the maximum average synchronization time is

$$\text{synchronization time} = 2NT = 2N^2t$$

where

$$T = \text{frame period of } Nt$$
$$N = \text{number of bits per frame}$$
$$t = \text{bit time}$$

For the T1 carrier, $N = 193$, $T = 125$ μs, and $t = 0.648$ μs; therefore, a maximum of 74,498 bits must be tested and the maximum average synchronization time is 48.25 ms.

Robbed Digit Framing

When a short frame time is used, added digit framing is very inefficient. This occurs in single-channel PCM systems such as those used in television terminals. An alternative solution is to replace the least significant bit of every nth frame with a framing bit. The parameter n is chosen as a compromise between reframe time and signal impairment. For $n = 10$, the SQR is impaired by only 1 dB. *Robbed digit framing* does not interrupt transmission, but instead, periodically replaces information bits with forced data errors to maintain clock synchronization. B6ZS and B3ZS are examples of systems that use robbed digit framing.

Added Channel Framing

Essentially, *added channel framing* is the same as added digit framing except that digits are added in groups or words instead of as individual bits. The CCITT multiplexing scheme previously discussed uses added channel framing. One of the 32 time slots in each frame is dedicated to a unique synchronizing sequence. The average frame synchronization time for added channel framing is

$$\text{synchronization time (bits)} = \frac{N^2}{2(2^L - 1)}$$

where

N = number of bits per frame
L = number of bits in the frame code

For the CCITT 32-channel system, $N = 256$ and $L = 8$. Therefore, the average number of bits needed to acquire frame synchronization is 128.5. At 2.048 Mbps, the synchronization time is approximately 62.7 μs.

Statistical Framing

With *statistical framing,* it is not necessary to either rob or add digits. With the Gray code, the second bit is a 1 in the central half of the code range and 0 at the extremes. Therefore, a signal that has a centrally peaked amplitude distribution generates a high probability of a 1 in the second digit. A mastergroup signal has such a distribution. With a mastergroup encoder, the probability that the second bit will be a 1 is 95%. For any other bit it is less than 50%. Therefore, the second bit can be used for a framing bit.

Unique Line Code Framing

With *unique line code framing,* the framing bit is different from the information bits. It is either made higher or lower in amplitude or of a different time duration. The earliest PCM/TDM systems used unique line code framing. D1 channel banks used framing pulses that were twice the amplitude of normal data bits. With unique line code framing, added digit or added word framing can be used with it or data bits can be used to simultaneously convey information and carry synchronizing signals. The advantage of unique line code framing is synchronization is immediate and automatic. The disadvantage is the additional processing requirements required to generate and recognize the unique framing bit.

BIT INTERLEAVING VERSUS WORD INTERLEAVING

When time-division multiplexing two or more PCM systems, it is necessary to interleave the transmissions from the various terminals in the time domain. Figure 5-22 shows two methods of interleaving PCM transmissions: *bit interleaving* and *word interleaving.*

T1 carrier systems use word interleaving; 8-bit samples from each channel are interleaved into a single 24-channel TDM frame. Higher-speed TDM systems and delta modulation systems use bit interleaving. The decision as to which type

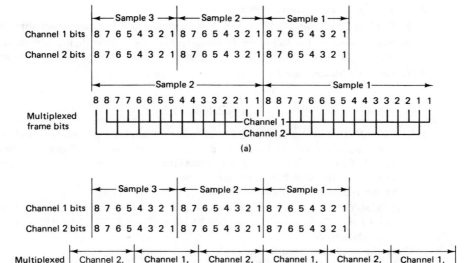

Figure 5-22 Interleaving: (a) bit; (b) word.

of interleaving to use is usually determined by the nature of the signals to be multiplexed.

QUESTIONS

5-1. Define *multiplexing*.

5-2. Describe time-division multiplexing.

5-3. Describe the Bell System T1 carrier system.

5-4. What is the purpose of the signaling bit?

5-5. What is frame synchronization? How is it achieved in a PCM/TDM system?

5-6. Describe the superframe format. Why is it used?

5-7. What is a codec? A combo chip?

5-8. What is a fixed-data-rate mode?

5-9. What is a variable-data-rate mode?

5-10. What is a DSX? What is it used for?

5-11. Explain *line coding*.

5-12. Briefly explain unipolar and bipolar transmission.

5-13. Briefly explain return-to-zero and nonreturn-to-zero transmission.

5-14. Contrast the bandwidth considerations of return-to-zero and nonreturn-to-zero transmission.

5-15. Contrast the clock recovery capabilities with return-to-zero and nonreturn-to-zero transmission.

5-16. Contrast the error detection and decoding capabilities of return-to-zero and nonreturn-to-zero transmission.

5-17. What is a regenerative repeater?

5-18. Explain B6ZS and B3ZS. When or why would you use one rather than the other?

5-19. Briefly explain the following framing techniques: added digit framing, robbed digit framing, added channel framing, statistical framing, and unique line code framing.

5-20. Contrast bit and word interleaving.

PROBLEMS

5-1. A PCM/TDM system multiplexes 24 voice band channels. Each sample is encoded into 7 bits and a framing bit is added to each frame. The sampling rate if 9000 samples/second. BPRZ-AMI encoding is the line format. Determine
   (a) the line speed in bits per second, and,
   (b) the minimum Nyquist bandwidth.

5-2. A PCM/TDM system multiplexes 32 voice band channels each with a bandwidth of 0 to 4 kHz. Each sample is encoded with an 8-bit PCM code. UPNRZ encoding is used. Determine
   (a) the minimum sample rate,
   (b) the line speed in bits per second, and
   (c) the minimum Nyquist bandwidth.

5-3. For the following bit sequence, draw the timing diagram for UPRZ, UPNRZ, BPRZ, BPNRZ, and BPRZ-AMI encoding:

bit stream: 1 1 1 0 0 1 0 1 0 1 1 0 0

5-4. Encode the following BPRZ-AMI data stream with B6ZS and B3ZS.

+ − 0 0 0 0 + − + 0 − 0 0 0 0 0 + − 0 0 + − + 0

6

FREQUENCY-DIVISION MULTIPLEXING

INTRODUCTION

In *frequency-division multiplexing* (FDM), multiple sources that originally occupied the same frequency spectrum are each converted to a different frequency band and transmitted simultaneously over a single transmission medium. Thus many relatively narrowband channels can be transmitted over a single wideband transmission system.

FDM is an analog multiplexing scheme; the information entering an FDM system is analog and it remains analog throughout transmission. An example of FDM is the AM commercial broadcast band, which occupies a frequency spectrum from 535 to 1605 kHz. Each station carries an intelligence signal with a bandwidth of 0 to 5 kHz. If the audio from each station were transmitted with their original frequency spectrum, it would be impossible to separate one station from another. Instead, each station amplitude modulates a different carrier frequency and produces a 10-kHz double-sideband signal. Because adjacent stations' carrier frequencies are separated by 10 kHz, the total commercial AM band is divided into 107 10-kHz frequency slots stacked next to each other in the frequency domain. To receive a particular station, a receiver is simply tuned to the frequency band associated with that station's transmissions. Figure 6-1 shows how commercial AM broadcast station signals are frequency-division multiplexed and transmitted over a single transmission medium (free space).

There are many other applications for FDM such as commercial FM and television broadcasting and high-volume telecommunications systems. Within any of the commercial broadcast bands, each station's transmissions are independent

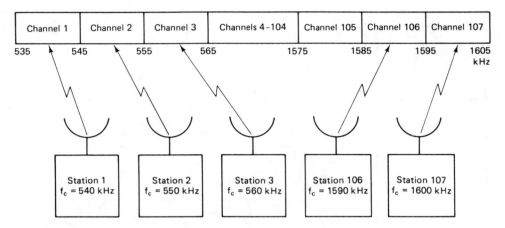

Figure 6-1 Frequency-division-multiplexing commercial AM broadcast band stations.

of all the other stations' transmissions. Consequently, the multiplexing (stacking) process is accomplished without any synchronization between stations. With a high-volume telephone communication system, many voice band telephone channels may originate from a common source and terminate in a common destination. The source and destination terminal equipment is most likely a high-capacity *electronic switching system* (ESS). Because of the possibility of a large number of narrowband channels originating and terminating at the same location, all multiplexing and demultiplexing operations must be synchronized.

AT&T's FDM HIERARCHY

Although AT&T is no longer the only long-distance common carrier in the United States, they still provide a vast majority of the long-distance services and if for no other reason than their overwhelming size, have essentially become the standards organization for the telephone industry in North America.

AT&T's nationwide communications network is subdivided into two classifications: *short haul* (short distance) and *long haul* (long distance). The T1 carrier explained in Chapter 5 is an example of a short-haul communications system.

Long-Haul Communications with FDM

Figure 6-2 shows AT&T's North American FDM Hierarchy for long-haul communications. Only a transmit terminal is shown, although a complete set of inverse functions must be performed at the receiving terminal.

Message Channel

The *message channel* is the basic building block of the FDM hierarchy. The basic message channel was originally intended for voice transmission, although it now includes any transmissions that utilize voice band frequencies (0 to 4 kHz) such as voice band data circuits. The basic voice band (VB) circuit is called a 3002 channel and is actually bandlimited to a 300- to 3000-Hz band, although for practical considerations, it is considered a 4-kHz channel. The basic 3002 channel can be subdivided into 24 narrower 3001 (telegraph) channels that have been frequency-division multiplexed to form a single 3002 channel.

Basic Group

A *group* is the next higher level in the FDM hierarchy above the basic message channel and is, consequently, the first multiplexing step for the message channels. A basic group is comprised of 12 voice band channels stacked on top of each other in the frequency domain. The 12-channel modulating block is called an *A-type* (analog) channel bank. The 12-channel *group* output of the A-type channel bank is the standard building block for most long-haul *broadband* communications systems. Additions and deletions in total system capacity are accomplished with a minimum of one group (12 VB channels). The A-type channel bank has generically progressed from the early A1 channel bank to the most recent A6 channel bank.

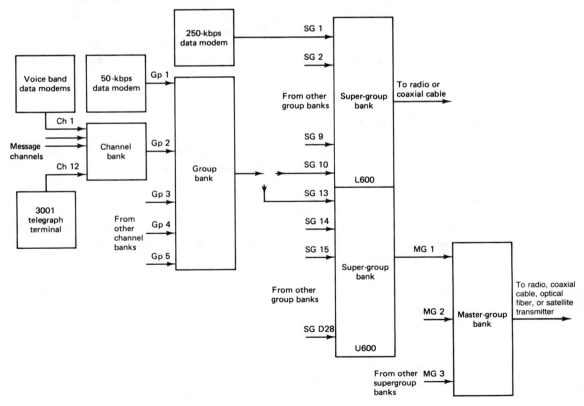

Figure 6-2 AT&T's long-haul FDM hierarchy.

Basic Supergroup

The next higher level in the FDM hierarchy shown in Figure 6-2 is the combination of five groups into a *supergroup*. The multiplexing of five groups is accomplished in a group bank. A single supergroup can carry information from 60 VB channels or handle high-speed data up to 250 kbps.

Basic Mastergroup

The next higher level in the FDM hierarchy is the basic *mastergroup*. A mastergroup is comprised of 10 supergroups (10 supergroups of five groups each = 600 VB channels). Supergroups are combined in supergroup banks to form mastergroups. There are two categories of mastergroups (U600 and L600) which occupy different frequency bands. The type of mastergroup used depends on the system capacity and whether the transmission medium is a coaxial cable, a microwave radio, an optical fiber, or a satellite trunsponder.

Larger Groupings

Master groups can be further multiplexed in mastergroup banks to form *jumbogroups, multi-jumbogroups,* and *superjumbogroups*. A basic FDM/FM microwave radio channel carries three mastergroups (1800 VB channels), a jumbogroup has 3600 VB channels, and a superjumbogroup has three jumbogroups (10,800 VB channels).

COMPOSITE BASEBAND SIGNAL

Baseband describes the modulating signal (intelligence) in a communications system. A single message channel is baseband. A group, supergroup, or master-group is also baseband. The composite baseband signal is the total intelligence signal prior to modulation of the final carrier. In Figure 6-2 the output of a channel bank is baseband. Also, the output of a group or supergroup bank is baseband. The final output of the FDM multiplexer is the *composite* (total) baseband. The formation of the composite baseband signal can include channel, group, super-group, and mastergroup banks, depending on the capacity of the system.

Formation of a Group

Figure 6-3a shows how a group is formed with an A-type channel bank. Each voice band channel is bandlimited with an antialiasing filter prior to modulating the channel carrier. FDM uses single-sideband suppressed carrier (SSBSC) modulation. The combination of the balanced modulator and the bandpass filter make up the SSBSC modulator. A balanced modulator is a double-sideband suppressed carrier modulator and the bandpass filter is tuned to the difference between the carrier and the input voice band frequencies (LSB). The ideal input

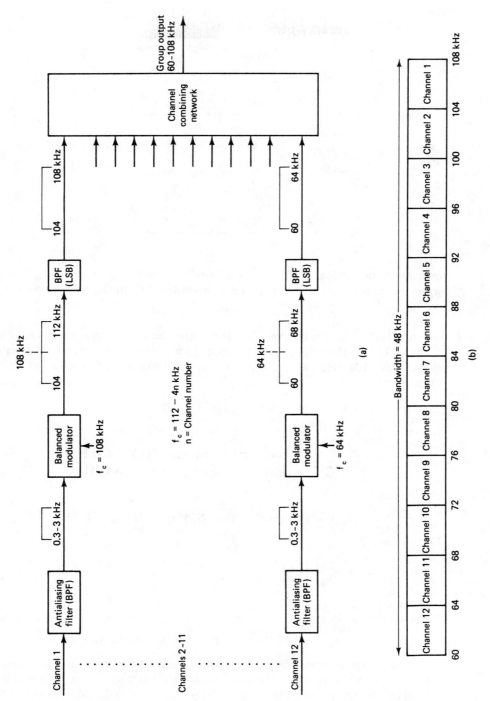

$f_c = 112 - 4n$ kHz
n = Channel number

(a)

Bandwidth = 48 kHz

(b)

Figure 6-3 Formation of a group: (a) A-type channel bank block diagram; (b) output spectrum.

247

TABLE 6-1   CHANNEL CARRIER FREQUENCIES

Channel	Carrier frequency (kHz)
1	108
2	104
3	100
4	96
5	92
6	88
7	84
8	80
9	76
10	72
11	68
12	64

frequency range for a single voice band channel is 0 to 4 kHz. The carrier frequencies for the channel banks are determined from the following expression:

$$f_c = 112 - 4n \text{ kHz}$$

where n is the channel number. Table 6-1 lists the carrier frequencies for channels 1 through 12. Therefore, for channel 1, a 0- to 4-kHz band of frequencies modulates a 108-kHz carrier. Mathematically, the output of the channel 1 bandpass filter is

$$f_{\text{out}} = f_c - f_i$$

where

f_c = channel carrier frequency $(112 - 4n \text{ kHz})$

f_i = channel frequency spectrum (0 to 4 kHz)

For channel 1:

$$f_{\text{out}} = 108 \text{ kHz} - (0 \text{ to } 4 \text{ kHz}) = 104 \text{ to } 108 \text{ kHz}$$

For channel 2:

$$f_{\text{out}} = 104 \text{ kHz} - (0 \text{ to } 4 \text{ kHz}) = 100 \text{ to } 104 \text{ kHz}$$

For channel 12:

$$f_{\text{out}} = 64 \text{ kHz} - (0 \text{ to } 4 \text{ kHz}) = 60 \text{ to } 64 \text{ kHz}$$

The outputs from the 12 A-type channel modulators are summed in the *linear* combiner to produce the total group spectrum shown in Figure 6-3b (60 to 108 kHz). Note that the total group bandwidth is equal to 48 kHz (12 channels × 4 kHz).

Formation of a Supergroup

Figure 6-4a shows how a supergroup is formed with a group bank and combining network. Five groups are combined to form a supergroup. The frequency spectrum for each group is 60 to 108 kHz. Each group is mixed with a different group carrier frequency in a balanced modulator then bandlimited with a bandpass filter tuned to the difference frequency band (LSB) to produce a SSBSC signal. The group carrier frequencies are derived from the following expression:

$$f_c = 372 + 48n \text{ kHz}$$

where n is the group number. Table 6-2 lists the carrier frequencies for groups 1 through 5. For group 1, a 60- to 108-kHz group signal modulates a 420-kHz group carrier frequency. Mathematically, the output of the group 1 bandpass filter is

$$f_{out} = f_c - f_i$$

where

f_c = group carrier frequency (372 + 48n kHz)
f_i = group frequency spectrum (60 to 108 kHz)

For group 1:

$$f_{out} = 420 \text{ kHz} - (60 \text{ to } 108 \text{ kHz}) = 312 \text{ to } 360 \text{ kHz}$$

For group 2:

$$f_{out} = 468 \text{ kHz} - (60 \text{ to } 108 \text{ kHz}) = 360 \text{ to } 408 \text{ kHz}$$

For group 5:

$$f_{out} = 612 \text{ kHz} - (60 \text{ to } 108 \text{ kHz}) = 504 \text{ to } 552 \text{ kHz}$$

The outputs from the five group modulators are summed in the linear combiner to produce the total supergroup spectrum shown in Figure 6-4b (312 to 552 kHz). Note that the total supergroup bandwidth is equal to 240 kHz (60 channels × 4 kHz).

TABLE 6-2   GROUP CARRIER FREQUENCIES

Group	Carrier frequency (kHz)
1	420
2	468
3	516
4	564
5	612

Composite Baseband Signal   **249**

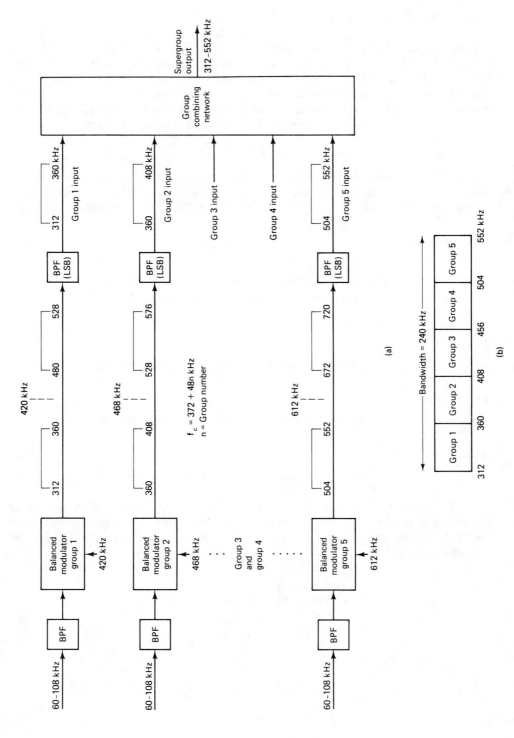

Figure 6-4 Formation of a supergroup: (a) group bank and combining network block diagram; (b) output spectrum.

Formation of a Mastergroup

There are two types of mastergroups: L600 and U600 type. The L600 mastergroup is used for low-capacity microwave systems, while the U600 mastergroup may be further multiplexed and used for higher-capacity microwave radio systems.

U600 Mastergroup. Figure 6-5a shows how a U600 mastergroup is formed with a supergroup bank and combining network. Ten supergroups are combined to form a mastergroup. The frequency spectrum for each supergroup is 312 to 552 kHz. Each supergroup is mixed with a different supergroup carrier frequency in a balanced modulator. The output is then bandlimited to the difference frequency band (LSB) to form a SSBSC signal. The 10 supergroup carrier frequencies are listed in Table 6-3. For supergroup 13, a 312- to 552-kHz supergroup band of frequencies modulates a 1116-kHz carrier frequency. Mathematically, the output from the supergroup 13 bandpass filter is

$$f_{\text{out}} = f_c - f_i$$

where

f_c = supergroup carrier frequency

f_i = supergroup frequency
spectrum (312 to 552 kHz)

For supergroup 13:

$$f_{\text{out}} = 1116 \text{ kHz} - (312 \text{ to } 552 \text{ kHz}) = 564 \text{ to } 804 \text{ kHz}$$

For supergroup 14:

$$f_{\text{out}} = 1364 \text{ kHz} - (312 \text{ to } 552 \text{ kHz}) = 812 \text{ to } 1052 \text{ kHz}$$

For supergroup D28:

$$f_{\text{out}} = 3396 \text{ kHz} - (312 \text{ to } 552 \text{ kHz}) = 2844 \text{ to } 3084 \text{ kHz}$$

The outputs from the 10 supergroup modulators are summed in the linear summer to produce the total mastergroup spectrum shown in Figure 6-4b (564 to 3084 kHz). Note that between any two adjacent supergroups there is a void band of frequencies that is not included within any supergroup band. These voids are called *guard bands*. The guard bands are necessary because the demultiplexing process is accomplished through filtering and down-converting. Without the guard bands, it would be difficult to separate one supergroup from an adjacent supergroup. The guard bands reduce the *quality factor* (Q) required to perform the necessary filtering. The guard band is 8 kHz between all supergroups except 18 and D25, where it is 56 kHz. Consequently, the bandwidth of a U600 mastergroup is 2520 kHz (564 to 3084 kHz), which is greater than is necessary to stack 600 voice band channels (600 × 4 kHz = 2400 kHz).

Guard bands were not necessary between adjacent groups because the group frequencies are sufficiently low and it is relatively easy to build bandpass filters to separate one group from another.

Composite Baseband Signal

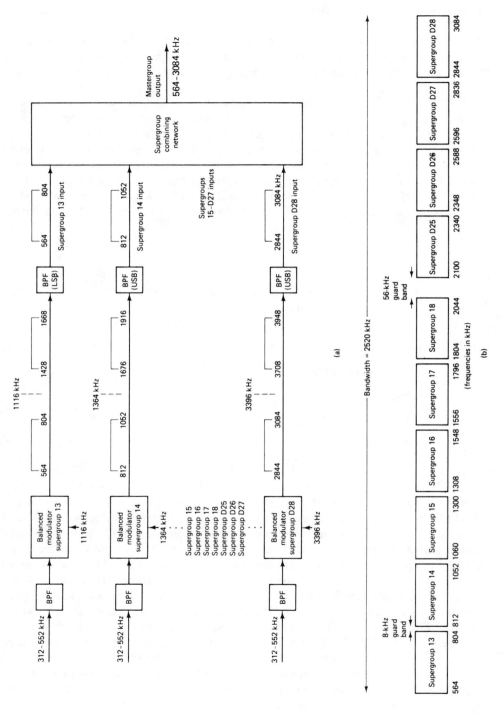

Figure 6-5 Formation of a U600 mastergroup: (a) supergroup bank and combining network block diagram; (b) output spectrum.

**TABLE 6-3 SUPERGROUP
CARRIER FREQUENCIES
FOR A U600
MASTERGROUP**

Supergroup	Carrier frequency (kHz)
13	1116
14	1364
15	1612
16	1860
17	2108
18	2356
D25	2652
D26	2900
D27	3148
D28	3396

In the channel bank, the antialiasing filter at the channel input passes a 0.3- to 3-kHz band. The separation between adjacent channel carrier frequencies is 4 kHz. Therefore, there is a 1300-Hz guard band between adjacent channels. This is shown in Figure 6-6.

L600 Mastergroup. With an L600 mastergroup, 10 supergroups are combined as with the U600 mastergroup except that the supergroup carrier frequencies are lower. Table 6-4 lists the supergroup carrier frequencies for a L600 mastergroup. With an L600 mastergroup, the composite baseband spectrum occupies a lower-frequency band than the U-type mastergroup (Figure 6-7). An L600 mastergroup is not further multiplexed. Therefore, the maximum channel capacity for a microwave or coaxial cable system using a single L600 mastergroup is 600 voice band channels.

Formation of a Radio Channel

A *radio channel* comprise either a single L600 mastergroup or up to three U600 mastergroups (1800 voice band channels). Figure 6-8 shows how an 1800-channel composite FDM baseband signal is formed for transmission over a single microwave radio channel. Mastergroup 1 is transmitted directly as is, while mastergroups 2 and 3 undergo an additional multiplexing step. The three mastergroups are summed in a mastergroup combining network to produce the output spectrum shown in Figure 6-8b. Note the 80-kHz guard band between adjacent mastergroups.

The system shown in Figure 6-8 can be increased from 1800 voice band channels to 1860 by adding an additional supergroup (supergroup 12) directly to mastergroup 1. The additional 312- to 552-kHz supergroup extends the composite output spectrum to 312 to 8284 kHz.

Composite Baseband Signal   253

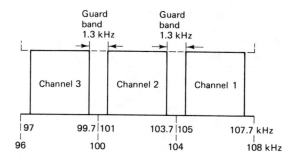

Figure 6-6 Channel guard bands.

Frequency Translation in FDM

Essentially, FDM is the process of transposing or translating a given input frequency band to some higher frequency band, where it is combined with other translated signals. With the L1860 FDM system shown in Figure 6-2, a single voice band channel may undergo as many as four frequency translations before it is transmitted. When troubleshooting an FDM system, it is necessary that the frequency band of a given channel be known at the various levels of multiplexing.

TABLE 6-4 SUPERGROUP CARRIER FREQUENCIES FOR A L600 MASTERGROUP

Supergroup	Carrier frequency (kHz)
1	612
2	Direct
3	1116
4	1364
5	1612
6	1860
7	2108
8	2356
9	2724
10	3100

Example 6-1

For a single-voice-band channel:

(a) Determine its frequency band at the output of the channel, group, supergroup, and mastergroup combiners when it is assigned to channel 4, group 2, supergroup 16, and mastergroup 2.

(b) Determine the frequency that a 1-kHz tone on the same channel would translate to.

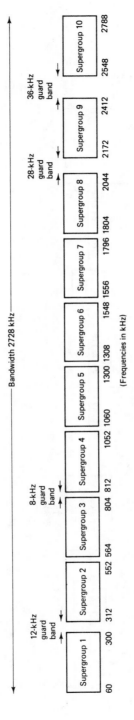

Figure 6-7 L600 mastergroup.

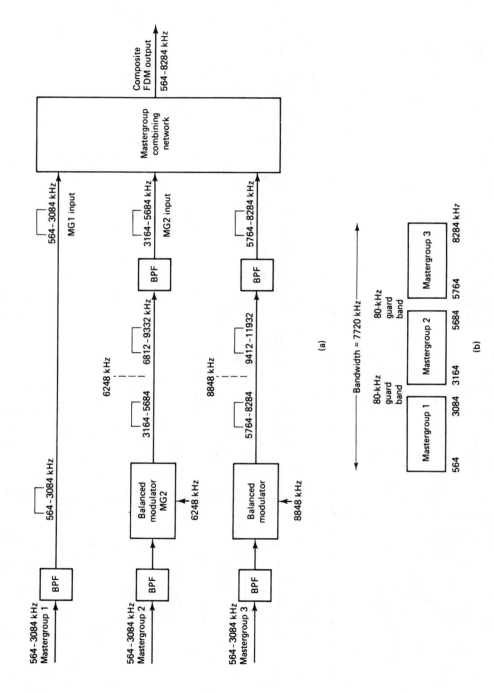

Figure 6-8 Three-mastergroup radio channel: (a) block diagram; (b) output spectrum.

Solution (a) For an ideal bandwidth of 0 to 4 kHz, the frequency band at the channel, group, supergroup, and master group combiners is determined as follows:

channel bank out = 96 kHz − (0 to 4 kHz) = 92 to 96 kHz
GP bank out = 468 kHz − (92 to 96 kHz) = 372 to 376 kHz
SG bank out = 1860 kHz − (372 to 376 kHz) = 1484 to 1488 kHz
MG bank out = 6248 kHz − (1484 to 1488 kHz) = 4760 to 4764 kHz

(b) For a 1-kHz test tone,
channel bank out = 96 kHz − 1 kHz = 95 kHz
GP bank out = 468 kHz − 95 kHz = 373 kHz
SG bank out = 1860 kHz − 373 kHz = 1487 kHz
MG bank out = 6248 kHz − 1487 kH = 4761 kHz

L CARRIERS

L carrier systems transmit frequency-division-multiplexed voice band signals over a coaxial cable for distances up to 4000 miles. L carriers have generically progressed from the early L1 and L3 systems to the high-capacity L4, L5, and L6 systems. L carrier systems combine many coaxial cables into a single tube and carry dozens of mastergroups and literally thousands of two-way simultaneous voice transmissions. In the near future, L cables are destined to be replaced by even higher-capacity optical fiber systems.

CARRIER SYNCHRONIZATION

With FDM, the receive channel, group, supergroup, and mastergroup carrier frequencies must be synchronized to the transmit carrier frequencies. If they are not synchronized, the recovered voice band signals will be offset in frequency from their original spectrum by the difference in the two carrier frequencies. FDM uses single-sideband suppressed carrier transmission. The carriers are suppressed in the balanced modulators at the transmit terminal and therefore cannot be recovered in the receive terminal directly from the composite baseband signal. Consequently, a carrier pilot frequency is transmitted together with the baseband signal for the purpose of carrier synchronization.

The channel, group, supergroup, and mastergroup carrier frequencies are all integral multiples of 4 kHz. Therefore, if the carrier frequencies at the transmit and receive terminals are derived from a single 4-kHz master oscillator, all of the transmit and receive carriers will be synchronized.

In an FDM communications system, one station is designated as the *master station*. Every other station in the system is a slave. That is, there is a single 4-kHz master oscillator from which all carrier frequencies in the system are derived. The 4-kHz master oscillator is multiplied to either a 64-, 312-, or 552-kHz pilot frequency, combined with the composite baseband signal, and transmitted to each slave station. The slave stations detect the pilot, divide it down to a 4-kHz base frequency, and synchronize their 4-kHz slave oscillators to it. Each slave station then multiplies the synchronous 4-kHz signal to produce synchronous channel, group, supergroup, and mastergroup carrier frequencies. If the master 4-kHz oscillator drifts in frequency, each slave station's 4-kHz oscillator tracks the frequency shift and the system remains synchronized.

D-Type Supergroups

With the U600 mastergroup, supergroups 25 through 28 are preceded by the letter "D." These supergroup carrier frequencies are derived in a slightly different fashion than the other carrier frequencies. Except for the D-supergroups, all carrier frequencies are generated through integer multiplication of the 4-kHz base frequency. The D-supergroups are generated through both multiplication and heterodyning (adding and subtracting). The supergroup 15- to 18-carrier frequencies are mixed with a 1040-kHz harmonic and the sum frequencies become the D25 to D28 carrier frequencies.

This method of deriving the higher supergroup carrier frequencies has no effect on the frequency offset introduced by frequency drift of the 4-kHz base oscillator. However, this technique reduces the amount of *phase jitter* (incidental phase modulation generally caused by ac ripple present in dc power supplies) in the higher supergroup carrier frequencies. When two frequencies with phase jitter are combined in a mixer, the total phase jitter in the sum frequency is less than the algebraic sum of the phase jitter of the two signals. Consequently, using D-type supergroup carriers has no effect on the frequency shift but reduces the magnitude of the total phase jitter in the higher supergroups. Before this technique was introduced, the voice band channels located in the higher supergroups could not be used for voice band data transmission when PSK modulation was used because the phase jitter caused excessive transmission errors.

Amplitude Regulation

Figure 6-9a shows the gain characteristics for an ideal transmission medium. For the ideal situation (Figure 6-9a), the gain for all baseband frequencies is the same. In a more practical situation, the gain is not the same for all frequencies (Figure 6-9b). Therefore, the demultiplexed voice band channels do not have the same amplitude characteristics as the original voice band signals had. This is called *amplitude distortion*. To reduce amplitude distortion, filters with the opposite characteristics as those introduced in the transmission medium can be added to the system, thus canceling the distortion. This is impractical because every transmission system has different characteristics and a special filter would have to be designed and built for each system.

Automatic gain devices (regulators) are used in the receiver demultiplexing equipment to compensate for amplitude distortion introduced in the transmission medium. Amplitude regulation is accomplished in several stages. First, the amplitude of each mastergroup is adjusted or regulated (mastergroup regulation; Figure 6-9c), then each supergroup within each mastergroup is regulated (super-

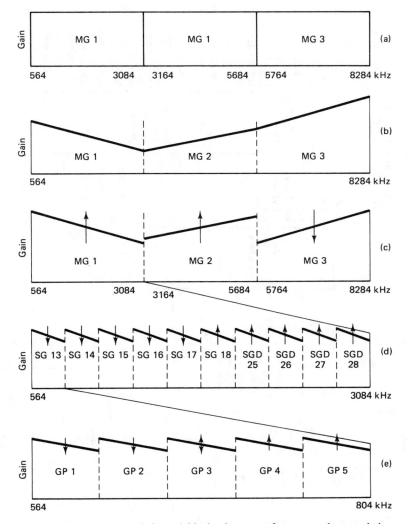

Figure 6-9 Gain characteristics: (a) ideal gain versus frequency characteristics; (b) amplitude distortion; (c) mastegroup regulation; (d) supergroup regulation; (e) group regulation.

group regulation; Figure 6-9d). The last stage of regulation is performed at a group level (group regulation; Figure 6-9e).

Regulation is performed by monitoring the power level of a mastergroup, supergroup, or group *pilot,* then regulating the entire frequency band associated with it, depending on the pilot level. Pilots are monitored rather than the actual signal level because the signal levels vary depending on how many channels are in use at a given time. A pilot is a continuous signal with a constant power level.

Figure 6-10 shows how the regulation pilots are nested within the composite baseband signal. Each group has a 104.08-kHz pilot added to it in the channel combining network. Consequently, each supergroup has five group pilots. The

Optical Fiber   259

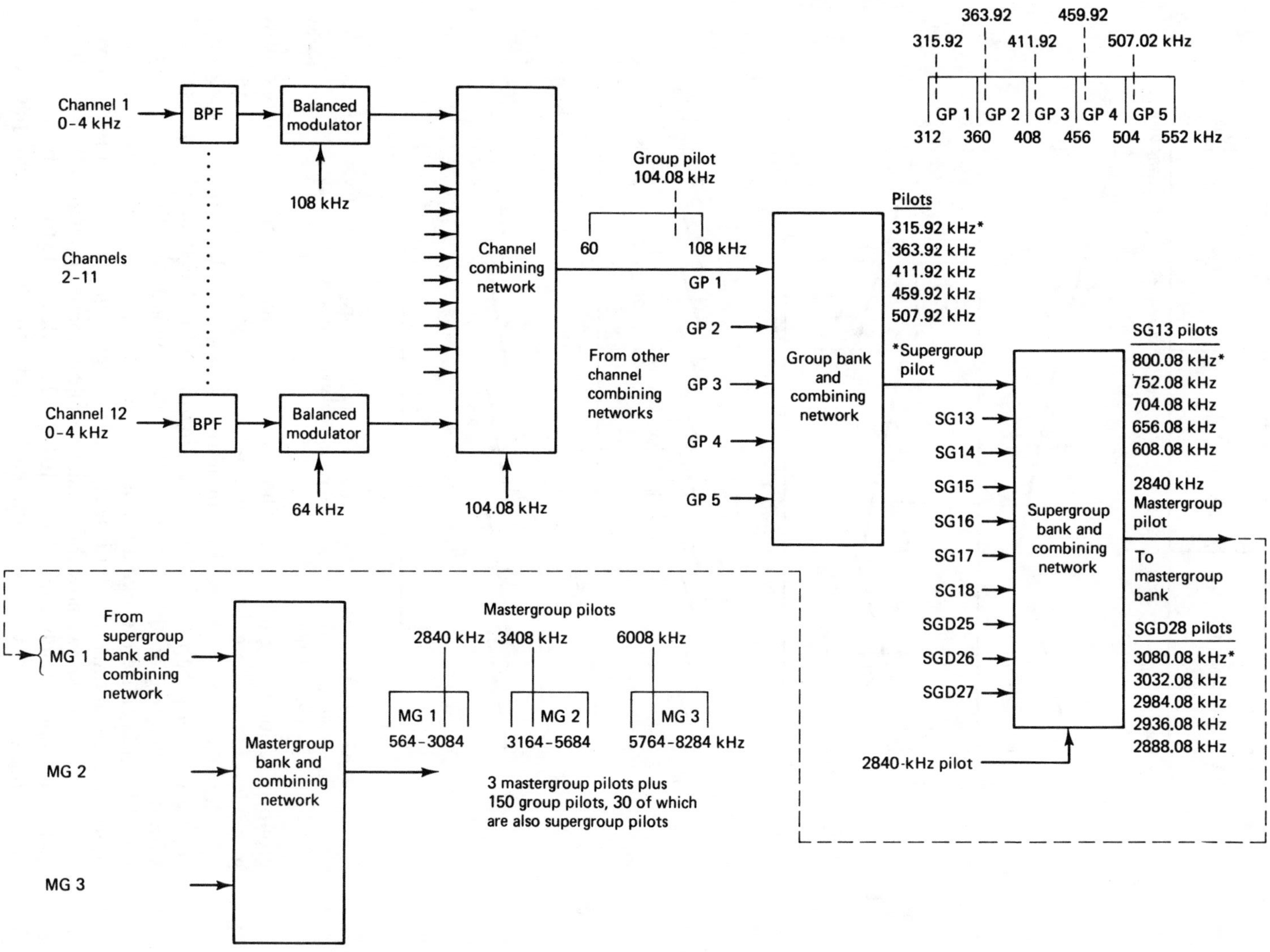

Figure 6-10 Pilot insertion.

group 1 pilot is also the supergroup pilot. Thus each mastergroup has 50 group pilots, of which 10 are also supergroup pilots. A separate 2840-kHz mastergroup pilot is added to each mastergroup in the supergroup combining network, making a total of 51 pilots per mastergroup.

Figure 6-11 is a partial block diagram for an FDM demultiplexer that shows how the pilots are monitored and used to separately regulate the mastergroups, supergroups, and groups automatically.

HYBRID DATA

With *hybrid* data it is possible to combine digitally encoded signals with FDM signals and transmit them as one composite baseband signal. There are four primary types of hybrid data: data under voice (DUV), data above voice (DAV), data above video (DAVID), and data in voice (DIV).

Data under Voice

Figure 6-12a shows the block diagram of AT&T's 1.544-Mbps *data under FDM voice* system. With the L1800 FDM system explained earlier in this chapter, the 0 to 564-kHz frequency spectrum is void of baseband signals. With FM transmission, the lower baseband frequencies realize the highest signal-to-noise ratios. Consequently, the best portion of the baseband spectrum was unused. DUV is a means of utilizing this spectrum for the transmission of digitally encoded signals. A T1 carrier system can be converted to a quasi-analog signal and then frequency-division multiplexed onto the lower portion of the FDM spectrum.

In Figure 6-12a, the *elastic store* removes timing jitter from the incoming data stream. The data are then *scrambled* to suppress the discrete high-power spectral components. The advantage of scrambling is the randomized data output spectrum is continuous and has a predictable effect on the FDM radio system. In other words, the data present a load to the system equivalent to adding additional FDM voice channels. The serial seven-level *partial response* encoder (correlative coder) compresses the data bandwidth and allows a 1.544-Mbps signal to be transmitted in a bandwidth less than 400 kHz. The low-pass filter performs the final spectral shaping of the digital information and suppresses the spectral power above 386 kHz. This prevents the DUV information from interfering with the 386-kHz pilot control tone. The DUV signal is preemphasized and combined with the L1800 baseband signal. The output spectrum is shown in Figure 6-12b.

AT&T uses DUV for *digital data service* (DDS). DDS is intended to provide a communications medium for the transfer of digital data from station to station without the use of a data modem. DDS circuits are guaranteed to average 99.5% error-free seconds at 56 kbps.

Data above Voice

Figure 6-13 shows the block diagram and frequency spectrum for a *data above voice* system. The advantage of DAV is for FDM systems that extend into the

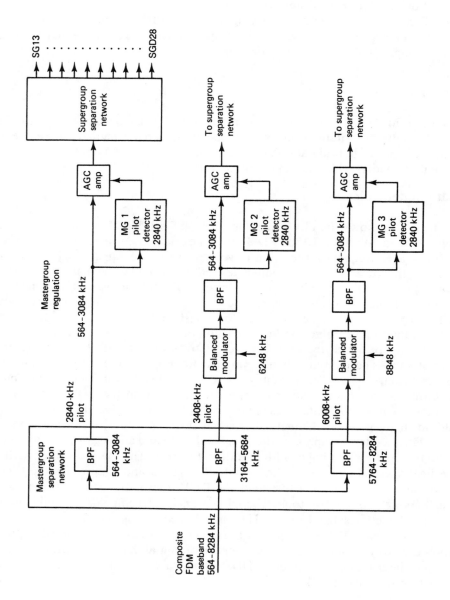

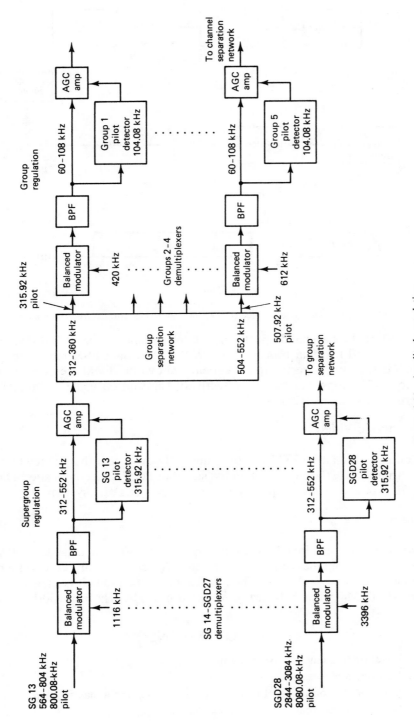

Figure 6-11 Amplitude regulation.

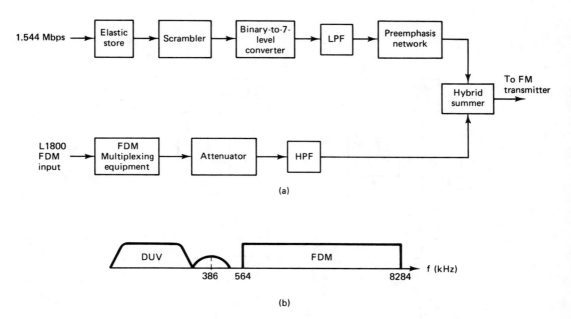

Figure 6-12 Data under voice (DUV): (a) block diagram; (b) frequency spectrum.

low end of the baseband spectrum; the low-frequency baseband does not have to be vacated for data transmission. With DAV, data PSK modulates a carrier which is then upconverted to a frequency above the FDM message. With DAV, up to 3.152 Mbps can be cost-effectively transmitted using existing FDM/FM microwave systems (Chapter 7).

Data above Video

Essentially, *data above video* is the same as DAV except that the lower baseband spectrum is a *vestigal sideband* video signal rather than a composite FDM signal. Figure 6-14 shows the frequency spectrum for a DAVID system.

Data in Voice

Data in voice, developed by Fujitsu of Japan, uses an eight-level PAM-VSB modulation technique with steep filtering. It uses a highly compressed partial response encoding technique which gives it a high bandwidth efficiency of nearly 5 bps/Hz (1.544-Mbps data are transmitted in a 344-kHz bandwidth).

QUESTIONS

6-1. Describe frequency-division multiplexing.

6-2. Describe a message channel.

6-3. Describe the formation of a group, a supergroup, and a mastergroup.

6-4. Define *baseband* and *composite baseband*.

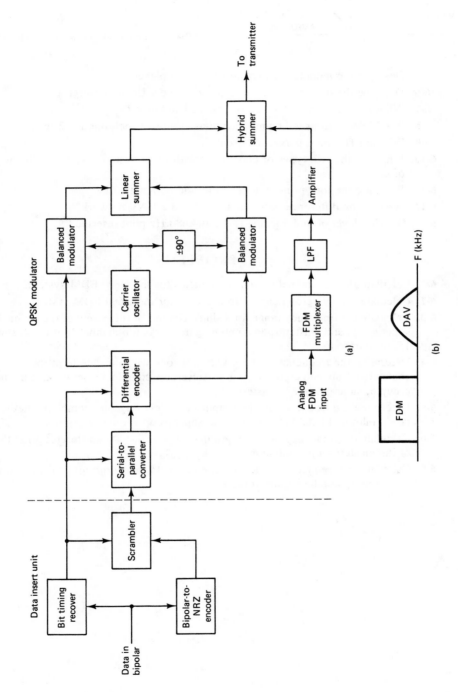

Figure 6-13 Data above voice (DAV): (a) block diagram; (b) frequency spectrum.

Vestigal SB video   QPSK
                     DAVID

f (Hz)   **Figure 6-14**   Data above video (DAVID).

6-5. Describe the modulators used in FDM multiplexers.

6-6. Describe the difference between an L600 and a U600 mastergroup.

6-7. What is a guard band? When is a guard band used?

6-8. Are FDM-multiplexed communications systems synchronous? Explain.

6-9. Why are D-type supergroups used?

6-10. What are the two types of pilots used with FDM systems, and what is the purpose of each?

6-11. What are the four primary types of hybrid data network?

6-12. What is the difference between a DUV and a DAV network?

6-13. At what level of multiplexing is the 104.08-kHz pilot inserted?

PROBLEMS

6-1. Calculate the 12 channel carrier frequencies for the U600 FDM system.

6-2. Calculate the five group carrier frequencies for the U600 FDM system.

6-3. Calculate the frequency range for a single channel at the output of the channel, group, supergroup, and mastergroup combining networks for channel 3, group 4, supergroup 15, mastergroup 2.

6-4. Determine the frequency that a 1-kHz test tone will translate to at the output of the channel, group, supergroup, and mastergroup combining networks for channel 5, group 5, supergroup 27, mastergroup 3.

6-5. Determine the frequency at the output of the mastergroup combining network for a group pilot of 104.08 kHz on group 2, supergroup 13, mastergroup 2.

6-6. Calculate the frequency range for group 4, supergroup 18, mastergroup 1 at the output of the mastergroup combining network.

6-7. Calculate the frequency range for supergroup 15, mastergroup 2 at the output of the mastergroup combining network.

7

MICROWAVE RADIO COMMUNICATIONS AND SYSTEM GAIN

INTRODUCTION

Presently, terrestrial (earth) *microwave radio relay systems* provide less than half of the total message circuit mileage in the United States. However, at one time microwave systems carried the bulk of long-distance communications for the public telephone network, military and governmental agencies, and specialized private communications networks. There are many different types of microwave systems that operate over distances varying from 15 to 4000 miles in length. *Intrastate* or *feeder service* systems are generally categorized as *short haul* because they are used for relatively short distances. *Long-haul* radio systems are those used for relatively long distances, such as interstate and backbone route applications. Microwave system capacities range from less than 12 voice band channels to more than 22,000. Early microwave radio systems carried frequency-division-multiplexed voice band circuits and used conventional, noncoherent frequency modulation techniques. More recently developed microwave systems carry pulse-code-modulated time-division-multiplexed voice band circuits and use more modern digital modulation techniques, such as phase shift keying and quadrature amplitude modulation. This chapter deals primarily with conventional FDM/FM microwave systems, and Chapter 8 deals with the more modern PCM/PSK techniques.

FREQUENCY VERSUS AMPLITUDE MODULATION

Frequency modulation (FM) is used in microwave radio systems rather than amplitude modulation (AM) because amplitude-modulated signals are more

267

sensitive to amplitude nonlinearities inherent in *wideband microwave amplifiers*. Frequency-modulated signals are relatively insensitive to this type of nonlinear distortion and can be transmitted through amplifiers that have compression or amplitude nonlinearity with little penalty. In addition, FM signals are less sensitive to random noise and can be propagated with lower transmit powers.

Intermodulation noise is a major factor when designing FM radio systems. In AM systems, intermodulation noise is caused by repeater amplitude nonlinearity. In FM systems, intermodulation noise is caused primarily by transmission gain and delay distortion. Consequently, in AM systems, intermodulation noise is a function of signal amplitude, but in FM systems it is a function of signal amplitude and the magnitude of the frequency deviation. Thus the characteristics of frequency-modulated signals are more suitable than amplitude-modulated signals for microwave transmission.

SIMPLIFIED FM MICROWAVE RADIO SYSTEM

A simplified block diagram of an FM microwave radio system is shown in Figure 7-1. The *baseband* is the composite signal that modulates the FM carrier and may comprise one or more of the following:

1. Frequency-division-multiplexed voice band channels
2. Time-division-multiplexed voice band channels
3. Broadcast-quality composite video or picturephone
4. Wideband data

FM Microwave Radio Transmitter

In the FM *microwave transmitter* shown in Figure 7-1a, a *preemphasis* network precedes the FM deviator. The preemphasis network is a high pass filter and thus provides an artificial boost in amplitude to the higher baseband frequencies. This allows the lower baseband frequencies to frequency modulate the IF carrier and the higher baseband frequencies to phase modulate it. This scheme assures a more uniform signal-to-noise ratio throughout the entire baseband spectrum. An FM deviator provides the modulation of the IF carrier which eventually becomes the main microwave carrier. Typically, IF carrier frequencies are between 60 and 80 MHz, with 70 MHz the most common. *Low-index* frequency modulation is used in the FM deviator. Typically, modulation indices are kept between 0.5 and 1. This produces a *narrowband* FM signal at the output of the deviator. Consequently, the IF bandwidth resembles conventional AM and is approximately equal to twice the highest baseband frequency.

The IF and its associated sidebands are up-converted to the microwave region by the AM mixer, microwave oscillator, and bandpass filter. Mixing, rather than multiplying, is used to translate the IF frequencies to RF frequencies because the modulation index is unchanged by the heterodyning process. Mul-

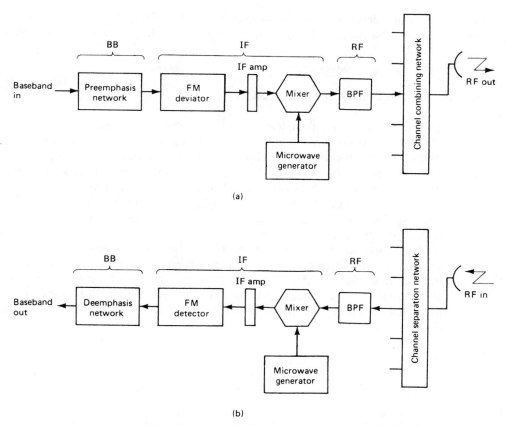

Figure 7-1 Simplified block diagram of an FM microwave radio system: (a) transmitter; (b) receiver.

tiplying the IF carrier would also multiply the frequency deviation and the modulation index, thus increasing the bandwidth. Typically, frequencies above 1000 MHz (1 GHz) are considered microwave frequencies. Presently, there are microwave systems operating with carrier frequencies up to approximately 18 GHz. The most common microwave frequencies currently being used are the 2-, 4-, 6-, 12-, and 14-GHz bands. The channel combining network provides a means of connecting more than one microwave transmitter to a single transmission line feeding the antenna.

FM Microwave Radio Receiver

In the FM microwave receiver shown in Figure 7-1b, the channel separation network provides the isolation and filtering necessary to separate individual microwave channels and direct them to their respective receivers. The bandpass filter, AM mixer, and microwave oscillator down-convert the RF microwave frequencies to IF frequencies and pass them on to the FM demodulator. The FM demodulator is a conventional, *noncoherent* FM detector (i.e., a discriminator

Simplified FM Microwave Radio System 269

or a ratio detector). At the output of the FM detector, a deemphasis network restores the baseband signal to its original amplitude versus frequency characteristics.

FM MICROWAVE RADIO REPEATERS

The permissible distance between an FM microwave transmitter and its associated microwave receiver depends on several system variables, such as transmitter output power, receiver noise threshold, terrain, atmospheric conditions, system capacity, reliability objectives, and performance expectations. Typically, this distance is between 15 and 40 miles. Longhaul microwave systems span distances considerably longer than this. Consequently, a single-hop microwave system, such as the one shown in Figure 7-1, is inadequate for most practical system applications. With systems that are longer than 40 miles or when geographical obstructions, such as a mountain, block the transmission path, *repeaters* are needed. A microwave repeater is a receiver and a transmitter placed back to back or in tandem with the system. A block diagram of a microwave repeater is shown in Figure 7-2. The repeater station receives a signal, amplifies and reshapes it, then retransmits the signal to the next repeater or terminal station downline from it.

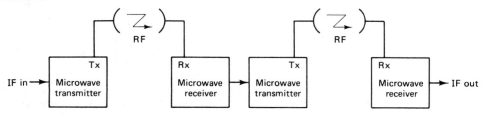

Figure 7-2 Microwave repeater.

Basically, there are two types of microwave repeaters: *baseband* and *IF* (Figure 7-3). IF repeaters are also called *heterodyne* repeaters. With an IF repeater (Figure 7-3a), the received RF carrier is down-converted to an IF frequency, amplified, reshaped, up-converted to an RF frequency, and then retransmitted. The signal is never demodulated below IF. Consequently, the baseband intelligence is unmodified by the repeater. With a baseband repeater (Figure 7-3b), the received RF carrier is down-converted to an IF frequency, amplified, filtered, and then further demodulated to baseband. The baseband signal, which is typically frequency-division-multiplexed voice band channels, is further demodulated to a mastergroup, supergroup, group, or even channel level. This allows the baseband signal to be reconfigured to meet the routing needs of the overall communications network. Once the baseband signal has been reconfigured, it FM modulates an IF carrier which is up-converted to an RF carrier and then retransmitted.

Figure 7-3c shows another baseband repeater configuration. The repeater demodulates the RF to baseband, amplifies and reshapes it, then modulates the FM carrier. With this technique, the baseband is not reconfigured. Essentially,

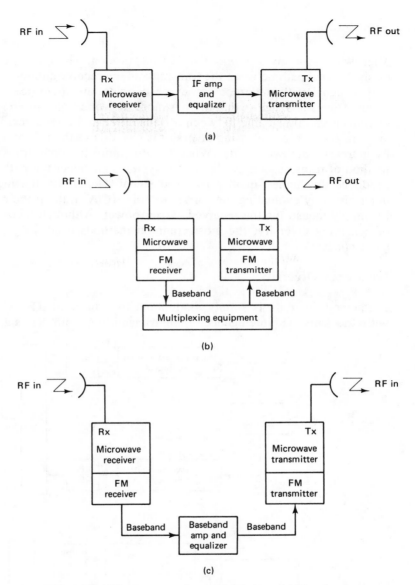

Figure 7-3 Microwave repeaters: (a) IF; (b) and (c) baseband.

this configuration accomplishes the same thing that an IF repeater accomplishes. The difference is that in a baseband configuration, the amplifier and equalizer act on baseband frequencies rather than IF frequencies. The baseband frequencies are generally less than 9 MHz, whereas the IF frequencies are in the range 60 to 80 MHz. Consequently, the filters and amplifiers necessary for baseband repeaters are simpler to design and less expensive than the ones required for IF repeaters. The disadvantage of a baseband configuration is the addition of the FM terminal equipment.

DIVERSITY

Microwave systems use *line-of-sight* transmission. There must be a direct, line-of-sight signal path between the transmit and the receive antennas. Consequently, if that signal path undergoes a severe degradation, a service interruption will occur. *Diversity* suggests that there is more than one transmission path or method of transmission available between a transmitter and a receiver. In a microwave system, the purpose of using diversity is to increase the reliability of the system by increasing its availability. When there is more than one transmission path or method of transmission available, the system can select the path or method that produces the highest-quality received signal. Generally, the highest quality is determined by evaluating the carrier-to-noise (C/N) ratio at the receiver input or by simply measuring the received carrier power. Although there are many ways of achieving diversity, the most common methods used are *frequency, space,* and *polarization.*

Frequency Diversity

Frequency diversity is simply modulating two different RF carrier frequencies with the same IF intelligence, then transmitting both RF signals to a given

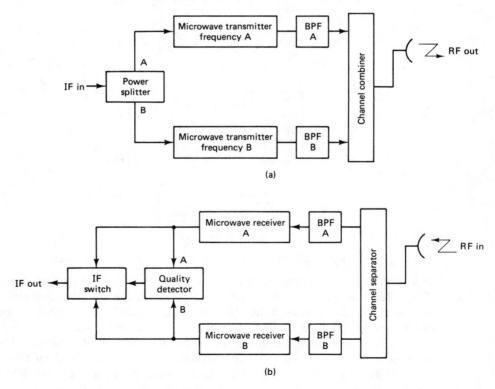

Figure 7-4 Frequency diversity microwave system: (a) transmitter; (b) receiver.

destination. At the destination, both carriers are demodulated, and the one that yields the better-quality IF signal is selected. Figure 7-4 shows a single-channel frequency-diversity microwave system.

In Figure 7-4a, the IF input signal is fed to a power splitter, which directs it to microwave transmitters A and B. The RF outputs from the two transmitters are combined in the channel-combining network and fed to the transmit antenna. At the receive end (Figure 7-4b), the channel separator directs the A and B RF carriers to their respective microwave receivers, where they are down-converted to IF. The quality detector circuit determines which channel, A or B, is the higher quality and directs that channel through the IF switch to be further demodulated to baseband. Many of the temporary, adverse atmospheric conditions that degrade an RF signal are frequency selective; they may degrade one frequency more than another. Therefore, over a given period of time, the IF switch may switch back and forth from receiver A to receiver B, and vice versa many times.

Space Diversity

With space diversity, the output of a transmitter is fed to two or more antennas that are physically separated by an appreciable number of wavelengths. Similarly, at the receiving end, there may be more than one antenna providing the input signal to the receiver. If multiple receiving antennas are used, they must also be separated by an appreciable number of wavelengths. Figure 7-5 shows a single-channel space-diversity microwave system.

When space diversity is used, it is important that the electrical distance from a transmitter to each of its antennas and to a receiver from each of its antennas is an equal multiple of wavelengths long. This is to ensure that when two or more signals of the same frequency arrive at the input to a receiver, they are in phase and additive. If received out of phase, they will cancel and, consequently, result in less received signal power than if simply one antenna system were used. Adverse atmospheric conditions are often isolated to a very small geographical area. With space diversity, there is more than one transmission path between a transmitter and a receiver. When adverse atmospheric conditions exist in one of the paths, it is unlikely that the alternate path is experiencing the same degradation. Consequently, the probability of receiving an acceptable signal is higher when space diversity is used than when no diversity is used. An alternate method of space diversity uses a single transmitting antenna and two receiving antennas separated vertically. Depending on the atmospheric conditions at a particular time, one of the receiving antennas should be receiving an adequate signal. Again, there are two transmission paths that are unlikely to be affected simultaneously by fading.

Polarization Diversity

With polarization diversity, a single RF carrier is propagated with two different electromagnetic polarizations (vertical and horizontal). Electromagnetic waves of different polarizations do not necessarily experience the same transmission

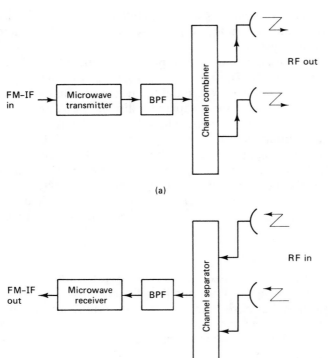

Figure 7-5 Space-diversity microwave system: (a) transmitter; (b) receiver.

impairments. Polarization diversity is generally used in conjunction with space diversity. One transmit/receive antenna pair is vertically polarized and the other is horizontally polarized. It is also possible to use frequency, space, and polarization diversity simultaneously.

PROTECTION SWITCHING

Radio path losses vary with atmospheric conditions. Over a period of time, the atmospheric conditions between transmitting and receiving antenna can vary significantly, causing a corresponding reduction in the received signal strength of 20, 30, 40, or more dB. This reduction in signal strength is referred to as a *radio fade*. *Automatic gain control circuits,* built into radio receivers, can compensate for fades of 25 to 40 dB, depending on the system design. However, when fades in excess of 40 dB occur, this is equivalent to a total loss of the received signal. When this happens, service continuity is lost. To avoid a service interruption during periods of deep fades or equipment failures, alternate facilities are temporarily made available in what is called a *protection switching* arrangement. Essentially, there are two types of protection switching arrangements: *hot standby* and *diversity*. With hot standby protection, each working radio channel has a dedicated backup or spare channel. With diversity protection, a single backup channel is made available to as many as 11 working channels. Hot standby systems offer 100% protection for each working radio channel. A diversity system offers 100% protection only to the first working channel that fails. If two radio channels fail at the same time, a service interruption will occur.

Hot Standby

Figure 7-6a shows a single-channel hot standby protection switching arrangement. At the transmitting end, the IF goes into a *head-end bridge,* which splits the signal power and directs it to the working and the spare (standby) microwave channels simultaneously. Consequently, both the working and standby channels are carrying the same baseband information. At the receiving end, the IF switch passes the IF signal from the working channel to the FM terminal equipment. The IF switch continuously monitors the received signal power on the working channel and if it fails, switches to the standby channel. When the IF signal on the working channel is restored, the IF switch resumes its normal position.

Diversity

Figure 7-6b shows a diversity protection switching arrangement. This system has two working channels (channel 1 and channel 2), one spare channel, and an *auxiliary* channel. The IF switch at the receive end continuously monitors the receive signal strength of both working channels. If either one should fail, the IF switch detects a loss of carrier and sends back to the transmitting station IF switch a VF (*voice frequency*) tone-encoded signal that directs it to switch the

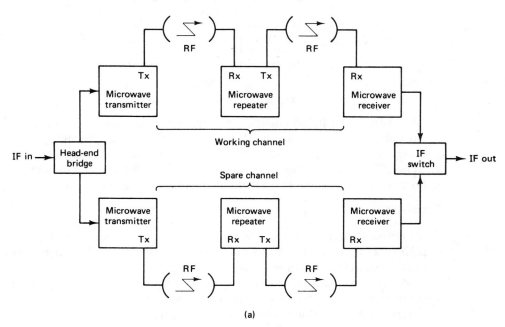

(a)

Figure 7-6 Microwave protection switching arrangements: (a) hot standby;

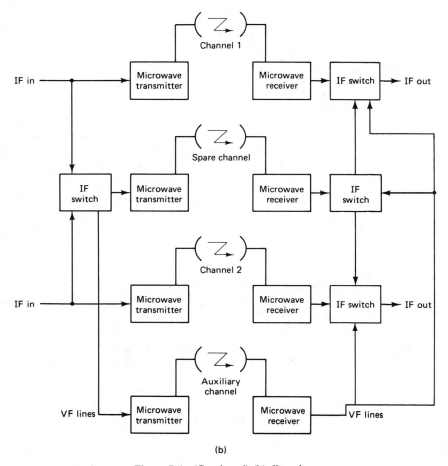

Channel 1

Spare channel

Channel 2

Auxiliary
channel

(b)

Figure 7-6 (Continued) (b) diversity.

IF signal from the failed channel onto the spare microwave channel. When the failed channel is restored, the IF switches resume their normal positions. The auxiliary channel simply provides a transmission path between the two IF switches. Typically, the auxiliary channel is a low-capacity low-power microwave radio that is designed to be used for a maintenance channel only.

Reliability

The number of repeater stations between protection switches depends on the *reliability objectives* of the system. Typically, there are between two and six repeaters between switching stations.

As you can see, diversity systems and protection switching arrangements are quite similar. The primary difference between the two is that diversity systems are permanent arrangements and are intended only to compensate for temporary, abnormal atmospheric conditions between only two selected stations in a system. Protection switching arrangements, on the other hand, compensate for both radio fades and equipment failures and may include from six to eight repeater stations between switches. Protection channels may also be used as temporary communication facilities, while routine maintenance is performed on a regular working channel. With a protection switching arrangement, all signal paths and radio equipment are protected. Diversity is used selectively, that is, only between stations that historically experience severe fading a high percentage of the time.

A statistical study of outage time (i.e., service interruptions) caused by radio fades, equipment failures, and maintenance is important in the design of a microwave radio system. From such a study, engineering decisions can be made on the type of diversity system and protection switching arrangement best suited for a particular application.

FM MICROWAVE RADIO STATIONS

Basically, there are two types of FM microwave stations: terminals and repeaters. *Terminal stations* are points in the system where baseband signals are either originated or terminated. *Repeater stations* are points in a system where baseband signals may be reconfigured or where RF carriers are simply "repeated" or amplified.

Terminal Station

Essentially, a terminal station consists of four major sections: the baseband, wire line entrance link (WLEL), FM-IF, and RF sections. Figure 7-7 shows the block diagram of the baseband, WLEL, and FM-IF sections. As mentioned previously, the baseband may be one of several different types of signals. For our example, frequency-division-multiplexed voice band channels are used.

Wire line entrance link (WLEL). Very often in large communications networks such as the American Telephone and Telegraph Company (AT&T), the building that houses the radio station is quite large. Consequently, it is desirable that similar equipment be physically placed at a common location (i.e., all FDM equipment in the same room). This simplifies alarm systems, providing dc power to the equipment, maintenance, and other general cabling requirements. Dissimilar equipment may be separated by a considerable distance. For example, the distance between the FDM multiplexing equipment and the FM-IF section is typically several hundred feet and in some cases several miles. For this reason a WLEL is required. A WLEL serves as the interface between the multiplex terminal equipment and the FM-IF equipment. A WLEL generally consists of an amplifier and an equalizer (which together compensate for cable transmission losses) and level-shaping devices commonly called pre- and deemphasis networks.

IF section. The FM terminal equipment shown in Figure 7-7 generates a frequency-modulated IF carrier. This is accomplished by mixing the outputs of two deviated oscillators that differ in frequency by the desired IF carrier. The

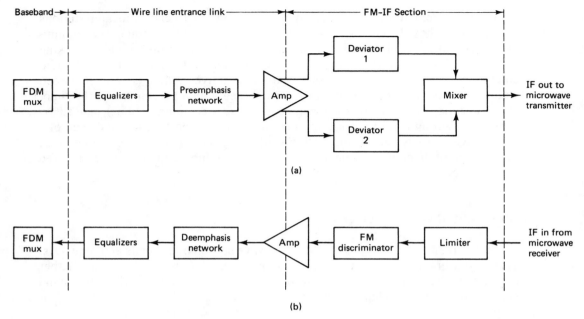

Figure 7-7 Microwave terminal station, baseband, wire line entrance link, and FM-1F: (a) transmitter; (b) receiver.

oscillators are deviated in phase opposition, which reduces the magnitude of phase deviation required of a single deviator by a factor of 2. This technique also reduces the deviation linearity requirements for the oscillators and provides for the partial cancellation of unwanted modulation products. Again, the receiver is a conventional noncoherent FM detector.

RF section. A block diagram of the RF section of a microwave terminal station is shown in Figure 7-8. The IF signal enters the transmitter (Figure 7-8a) through a protection switch. The IF and compression amplifiers help keep the IF signal power constant and at approximately the required input level to the transmit modulator (*transmod*). A transmod is a balanced modulator that when used in conjunction with a microwave generator, power amplifier, and bandpass filter, up-converts the IF carrier to an RF carrier and amplifies the RF to the desired output power. Power amplifiers for microwave radios must be capable of amplifying very high frequencies and passing very wide bandwidth signals. *Klystron tubes, traveling-wave tubes* (TWTs), and *IMPATT* (*imp*act/*a*valanche and *T*ransit *T*ime) diodes are several of the devices currently being used in microwave power amplifiers. Because high-gain antennas are used and the distance between microwave stations is relatively short, it is not necessary to develop a high output power from the transmitter output amplifiers. Typical gains for microwave antennas range from 40 to 80 dB, and typical transmitter output powers are between 0.5 and 10 W.

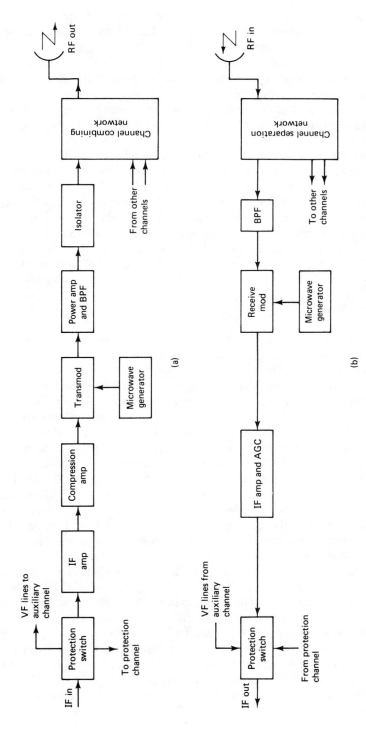

Figure 7-8 Microwave terminal station: (a) transmitter; (b) receiver.

279

A *microwave generator* provides the RF carrier input to the up-converter. It is called a microwave generator rather than an oscillator because it is difficult to construct a stable circuit that will oscillate in the gigahertz range. Instead, a crystal-controlled oscillator operating in the range 5 to 25 MHz is used to provide a base frequency that is multiplied up to the desired RF carrier frequency.

An *isolator* is a unidirectional device often made from a ferrite material. The isolator is used in conjunction with a channel-combining network to prevent the output of one transmitter from interfering with the output of another transmitter.

The RF receiver (Figure 7-8b) is essentially the same as the transmitter except that it works in the opposite direction. However, one difference is the presence of an IF amplifier in the receiver. This IF amplifier has an *automatic gain control* (AGC) circuit. Also, very often, there are no RF amplifiers in the receiver. Typically, a very sensitive, low-noise-balanced demodulator is used for the receive demodulator (receive mod). This eliminates the need for an RF amplifier and improves the overall signal-to-noise ratio. When RF amplifiers are required, high-quality, *low-noise amplifiers* (LNAs) are used. Examples of commonly used LNAs are tunnel diodes and parametric amplifiers.

Repeater Station

Figure 7-9 shows the block diagram of a microwave IF repeater station. The received RF signal enters the receiver through the channel separation network and bandpass filter. The receive mod down-converts the RF carrier to IF. The IF AMP/AGC and equalizer circuits amplify and reshape the IF. The equalizer compensates for *gain versus frequency nonlinearities* and *envelope delay distortion* introduced in the system. Again, the transmod up-converts the IF to RF for retransmission. However, in a repeater station, the method used to generate the RF microwave carrier frequencies is slightly different from the method used in a terminal station. In the IF repeater, only one microwave generator is required to supply both the transmod and the receive mod with an RF carrier signal. The microwave generator, shift oscillator, and shift modulator allow the repeater to receive one RF carrier frequency, down-convert it to IF, and then up-convert the IF to a different RF carrier frequency (Figure 7-10a). It is possible for station C to receive the transmissions from both station A and station B simultaneously (this is called *multihop interference*). This can occur only when three stations are placed in a geographical straight line in the system. To prevent this from occurring, the allocated bandwidth for the system is divided in half, creating a low-frequency and a high-frequency band. Each station, in turn, alternates from a low-band to a high-band transmit carrier frequency (Figure 7-10b). If a transmission from station A is received by station C, it will be rejected in the channel separation network and cause no interference. This arrangement is called a high/low microwave repeater system. The rules are simple: If a repeater station receives a low-band RF carrier, it retransmits a high-band RF carrier, and vice versa. The only time that multiple carriers of the same frequency can be received

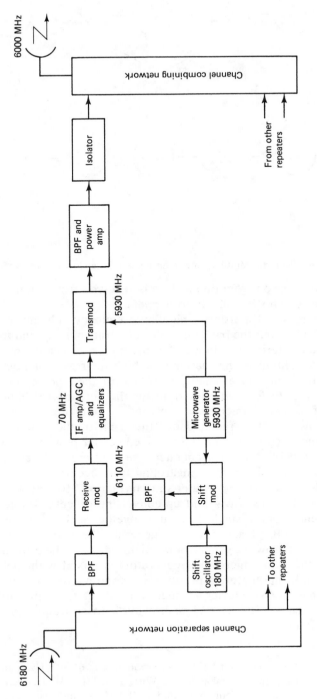

Figure 7-9 Microwave IF repeater station.

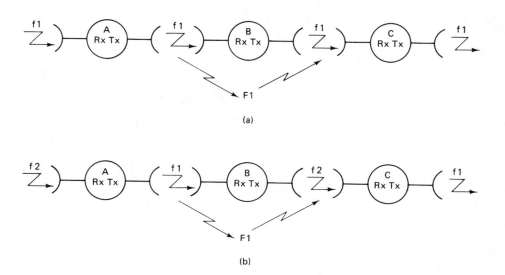

Figure 7-10 (a) Multihop interference and (b) high/low microwave system.

is when a transmission from one station is received from another station that is three hops away. This is unlikely to happen.

Another reason for using a high/low-frequency scheme is to prevent the power that "leaks" out the back and sides of a transmit antenna from interferring with the signal entering the input of a nearby receive antenna. This is called *ringaround*. All antennas, no matter how high their gain or how directive their radiation pattern, radiate a small percentage of their power out the back and sides; giving a finite *front-to-back* ratio for the antenna. Although the front-to-back ratio of a typical microwave antenna is quite high, the relatively small amount of power that is radiated out the back of the antenna may be quite substantial compared to the normal received carrier power in the system. If the transmit and receive carrier frequencies are different, filters in the receiver separation network will prevent ringaround from occurring.

A high/low microwave repeater station (Figure 7-10b) needs two microwave carrier supplies for the down- and up-converting process. Rather than use two microwave generators, a single generator together with a shift oscillator, a shift modulator, and a bandpass filter can generate the two required signals. One output from the microwave generator is fed directly into the transmod and another output (from the same microwave generator) is mixed with the shift oscillator signal in the shift modulator to produce a second microwave carrier frequency. The second microwave carrier frequency is offset from the first by the shift oscillator frequency. The second microwave carrier frequency is fed into the receive modulator.

Example 7-1

In Figure 7-9 the received RF carrier frequency is 6180 MHz, and the transmitted RF carrier frequency is 6000 MHz. With a 70-MHz IF frequency, a 5930-MHz microwave generator frequency, and a 180-MHz shift oscillator frequency, the output filter of the shift mod must be tuned to 6110 MHz. This is the sum of the microwave generator and the shift oscillator frequencies (5930 MHz + 180 MHz = 6110 MHz).

This process does not reduce the number of oscillators required, but it is simpler and cheaper to build one microwave generator and one relatively low-frequency shift oscillator than to build two microwave generators. This arrangement also provides a certain degree of synchronization between repeaters. The obvious disadvantage of the high/low scheme is that the number of channels available in a given bandwidth is cut in half.

Figure 7-11 shows a high/low-frequency plan with eight channels (four high-band and four low-band). Each channel occupies a 29.7-MHz bandwidth. The west terminal transmits the low-band frequencies and receives the high-band frequencies. Channel 1 and 3 (Figure 7-11a) are designated as *V channels*. This means that they are propagated with vertical polarization. Channels 2 and 4 are designated as H or horizontally polarized channels. This is not a polarization diversity system. Channels 1 through 4 are totally independent of each other; they carry different baseband information. The transmission of *orthogonally* polarized carriers (90° out of phase) further enhances the isolation between the transmit and receive signals. In the west-to-east direction, the repeater receives the low-band and transmits the high-band frequencies. After channel 1 is received and down-converted to IF, it is up-converted to a different RF frequency and a different polarization for retransmission. The low-band channel 1 corresponds to the high-band channel 11, channel 2 to channel 12, and so on. The east-to-west direction (Figure 7-11b) propagates the high- and low-band carriers in the sequence opposite to the west-to-east system. The polarizations are also reversed. If some of the power from channel 1 of the west terminal were to propagate directly to the east terminal receiver, it has a different frequency and polarization than channel 11's transmissions. Consequently, it would not interfere with the reception of channel 11 (no multihop interference). Also, note that none of the transmit or receive channels at the repeater station has both the same frequency and polarization. Consequently, the interference from the transmitters to the receivers due to ringaround is insignificant.

PATH CHARACTERISTICS

The normal *propagation paths* between two radio antennas in a microwave radio system is shown in Figure 7-12. The *free-space path* is the *line-of-sight path* directly between the transmit and receive antennas (this is also called the *direct wave*). The *ground-reflected wave* is the portion of the transmit signal that is reflected off the earth's surface and captured by the receive antenna. The *surface wave* consists of the electric and magnetic fields associated with the currents induced in the earth's surface. The magnitude of the surface wave depends on the characteristics of the earth's surface and the electromagnetic polarization of the wave. The sum of these three paths (taking into account their amplitude and

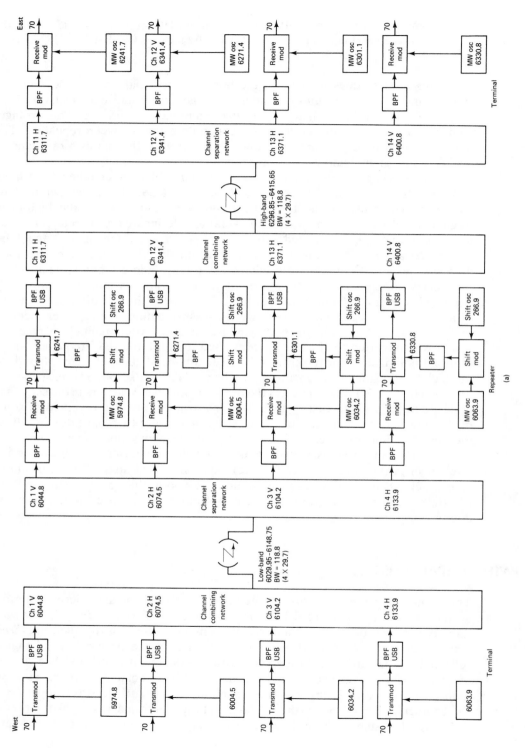

(a)

284

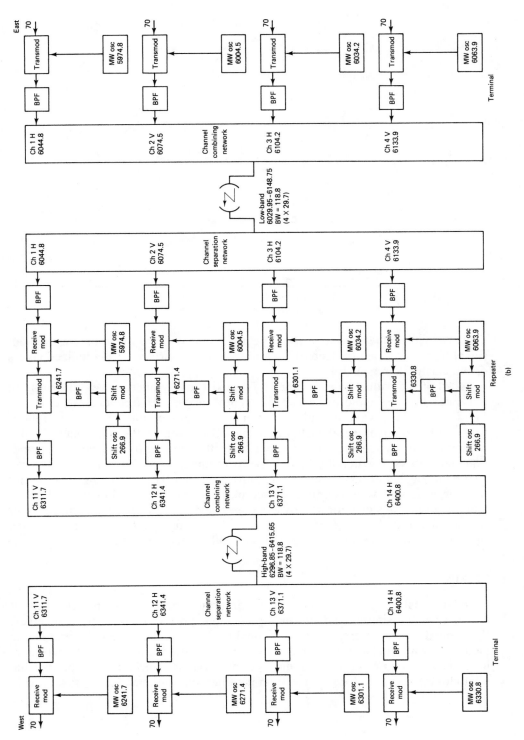

Figure 7-11 Eight-channel high/low frequency plan: (a) west to east; (b) east to west. All frequencies in megahertz.

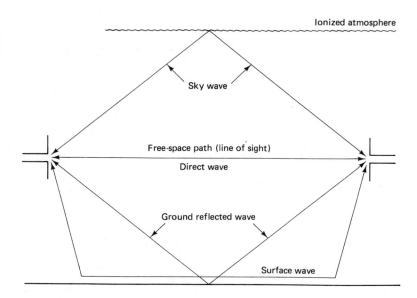

Figure 7-12 Propagation paths.

phase) is called the *ground wave*. The *sky wave* is the portion of the transmit signal that is returned (reflected) back to the earth's surface by the ionized layers of the earth's atmosphere.

All of the paths shown in Figure 7-12 exist in any microwave radio system, but some are negligible in certain frequency ranges. At frequencies below 1.5 MHz, the surface wave provides the primary coverage, and the sky wave helps to extend this coverage at night when the absorption of the ionosphere is at a minimum. For frequencies above about 30 to 50 MHz, the free-space and ground-reflected paths are generally the only paths of importance. The surface wave can also be neglected at these frequencies, provided that the antenna heights are not too low. The sky wave is only a source of occasional long-distance interference and not a reliable signal for microwave communications purposes. In this chapter the surface and sky-wave propagations are neglected, and attention is focused on those phenomena that affect the direct and reflected waves.

SYSTEM GAIN

In its simplest form, *system gain* is the difference between the nominal output power of a transmitter and the minimum input power required by a receiver. System gain must be greater than or equal to the sum of all the gains and losses incurred by a signal as it propagates from a transmitter to a receiver. In essence, it represents the net loss of a radio system. System gain is used to predict the reliability of a system for given system parameters. Mathematically, system gain is

$$G_s = P_t - C_{\min}$$

where

G_s = system gain (dB)
P_t = transmitter output power (dBm)
C_{min} = minimum receiver input power for a given quality objective (dBm)

and where

$$P_t - C_{min} \geq \text{losses} + \text{gains}$$

Gains:

A_t = transmit antenna gain (dB) relative to an isotropic radiator
A_r = receive antenna gain (dB) relative to an isotropic radiator

Losses:

L_p = free-space path loss between antennas (dB)

L_f = waveguide feeder loss (dB) between the distribution network (channel combining network or channel separation network) and its respective antenna (see Table 7-1)

L_b = total coupling or branching loss (dB) in the circulators, filters, and distribution network between the output of a transmitter or the input to a receiver and its respective waveguide feed (see Table 7-1)

FM = fade margin for a given reliability objective

Mathematically, system gain is

$$G_s = P_t - C_{min} \geq \text{FM} + L_p + L_f + L_b - A_t - A_r \qquad (7\text{-}1)$$

TABLE 7-1 SYSTEM GAIN PARAMETERS

Frequency (GHz)	Feeder loss, L_f		Branching loss (dB) Diversity:		Antenna gain, A_t or A_r	
	Type	Loss (dB/100 m)	Frequency	Space	Size (m)	Gain (dB)
1.8	Air-filled coaxial cable	5.4	5	2	1.2	25.2
					2.4	31.2
					3.0	33.2
					3.7	34.7
7.4	EWP 64 eliptical waveguide	4.7	3	2	1.5	38.8
					2.4	43.1
					3.0	44.8
					3.7	46.5
8.0	EWP 69 eliptical waveguide	6.5	3	2	2.4	43.8
					3.0	45.6
					3.7	47.3
					4.8	49.8

where all values are expressed in dB or dBm. Because system gain is indicative of a net loss, the losses are represented with positive dB values and the gains are represented with negative dB values. Figure 7-13 shows an overall microwave system diagram and indicates where the respective losses and gains are incurred.

Free-Space Path Loss

Free-space path loss is defined as the loss incurred by an electromagnetic wave as it propagates in a straight line through a vacuum with no absorption or reflection of energy from nearby objects. The expression for free-space path loss is given as

$$L_p = \left(\frac{4\pi D}{\lambda}\right)^2 = \left(\frac{4\pi f D}{c}\right)^2$$

where

$\quad L_p$ = free-space path loss
$\quad D$ = distance
$\quad f$ = frequency
$\quad \lambda$ = wavelength
$\quad c$ = velocity of light in free space (3×10^8 m/s)

Converting to dB yields

$$L_p\,(\text{dB}) = 20\log\frac{4\pi f D}{c} = 20\log\frac{4\pi}{c} + 20\log f + 20\log D$$

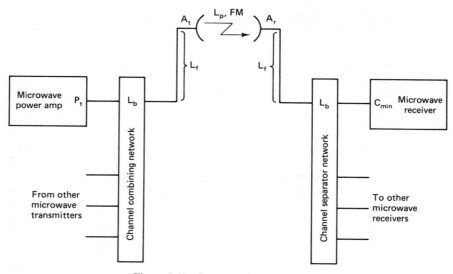

Figure 7-13 System gains and losses.

When the frequency is given in MHz and the distance in km,

$$L_p \text{ (dB)} = 20 \log \frac{4\pi(10)^6 (10)^3}{3 \times 10^8} + 20 \log f \text{(MHz)} + 20 \log D \text{ (km)}$$
$$= 32.4 + 20 \log f \text{(MHz)} + 20 \log D \text{ (km)}$$

(7-2)

When the frequency is given in GHz and the distance in km,

$$L_p \text{ (dB)} = 92.4 + 20 \log f \text{ (GHz)} + 20 \log D \text{ (km)} \tag{7-3}$$

Similar conversions can be made using distance in miles, frequency in kHz, and so on.

Example 7-2

For a carrier frequency of 6 GHz and a distance of 50 km, determine the free-space path loss.

Solution

$$L_p \text{ (dB)} = 32.4 + 20 \log 6000 + 20 \log 50$$
$$= 32.4 + 75.6 + 34$$
$$= 142 \text{ dB}$$

or

$$L_p \text{ (dB)} = 92.4 + 20 \log 6 + 20 \log 50$$
$$= 92.4 + 15.6 + 34$$
$$= 142 \text{ dB}$$

Fade Margin

Essentially, *fade margin* is a "fudge factor" included in the system gain equation that considers the nonideal and less predictable characteristics of radio-wave propagation, such as *multipath propagation* (*multipath loss*) and *terrain sensitivity*. These characteristics cause temporary, abnormal atmospheric conditions that alter the free-space path loss and are usually detrimental to the overall system performance. Fade margin also considers system reliability objectives. Thus fade margin is included in the system gain equation as a loss.

Solving the Barnett–Vignant reliability equations for a specified annual system availability for an unprotected, nondiversity system yields the following expression:

$$\text{FM} = \underbrace{30 \log D}_{\substack{\text{multipath} \\ \text{effect}}} + \underbrace{10 \log (6ABf)}_{\substack{\text{terrain} \\ \text{sensitivity}}} - \underbrace{10 \log (1 - R)}_{\substack{\text{reliability} \\ \text{objectives}}} - \underbrace{70}_{\text{constant}} \tag{7-4}$$

System Gain

where

> FM = fade margin (dB)
> D = distance (km)
> f = frequency (GHz)
> R = reliability expressed as a decimal (i.e., 99.99% = 0.9999 reliability)
> $1 - R$ = reliability objective for a one-way 400-km route
> A = roughness factor
>   = 4 over water or a very smooth terrain
>   = 1 over an average terrain
>   = 0.25 over a very rough, mountainous terrain
> B = factor to convert a worst-month probability to an annual probability
>   = 1 to convert an annual availability to a worst-month basis
>   = 0.5 for hot humid areas
>   = 0.25 for average inland areas
>   = 0.125 for very dry or mountainous areas

Example 7-3

Consider a space-diversity microwave radio system operating at an RF carrier frequency of 1.8 GHz. Each station has a 2.4-m-diameter parabolic antenna that is fed by 100 m of air-filled coaxial cable. The terrain is smooth and the area has a humid climate. The distance between stations is 40 km. A reliability objective of 99.99% is desired. Determine the system gain.

Solution   Substituting into Equation 7-4, we find that the fade margin is

$$\text{FM} = 30 \log 40 + 10 \log (6)(4)(0.5)(1.8) - 10 \log (1 - 0.9999) - 70$$

$$= 48.06 + 13.34 - (-40) - 70$$

$$= 48.06 + 13.34 + 40 - 70$$

$$= 31.4 \, \text{dB}$$

Substituting into Equation 7-3, we obtain path loss

$$L_p = 92.4 + 20 \log 1.8 + 20 \log 40$$

$$= 92.4 + 5.11 + 32.04$$

$$= 129.55 \, \text{dB}$$

From Table 7-1,

$$L_b = 4 \, \text{dB} \, (2 + 2 = 4)$$

$$L_f = 10.8 \, \text{dB} \, (100 \, \text{m} + 100 \, \text{m} = 200 \, \text{m})$$

$$A_t = A_r = 31.2 \, \text{dB}$$

Substituting into Equation 7-1 gives us system gain

$$G_s = 31.4 + 129.55 + 10.8 + 4 - 31.2 - 31.2 = 113.35 \, \text{dB}$$

The results indicate that for this system to perform at 99.99% reliability with the given terrain, distribution networks, transmission lines, and antennas, the transmitter output power must be at least 113.35 dB more than the minimum receive signal level.

Receiver Threshold

Carrier-to-noise (*C/N*) is probably the most important parameter considered when evaluating the performance of a microwave communications system. The minimum wideband carrier power (C_{min}) at the input to a receiver that will provide a usable baseband output is called the receiver *threshold* or, sometimes, receiver *sensitivity*. The receiver threshold is dependent on the wideband noise power present at the input of a receiver, the noise introduced within the receiver, and the noise sensitivity of the baseband detector. Before C_{min} can be calculated, the input noise power must be determined. The input noise power is expressed mathematically as

$$N = KTB$$

where

$$N = \text{noise power}$$
$$K = \text{Boltzmann's constant } (1.38 \times 10^{-23} \text{ J/K})$$
$$T = \text{equivalent noise temperature of the receiver (K)}$$
$$\text{(room temperature} = 290 \text{ K)}$$
$$B = \text{noise bandwidth (Hz)}$$

Expressed in dBm,

$$N \text{ (dBm)} = 10 \log \frac{KTB}{0.001} = 10 \log \frac{KT}{0.001} + 10 \log B$$

For a 1-Hz bandwidth at room temperature,

$$N = 10 \log \frac{(1.38 \times 10^{-23})(290)}{0.001} + 10 \log 1$$
$$= -174 \text{ dBm}$$

Thus

$$N \text{ (dBm)} = -174 \text{ dBm} + 10 \log \text{B} \qquad (7\text{-}5)$$

Example 7-4

For an equivalent noise bandwidth of 10 MHz, determine the noise power.

Solution   Substituting into Equation 7-5 yields

$$N = -174 \text{ dBm} + 10 \log (10 \times 10^6)$$
$$= -174 \text{ dBm} + 70 \text{ dB} = -104 \text{ dBm}$$

If the minimum *C/N* requirement for a receiver with a 10-MHz noise bandwidth is 24 dB, the minimum receive carrier power is

$$C_{min} = \frac{C}{N} \text{(dB)} + N \text{ (dB)}$$

$$= 24 \text{ dB} + (-104 \text{ dBm}) = -80 \text{ dBm}$$

For a system gain of 113.35 dB, it would require a minimum transmit carrier power (P_t) of

$$P_t = G_s + C_{min}$$
$$= 113.35\ dB + (-80\ dBm) = 33.35\ dBm$$

This indicates that a minimum transmit power of 33.35 dBm (2.16 W) is required to achieve a carrier-to-noise ratio of 24 dB with a system gain of 113.35 dB and a bandwidth of 10 MHz.

Carrier-to-Noise versus Signal-to-Noise

Carrier-to-noise (C/N) is the ratio of the wideband "carrier" (actually, not just the carrier, but rather the carrier and its associated sidebands) to the wideband noise power (the noise bandwidth of the receiver). C/N can be determined at an RF or an IF point in the receiver. Essentially, C/N is a *predetection* (before the FM demodulator) signal-to-noise ratio. Signal-to-noise (S/N) is a *postdetection* (after the FM demodulator) ratio. At a baseband point in the receiver, a single voice band channel can be separated from the rest of the baseband and measured independently. At an RF or IF point in the receiver, it is impossible to separate a single voice band channel from the composite FM signal. For example, a typical bandwidth for a single microwave channel is 30 MHz. The bandwidth of a voice band channel is 4 kHz. C/N is the ratio of the power of the composite RF signal to the total noise power in the 30-MHz bandwidth. S/N is the ratio of the signal power of a single voice band channel to the noise power in a 4-kHz bandwidth.

Noise Figure

In its simplest form, *noise figure* (F) is the signal-to-noise ratio of an ideal noiseless device divided by the S/N ratio at the output of an amplifier or a receiver. In a more practical sense, noise figure is defined as the ratio of the S/N ratio at the input to a device divided by the S/N ratio at the output. Mathematically, noise figure is

$$F = \frac{(S/N)_{in}}{(S/N)_{out}} \quad \text{and} \quad F(dB) = 10 \log \frac{(S/N)_{in}}{(S/N)_{out}}$$

Thus noise figure is a ratio of ratios. The noise figure of a totally noiseless device is unity or 0 dB. Remember, the noise present at the input to an amplifier is amplified by the same gain as the signal. Consequently, only noise added within the amplifier can decrease the signal-to-noise ratio at the output and increase the noise figure. (Keep in mind, the higher the noise figure, the worse the S/N ratio at the output).

Essentially, noise figure indicates the relative increase of the noise power to the increase in signal power. A noise figure of 10 means that the device added sufficient noise to reduce the S/N ratio by a factor of 10, or the noise power increased tenfold in respect to the increase in signal power.

When two or more amplifiers or devices are cascaded together (Figure 7-14), the total noise figure (NF) is an accumulation of the individual noise figures. Mathematically, the total noise figure is

$$NF = F_1 + \frac{F_2 - 1}{A_1} + \frac{F_3 - 1}{A_1 A_2} + \frac{F_4 - 1}{A_1 A_2 A_3} \quad \text{etc.} \quad (7\text{-}6)$$

where

$$NF = \text{total noise figure}$$
$$F_1 = \text{noise figure of amplifier 1}$$
$$F_2 = \text{noise figure of amplifier 2}$$
$$F_3 = \text{noise figure of amplifier 3}$$
$$A_1 = \text{gain of amplifier 1}$$
$$A_2 = \text{gain of amplifier 2}$$

Note: In equation 7-6 noise figures and gains are expressed as absolute values rather than in dB.

It can be seen that the noise figure of the first amplifier (F1) contributes the most toward the overall noise figure. The noise introduced in the first stage is amplified by each of the succeeding amplifiers. Therefore, when compared to the noise introduced in the first stage, the noise added by each succeeding amplifier is effectively reduced by a factor equal to the product of the gains of the preceding amplifiers.

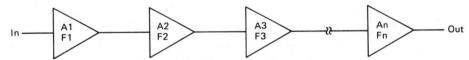

Figure 7-14 Total noise figure.

When precise noise calculations (0.1 dB or less) are necessary, it is generally more convenient to express noise figure in terms of noise temperature or equivalent noise temperature rather than as an absolute power (Chapter 8). Because noise power (N) is proportional to temperature, the noise present at the input to a device can be expressed as a function of the device's environmental temperature (T) and its equivalent noise temperature (T_e). To convert noise figure to a term dependent on temperature only, refer to Figure 7-15.

Let

$$N_d = \text{noise power added by a single amplifier}$$

Then

$$N_d = KT_e B$$

where T_e is the equivalent noise temperature. Let

$$N_o = \text{total output noise power of an amplifier}$$
$$N_i = \text{total input noise power of an amplifier}$$
$$A = \text{gain of an amplifier}$$

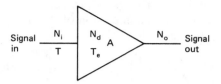

Figure 7-15 Noise figure as a function of temperature.

Therefore,

$$N_o \quad \text{may be expressed as}$$
$$N_o = AN_i + AN_d$$

and

$$N_o = AKTB + AKT_e B$$

Simplifying yields

$$N_o = AKB\,(T + T_e)$$

and the overall noise figure (NF) equals

$$NF = \frac{(S/N)_{\text{in}}}{(S/N)_{\text{out}}} = \frac{S/N_i}{AS/N_o} = \frac{N_o}{AN_i} = \frac{AKB\,(T + T_e)}{AKTB}$$

$$= \frac{T + T_e}{T} = 1 + \frac{T_e}{T}$$

(7-7)

Example 7-5

In Figure 7-14, let $F_1 = F_2 = F_3 = 3$ dB and $A_1 = A_2 = A_3 = 10$ dB. Solve for the total noise figure.

Solution   Substituting into Equation 7-6 (*Note:* All gains and noise figures have been converted to absolute values) yields

$$NF = F_1 + \frac{F_2 - 1}{A_1} + \frac{F_3 - 1}{A_1 A_2}$$

$$= 2 + \frac{2 - 1}{10} + \frac{2 - 1}{100}$$

$$= 2.11 \text{ or } 10 \log 2.11 = 3.24 \text{ dB}$$

An overall noise figure of 3.24 dB indicates that the S/N ratio at the output of A3 is 3.24 dB less than the S/N ratio at the input to A1.

The noise figure of a receiver must be considered when determining C_{min}. The noise figure is included in the system gain equation as an equivalent loss. (Essentially, a gain in the total noise power is equivalent to a corresponding loss in the signal power.)

Example 7-6

Refer to Figure 7-16. For a system gain of 112 dB, a total noise figure of 6.5 dB, an input noise power of -104 dBm, and a minimum $(S/N)_{\text{out}}$ of the FM demodulator of 32 dB, determine the minimum receive carrier power and the minimum transmit power.

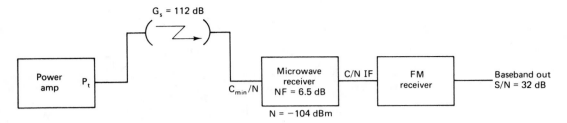

Figure 7-16 System gain example.

Solution To achieve a S/N ratio of 32 dB out of the FM demodulator, an input C/N of 15 dB is required (17 dB of improvement due to FM quieting). Solving for the receiver input carrier-to-noise ratio gives

$$\frac{C_{\min}}{N} = \frac{C}{N} + NF = 15\,dB + 6.5\,dB = 21.5\,dB$$

Thus

$$C_{\min} = \frac{C_{\min}}{N} + N$$

$$= 21.5\,dB + (-104\,dBm) = -82.5\,dBm$$

$$P_t = G_s + C_{\min}$$

$$= 112\,dB + (-82.5\,dBm) = 29.5\,dBm$$

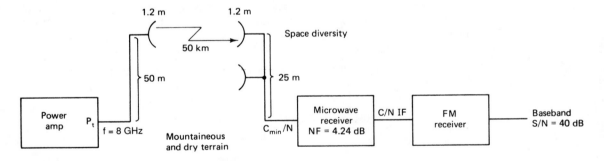

Reliability objective = 99.999%
Bandwidth = 6.3 MHz

Figure 7-17 System gain example.

Example 7-7

For the system shown in Figure 7-17, determine the following: G_s, $C_{\min}/N$, $C_{\min}$, N, G_s, and P_t.

Solution The minimum C/N at the input to the FM receiver is 23 dB.

$$\frac{C_{\min}}{N} = \frac{C}{N} + NF$$

$$= 23\,dB + 4.24\,dB = 27.24\,dB$$

System Gain

Substituting into Equation 7-5 yields

$$N = -174\,\text{dBm} + 10\log B$$

$$= -174\,\text{dBm} + 68\,\text{dB} = -106\,\text{dBm}$$

$$C_{\text{min}} = \frac{C_{\text{min}}}{N} + N$$

$$= 27.24\,\text{dB} + (-106\,\text{dBm}) = -78.76\,\text{dBm}$$

Substituting into Equation 7-4 gives us

$$FM = 30\log 50 + 10\log\left[(6)(0.25)(0.125)(8)\right]$$

$$-10\log(1 - 0.99999) - 70$$

$$= 32.76\,\text{dB}$$

Substituting into Equation 7-3, we have

$$L_p = 92.4\,\text{dB} + 20\log 8 + 20\log 50$$

$$= 92.4\,\text{dB} + 18.06\,\text{dB} + 33.98\,\text{dB} = 144.44\,\text{dB}$$

From Table 7-1,

$$L_b = 4\,\text{dB}$$

$$L_f = 0.75\,(6.5\,\text{dB}) = 4.875\,\text{dB}$$

$$A_t = A_r = 37.8\,\text{dB}$$

Note: The gain of an antenna increases or decreases proportional to the square of its diameter (i.e., if its diameter changes by a factor of 2, its gain changes by a factor of 4 which is 6 dB).

Substituting into Equation 7-1 yields

$$G_s = 32.76 + 144.44 + 4.875 + 4 - 37.8 - 37.8 = 110.475\,\text{dB}$$

$$P_t = G_s + C_{\text{min}}$$

$$= 110.475\,\text{dB} + (-78.76\,\text{dBm}) = 31.715\,\text{dBm}$$

QUESTIONS

7-1. What constitutes a short-haul microwave system? A long-haul microwave system?

7-2. Describe the baseband signal for a microwave system.

7-3. Why do FDM/FM microwave systems use low-index FM?

7-4. Describe a microwave repeater. Contrast baseband and IF repeaters.

7-5. Define *diversity*. Describe the three most commonly used diversity schemes.

7-6. Describe a protection switching arrangement. Contrast the two types of protection switching arrangements.

7-7. Briefly describe the four major sections of a microwave terminal station.

7-8. Define *ringaround*.

7-9. Briefly describe a high/low microwave system.

7-10. Define *system gain*.

7-11. Define the following terms: free-space path loss, branching loss, and feeder loss.

7-12. Define *fade margin*. Describe multipath losses, terrain, sensitivity, and reliability objectives and how they affect fade margin.

7-13. Define *receiver threshold*.

7-14. Contrast carrier-to-noise ratio and signal-to-noise ratio.

7-15. Define *noise figure*.

PROBLEMS

7-1. Calculate the noise power at the input to a receiver that has a radio carrier frequency of 4 GHz and a bandwidth of 30 MHz (assume room temperature).

7-2. Determine the path loss for a 3.4-GHz signal propagating 20,000 m.

7-3. Determine the fade margin for a 60-km microwave hop. The RF carrier frequency is 6 GHz, the terrain is very smooth and dry, and the reliability objective is 99.95%.

7-4. Determine the noise power for a 20-MHz bandwidth at the input to a receiver with an input noise temperature of 290°C.

7-5. For a system gain of 120 dB, a minimum input C/N of 30 dB, and an input noise power of -115 dBm, determine the minimum transmit power (P_t).

7-6. Determine the amount of loss contributed to a reliability objective of 99.98%.

7-7. Determine the terrain sensitivity loss for a 4-GHz carrier that is propagating over a very dry, mountainous area.

7-8. A frequency-diversity microwave system operates at an RF carrier frequency of 7.4 GHz. The IF is a low-index frequency-modulated subcarrier. The baseband signal is the 1800-channel FDM system described in Chapter 6 (564 to 8284 kHz). The antennas are 4.8-m-diameter parabolic dishes. The feeder lengths are 150 m at one station and 50 m at the other station. The reliability objective is 99.999%. The system propagates over an average terrain that has a very dry climate. The distance between stations is 50 km. The minimum carrier-to-noise ratio at the receiver input is 30 dB. Determine the following: fade margin, antenna gain, free-space path loss, total branching and feeder losses, receiver input noise power, $C_{\min}$, minimum transmit power, and system gain.

7-9. Determine the overall noise figure for a receiver that has two RF amplifiers each with a noise figure of 6 dB and a gain of 10 dB, a mixer down-converter with a noise figure of 10 dB, and a conversion gain of -6 dB, and 40 dB of IF gain with a noise figure of 6 dB.

7-10. A microwave receiver has a total input noise power of -102 dBm and an overall noise figure of 4 dB. For a minimum C/N ratio of 20 dB at the input to the FM detector, determine the minimum receive carrier power.

8

SATELLITE COMMUNICATIONS

INTRODUCTION

In the early 1960s, the American Telephone and Telegraph Company (AT&T) released studies indicating that a few powerful satellites of advanced design could handle more traffic than the entire AT&T long-distance communications network. The cost of these satellites was estimated to be only a fraction of the cost of equivalent terrestrial microwave facilities. Unfortunately, because AT&T was a utility, government regulations prevented them from developing the satellite systems. Smaller and much less lucrative corporations were left to develop the satellite systems, and AT&T continued to invest billions of dollars each year in conventional terrestrial microwave systems. Because of this, early developments in satellite technology were slow in coming.

Throughout the years the prices of most goods and services have increased substantially; however, satellite communications services have become more affordable each year. In most instances, satellite systems offer more flexibility than submarine cables, buried underground cables, line-of-sight microwave radio, tropospheric scatter radio, or optical fiber systems.

Essentially, a satellite is a radio repeater in the sky (*transponder*). A satellite system consists of a transponder, a ground-based station to control its operation, and a user network of earth stations that provide the facilities for transmission and reception of communications traffic through the satellite system. Satellite transmissions are categorized as either *bus* or *payload*. The bus includes control mechanisms that support the payload operation. The payload is the actual user information that is conveyed through the system. Although in recent years new

298

data services and television broadcasting are more and more in demand, the transmission of conventional speech telephone signals (in analog or digital form) is still the bulk of the satellite payload.

HISTORY OF SATELLITES

The simplest type of satellite is a *passive reflector,* a device that simply "bounces" a signal from one place to another. The moon is a natural satellite of the earth and, consequently, in the late 1940s and early 1950s, became the first satellite transponder. In 1954, the U.S. Navy successfully transmitted the first messages over this earth-to-moon-to-earth relay. In 1956, a relay service was established between Washington, D.C., and Hawaii and, until 1962, offered reliable long-distance communications. Service was limited only by the availability of the moon.

In 1957, Russia launched *Sputnik I,* the first *active* earth satellite. An active satellite is capable of receiving, amplifying, and retransmitting information to and from earth stations. *Sputnik I* transmitted telemetry information for 21 days. Later in the same year, the United States launched *Explorer I,* which transmitted telemetry information for nearly 5 months.

In 1958, NASA launched *Score,* a 150-pound conical-shaped projectory. With an on-board tape recording, *Score* rebroadcasted President Eisenhower's 1958 Christmas message. *Score* was the first artificial satellite used for relaying terrestrial communications. *Score* was a *delayed repeater satellite*; it received transmissions from earth stations, stored them on magnetic tape, and rebroadcasted them to ground stations farther along in its orbit.

In 1960, NASA in conjunction with Bell Telephone Laboratories and the Jet Propulsion Laboratory launched *Echo,* a 100-ft-diameter plastic balloon with an aluminum coating. *Echo* passively reflected radio signals from a large earth antenna. *Echo* was simple and reliable but required extremely high power transmitters at the earth stations. The first transatlantic transmission using a satellite transponder was accomplished using *Echo.* Also in 1960, the Department of Defense launched *Courier. Courier* transmitted 3 W of power and lasted only 17 days.

In 1962, AT&T launched *Telstar I,* the first satellite to receive and transmit simultaneously. The electronic equipment in *Telstar I* was damaged by radiation from the newly discovered Van Allen belts and, consequently, lasted only a few weeks. *Telstar II* was electronically identical to *Telstar I,* but it was made more radiation resistant. *Telstar II* was successfully launched in 1963. It was used for telephone, television, facsimile, and data transmissions. The first successful transatlantic transmission of video was accomplished with *Telstar II.*

Early satellites were both of the passive and active type. Again, a passive satellite is one that simply reflects a signal back to earth; there are no gain devices on board to amplify or repeat the signal. An active satellite is one that electronically repeats a signal back to earth (i.e., receives, amplifies, and retransmits the signal). An advantage of passive satellites is that they do not require sophisticated electronic equipment on board, although they are not necessarily void of power.

Some passive satellites require a *radio beacon transmitter* for tracking and ranging purposes. A beacon is a continuously transmitted unmodulated carrier that an earth station can lock onto and use to align its antennas or to determine the exact location of the satellite. A disadvantage of passive satellites is their inefficient use of transmitted power. With *Echo,* for example, only 1 part in every 10^{18} of the earth station transmitted power was actually returned to the earth station receiving antenna.

ORBITAL SATELLITES

The satellites mentioned thus far are called *orbital* or *nonsynchronous* satellites. Nonsynchronous satellites rotate around the earth in a low-altitude elliptical or circular pattern. If the satellite is orbiting in the same direction as the earth's rotation and at an angular velocity greater than that of the earth, this is called a *prograde orbit.* If the satellite is orbiting in the opposite direction as the earth's rotation or in the same direction but at an angular velocity less than that of earth, this is called a *retrograde orbit.* Consequently, nonsynchronous satellites are continuously either gaining or falling back on earth and do not remain stationary to any particular point on earth. Thus nonsynchronous satellites have to be used when available, which may be as short a period of time as 15 minutes per orbit. Another disadvantage of orbital satellites is the need for complicated and expensive tracking equipment at the earth stations. Each earth station must locate the satellite as it comes into view on each orbit and then lock its antenna onto the satellite and track it as it passes overhead. A major advantage of orbital satellites is that propulsion rockets are not required on board the satellites to keep them in their respective orbits.

One of the more interesting orbital satellite systems is the Soviet *Molniya* system. This is also spelled *Molnya* and *Molnia,* which means "lightning" in Russian (in colloquial Russian it means "news flash"). The Molniya satellites are used for television broadcasting and are presently the only nonsynchronous-orbit commercial satellite system in use. Molniya uses a highly elliptical orbit with *apogee* at about 40,000 km and *perigee* at about 1000 km (see Figure 8-1). The apogee is the farthest distance from earth a satellite orbit reaches, the perigee is

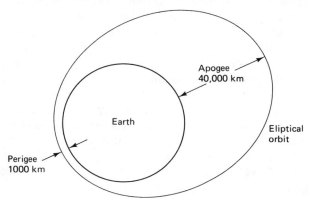

the minimum distance, and the *line of apsides* is the line joining the perigee and apogee through the center of the earth. With the *Molniya* system, the apogee is reached while over the northern hemisphere and the perigee while over the southern hemisphere. The size of the ellipse was chosen to make its period exactly one-half of a sidereal day (the time it takes the earth to rotate back to the same constellation). Because of its unique orbital pattern, the *Molniya* satellite is synchronous with the rotation of the earth. During its 12-h orbit, it spends about 11 h over the north hemisphere.

GEOSTATIONARY SATELLITES

Geostationary or *geosynchronous* satellites are satellites that orbit in a circular pattern with an angular velocity equal to that of earth. Consequently, they remain in a fixed position in respect to a given point on earth. An obvious advantage is they are available to all the earth stations within their *shadow* 100% of the time. The shadow of a satellite includes all earth stations that have a line-of-sight path to it and lie within the radiation pattern of the satellite's antennas. An obvious disadvantage is they require sophisticated and heavy propulsion devices on board to keep them in a fixed orbit. The orbital time of a geosynchronous satellite is 24 h, the same as earth.

Syncom I, launched in February 1963, was the first attempt to place a geosynchronous satellite into orbit. *Syncom I* was lost during orbit injection. *Syncom II* and *Syncom III* were successfully launched in February 1963 and August 1964, respectively. The *Syncom III* satellite was used to broadcast the 1964 Olympic Games from Tokyo. The *Syncom* projects demonstrated the feasibility of using geosynchronous satellites.

Since the *Syncom* projects, a number of nations and private corporations have successfully launched satellites that are currently being used to provide national as well as regional and international global communications. There are more than 80 satellite communications systems operating in the world today. They provide worldwide fixed common-carrier telephone and data circuits; point-to-point cable television (CATV); network television distribution; music broadcasting; mobile telephone service; and private networks for corporations, governmental agencies, and military applications.

In 1964 a commercial global satellite network known as *Intelsat* (International Telecommunications Satellite Organization) was established. Intelsat is owned and operated by a consortium of more than 100 countries. Intelsat is managed by the designated communications entities in their respective countries. The first Intelsat satellite was *Early Bird 1,* which was launched in 1965 and provided 480 voice channels. From 1966 to 1987, a series of satellites designated *Intelsat II, III, IV, V,* and *VI* were launched. *Intelsat VI* has a capacity of 80,000 voice channels.

Domestic satellites (*domsats*) are used to provide satellite services within a single country. In the United States, all domsats are situated in geostationary orbit. Table 8-1 is a partial list of current international and domestic satellite systems and their primary payload.

Geostationary Satellites

TABLE 8-1 CURRENT SATELLITE COMMUNICATIONS SYSTEMS

Characteristic System					
	Westar	*Intelsat V*	*SBS*	*Fleet-satcom*	*ANIK-D*
Operator	Western Union Telegraph	Intelsat	Satellite Business Systems	U.S. Dept. of Defense	Telsat Canada
Frequency band	C	C and Ku	Ku	UHF, X	C, Ku
Coverage	Consus	Global, zonal, spot	Consus	Global	Canada, northern U.S.
Number of transponders	12	21	10	12	24
Transponder BW (MHz)	36	36–77	43	0.005–0.5	36
EIRP (dBW)	33	23.5–29	40–43.7	26–28	36
Multiple Access	FDMA, TDMA	FDMA, TDMA, reuse	TDMA	FDMA	FDMA
Modulation	FM, QPSK	FDM/FM, QPSK	QPSK	FM, QPSK	FDM, FM, FM/TVD, SCPC
Service	Fixed tele, TTY	Fixed tele, TVD	Fixed tele, TVD	Mobile military	Fixed tele

C-band: 3.4–6.425 GHz
Ku-band: 10.95–14.5 GHz
X-band: 7.25–8.4 GHz

TTY   Teletype
TVD   TV distribution
FDMA   Frequency-division multiple access
TDMA   Time-division multiple access
Consus   Continental United States

ORBITAL PATTERNS

Once projected, a satellite remains in orbit because the centrifugal force caused by its rotation around the earth is counterbalanced by the earth's gravitational pull. The closer to earth the satellite rotates, the greater the gravitational pull and the greater the velocity required to keep it from being pulled to earth. Low-altitude satellites that orbit close to earth (100 to 300 miles in height) travel at approximately 17,500 miles per hour. At this speed, it takes approximately $1\frac{1}{2}$ h to rotate around the entire earth. Consequently, the time that the satellite is in line of sight of a particular earth station is only $\frac{1}{4}$ h or less per orbit. Medium-altitude satellites (6000 to 12,000 miles in height) have a rotation period of 5 to 12 h and remain in line of sight of a particular earth station for 2 to 4 h per orbit. High-altitude, geosynchronous satellites (19,000 to 25,000 miles in height) travel at approximately 6879 miles per hour and have a rotation period of 24 h, exactly the same as the earth. Consequently, they remain in a *fixed* position in respect to a given earth station and have a 24-h availability time. Figure 8-2 shows a low-, medium-, and high-altitude satellite orbit. It can be seen that three equally spaced, high-altitude geosynchronous satellites rotating around the earth above the equator can cover the entire earth except for the unpopulated areas of the north and south poles.

Figure 8-3 shows the three paths that a satellite may take as it rotates around the earth. When the satellite rotates in an orbit above the equator, it is called an *equatorial orbit*. When the satellite rotates in an orbit that takes it over the north and south poles, it is called a *polar orbit*. Any other orbital path is called an *inclined orbit*. An *ascending node* is the point where the orbit crosses the equatorial plane going from south to north, and a *descending node* is the point where the orbit crosses the equatorial plane going from north to south. The line joining the ascending and descending nodes through the center of earth is called the *line of nodes*.

It is interesting to note that 100% of the earth's surface can be covered with a single satellite in a polar orbit. The satellite is rotating around the earth in a longitudinal orbit while the earth is rotating on a latitudinal axis. Consequently, the satellite's radiation pattern is a diagonal spiral around the earth which somewhat resembles a barber pole. As a result, every location on earth lies within the radiation pattern of the satellite twice each day.

SUMMARY

Advantages of Geosynchronous Orbits

1. The satellite remains almost stationary in respect to a given earth station. Consequently, expensive tracking equipment is not required at the earth stations.

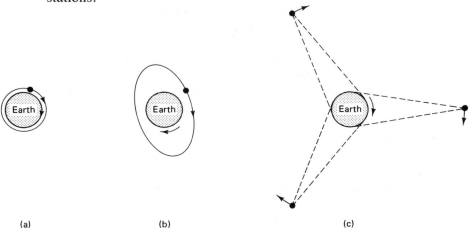

(a)   (b)   (c)

Figure 8-2 Satellite orbits: (a) low altitude (circular orbit, 100–300 mi); (b) medium altitude (elliptical orbit, 6000 to 12,000 mi); (c) high altitude (geosynchronous orbit, 19,000 to 25,000 mi).

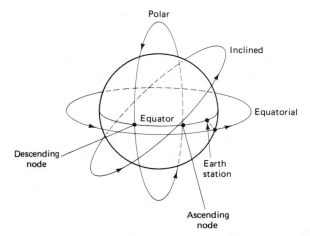

Polar

Inclined

Equatorial

Equator

Descending
node

Earth
station

Ascending
node

Figure 8-3 Satellite orbits.

2. There is no need to switch from one satellite to another as they orbit overhead. Consequently, there are no breaks in transmission because of the switching times.

3. High-altitude geosynchronous satellites can cover a much larger area of the earth than their low-altitude orbital counterparts.

4. The effects of Doppler shift are negligible.

Disadvantages of Geosynchronous Orbits

1. The higher altitudes of geosynchronous satellites introduce much longer propagation times. The round-trip propagation delay between two earth stations through a geosynchronous satellite is 500 to 600 ms.

2. Geosynchronous satellites require higher transmit powers and more sensitive receivers because of the longer distances and greater path losses.

3. High-precision spacemanship is required to place a geosynchronous satellite into orbit and to keep it there. Also, propulsion engines are required on board the satellites to keep them in their respective orbits.

LOOK ANGLES

To orient an earth station antenna toward a satellite, it is necessary to know the *elevation angle* and *azimuth* (Figure 8-4). These are called the *look angles*.

Angle of Elevation

The angle of elevation is the angle formed between the plane of a wave radiated from an earth station antenna and the horizon, or the angle subtended at the

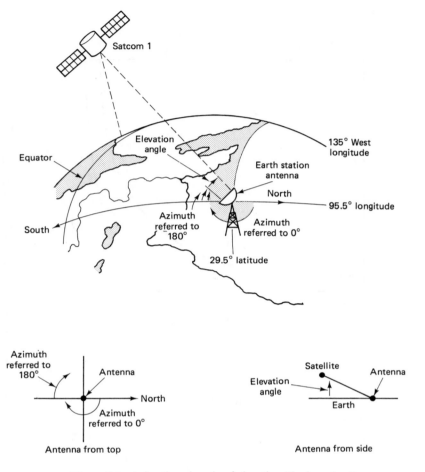

Figure 8-4 Azimuth and angle of elevation "look angles."

earth station antenna between the satellite and the earth's horizon. The smaller the angle of elevation, the greater the distance a propagated wave must pass through the earth's atmosphere. As with any wave propagated through the earth's atmosphere, it suffers absorption and may also be severely contaminated by noise. Consequently, if the angle of elevation is too small and the distance the wave is within the earth's atmosphere is too long, the wave may deteriorate to a degree that it provides inadequate transmission. Generally, 5° is considered as the minimum acceptable angle of elevation. Figure 8-5 shows how the angle of elevation affects the signal strength of a propagated wave due to normal atmospheric absorption, absorption due to thick fog, and absorption due to a heavy rain. It can be seen that the 14/12-GHz band (Figure 8-5b) is more severely affected than the 6/4-GHz band (Figure 8-5a). This is due to the smaller wavelengths associated with the higher frequencies. Also, at elevation angles less than 5°, the attenuation increases rapidly.

Look Angles   **305**

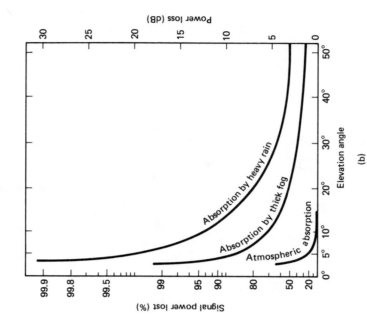

(b)

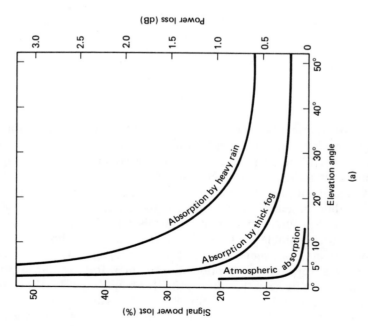

(a)

Figure 8-5 Attenuation due to atmospheric absorption: (a) 6/4-GHz band; (b) 14/12-GHz band.

Azimuth

Azimuth is defined as the horizontal pointing angle of an antenna. It is measured in a clockwise direction in degrees from true north. The angle of elevation and the azimuth both depend on the latitude of the earth station and the longitude of both the earth station and the orbiting satellite. For a geosynchronous satellite in an equatorial orbit, the procedure is as follows: From a good map, determine the longitude and latitude of the earth station. From Table 8-2, determine the longitude of the satellite of interest. Calculate the difference, in degrees (ΔL), between the longitude of the satellite and the longitude of the earth station. Then, from Figure 8-6, determine the azimuth and elevation angle for the antenna. Figure 8-6 is for a geosynchronous satellite in an equatorial orbit.

Example 8-1

An earth station is located at Houston, Texas, which has a longitude of 95.5°W and a latitude of 29.5°N. The satellite of interest is RCA's *Satcom 1,* which has a longitude of 135°W. Determine the azimuth and elevation angle for the earth station antenna.

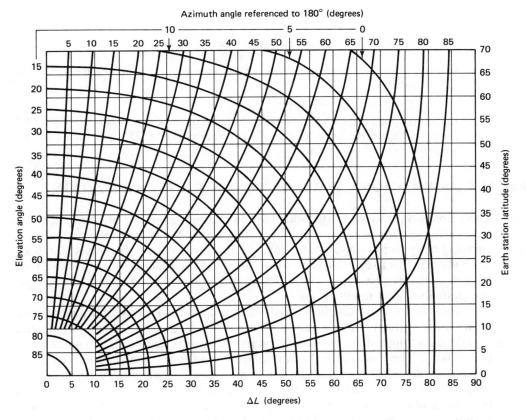

Figure 8-6 Azimuth and elevation angle for earth stations located in the northern hemisphere (referred to 180°).

**TABLE 8-2
LONGITUDINAL
POSITION OF
SEVERAL CURRENT
SYNCHRONOUS
SATELLITES
PARKED IN AN
EQUATORIAL ARC[a]**

Satellite	Longitude (°W)
Satcom I	135
Satcom V	143
ANIK I	104
Westar I	99
Westar II	123.5
Westar III	91
Westar IV	98.5
Westar V	119.5
RCA	126
Mexico	116.5
Galaxy	74
Telstar	96

[a]0° Latitude.

Solution First determine the difference between the longitude of the earth station and the satellite.

$$\Delta L = 135° - 95.5° = 39.5°$$

Locate the intersection of ΔL and the latitude of the earth station on Figure 8-6. From the figure the angle of elevation is approximately 35°, and the azimuth is approximately 59° west of south.

ORBITAL CLASSIFICATIONS, SPACING, AND FREQUENCY ALLOCATION

There are two primary classifications for communications satellites: *spinners* and *three-axis stabilizer satellites*. Spinner satellites use the angular momentum of its spinning body to provide roll and yaw stabilization. With a three-axis stabilizer, the body remains fixed relative to the earth's surface while an internal subsystem provides roll and yaw stabilization. Figure 8-7 shows the two main classifications of communications satellites.

Geosynchronous satellites must share a limited space and frequency spectrum within a given arc of a geostationary orbit. Each communications satellite is assigned a longitude in the geostationary arc approximately 22,300 miles above the equator. The position in the slot depends on the communications frequency band used. Satellites operating at or near the same frequency must be sufficiently separated in space to avoid interfering with each other (Figure 8-8). There is a realistic limit to the number of satellite structures that can be stationed (*parked*) within a given area in space. The required *spatial separation* is dependent on the following variables:

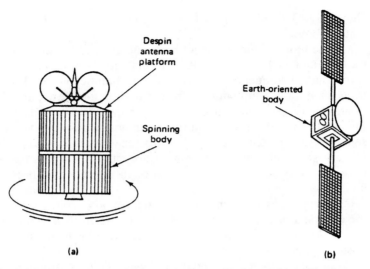

Figure 8-7 Satellite classes: (a) spinner; (b) three-axis stabilized.

1. Beamwidths and sidelobe radiation of both the earth station and satellite antennas
2. RF carrier frequency
3. Encoding or modulation technique used
4. Acceptable limits of interference
5. Transmit carrier power

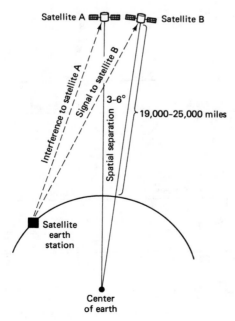

Figure 8-8 Spatial separation of satellites in geosynchronous orbit.

Orbital Classifications, Spacing, and Frequency Allocation   **309**

Generally, 3 to 6° of spatial separation is required depending on the variables stated above.

The most common carrier frequencies used for satellite communications are the 6/4- and 14/12-GHz bands. The first number is the up-link (earth station-to-transponder) frequency, and the second number is the down-link (transponder-to-earth station) frequency. Different up-link and down-link frequencies are used to prevent ringaround from occurring (Chapter 7). The higher the carrier frequency, the smaller the diameter required of an antenna for a given gain. Most domestic satellites use the 6/4-GHz band. Unfortunately, this band is also used extensively for terrestrial microwave systems. Care must be taken when designing a satellite network to avoid interference from or interference with established microwave links.

Certain positions in the geosynchronous orbit are in higher demand than the others. For example, the mid-Atlantic position which is used to interconnect North America and Europe is in exceptionally high demand. The mid-Pacific position is another.

The frequencies allocated by WARC (World Administrative Radio Conference) are summarized in Figure 8-9. Table 8-3 shows the bandwidths available for various services in the United States. These services include *fixed-point* (between earth stations located at fixed geographical points on earth), *broadcast* (wide-area coverage), *mobile* (ground-to-aircraft, ships, or land vehicles), and *intersatellite* (satellite-to-satellite cross-links).

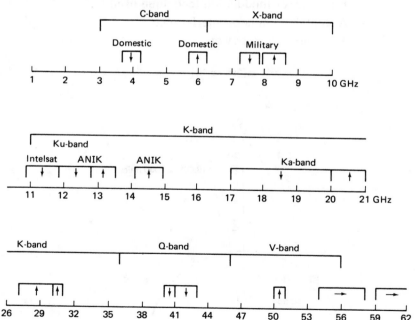

Figure 8-9 WARC satellite frequency assignments.

**TABLE 8-3   RF SATELLITE BANDWIDTHS
AVAILABLE IN THE UNITED STATES**

| Band | Frequency band (GHz) | | Bandwidth (MHz) |
	Up-link	Down-link	
C	5.9–6.4	3.7–4.2	500
X	7.9–8.4	7.25–7.75	500
Ku	14–14.5	11.7–12.2	500
Ka	27–30	17–20	—
	30–31	20–21	—
V	50–51	40–41	1000
Q	—	41–43	2000
V	54–58		3900
(ISL)	59–64		5000

RADIATION PATTERNS: FOOTPRINTS

The area of the earth covered by a satellite depends on the location of the satellite in its geosynchronous orbit, its carrier frequency, and the gain of its antennas. Satellite engineers select the antenna and carrier frequency for a particular spacecraft to concentrate the limited transmitted power on a specific area of the earth's surface. The geographical representation of a satellite antenna's radiation pattern is called a *footprint* (Figure 8-10). The contour lines represent limits of equal receive power density.

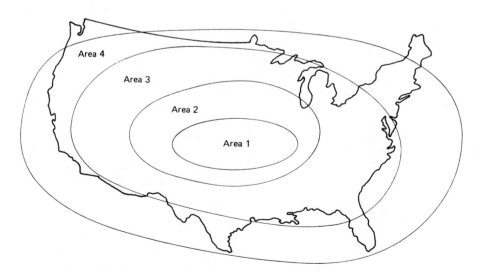

Figure 8-10   Satellite antenna radiation patterns ("footprints").

The radiation pattern from a satellite antenna may be categorized as either *spot, zonal,* or *earth* (Figure 8-11). The radiation patterns of earth coverage antennas have a beamwidth of approximately 17° and include coverage of approximately one-third of the earth's surface. Zonal coverage includes an area less than one-third of the earth's surface. Spot beams concentrate the radiated power in a very small geographic area.

Reuse

When an allocated frequency band is filled, additional capacity can be achieved by *reuse* of the frequency spectrum. By increasing the size of an antenna (i.e., increasing the antenna gain) the beamwidth of the antenna is also reduced. Thus different beams of the same frequency can be directed to different geographical areas of the earth. This is called frequency reuse. Another method of frequency reuse is to use dual polarization. Different information signals can be transmitted to different earth station receivers using the same band of frequencies simply by orienting their electromagnetic polarizations in an orthogonal manner (90° out of phase). Dual polarization is less effective because the earth's atmosphere has a tendency to reorient or repolarize an electromagnetic wave as it passes through. Reuse is simply another way to increase the capacity of a limited bandwidth.

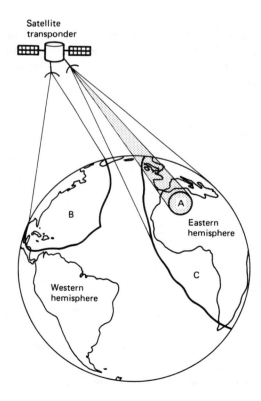

Figure 8-11   Beams: A, spot; B, zonal; C, earth.

SATELLITE SYSTEM LINK MODELS

Essentially, a satellite system consists of three basic sections: the uplink, the satellite transponder, and the downlink.

Uplink Model

The primary component within the *uplink* section of a satellite system is the earth station transmitter. A typical earth station transmitter consists of an IF modulator, an IF-to-RF microwave up-converter, a high-power amplifier (HPA), and some means of bandlimiting the final output spectrum (i.e., an output bandpass filter). Figure 8-12 shows the block diagram of a satellite earth station transmitter. The IF modulator converts the input baseband signals to either an FM, a PSK, or a QAM modulated intermediate frequency. The up-converter (mixer and bandpass filter) converts the IF to an appropriate RF carrier frequency. The HPA provides adequate input sensitivity and output power to propagate the signal to the satellite transponder. HPAs commonly used are klystons and traveling-wave tubes.

Transponder

A typical *satellite transponder* consists of an input bandlimiting device (BPF), an input *low-noise amplifier* (LNA), a *frequency translator,* a low-level power amplifier, and an output bandpass filter. Figure 8-13 shows a simplified block diagram of a satellite transponder. This transponder is an RF-to-RF repeater. Other transponder configurations are IF and baseband repeaters similar to those used in microwave repeaters. In Figure 8-13, the input BPF limits the total noise applied to the input of the LNA. (A common device used as an LNA is a tunnel diode.) The output of the LNA is fed to a frequency translator (a shift oscillator and a BPF) which converts the high-band uplink frequency to the low-band

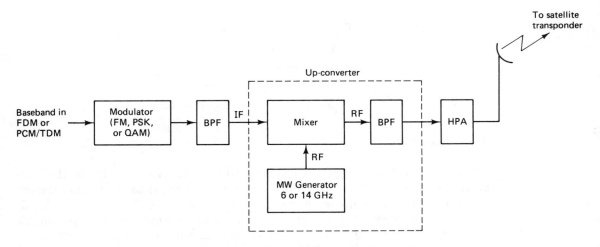

Figure 8-12 Satellite uplink model.

Satellite System Link Models

313

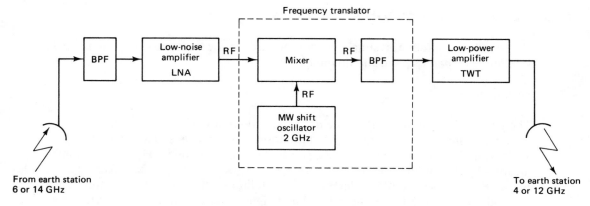

Figure 8-13 Satellite transponder.

downlink frequency. The low-level power amplifier, which is commonly a traveling-wave tube, amplifies the RF signal for transmission through the downlink to the earth station receivers. Each RF satellite channel requires a separate transponder.

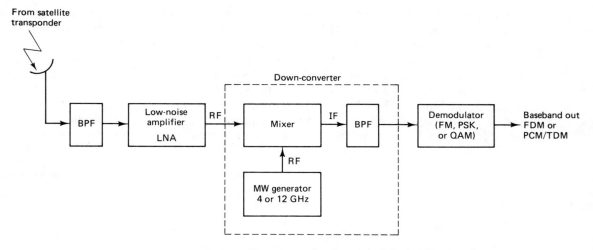

Figure 8-14 Satellite downlink model.

Downlink Model

An earth station receiver includes an input BPF, an LNA, and an RF-to-IF down-converter. Figure 8-14 shows a block diagram of a typical earth station receiver. Again, the BPF limits the input noise power to the LNA. The LNA is a highly sensitive, low-noise device such as a tunnel diode amplifier or a parametric amplifier. The RF-to-IF down-converter is a mixer/bandpass filter combination which converts the received RF signal to an IF frequency.

Cross-Links

Occasionally, there is an application where it is necessary to communicate between satellites. This is done using *satellite cross-links* or *intersatellite links* (ISLs), shown in Figure 8-15. A disadvantage of using an ISL is that both the transmitter and receiver are *spacebound*. Consequently, both the transmitter's output power and the receiver's input sensitivity are limited.

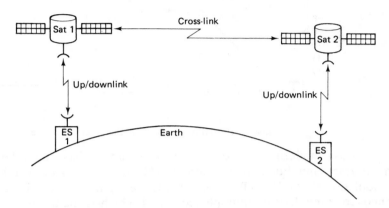

Figure 8-15   Intersatellite link.

SATELLITE SYSTEM PARAMETERS

Transmit Power and Bit Energy

High-power amplifiers used in earth station transmitters and the traveling-wave tubes typically used in satellite transponders are *nonlinear devices*; their gain (output power-versus-input power) is dependent on input signal level. A typical input/output power characteristic curve is shown in Figure 8-16. It can be seen that as the input power is reduced by 5 dB, the output power is reduced by only 2 dB. There is an obvious *power compression*. To reduce the amount of intermodulation distortion caused by the nonlinear amplification of the HPA, the input power must be reduced (*backed off*) by several dB. This allows the HPA to operate in a more *linear* region. The amount the input level is backed off is equivalent to a loss and is appropriately called *back-off loss* (L_{bo}).

To operate as efficiently as possible, a power amplifier should be operated as close as possible to saturation. The *saturated output power* is designated P_o (sat) or simply P_t. The output power of a typical satellite earth station transmitter is much higher than the output power from a terrestrial microwave power amplifier. Consequently, when dealing with satellite systems, P_t is generally expressed in dBW (decibels in respect to 1 W) rather than in dBm (decibels in respect to 1 mW).

Satellite System Parameters   **315**

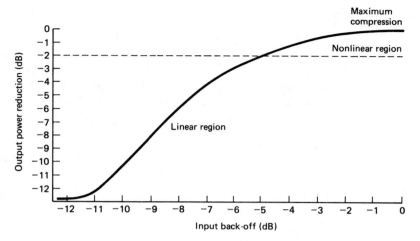

Figure 8-16 HPA input/output characteristic curve.

Most modern satellite systems use either phase shift keying (PSK) or quadrature amplitude modulation (QAM) rather than conventional frequency modulation (FM). With PSK and QAM, the input baseband is generally a PCM-encoded, time-division-multiplexed signal which is digital in nature. Also, with PSK and QAM, several bits may be encoded in a single transmit signaling element (baud). Consequently, a parameter more meaningful than carrier power is *energy per bit* (E_b). Mathematically, E_b is

$$E_b = P_t T_b \qquad (8\text{-}1a)$$

where

E_b = energy of a single bit (J/bit)

P_t = total carrier power (W)

T_b = time of a single bit (s)

or because $T_b = 1/f_b$, where f_b is the bit rate in bits per second.

$$E_b = \frac{P_t}{f_b} \qquad (8\text{-}1b)$$

Example 8-2

For a total transmit power (P_t) of 1000 W, determine the energy per bit (E_b) for a transmission rate of 50 Mbps.

Solution

$$T_b = \frac{1}{f_b} = \frac{1}{50 \times 10^6 \text{ bps}} = 0.02 \times 10^{-6} \text{ s}$$

(It appears that the units for T_b should be s/bit but the per bit is implied in the definition of T_b, time of bit.)

Substituting into Equation 8-1a yields

$$E_b = 1000 \text{ J/s } (0.02 \times 10^{-6} \text{ s/bit}) = 20 \text{ } \mu\text{J/bit}$$

(Again the units appear to be J/bit, but the per bit is implied in the definition of E_b, energy per bit.)

$$E_b = \frac{1000 \text{ J/s}}{50 \times 10^6 \text{ bps}} = 20 \text{ } \mu\text{J}$$

Expressed as a log,

$$E_b = 10 \log (20 \times 10^{-6}) = -47 \text{ dBJ}$$

It is common to express P_t in dBW and E_b in dBW/bps. Thus

$$P_t = 10 \log 1000 = 30 \text{ dBW}$$

$$E_b = P_t - 10 \log f_b$$

$$= P_t - 10 \log(50 \times 10^6)$$

$$= 30 \text{ dBW} - 77 \text{ dB} = -47 \text{ dBW/bps}$$

or simply -47 dBW.

Effective Isotropic Radiated Power

Effective isotropic radiated power (EIRP) is defined as an equivalent transmit power and is expressed mathematically as

$$\text{EIRP} = P_r A_t$$

where

> EIRP = effective isotropic radiated power (W)
> P_r = total power radiated from an antenna (W)
> A_t = transmit antenna gain (W/W or a unitless ratio)

Expressed as a log,

$$\text{EIRP (dBW)} = P_r \text{ (dBW)} + A_t \text{ (dB)}$$

In respect to the transmitter output,

$$P_r = P_t - L_{\text{bo}} - L_{bf}$$

Thus

$$\text{EIRP} = P_t - L_{\text{bo}} - L_{bf} + A_t \tag{8-2}$$

where

> P_t = actual power output of the transmitter (dBW)
> L_{bo} = back-off losses of HPA (dB)
> L_{bf} = total branching and feeder loss (dB)
> A_t = transmit antenna gain (dB)

Example 8-3

For an earth station transmitter with an output power of 40 dBW (10,000 W), a

Satellite System Parameters **317**

back-off loss of 3 dB, a total branching and feeder loss of 3 dB, and a transmit antenna gain of 40 dB, determine the EIRP.

Solution   Substituting into Equation 8-2 yields

$$EIRP = P_t - L_{bo} - L_{bf} + A_t$$

$$= 40\,dBW - 3\,dB - 3\,dB + 40\,dB = 74\,dBW$$

Equivalent Noise Temperature

With terrestrial microwave systems, the noise introduced in a receiver or a component within a receiver was commonly specified by the parameter noise figure. In satellite communications systems, it is often necessary to differentiate or measure noise in increments as small as a tenth or a hundredth of a decibel. Noise figure, in its standard form, is inadequate for such precise calculations. Consequently, it is common to use *environmental temperature* (T) and *equivalent noise temperature* (T_e) when evaluating the performance of a satellite system. In Chapter 7 total noise power was expressed mathematically as

$$N = KTB$$

Rearranging and solving for T gives us

$$T = \frac{N}{KB}$$

where

$$N = \text{total noise power (W)}$$
$$K = \text{Boltzmann's constant (J/K)}$$
$$B = \text{bandwidth (Hz)}$$
$$T = \text{temperature of the environment (K)}$$

Again from Chapter 7 (Equation 7-7),

$$NF = 1 + \frac{T_e}{T}$$

where

$$T_e = \text{equivalent noise temperature (K)}$$
$$NF = \text{noise figure (absolute value)}$$
$$T = \text{temperature of the environment (K)}$$

Rearranging Equation 7-7, we have

$$T_e = T(NF - 1)$$

Typically, equivalent noise temperatures of the receivers used in satellite transponders are about 1000 K. For earth station receivers T_e values are between

20 and 1000 K. Equivalent noise temperature is generally more useful when expressed logarithmically with the unit of dBK, as follows:

$$T_e \text{ (dBK)} = 10 \log T_e$$

For an equivalent noise temperature of 100 K, T_e (dBK) is

$$T_e \text{ (dBK)} = 10 \log 100 \text{ or } 20 \text{ dBK}$$

Equivalent noise temperature is a hypothetical value that can be calculated but cannot be measured. Equivalent noise temperature is often used rather than noise figure because it is a more accurate method of expressing the noise contributed by a device or a receiver when evaluating its performance. Essentially, equivalent noise temperature (T_e) is the noise present at the input to a device or amplifier plus the noise added internally by that device. This allows us to analyze the noise characteristics of a device by simply evaluating an equivalent input noise temperature. As you will see in subsequent discussions, T_e is a very useful parameter when evaluating the performance of a satellite system.

Example 8-4

Convert noise figures of 4 and 4.01 to equivalent noise temperatures. Use 300 K for the environmental temperature.

Solution Substituting into Equation 7-7 yields

$$T_e = T(\text{NF} - 1)$$

For NF = 4:

$$T_e = 300(4 - 1) = 900 \text{ K}$$

For NF = 4.01:

$$T_e = 300(4.01 - 1) = 903 \text{ K}$$

It can be seen that the 3° difference in the equivalent temperatures is 300 times as large as the difference between the two noise figures. Consequently, equivalent noise temperature is a more accurate way of comparing the noise performances of two receivers or devices.

Noise Density

Simply stated, *noise density* (N_0) is the total noise power normalized to a 1-Hz bandwidth, or the noise power present in a 1-Hz bandwidth. Mathematically, noise density is

$$N_0 = \frac{N}{B} \quad \text{or} \quad KT_e \tag{8-3a}$$

where

N_0 = noise density (W/Hz) (N_0 is generally expressed as simply watts; the per hertz is implied in the definition of N_0)

Satellite System Parameters

N = total noise power (W)

B = bandwidth (Hz)

K = Boltzmann's constant (J/K)

T_e = equivalent noise temperature (K)

Expressed as a log,

$$N_0 \,(\text{dBW/Hz}) = 10 \log N - 10 \log B \qquad (8\text{-}3\text{b})$$

$$= 10 \log K + 10 \log T_e \qquad (8\text{-}3\text{c})$$

Example 8-5

For an equivalent noise bandwidth of 10 MHz and a total noise power of 0.0276 pW, determine the noise density and equivalent noise temperature.

Solution Substituting into Equation 8-3a, we have

$$N_0 = \frac{N}{B} = \frac{276 \times 10^{-16}\,\text{W}}{10 \times 10^6\,\text{Hz}} = 276 \times 10^{-23}\,\frac{\text{W}}{\text{Hz}}$$

or simply, 276×10^{-23} W.

$$N_0 = 10 \log (276 \times 10^{-23}) = -205.6 \text{ dBW/Hz}$$

or simply -205.6 dBW. Substituting into Equation 8-3b gives us

$$N_0 = N \,(\text{dBW}) - B \,(\text{dB/Hz})$$

$$= -135.6 \,\text{dBW} - 70 \,(\text{dB/Hz}) = -205.6 \,\text{dBW}$$

Rearranging Equation 8-3a and solving for equivalent noise temperature yields

$$T_e = \frac{N_0}{K}$$

$$= \frac{276 \times 10^{-23}\,\text{J/cycle}}{1.38 \times 10^{-23}\,\text{J/K}} = 200 \text{ K/cycle}$$

$$= 10 \log 200 = 23 \text{ dBK}$$

$$= N_0 \,(\text{dBW}) - 10 \log K$$

$$= -205.6 \,\text{dBW} - (-228.6 \,\text{dBWK}) = 23 \text{ dBK}$$

Carrier-to-Noise Density Ratio

C/N_0 is the average wideband carrier power-to-noise density ratio. The *wideband carrier power* is the combined power of the carrier and its associated sidebands. The noise is the thermal noise present in a normalized 1-Hz bandwidth. The carrier-to-noise density ratio may also be written as a function of noise temperature. Mathematically, C/N_0 is

$$\frac{C}{N_0} = \frac{C}{KT_e} \qquad (8\text{-}4\text{a})$$

Expressed as a log,

$$\frac{C}{N_0}(dB) = C(dBW) - N_0(dBW) \qquad (8\text{-}4b)$$

Energy of Bit-to-Noise Density Ratio

E_b/N_0 is one of the most important and most often used parameters when evaluating a digital radio system. The E_b/N_0 ratio is a convenient way to compare digital systems that use different transmission rates, modulation schemes, or encoding techniques. Mathematically, E_b/N_0 is

$$\frac{E_b}{N_0} = \frac{C/f_b}{N/B} = \frac{CB}{Nf_b} \qquad (8\text{-}5)$$

E_b/N_0 is a convenient term used for digital system calculations and perform-ance comparisons, but in the real world, it is more convenient to measure the wideband carrier power-to-noise density ratio and convert it to E_b/N_0. Rearranging Equation 8-5 yields the following expression:

$$\frac{E_b}{N_0} = \frac{C}{N} \times \frac{B}{f_b}$$

The E_b/N_0 ratio is the product of the carrier-to-noise ratio (C/N) and the noise bandwidth-to-bit ratio (B/f_b). Expressed as a log,

$$\frac{E_b}{N_0}(dB) = \frac{C}{N}(dB) + \frac{B}{f_b}(dB) \qquad (8\text{-}6)$$

The energy per bit (E_b) will remain constant as long as the total wideband carrier power (C) and the transmission rate (bps) remain unchanged. Also, the noise density (N_0) will remain constant as long as the noise temperature remains constant. The following conclusion can be made: For a given carrier power, bit rate, and noise temperature, the E_b/N_0 ratio will remain constant regardless of the encoding technique, modulation scheme, or bandwidth used.

Figure 8-17 graphically illustrates the relationship between an expected probability of error $P(e)$ and the minimum C/N ratio required to achieve the $P(e)$. The C/N specified is for the minimum double-sided Nyquist bandwidth. Figure 8-18 graphically illustrates the relationship between an expected $P(e)$ and the minimum E_b/N_0 ratio required to achieve that $P(e)$.

A $P(e)$ of 10^{-5} ($1/10^5$) indicates a probability that 1 bit will be in error for every 100,000 bits transmitted. $P(e)$ is analogous to the bit error rate (BER).

Example 8-6

A coherent binary phase-shift-keyed (BPSK) transmitter operates at a bit rate of 20 Mbps. For a probability of error $P(e)$ of 10^{-4}:

(a) Determine the minimum theoretical C/N and E_b/N_0 ratios for a receiver bandwidth equal to the minimum double-sided Nyquist bandwidth.

Satellite System Parameters   **321**

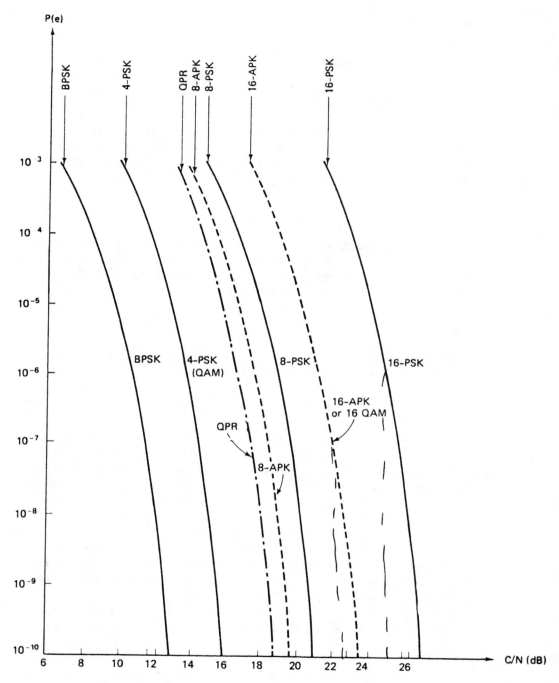

Figure 8-17 *P(e)* performance of *M*-ary PSK, QAM, QPR, and *M*-ary APK coherent systems. The rms *C/N* is specified in the double-sided Nyquist bandwidth.

Satellite Communications   Chap. 8

(b) Determine the C/N if the noise is measured at a point prior to the bandpass filter, where the bandwidth is equal to twice the Nyquist bandwidth.

(c) Determine the C/N if the noise is measured at a point prior to the bandpass filter where the bandwidth is equal to three times the Nyquist bandwidth.

Solution (a) With BPSK, the minimum bandwidth is equal to the bit rate, 20 MHz. From Figure 8-17, the minimum C/N is 8.8 dB. Substituting into Equation 8-6 gives us

$$\frac{E_b}{N_0}(\text{dB}) = \frac{C}{N}(\text{dB}) + \frac{B}{f_b}(\text{dB})$$

$$= 8.8\,\text{dB} + 10\log\frac{20 \times 10^6}{20 \times 10^6}$$

$$= 8.8\,\text{dB} + 0\,\text{dB} = 8.8\,\text{db}$$

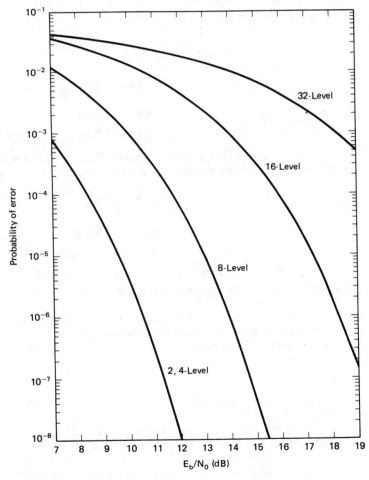

Figure 8-18 Probability of error $P(e)$ versus E_b/N_0 ratio for various digital modulation schemes.

Satellite System Parameters

Note: The minimum E_b/N_0 equals the minimum C/N when the receiver noise bandwidth equals the minimum Nyquist bandwidth. The minimum E_b/N_0 of 8.8 can be verified from Figure 8-18.

What effect does increasing the noise bandwidth have on the minimum C/N and E_b/N_0 ratios? The wideband carrier power is totally independent of the noise bandwidth. Similarly, an increase in the bandwidth causes a corresponding increase in the noise power. Consequently, a decrease in C/N is realized that is directly proportional to the increase in the noise bandwidth. E_b is dependent on the wideband carrier power and the bit rate only. Therefore, E_b is unaffected by an increase in the noise bandwidth. N_0 is the noise power normalized to a 1-Hz bandwidth and, consequently, is also unaffected by an increase in the noise bandwidth.

(b) Since E_b/N_0 is independent of bandwidth, measuring the C/N at a point in the receiver where the bandwidth is equal to twice the minimum Nyquist bandwidth has absolutely no effect on E_b/N_0. Therefore, E_b/N_0 becomes the constant in Equation 8-6 and is used to solve for the new value of C/N. Rearranging Equation 8-6 and using the calculated E_b/N_0 ratio, we have

$$\frac{C}{N}(\text{dB}) = \frac{E_b}{N_0}(\text{dB}) - \frac{B}{f_b}(\text{dB})$$

$$= 8.8\,\text{dB} - 10\log\frac{40 \times 10^6}{20 \times 10^6}$$

$$= 8.8\,\text{dB} - 10\log 2$$

$$= 8.8\,\text{dB} - 3\,\text{dB} = 5.8\,\text{dB}$$

(c) Measuring the C/N ratio at a point in the receiver where the bandwidth equals three times the minimum bandwidth yields the following results for C/N.

$$\frac{C}{N} = \frac{E_b}{N_0} - 10\log\frac{60 \times 10^6}{20 \times 10^6}$$

$$= 8.8\,\text{dB} - 10\log 3$$

$$= 4.03\,\text{dB}$$

The C/N ratios of 8.8, 5.8, and 4.03 dB indicate the C/N ratios that would be measured at the three specified points in the receiver to achieve the desired minimum E_b/N_0 and $P(e)$.

Because E_b/N_0 cannot be directly measured to determine the E_b/N_0 ratio, the wideband carrier-to-noise ratio is measured and then substituted into Equation 8-6. Consequently, to accurately determine the E_b/N_0 ratio, the noise bandwidth of the receiver must be known.

Example 8-7

A coherent 8-PSK transmitter operates at a bit rate of 90 Mbps. For a probability of error of 10^{-5}:

(a) Determine the minimum theoretical C/N and E_b/N_0 ratios for a receiver bandwidth equal to the minimum double-sided Nyquist bandwidth.

(b) Determine the C/N if the noise is measured at a point prior to the bandpass filter where the bandwidth is equal to twice the Nyquist bandwidth.

(c) Determine the C/N if the noise is measured at a point prior to the bandpass filter where the bandwidth is equal to three times the Nyquist bandwidth.

Solution (a) 8-PSK has a bandwidth efficiency of 3 bps/Hz and, consequently, requires a minimum bandwidth of one-third the bit rate or 30 MHz. From Figure 8-17, the minimum C/N is 18.5 dB. Substituting into Equation 8-6, we obtain

$$\frac{E_b}{N_0}(\text{dB}) = 18.5\,\text{dB} + 10\log\frac{30\,\text{MHz}}{90\,\text{Mbps}}$$

$$= 18.5\,\text{dB} + (-4.8\,\text{dB}) = 13.7\,\text{db}$$

(b) Rearranging Equation 8-6 and substituting for E_b/N_0 yields

$$\frac{C}{N}(\text{dB}) = 13.7\,(\text{dB}) - 10\log\frac{60\,\text{MHz}}{90\,\text{Mbps}}$$

$$= 13.7\,\text{dB} - (-1.77\,\text{dB}) = 15.47\,\text{dB}$$

(c) Again, rearranging Equation 8-6 and substituting for E_b/N_0 gives us

$$\frac{C}{N}(\text{dB} = 13.7\,(\text{dB}) - 10\log\frac{90\,\text{MHz}}{90\,\text{Mbps}}$$

$$= 13.7\,\text{dB} - 0\,\text{dB} = 13.7\,\text{dB}$$

It should be evident from Examples 8-6 and 8-7 that the E_b/N_0 and C/N ratios are equal only when the noise bandwidth is equal to the bit rate. Also, as the bandwidth at the point of measurement increases, the C/N decreases.

When the modulation scheme, bit rate, bandwidth, and C/N ratios of two digital radio systems are different; it is often difficult to determine which system has the lower probability of error. Because E_b/N_0 is independent of bit rate, bandwidth, and modulation scheme; it is a convenient common denominator to use for comparing the probability of error performance of two digital radio systems.

Example 8-8

Compare the performance characteristics of the two digital systems listed below, and determine which system has the lower probability of error.

	QPSK	8-PSK
Bit rate	40 Mbps	60 Mbps
Bandwidth	1.5 × minimum	2 × minimum
C/N	10.75 dB	13.76 dB

Solution Substituting into Equation 8-6 for the QPSK system gives us

$$\frac{E_b}{N_0}(\text{dB}) = \frac{C}{N}(\text{dB}) + 10\log\frac{B}{f_b}$$

$$= 10.75\,\text{dB} + 10\log\frac{1.5 \times 20\,\text{MHz}}{40\,\text{Mbps}}$$

$$= 10.75\,\text{dB} + (-1.25\,\text{dB})$$

$$= 9.5\,\text{dB}$$

From Figure 8-18, the $P(e)$ is 10^{-4}.

Satellite System Parameters

Substituting into Equation 8-6 for the 8-PSK system gives us

$$\frac{E_b}{N_0}(\text{dB}) = 13.76\,\text{dB} + 10\log\frac{2 \times 20\,\text{MHz}}{60\,\text{Mbps}}$$

$$= 13.76\,\text{dB} + (-1.76\,\text{dB})$$

$$= 12\,\text{dB}$$

From Figure 8-18, the $P(e)$ is 10^{-3}.

Although the QPSK system has a lower C/N and E_b/N_0 ratio, the $P(e)$ of the QPSK system is 10 times lower (better) than the 8-PSK system.

Gain-to-Equivalent Noise Temperature Ratio

Essentially, *gain-to-equivalent noise temperature ratio* (G/T_e) is a figure of merit used to represent the quality of a satellite or an earth station receiver. The G/T_e of a receiver is the ratio of the receive antenna gain to the equivalent noise temperature (T_e) of the receiver. Because of the extremely small receive carrier powers typically experienced with satellite systems, very often an LNA is physically located at the feedpoint of the antenna. When this is the case, G/T_e is a ratio of the gain of the receiving antenna plus the gain of the LNA to the equivalent noise temperature. Mathematically, gain-to-equivalent noise temperature ratio is

$$\frac{G}{T_e} = \frac{A_r + A(\text{LNA})}{T_e} \tag{8-7}$$

Expressed in logs, we have

$$\frac{G}{T_e}(\text{dBK}^{-1}) = A_r\,(\text{dB}) + A(\text{LNA})(\text{dB}) - T_e\,(\text{dBK}^{-1}) \tag{8-8}$$

G/T_e is a very useful parameter for determining the E_b/N_0 and C/N ratios at the satellite transponder and earth station receivers. G/T_e is essentially the only parameter required at a satellite or an earth station receiver when completing a link budget.

Example 8-9

For a satellite transponder with a receiver antenna gain of 22 dB, an LNA gain of 10 dB, and an equivalent noise temperature of 22 dBK^{-1}; determine the G/T_e figure of merit.

Solution Substituting into Equation 8-8 yields

$$\frac{G}{T_e}(\text{dBK}^{-1}) = 22\,\text{dB} + 10\,\text{dB} - 22\,\text{dBK}^{-1}$$

$$= 10\,\text{dBK}^{-1}$$

SATELLITE SYSTEM LINK EQUATIONS

The error performance of a digital satellite system is quite predictable. Figure 8-19 shows a simplified block diagram of a digital satellite system and identifies the various gains and losses that may affect the system performance. When evaluating the performance of a digital satellite system, the uplink and downlink parameters are first considered separately, then the overall performance is determined by combining them in the appropriate manner. Keep in mind, a digital microwave or satellite radio simply means the original and demodulated baseband signals are digital in nature. The RF portion of the radio is analog; that is, FSK, PSK, QAM, or some other higher-level modulation riding on an analog microwave carrier.

LINK EQUATIONS

The following *link equations* are used to separately analyze the uplink and the downlink sections of a single radio-frequency carrier satellite system. These equations consider only the ideal gains and losses and effects of thermal noise associated with the earth station transmitter, earth station receiver, and the satellite transponder. The nonideal aspects of the system are discussed later in this chapter.

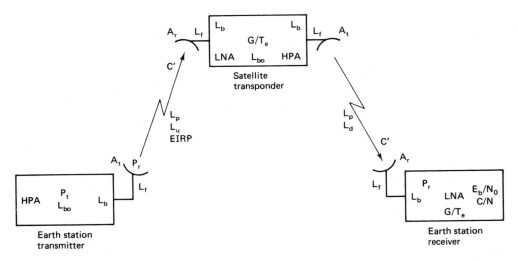

Figure 8-19 Overall satellite system showing the gains and losses incurred in both the uplink and downlink sections. HPA, High-power amplifier; P_t, HPA output power; L_{bo}, back-off loss; L_f, feeder loss; L_b, branching loss; A_t, transmit antenna gain; P_r, total radiated power = $P_t - L_{bo} - L_b - L_f$; EIRP, effective isotropic radiated power = $P_r A_t$; L_u, additional uplink losses due to atmosphere; L_p, path loss; A_r, receive antenna gain; G/T_e, gain-to-equivalent noise ratio; L_d, additional downlink losses due to atmosphere; LNA, low-noise amplifier; C/T_e, carrier-to-equivalent noise ratio; C/N_0, carrier-to-noise density ratio; E_b/N_0, energy of bit-to-noise density ratio; C/N, carrier-to-noise ratio.

Link Equations   **327**

Uplink Equation

$$\frac{C}{N_0} = \frac{A_t P_r (L_p L_u) A_r}{K T_e} = \frac{A_t P_r (L_p L_u)}{K} \times \frac{G}{T_e}$$

where L_d and L_u are the additional uplink and downlink atmospheric losses, respectively. The uplink and downlink signals must pass through the earth's atmosphere, where they are partially absorbed by the moisture, oxygen, and particulates in the air. Depending on the elevation angle, the distance the RF signal travels through the atmosphere varies from one earth station to another. Because L_p, L_u, and L_d represent losses, they are decimal values less than 1. G/T_e is the receiving antenna gain divided by the equivalent input noise temperature.

Expressed as a log,

$$\frac{C}{N_0} = \underbrace{10 \log A_t P_r}_{\substack{\text{EIRP} \\ \text{earth} \\ \text{station}}} - \underbrace{20 \log \left(\frac{4\pi D}{\lambda} \right)}_{\substack{\text{free-space} \\ \text{path loss}}} + \underbrace{10 \log \left(\frac{G}{T_e} \right)}_{\substack{\text{satellite} \\ G/T_e}} - \underbrace{10 \log L_u}_{\substack{\text{additional} \\ \text{atmospheric} \\ \text{losses}}} - \underbrace{10 \log K}_{\substack{\text{Boltzmann's} \\ \text{constant}}}$$

$$= \text{EIRP (dBW)} - L_p\,(\text{dB}) + \frac{G}{T_e}\,(\text{dBK}^{-1}) - L_u\,(\text{dB}) - K\,(\text{dBWK})$$

Downlink Equation

$$\frac{C}{N_0} = \frac{A_t P_r (L_p L_d) A_r}{K T_e} = \frac{A_t A_r (L_p L_d)}{K} \times \frac{G}{T_e}$$

Expressed as a log

$$\frac{C}{N_0} = \underbrace{10 \log A_t P_r}_{\substack{\text{EIRP} \\ \text{satellite}}} - \underbrace{20 \log \left(\frac{4\pi D}{\lambda} \right)}_{\substack{\text{free-space} \\ \text{path loss}}} + \underbrace{10 \log \left(\frac{G}{T_e} \right)}_{\substack{\text{earth station} \\ G/T_e}} - \underbrace{10 \log L_d}_{\substack{\text{additional} \\ \text{atmospheric} \\ \text{losses}}} - \underbrace{10 \log K}_{\substack{\text{Boltzmann's} \\ \text{constant}}}$$

$$= \text{EIRP (dBW)} - L_p\,(\text{dB}) + \frac{G}{T_e}\,(\text{dBK}^{-1}) - L_d\,(\text{dB}) - K\,(\text{dBWK})$$

LINK BUDGET

Table 8-4 lists the system parameters for three typical satellite communication systems. The systems and their parameters are not necessarily for an existing or future system; they are hypothetical examples only. The system parameters are used to construct a *link budget*. A link budget identifies the system parameters and is used to determine the projected C/N and E_b/N_0 ratios at both the satellite and earth station receivers for a given modulation scheme and desired $P(e)$.

TABLE 8-4 SYSTEM PARAMETERS FOR THREE HYPOTHETICAL SATELLITE SYSTEMS

	System A: 6/4 GHz, earth coverage QPSK modulation, 60 Mbps	System B: 14/12 GHz, earth coverage 8-PSK modulation, 90 Mbps	System C: 14/12 GHz, earth coverage 8-PSK modulation, 120 Mbps
Uplink			
Transmitter output power (saturation, dBW)	35	25	33
Earth station back-off loss (dB)	2	2	3
Earth station branching and feeder loss (dB)	3	3	4
Additional atmospheric (dB)	0.6	0.4	0.6
Earth station antenna gain (dB)	55	45	64
Free-space path loss (dB)	200	208	206.5
Satellite receive antenna gain (dB)	20	45	23.7
Satellite branching and feeder loss (dB)	1	1	0
Satellite equivalent noise temperature (K)	1000	800	800
Satellite G/T_e (dBK^{-1})	-10	16	-5.3
Downlink			
Transmitter output power (saturation, dBW)	18	20	30.8
Satellite back-off loss (dB)	0.5	0.2	0.1
Satellite branching and feeder loss (dB)	1	1	0.5
Additional atmospheric loss (dB)	0.8	1.4	0.4
Satellite antenna gain (dB)	16	44	10
Free-space path loss (dB)	197	206	205.6
Earth station receive antenna gain (dB)	51	44	62
Earth station branching and feeder loss (dB)	3	3	0
Earth station equivalent noise temperature (K)	250	1000	270
Earth station G/T_e (dBK^{-1})	27	14	37.7

Example 8-10

Complete the link budget for a satellite system with the following parameters.

Uplink

1. Earth station transmitter output power   33 dBW
   at saturation, 2000 W

2. Earth station back-off loss   3 dB

3. Earth station branching and feeder losses   4 dB

4. Earth station transmit antenna gain (from   64 dB
   Figure 8-20, 15 m at 14 GHz)

5. Additional uplink atmospheric losses   0.6 dB

Link Budget   329

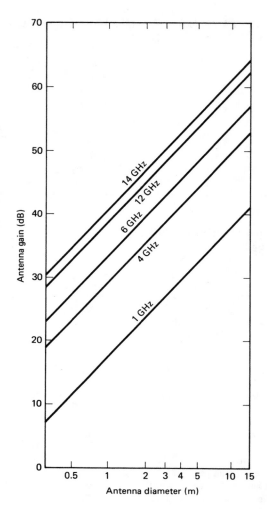

Figure 8-20 Antenna gain based on the gain equation for a parabolic antenna:

$$A \text{ (dB)} = 10 \log \eta \, (\pi D/\lambda)^2$$

where D is the antenna diameter, λ = the wavelength, and η = the antenna efficiency. Here η = 0.55. To correct for a 100% efficient antenna, add 2.66 dB to the value.

6.	Free-space path loss (from Figure 8-21, at 14 GHz)	206.5 dB
7.	Satellite receiver G/T_e ratio	−5.3 dBK^{-1}
8.	Satellite branching and feeder losses	0 dB
9.	Bit rate	120 Mbps
10.	Modulation scheme	8-PSK

Downlink

1.	Satellite transmitter output power at saturation 10 W	10 dBW

2. Satellite back-off loss	0.1 dB
3. Satellite branching and feeder losses	0.5 dB
4. Satellite transmit antenna gain (from Figure 8-20, 0.37 m at 12 GHz)	30.8 dB
5. Additional downlink atmospheric losses	0.4 dB
6. Free-space path loss (from Figure 8-21, at 12 GHz)	205.6 dB
7. Earth station receive antenna gain (15 m, 12 GHz)	62 dB
8. Earth station branching and feeder losses	0 dB
9. Earth station equivalent noise temperature	270 K
10. Earth station G/T_e ratio	37.7 dBK^{-1}
11. Bit rate	120 Mbps
12. Modulation scheme	8-PSK

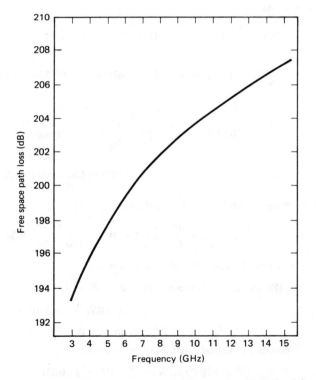

Elevation angle correction:	
Angle	+dB
90°	0
45°	0.44
0°	1.33

Figure 8-21 Free-space path loss (L_p) determined from

$$L_p = 183.5 + 20 \log f \text{ (GHz)}$$

Elevation angle = 90°, distance = 35,930 km.

Link Budget

Solution *Uplink budget:* Expressed as a log,

$$\text{EIRP (earth station)} = P_t + A_t - L_{bo} - L_{bf}$$

$$= 33\,\text{dBW} + 64\,\text{dB} - 3\,\text{dB} - 4\,\text{dB} = 90\,\text{dBW}$$

Carrier power density at the satellite antenna:

$$C' = \text{EIRP (earth station)} - L_p - L_u$$

$$= 90\,\text{dBw} - 206.5\,\text{dB} - 0.6\,\text{dB} = -117.1\,\text{dBW}$$

C/N_0 at the satellite:

$$\frac{C}{N_0} = \frac{C}{KT_e} = \frac{C}{T_e} \times \frac{1}{K} \quad \text{where } \frac{C}{T_e} = C' \times \frac{G}{T_e}$$

Thus

$$\frac{C}{N_0} = C' \times \frac{G}{T_e} \times \frac{1}{K}$$

Expressed as a log,

$$\frac{C}{N_0}\,(\text{dB}) = C'\,(\text{dBW}) + \frac{G}{T_e}\,(\text{dBK}^{-1}) - 10\log(1.38 \times 10^{-23})$$

$$\frac{C}{N_0} = -117.1\,\text{dBW} + (-5.3\,\text{dBK}^{-1}) - (-228.6\,\text{dBWK}) = 106.2\,\text{dB}$$

Thus

$$\frac{E_b}{N_0}\,(\text{dB}) = \frac{C/f_b}{N_0}\,(\text{dB}) = \frac{C}{N_0}\,(\text{dB}) - 10\log f_b$$

$$\frac{E_b}{N_0} = 106.2\,\text{dB} - 10\,(\log 120 \times 10^6) = 25.4\,\text{dB}$$

and for a minimum bandwidth system,

$$\frac{C}{N} = \frac{E_b}{N_0} - \frac{B}{f_b} = 25.4 - 10\log\frac{40 \times 10^6}{120 \times 10^6} = 30.2\,\text{dB}$$

Downlink budget: Expressed as a log,

$$\text{EIRP (satellite transponder)} = P_t + A_t - L_{bo} - L_{bf}$$

$$= 10\,\text{dBW} + 30.8\,\text{dB} - 0.1\,\text{dB} - 0.5\,\text{dB}$$

$$= 40.2\,\text{dBW}$$

Carrier power density at earth station antenna:

$$C' = \text{EIRP (dBW)} - L_p\,(\text{dB}) - L_d\,(\text{dB})$$

$$= 40.2\,\text{dBW} - 205.6\,\text{dB} - 0.4\,\text{dB} = -165.8\,\text{dBW}$$

C/N_0 at the earth station receiver:

$$\frac{C}{N_0} = \frac{C}{KT_e} = \frac{C}{T_e} \times \frac{1}{K} \quad \text{where } \frac{C}{T_e} = C' \times \frac{G}{T_e}$$

Thus

$$\frac{C}{N_0} = C' \times \frac{G}{T_e} \times \frac{1}{K}$$

Expressed as a log,

$$\frac{C}{N_0}(\text{dB}) = C'(\text{dBW}) + \frac{G}{T_e}(\text{dBK}^{-1}) - 10\log(1.38 \times 10^{-23})$$

$$= -165.8\,\text{dBW} + (37.7\,\text{dBK}^{-1}) - (-228.6\,\text{dBWK}) = 100.5\,\text{dB}$$

An alternative method of solving for C/N_0 is

$$\frac{C}{N_0}(\text{dB}) = C'(\text{dBW}) + A_r(\text{dB}) - T_e(\text{dBK}^{-1}) - K(\text{dBWK})$$

$$= -165.8\,\text{dBW} + 62\,\text{dB} - 10\log 270 - (-228.6\,\text{dBWK})$$

$$\frac{C}{N_0} = -165.8\,\text{dBW} + 62\,\text{dB} - 24.3\,\text{dBK}^{-1} + 228.6\,\text{dBWK} = 100.5\,\text{dB}$$

$$\frac{E_b}{N_0}(\text{dB}) = \frac{C}{N_0}(\text{dB}) - 10\log f_b$$

$$= 100.5\,\text{dB} - 10\log(120 \times 10^6)$$

$$= 100.5\,\text{dB} - 80.8\,\text{dB} = 19.7\,\text{dB}$$

and for a minimum bandwidth system,

$$\frac{C}{N} = \frac{E_b}{N_0} - \frac{B}{f_b} = 19.7 - 10\log\frac{40 \times 10^6}{120 \times 10^6} = 24.5\,\text{dB}$$

With careful analysis and a little algebra, it can be shown that the overall energy of bit-to-noise density ratio (E_b/N_0), which includes the combined effects of the uplink ratio $(E_b/N_0)_u$ and the downlink ratio $(E_b/N_0)_d$, is a standard product over the sum relationship and is expressed mathematically as

$$\frac{E_b}{N_0}(\text{overall}) = \frac{(E_b/N_0)_u \, (E_b/N_0)_d}{(E_b/N_0)_u + (E_b/N_0)_d} \tag{8-9}$$

where all E_b/N_0 ratios are in absolute values. For Example 8-10, the overall E_b/N_0 ratio is

$$\frac{E_b}{N_0}(\text{overall}) = \frac{(346.7)(93.3)}{346.7 + 93.3} = 73.5$$

$$= 10\log 73.5 = 18.7\,\text{dB}$$

As with all product-over-sum relationships, the smaller of the two numbers dominates. If one number is substantially smaller than the other, the overall result is approximately equal to the smaller of the two numbers.

The system parameters used for Example 8-10 were taken from system C in Table 8-4. A complete link budget for the system is shown in Table 8-5.

Link Budget 333

TABLE 8-5   LINK BUDGET FOR EXAMPLE 8-10

Uplink

1. Earth station transmitter output power at saturation, 2000 W	33 dBW
2. Earth station back-off loss	3 dB
3. Earth station branching and feeder losses	4 dB
4. Earth station transmit antenna gain	64 dB
5. Earth station EIRP	90 dBW
6. Additional uplink atmospheric losses	0.6 dB
7. Free-space path loss	206.5 dB
8. Carrier power density at satellite	-117.1 dBW
9. Satellite branching and feeder losses	0 dB
10. Satellite G/T_e ratio	-5.3 dBK^{-1}
11. Satellite C/T_e ratio	-122.4 dBWK^{-1}
12. Satellite C/N_0 ratio	106.2 dB
13. Satellite C/N ratio	30.2 dB
14. Satellite E_b/N_0 ratio	25.4 dB
15. Bit rate	120 Mbps
16. Modulation scheme	8-PSK

Downlink

1. Satellite transmitter output power at saturation, 10 W	10 dBW
2. Satellite back-off loss	0.1 dB
3. Satellite branching and feeder losses	0.5 dB
4. Satellite transmit antenna gain	30.8 dB
5. Satellite EIRP	40.2 dBW
6. Additional downlink atmospheric losses	0.4 dB
7. Free-space path loss	205.6 dB
8. Earth station receive antenna gain	62 dB
9. Earth station equivalent noise temperature	270 K
10. Earth station branching and feeder losses	0 dB
11. Earth station G/T_e ratio	37.7 dBK^{-1}
12. Carrier power density at earth station	-165.8 dBW
13. Earth station C/T_e ratio	-128.1 dBWK^{-1}
14. Earth station C/N_0 ratio	100.5 dB
15. Earth station C/N ratio	24.5 dB
16. Earth station E_b/N_0 ratio	19.7 dB
17. Bit rate	120 Mbps
18. Modulation scheme	8-PSK

NONIDEAL SYSTEM PARAMETERS

Additional *nonideal parameters* include the following impairments: AM/AM conversion and AM/PM conversion, which result from nonlinear amplification in HPAs and limiters; *pointing error,* which occurs when the earth station and satellite antennas are not exactly aligned; *phase jitter,* which results from imperfect carrier recovery in receivers; *nonideal filtering,* due to the imperfections introduced in bandpass filters; *timing error,* due to imperfect clock recovery in receivers; and *frequency translation errors* introduced in the satellite transponders. The degradation caused by the preceding impairments effectively reduces the E_b/N_0 ratios determined in the link budget calculations. Consequently, they have to be included in the link budget as equivalent losses. An in-depth coverage of the nonideal parameters is beyond the intent of this text.

QUESTIONS

8-1. Briefly describe a satellite.

8-2. What is a passive satellite? An active satellite?

8-3. Contrast nonsynchronous and synchronous satellites.

8-4. Define *prograde* and *retrograde*.

8-5. Define *apogee* and *perigee*.

8-6. Briefly explain the characteristics of low-, medium-, and high-altitude satellite orbits.

8-7. Explain equatorial, polar, and inclined orbits.

8-8. Contrast the advantages and disadvantages of geosynchronous satellites.

8-9. Define *look angles, angle of elevation,* and *azimuth.*

8-10. Define *satellite spatial separation* and list its restrictions.

8-11. Describe a "footprint."

8-12. Describe spot, zonal, and earth coverage radiation patterns.

8-13. Explain *reuse*.

8-14. Briefly describe the functional characteristics of an uplink, a transponder, and a downlink model for a satellite system.

8-15. Define *back-off loss* and its relationship to saturated and transmit power.

8-16. Define *bit energy*.

8-17. Define *effective isotropic radiated power*.

8-18. Define *equivalent noise temperature*.

8-19. Define *noise density*.

8-20. Define *carrier-to-noise density ratio* and *energy of bit-to-noise density ratio*.

8-21. Define *gain-to-equivalent noise temperature ratio*.

8-22. Describe what a satellite link budget is and how it is used.

PROBLEMS

8-1. An earth station is located at Houston, Texas, which has a longitude of 99.5° and a latitude of 29.5° north. The satellite of interest is Satcom 2. Determine the look angles for the earth station antenna.

8-2. A satellite system operates at 14-GHz uplink and 11-GHz downlink and has a projected $P(e)$ of 10^{-7}. The modulation scheme is 8-PSK, and the system will carry 120 Mbps. The equivalent noise temperature of the receiver is 400 K, and the receiver noise bandwidth is equal to the minimum Nyquist frequency. Determine the following parameters: minimum theoretical C/N ratio, minimum theoretical E_b/N_0 ratio, noise density, total receiver input noise, minimum receive carrier power, and the minimum energy per bit at the receiver input.

8-3. A satellite system operates at 6-GHz uplink and 4-GHz downlink and has a projected $P(e)$ of 10^{-6}. The modulation scheme is QPSK and the system will carry 100 Mbps. The equivalent receiver noise temperature is 290 K, and the receiver noise bandwidth is equal to the minimum Nyquist frequency. Determine the C/N ratio that would be measured at a point in the receiver prior to the BPF where the bandwidth is equal to **(a)** $1\frac{1}{2}$ times the minimum Nyquist frequency, and **(b)** 3 times the minimum Nyquist frequency.

8-4. Which system has the best projected BER?
(a) 8-QAM, $C/N = 15$ dB, $B = 2f_N$, $f_b = 60$ Mbps.
(b) QPSK, $C/N = 16$ dB, $B = f_N$, $f_b = 40$ Mbps.

8-5. An earth station satellite transmitter has an HPA with a rated saturated output power of 10,000 W. The back-off ratio is 6 dB, the branching loss is 2 dB, the feeder loss is 4 dB, and the antenna gain is 40 dB. Determine the actual radiated power and the EIRP.

8-6. Determine the total noise power for a receiver with an input bandwidth of 20 MHz and an equivalent noise temperature of 600 K.

8-7. Determine the noise density for Problem 8-6.

8-8. Determine the minimum C/N ratio required to achieve a $P(e)$ of 10^{-5} for an 8-PSK receiver with a bandwidth equal to f_N.

8-9. Determine the energy of bit-to-noise density ratio when the receiver input carrier power is -100 dBW, the receiver input noise temperature is 290 K, and a 60-Mbps transmission rate is used.

8-10. Determine the carrier-to-noise density ratio for a receiver with a -70-dBW input carrier power, an equivalent noise temperature of 180 K, and a bandwidth of 20 MHz.

8-11. Determine the minimum C/N ratio for an 8-PSK system when the transmission rate is 60 Mbps, the minimum energy of bit-to-noise density ratio is 15 dB, and the receiver bandwidth is equal to the minimum Nyquist frequency.

8-12. For an earth station receiver with an equivalent input temperature of 200 K, a noise bandwidth of 20 MHz, a receive antenna gain of 50 dB, and a carrier frequency of 12 GHz, determine the following: G/T_e, N_0, and N.

8-13. For a satellite with an uplink E_b/N_0 of 14 dB and a downlink E_b/N_0 of 18 dB, determine the overall E_b/N_0 ratio.

8-14. Complete the following link budget:

Uplink Parameters

1. Earth station transmitter output power at saturation, 1 kW
2. Earth station back-off loss, 3 dB
3. Earth station total branching and feeder losses, 3 dB
4. Earth station transmit antenna gain for a 10-m parabolic dish at 14 GHz
5. Free-space path loss for 14 GHz
6. Additional uplink losses due to the earth's atmosphere, 0.8 dB
7. Satellite transponder G/Te, -4.6 dBK
8. Transmission bit rate, 90 Mbps, 8-PSK

Downlink Parameters

1. Satellite transmitter output power at saturation, 10 W
2. Satellite transmit antenna gain for a 0.5-m parabolic dish at 12 GHz
3. Satellite modulation back-off loss, 0.8 dB
4. Free-space path loss for 12 GHz
5. Additional downlink losses due to earth's atmosphere, 0.6 dB
6. Earth station receive antenna gain for a 10-m parabolic dish at 12 GHz
7. Earth station equivalent noise temperature, 200 K
8. Earth station branching and feeder losses, 0 dB
9. Transmission bit rate, 90 Mbps, 8-PSK

9

SATELLITE MULTIPLE-ACCESS ARRANGEMENTS

INTRODUCTION

In Chapter 8 we analyzed the link parameters of *single-channel satellite transponders*. In this chapter, we will extend the discussion of satellite communications to systems designed for *multiple carriers*. Whenever multiple carriers are utilized in satellite communications, it is necessary that a *multiple-accessing format* be established over the system. This format allows for a distinct separation between the uplink and downlink transmissions to and from a multitude of different earth stations. Each format has its own specific characteristics, advantages, and disadvantages.

FDM/FM SATELLITE SYSTEMS

Figure 9-1a shows a single-link (two earth stations) *fixed-frequency* FDM/FM system using a single satellite transponder. With earth coverage antennas and for full-duplex operation, each link requires two RF satellite channels (i.e., four RF carrier frequencies, two uplink and two downlink). In Figure 9-1a, earth station 1 transmits on a high-band carrier (f11, f12, f13, etc.) and receives on a low-band carrier (f1, f2, f3, etc.). To avoid interfering with earth station 1, earth station 2 must transmit and receive on different RF carrier frequencies. The RF carrier frequencies are fixed and the satellite transponder is simply an RF-to-RF repeater that provides the uplink/downlink frequency translation. This arrangement is economically impractical and extremely inefficient as well. Additional earth stations can communicate through different transponders within the same satellite

338

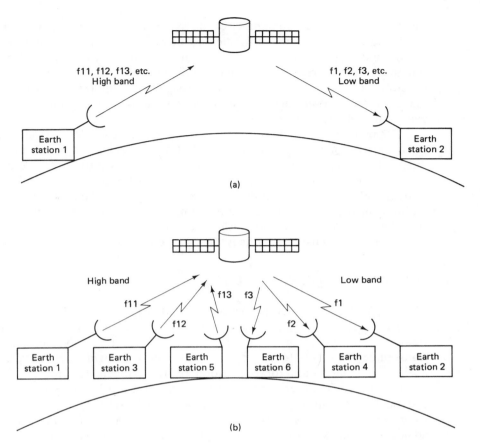

Figure 9-1 Fixed-frequency earth station satellite system: (a) single link: (b) multiple link.

structure (Figure 9-1b). Each additional link requires four more RF carrier frequencies. It is unlikely that any two-point link would require the capacity available in an entire RF satellite channel. Consequently, most of the available bandwidth is wasted. Also, with this arrangement, each earth station can communicate with only one other earth station. The RF satellite channels are fixed between any two earth stations; thus the voice band channels from each earth station are committed to a single destination.

In a system where three or more earth stations wish to communicate with each other, fixed-frequency or *dedicated channel* systems such as those shown in Figure 8-1 are inadequate; a method of *multiple accessing* is required. That is, each earth station using the satellite system has a means of communicating with each of the other earth stations in the system through a common satellite transponder. Multiple accessing is sometimes called *multiple destination* because the transmissions from each earth station are received by all the other earth stations in the system. The voice band channels between any two earth stations may be *preassigned* (*dedicated*) or *demand-assigned* (*switched*). When preas-

FDM/FM Satellite Systems **339**

signment is used, a given number of the available voice band channels from each earth station are assigned a dedicated destination. With demand assignment, voice band channels are assigned on an as-needed basis. Demand assignment provides more versatility and more efficient use of the available frequency spectrum. On the other hand, demand assignment requires a control mechanism that is common to all the earth stations to keep track of channel routing and the availability of each voice band channel.

Remember, in an FDM/FM satellite system, each RF channel requires a separate transponder. Also, with FDM/FM transmissions, it is impossible to differentiate (separate) multiple transmissions that occupy the same bandwidth. Fixed-frequency systems may be used in a multiple-access configuration by switching the RF carriers at the satellite, reconfiguring the baseband signals with multiplexing/demultiplexing equipment on board the satellite, or by using multiple spot beam antennas (reuse). All three of these methods require relatively complicated, expensive, and heavy hardware on the spacecraft.

ANIK-D COMMUNICATIONS SATELLITE

The *ANIK-D* communications satellite is a domsat satellite that was launched in August 1982. *ANIK-D* is operated by Telsat Canada. Figure 9-2 shows the frequency and polarization plan for the *ANIK-D* satellite system. There are 12 transponder channels (each approximately 36 MHz wide). However, by using horizontal polarization for one group of 12 channels (group A) and vertical polarization for another group of 12 channels (group B), a total of 24 channels can occupy a bandwidth of approximately 500 MHz. This scheme is called *frequency reuse* and is possible by using *orthogonal polarization* and spacing adjacent channels 20 MHz apart. There are 12 primary channels and 12 spare or preemptible channels.

MULTIPLE ACCESSING

Figure 9-3 shows the three most commonly used multiple accessing arrangements: frequency-division multiple accessing (FDMA), time-division multiple accessing (TDMA), and code-division multiple accessing (CDMA). With FDMA, each earth station's transmissions are assigned specific uplink and downlink frequency bands within an allotted satellite channel bandwidth; they may be preassigned or demand assigned. Consequently, transmissions from different earth stations are separated in the frequency domain. With TDMA, each earth station transmits a short burst of information during a specific time slot (*epoch*) within a TDMA frame. The bursts must be synchronized so that each station's *burst* arrives at the satellite at a different time. Consequently, transmissions from different earth stations are separated in the time domain. With CDMA, all earth stations transmit within the same frequency band and, for all practical purposes, have no limitation on when they may transmit or on which carrier frequency. Carrier separation is accomplished with *envelope encryption/decryption* techniques.

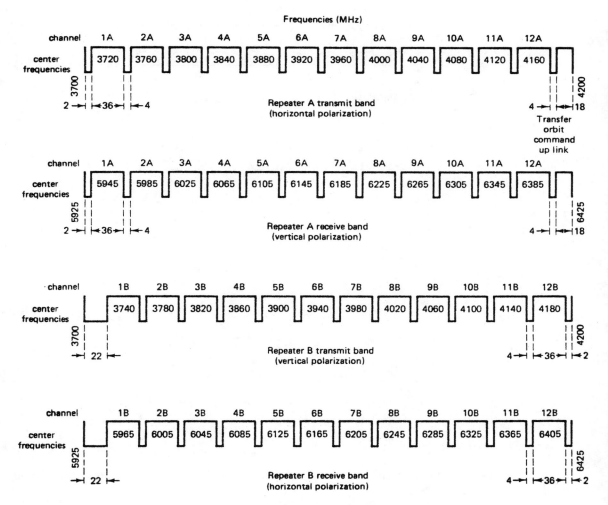

Figure 9-2 *ANIK-D* frequency and polarization plan.

Frequency-Division Multiple Access

Frequency-division multiple access (FDMA) is a method of multiple accessing where a given RF channel bandwidth is divided into smaller frequency bands called *subdivisions*. Each subdivision is used to carry one voice band channel. A control mechanism is used to ensure that no two earth stations transmit on the same subdivision at the same time. Essentially, the control mechanism designates a receive station for each of the subdivisions. In demand-assignment systems, the control mechanism is also used to establish or terminate the voice band links between the source and destination earth stations. Consequently, any of the subdivisions may be used by any of the participating earth stations at any given time. Typically, each subdivision is used to carry a single 4-kHz voice band

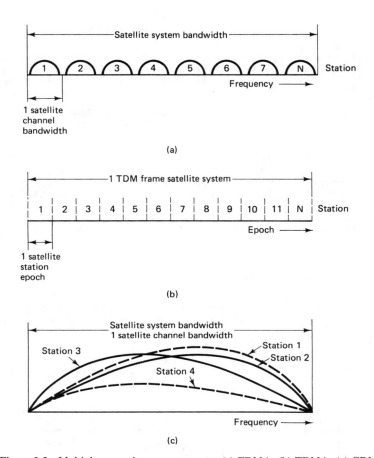

Figure 9-3 Multiple-accessing arrangements: (a) FDMA; (b) TDMA; (c) CDMA.

channel, but occasionally, groups, supergroups, or even mastergroups are assigned a larger subdivision.

SPADE system. The first FDMA demand-assignment system for satellites was developed by Comsat for use on the *Intelsat IV* satellite. This system was called *SPADE* (single-channel-per-carrier PCM multiple-access demand assignment equipment). Figures 9-4 and 9-5 show the block diagram and IF frequency assignments for SPADE, respectively.

With SPADE, 800 PCM-encoded voice band channels separately QPSK modulate an IF carrier frequency (hence the name *single carrier per channel*, SCPC). Each 4-kHz voice band channel is sampled at an 8-kHz rate and converted to an 8-bit PCM code. This produces a 64-kbps PCM code for each voice band channel. The PCM code from each voice band channel QPSK modulates a different IF carrier frequency. With QPSK, the minimum required bandwidth is equal to one-half the input bit rate. Consequently, the output of each QPSK modulator requires a minimum bandwidth of 32 kHz. Each channel is allocated a 45-kHz bandwidth, which allows for a 13-kHz guard band between each frequency-division-multiplexed channel. The IF carrier frequencies begin at 52.0225 MHz (low-band channel 1) and increase in 45-kHz steps to 87.9775 MHz (high-band channel 400). The entire 36-MHz band (52 to 88 MHz) is divided in half, producing two 400-channel bands (a low-band and a high-band). For full-duplex operation, four hundred 45-kHz channels are used for one direction of transmission and 400 are used for the opposite direction. Also, channels 1, 2, and 400 from each band are left permanently vacant. This reduces the number of usable full-duplex voice band channels to 397. The 6-GHz C-band extends from 5.725 to 6.425 GHz (700 MHz). This allows for approximately nineteen 36-MHz RF channels per system. Each RF channel has a capacity of 397 full-duplex voice band channels.

Each RF channel (Figure 9-5) has a 160-kHz *common signaling channel* (CSC). The CSC is a time-division-multiplexed transmission that is frequency-division multiplexed onto the IF spectrum below the QPSK-encoded voice band channels. Figure 9-6 shows the TDM frame structure for the CSC. The total frame time is 50 ms, which is subdivided into fifty 1-ms epochs. Each earth station transmits on the CSC channel only during its preassigned 1-ms time slot. The CSC signal is a 128-bit binary code. To transmit a 128-bit code in 1 ms, a transmission rate of 128 kbps is required. The CSC code is used for establishing and disconnecting voice band links between two earth station users when demand-assignment channel allocation is used.

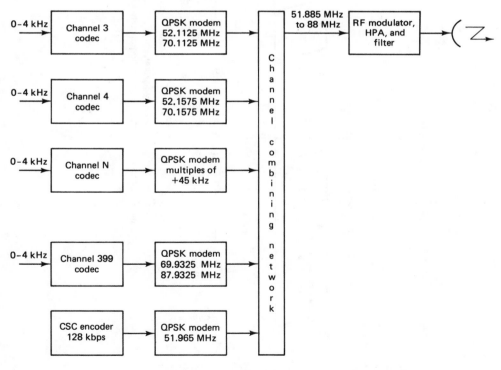

Figure 9-4 FDMA, SPADE earth station transmitter.

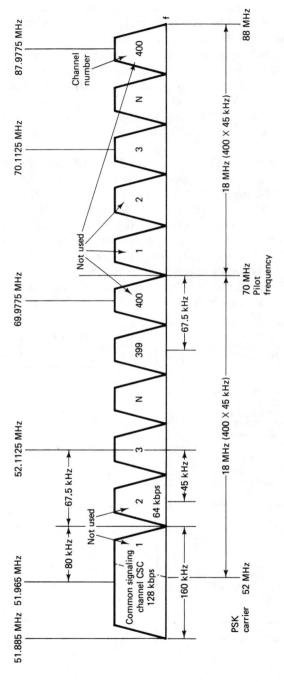

Figure 9-5 Carrier frequency assignments for the Intelsat single channel-per-carrier PCM multiple access demand assignments equipment (SPADE).

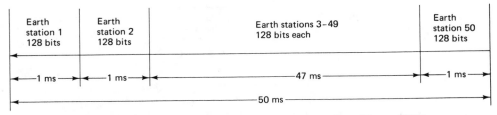

128 bits/1 ms × 1000 ms/1 s = 128 kbps or 6400 bits/frame × 1 frame/50 ms = 128 kbps

Figure 9-6 FDMA, SPADE common signaling channel (CSC).

Example 9-1

For the system shown in Figure 9-7, a user earth station in New York wishes to establish a voice band link between itself and London. New York randomly selects an idle voice band channel. It then transmits a binary-coded message to London on the CSC channel during its respective time slot, requesting that a link be established on the randomly selected channel. London responds on the CSC channel during its time slot with a binary code, either confirming or denying the establishment of the voice band link. The link is disconnected in a similar manner when the users are finished.

The CSC channel occupies a 160-kHz bandwidth, which includes the 45 kHz for low-band channel 1. Consequently, the CSC channel extends from 51.885 MHz to 52.045 MHz. The 128-kbps CSC binary code QPSK modulates a 51.965-MHz carrier. The minimum bandwidth required for the CSC channel is 64 kHz; this results in a 48-kHz guard band on either side of the CSC signal.

With FDMA, each earth station may transmit simultaneously within the same 36-MHz RF spectrum, but on different voice band channels. Consequently, simultaneous transmissions of voice band channels from all earth stations within the satellite network are interleaved in the frequency domain in the satellite transponder. Transmissions of CSC signals are interleaved in the time domain.

An obvious disadvantage of FDMA is that carriers from multiple earth stations may be present in a satellite transponder at the same time. This results in cross-modulation distortion between the various earth station transmissions. This is alleviated somewhat by shutting off the IF subcarriers on all unused 45-kHz voice band channels. Because balanced modulators are used in the generation of QPSK, carrier suppression is inherent. This also reduces the power load on a system and increases its capacity by reducing the idle channel power.

Time-Division Multiple Access

Time-division multiple access (TDMA) is the predominant multiple-access method used today. It provides the most efficient method of transmitting digitally modulated carriers (PSK). TDMA is a method of time-division multiplexing digitally modulated carriers between participating earth stations within a satellite network through a common satellite transponder. With TDMA, each earth station transmits a short *burst* of a digitally modulated carrier during a precise time slot

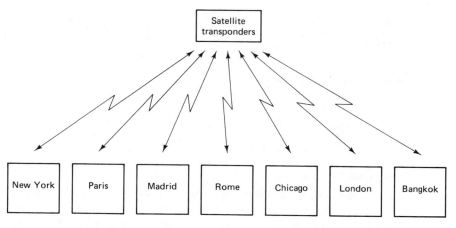

Figure 9-7 Diagram of the system for Example 9-1.

(epoch) within a TDMA frame. Each station's burst is synchronized so that it arrives at the satellite transponder at a different time. Consequently, only one earth station's carrier is present in the transponder at any given time, thus avoiding a collision with another station's carrier. The transponder is an RF-to-RF repeater that simply receives the earth station transmissions, amplifies them, and then retransmits them in a down-link beam which is received by all the participating earth stations. Each earth station receives the bursts from all other earth stations and must select from them the traffic destined only for itself.

Figure 9-8 shows a basic TDMA frame. Transmissions from all earth stations are synchronized to a *reference burst*. Figure 9-8 shows the reference burst as a separate transmission, but it may be the *preamble* which precedes a reference

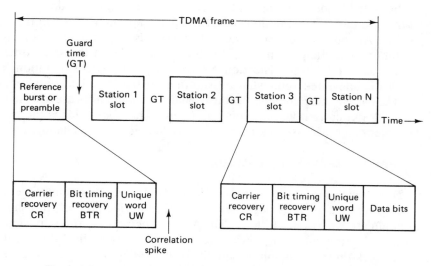

Figure 9-8 Basic time-division-multiple accessing (TDMA) frame.

Satellite Multiple-Access Arrangements **Chap. 9**

station's transmission of data. Also, there may be more than one synchronizing reference burst.

The reference burst contains a *carrier recovery sequence* (CRS) from which all receiving stations recover a frequency and phase coherent carrier for PSK demodulation. Also included in the reference burst is a binary sequence for *bit timing recovery* (BTR, i.e., clock recovery). At the end of each reference burst, a *unique word* (UW) is transmitted. The UW sequence is used to establish a precise time reference that each of the earth stations use to synchronize the transmission of its burst. The UW is typically a string of successive binary 1's terminated with a binary 0. Each earth station receiver demodulates and integrates the UW sequence. Figure 9-9 shows the result of the integration process. The integrator and threshold detector are designed so that the threshold voltage is reached precisely when the last bit of the UW sequence is integrated. This generates a *correlation spike* at the output of the threshold detector at the exact time the UW sequence ends.

Each earth station synchronizes the transmission of its carrier to the occurrence of the UW correlation spike. Each station waits a different length of time before it begins transmitting. Consequently, no two stations will transmit carrier at the same time. Note the *guard time* (GT) between transmissions from successive stations. This is analogous to a guard band in a frequency-division-multiplexed system. Each station precedes the transmission of data with a *preamble*. The preamble is logically equivalent to the reference burst. Because each station's transmissions must be received by all other earth stations, all stations must recover carrier and clocking information prior to demodulating the

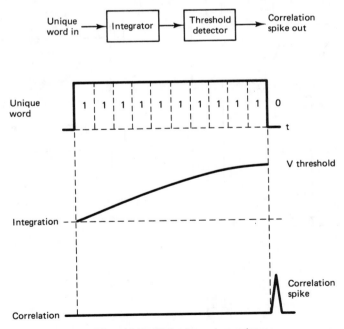

Figure 9-9 Unique word correlator.

Multiple Accessing

data. If demand assignment is used, a common signaling channel must also be included in the preamble.

CEPT primary multiplex frame.   Figures 9-10 and 9-11 show the block diagram and timing sequence for the CEPT primary multiplex frame respectively (CEPT—Conference of European Postal and Telecommunications Administrations; the CEPT sets many of the European telecommunications standards). This is a commonly used TDMA frame format for digital satellite systems.

Essentially, TDMA is a *store-and-forward* system. Earth stations can transmit only during their specified time slot, although the incoming voice band signals are continuous. Consequently, it is necessary to sample and store the voice band signals prior to transmission. The CEPT frame is made up of 8-bit PCM encoded samples from 16 independent voice band channels. Each channel has a separate codec that samples the incoming voice signals at a 16-kHz rate and converts those samples to an 8-bit binary code. This results in 128-kbps transmitted at a 2.048 MHz rate from each voice channel codec. The sixteen 128-kbps transmissions are time-division multiplexed into a subframe that contains one 8-bit sample from each of the 16 channels (128 bits). It requires only 62.5 μs

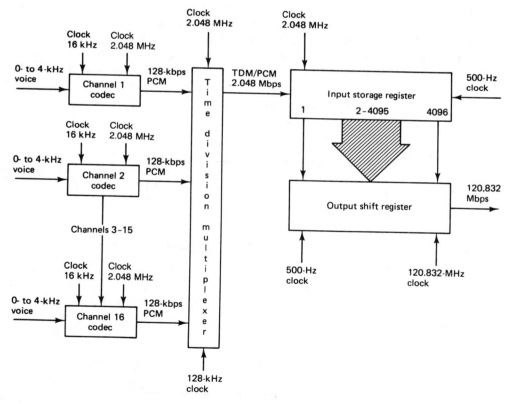

Figure 9-10   TDMA, CEPT primary multiplex frame transmitter.

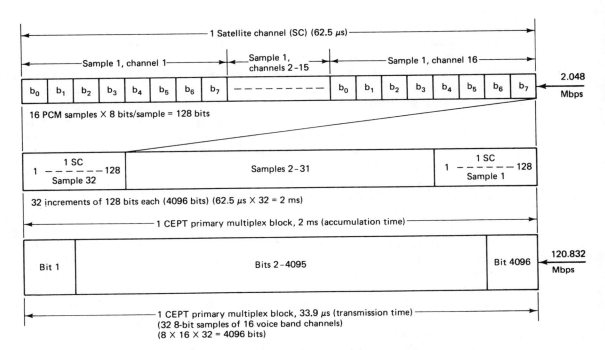

Figure 9-11 TDMA, CEPT primary multiplex frame.

to accumulate the 128 bits (2.048-Mbps transmission rate). The CEPT multiplex format specifies a 2-ms frame time. Consequently, each earth station can transmit only once every 2 ms and therefore must store the PCM-encoded samples. The 128 bits accumulated during the first sample of each voice band channel are stored in a holding register while a second sample is taken from each channel and converted into another 128-bit *subframe*. This 128-bit sequence is stored in the holding register behind the first 128 bits. The process continues for 32 subframes (32 × 62.5 μs = 2 ms). After 2 ms, thirty-two 8-bit samples have been taken from each of 16 voice band channels for a total of 4096 bits (32 × 8 × 16 = 4096). At this time, the 4096 bits are transferred to an output shift register for transmission. Because the total TDMA frame is 2 ms long and during this 2-ms period each of the participating earth stations must transmit at different times, the individual transmissions from each station must occur in a significantly shorter time period. In the CEPT frame, a transmission rate of 120.832 Mbps is used. This rate is the fifty-ninth multiple of 2.048 Mbps. Consequently, the actual transmission of the 4096 accumulated bits takes approximately 33.9 μs. At the earth station receivers, the 4096 bits are stored in a holding register and shifted a 2.048-Mbps rate. Because all the clock rates (500 Hz, 16 kHz, 128 kHz, 2.048 MHz, and 120.832 MHz) are synchronized, the PCM codes are accumulated, stored, transmitted, received, and then decoded in perfect synchronization. To the users, the voice transmission is a continuous process.

There are several advantages of TDMA over FDMA. The first, and probably the most significant, is that with TDMA only the carrier from one earth station

Multiple Accessing

is present in the satellite transponder at any given time, thus reducing intermodulation distortion. Second, with FDMA, each earth station must be capable of transmitting and receiving on a multitude of carrier frequencies to achieve multiple accessing capabilities. Third, TDMA is much better suited to the transmission of digital information than FDMA. Digital signals are naturally acclimated to storage, rate conversions, and time-domain processing than their analog counterparts.

The primary disadvantage of TDMA as compared to FDMA is that in TDMA precise synchronization is required. Each earth station's transmissions must occur during an exact time slot. Also, bit and frame timing must be achieved and maintained with TDMA.

Code-Division Multiple Access (Spread-Spectrum Multiple Accessing)

With FDMA, earth stations are limited to a specific bandwidth within a satellite channel or system but have no restriction on when they can transmit. With TDMA, earth station's transmissions are restricted to a precise time slot but have no restriction on what frequency or bandwidth they may use within a specified satellite system or channel allocation. With *code-division multiple access* (CDMA), there are no restrictions on time or bandwidth. Each earth station transmitter may transmit whenever it wishes and can use any or all of the bandwidth allocated a particular satellite system or channel. Because there is no limitation on the bandwidth, CDMA is sometimes referred to as *spread-spectrum multiple access*; transmissions can spread throughout the entire allocated bandwidth spectrum. Transmissions are separated through envelope encryption/decryption techniques. That is, each earth station's transmissions are encoded with a unique binary word called a *chip code*. Each station has a unique chip code. To receive a particular earth station's transmission, a receive station must know the chip code for that station.

Figure 9-12 shows the block diagram of a CDMA encoder and decoder. In the encoder (Figure 9-12a), the input data (which may be PCM-encoded voice band signals or raw digital data) is multiplied by a unique chip code. The product code PSK modulates an IF carrier which is up-converted to RF for transmission. At the receiver (Figure 9-12b), the RF is down-converted to IF. From the IF, a coherent PSK carrier is recovered. Also, the chip code is acquired and used to synchronize the receive station's code generator. Keep in mind, the receiving station knows the chip code but must generate a chip code that is synchronous in time with the receive code. The recovered synchronous chip code multiplies the recovered PSK carrier and generates a PSK modulated signal that contains the PSK carrier plus the chip code. The received IF signal that contains the chip code, the PSK carrier, and the data information is compared to the received IF signal in the *correlator*. The function of the correlator is to compare the two signals and recover the original data. Essentially, the correlator subtracts the recovered PSK carrier + chip code from the received PSK carrier + chip code + data. The resultant is the data.

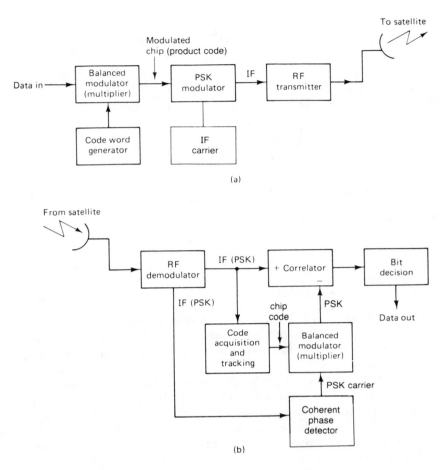

Figure 9-12 Code-division multiple access (CDMA): (a) encoder; (b) decoder.

The correlation is accomplished on the analog signals. Figure 9-13 shows how the encoding and decoding is accomplished. Figure 9-13a shows the correlation of the correctly received chip code. A $+1$ indicates an in-phase carrier and a -1 indicates an out-of-phase carrier. The chip code is multiplied by the data (either $+1$ or -1). The product is either an in-phase code or one that is 180° out of phase with the chip code. In the receiver, the recovered synchronous chip code is compared in the correlator to the received signaling elements. If the phases are the same, a $+1$ is produced; if they are 180° out of phase, a -1 is produced. It can be seen that if all the recovered chips correlate favorably with the incoming chip code, the output of the correlator will be a $+6$ (which is the case when a logic 1 is received). If all the code chips correlate 180° out of phase, a -6 is generated (which is the case when a logic 0 is received). The bit decision circuit is simply a threshold detector. Depending on whether a $+6$ or -6 is generated, the threshold detector will output a logic 1 or a logic 0, respectively.

Multiple Accessing

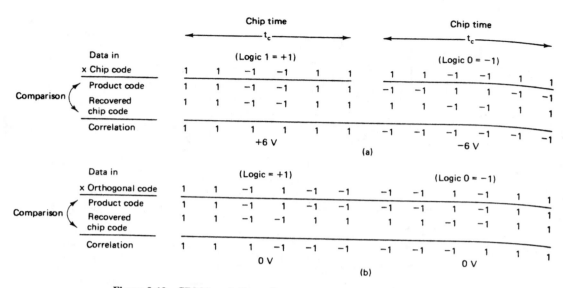

Figure 9-13 CDMA code/data alignment: (a) correct code; (b) orthogonal code.

As the name implies, the correlator looks for a correlation (similarity) between the incoming coded signal and the recovered chip code. When a correlation occurs, the bit decision circuit generates the corresponding logic condition.

With CDMA, all earth stations within the system may transmit on the same frequency at the same time. Consequently, an earth station receiver may be receiving coded PSK signals simultaneously from more than one transmitter. When this is the case, the job of the correlator becomes considerably more difficult. The correlator must compare the recovered chip code with the entire received spectrum and separate from it only the chip code from the desired earth station transmitter. Consequently, the chip code from one earth station must not correlate with the chip codes from any of the other earth stations.

Figure 9-13b shows how such a coding scheme is achieved. If half of the chips within a code were made the same and half were made exactly the opposite, the resultant would be zero cross correlation between chip codes. Such a code is called an *orthogonal code*. In Figure 9-13b it can be seen that when the orthogonal code is compared with the original chip code, there is no correlation (i.e., the sum of the comparison is zero). Consequently, the orthogonal code, although received simultaneously with the desired chip code, had absolutely no effect on the correlation process. For this example, the orthogonal code is received in exact time synchronization with the desired chip code; this is not always the case. For systems that do not have time synchronous transmissions, codes must be developed where there is no correlation between one station's code and any phase of another station's code. For more than two participating earth stations, this is impossible to do. A code set has been developed called the *Gold code*. With the Gold code, there is a minimum correlation between different chips' codes. For a reasonable number of users, it is impossible to achieve perfect

Satellite Multiple-Access Arrangements   Chap. 9

orthogonal codes. You can design only for a minimum *cross correlation* between chips.

One of the advantages of CDMA was that the entire bandwidth of a satellite channel or system may be used for each transmission from every earth station. For our example, the chip rate was six times the original bit rate. Consequently, the actual transmission rate of information was one-sixth of the PSK modulation rate, and the bandwidth required is six times that required to simply transmit the original data as binary. Because of the coding inefficiency resulting from transmitting chips for bits, the advantage of more bandwidth is partially offset and is thus less of an advantage. Also, if the transmission of chips from the various earth stations must be synchronized, precise timing is required for the system to work. Therefore, the disadvantage of requiring time synchronization in TDMA systems is also present with CDMA. In short, CDMA is not all that it is cracked up to be. The only significant advantage of CDMA is immunity to interference (jamming), which makes CDMA ideally suited for military applications.

FREQUENCY HOPPING

Frequency hopping is a form of CDMA where a digital code is used to continually change the frequency of the carrier. With frequency hopping, the total available bandwidth is partitioned into smaller frequency bands and the total transmission time is subdivided into smaller time slots. The idea is to transmit within a limited frequency band for only a short period of time, then switch to another frequency band, and so on. This process continues indefinitely. The frequency hopping pattern is determined by a binary code. Each station uses a different code sequence. A typical *hopping pattern* (*frequency-time matrix*) is shown in Figure 9-14.

With frequency hopping, each earth station within a CDMA network is assigned a different frequency hopping pattern. Each transmitter switches (hops) from one frequency band to the next according to their assigned pattern. With frequency hopping, each station uses the entire RF spectrum but never occupies more than a small portion of that spectrum at any one time.

FSK is the modulation scheme most commonly used with frequency hopping. When it is a given station's turn to transmit, it sends one of the two frequencies (either mark or space) for the particular band in which it is transmitting. The number of stations in a given frequency hopping system is limited by the number of unique hopping patterns that can be generated.

CHANNEL CAPACITY

Essentially, there are two methods used to interface terrestrial voice band channels with satellite channels: digital noninterpolated interfaces (DNI) and digital speech interpolated interfaces (DSI).

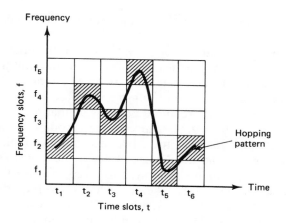

(a)

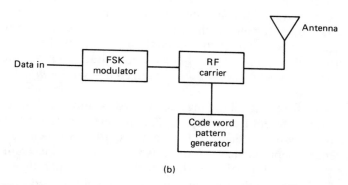

(b)

Figure 9-14 Frequency hopping: (a) frequency time-hopping matrix;
(b) frequency hopping transmitter.

Digital Noninterpolated Interfaces

A *digital noninterpolated interface* assigns an individual terrestrial channel (TC)
to a particular satellite channel (SC) for the duration of the call. A DNI system
can carry no more traffic than the number of satellite channels it has. Once a TC
has been assigned an SC, the SC is unavailable to the other TCs for the duration
of the call. DNI is a form of preassignment; each TC has a permanent dedicated
SC.

Digital Speech Interpolated Interfaces

A *digital speech interpolated interface* assigns a terrestrial channel to a satellite channel only when speech energy is present on the TC. DSI interfaces have *speech detectors* that are similar to *echo suppressors*; they sense speech energy, then seize an SC. Whenever a speech detector senses energy on a TC, the TC is assigned to an SC. The SC assigned is randomly selected from the idle SCs. On a given TC, each time speech energy is detected, the TC could be assigned to a different SC. Therefore, a single TC can use several SCs for a single call. For demultiplexing purposes, the TC/SC assignment information must be conveyed to the receive terminal. This is done on a common signaling channel similar to the one used on the SPADE system. DSI is a form of demand assignment; SCs are randomly assigned on an as-needed basis.

With DSI it is apparent that there is a *channel compression*; there can be more TCs assigned than there are SCs. Generally, a TC:SC ratio of 2:1 is used. For a full-duplex (two-way simultaneous) communication circuit, there is speech in each direction 40% of the time, and for 20% of the time the circuit is idle in both directions. Therefore, a DSI gain slightly more than 2 is realized. The DSI gain is affected by a phenomenon called *competitive clipping*. Competitive clipping is when speech energy is detected on a TC and there is no SC to assign it to. During the *wait* time, speech information is lost. Competitive clipping is not noticed by a subscriber if its duration is less than 50 ms.

To further enhance the channel capacity, a technique called *bit stealing* is used. With bit stealing, channels can be added to fully loaded systems by stealing bits from the in-use channels. Generally, an overload channel is generated by stealing the least significant bit from seven other satellite channels. Bit stealing results in eight channels with 7-bit resolution for the time that the *overload channel* is in use. Consequently, bit stealing results in a lower SQR than normal.

Time-Assignment Speech Interpolation

Time-assignment speech interpolation (TASI) is a form of analog channel compression that has been used for suboceanic cables for many years. TASI is very similar to DSI except that the signals interpolated are analog rather than digital. TASI also uses a 2:1 compression ratio. TASI was also the first means used to scramble voice for military security. TASI is similar to a packet data network; the voice message is chopped up into smaller segments comprised of sounds or portions of sounds. The sounds are sent through the network as separate bundles of energy, then put back together at the receive end to reform the original voice message.

QUESTIONS

9-1. Discuss the drawbacks of using FDM/FM modulation for statellite multiple-accessing systems.

9-2. Contrast *preassignment* and *demand assignment*.

9-3. What are the three most common multiple-accessing arrangements used with satellite systems?

9-4. Briefly describe the multiple-accessing arrangements listed in Question 9.3.

9-5. Briefly describe the operation of Comsat's *Spade* system.

9-6. What is meant by *single carrier per channel*?

9-7. What is a common signaling channel, and how is it used?

9-8. Describe what a reference burst is for TDMA and explain the following terms: preamble, carrier recovery sequence, bit timing recovery, unique word, and correlation spike.

9-9. Describe guard time.

9-10. Briefly describe the operation of the CEPT primary multiplex frame.

9-11. What is a store-and-forward system?

9-12. What is the primary advantage of TDMA as compared to FDMA?

9-13. What is the primary advantage of FDMA as compared to TDMA?

9-14. Briefly describe the operation of a CDMA multiple-accessing system.

9-15. Describe a chip code.

9-16. Describe what is meant by an orthogonal code.

9-17. Describe cross correlation.

9-18. What are the advantages of CDMA as compared to TDMA and FDMA?

9-19. What are the disadvantages of CDMA?

9-20. What is a Gold code?

9-21. Describe frequency hopping.

9-22. What is a frequency-time matrix?

9-23. Describe digital noninterpolated interfaces.

9-24. Describe digital speech interpolated interfaces.

9-25. What is channel compression, and how is it accomplished with a DSI system?

9-26. Describe competitive clipping.

9-27. What is meant by *bit stealing*?

9-28. Describe time-assignment speech interpolation.

PROBLEMS

9-1. How many satellite transponders are required to interlink six earth stations with FDM/FM modulation?

9-2. For the *Spade* system, what are the carrier frequencies for channel 7? What are the allocated passbands for channel 7? What are the actual passband frequencies (excluding guard bands) required?

9-3. If a 512-bit preamble precedes each CEPT station's transmission, what is the maximum number of earth stations that can be linked together with a single satellite transponder?

9-4. Determine an orthogonal code for the following chip code (101010). Prove that your selection will not produce any cross correlation for an in-phase comparison. Determine the cross correlation for each out-of-phase condition that is possible.

10

FIBER OPTIC COMMUNICATIONS

INTRODUCTION

During the past 10 years, the electronic communications industry has experienced many remarkable and dramatic changes. A phenomenal increase in voice, data, and video communications has caused a corresponding increase in the demand for more economical and larger capacity communications systems. This has caused a technical revolution in the electronic communications industry. Terrestrial microwave systems have long since reached their capacity, and satellite systems can provide, at best, only a temporary relief to the ever-increasing demand. It is obvious that economical communications systems that can handle large capacities and provide high-quality service are needed.

Communications systems that use light as the carrier of information have recently received a great deal of attention. As we shall see later in this chapter, propagating light waves through the earth's atmosphere is difficult and impractical. Consequently, systems that use glass or plastic fiber cables to "contain" a light wave and guide it from a source to a destination are presently being investigated at several prominent research and development laboratories. Communications systems that carry information through a *guided fiber cable* are called *fiber optic systems*.

The *information-carrying capacity* of a communications system is directly proportional to its bandwidth; the wider the bandwidth, the greater its information-carrying capacity. For comparison purposes, it is common to express the bandwidth of a system as a percentage of its carrier frequency. For instance, a VHF radio system operating at 100 MHz has a bandwidth equal to 10 MHz (i.e.,

10% of the carrier frequency). A microwave radio system operating at 6 GHz with a bandwidth equal to 10% of its carrier frequency would have a bandwidth equal to 600 MHz. Thus the higher the carrier frequency, the wider the bandwidth possible and consequently, the greater the information-carrying capacity. Light frequencies used in fiber optic systems are between 10^{14} and 10^{15} Hz (100,000 to 1,000,000 GHz). Ten percent of 1,000,000 GHz is 100,000 GHz. To meet today's communications needs or the needs of the foreseeable future, 100,000 GHz is an excessive bandwidth. However, it does illustrate the capabilities of optical fiber systems.

HISTORY OF FIBER OPTICS

In 1880, Alexander Graham Bell experimented with an apparatus he called a *photophone*. The photophone was a device constructed from mirrors and selenium detectors that transmitted sound waves over a beam of light. The photophone was awkward, unreliable, and had no real practical application. Actually, visual light was a primary means of communicating long before electronic communications came about. Smoke signals and mirrors were used ages ago to convey short, simple messages. Bell's contraption, however, was the first attempt at using a beam of light for carrying information.

Transmission of light waves for any useful distance through the earth's atmosphere is impractical because water vapor, oxygen, and particulates in the air absorb and attenuate the ultrahigh light frequencies. Consequently, the only practical type of optical communications system is one that uses a fiber guide. In 1930, J. L. Baird, an English scientist, and C. W. Hansell, a scientist from the United States, were granted patents for scanning and transmitting television images through uncoated fiber cables. A few years later a German scientist named H. Lamm successfully transmitted images through a single glass fiber. At that time, most people considered fiber optics more of a toy or a laboratory stunt and consequently, it was not until the early 1950s that any substantial breakthrough was made in the field of fiber optics.

In 1951, A. C. S. van Heel of Holland and H. H. Hopkins and N. S. Kapany of England experimented with light transmission through *bundles* of fibers. Their studies led to the development of the *flexible fiberscope,* which is used extensively in the medical field. It was Kapany who coined the term "fiber optics" in 1956.

In 1958, Charles H. Townes, an American, and Arthur L. Schawlow, a Canadian, wrote a paper describing how it was possible to use stimulated emission for amplifying light waves (laser) as well as microwaves (the maser). Two years later, Theodore H. Maiman, a scientist with Hughes Aircraft Company, built the first optical maser.

The *laser* (*l*ight *a*mplification by *s*timulated *e*mission of *r*adiation) was invented in 1960. The laser's relatively high output power, high frequency of operation, and capability of carrying an extremely wide bandwidth signal make it ideally suited for high-capacity communications systems. The invention of the laser greatly accelerated research efforts in fiber optic communications, although it was not until 1967 that K. C. Kao and G. A. Bockham of the Standard Telecommunications Laboratory in England proposed a new communications medium using *cladded* fiber cables.

The fiber cables available in the 1960s were extremely *lossy* (more than 1000 dB/km), which limited optical transmissions to short distances. In 1970, Kapron, Keck, and Maurer of Corning Glass Works in Corning, New York, developed an optical fiber with losses less than 2 dB/km. That was the "big" breakthrough needed to permit practical fiber optics communications systems. Since 1970, fiber optics technology has grown exponentially. Recently, Bell Laboratories successfully transmitted 1 billion bps through a fiber cable for 600 miles without a regenerator.

In the late 1970s and early 1980s, the refinement of optical cables and the development of high-quality, affordable light sources and detectors have opened the door to the development of high-quality, high-capacity, and efficient fiber optics communications systems. The branch of electronics that deals with light is called *optoelectronics*.

OPTICAL FIBERS VERSUS METALLIC CABLE FACILITIES

Communications through glass or plastic fiber cables has several overwhelming advantages over communications using conventional *metallic* or *coaxial* cable facilities.

Advantages of Fiber Systems

1. Fiber systems have a greater capacity due to the inherently larger bandwidths available with optical frequencies. Metallic cables exhibit capacitance between and inductance along their conductors. These properties cause them to act like low-pass filters which limit their transmission frequencies and bandwidths.

2. Fiber systems are immune to crosstalk between cables caused by *magnetic induction*. Glass or plastic fibers are nonconductors of electricity and therefore do not have a magnetic field associated with them. In metallic cables, the primary cause of crosstalk is magnetic induction between conductors located near each other.

3. Fiber cables are immune to *static* interference caused by lightning, electric motors, fluorescent lights, and other electrical noise sources. This immunity is also attributable to the fact that optical fibers are nonconductors of electricity. Also, fiber cables do not radiate energy and therefore cannot cause interference with other communications systems. This characteristic makes fiber systems ideally suited to military applications, where the effects of nuclear weapons (EMP—electromagnetic pulse interference) has a devastating effect on conventional communications systems.

4. Fiber cables are more resistive to environmental extremes. They operate

over a larger temperature variation than their metallic counterparts, and fiber cables are affected less by corrosive liquids and gases.

5. Fiber cables are safer and easier to install and maintain. Because glass and plastic fibers are nonconductors, there are no electrical currents or voltages associated with them. Fibers can be used around volatile liquids and gases without worrying about their causing explosions or fires. Fibers are smaller and much more lightweight than their metallic counterparts. Consequently, they are easier to work with. Also, fiber cables require less storage space and are cheaper to transport.

6. Fiber cables are more secure than their copper counterparts. It is virtually impossible to tap into a fiber cable without the user knowing about it. This is another quality attractive for military applications.

7. Although it has not yet been proven, it is projected that fiber systems will last longer than metallic facilities. This assumption is based on the higher tolerances that fiber cables have to changes in the environment.

8. The long-term cost of a fiber optic system is projected to be less than that of its metallic counterpart.

Disadvantages of Fiber Systems

At the present time, there are few disadvantages of fiber systems. The only significant disadvantage is the higher initial cost of installing a fiber system, although in the future it is believed that the cost of installing a fiber system will be reduced dramatically. Another disadvantage of fiber systems is the fact that they are unproven; there are no systems that have been in operation for an extended period of time.

ELECTROMAGNETIC SPECTRUM

The total electromagnetic frequency spectrum is shown in Figure 10-1. It can be seen that the frequency spectrum extends from the *subsonic* frequencies (a few

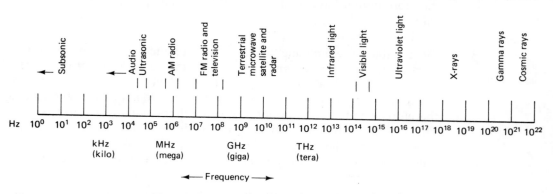

Figure 10-1 Electromagnetic frequency spectrum.

Fiber Optic Communications   **Chap. 10**

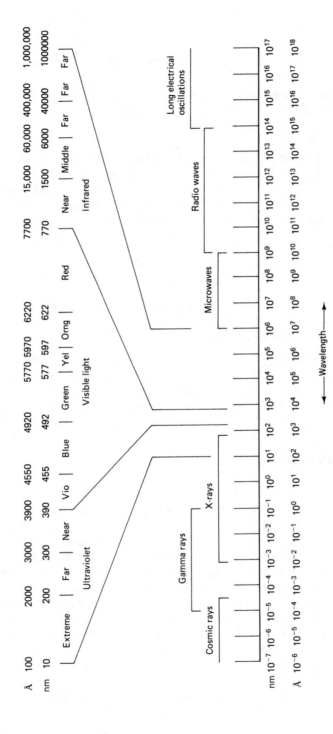

Figure 10-2 Electromagnetic wavelength spectrum.

hertz) to *cosmic rays* (10^{22} Hz). The frequency spectrum can be divided into three general bands:

1. *Infrared:* band of light wavelengths that are too long to be seen by the human eye
2. *Visible:* band of light wavelengths that the human eye will respond to
3. *Ultraviolet:* band of light wavelengths that are too short to be seen by the human eye

When dealing with ultrahigh-frequency electromagnetic waves, such as light, it is common to use units of *wavelength* rather than frequency. Wavelength is the length of the wave that one cycle of an electromagnetic wave occupies in space. The length of a wavelength depends on the frequency of the wave and the velocity of light. Mathematically, wavelength is

$$\lambda = \frac{c}{f} \qquad (10\text{-}1)$$

where

λ = wavelength (Greek lowercase letter lambda)
c = velocity of light (300,000,000 m/s)
f = frequency

With very high frequencies, wavelength is often stated in *microns* (1 micron = 0.000001 meter) or *nanometers* (1 nanometer = 10^{-9} meter or 0.001 micron). However, when describing the optical spectrum, the unit *angstrom* (Å) is often used to express wavelength (1 Å = 10^{-10} meter or 0.0001 micron). Figure 10-2 shows the total electromagnetic wave length spectrum.

OPTICAL FIBER COMMUNICATIONS SYSTEM

Figure 10-3 shows a simplified block diagram of a optical fiber communications link. The three primary building blocks of the link are the *transmitter,* the *receiver,* and the *fiber guide.* The transmitter consists of an analog or digital interface, a voltage-to-current converter, a light source, and a source-to-fiber light coupler. The fiber guide is either an ultra-pure glass or plastic cable. The receiver includes a fiber-to-light detector coupling device, a photo detector, a current-to-voltage converter, an amplifier, and an analog or digital interface.

In an optical fiber transmitter, the light source can be modulated by a digital or an analog signal. For analog modulation, the input interface matches impedances and limits the input signal amplitude. For digital modulation, the original source may already be in digital form or, if in analog form, it must be converted to a digital pulse stream. For the latter case, an analog-to-digital converter must be included in the interface.

The voltage-to-current converter serves as an electrical interface between the input circuitry and the light source. The light source is either a light-emitting

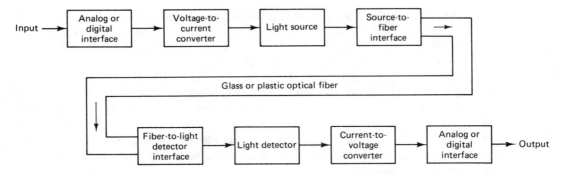

Figure 10-3 Fiber optic communications link.

diode (LED) or an injection laser diode (ILD). The amount of light emitted by either an LED or an ILD is proportional to the amount of drive current. Thus the voltage-to-current converter converts an input signal voltage to a current which is used to drive the light source.

The source-to-fiber coupler is a mechanical interface. Its function is to couple the light emitted by the source into the optical fiber cable. The optical fiber consists of a glass or plastic fiber core, a cladding, and a protective jacket. The fiber-to-light detector coupling device is also a mechanical coupler. Its function is to couple as much light as possible from the fiber cable into the light detector.

The light detector is very often either a PIN (*p*ositive-*i*ntrinsic-*n*egative) diode or an APD (*a*valanche *p*hoto*d*iode). Both the APD and the PIN diode convert light energy to current. Consequently, a current-to-voltage converter is required. The current-to-voltage converter transforms changes in detector current to changes in output signal voltage.

The analog or digital interface at the receiver output is also an electrical interface. If analog modulation is used, the interface matches impedances and signal levels to the output circuitry. If digital modulation is used, the interface must include a digital-to-analog converter.

OPTICAL FIBERS

Fiber Types

Essentially, there are three varieties of optical fibers available today. All three varieties are constructed of either glass, plastic, or a combination of glass and plastic. The three varieties are:

1. Plastic core and cladding
2. Glass core with plastic cladding (often called PCS fiber, plastic-clad silica)
3. Glass core and glass cladding (often called SCS, silica-clad silica)

Optical Fibers   363

Presently, Bell Laboratories is investigating the possibility of using a fourth variety that uses a *nonsilicate* substance, *zinc chloride*. Preliminary experiments have indicated that fibers made of this substance will be as much as 1000 times as efficient as glass, their silica-based counterpart.

Plastic fibers have several advantages over glass fibers. First, plastic fibers are more flexible and, consequently, more rugged than glass. They are easy to install, can better withstand stress, are less expensive, and weigh approximately 60% less than glass. The disadvantage of plastic fibers is their high attenuation characteristic; they do not propagate light as efficiently as glass. Consequently, plastic fibers are limited to relatively short runs, such as within a single building or a building complex.

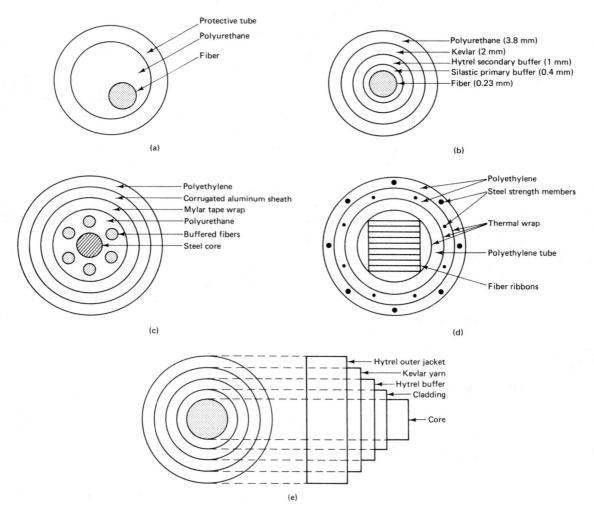

Figure 10-4 Fiber optic cable configurations: (a) loose tube construction; (b) constrained fiber; (c) multiple strands; (d) telephone cable; (e) plastic-clad silica cable.

Fibers with glass cores exhibit low attenuation characteristics. However, PCS fibers are slightly better than SCS fibers. Also, PCS fibers are less affected by radiation and are therefore more attractive to military applications. SCS fibers have the best propagation characteristics and they are easier to terminate than PCS fibers. Unfortunately, SCS cables are the least rugged, and they are more susceptible to increases in attenuation when exposed to radiation.

The selection of a fiber for a given application is a function of specific system requirements. There are always trade-offs based on the economics and logistics of a particular application.

Fiber Construction

There are many different cable designs available today. Figure 10-4 shows examples of several fiber optic cable configurations. Depending on the configuration, the cable may include a *core,* a *cladding,* a *protective tube, buffers, strength members,* and one or more *protective jackets.*

With the *loose* tube construction (shown in Figure 10-4a) each fiber is contained in a protective tube. Inside the protective tube, a polyurethane compound encapsules the fiber and prevents the intrusion of water.

Figure 10-4b shows the construction of a *constrained* optical fiber cable. Surrounding the fiber cable are a primary and a secondary buffer. The buffer jackets provide protection for the fiber from external mechanical influences which could cause fiber breakage or excessive optical attenuation. Kelvar is a yarn-type material that increases the tensile strength of the cable. Again, an outer protective tube is filled with polyurethane, which prevents moisture from coming into contact with the fiber core.

Figure 10-4c shows a *multiple-strand* configuration. To increase the tensile strength, a steel central member and a layer of Mylar tape wrap are included in the package. Figure 10-4d shows a *ribbon* configuration, which is frequently seen in telephone systems using fiber optics. Figure 10-4e shows both the end and side views of a plastic-clad silica cable.

The type of cable construction used depends on the performance requirements of the system and both the economic and environmental constraints.

LIGHT PROPAGATION

The Physics of Light

Although the performance of optical fibers can be analyzed completely by application of Maxwell's equations, this is necessarily complex. For most practical applications, Maxwell's equations may be substituted by the application of *geometric ray tracing,* which will yield a sufficiently detailed analysis.

An atom has several energy levels or states, the lowest of which is the ground state. Any energy level above the ground state is called an *excited state.* If an atom in one energy level decays to a lower energy level, the loss of energy (in electron volts) is emitted as a photon. The energy of the photon is equal to the difference between the energy of the two energy levels. The process of decay from one energy level to another energy level is called *spontaneous decay* or *spontaneous emission.*

Atoms can be irradiated by a light source whose energy is equal to the difference between the ground level and an energy level. This can cause an electron to change from one energy level to another by absorbing light energy. The process of moving from one energy level to another is called *absorption.* When making the transition from one energy level to another, the atom absorbs a packet of energy called a *photon.* This process is similar to that of emission.

The energy absorbed or emitted (photon) is equal to the difference between the two energy levels. Mathematically,

$$E_2 - E_1 = E_p \tag{10-2}$$

where E_p is the energy of the photon. Also,

$$E_p = hf \tag{10-3}$$

where

$$h = \text{Planck's constant}$$

$$= 6.625 \times 10^{34} \text{ J-s}$$

Photon energy may also be expressed in terms of wavelength. Substituting Equation 10-1 into Equation 10-3 yields

$$E_p = hf \tag{10-4}$$

$$= \frac{hc}{\lambda}$$

Velocity of Propagation

Electromagnetic energy, such as light, travels at approximately 300,000,000 m/s (186,000 miles per second) in free space. Also, the velocity of propagation is the same for all light frequencies in free space. However, it has been demonstrated that in materials more dense than free space, the velocity is reduced. When the velocity of an electromagnetic wave is reduced as it passes from one medium to another medium of a denser material, the light ray is *refracted* (bent) toward the normal. Also, in materials more dense than free space, all light frequencies do not propagate at the same velocity.

Refraction

Figure 10-5a shows how a light ray is refracted as it passes from a material of a given density into a less dense material. (Actually, the light ray is not bent, but rather, it changes direction at the interface.) Figure 10-5b shows how sunlight, which contains all light frequencies, is affected as it passes through a material more dense than free space. Refraction occurs at both air/glass interfaces. The

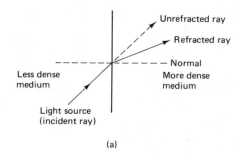

(a)

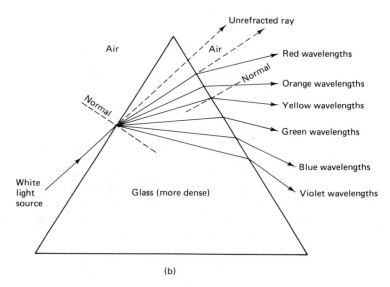

(b)

Figure 10-5 Refraction of light: (a) light refraction; (b) prismatic refraction.

violet wavelengths are refracted the most, and the red wavelengths are refracted the least. The spectral separation of white light in this manner is called *prismatic refraction*. It is this phenomenon that causes rainbows; water droplets in the atmosphere act like small prisms that split the white sunlight into the various wavelengths, creating a visible spectrum of color.

Refractive Index

The amount of bending or refraction that occurs at the interface of two materials of different densities is quite predictable and depends on the *refractive index* (also called *index of refraction*) of the two materials. The refractive index is simply the ratio of the velocity of propagation of a light ray in free space to the velocity of propagation of a light ray in a given material. Mathematically, the refractive index is

$$n = \frac{c}{v}$$

Light Propagation

TABLE 10-1 TYPICAL INDEXES OF REFRACTION

Medium	Index of refraction[a]
Vacuum	1.0
Air	1.0003 ($\approx$1.0)
Water	1.33
Ethyl alcohol	1.36
Fused quartz	1.46
Glass fiber	1.5–1.9
Diamond	2.0–2.42
Silicon	3.4
Gallium-arsenide	3.6

[a]Index of refraction is based on a wavelength of light emitted from a sodium flame (5890 Å).

where

c = speed of light in free space
v = speed of light in a given material

Although the refractive index is also a function of frequency, the variation in most applications is insignificant and therefore omitted from this discussion. The indexes of refraction of several common materials are given in Table 10-1.

How a light ray reacts when it meets the interface of two transmissive materials that have different indexes of refraction can be explained with *Snell's law*. Snell's law simply states:

$$n_1 \sin \theta_1 = n_2 \sin \theta_2 \qquad (10\text{-}5)$$

where

n_1 = refractive index of material 1
n_2 = refractive index of material 2
θ_1 = angle of incidence
θ_2 = angle of refraction

A refractive index model for Snell's law is shown in Figure 10-6. At the interface, the incident ray may be refracted toward the normal or away from it, depending on whether n_1 is less than or greater than n_2.

Figure 10-7 shows how a light ray is refracted as it travels from a more dense (higher refractive index) material into a less dense (lower refractive index) material. It can be seen that the light ray changes direction at the interface, and the angle of refraction is greater than the angle of incidence. Consequently, when a light ray enters a less dense material, the ray bends away from the normal. The normal is simply a line drawn perpendicular to the interface at the point where the incident ray strikes the interface. Similarly, when a light ray enters a more dense material, the ray bends toward the normal.

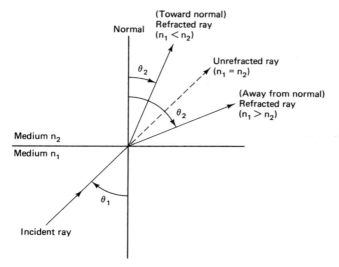

Figure 10-6 Refractive model for Snell's law.

Example 10-1

In Figure 10-7, let medium 1 be glass and medium 2 be ethyl alcohol. For an angle of incidence of 30°, determine the angle of refraction.

Solution From Table 10-1,

$$n_1 \text{ (glass)} = 1.5$$

$$n_2 \text{ (ethyl alcohol)} = 1.36$$

Rearranging Equation 10-5 and substituting for n_1, n_2, and θ_1 gives us

$$\frac{n_1}{n_2} \sin \theta_1 = \sin \theta_2$$

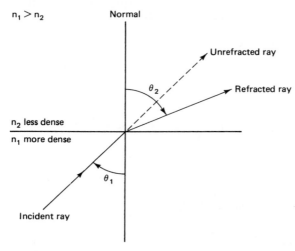

Figure 10-7 Light ray refracted away from the normal.

Light Propagation

369

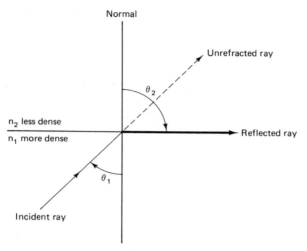

Normal

Unrefracted ray

θ_2

n_2 less dense

n_1 more dense

Reflected ray

θ_1

Incident ray

Figure 10-8   Critical angle reflection.

$$\frac{1.5}{1.36} \sin 30 = 0.5514 = \sin \theta_2$$

$$\theta_2 = \sin^{-1} 0.5514 = 33.47°$$

The result indicates that the light ray refracted (bent) or changed direction by 3.47° at the interface. Because the light was traveling from a more dense material into a less dense material, the ray bent away from the normal.

Critical Angle

Figure 10-8 shows a condition in which an *incident ray* is at an angle such that the angle of refraction is 90° and the refracted ray is along the interface. (It is important to note that the light ray is traveling from a medium of higher refractive index to a medium with a lower refractive index.) Again, using Snell's law,

$$\sin \theta_1 = \frac{n_2}{n_1} \sin \theta_2$$

With $\theta_2 = 90°$,

$$\sin \theta_1 = \frac{n_2}{n_1}(1) \qquad \text{or} \qquad \sin \theta_1 = \frac{n_2}{n_1}$$

and

$$\sin^{-1} \frac{n_2}{n_1} = \theta_1 = \theta_c \qquad (10\text{-}6)$$

where θ is the critical angle.

The *critical angle* is defined as the minimum angle of incidence at which a light ray may strike the interface of two media and result in an angle of refraction of 90° or greater. (This definition pertains only when the light ray is traveling from a more dense medium into a less dense medium.) If the angle of refraction is 90° or greater, the light ray is not allowed to penetrate the less dense material. Consequently, total reflection takes place at the interface, and the angle of reflection is equal to the angle of incidence. Figure 10-9 shows a comparison of the angle of refraction and the angle of reflection when the angle of incidence is less than or more than the critical angle.

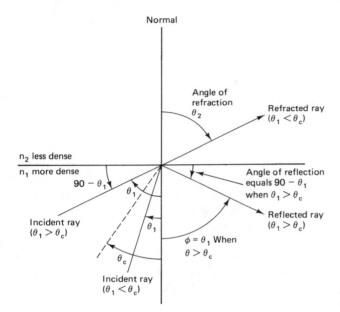

Figure 10-9 Angle of reflection and refraction.

PROPAGATION OF LIGHT THROUGH AN OPTICAL FIBER

Light can be propagated down an optical fiber cable by either reflection or refraction. How the light is propagated depends on the *mode of propagation* and the *index profile* of the fiber.

Mode of Propagation

In fiber optics terminology, the word *mode* simply means path. If there is only one path for light to take down the cable, it is called *single mode*. If there is more than one path, it is called *multimode*. Figure 10-10 shows single and multimode propagation of light down an optical fiber.

Propagation of Light through an Optical Fiber 371

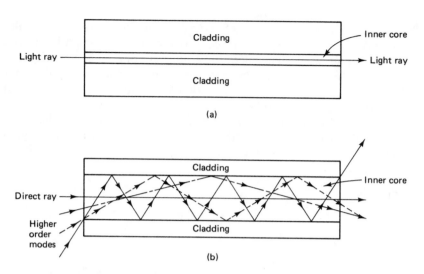

Figure 10-10 Modes of propagation: (a) single mode; (b) multimode.

Index Profile

The index profile of an optical fiber is a graphical representation of the refractive index of the core. The refractive index is plotted on the horizontal axis and the radial distance from the core axis is plotted on the vertical axis. Figure 10-11 shows the core index profiles of three types of fiber cables.

There are two basic types of index profiles: step and graded. A *step-index fiber* has a central core with a uniform refractive index. The core is surrounded by an outside cladding with a uniform refractive index less than that of the central core. From Figure 10-11 it can be seen that in a step-index fiber there is an abrupt change in the refractive index at the core/cladding interface. In a *graded-index fiber* there is no cladding, and the refractive index of the core is nonuniform; it is highest at the center and decreases gradually toward the outer edge.

OPTICAL FIBER CONFIGURATIONS

Essentially, there are three types of optical fiber configurations: single-mode step-index, multimode step-index, and multimode graded-index.

Single-Mode Step-Index Fiber

A *single-mode step-index fiber* has a central core that is sufficiently small so that there is essentially only one path that light may take as it propagates down the cable. This type of fiber is shown in Figure 10-12. In the simplest form of single-mode step-index fiber, the outside cladding is simply air (Figure 10-12a). The refractive index of the glass core (n_1) is approximately 1.5, and the refractive index of the air cladding (n_0) is 1. The large difference in the refractive indexes results in a small critical angle (approximately 42°) at the glass/air interface. Consequently, the fiber will accept light from a wide aperture. This makes it relatively easy to couple light from a source into the cable. However, this type of fiber is typically very weak and of limited practical use.

A more practical type of single-mode step-index fiber is one that has a cladding other than air (Figure 10-12b). The refractive index of the cladding (n_2) is slightly less than that of the central core (n_1) and is uniform throughout the cladding. This type of cable is physically stronger than the air-clad fiber, but the critical angle is also much higher (approximately 77°). This results in a small acceptance angle and a narrow source-to-fiber aperture, making it much more difficult to couple light into the fiber from a light source.

With both types of single-mode step-index fibers, light is propagated down the fiber through reflection. Light rays that enter the fiber propagate straight down the core or, perhaps, are reflected once. Consequently, all light rays follow approximately the same path down the cable and take approximately the same amount of time to travel the length of the cable. This is one overwhelming advantage of single-mode step-index fibers and will be explained in more detail later.

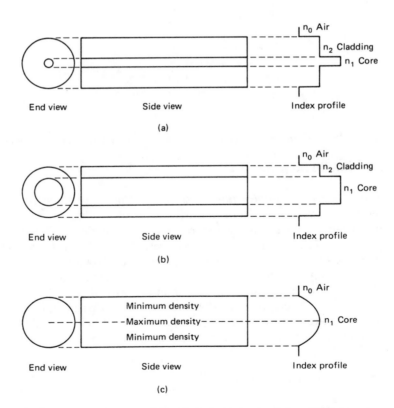

Figure 10-11   Core index profiles: (a) single-mode step index; (b) multimode step index; (c) multimode graded index.

Optical Fiber Configurations 373

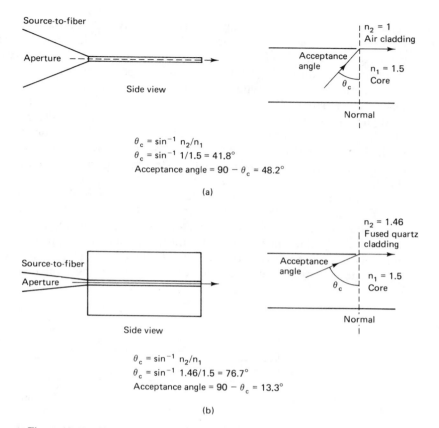

$$\theta_c = \sin^{-1} n_2/n_1$$
$$\theta_c = \sin^{-1} 1/1.5 = 41.8°$$
$$\text{Acceptance angle} = 90 - \theta_c = 48.2°$$

(a)

$$\theta_c = \sin^{-1} n_2/n_1$$
$$\theta_c = \sin^{-1} 1.46/1.5 = 76.7°$$
$$\text{Acceptance angle} = 90 - \theta_c = 13.3°$$

(b)

Figure 10-12 Single-mode step-index fibers: (a) air cladding (b) glass cladding.

Multimode Step-Index Fiber

A *multimode step-index fiber* is shown in Figure 10-13. It is similar to the single-mode configuration except that the center core is much larger. This type of fiber has a large light-to-fiber aperture and, consequently, allows more light to enter the cable. The light rays that strike the core/cladding interface at an angle greater than the critical angle (ray A) are propagated down the core in a zigzag fashion, continuously reflecting off the interface boundary. Light rays that strike the core/cladding interface at an angle less than the critical angle (ray B) enter the cladding and are lost. It can be seen that there are many paths that a light ray may follow as it propagates down the fiber. As a result, all light rays do not follow the same path and, consequently, do not take the same amount of time to travel the length of the fiber.

Multimode Graded-Index Fiber

A *multimode graded-index fiber* is shown in Figure 10-14. A multimode graded-index fiber is characterized by a central core that has a refractive index that is

Fiber Optic Communications   **Chap. 10**

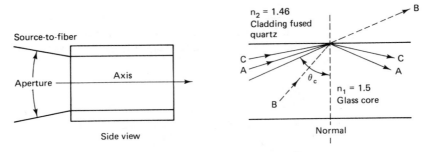

Figure 10-13 Multimode step-index fiber.

nonuniform; it is maximum at the center and decreases gradually toward the outer edge. Light is propagated down this type of fiber through refraction. As a light ray propagates diagonally across the core, it is continually intersecting a less-dense-to-more-dense interface. Consequently, the light rays are constantly being refracted, which results in a continuous bending of the light rays. Light enters the fiber at many different angles. As they propagate down the fiber, the light rays that travel in the outermost area of the fiber travel a greater distance than the rays traveling near the center. Because the refractive index decreases with distance from the center and the velocity is inversely proportional to the refractive index, the light rays traveling farthest from the center propagate at a higher velocity. Consequently, they take approximately the same amount of time to travel the length of the fiber.

COMPARISON OF THE THREE TYPES OF OPTICAL FIBERS

Single-Mode Step-Index Fiber

Advantages

1. There is minimum dispersion. Because all rays propagating down the fiber take approximately the same path, they take approximately the same amount of time to travel down the cable. Consequently, a pulse of light entering the cable can be reproduced at the receiving end very accurately.

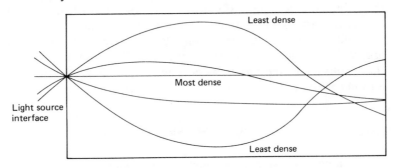

Figure 10-14 Multimode graded-index fiber.

Comparison of the Three Types of Optical Fibers 375

2. Because of the high accuracy in reproducing transmitted pulses at the receive end, larger bandwidths and higher information transmission rates are possible with single-mode step-index fibers than with the other types of fibers.

Disadvantages

1. Because the central core is very small, it is difficult to couple light into and out of this type of fiber. The source-to-fiber aperture is the smallest of all the fiber types.
2. Again, because of the small central core, a highly directive light source such as a laser is required to couple light into a single-mode step-index fiber.
3. Single-mode step-index fibers are expensive and difficult to manufacture.

Multimode Step-Index Fiber

Advantages

1. Multimode step-index fibers are inexpensive and simple to manufacture.
2. It is easy to couple light into and out of multimode step-index fibers; they have a relatively large source-to-fiber aperture.

Disadvantages

1. Light rays take many different paths down the fiber, which results in large differences in their propagation times. Because of this, rays traveling down this type of fiber have a tendency to spread out. Consequently, a pulse of light propagating down a multimode step-index fiber is distorted more than with the other types of fibers.
2. The bandwidth and rate of information transfer possible with this type of cable are less than the other types.

Multimode Graded-Index Fiber

Essentially, there are no outstanding advantages or disadvantages of this type of fiber. Multimode graded-index fibers are easier to couple light into and out of than single-mode step-index fibers but more difficult than multimode step-index fibers. Distortion due to multiple propagation paths is greater than in single-mode step-index fibers but less than in multimode step-index fibers. Graded-index fibers are easier to manufacture than single-mode step-index fibers but more difficult than multimode step-index fibers. The multimode graded-index fiber is considered an intermediate fiber compared to the other types.

ACCEPTANCE ANGLE AND ACCEPTANCE CONE

In previous discussions, the *source-to-fiber aperture* was mentioned several times, and the *critical* and *acceptance* angles at the point where a light ray strikes the

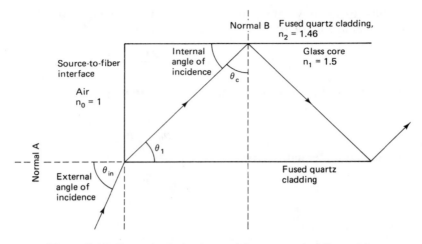

Figure 10-15 Ray propagation into and down an optical fiber cable.

core/cladding interface were explained. The following discussion deals with the light-gathering ability of the fiber, the ability to couple light from the source into the fiber cable.

Figure 10-15 shows the source end of a fiber cable. When light rays enter the fiber, they strike the air/glass interface at normal A. The refractive index of air is 1 and the refractive index of the glass core is 1.5. Consequently, the light entering at the air/glass interface propagates from a less dense medium into a more dense medium. Under these conditions and according to Snell's law, the light rays will refract toward the normal. This causes the light rays to change direction and propagate diagonally down the core at an angle (θ_c) which is different than the external angle of incidence at the air/glass interface (θ_{in}). In order for a ray of light to propagate down the cable, it must strike the internal core/cladding interface at an angle that is greater than the critical angle (θ_c).

Applying Snell's law to the external angle of incidence yields the following expression:

$$n_0 \sin \theta_{in} = n_1 \sin \theta_1 \qquad (10\text{-}7)$$

and

$$\theta_1 = 90 - \theta_c$$

Thus

$$\sin \theta_1 = \sin (90 - \theta_c) = \cos \theta_c \qquad (10\text{-}8)$$

Substituting Equation 10-8 into Equation 10-7 yields the following expression:

$$n_0 \sin \theta_{in} = n_1 \cos \theta_c$$

Rearranging and solving for $\sin \theta_{in}$ gives us

$$\sin \theta_{in} = \frac{n_1}{n_0} \cos \theta_c \qquad (10\text{-}9)$$

Acceptance Angle and Acceptance Cone

Figure 10-16 shows the geometric relationship of Equation 10-9.

From Figure 10-16 and using the Pythagorean theorem, we obtain

$$\cos \theta_c = \frac{\sqrt{n_1^2 - n_2^2}}{n_1} \tag{10-10}$$

Substituting Equation 10-10 into Equation 10-9 yields

$$\sin \theta_{in} = \frac{n_1}{n_0} \frac{\sqrt{n_1^2 - n_2^2}}{n_1}$$

Reducing the equation gives

$$\sin \theta_{in} = \frac{\sqrt{n_1^2 - n_2^2}}{n_0} \tag{10-11}$$

and

$$\theta_{in} = \sin^{-1} \frac{\sqrt{n_1^2 - n_2^2}}{n_0} \tag{10-12}$$

Because light rays generally enter the fiber from an air medium, n_0 equals 1. This simplifies Equation 10-12 to

$$\theta_{in(max)} = \sin^{-1} \sqrt{n_1^2 - n_2^2} \tag{10-13}$$

θ_{in} is called the *acceptance angle* or *acceptance cone* half-angle. It defines the maximum angle in which external light rays may strike the air/fiber interface and still propagate down the fiber with a response that is no greater than 10 dB down from the peak value. Rotating the acceptance angle around the fiber axis describes the acceptance cone of the fiber. This is shown in Figure 10-17.

Numerical Aperture

Numerical aperture (NA) is a figure of merit that is used to measure the light-gathering or light-collecting ability of an optical fiber. The larger the magnitude of NA, the greater the amount of light accepted by the fiber from the external light source. For a step-index fiber, numerical aperture is mathematically defined as the sine of the acceptance half-angle. Thus

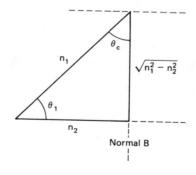

Figure 10-16 Geometric relationship of Equation 10-9.

Fiber Optic Communications   Chap. 10

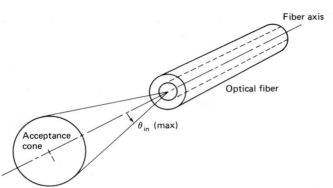

Fiber axis

Optical fiber

θ_{in} (max)

Acceptance
cone

Figure 10-17 Acceptance cone of a fiber cable.

$$NA = \sin \theta_{in}$$

and

$$NA = \sqrt{n_1^2 - n_2^2} \qquad (10\text{-}14)$$

Also,

$$\sin^{-1} NA = \theta_{in}$$

For a graded index, NA is simply the sin of the critical angle:

$$NA = \sin \theta_c$$

Example 10-2

For this example refer to Figure 10-15. For a multimode step-index fiber with a glass core ($n_1 = 1.5$) and a fused quartz cladding ($n_2 = 1.46$), determine the critical angle (θ_c), acceptance angle (θ_{in}), and numerical aperture. The source-to-fiber media is air.

Solution   Substituting into Equation 10-6, we have

$$\theta_c = \sin^{-1}\frac{n_2}{n_1} = \sin^{-1}\frac{1.46}{1.5} = 76.7°$$

Substituting into Equation 10-13 yields

$$\theta_{in} = \sin^{-1}\sqrt{n_1^2 - n_2^2} = \sin^{-1}\sqrt{1.5^2 - 1.46^2}$$

$$= 20.2°$$

Substituting into Equation 10-14 gives us

$$NA = \sin \theta_{in} = \sin 20.2$$

$$= 0.344$$

LOSSES IN OPTICAL FIBER CABLES

Transmission losses in optical fiber cables are one of the most important characteristics of the fiber. Losses in the fiber result in a reduction in the light

Losses in Optical Fiber Cables   **379**

power and thus reduce the system bandwidth, information transmission rate, efficiency, and overall system capacity. The predominant fiber losses are as follows:

1. Absorption losses
2. Material or Rayleigh scattering losses
3. Chromatic or wavelength dispersion
4. Radiation losses
5. Modal dispersion
6. Coupling losses

Absorption Losses

Absorption loss in optical fibers is analogous to power dissipation in copper cables; impurities in the fiber absorb the light and convert it to heat. The ultrapure glass used to manufacture optical fibers is approximately 99.9999% pure. Still, absorption losses between 1 and 1000 dB/km are typical. Essentially, there are three factors that contribute to the absorption losses in optical fibers: ultraviolet absorption, infrared absorption, and ion resonance absorption.

Ultraviolet absorption. Ultraviolet absorption is caused by valence electrons in the silica material from which fibers are manufactured. Light *ionizes* the valence electrons into conduction. The ionization is equivalent to a loss in the total light field and, consequently, contributes to the transmission losses of the fiber.

Infrared absorption. Infrared absorption is a result of *photons* of light that are absorbed by the atoms of the glass core molecules. The absorbed photons are converted to random mechanical vibrations typical of heating.

Ion resonance absorption. Ion resonance absorption is caused by OH^- ions in the material. The source of the OH^- ions is water molecules that have been trapped in the glass during the manufacturing process. Ion absorption is also caused by iron, copper, and chromium molecules.

Figure 10-18 shows typical losses in optical fiber cables due to ultraviolet, infrared, and ion resonance absorption.

Material or Rayleigh Scattering Losses

During the manufacturing process, glass is extruded (drawn into long fibers of very small diameter). During this process, the glass is in a plastic state (not liquid and not solid). The tension applied to the glass during this process causes the cooling glass to develop submicroscopic irregularities that are permanently formed in the fiber. When light rays that are propagating down a fiber strike one of these impurities, they are *diffracted*. Diffraction causes the light to disperse or spread

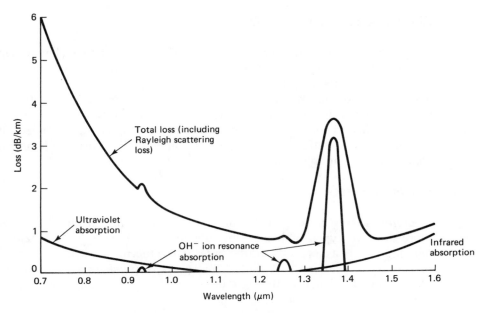

Figure 10-18 Absorption losses in optical fibers.

out in many directions. Some of the diffracted light continues down the fiber and some of it escapes through the cladding. The light rays that escape represent a loss in light power. This is called *Rayleigh scattering loss*. Figure 10-19 graphically shows the relationship between wavelength and Rayleigh scattering loss.

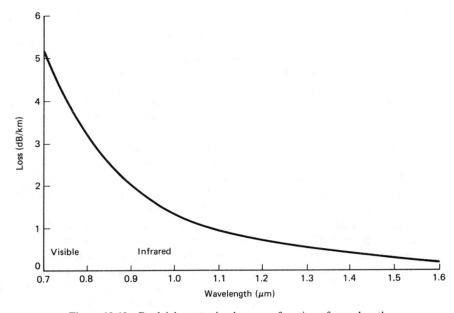

Figure 10-19 Rayleigh scattering loss as a function of wavelength.

Losses in Optical Fiber Cables   **381**

Chromatic or Wavelength Dispersion

As stated previously, the refractive index of a material is wavelength dependent. Light-emitting diodes (LEDs) emit light that contains a combination of wavelengths. Each wavelength within the composite light signal travels at a different velocity. Consequently, light rays that are simultaneously emitted from an LED and propagated down an optical fiber do not arrive at the far end of the fiber at the same time. This results in a distorted receive signal and is called *chromatic distortion*. Chromatic distortion can be eliminated by using a monochromatic source such as an injection laser diode (ILD).

Radiation Losses

Radiation losses are caused by small bends and kinks in the fiber. Essentially, there are two types of bends: microbends and constant-radius bends. *Microbending* occurs as a result of differences in the thermal contraction rates between the core and cladding material. A microbend represents a discontinuity in the fiber where Rayleigh scattering can occur. *Constant-radius bends* occur when fibers are bent during handling or installation.

Modal Dispersion

Modal dispersion or *pulse spreading,* is caused by the difference in the propagation times of light rays that take different paths down a fiber. Obviously, modal dispersion can occur only in multimode fibers. It can be reduced considerably by using graded-index fibers and almost entirely eliminated by using single-mode step-index fibers.

Modal dispersion can cause a pulse of light energy to spread out as it propagates down a fiber. If the pulse spreading is sufficiently severe, one pulse may fall back on top of the next pulse (this is an example of intersymbol interference). In a multimode step-index fiber, a light ray that propagates straight down the axis of the fiber takes the least amount of time to travel the length of the fiber. A light ray that strikes the core/cladding interface at the critical angle will undergo the largest number of internal reflections and, consequently, take the longest time to travel the length of the fiber.

Figure 10-20 shows three rays of light propagating down a multimode step-index fiber. The lowest-order mode (ray 1) travels in a path parallel to the axis of the fiber. The middle-order mode (ray 2) bounces several times at the interface before traveling the length of the fiber. The highest-order mode (ray 3) makes many trips back and forth across the fiber as it propagates the entire length. It can be seen that ray 3 travels a considerably longer distance than ray 1 as it propagates down the fiber. Consequently, if the three rays of light were emitted into the fiber at the same time and represented a pulse of light energy, the three rays would reach the far end of the fiber at different times and result in a spreading out of the light energy in respect to time. This is called modal dispersion and results in a stretched pulse which is also reduced in amplitude at the output of

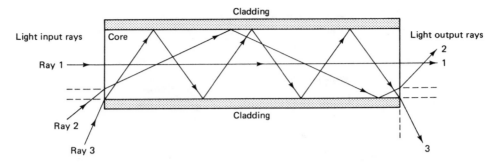

Figure 10-20 Light propagation down a multimode step-index fiber.

the fiber. All three rays of light propagate through the same material at the same velocity, but ray 3 must travel a longer distance and, consequently, takes a longer period of time to propagate down the fiber.

Figure 10-21 shows light rays propagating down a single-mode step-index fiber. Because the radial dimension of the fiber is sufficiently small, there is only a single path for each of the rays to follow as they propagate down the length of the fiber. Consequently, each ray of light travels the same distance in a given period of time and the light rays have exactly the same time relationship at the far end of the fiber as they had when they entered the cable. The result is no *modal dispersion* or *pulse stretching*.

Figure 10-22 shows light propagating down a multimode graded-index fiber. Three rays are shown traveling in three different modes. Each ray travels a different path but they all take approximately the same amount of time to propagate the length of fiber. This is because the refractive index of the fiber decreases with distance from the center, and the velocity at which a ray travels is inversely proportional to the refractive index. Consequently, the farther rays 2 and 3 travel from the center of the fiber, the faster they propagate.

Figure 10-23 shows the relative time/energy relationship of a pulse of light as it propagates down a fiber cable. It can be seen that as the pulse propagates down the fiber, the light rays that make up the pulse spread out in time, which causes a corresponding reduction in the pulse amplitude and stretching of the pulse width. It can also be seen that as light energy from one pulse falls back in time, it will interfere with the next pulse. This is called *pulse spreading* or *pulse-width dispersion* and causes errors in digital transmission.

Figure 10-24a shows a unipolar return-to-zero (UPRZ) digital transmission. With UPRZ transmission (assuming a very narrow pulse) if light energy from

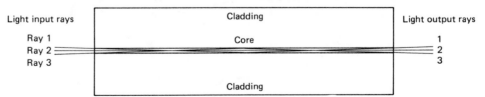

Figure 10-21 Light propagation down a single-mode step-index fiber.

Losses in Optical Fiber Cables 383

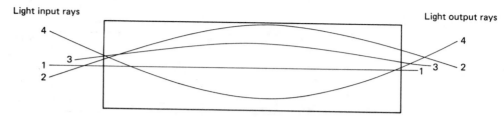

Figure 10-22 Light propagation down a multimode graded-index fiber.

pulse A were to fall back (*spread*) one bit time (T_b), it would interfere with pulse B and change what was a logic 0 to a logic 1. Figure 10-24b shows a unipolar nonreturn-to-zero (UPNRZ) digital transmission where each pulse is equal to the bit time. With UPNRZ transmission, if energy from pulse A were to fall back one-half of a bit time, it would interfere with pulse B. Consequently, UPRZ transmissions can tolerate twice as much delay or spread as UPNRZ transmissions.

The difference between the absolute delay times of the fastest and slowest rays of light propagating down a fiber is called the *pulse-spreading constant* (Δt) and is generally expressed in nanoseconds per kilometer (ns/km). The total pulse spread (ΔT) is then equal to the pulse spreading constant (Δt) times the total fiber length (L). Mathematically, ΔT is

$$\Delta T \, (\text{ns}) = \Delta t \left(\frac{\text{ns}}{\text{km}} \right) \times L \, (\text{km}) \qquad (10\text{-}15)$$

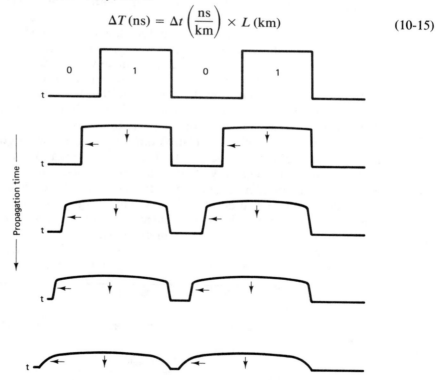

Figure 10-23 Pulse-width dispersion in an optical fiber cable.

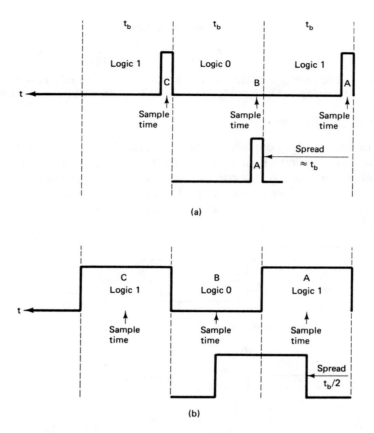

Figure 10-24 Pulse spreading of digital transmissions: (a) UPRZ; (b) UPNRZ.

For UPRZ transmissions, the maximum data transmission rate in bits per second (bps) is expressed as

$$f_b \, (\text{bps}) = \frac{1}{\Delta t \times L} \qquad (10\text{-}16)$$

and for UPNRZ transmissions, the maximum transmission rate is

$$f_b \, (\text{bps}) = \frac{1}{2 \, \Delta t \times L} \qquad (10\text{-}17)$$

Example 10-3

For an optical fiber 10 km long with a pulse-spreading constant of 5 ns/km, determine the maximum digital transmission rates for (a) return-to-zero, and (b) nonreturn-to-zero transmissions.

Solution　(a) Substituting into Equation 10-16 yields

$$f_b = \frac{1}{5 \, \text{ns/km} \times 10 \, \text{km}} = 20 \, \text{Mbps}$$

Losses in Optical Fiber Cables

(b) Substituting into Equation 10-17 yields

$$f_b = \frac{1}{(2 \times 5 \text{ ns/km}) \times 10 \text{ km}} = 10 \text{ Mbps}$$

The results indicate that the digital transmission rate possible for this optical fiber is twice as high (20 Mbps versus 10 Mbps) for UPRZ as for UPNRZ transmission.

Coupling Losses

In fiber cables coupling losses can occur at any of the following three types of optical junctions: light source-to-fiber connections, fiber-to-fiber connections, and fiber-to-photodetector connections. Junction losses are most often caused by one of the following alignment problems: lateral misalignment, gap misalignment, angular misalignment, and imperfect surface finishes. These impairments are shown in Figure 10-25.

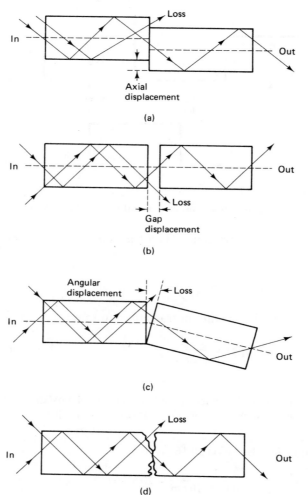

Figure 10-25 Fiber alignment impairments: (a) lateral misalignment; (b) gap displacement; (c) angular misalignment; (d) surface finish.

Fiber Optic Communications   Chap. 10

Lateral misalignment. This is shown in Figure 10-25a and is the lateral or axial displacement between two pieces of adjoining fiber cables. The amount of loss can be from a couple of tenths of a decibel to several decibels. This loss is generally negligible if the fiber axes are aligned to within 5% of the smaller fiber's diameter.

Gap misalignment. This is shown in Figure 10-25b and is sometimes called *end separation*. When *splices* are made in optical fibers, the fibers should actually touch. The farther apart the fibers are, the greater the loss of light. If two fibers are joined with a connector, the ends should not touch. This is because the two ends rubbing against each other in the connector could cause damage to either or both fibers.

Angular misalignment. This is shown in Figure 10-25c and is sometimes called *angular displacement*. If the angular displacement is less than 2°, the loss will be less than 0.5 dB.

Imperfect surface finish. This is shown in Figure 10-25d. The ends of the two adjoining fibers should be highly polished and fit together squarely. If the fiber ends are less than 3° off from perpendicular, the losses will be less than 0.5 dB.

LIGHT SOURCES

Essentially, there are two devices commonly used to generate light for fiber optic communications systems: light-emitting diodes (LEDs) and injection laser diodes (ILDs). Both devices have advantages and disadvantages and selection of one device over the other is determined by system requirements.

Light-Emitting Diodes

Essentially, a *light-emitting diode* (LED) is simply a P-N junction diode. It is usually made from a semiconductor material such as aluminum-gallium-arsenide (AlGaAs) or gallium-arsenide-phosphide (GaAsP). LEDs emit light by spontaneous emission; light is emitted as a result of the recombination of electrons and holes. When forward biased, minority carriers are injected across the *p-n* junction. Once across the junction, these minority carriers recombine with majority carriers and give up energy in the form of light. This process is essentially the same as in a conventional diode except that in LEDs certain semiconductor materials and dopants are chosen such that the process is radiative; a photon is produced. A photon is a quantum of electromagnetic wave energy. Photons are particles that travel at the speed of light but at rest have no mass. In conventional semiconductor diodes (germanium and silicon, for example), the process is primarily nonradiative and no photons are generated. The energy gap of the material used to construct an LED determines whether the light emitted by it is invisible or visible and of what color.

The simplest LED structures are homojunction, epitaxially grown, or single-diffused devices and are shown in Figure 10-26. *Epitaxially grown LEDs* are generally constructed of silicon-doped gallium-arsenide (Figure 10-26a). A typical wavelength of light emitted from this construction is 940 nm, and a typical output power is approximately 3 mW at 100 mA of forward current. *Planar diffused* (*homojunction*) *LEDs* (Figure 10-26b) output approximately 500 μW at a wavelength of 900 nm. The primary disadvantage of homojunction LEDs is the nondirectionality of their light emission, which makes them a poor choice as a light source for fiber optic systems.

The *planar heterojunction LED* (Figure 10-27) is quite similar to the epitaxially grown LED except that the geometry is designed such that the forward current is concentrated to a very small area of the active layer. Because of this the planar heterojunction LED has several advantages over the homojunction type. They are:

1. The increase in current density generates a more brilliant light spot.
2. The smaller emitting area makes it easier to couple its emitted light into a fiber.
3. The small effective area has a smaller capacitance, which allows the planar heterojunction LED to be used at higher speeds.

Burrus etched-well surface-emitting LED.   For the more practical applications, such as telecommunications, data rates in excess of 100 Mbps are required. For these applications, the etched-well LED was developed. Burrus and Dawson of Bell Laboratories developed the etched-well LED. It is a surface-emitting LED and is shown in Figure 10-28. The Burrus etched-well LED emits light in many directions. The etched well helps concentrate the emitted light to a very small area. Also, domed lenses can be placed over the emitting surface to direct the light into a smaller area. These devices are more efficient than the standard surface emitters and they allow more power to be coupled into the optical fiber, but they are also more difficult and expensive to manufacture.

Edge-emitting LED.   The edge-emitting LED, which was developed by RCA, is shown in Figure 10-29. These LEDs emit a more directional light pattern

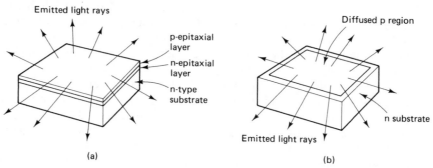

Figure 10-26 Homojunction LED structures: (a) silicon-doped gallium arsenide; (b) planar diffused.

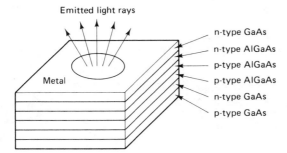

Figure 10-27 Planar heterojunction LED.

than do the surface-emitting LEDs. The construction is similar to the planar and Burrus diodes except that the emitting surface is a stripe rather than a confined circular area. The light is emitted from an active stripe and forms an elliptical beam. Surface-emitting LEDs are more commonly used than edge emitters because they emit more light. However, the coupling losses with surface emitters are greater and they have narrower bandwidths.

The *radiant* light power emitted from an LED is a linear function of the forward current passing through the device (Figure 10-30). It can also be seen that the optical output power of an LED is, in part, a function of the operating temperature.

Injection Laser Diode

The word *laser* is an acronym for *l*ight *a*mplification by *s*timulated *e*mission of *r*adiation. Lasers are constructed from many different materials, including gases, liquids, and solids, although the type of laser used most often for fiber optic communications is the semiconductor laser.

The *injection laser diode* (ILD) is similar to the LED. In fact, below a certain threshold current, an ILD acts like an LED. Above the threshold current, an ILD oscillates; lasing occurs. As current passes through a forward-biased *p-n* junction diode, light is emitted by spontaneous emission at a frequency determined by the energy gap of the semiconductor material. When a particular current level is reached, the number of minority carriers and photons produced

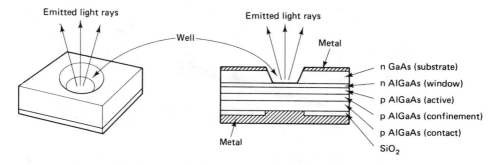

Figure 10-28 Burrus etched-well surface-emitting LED.

Light Sources

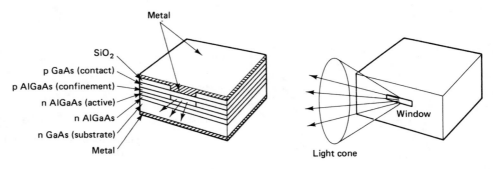

Figure 10-29 Edge-emitting LED.

on either side of the *p-n* junction reaches a level where they begin to collide with already excited minority carriers. This causes an increase in the ionization energy level and makes the carriers unstable. When this happens, a typical carrier recombines with an opposite type of carrier at an energy level that is above its normal before-collision value. In the process, two photons are created; one is stimulated by another. Essentially, a gain in the number of photons is realized. For this to happen, a large forward current that can provide many carriers (holes and electrons) is required.

The construction of an ILD is similar to that of an LED (Figure 10-31) except that the ends are highly polished. The mirror-like ends trap the photons in the active region and, as they reflect back and forth, stimulate free electrons to recombine with holes at a higher-than-normal energy level. This process is called *lasing*.

The radiant output light power of a typical ILD is shown in Figure 10-32. It can be seen that very little output power is realized until the threshold current is reached; then lasing occurs. After lasing begins, the optical output power increases dramatically, with small increases in drive current. It can also be seen that the magnitude of the optical output power of the ILD is more dependent on operating temperature than is the LED.

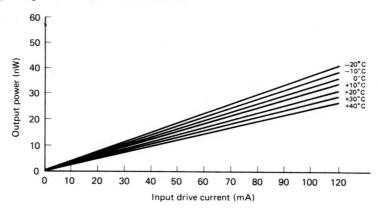

Figure 10-30 Output power versus forward current and operating temperature for an LED.

Fiber Optic Communications   **Chap. 10**

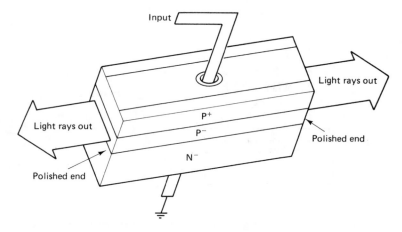

Figure 10-31 Injection laser diode construction.

Figure 10-33 shows the light radiation patterns typical of an LED and an ILD. Because light is radiated out the end of an ILD in a narrow concentrated beam, it has a more direct radiation pattern.

Advantages of ILDs
1. Because ILDs have a more direct radiation pattern, it is easier to couple their light into an optical fiber. This reduces the coupling losses and allows smaller fibers to be used.
2. The radiant output power from an ILD is greater than that for an LED. A typical output power for an ILD is 5 mW (7 dBm) and 0.5 mW (-3 dBm) for LEDs. This allows ILDs to provide a higher drive power and to be used for systems that operate over longer distances.
3. ILDs can be used at higher bit rates than can LEDs.
4. ILDs generate monochromatic light, which reduces chromatic or wavelength dispersion.

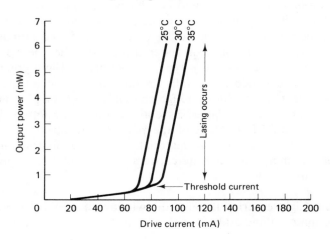

Figure 10-32 Output power versus forward current and temperature for an ILD.

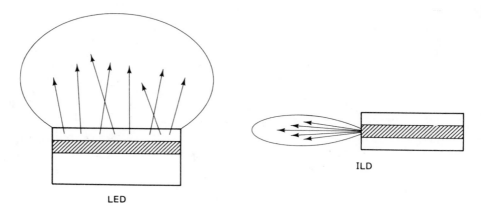

Figure 10-33 LED and ILD radiation patterns.

Disadvantages of ILDs

1. ILDs are typically on the order of 10 times more expensive than LEDs.
2. Because ILDs operate at higher powers, they typically have a much shorter lifetime than LEDs.
3. IDLs are more temperature dependent than LEDs.

LIGHT DETECTORS

There are two devices that are commonly used to detect light energy in fiber optic communications receivers; PIN (positive-intrinsic-negative) diodes and APD (avalanche photodiodes).

PIN Diodes

A *PIN diode* is a *depletion-layer photodiode* and is probably the most common device used as a light detector in fiber optic communications systems. Figure 10-34 shows the basic construction of a PIN diode. A very lightly doped (almost pure or intrinsic) layer of *n*-type semiconductor material is sandwiched between the junction of the two heavily doped *n*- and *p*-type contact areas. Light enters the device through a very small window and falls on the carrier-void intrinsic material. The intrinsic material is made thick enough so that most of the photons that enter the device are absorbed by this layer. Essentially, the PIN photodiode operates just the opposite of an LED. Most of the photons are absorbed by electrons in the valence band of the intrinsic material. When the photons are absorbed, they add sufficient energy to generate carriers in the depletion region and allow current to flow through the device.

Photoelectric effect. Light entering through the window of a PIN diode is absorbed by the intrinsic material and adds enough energy to cause electrons to move from the valence band into the conduction band. The increase in the number of electrons that move into the conduction band is matched by an increase in the number of holes in the valence band. To cause current to flow in a photodiode, sufficient light must be absorbed to give valence electrons enough energy to jump the energy gap. The energy gap for silicon is 1.12 eV (electron volts). Mathematically, the operation is as follows.

For silicon, the energy gap (E_g) equals 1.12 eV:

$$1 \text{ eV} = 1.6 \times 10^{-19} \text{ J}$$

Thus the energy gap for silicon is

$$E_g = (1.12 \text{ eV}) \left(1.6 \times 10^{-19} \frac{\text{J}}{\text{eV}} \right) = 1.792 \times 10^{-19} \text{ J}$$

and

$$\text{energy } (E) = hf$$

where

$$h = \text{Planck's constant} = 6.6256 \times 10^{-34 \text{ J/Hz}}$$

$$f = \text{frequency (Hz)}$$

Rearranging and solving for f yields

$$f = \frac{E}{h}$$

For a silicon photodiode,

$$f = \frac{1.792 \times 10^{-19} \text{ J}}{6.6256 \times 10^{-34} \text{ J/Hz}}$$

$$= 2.705 \times 10^{14} \text{ Hz}$$

Converting to wavelength yields

$$\lambda = \frac{c}{f} = \frac{3 \times 10^8 \text{ m/s}}{2.705 \times 10^{14} \text{ Hz}} = 1109 \text{ nm/cycle}$$

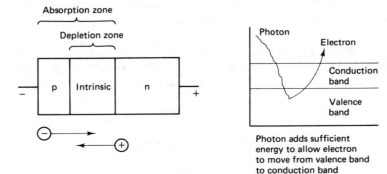

Figure 10-34 PIN photodiode construction.

Consequently, light wavelengths of 1109 nm or shorter, or light frequencies of 2.705×10^{14} Hz or higher, are required to generate enough electrons to jump the energy gap of a silicon photodiode.

Avalanche Photodiodes

Figure 10-35 shows the basic construction of an *avalanche photodiode* (APD). An APD is a *pipn* structure. Light enters the diode and is absorbed by the thin, heavily doped *n*-layer. This causes a high electric field intensity to be developed across the *i-p-n* junction. The high reverse-biased field intensity causes impact ionization to occur near the breakdown voltage of the junction. During impact ionization, a carrier can gain sufficient energy to ionize other bound electrons. These ionized carriers, in turn, cause more ionizations to occur. The process continues like an avalanche and is, effectively, equivalent to an internal gain or carrier multiplication. Consequently, APDs are more sensitive than PIN diodes and require less additional amplification. The disadvantages of APDs are relatively long transit times and additional internally generated noise due to the avalanche multiplication factor.

Characteristics of Light Detectors

The most important characteristics of light detectors are:

Responsivity. This is a measure of the conversion efficiency of a photo-detector. It is the ratio of the output current of a photodiode to the input optical power and has the unit of amperes/watt. Responsivity is generally given for a particular wavelength or frequency.

Dark current. This is the leakage current that flows through a photodiode with no light input. Dark current is caused by thermally generated carriers in the diode.

Transit time. This is the time it takes a light-induced carrier to travel across the depletion region. This parameter determines the maximum bit rate possible with a particular photodiode.

Spectral response. This parameter determines the range or system length that can be achieved for a given wavelength. Generally, relative spectral response is graphed as a function of wavelength or frequency. Figure 10-36 is an illustrative

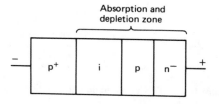

Figure 10-35 Avalanche photodiode construction.

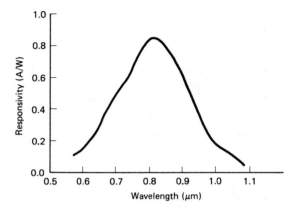

Figure 10-36 Spectral response curve.

example of a spectral response curve. It can be seen that this particular photodiode more efficiently absorbs energy in the range 800 to 820 nm.

LASERS

Laser technology deals with the concentration of light into very small, powerful beams. The word *laser* is an acronym derived from the initials of the term "*l*ight *a*mplification by *s*timulated *e*mission of *r*adiation." The acronym was chosen when technology shifted from microwaves to light waves.

The first laser was developed by Theodore H. Maiman, a scientist who worked for Hughes Aircraft Company in California. Maiman directed a beam of light into ruby crystals with a xenon flashlamp and measured emitted radiation from the ruby. He discovered that when the emitted radiation increased beyond threshold it caused emitted radiation to become extremely intense and highly directional. Uranium lasers were developed in 1960 along with other rare-earth materials. Also in 1960, A. Javin of Bell Laboratories developed the helium laser. Semiconductor lasers (injection laser diodes) were manufactured in 1962 by General Electric, IBM, and Lincoln Laboratories.

Laser Types

Basically, there are four types of lasers: gas, liquid, solid, and semiconductor.

1. Gas lasers. Gas lasers use a mixture of helium and neon enclosed in a glass tube. A flow on coherent (one frequency) light waves is emitted through the output coupler when an electric current is discharged into the gas. The continuous light-wave output is monochromatic (one color).

2. Liquid lasers. Liquid lasers use organic dyes enclosed in a glass tube for an active medium. Dye is circulated into the tube with a pump. A powerful pulse of light excites the organic dye.

3. Solid lasers. Solid lasers use a solid, cylindrical crystal such as ruby for

Lasers 395

the active medium. Each end of the ruby is polished and parallel. The ruby is excited by a tungsten lamp tied to an alternating-current power supply. The output from the laser is a continuous wave.

4. Semiconductor lasers. Semiconductor lasers are made from semiconductor *p-n* junctions and are commonly called *injection laser diodes* (ILDs). The excitation mechanism is a direct-current power supply which controls the amount of current to the active medium. The output light from an ILD is easily modulated, making it very useful in many electronic communications applications.

Laser Characteristics

All types of lasers have several common characteristics: (1) they all use an active material to convert energy into laser light, (2) a pumping source to provide power or energy, (3) optics to direct the beam through the active material to be amplified, (4) optics to direct the beam into a narrow powerful cone of divergence, (5) a feedback mechanism to provide continuous operation, and (6) an output coupler to transmit power out of the laser.

The radiance of a laser is extremely intense and directional. When focused into a fine hairlike beam, it can concentrate all its power into the narrow beam. If the beam of light were allowed to diverge, it would lose most of its power.

Laser Construction

Figure 10-37 shows the construction of a basic laser. A power source is connected to a flashtube that is coiled around a glass tube that holds the active medium. One end of the glass tube is a polished mirror face for 100% internal reflection. The flashtube is energized by a trigger pulse and produces a high-level burst of light (similar to a flashbulb). The flash causes the chromium atoms within the active crystalline structure to become excited. The process of pumping raises the level of the chromium atoms from ground state to an excited energy state. The ions then decay, falling to an intermediate energy level. When the population of ions in the intermediate level is greater than the ground state, a population inversion occurs. The population inversion causes laser action (lasing) to occur. After a period of time, the excited chromium atoms will fall to the ground energy level. At this time, photons are emitted. A photon is a pocket of light caused by radiant energy. The emitted photons strike atoms and two other photons are emitted (hence the term "stimulated emission"). The frequency of the energy determines the strength of the photons; higher frequencies cause greater strength photons.

Laser Applications

Since its inception, lasers have become commonly used devices for both commercial and industrial applications. Lasers are used in electronics communications, holography, medicine, direction finding, and manufacturing.

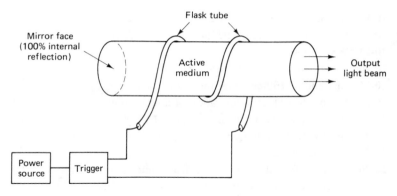

Figure 10-37 Laser construction.

In electronics communications, lasers are used in audio, radio, and television transmission. Laser beams have a very narrow bandwidth and are highly directional. Modulated light is a necessity for optical fiber applications. In medicine, ruby lasers are used for precise applications such as eye surgery. Argon ion lasers are replacing scalpels. The military uses lasers for distance measuring and surveying. In manufacturing, the laser is used for holography to detect stains and measure irregular objects. High-power lasers are used to cut reams of cloth and drill fine holes. Because of its narrow beamwidth, laser can be used to cut fabric within the accuracy of a single thread. There is really no end in sight for the application for lasers.

QUESTIONS

10-1. Define a fiber optic system.

10-2. What is the relationship between information capacity and bandwidth?

10-3. What development in 1951 was a substantial breakthrough in the field of fiber optics? In 1960? In 1970?

10-4. Contrast the advantages and disadvantages of fiber optic cables and metallic cables.

10-5. Outline the primary building blocks of a fiber optic system.

10-6. Contrast glass and plastic fiber cables.

10-7. Briefly describe the construction of a fiber optic cable.

10-8. Define the following terms: velocity of propagation, refraction, and refractive index.

10-9. State Snell's law for refraction and outline its significance in fiber optic cables.

10-10. Define *critical angle*.

10-11. Describe what is meant by mode of operation; by index profile.

10-12. Describe a step-index fiber cable; a graded-index cable.

10-13. Contrast the advantages and disadvantages of step-index, graded-index, single-mode propagation, and multimode propagation.

10-14. Why is single-mode propagation impossible with graded-index fibers?

10-15. Describe the source-to-fiber aperture.

10-16. What are the acceptance angle and the acceptance cone for a fiber cable?

10-17. Define *numerical aperture.*

10-18. List and briefly describe the losses associated with fiber cables.

10-19. What is *pulse spreading?*

10-20. Define *pulse spreading constant.*

10-21. List and briefly describe the various coupling losses.

10-22. Briefly describe the operation of a light-emitting diode.

10-23. What are the two primary types of LEDs?

10-24. Briefly describe the operation of an injection laser diode.

10-25. What is lasing?

10-26. Contrast the advantages and disadvantages of ILDs and LEDs.

10-27. Briefly describe the function of a photodiode.

10-28. Describe the photoelectric effect.

10-29. Explain the difference between a PIN diode and an APD.

10-30. List and describe the primary characteristics of light detectors.

PROBLEMS

10-1. Determine the wavelengths in nanometers and angstroms for the following light frequencies.
(a) 3.45×10^{14} Hz
(b) 3.62×10^{14} Hz
(c) 3.21×10^{14} Hz

10-2. Determine the light frequency for the following wavelengths.
(a) 670 nm
(b) 7800 Å
(c) 710 nm

10-3. For a glass ($n = 1.5$)/quartz ($n = 1.38$) interface and an angle of incidence of 35°, determine the angle of refraction.

10-4. Determine the critical angle for the fiber described in Problem 10-3.

10-5. Determine the acceptance angle for the cable described in Problem 10-3.

10-6. Determine the numerical aperture for the cable described in Problem 10-3.

10-7. Determine the maximum bit rate for RZ and NRZ encoding for the following pulse-spreading constants and cable lengths.
(a) $\Delta t = 10$ ns/m, $L = 100$ m
(b) $\Delta t = 20$ ns/m, $L = 1000$ m
(c) $\Delta t = 2000$ ns/km, $L = 2$ km

10-8. Determine the lowest light frequency that can be detected by a photodiode with an energy gap = 1.2 eV.

SOLUTIONS TO ODD-NUMBERED PROBLEMS

CHAPTER 1

1-1. 10 megabaud; minimum bandwidth = 40 MHz

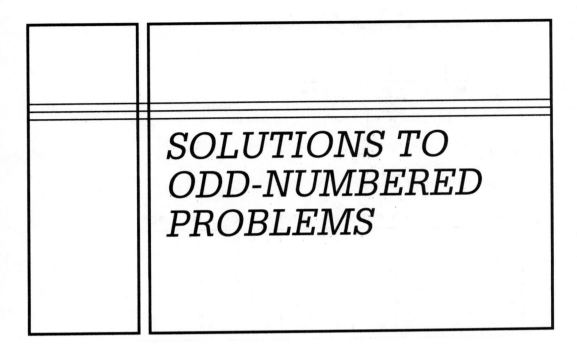

Output spectrum

1-3.

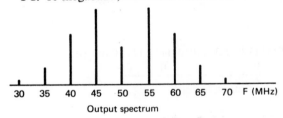

I	Q	Output expression
0	0	$-\sin \omega_c t + \cos \omega_c t$
0	1	$-\sin \omega_c t - \cos \omega_c t$
1	0	$+\sin \omega_c t + \cos \omega_c t$
1	1	$+\sin \omega_c t - \cos \omega_c t$

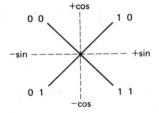

1-5. 6.67 megabaud; minimum bandwidth = 6.67 MHz

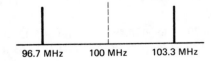

Solutions to Odd-Numbered Problems

1-7. 5 megabaud; minimum bandwidth = 5 MHz

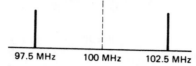

97.5 MHz   100 MHz   102.5 MHz

1-9. **(a)** 2 bps/Hz   **(b)** 3 bps/Hz   **(c)** 4 bps/Hz

CHAPTER 2

2-1.

	D	A	T	A	Sp		C	O	M	M	U	N	I	C	A	T	I	O	N	S		ETX	BCS
b_0	0	1	0	1	0		1	1	1	1	1	0	1	1	1	0	1	1	0	1		1	0
b_1	0	0	0	0	0		1	1	0	0	0	1	0	1	0	0	0	1	1	1		1	0
b_2	1	0	1	0	0		0	1	1	1	1	1	0	0	0	1	0	1	1	0		0	0
b_3	0	0	0	0	0		0	1	1	1	0	1	1	0	0	0	1	1	1	0		0	0
b_4	0	0	1	0	0		0	0	0	0	1	0	0	0	0	1	0	0	0	1		0	0
b_5	0	0	0	0	1		0	0	0	0	0	0	0	0	0	0	0	0	0	0		0	1
b_6	1	1	1	1	0		1	1	1	1	1	1	1	1	1	1	1	1	1	1		0	0
VRC	1	1	0	1	0		0	0	1	1	1	1	0	0	1	0	0	0	1	1		1	1

2-3. Four Hamming bits

CHAPTER 3

3-1. 10111000 binary or B8H

3-3. 1110001000011111 11110011111 0100111101011111 11111 1001011

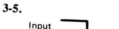

inserted zeros

3-5.

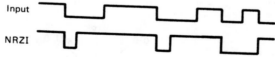

Input

NRZI

CHAPTER 4

4-1. **(a)** 8 kHz   **(b)** 20 kHz

4-3. 10 kHz

4-5. 511 or 54 dB

4-7. **(a)** −2.12 V   **(b)** +0.12 V   **(c)** +0.04 V   **(d)** −2.52 V   **(e)** 0 V

4-9. Resolution = 0.01 V, Qe = 0.005 V

4-11. **(a)** +0.01 to +0.03 V
(b) −0.01 to 0 V
(c) +20.47 to +20.49
(d) −20.47 to −20.49
(e) +5.13 to +5.15 V
(f) +13.63 to +13.65

Solutions to Odd-Numbered Problems

CHAPTER 5

5-1. (a) 1.521 Mbps
(b) 760.5 kHz

5-3.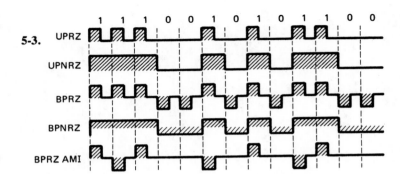

CHAPTER 6

6-1. Ch 1, 108 kHz; Ch 2, 104 kHz; Ch 3, 100 kHz; Ch 4, 96 kHz; Ch 5, 92 kHz; Ch 6, 88 kHz; Ch 7, 84 kHz; Ch 8, 80 kHz; Ch 9, 76 kHz; Ch 10, 72 kHz; Ch 11, 68 kHz; Ch 12, 64 kHz

6-3. Ch = 96 to 100 kHz, GP = 464 to 468 kHz, SG = 1144 to 1148 kHz, MG = 5100 to 5104 kHz

6-5. 5495.92 kHz   **6-7.** 4948 to 5188 kHz

CHAPTER 7

7-1. −99.23 dBm   **7-7.** −1.25 dB
7-3. 28.9 dB   **7-9.** 6.58 dB
7-5. 35 dBm

CHAPTER 8

8-1. Elevation angle = 51°, azimuth = 33° west of south
8-3. (a) 11.74 dB   (b) 8.74 dB
8-5. Radiated power = 28 dBW, EIRP = 68 dBW
8-7. −200.8 dBW   **8-11.** 19.77 dB
8-9. 26.18 dB   **8-13.** 12.5 dB

CHAPTER 9

9-1. 15 transponders   **9-3.** 44 stations

CHAPTER 10

10-1. (a) 869 nm, 8690 Å   **10-7.** (a) RZ = 1 Mbps, NRZ = 500 kbps
(b) 828 nm, 8280 Å   (b) RZ = 50 kbps, NRZ = 25 kbps
(c) 935 nm, 9350 Å   (c) RZ = 250 kbps, NRZ = 125 kbps
10-3. 38.57°
10-5. 36°

INDEX

A

Abort sequence, 140
Absolute phase encoding, 43
Absorption, 366
Absorption loss, 380
Acceptance angle, 376, 378
Acceptance cone, 369, 376, 378
Acknowledgement sequence, 120, 125
Acquisition time, 164
Active state, 129
Adaptive delta modulation PCM, 193
Added channel framing, 239
Added digit framing, 239
Address field, 130
Advanced data communications control procedures (ADCCP), 146
A-law companding, 181
Aliasing distortion, 167
Alternate mark inversion, 233
American National Standards Institute (ANSI), 63
Amplitude modulation (AM), 1, 267
Amplitude regulation, 258

Analog, 1
Analog companding, 179
Analog-to-digital converters (ADCs), 32, 164
Angle of elevation, 304
Angle of incidence, 368
Angstrom, 362
Angular misalignment, 387
ANIK-D satellite, 340
ANSI, 63
ANSI 3.66, 146
Answer channel, 108
Aperture distortion, 164
Aperture time, 164
Apogee, 300
Applications layer, 119
ARQ code, 76
Ascending node, 303
ASCII code, 70
Asynchronous data format, 84
Asynchronous disconnect mode, 142
Asynchronous modems, 106
Asynchronous protocols, 118
Asynchronous response mode, 142

Automatic request for retransmission (ARQ), 82, 119, 131, 148
AT&T's FDM Hierarchy, 244
Avalanche photodiodes, 394
Azimuth, 304, 307

B

Back-off algorithm, 158
Back-off loss, 315
Balanced operation, 143
Balanced ring modulator, 11
Bandwidth efficiency, 41
Baseband, 246
Basic group, 245
Basic supergroup, 246
Baud, 5
Baudot, Emile, 62, 69
Baudot code, 68
Beacon, 139, 300
Bessel function, 8
Binary FSK, 4
Binary phase shift keying (BPSK), 11
Binary synchronous communications, 122
Biphase modulation, 11
Bipolar, 232
Bipolar-return-to-zero alternate mark inversion (BPRZ AMI), 233, 236
Bisync, 122
Bit, 2
  energy, 315
  error rate (BER), 47
  interleaving, 240
  oriented protocol (BOP), 129
  rate, 5
  stealing, 355
Blinding character, 121
Block, 126
Block check character (BCC), 78
Block check sequence (BCS), 78
Blocking, 144
Block of data, 78

Broadband communications, 245
Broadcast address, 121
B6ZS, 237
B3ZS, 238
Burst, 340, 345
Bus topology, 67

C

Call request packet, 148
Cambridge ring, 154
Carrier recovery, 42
Carrier recovery sequence (CRS), 347
Carrier sense, multiple access with collision detection (CSMA/CD), 153
Carrier synchronization, 257
Carrier-to-noise density ratio (C/N$_o$), 320
Carrier-to-noise density power ratio (C/N), 47, 291, 293
CCITT, 63, 117
CCITT international alphabet number 2, 69
CCITT time division multiplexed carrier system, 211
Centralized network, 86
CEPT, 348
CEPT primary multiplex frame, 348
Channel accessing, 153
Channel capacity, 353
Channel compression, 355
Character codes, 68
Character languages, 68
  ARQ, 76
  ASCII, 70
  Baudot, 68
  EBCDIC, 72
Character oriented protocol, 119
Character parity, 77
Character sets, 68
Character synchronization, 84, 122, 129

Checkpointing, 148
Chip code, 350
Chromatic dispersion, 382
Circuit switching, 143
Cladded fiber cables, 359
Clearing character, 120
Clear to send (CTS), 97, 99
Clock recovery, 47, 110, 233
Cluster, 124
Codec, 164, 206, 212
Code division multiple-accessing
    (CDMA), 340, 350
Coding efficiency, 174
Coding methods, 178
Coherent carrier recovery, 15
Collision, 153
Collision enforcement consensus
    procedure, 158
Collision interval, 157
Collision window, 157
Combo chips, 212
Common signaling channel (CSC),
    343
Companding, 178
    analog, 179
    digital, 181
Competitive clipping, 355
Composite baseband, 246
Compressed code, 181
Compressing, 178
Compromise equalizers, 113
Configure command/response,
    138
Connecting medium, 152
Constellation diagram, 12
Continuous phase frequency-shift
    keying (CPFSK), 9
Control field, 131
Conversion time, 164
Correlation spike, 347
Correlator, 350
Costas loop, 43, 44
Coupling losses, 287, 386
Critical angle, 370
Cross-links, 314
Cyclic redundancy checking, 79

D

Dark current, 394
Data, 61
Data above video (DAVID), 264
Data above voice (DAV), 261
Data communications, 61
    circuit configurations, 66
    circuits, 63
    codes, 68
    hardware, 86
    link, 86
Data communications equipment
    (DCE), 65
Datagram, 148
Data in voice (DIV), 264
Data link control (DLC) characters,
    68, 121
Data link escape, 128
Data link layer, 118
Data link protocol, 116
Data modem, 86, 105
Dataphones, 106
Datasets, 106
Data set ready (DSR), 97, 99
Data terminal, 230
Data terminal equipment (DTE), 65,
    87
Data terminal ready (DTR), 97,
    99
Data transfer packet, 150
Data under voice (DUV), 261
dc wandering, 233
Delayed repeater, 299
Delimiting sequence, 129, 141
Delta modulation PCM, 191
Demand assigned, 339
Descending node, 303
Descramblers, 111
Deviation ratio, 7
Device address, 123
Dibits, 17
Differential binary phase shift keying
    (DBPSK), 45
Differential phase shift keying
    (DPSK), 45

Differential pulse code modulation (DPCM), 194
Digit, 2
Digital, 1
Digital biphase, 234
Digital communications, 2
Digital communications systems, 1
Digital crossconnect (DSX), 227
Digital data service (DDS), 261
Digital multiplexing, 203
Digital noninterpolated interfaces (DNI), 353, 354
Digital radio, 2, 4
Digital signals (DS), 227
Digital speech interpolated interfaces (DSI), 353, 355
Digital-to-analog converters (DACs), 26, 164
Digital transmission, 2, 161
Digit-at-a time coding, 178
Diphase, 234
Direct distance, dialing (DDD), 104
Diversity, 272, 275
Domsats, 301
Driver, 95
Droop, 165
D-type channel banks, 206
    D4, 210
D-type supergroups, 258
Duplex, 66
Duty cycle, 231
Dynamic range, 172

E

Earth coverage, 312
EBCDIC code, 72
Echo suppressors, 353
Effective isotropic radiated power, 317
8-phase PSK, 25
8-QAM, 33
Elastic stores, 261

Electromagnetic pulse interference (EMP), 359
Electromagnetic spectrum, 360
    frequency, 360
    wavelength, 361
Electronic Industries Association (EIA), 63, 94
Electronic switching systems (ESS), 104
Electron volt, 393
Elevation angle, 304
Energy gap, 393
Energy per bit (E_b), 49, 315, 316
Energy per bit-to-noise power density ratio (E_b/N_o), 47, 50, 320
Envelope encription/decryption, 340
Epoch, 340, 346
Equalizers, 113, 197
Equatorial orbit, 303
Equivalent noise temperature, 318
Error control, 75
Error correction, 81
    Forward error correction (FEC), 82
    Retransmission, 82
    Symbol substitution, 81
Error detection, 75, 234
    Block check sequence (BCC), 78, 125
    Cyclic redundancy checking (CRC), 79, 148
    Exact count encoding, 75
    Frame check sequence (FCS), 137, 142
    Redundancy, 75, 123
    Longitudinal redundancy checking (LRC), 78, 126
    Parity, 75
    Vertical redundancy checking (VRC), 77, 119
Ethernet, 154
Exact count code, 76
Expanding, 178
Extending addressing, 141
Eye patterns, 198

F

Fade margin, 287, 289
FDM/FM satellite systems, 338
FDM hierarchy, 245
Feeder losses, 287
Feeder services, 267
Fiber guide, 362
Fiber losses, 380
Fiber optic communications, 357
Fiber optics
  advantages, 359
  disadvantages, 360
  history, 358
  light propagation, 365
  optical fibers, 363
Fiber optic system, 357
Fibers, 359
Final/final not bit, 132
Fixed data rate mode, 217
Fixed-frequency FDM/FM, 338
Flag, 129
Flag field, 129
Flat top sampling, 165
Flexible fiberscope, 358
Folded binary code, 169
Foldover distortion, 167
Footprints, 311
Format character, 123
Format identifier, 150
Forward error correction (FEC), 82
Four-wire, 68
Frame, 129
Frame check sequence (FCS), 137,
  142
Frame synchronization, 238
Frame time, 204
Framing bit, 205
Free space path, 283
Free space path loss, 287, 288
Frequency deviation, 7
Frequency diversity, 272
Frequency division multiple-access-
  ing (FDMA), 340, 341
Frequency division multiplexing
  (FDM), 203, 243

Frequency hopping, 353
Frequency modulation (FM), 1, 267
  low index, 268
Frequency shift keying (FSK), 4
  error performance, 56
Frequency translation, 254
Front end processor (FEP), 87
Front-to-back ratio, 282
Full duplex (FDX), 66
Full/Full duplex (F/FDX), 67
Function descriptor, 138

G

Gain-to-equivalent noise temperature
  ratio (G/T_e), 326
Gap misalignment, 387
Gateway protocol, 146
General poll, 123
Geometric wave tracing, 365
Geostationary satellite, 301, 303
Geosynchronous satellite, 301, 303
Go-ahead sequence, 137
Gold code, 352
Graded index fiber, 372
Granular noise, 193
Gray code, 27
Ground reflected wave, 283
Group, 245, 246
Group address, 121
Guard band, 251
Guard time, 347
Guided fiber cables, 357

H

Half duplex (HDX), 66
Hamming bits, 82
Hamming code, 82
Handshake, 125
Hartley's law, 2
Heading sequence, 122
h-factor, 106
High-level data link control (HDLC),
  141

High power amplifier (HPA), 313, 315
Hold-and-forward network, 144
Hopping pattern, 353
Horizontal pointing angle, 307
Horizontal redundancy checking (HRC), 126
Host station, 86
Hot standby diversity, 275
Hybrid data, 261

I

I-channel, 17
Idle channel noise, 177
Idle line ones, 84
Idle state, 129
IEEE, 63, 154
    Standard 802.3, 154
    Standard 802.5, 154
IF bandwidth, 8
IMPATT diodes, 278
Imperfect surface finish, 387
Incident ray, 370
Inclined orbit, 303
Index of refraction, 367
Index profile, 372
Information, 1, 61
Information capacity, 2
Information carring capacity, 357
Information density, 41
Information field, 129
Information frame, 131
Infrared absorption, 380
Initialization mode, 134
Initial program logic (IPL), 135
Injection laser diode (ILD), 363, 389
Intelsat, 301
International Standards Organization (ISO), 53
Intersymbol interference, 196
Invert-on-zero encoding, 140
Ion resonance absorption, 380
ISO, 63, 117
ISO 3309-1976 (E), 141

ISO 4335-1979 (E), 142
ISO 7890-1985 (E), 143
Isochronous transmission, 109

J

Jumbogroups, 246

K

Klystron, 278

L

Lasser, 358, 395
Lateral misalignment, 387
L carriers, 257
Leading pad, 123
Level-at-a time coding, 178
Light detectors, 392
Light emitting diode (LED), 363, 387
Light propagation, 365
Light sources, 387
Linear PCM codes, 176
Linear quantizer, 170
Line control unit (LCU), 86, 116, 87
Line encoding, 231
    BPNRZ, 232
    BPRZ, 232
    BPRZ AMI, 232
    UPNRZ, 232, 384
    UPRZ, 232, 383
Line of apsides, 301
Line of sight, 272, 283, 298
Line turnaround, 117
Line turnaround character, 123
Link access procedure balanced (LAPB), 147
Link budget, 328
Link equations, 327
Local area networks (LANs), 151
Local area network controller for Ethernet (LANCE), 157
Logical channel identifier (LCI), 150
Log-PCM codes, 180

Long haul communications, 244
Longitudinal currents, 101
Longitudinal redundancy checking
    (LRC), 126
Look angles, 304
Loop (SDLC), 137
Loop topology, 66
Low noise amplifier (LNA), 313, 314

M

Major pulse lobe, 197
Manchester coding, 155, 234
Mark frequency, 5
M-ary encoding, 16
Material scattering loss, 380
Maximum distance code, 27
Maxwell's equations, 365
Master, 116
Mastergroup, 246, 251
Master station, 257
Mesh topology, 66
Message abort, 140
Message channel, 244
Message parity, 78
Message switching, 144
Message synchronization, 84
Metallic currents, 101
Microbending, 382
Micron, 362
Microwave system, 268
    transmitter, 268
    radio stations, 277
    receiver, 269
    repeaters, 270
Midrise quantization, 177
Midtread quantization, 177
Minimum Nyquist bandwidth, 8
Minimum shift keying FSK (MSK),
    9
Modal dispersion, 382
Mode of propagation, 371
Modem, 57, 65, 86, 105
Modem synchronization, 109
Modulation index, 7

Morse code, 62
Morse, Samuel F. B., 62
Muldems, 227
Multicast address, 155
Multidrop topology, 66
Multiframe alignment, 208
Multihop interference, 280
Multijumbo groups, 246
Multimode, 371
Multimode graded-index fiber, 372
Multipath propagation loss, 289
Multiple-accessing, 338, 340
    CDMA, 340, 350
    FDMA, 340, 341
    TDMA, 340, 345
Multiple-destination, 339
Multiplexing, 203
Multipoint circuit, 66

N

Nanometere, 362
Narrowband FM, 268
Natural sampling, 165
Network architecture, 116
Network layer, 118
Network protocol, 116
Noise figure, 292
Noise margin, 95
Noise power density (N_o), 49, 319
Noncontinuous FSK, 10
Nonlinear PCM codes, 176
Nonreturn-to-zero (NRZ), 196
Nonreturn-to-zero inverted (NRZI),
    140
Nonsynchronous satellite, 301
Normal disconnect mode, 134
Normal response mode, 134
North American digital hierarchy,
    227
NRZ, 196, 231
NRZI encoding, 140
Numbered frames (ns/nr), 131
Numerical aperture, 378
Nyquist bandwidth, 8

Nyquist sample rate, 167
Nyquist sample theorem, 167

O

Offset keyed QPSK, 24
Offset QPSK (OQPSK), 24
One-way only, 66
Open systems interconnection, 117
Operating modes, 121
Optical electronics, 359
Optical fiber communications system, 362
Optical fiber configurations, 364
Optical fibers, 359, 363
    losses, 379
    multimode graded-index, 374, 376
    multimode step-index, 374, 376
    single-mode step-index, 372, 375
Orbital classifications, 308
Orbital patterns, 302
Originate channel, 108
Orthogonal code, 352
OSI, 117
Overload distortion, 169

P

Packet assembler/disassembler
    (PAD), 146
Packet mode, 146
Packets, 144, 147
Packet switching, 144
Packet-switching network, 143
PAD character, 123
Parallel data transmission, 65
Parametric amplifier, 314
Parity, 75
Parked, 308
Passive reflector, 298
Passive satellite, 299
Path characteristics, 283
Payload, 298
PCM codes, 168
Peak limiting, 169

Percentage error, 188
Perigee, 300
Permanent virtual circuit, 148
Phase locked loop (PLL), 9
Phase modulation (PM), 1
Phase referencing, 42
Phase reversal keying (PRK), 11
Phase shift keying (PSK), 4, 11
    BPSK, 11
    DPSK, 45
    8-PSK, 25
    error performance, 52
    OQPSK, 24
    16-PSK, 32
    QPSK, 17
Photoelectric effect, 392
Photon, 366
Photophone, 358
Physical address, 155
Physical layer, 118
Picturephone terminal, 229
Pilot, 259
PIN diodes, 392
Point-to-point topology, 66
Polarization diversity, 273
Polar orbit, 303
Poll/poll not bit, 132
Polling, 117
Power compression, 315
Preamble, 346
Preassigned channel, 339
Preemphasis network, 268
Presentation layer, 119
Primary station, 63, 86
Prismatic refraction, 367
Private line, 104
Probability of error P(e), 47, 322
Product modulator, 12
Prograde orbit, 300
Propagation of light, 371
Protection switching, 274
Protocol, 116
    asynchronous, 119
    bisync, 122
    bit oriented (BOP), 129
    character oriented, 119

HDLC, 141
SDLC, 122, 129
single-packet-per-segment, 148
synchronous, 122
Public data network (PDN), 143
Public telephone network (PTN), 104
Pulse amplitude modulation (PAM),
    26, 163
Pulse code modulation (PCM), 163
adaptive delta modulation, 193
codes, 168
delta PCM, 191
differential PCM, 194
Pulse modulation, 162
Pulse position modulation (PPM),
    163
Pulse spreading, 382
Pulse spreading constant, 384
Pulse stretching, 383
Pulse transmission, 195
Pulse width dispersion, 383
Pulse width modulation (PWM), 163

Q

Q-channel, 17
Quadbits, 36
Quadrature amplitude modulation
    (QAM), 4, 32
8-QAM, 33
error performance, 55
16-QAM, 36
Quadrature PSK (QPSK), 17
Quantization error, 170
Quantization interval, 169
Quantization noise, 170
Quantization range, 169
Quantizing, 169
Quaternary phase shift keying
    (QPSK), 17

R

Radiation losses, 382
Raditiation patterns, 311

Radio channel, 253
Rayleigh scattering loss, 380
Receiver sensitivity, 291
Receiver threshold, 291
Redundancy, 122, 123
Reference burst, 346
Refracted, 366
Refraction, 366
Refraction index, 367
Reliability objectives, 289
Remodulator, 43, 44
Repeaters, 270
Repeater station, 280
Request to send (RTS), 97, 99
Resolution, 169
Responsivity, 394
Rest frequency, 5
Retransmisison, 82
Retrograde orbit, 300
Return-to-zero (RZ), 231
Reuse, 312, 340
Reverse interrupt (RVI), 125
Ringaround, 282
Ring modulator, 11
Ring topology, 66
Ringing tails, 195
RLSD, 123
Robbed digit framing, 239
RS-422A, 94, 101, 146
RS 423A, 94, 101, 146
RS-449A, 100
RS, 232C, 94, 146
RZ, 231

S

Sample and hold circuit, 163, 164
Sampling rate, 167
Satellites
  ANIK-D, 340
  broadcast, 310
  CEPT primary multiplex frame,
    348
  code division multiple-accessing
    (CDMA), 340, 350
  cross-links, 314

Satellites (*cont.*)
downlink model, 314
FDM/FM satellite systems, 338
fixed-frequency, 338
fixed point, 310
frequency division multiple-accessing (FDMA), 340, 341
frequency hopping, 353
geostationary, 301
geosynchronous, 301, 303
intersatellite, 310, 314
link budget, 328
link equations, 327
mobile, 310
multiple-accessing, 338, 340
nonideal system parameters,
334
nonsynchronous, 300
orbital, 300
passive, 299
single-channel satellite transponders, 338
SPADE, 342
spread spectrum multiple-accessing, 350
Time division multiple-accessing
(TDMA), 340, 345
uplink model, 313
Saturated output power, 315
Scramblers, 111
SDLC loop 137
Secondary lobes, 195
Secondary station, 63, 86
Selection sequence, 120
Selective calling system (8A1/8B1),
119
Serial data transmission, 65
Serial interfaces, 94
RS-422A, 94, 101, 146
RS-423A, 94, 101, 146
RS-449A, 100
RS-232C, 94, 146
Session layer, 119
Setup time, 143
Seven layer model, 117
Shadow, 301

Shannon limit for information capac-
ity, 2, 4
Shift register mode, 220
Signal state-space diagram, 12
Signal-to-distortion ratio, 175
Signal-to-noise ratio, 292
Signal-to-quantization noise ratio
(SQR), 175
Sign-magnitude PCM codes, 168
Simplex, 66, 163
Single mode, 371
Single mode step-index fiber, 372
Single-packet-per-segment protocol,
148
Sin x/x function, 195
16-PSK, 32
16-QAM, 36
Skywave, 286
Slave station, 116
Slope overload, 192
Snell's law, 377
Spacebound, 315
Space diversity, 273
Space frequency, 5
SPADE, 342
Spatial separation, 308
Specific poll, 123
Spectral response, 394
Spectrical null, 195
Spinners, 308
Spontaneous decay, 366
Spontaneous emission, 366
Spot coverage, 312
Spread spectrum multiple-accessing,
350
Squaring loop, 43
Stand alone station, 120
Standards council of Canada (SCC),
63
Standards organizations for data
communications, 62
Star topology, 66
Start/stop bits, 84
Start/stop mode, 145
Station polling address, 120, 123
Station selection address, 124

Statistical framing, 240
Step-index fiber, 372
Storage time, 164
Store-and-forward network, 144
Store-and-forward system, 348
Superframe format, 207
Supergroup, 246, 249
    D-type, 258
Supervisory frame, 133
Supervisory signaling, 221
Surface wave, 283
Symbol substitution, 81, 119
Sync character, 85, 122
Synchronization, 84
    carrier, 42, 257
    character, 84
    clock, 47
Synchronous data format, 85
Synchronous data link control
        (SDLC), 122, 129
    frame format, 130
    SDLC loop operation, 137
Synchronous mode, 145
Synchronous modems, 108
Synchronous protocol, 122
System gain, 286

T

T carriers, 204, 210, 227, 235
    T1, 204, 227, 235
    T1C, 210, 235
    T2, 227, 237
    T3, 238
    T4M, 238
    T5, 238
Telegraph, 62
Telex code, 68
Terminator, 95
Terrain sensitivity, 289
Thermal noise power, 48, 291
Three axis stabilizers, 308
Time assigned speech interpolation
        (TASI), 355
Time division multiple-accessing,
        (TDMA), 340, 345

Time division multiplexing (TDM),
        203
Token passing, 154
Topology, 66, 151
Trailing pad, 123
Training sequence, 99, 109, 110
Transactional switch, 144
Transient state, 129
Transit time, 394
Transmission media, 104
Transmission modes, 66
Transmit power, 315
Transmod, 278
Transparency, 128, 139
Transparent switch, 144
Transponder, 298, 313
Transport layer, 119
Traveling wave tube (TWT), 278
Tribits, 25
Tunnel diode, 314
Turnaround sequence, 137
Two-point circuit, 66
Two-way alternate, 66
Two-way simultaneous, 66
Two-wire, 67

U

UART, 87
Ultraviolet absorption, 380
Unbalanced operation, 143
Unipolar, 232
Unique line code framing, 240
Unique word, 347
Unnumbered frame, 134
Unnumbered information, 134
User to network interface, 146
USRT, 87, 92

V

V.24, 94
V.28, 94
V.41, 79
Value added network (VAN), 143

Variable data rate mode, 220
Velocity of propagation, 366
Vertical redundancy checking, 119
Virtual call, 148
Vocoders, 189
    channel, 190
    format, 190
    linear predictive, 190
Voltage controlled oscillator (VCO),
    6
Voice band circuit, 105

W

WARC, 310
Wavelength, 362
Wavelength dispersion, 382
Wire line entrance link (WLEL), 277
Word-at-a time coding, 178
Word interleaving, 240
World Administrative Radio Confer-
    ence (WARC), 310
Wrap, 139

X

X.1, 145, 152
X.75, 146, 152
X.3, 152
X.20bis, 152
X.21bis, 102, 152
X.28, 152
X.25, 146, 148, 151, 152
X.25 packet format, 148, 152
X.29, 152
X.21, 102, 146, 152
X.27, 103, 146, 152
X.26, 103, 146, 152
X.2, 152
X.121, 152

Z

Zero bit insertion, 140
Zero insertion, 140
Zero stuffing, 140
Zonal coverage, 312